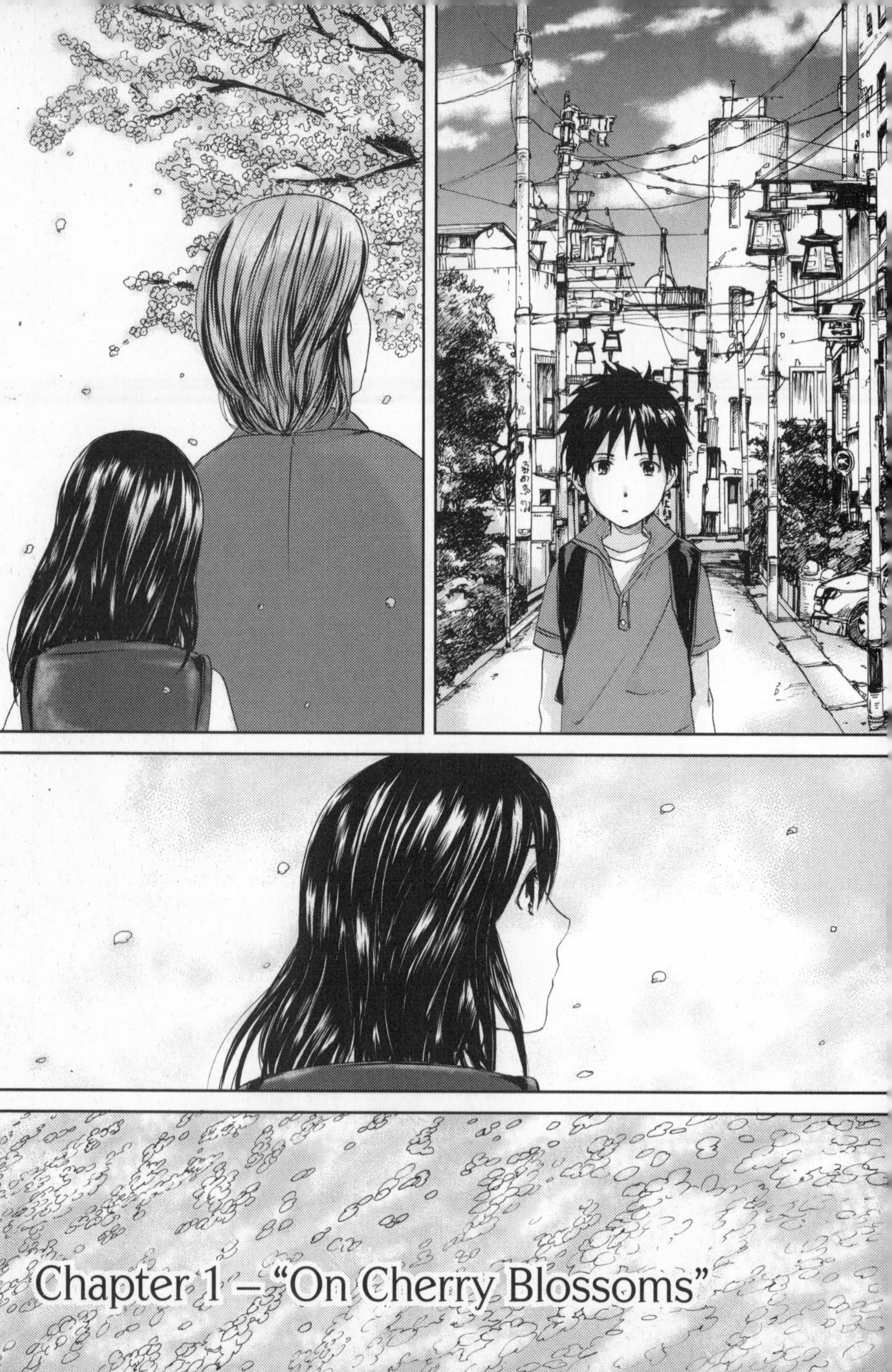
Chapter 1 – "On Cherry Blossoms"

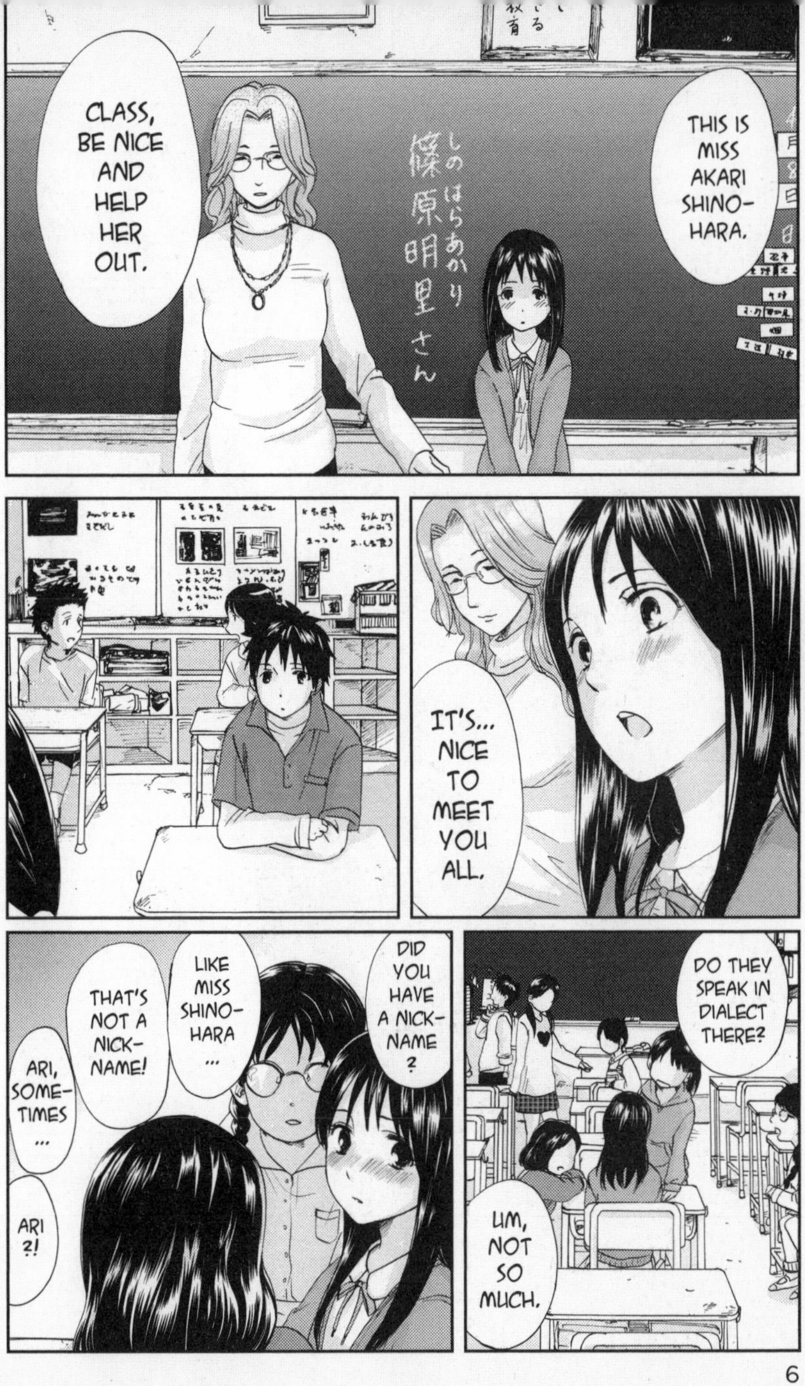
THIS IS MISS AKARI SHINO-HARA.
しのはらあかり
篠原明里さん
CLASS, BE NICE AND HELP HER OUT.
IT'S... NICE TO MEET YOU ALL.
DO THEY SPEAK IN DIALECT THERE?
UM, NOT SO MUCH.
DID YOU HAVE A NICK-NAME?
LIKE MISS SHINO-HARA...
THAT'S NOT A NICK-NAME!
ARI, SOME-TIMES...
ARI?!

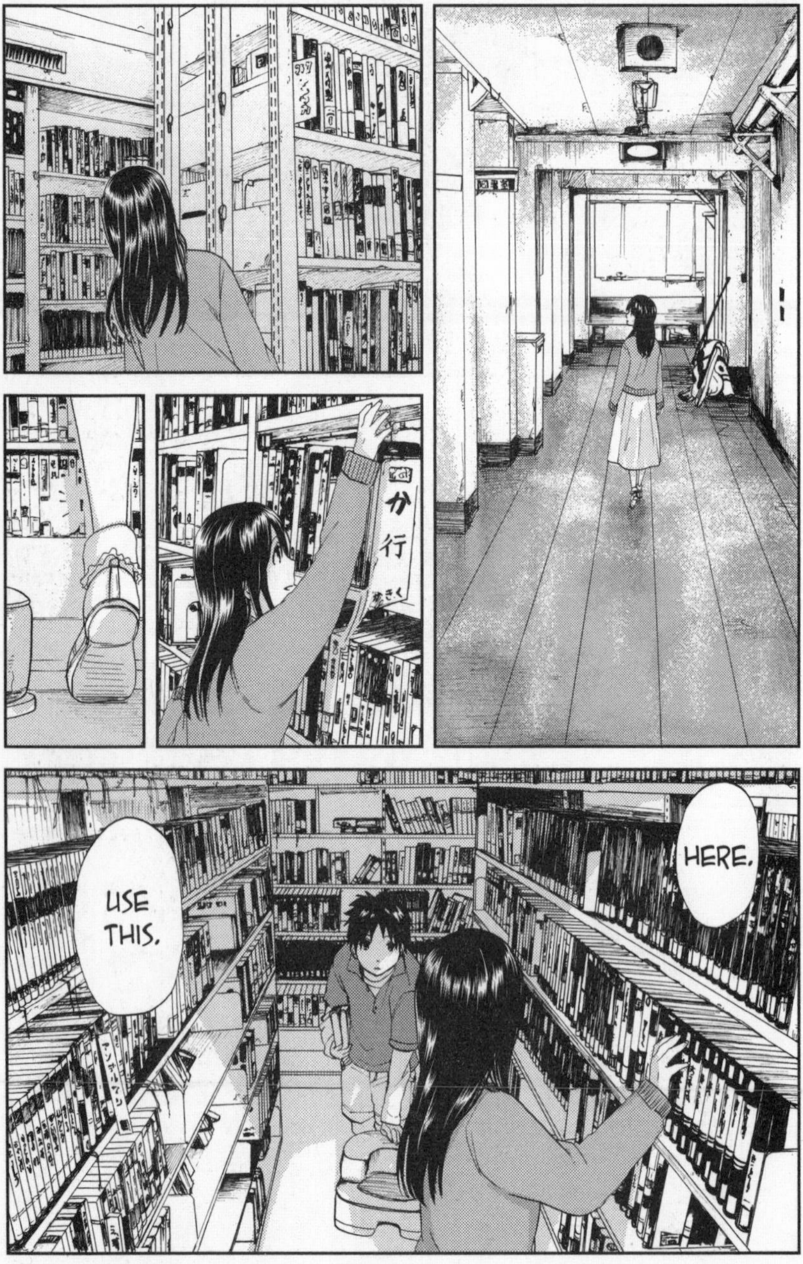
か行
HERE.
USE THIS.

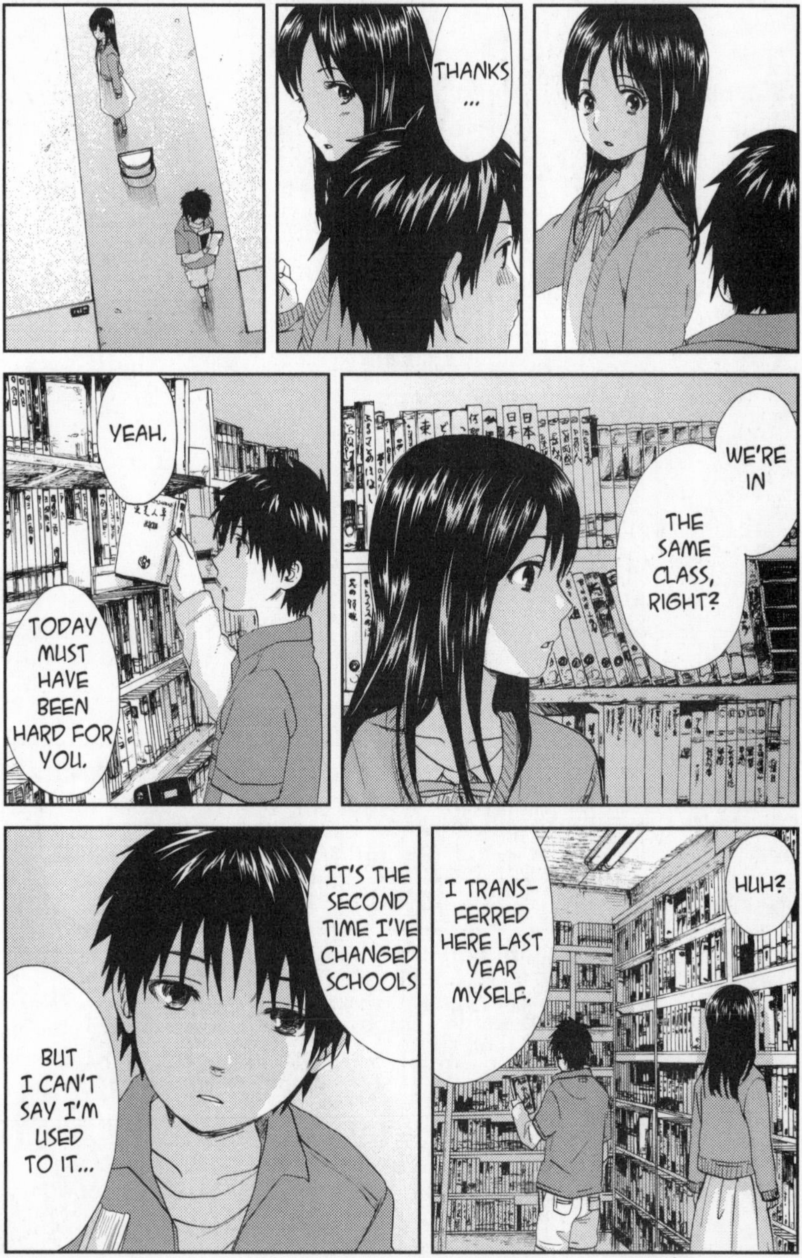
THANKS ...
WE'RE IN THE SAME CLASS, RIGHT?
YEAH.
TODAY MUST HAVE BEEN HARD FOR YOU.
HUH?
I TRANS-FERRED HERE LAST YEAR MYSELF.
IT'S THE SECOND TIME I'VE CHANGED SCHOOLS
BUT I CAN'T SAY I'M USED TO IT...

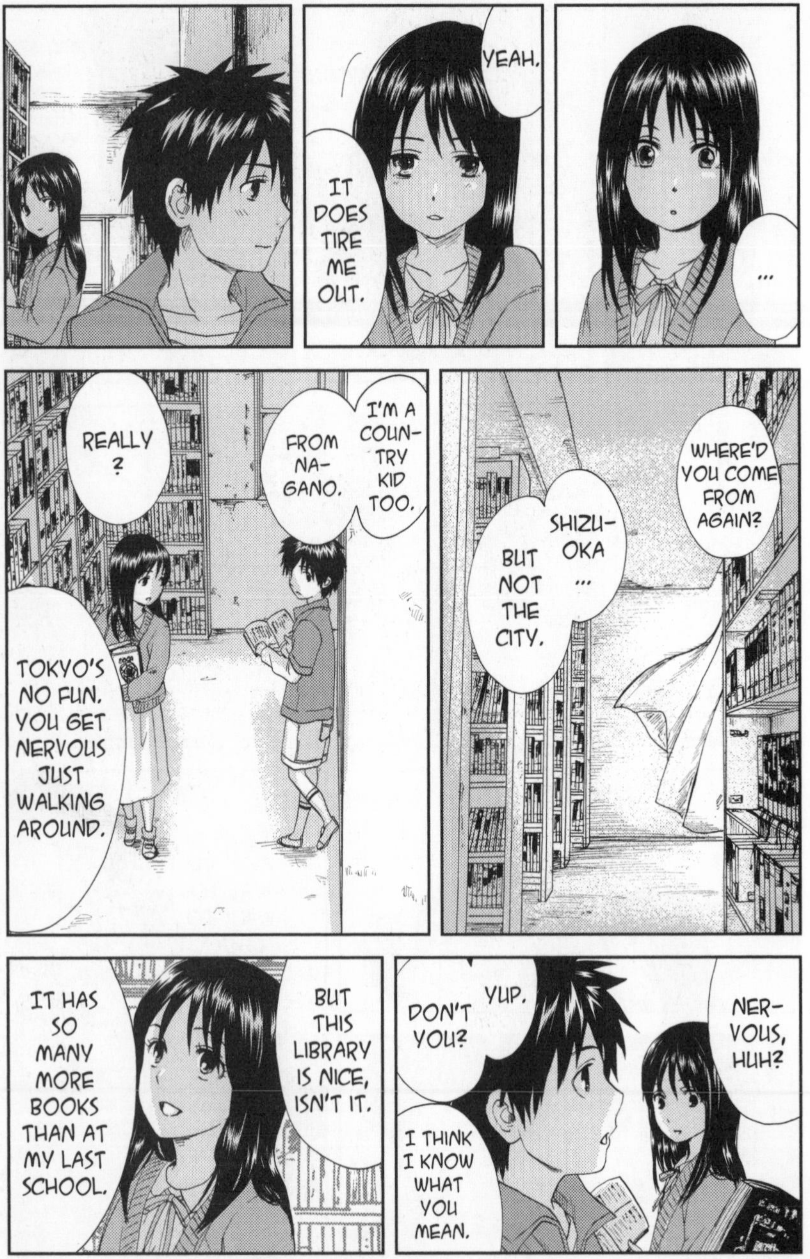
...
YEAH,
IT DOES TIRE ME OUT.
WHERE'D YOU COME FROM AGAIN?
SHIZU-OKA ...
BUT NOT THE CITY.
I'M A COUNTRY KID TOO.
FROM NA-GANO.
REALLY ?
TOKYO'S NO FUN. YOU GET NERVOUS JUST WALKING AROUND.
NER-VOUS, HUH?
YUP.
DON'T YOU?
I THINK I KNOW WHAT YOU MEAN.
BUT THIS LIBRARY IS NICE, ISN'T IT.
IT HAS SO MANY MORE BOOKS THAN AT MY LAST SCHOOL.

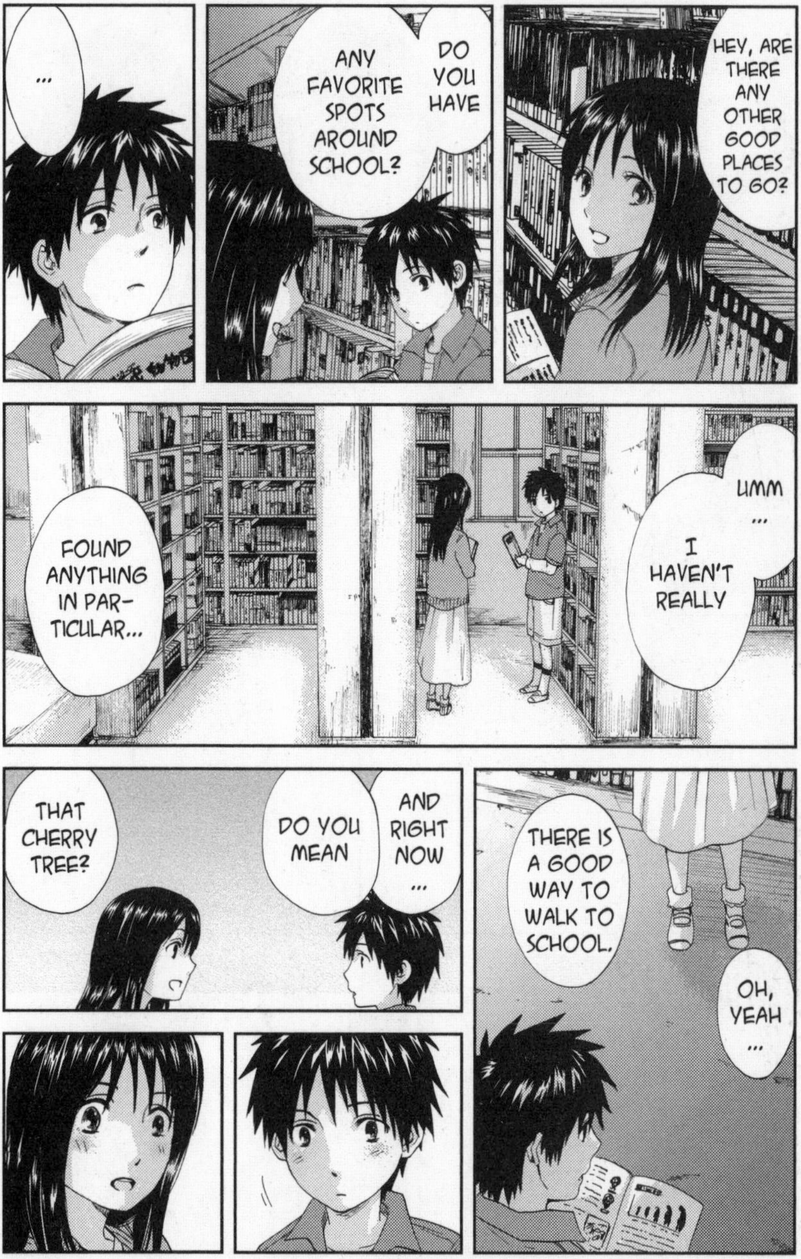
HEY, ARE THERE ANY OTHER GOOD PLACES TO GO?
DO YOU HAVE
ANY FAVORITE SPOTS AROUND SCHOOL?
...
UMM ...
I HAVEN'T REALLY
FOUND ANYTHING IN PAR-TICULAR...
THERE IS A GOOD WAY TO WALK TO SCHOOL.
OH, YEAH ...
AND RIGHT NOW ...
DO YOU MEAN
THAT CHERRY TREE?

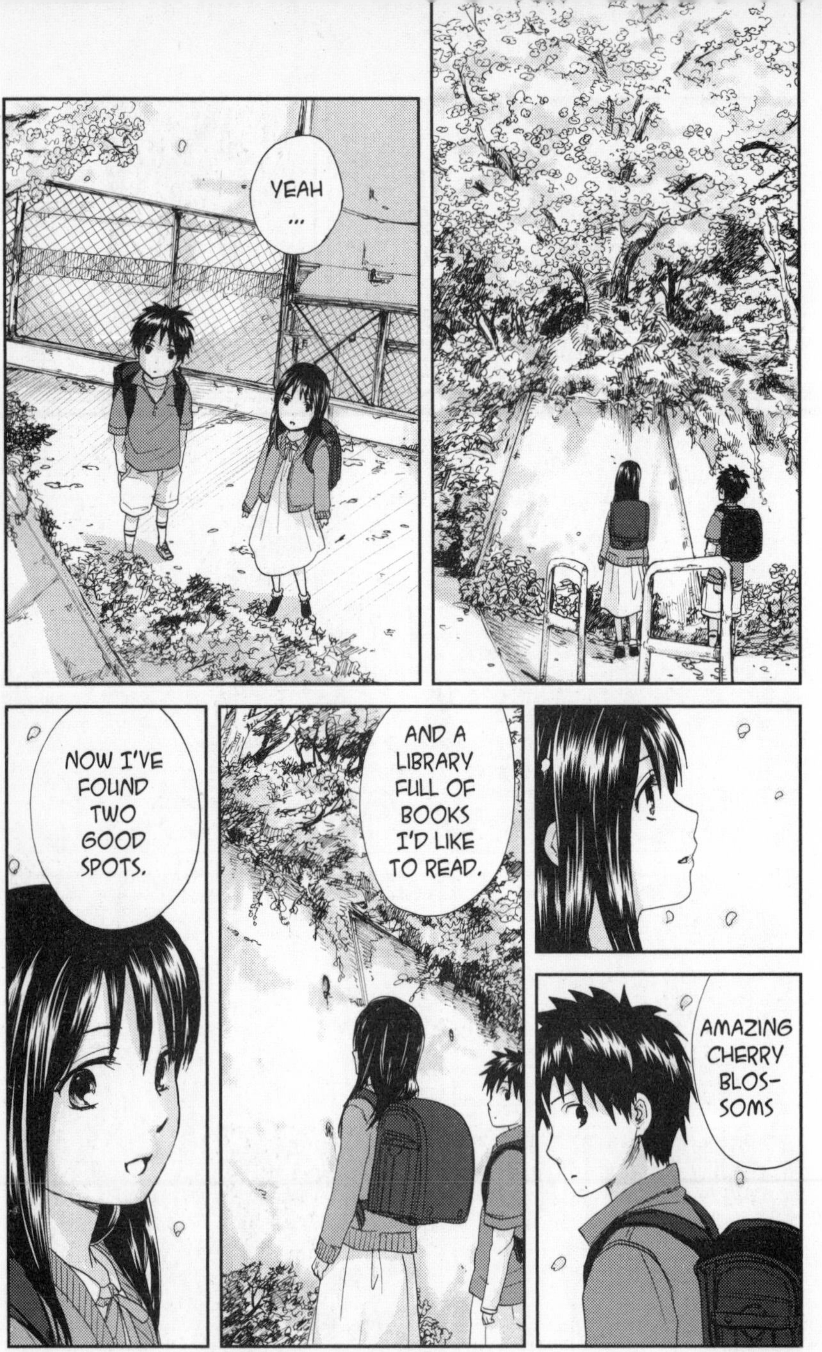
YEAH ...
AMAZING CHERRY BLOS-SOMS
AND A LIBRARY FULL OF BOOKS I'D LIKE TO READ.
NOW I'VE FOUND TWO GOOD SPOTS.

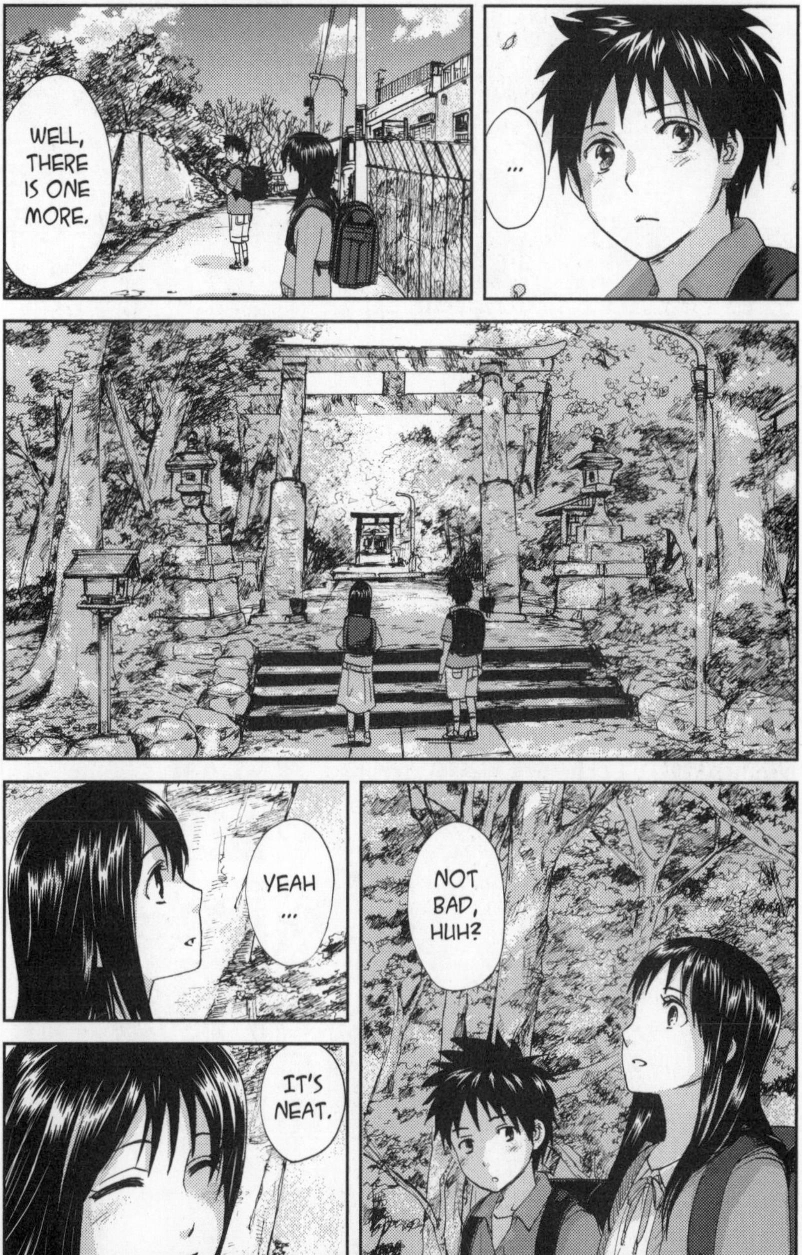
...
WELL, THERE IS ONE MORE.
NOT BAD, HUH?
YEAH ...
IT'S NEAT.

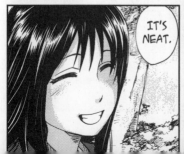

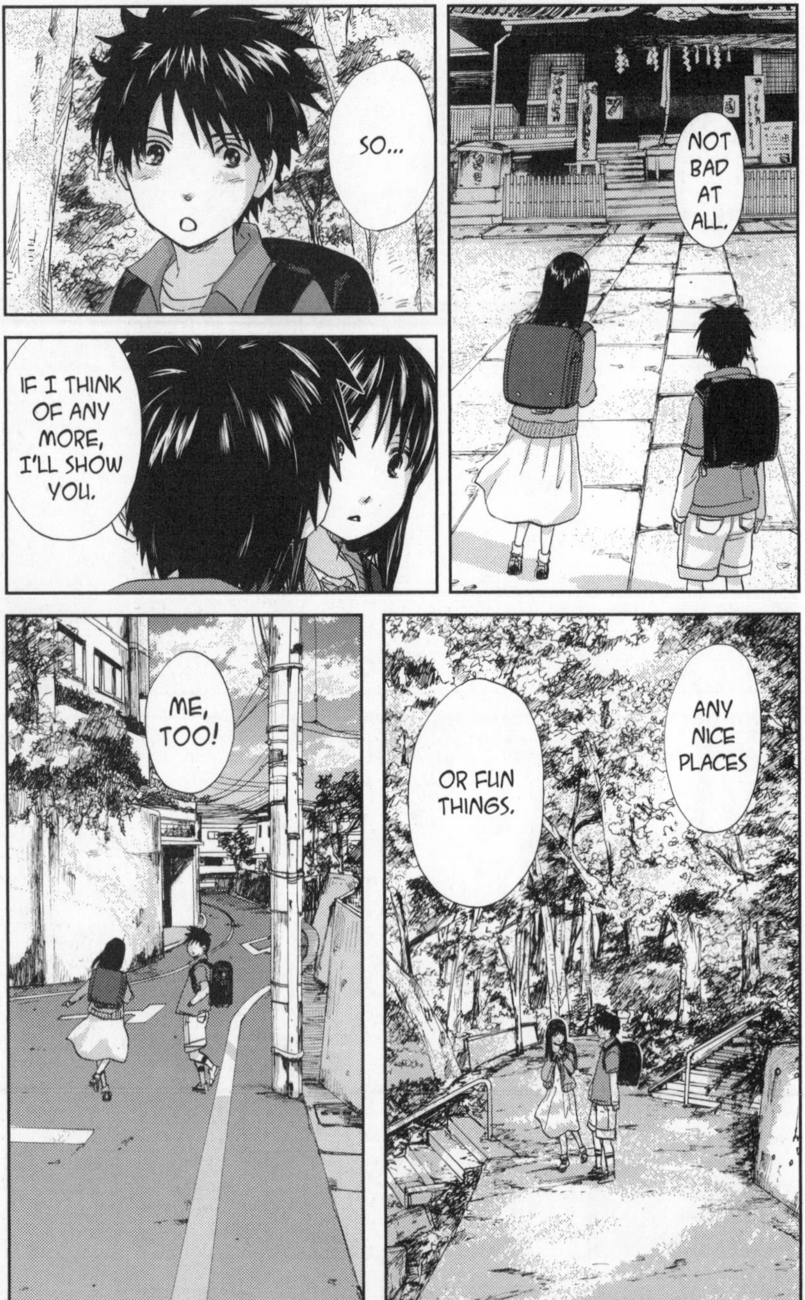
NOT BAD AT ALL.
SO...
IF I THINK OF ANY MORE, I'LL SHOW YOU.
ANY NICE PLACES
OR FUN THINGS.
ME, TOO!

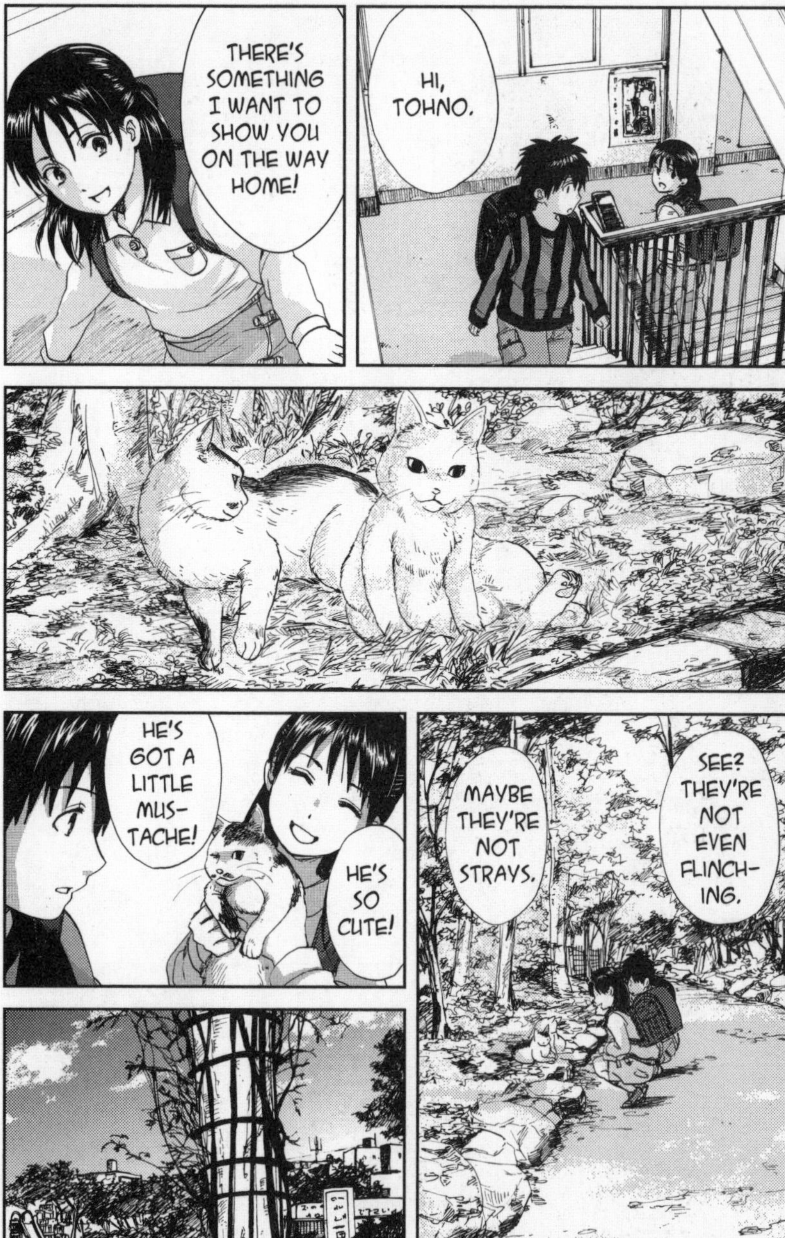
HI, TOHNO.
THERE'S SOMETHING I WANT TO SHOW YOU ON THE WAY HOME!
SEE? THEY'RE NOT EVEN FLINCH-ING.
MAYBE THEY'RE NOT STRAYS.
HE'S SO CUTE!
HE'S GOT A LITTLE MUS-TACHE!

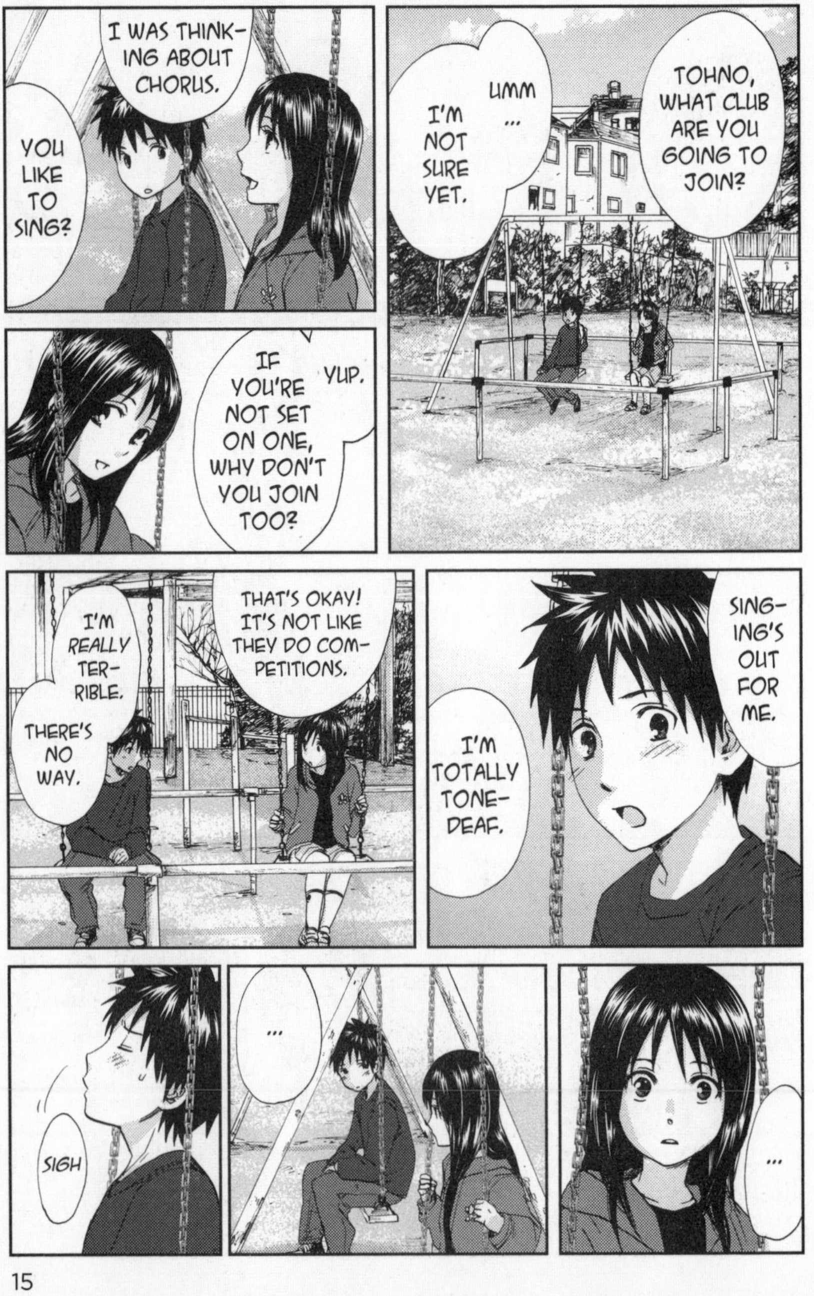
TOHNO, WHAT CLUB ARE YOU GOING TO JOIN?
UMM ...
I'M NOT SURE YET.
I WAS THINKING ABOUT CHORUS.
YOU LIKE TO SING?
YUP.
IF YOU'RE NOT SET ON ONE, WHY DON'T YOU JOIN TOO?
SINGING'S OUT FOR ME.
I'M TOTALLY TONE-DEAF.
THAT'S OKAY! IT'S NOT LIKE THEY DO COMPETITIONS.
I'M REALLY TERRIBLE.
THERE'S NO WAY.
...
...
SIGH

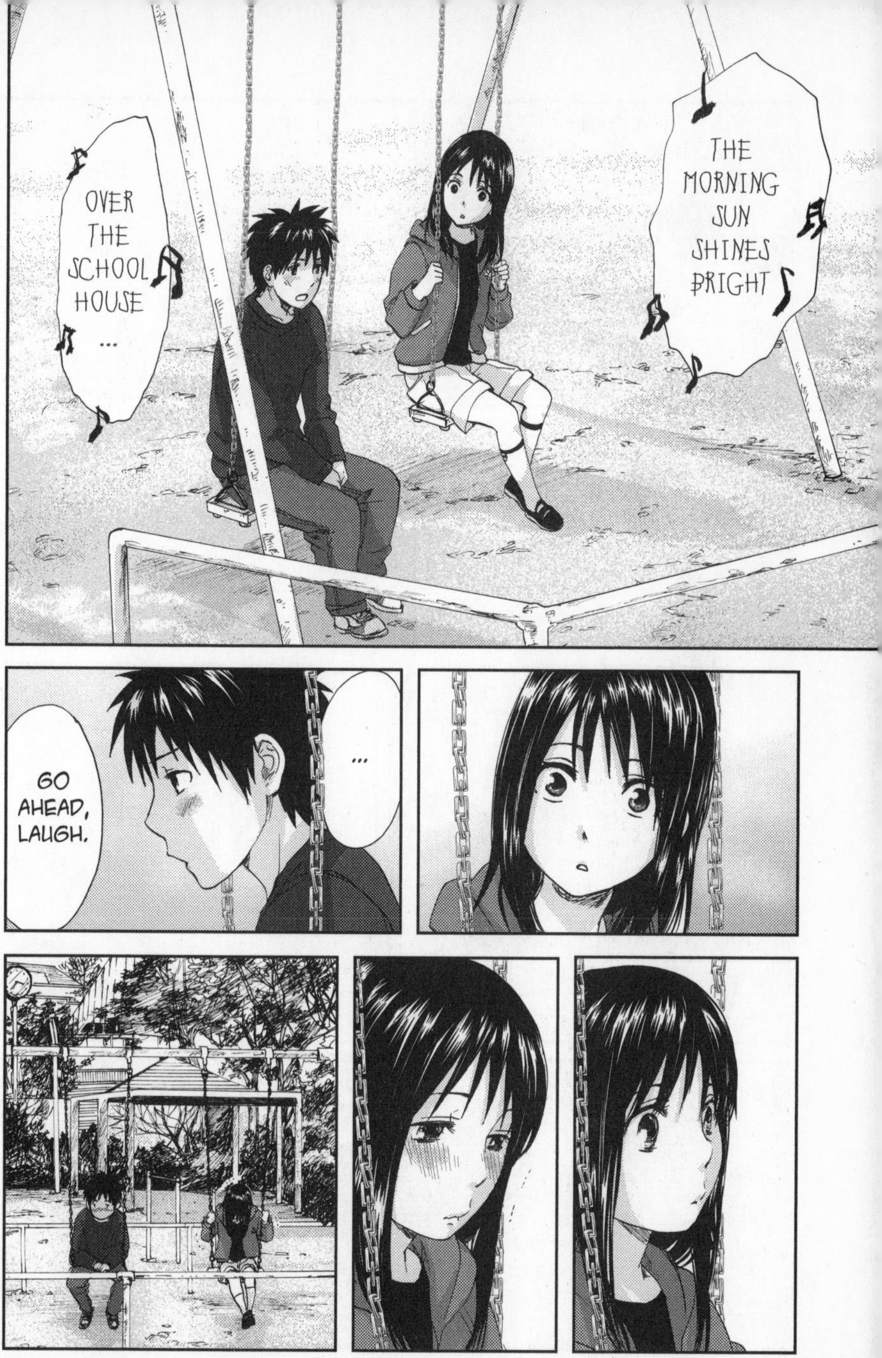
THE MORNING SUN SHINES BRIGHT
OVER THE SCHOOL HOUSE ...
...
GO AHEAD, LAUGH.

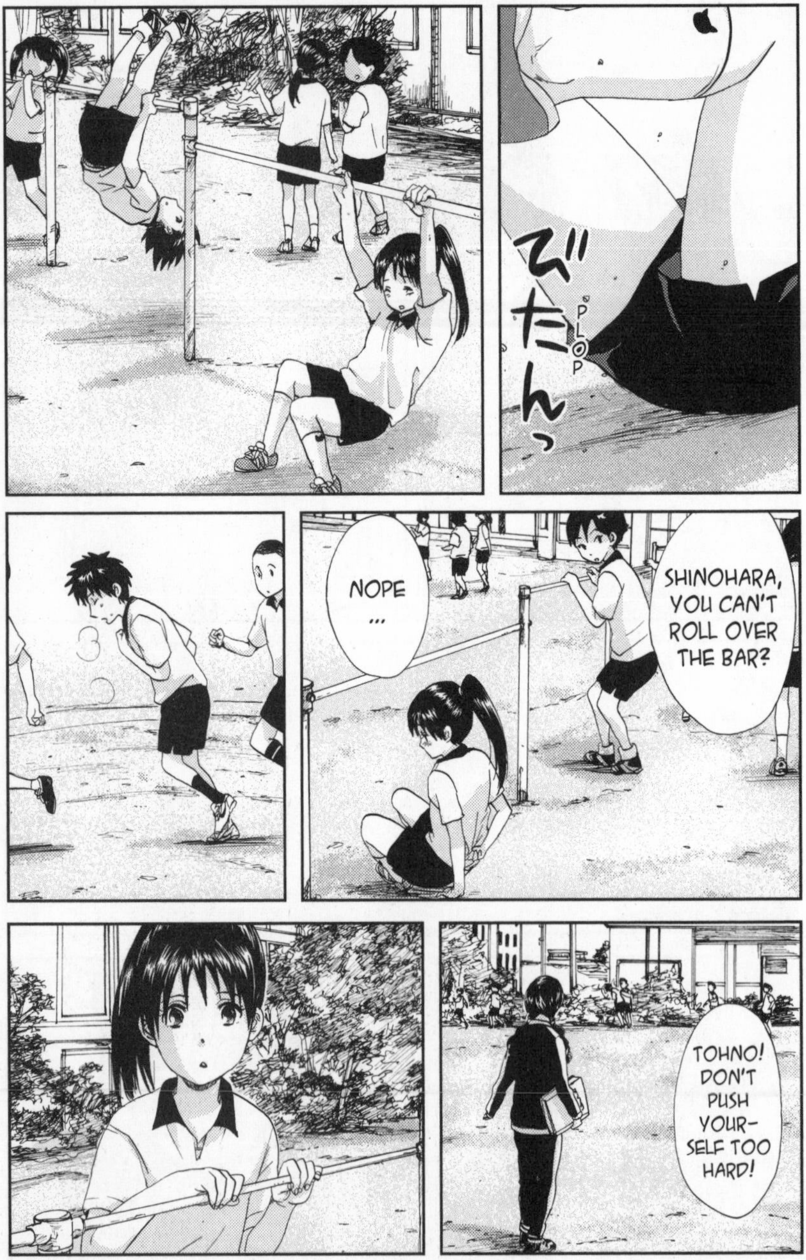
びたんっ
PLOP
SHINOHARA, YOU CAN'T ROLL OVER THE BAR?
NOPE ...
TOHNO! DON'T PUSH YOUR-SELF TOO HARD!

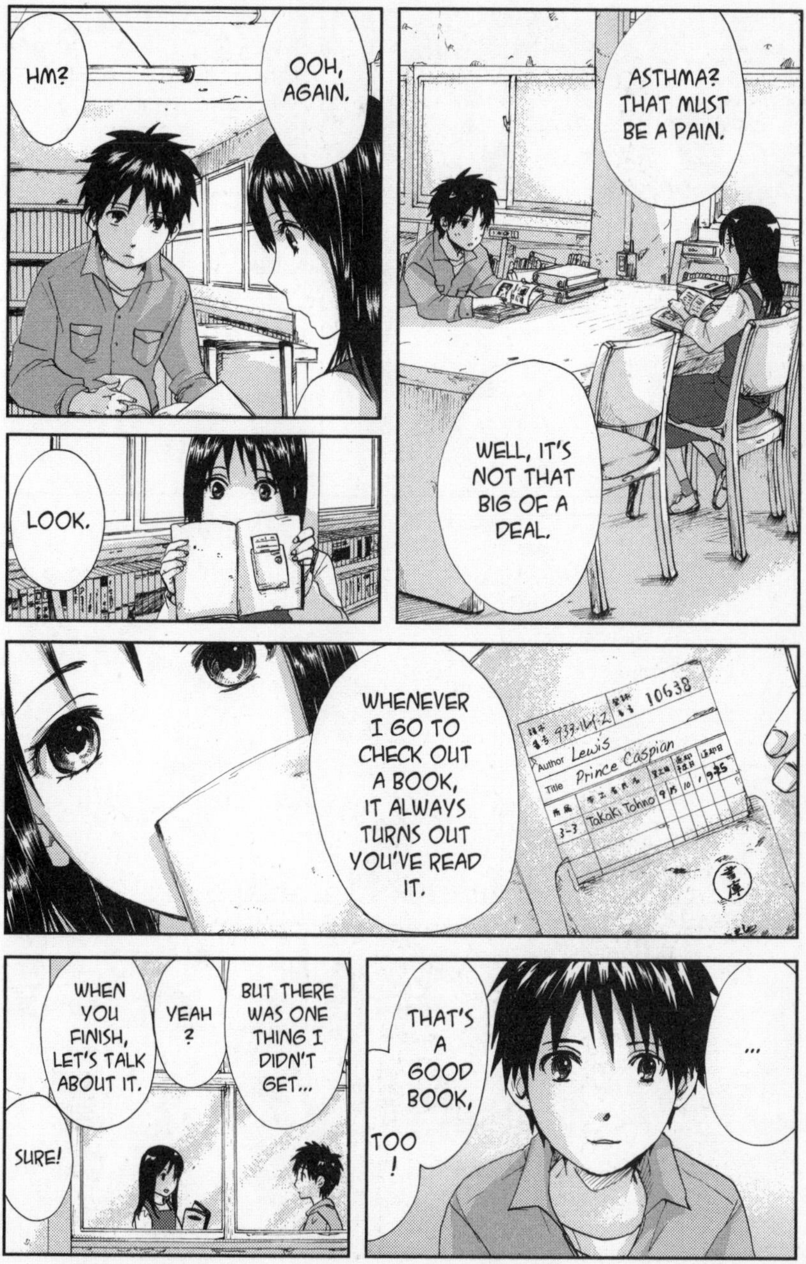
ASTHMA? THAT MUST BE A PAIN.
WELL, IT'S NOT THAT BIG OF A DEAL.
OOH, AGAIN.
HM?
LOOK.
WHENEVER I GO TO CHECK OUT A BOOK, IT ALWAYS TURNS OUT YOU'VE READ IT.
10638
Author Lewis
Title Prince Caspian
3-3 Takaki Tohno
...
THAT'S A GOOD BOOK, TOO!
BUT THERE WAS ONE THING I DIDN'T GET...
YEAH?
WHEN YOU FINISH, LET'S TALK ABOUT IT.
SURE!

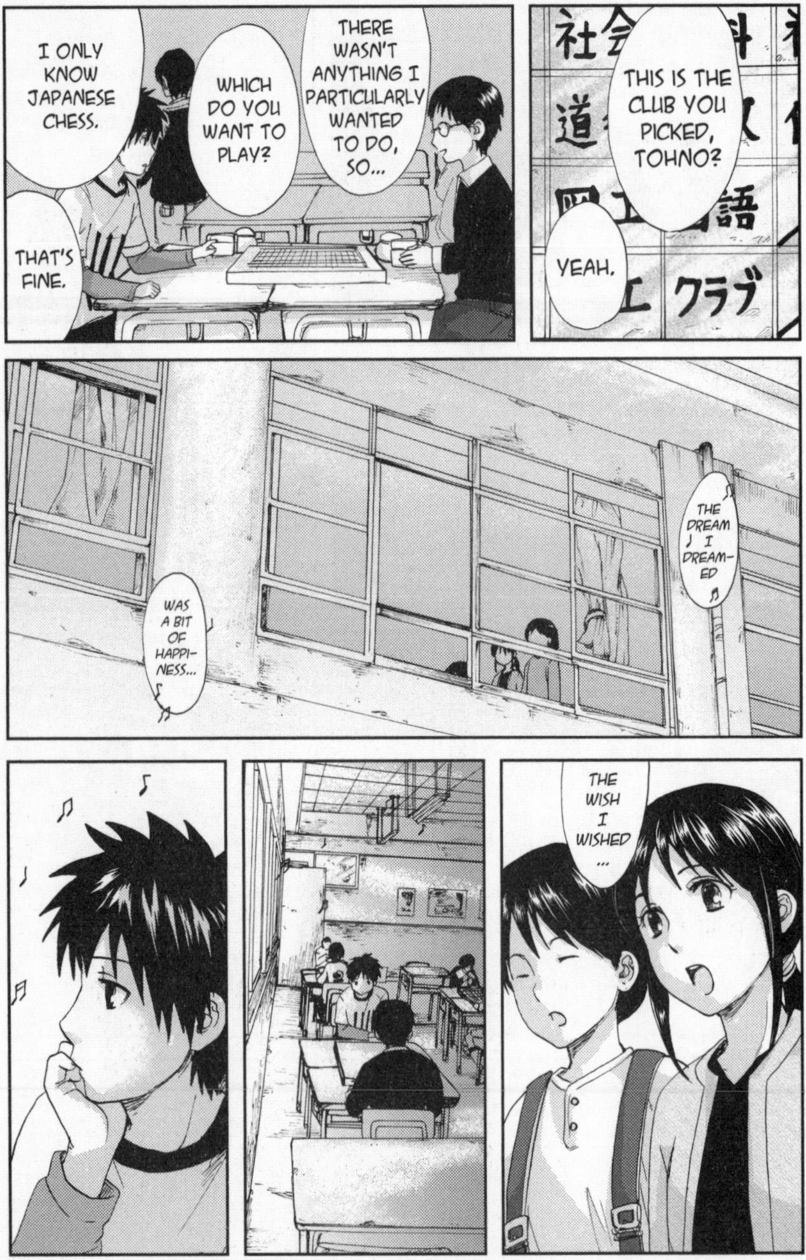
THIS IS THE CLUB YOU PICKED, TOHNO?
YEAH.
THERE WASN'T ANYTHING I PARTICULARLY WANTED TO DO, SO...
WHICH DO YOU WANT TO PLAY?
I ONLY KNOW JAPANESE CHESS.
THAT'S FINE.
THE DREAM I DREAM-ED
WAS A BIT OF HAPPI-NESS...
THE WISH I WISHED ...

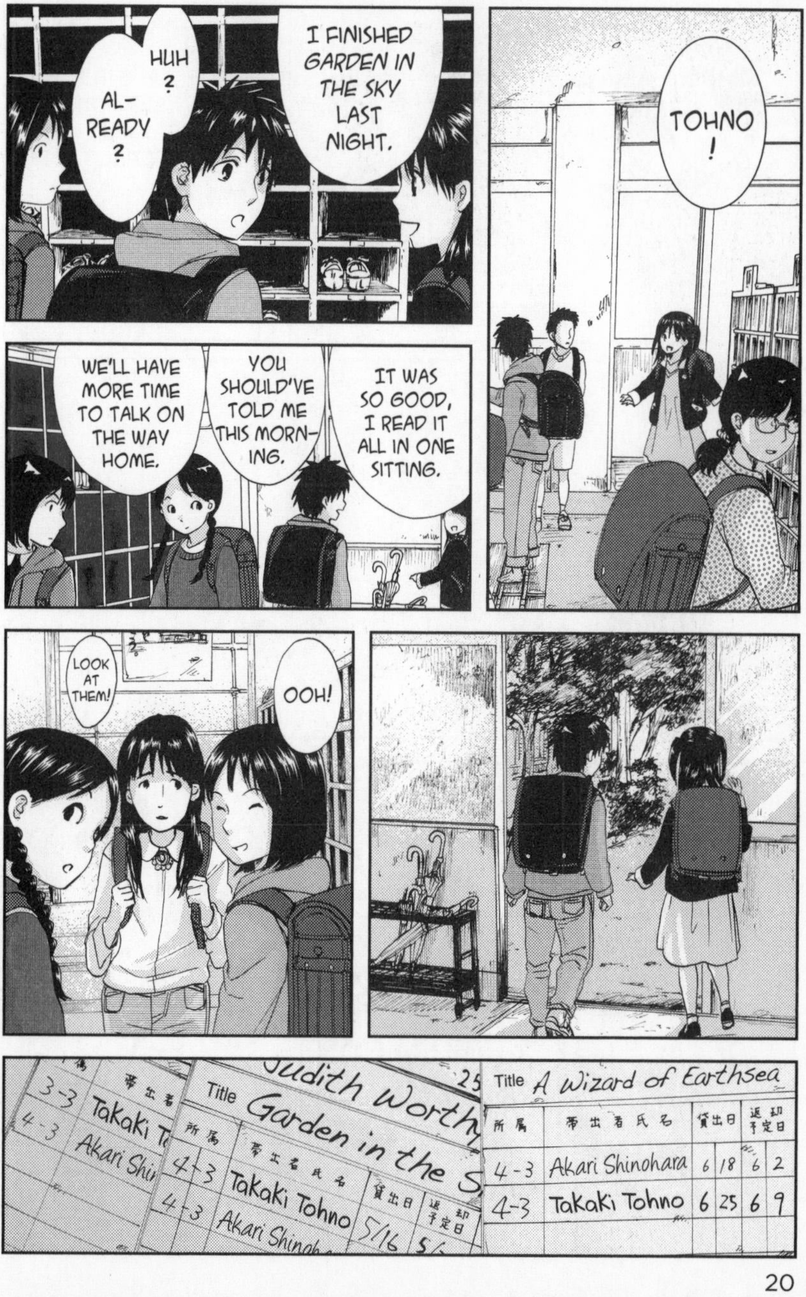
TOHNO!
I FINISHED GARDEN IN THE SKY LAST NIGHT.
HUH? AL-READY?
IT WAS SO GOOD, I READ IT ALL IN ONE SITTING.
YOU SHOULD'VE TOLD ME THIS MORN-ING.
WE'LL HAVE MORE TIME TO TALK ON THE WAY HOME.
OOH!
LOOK AT THEM!
Title A Wizard of Earthsea
所属 帯出者氏名 貸出日 返却予定日
4-3 Akari Shinohara 6 18 6 2
4-3 Takaki Tohno 6 25 6 9
Title Garden in the S
所属 帯出者氏名 貸出日 返却予定日
4-3 Takaki Tohno 5/16
4-3 Akari Shinoh
udith Worth
25
3-3 Takaki To
4-3 Akari Shi

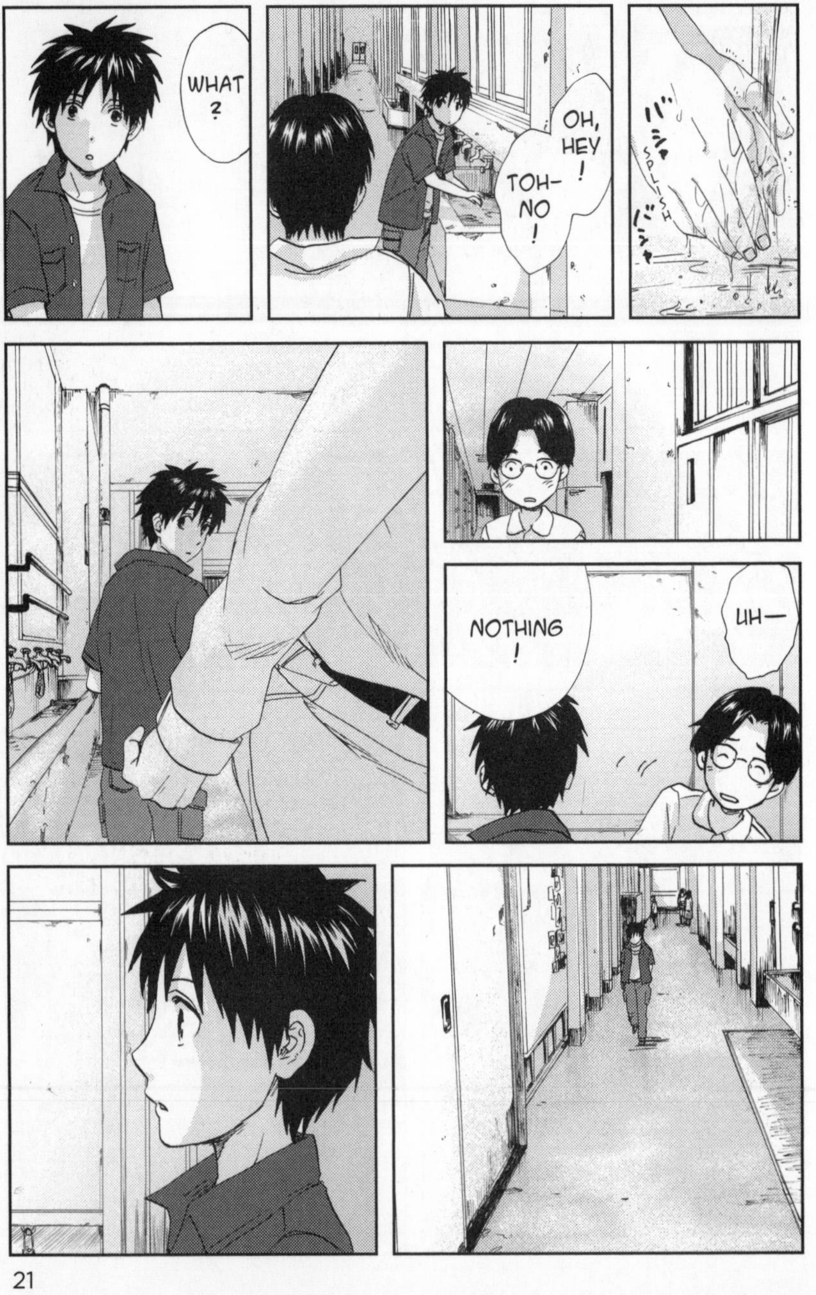
バシャ
SPLISH
バシャ
OH, HEY!
TOH-NO!
WHAT?
UH—
NOTHING!

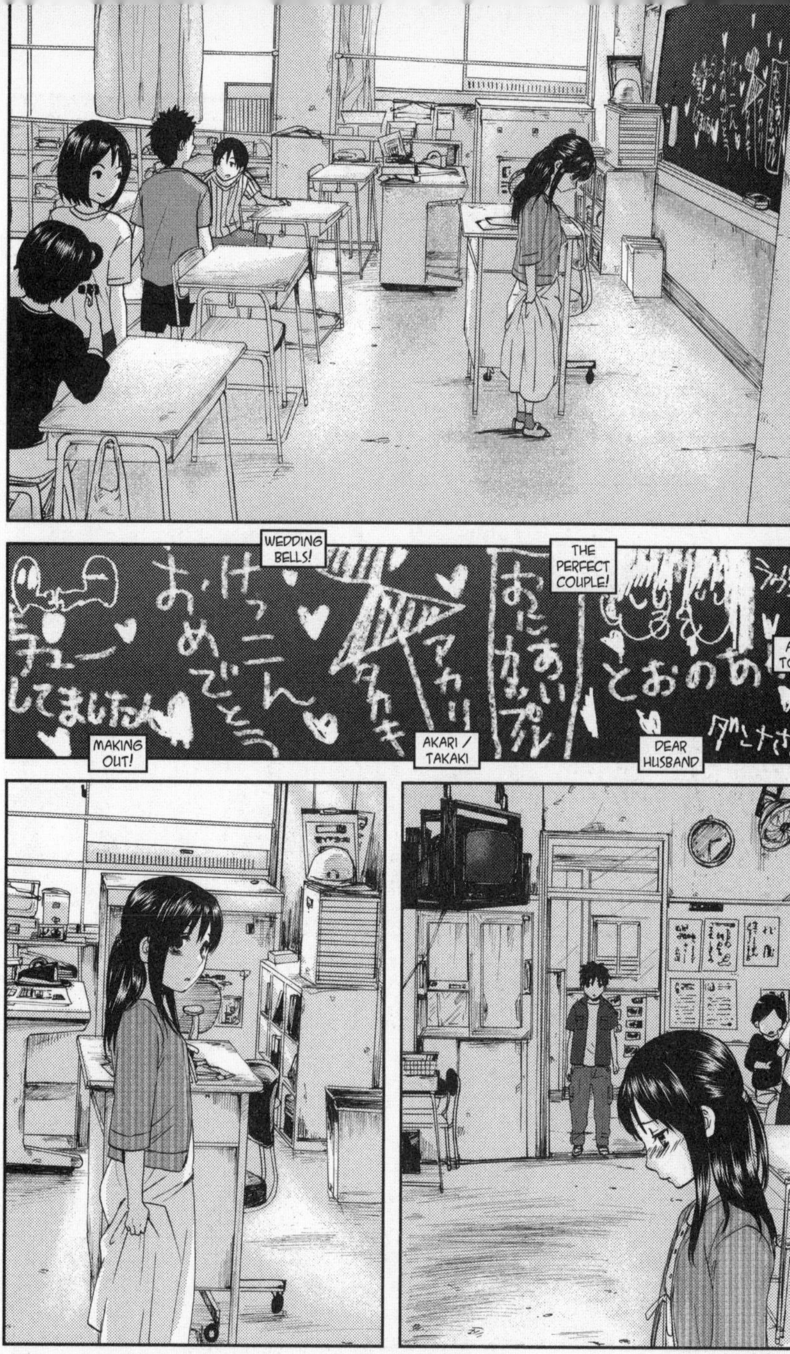
AKARI TOHNO
DEAR HUSBAND
THE PERFECT COUPLE!
AKARI / TAKAKI
WEDDING BELLS!
MAKING OUT!

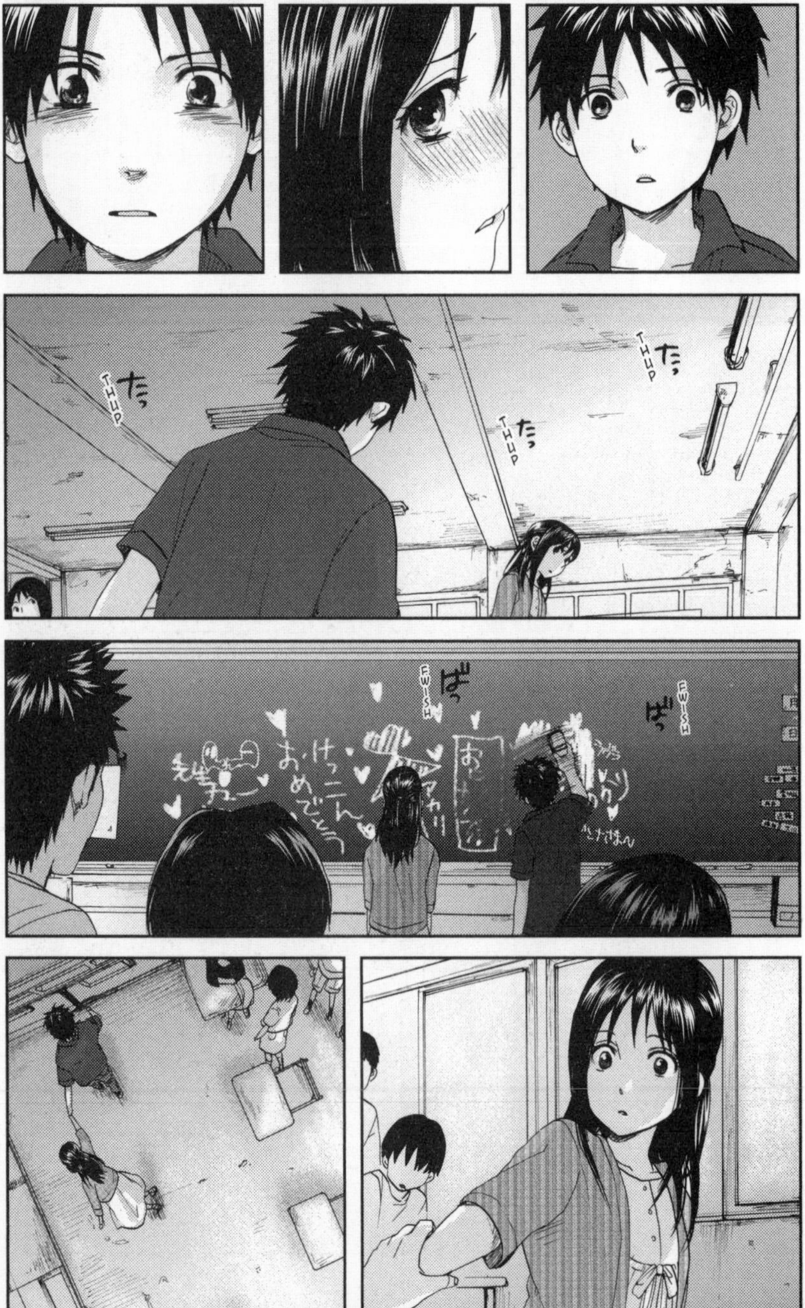
THUP
たっ
THUP
たっ
THUP
たっ
FWISH
ばっ
FWISH
ばっ
アカリ

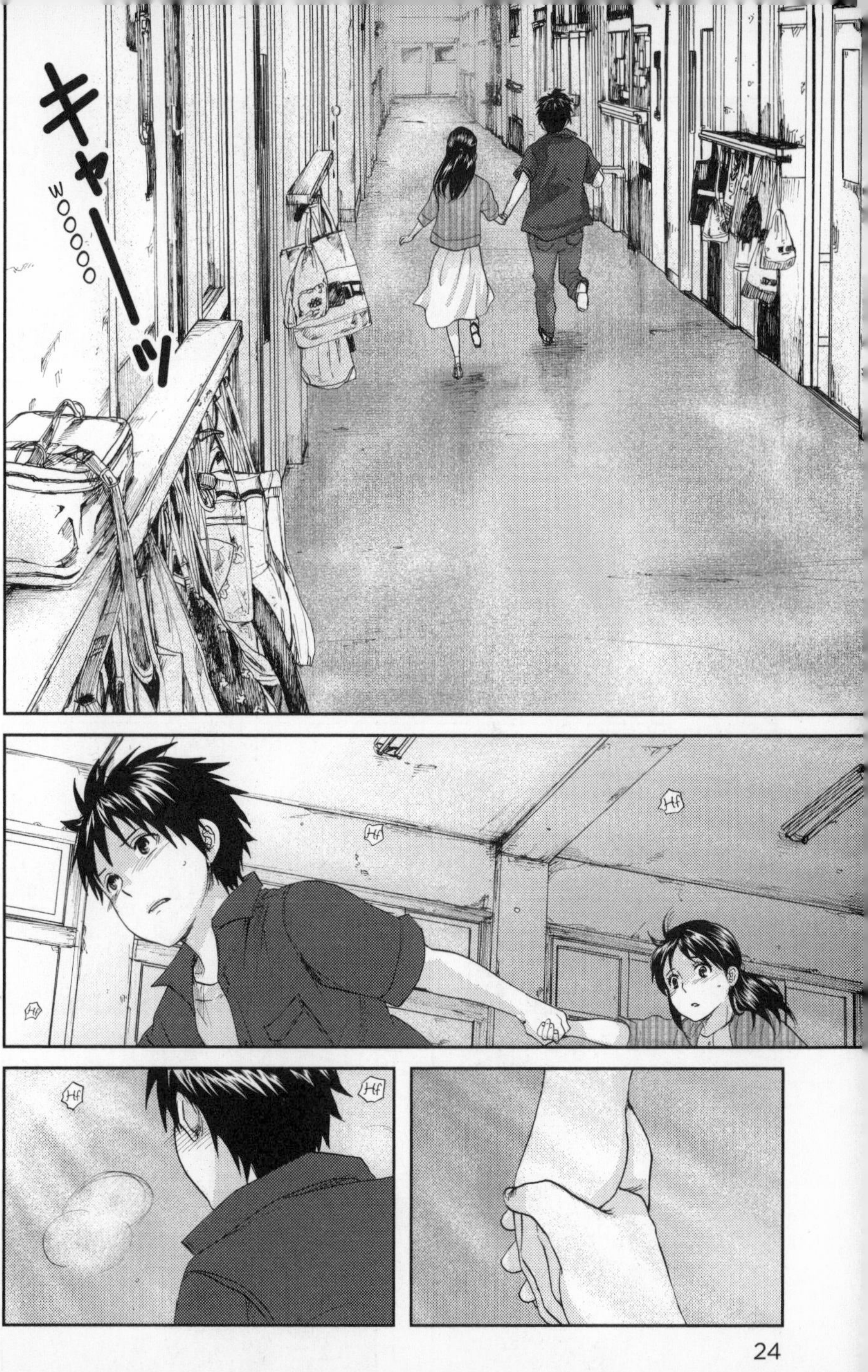
キャーーッ
WOOOOOO
Hf
Hf
Hf
Hf
Hf

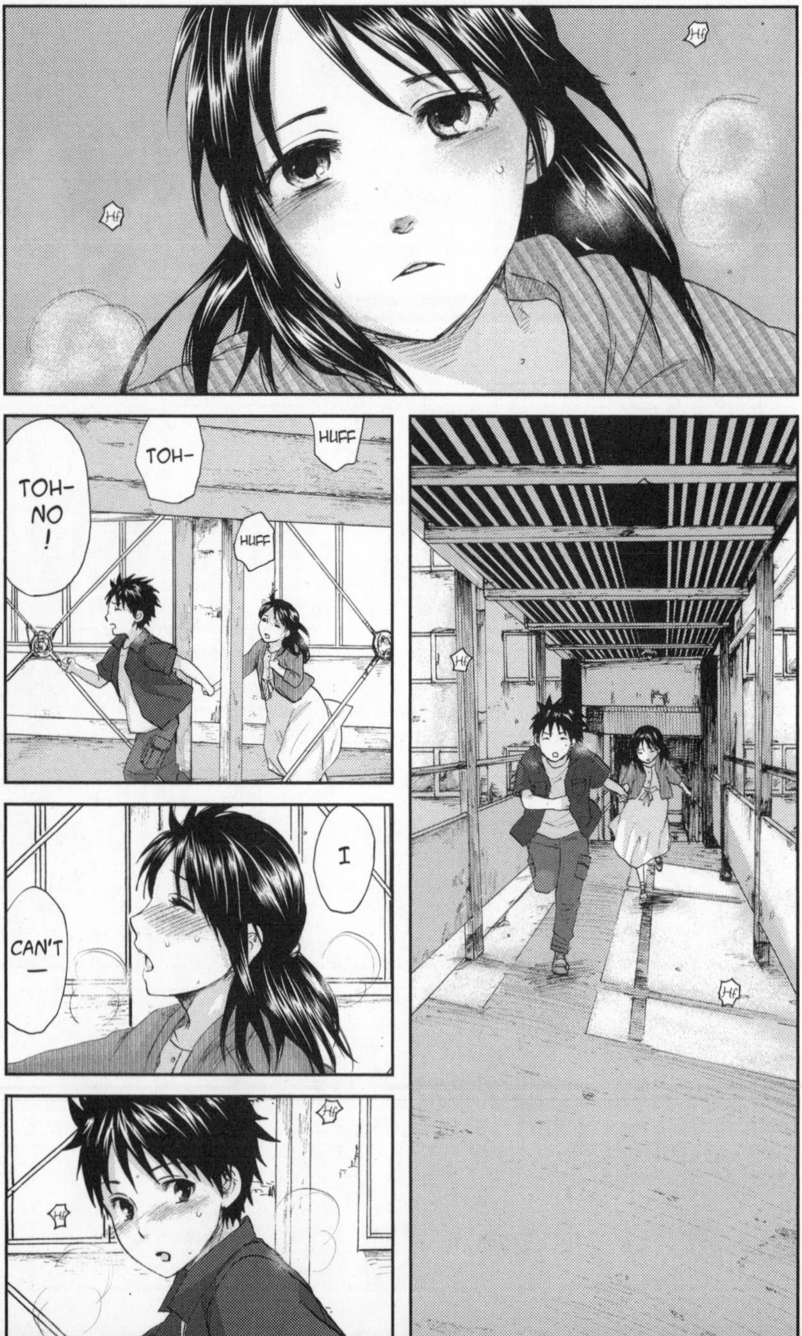
Hf
Hf
Hf
Hf
HUFF
TOH-
TOH-NO!
HUFF
I CAN'T —
Hf
Hf

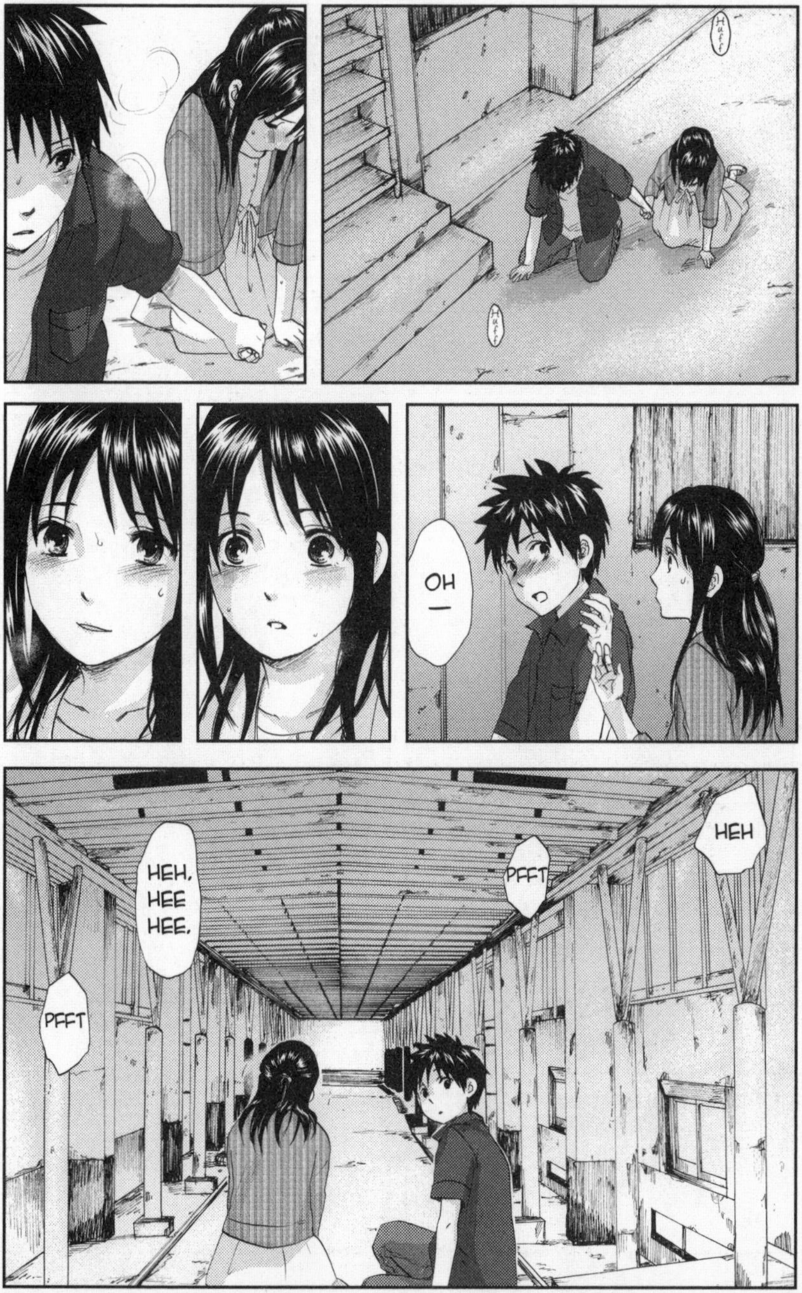
Huff
Huff
OH —
HEH
PFFT
HEH, HEE HEE.
PFFT

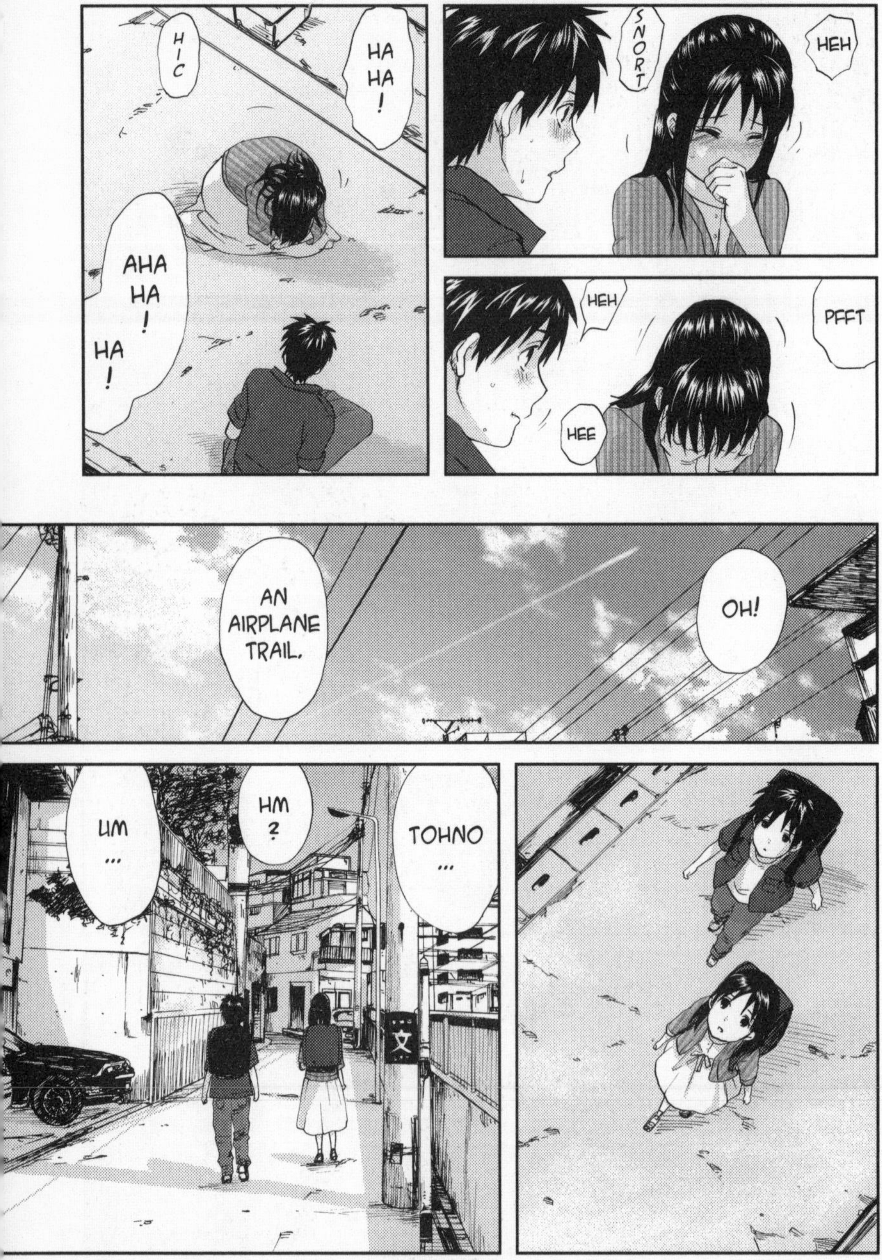
HEH
SNORT
PFFT
HEH
HEE
HA HA!
HIC
AHA HA! HA!
OH!
AN AIRPLANE TRAIL.
TOHNO ...
HM?
UM ...

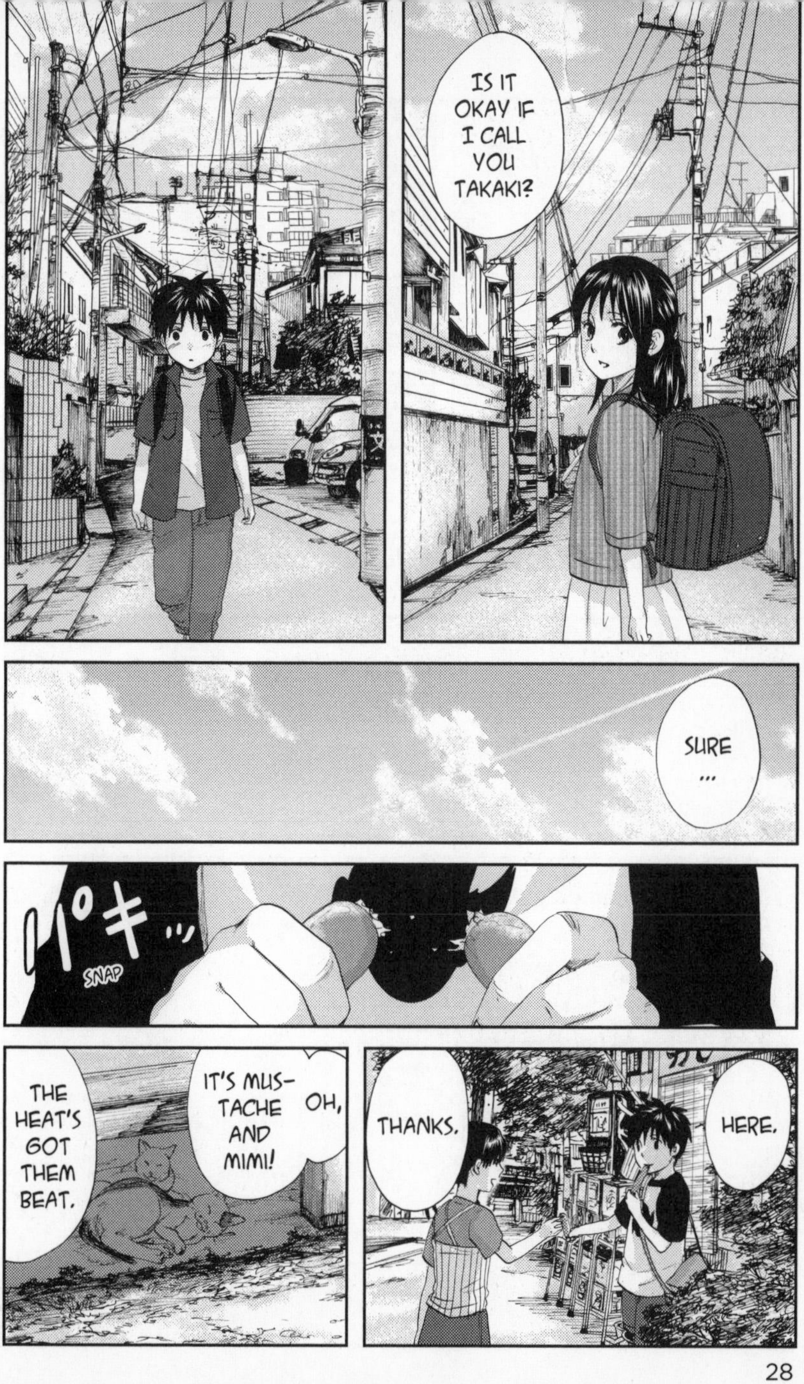
IS IT OKAY IF I CALL YOU TAKAKI?
SURE ...
パキッ
SNAP
HERE.
THANKS.
OH, IT'S MUS-TACHE AND MIMI!
THE HEAT'S GOT THEM BEAT.

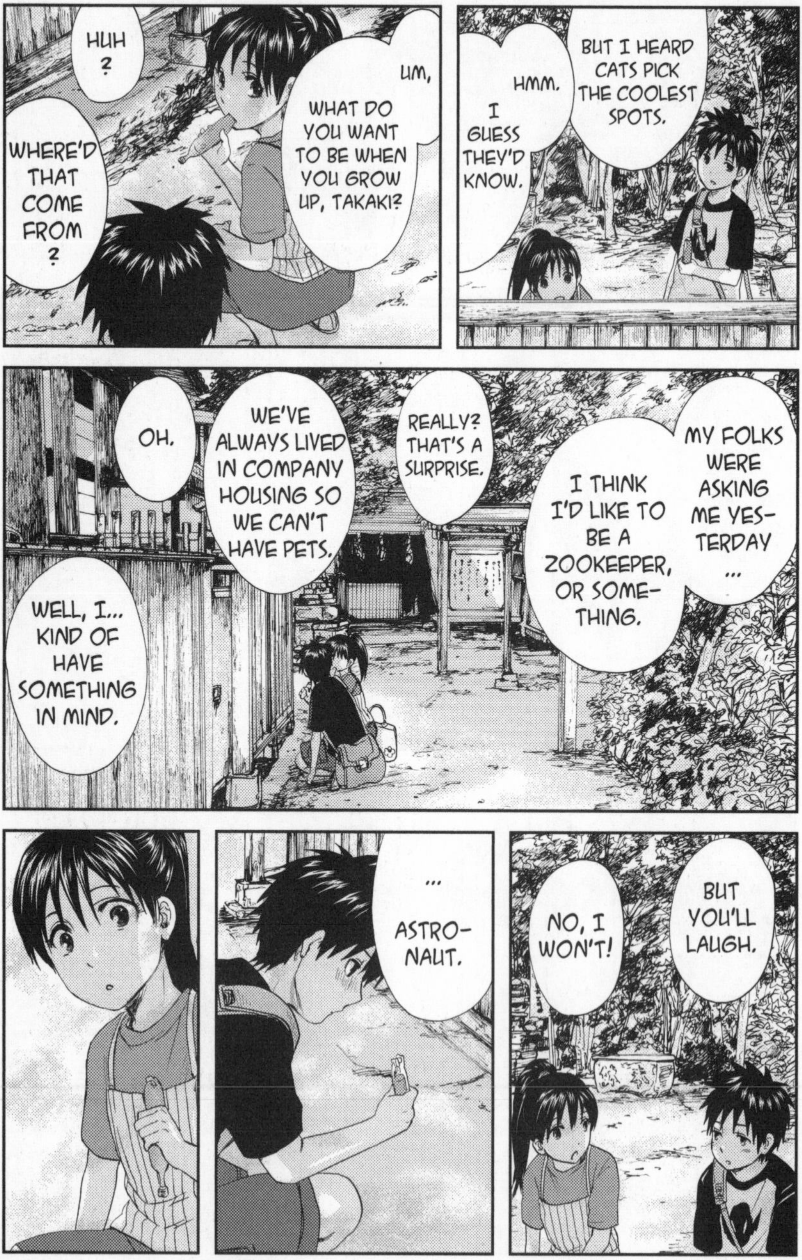
BUT I HEARD CATS PICK THE COOLEST SPOTS.
HMM.
I GUESS THEY'D KNOW.
UM,
WHAT DO YOU WANT TO BE WHEN YOU GROW UP, TAKAKI?
HUH?
WHERE'D THAT COME FROM?
MY FOLKS WERE ASKING ME YES-TERDAY...
I THINK I'D LIKE TO BE A ZOOKEEPER, OR SOME-THING.
REALLY? THAT'S A SURPRISE.
WE'VE ALWAYS LIVED IN COMPANY HOUSING SO WE CAN'T HAVE PETS.
OH.
WELL, I... KIND OF HAVE SOMETHING IN MIND.
BUT YOU'LL LAUGH.
NO, I WON'T!
...
ASTRO-NAUT.

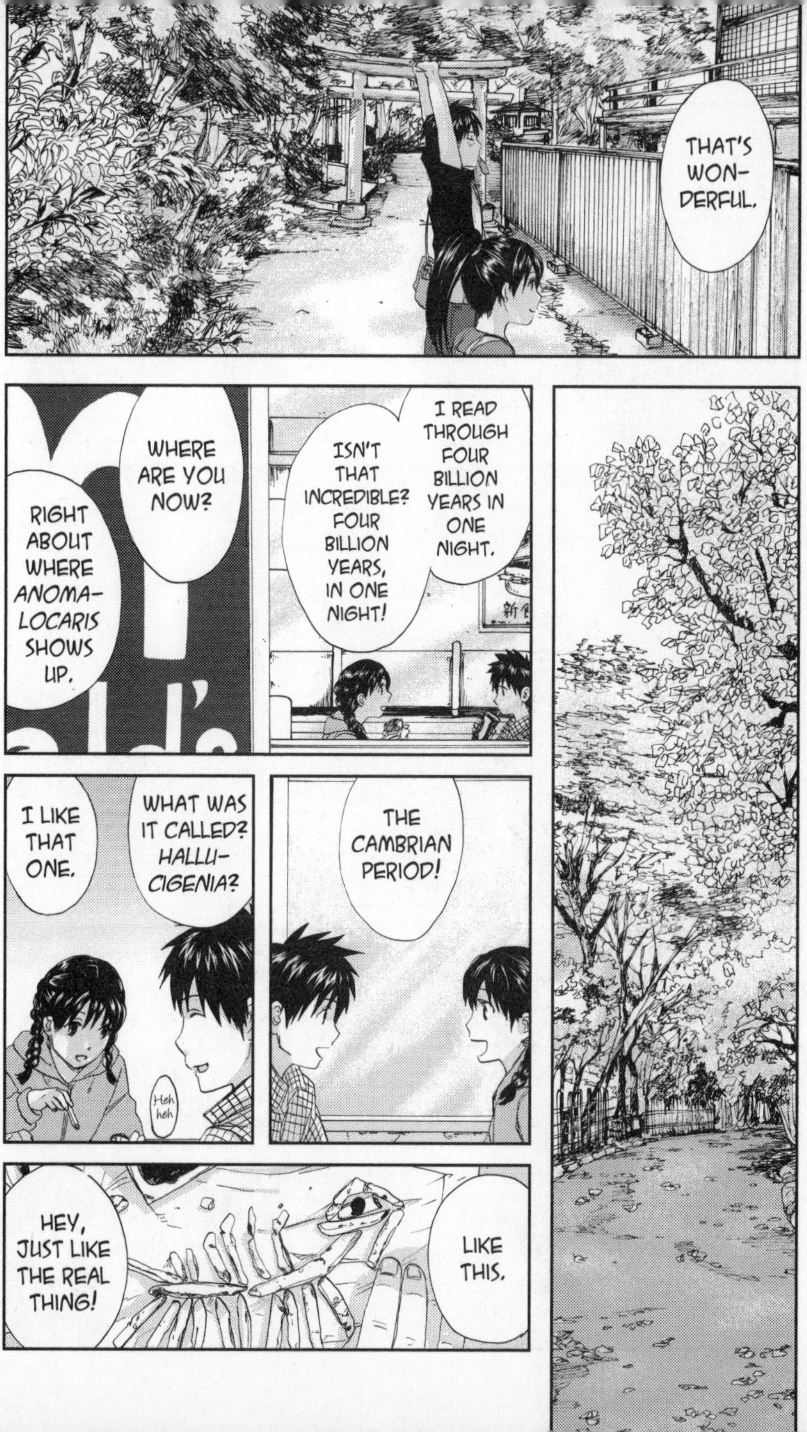
THAT'S WON-DERFUL.
I READ THROUGH FOUR BILLION YEARS IN ONE NIGHT.
ISN'T THAT INCREDIBLE? FOUR BILLION YEARS, IN ONE NIGHT!
WHERE ARE YOU NOW?
RIGHT ABOUT WHERE ANOMA-LOCARIS SHOWS UP.
THE CAMBRIAN PERIOD!
WHAT WAS IT CALLED? HALLU-CIGENIA?
I LIKE THAT ONE.
Heh heh
LIKE THIS.
HEY, JUST LIKE THE REAL THING!

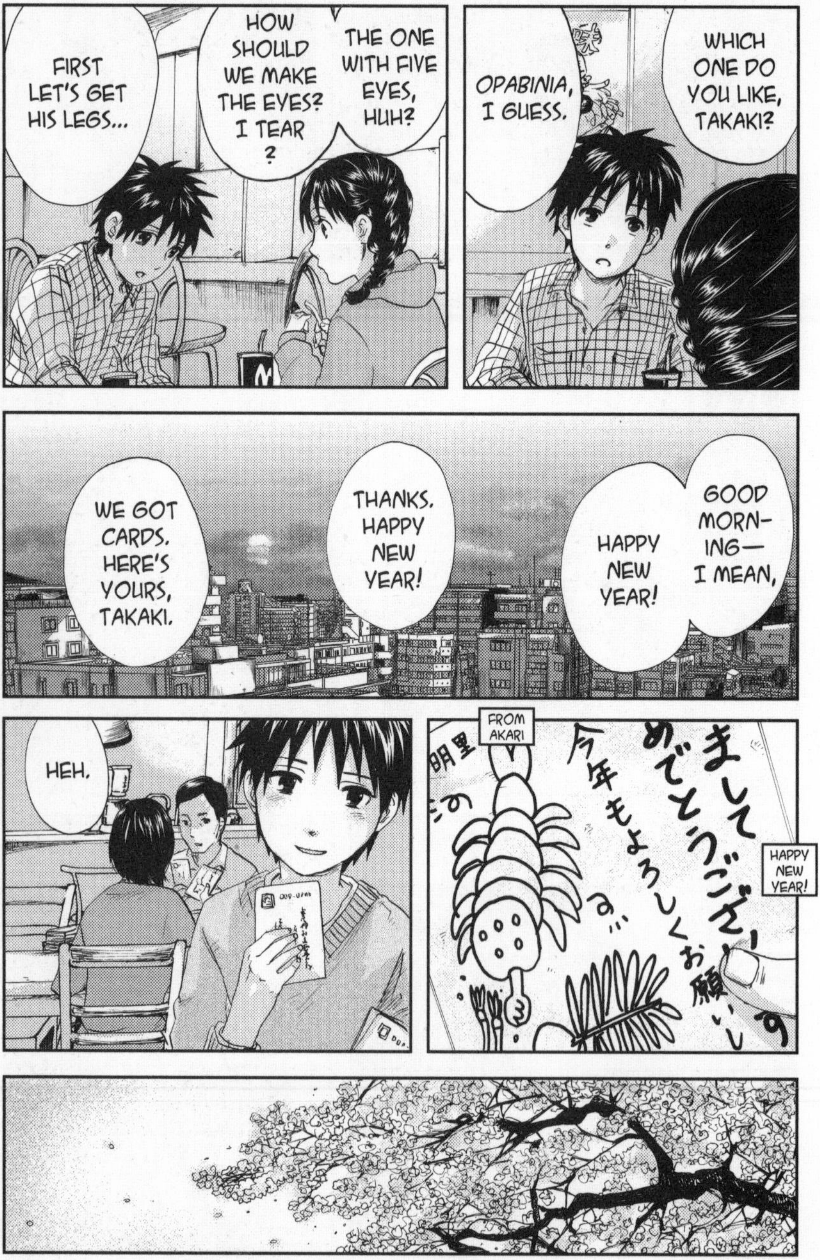
WHICH ONE DO YOU LIKE, TAKAKI?
OPABINIA, I GUESS.
THE ONE WITH FIVE EYES, HUH?
HOW SHOULD WE MAKE THE EYES? I TEAR ?
FIRST LET'S GET HIS LEGS...
GOOD MORNING— I MEAN,
HAPPY NEW YEAR!
THANKS. HAPPY NEW YEAR!
WE GOT CARDS. HERE'S YOURS, TAKAKI.
まして
めでとうござ
今年もよろしくお願いし
ます
明里
FROM AKARI
HAPPY NEW YEAR!
HEH.

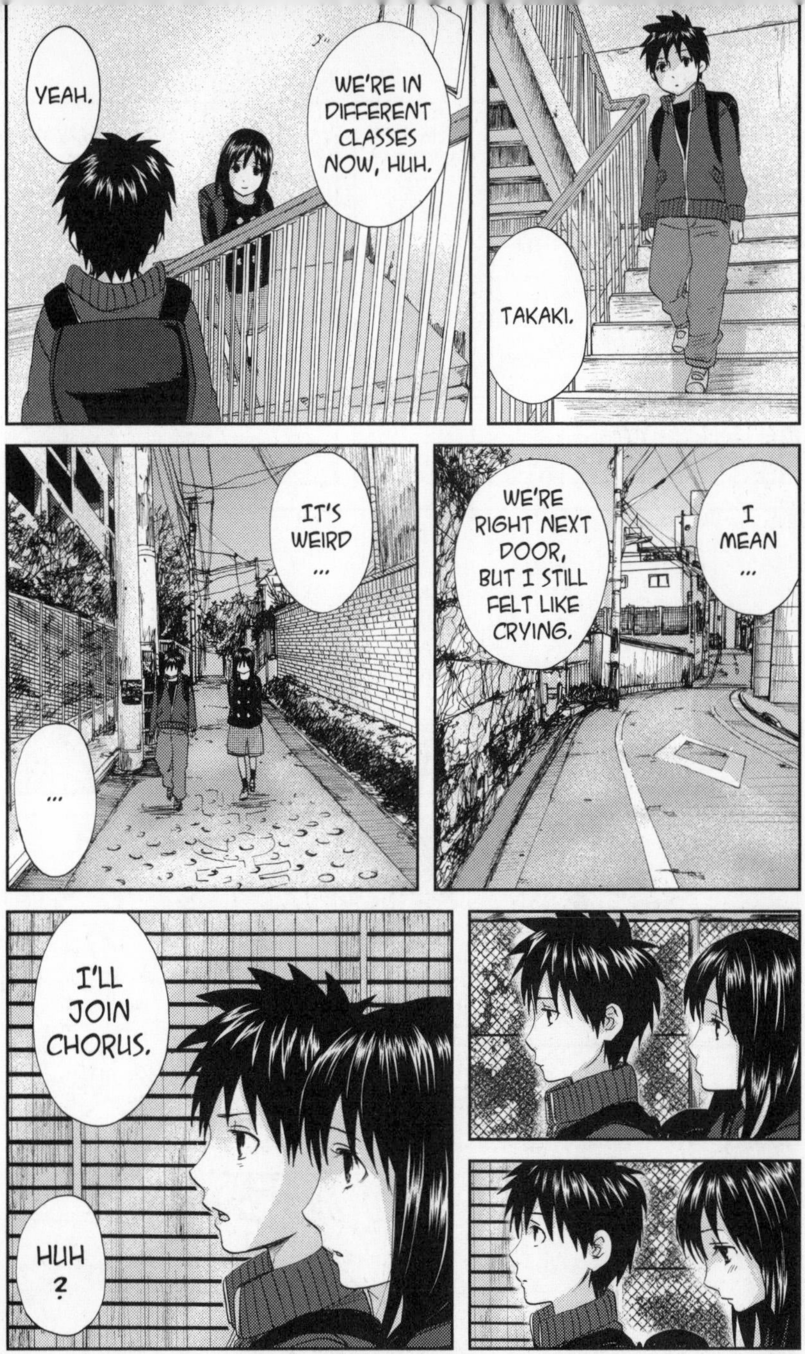
TAKAKI.
WE'RE IN DIFFERENT CLASSES NOW, HUH.
YEAH.
I MEAN ...
WE'RE RIGHT NEXT DOOR, BUT I STILL FELT LIKE CRYING.
IT'S WEIRD ...
...
I'LL JOIN CHORUS.
HUH ?

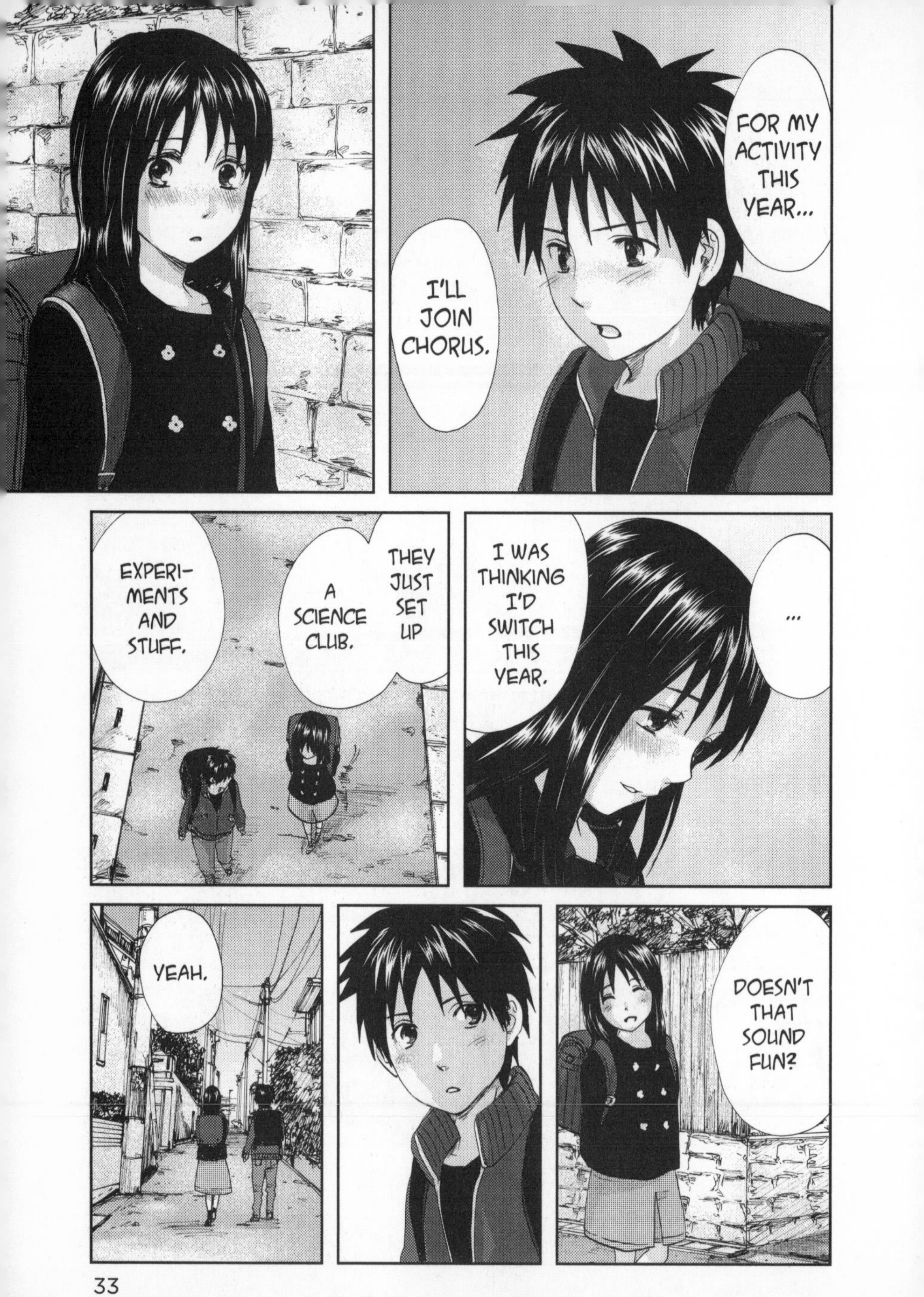
FOR MY ACTIVITY THIS YEAR...
I'LL JOIN CHORUS.
...
I WAS THINKING I'D SWITCH THIS YEAR.
THEY JUST SET UP
A SCIENCE CLUB.
EXPERI-MENTS AND STUFF.
DOESN'T THAT SOUND FUN?
YEAH.

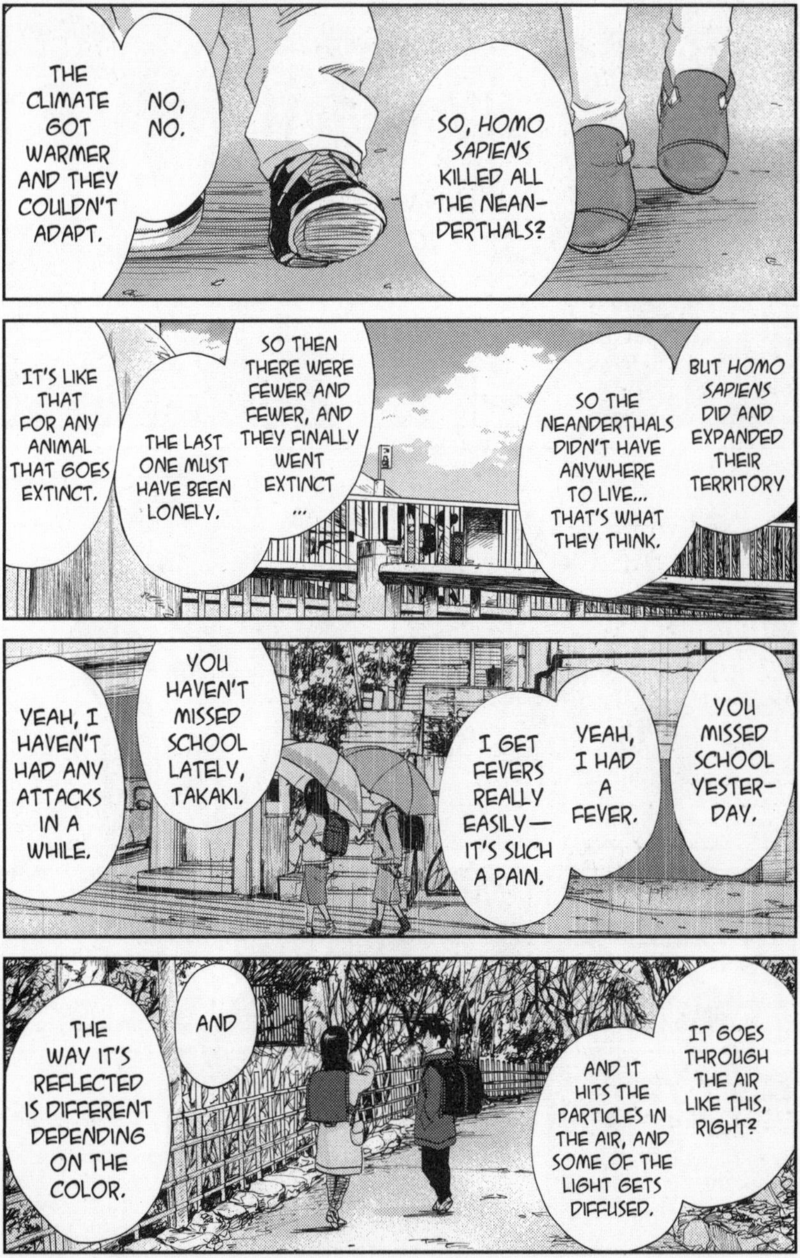
SO, HOMO SAPIENS KILLED ALL THE NEAN-DERTHALS?
NO, NO.
THE CLIMATE GOT WARMER AND THEY COULDN'T ADAPT.
BUT HOMO SAPIENS DID AND EXPANDED THEIR TERRITORY
SO THE NEANDERTHALS DIDN'T HAVE ANYWHERE TO LIVE... THAT'S WHAT THEY THINK.
SO THEN THERE WERE FEWER AND FEWER, AND THEY FINALLY WENT EXTINCT ...
THE LAST ONE MUST HAVE BEEN LONELY.
IT'S LIKE THAT FOR ANY ANIMAL THAT GOES EXTINCT.
YOU MISSED SCHOOL YESTER-DAY.
YEAH, I HAD A FEVER.
I GET FEVERS REALLY EASILY— IT'S SUCH A PAIN.
YOU HAVEN'T MISSED SCHOOL LATELY, TAKAKI.
YEAH, I HAVEN'T HAD ANY ATTACKS IN A WHILE.
IT GOES THROUGH THE AIR LIKE THIS, RIGHT?
AND IT HITS THE PARTICLES IN THE AIR, AND SOME OF THE LIGHT GETS DIFFUSED.
AND
THE WAY IT'S REFLECTED IS DIFFERENT DEPENDING ON THE COLOR.

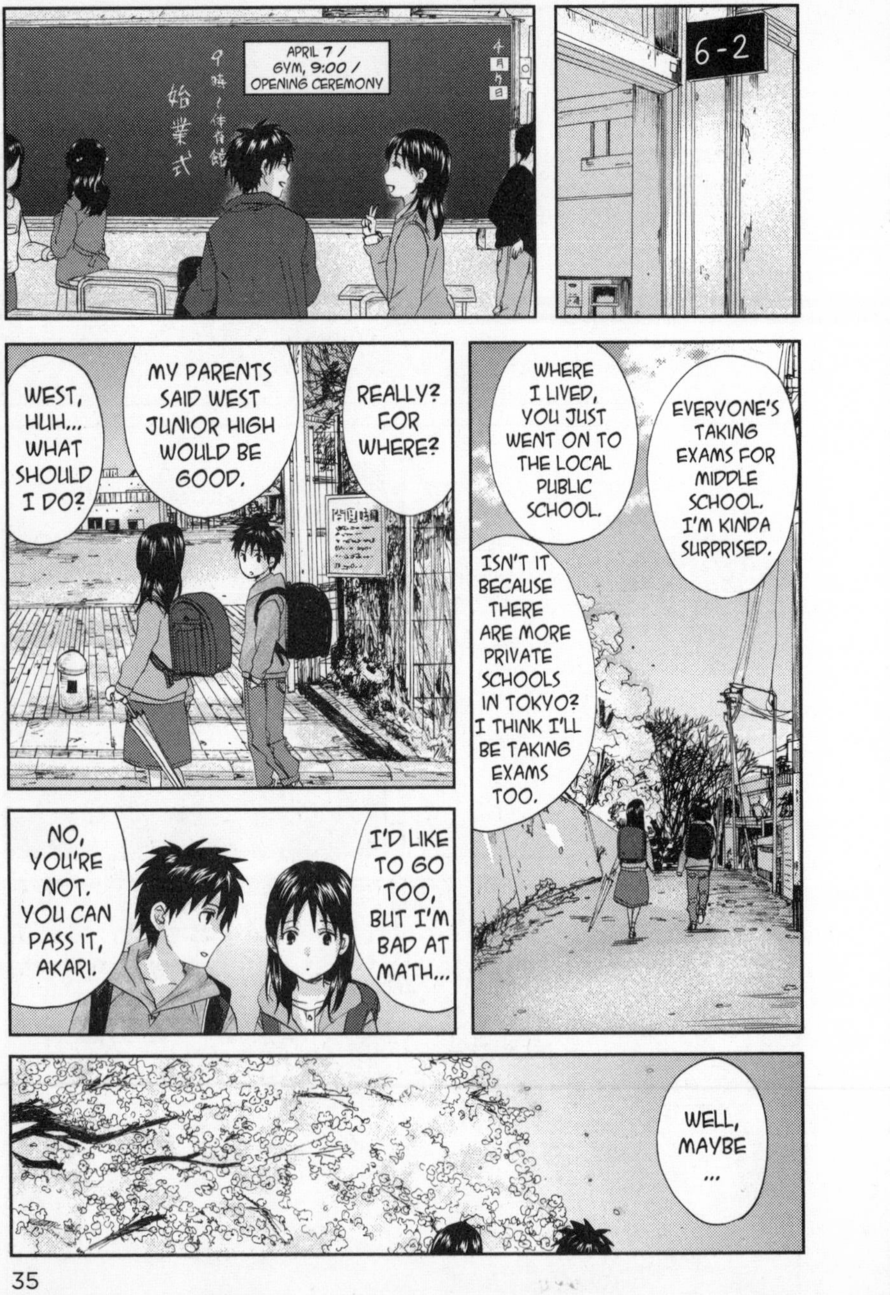
6-2
APRIL 7 / GYM, 9:00 / OPENING CEREMONY
4月7日
9時/体育館
始業式
EVERYONE'S TAKING EXAMS FOR MIDDLE SCHOOL. I'M KINDA SURPRISED.
WHERE I LIVED, YOU JUST WENT ON TO THE LOCAL PUBLIC SCHOOL.
ISN'T IT BECAUSE THERE ARE MORE PRIVATE SCHOOLS IN TOKYO? I THINK I'LL BE TAKING EXAMS TOO.
REALLY? FOR WHERE?
MY PARENTS SAID WEST JUNIOR HIGH WOULD BE GOOD.
WEST, HUH... WHAT SHOULD I DO?
I'D LIKE TO GO TOO, BUT I'M BAD AT MATH...
NO, YOU'RE NOT. YOU CAN PASS IT, AKARI.
WELL, MAYBE ...

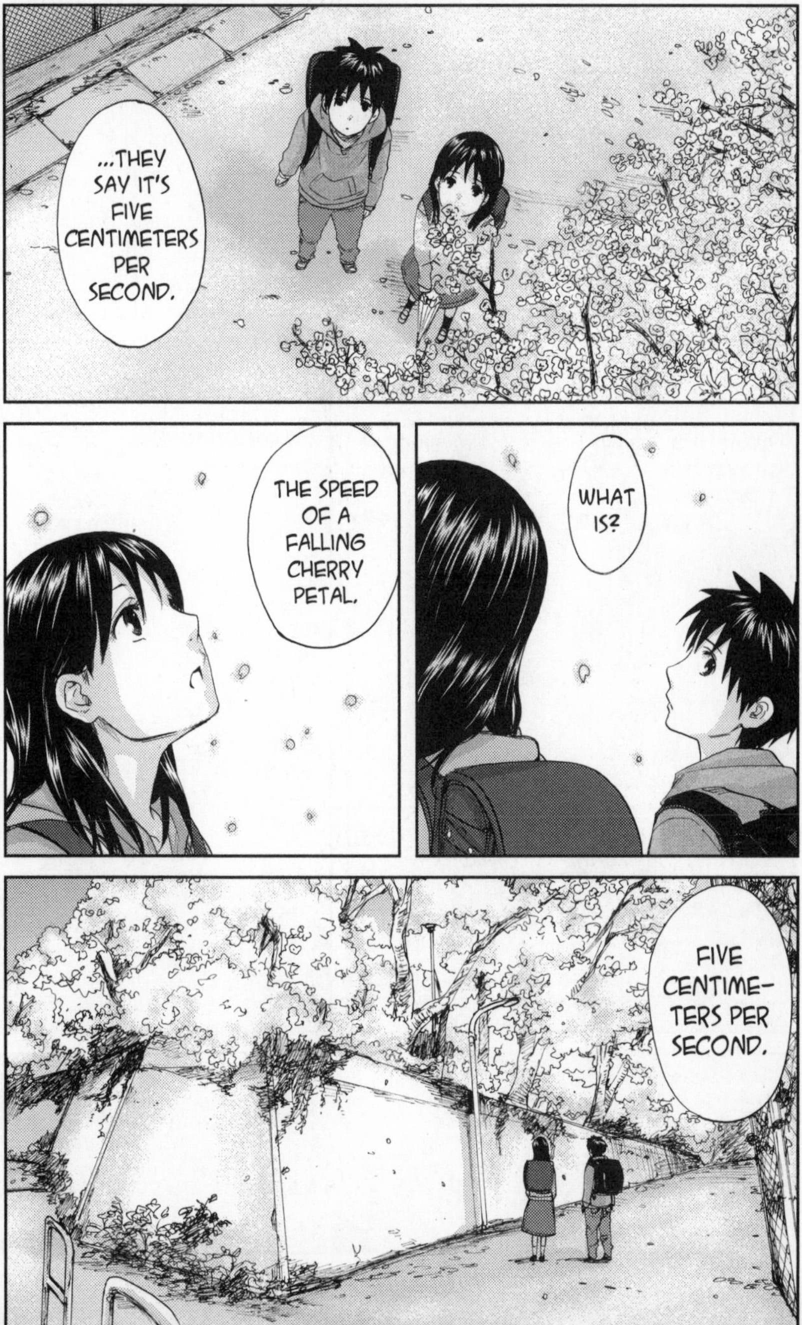
...THEY SAY IT'S FIVE CENTIMETERS PER SECOND.
WHAT IS?
THE SPEED OF A FALLING CHERRY PETAL.
FIVE CENTIME-TERS PER SECOND.

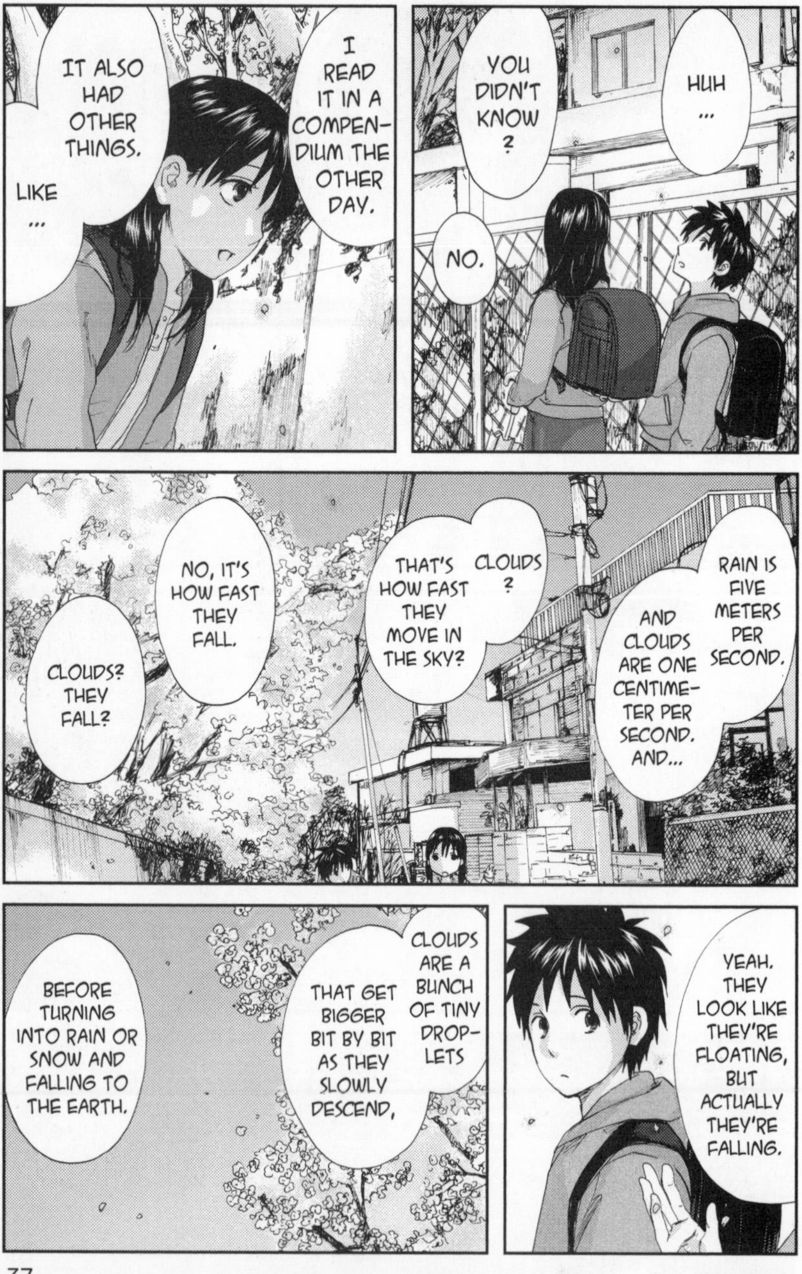
HUH ...
YOU DIDN'T KNOW?
NO.
I READ IT IN A COMPENDIUM THE OTHER DAY.
IT ALSO HAD OTHER THINGS.
LIKE ...
RAIN IS FIVE METERS PER SECOND.
AND CLOUDS ARE ONE CENTIMETER PER SECOND. AND...
CLOUDS?
THAT'S HOW FAST THEY MOVE IN THE SKY?
NO, IT'S HOW FAST THEY FALL.
CLOUDS? THEY FALL?
YEAH. THEY LOOK LIKE THEY'RE FLOATING, BUT ACTUALLY THEY'RE FALLING.
CLOUDS ARE A BUNCH OF TINY DROPLETS
THAT GET BIGGER BIT BY BIT AS THEY SLOWLY DESCEND,
BEFORE TURNING INTO RAIN OR SNOW AND FALLING TO THE EARTH.

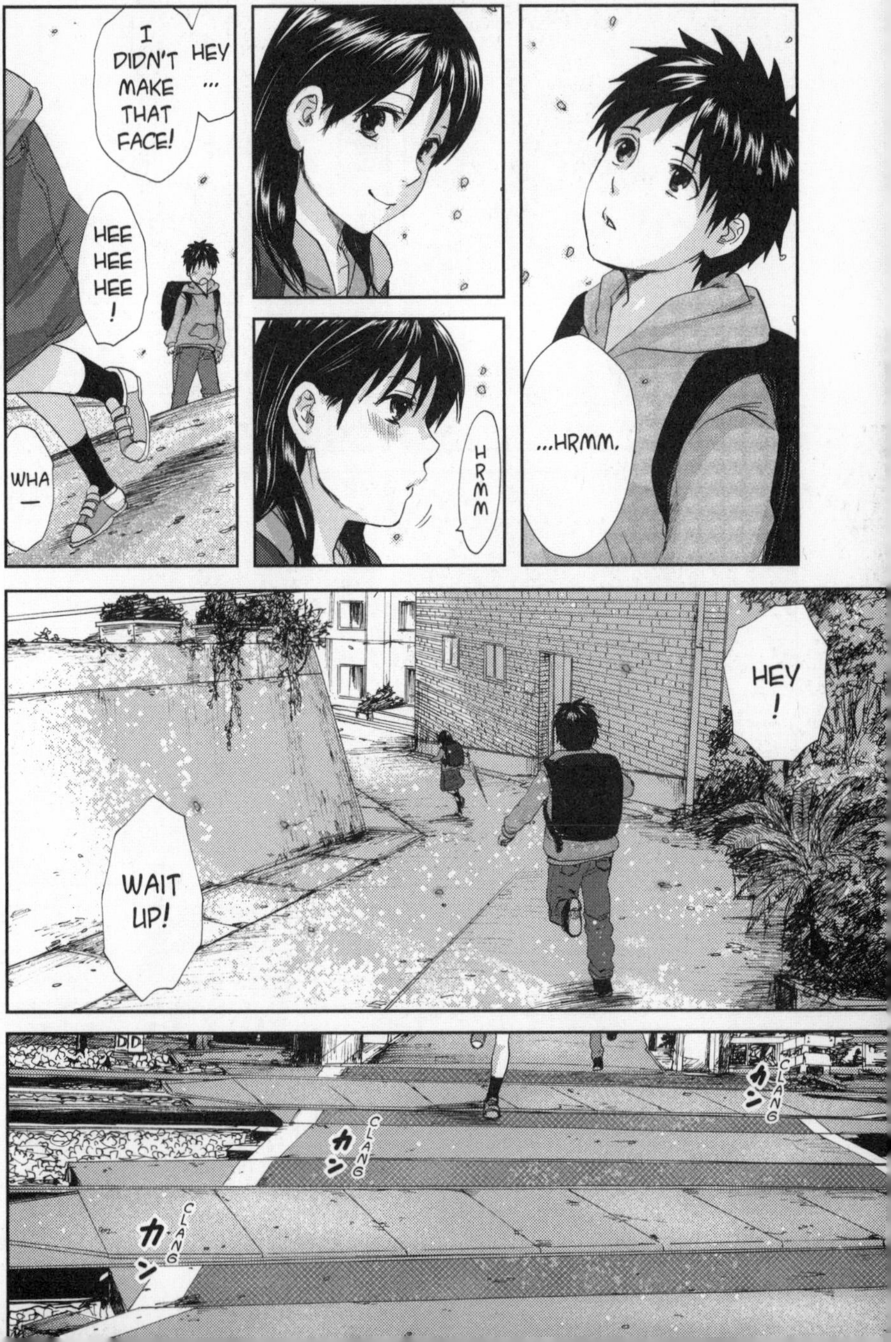
...HRMM.
HRMM
HEY ...
I DIDN'T MAKE THAT FACE!
HEE HEE HEE!
WHA —
HEY!
WAIT UP!
カン CLANG
カン CLANG
カン CLANG

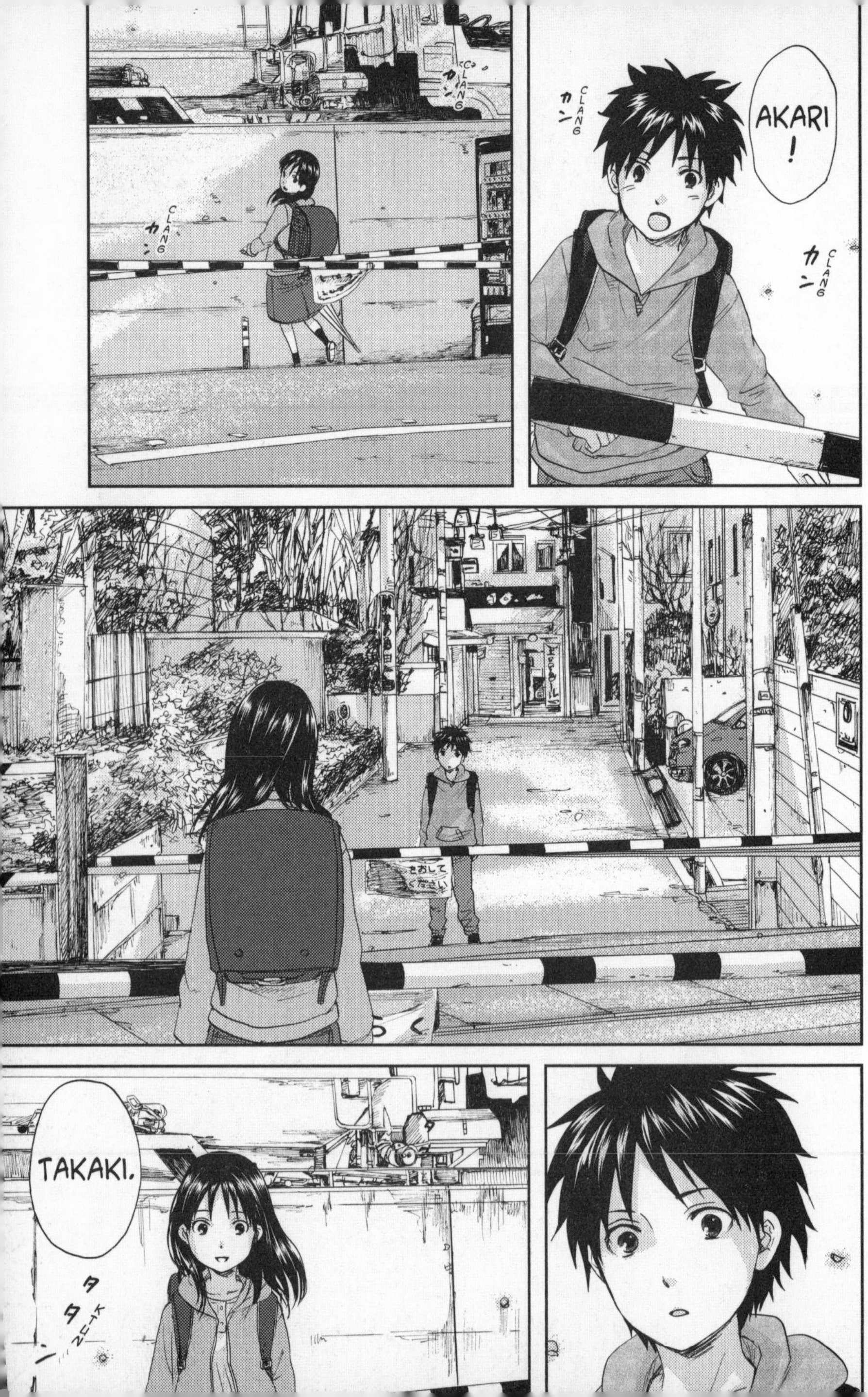
AKARI!
CLANG カン
CLANG カン
CLANG カン
CLANG カン
TAKAKI.
KTUN タタン

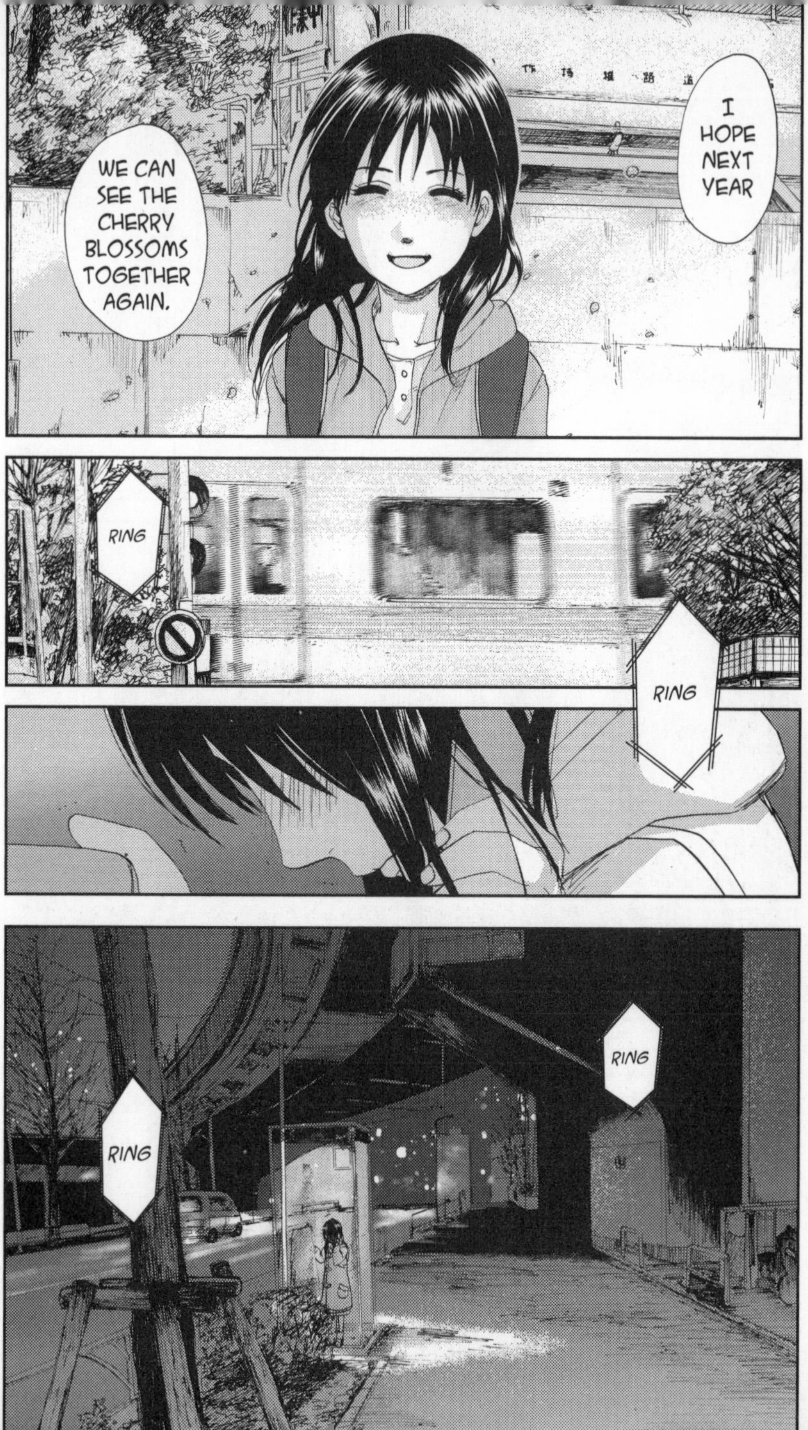
I HOPE NEXT YEAR
WE CAN SEE THE CHERRY BLOSSOMS TOGETHER AGAIN.
RING
RING
RING
RING

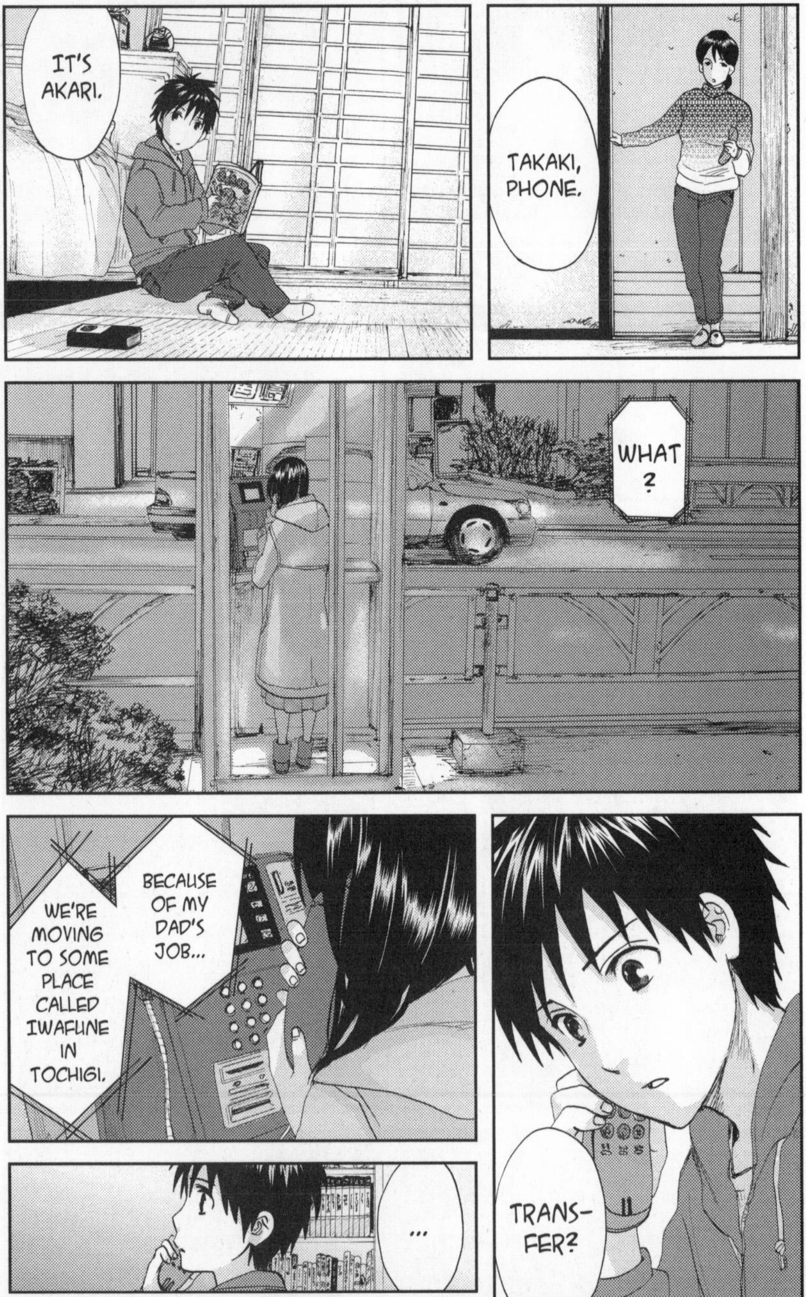
TAKAKI, PHONE.
IT'S AKARI.
WHAT?
TRANSFER?
BECAUSE OF MY DAD'S JOB...
WE'RE MOVING TO SOME PLACE CALLED IWAFUNE IN TOCHIGI.
...

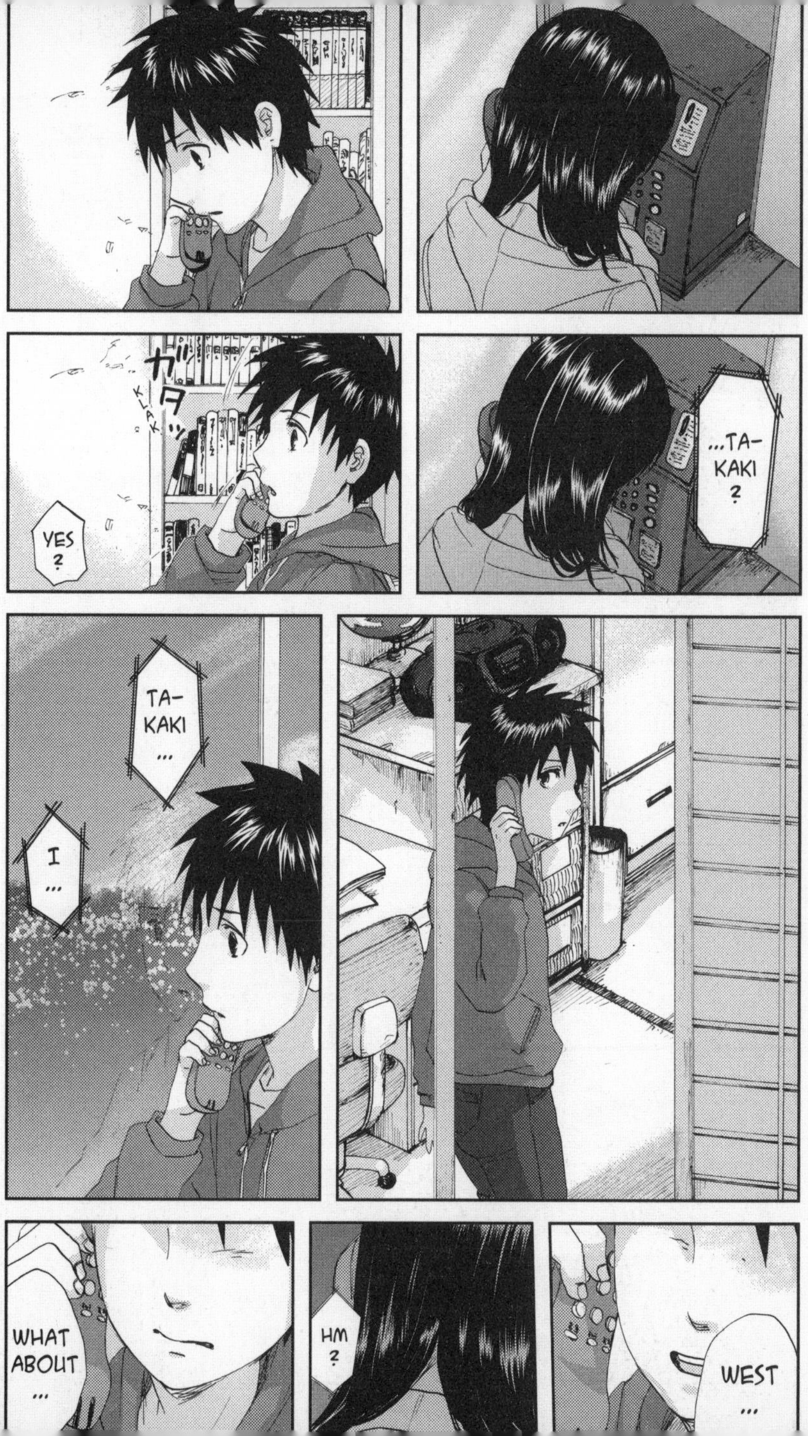
...TA-KAKI?
ガタッ
KLAK
YES?
TA-KAKI ...
I ...
WEST ...
HM?
WHAT ABOUT ...

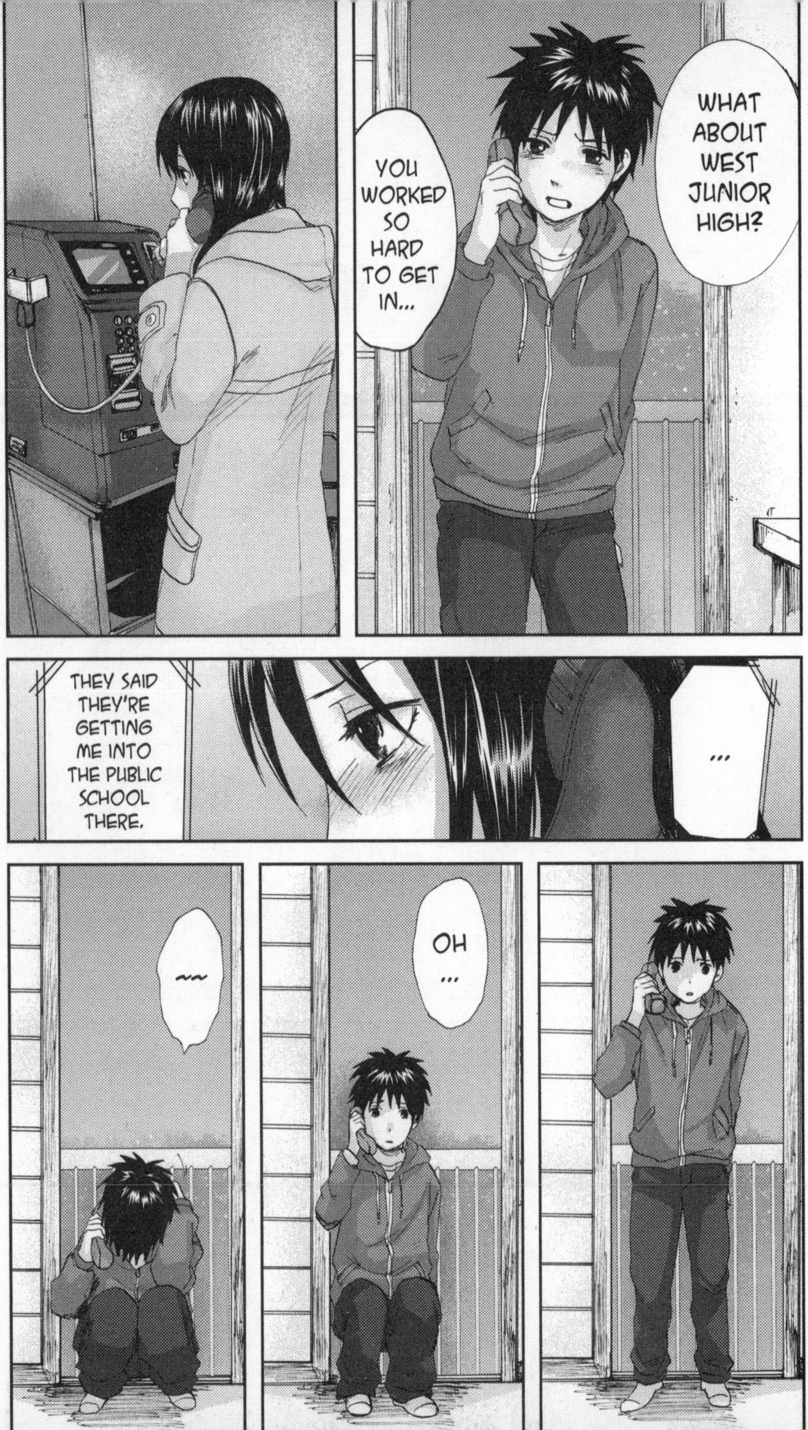
WHAT ABOUT WEST JUNIOR HIGH?
YOU WORKED SO HARD TO GET IN...
...
THEY SAID THEY'RE GETTING ME INTO THE PUBLIC SCHOOL THERE.
OH ...
~~

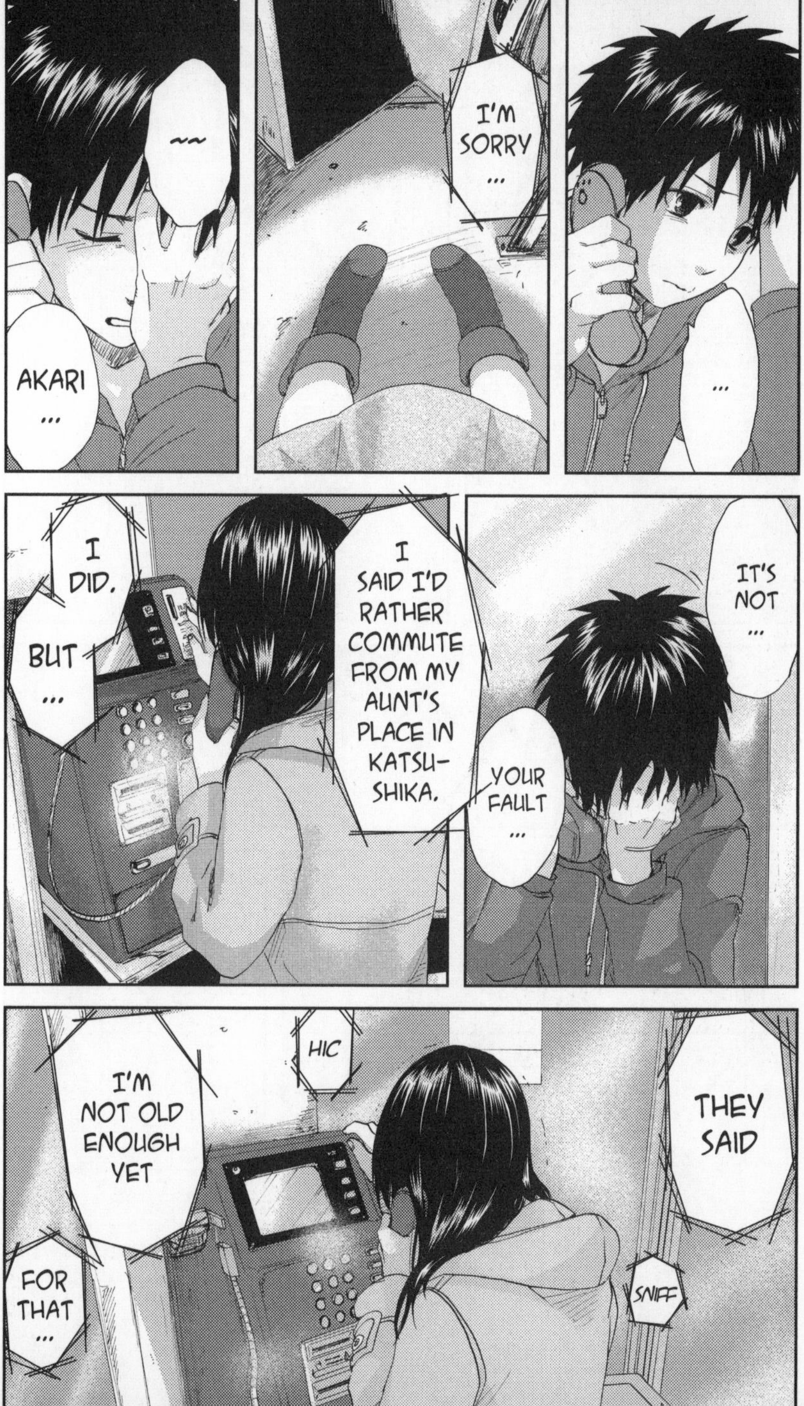
...
I'M SORRY ...
~~
AKARI ...
IT'S NOT ...
YOUR FAULT ...
I SAID I'D RATHER COMMUTE FROM MY AUNT'S PLACE IN KATSU-SHIKA.
I DID.
BUT ...
THEY SAID
SNIFF
HIC
I'M NOT OLD ENOUGH YET
FOR THAT ...

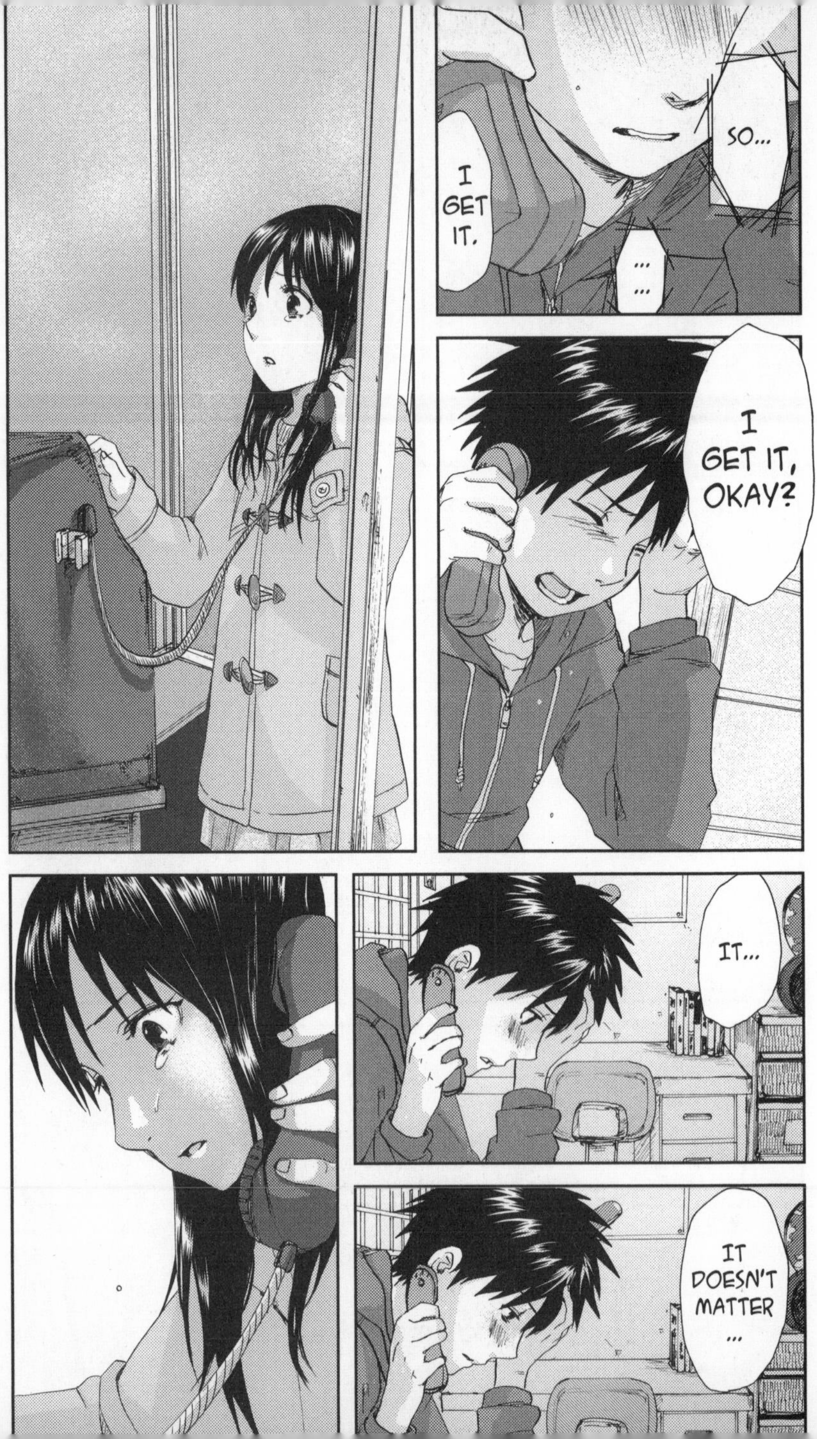
SO...
I GET IT.
... ...
I GET IT, OKAY?
IT...
IT DOESN'T MATTER ...

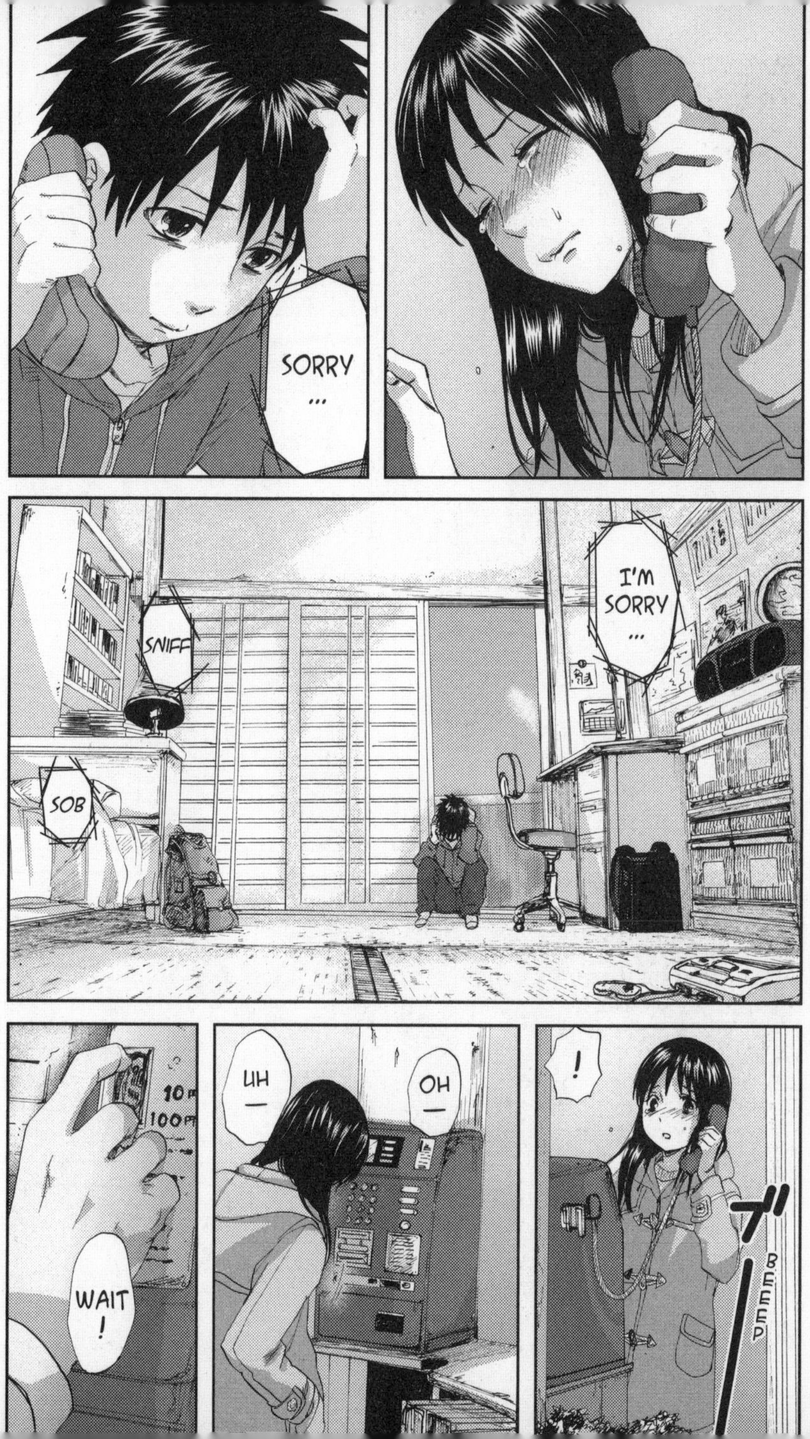
SORRY ...
I'M SORRY ...
SNIFF
SOB
!
ブ
BEEEP
OH —
UH —
WAIT !

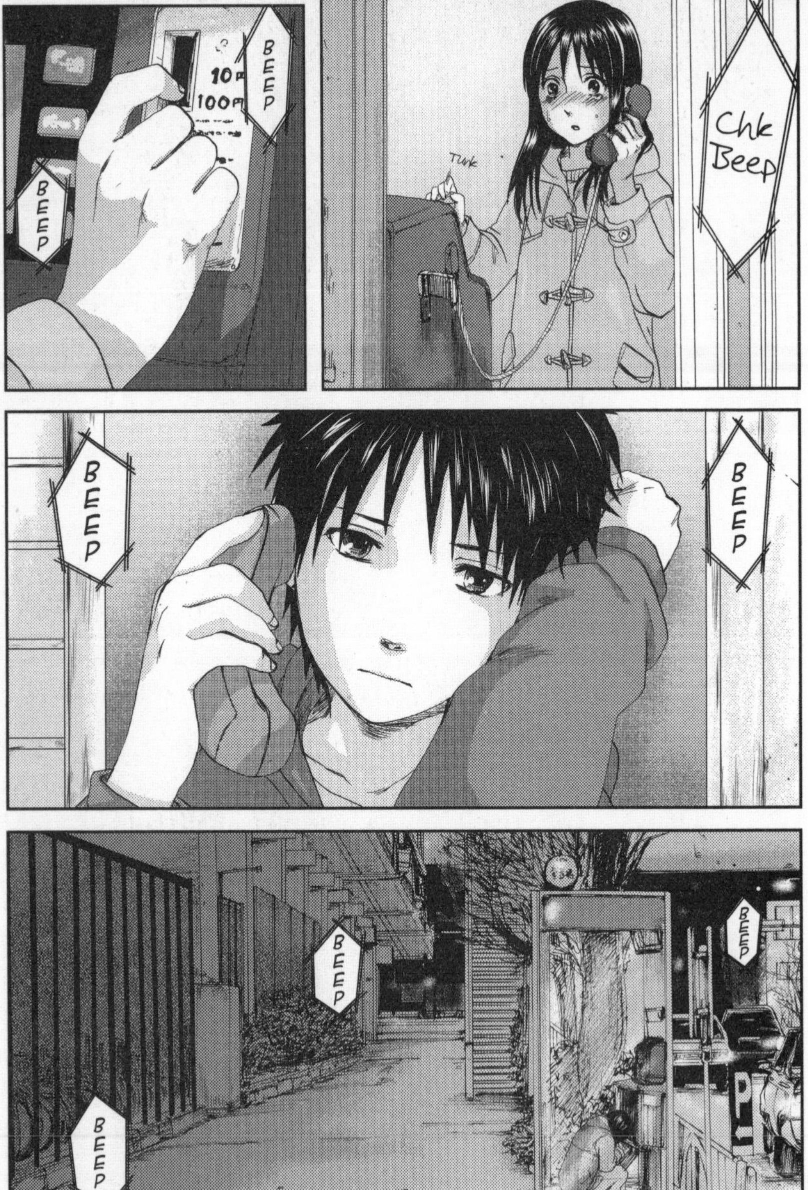
Chk Beep
Tunk
BEEP BEEP
BEEP BEEP
BEEP BEEP
BEEP BEEP
BEEP
BEEP BEEP
BEEP BEEP

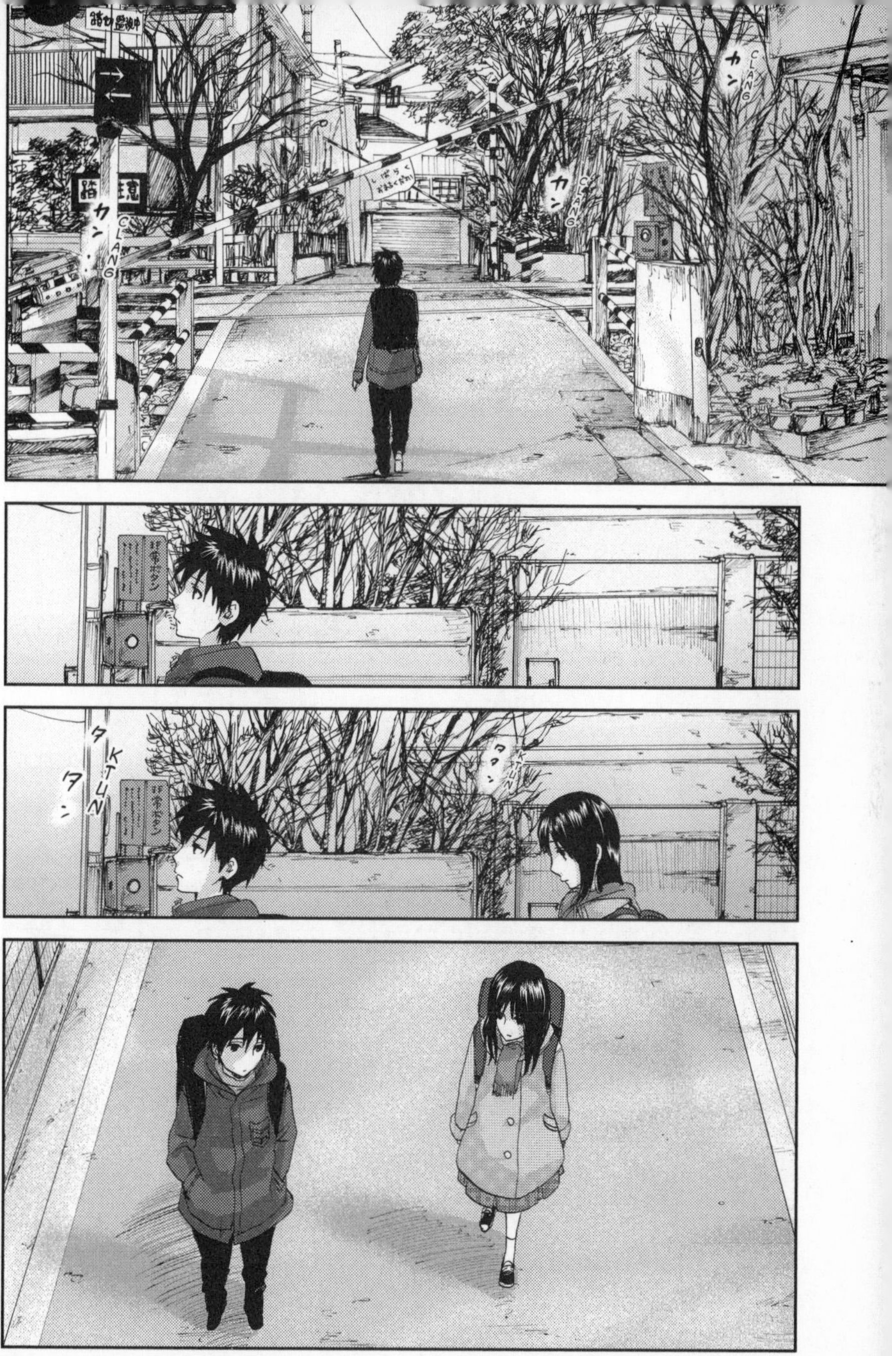
カン
CLANG
カン
CLANG
カン・・
CLANG
タタン
KTUN
タタン
KTUN

...HI.
非常ボタン
ゴトン
KTUN
HI...
ゴトン
KTUN
ゴトン
KTUN
ゴトン
KTUN
ゴトン
KTUN
ゴトン
KTUN
ゴトン
KTUN
ゴトン
KTUN
ゴトン
KTUN
ゴトン
KTUN

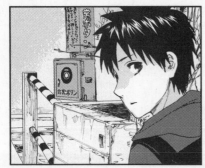

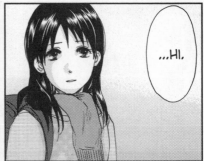

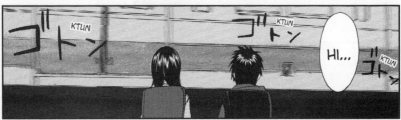

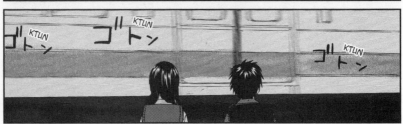

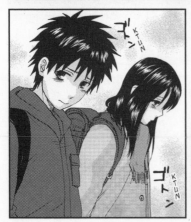

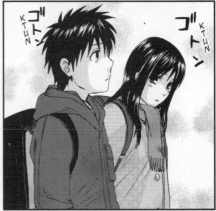

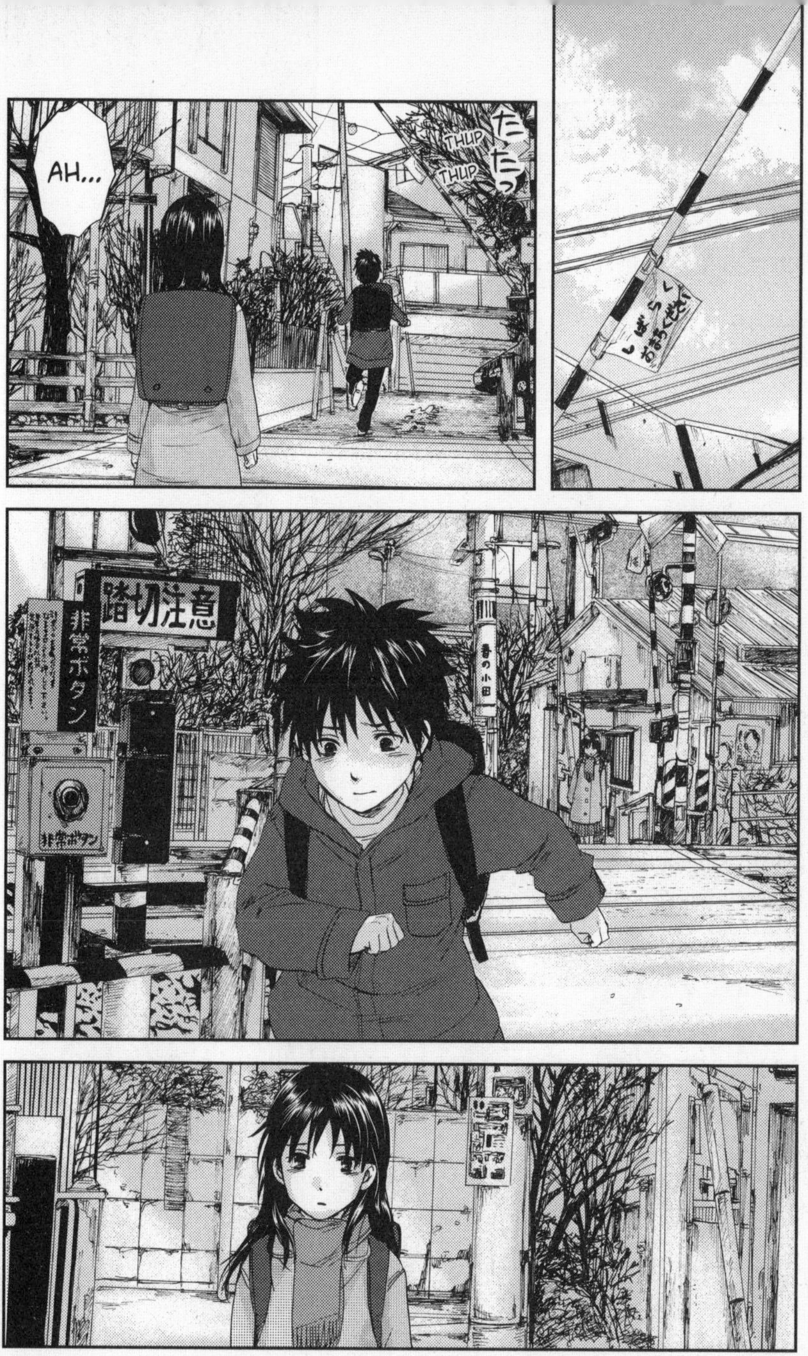
たたっ
THUP THUP
AH...
踏切注意
非常ボタン
非常ボタン

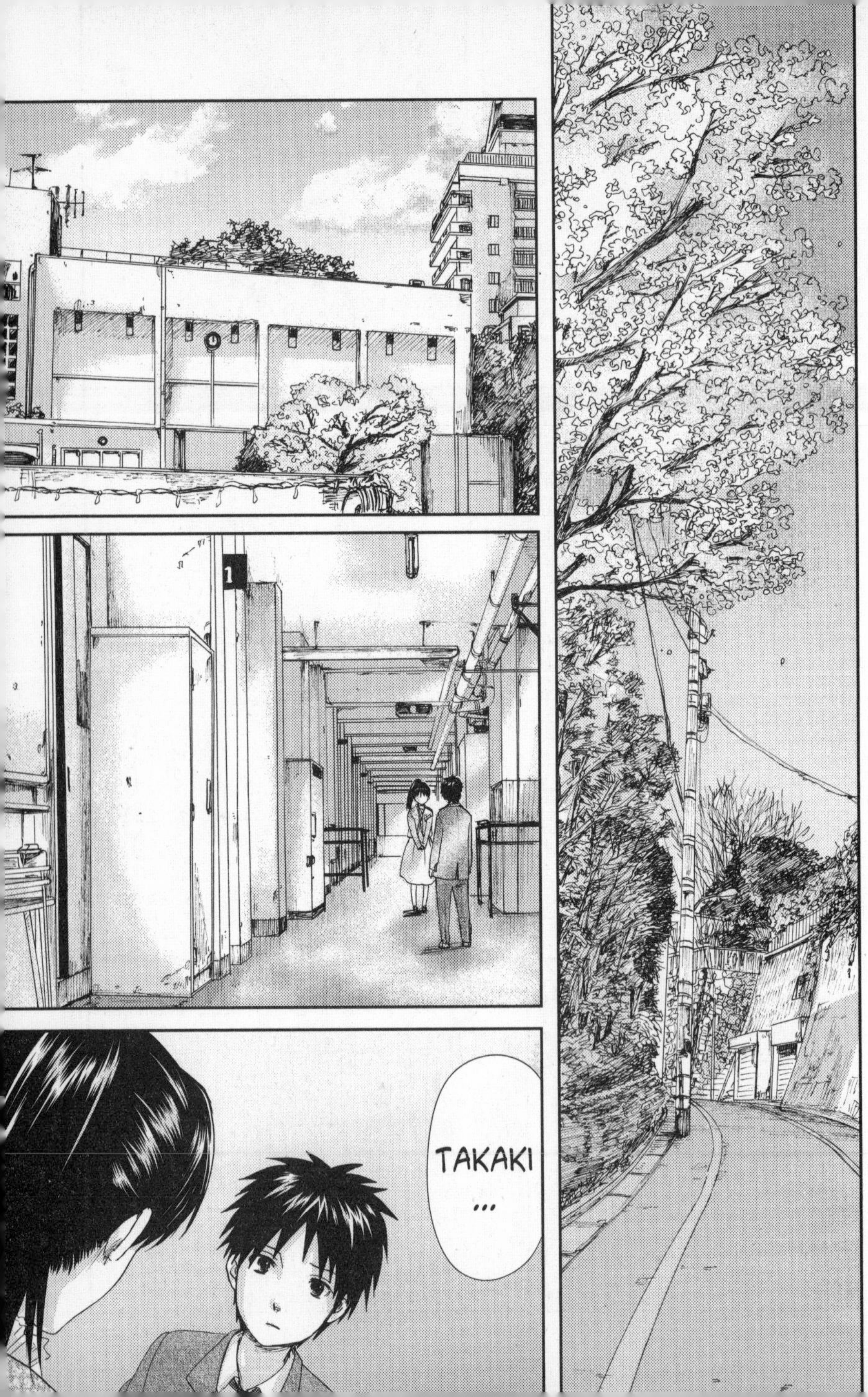
1
TAKAKI
...

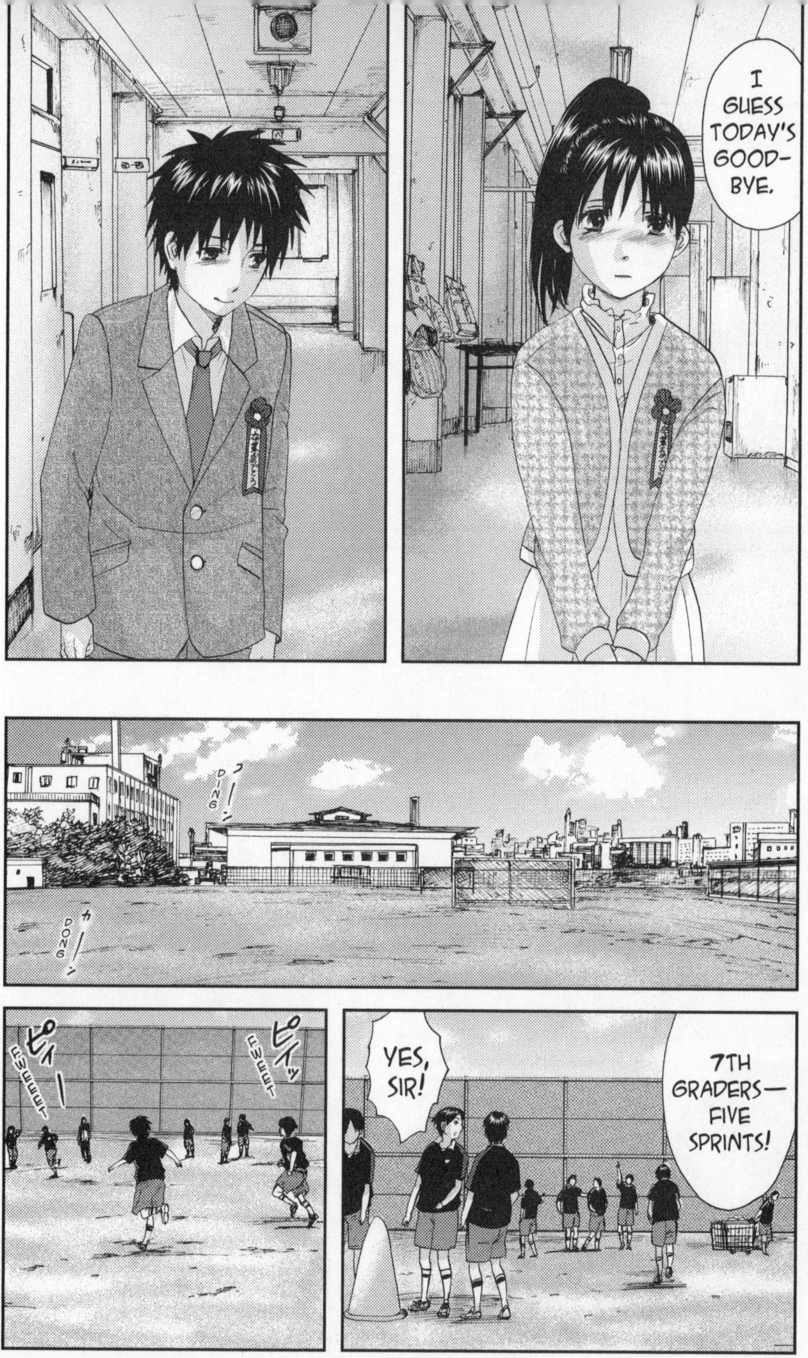
I GUESS TODAY'S GOOD-BYE.
DING
DONG
7TH GRADERS— FIVE SPRINTS!
YES, SIR!
FWEET
FWEEEET

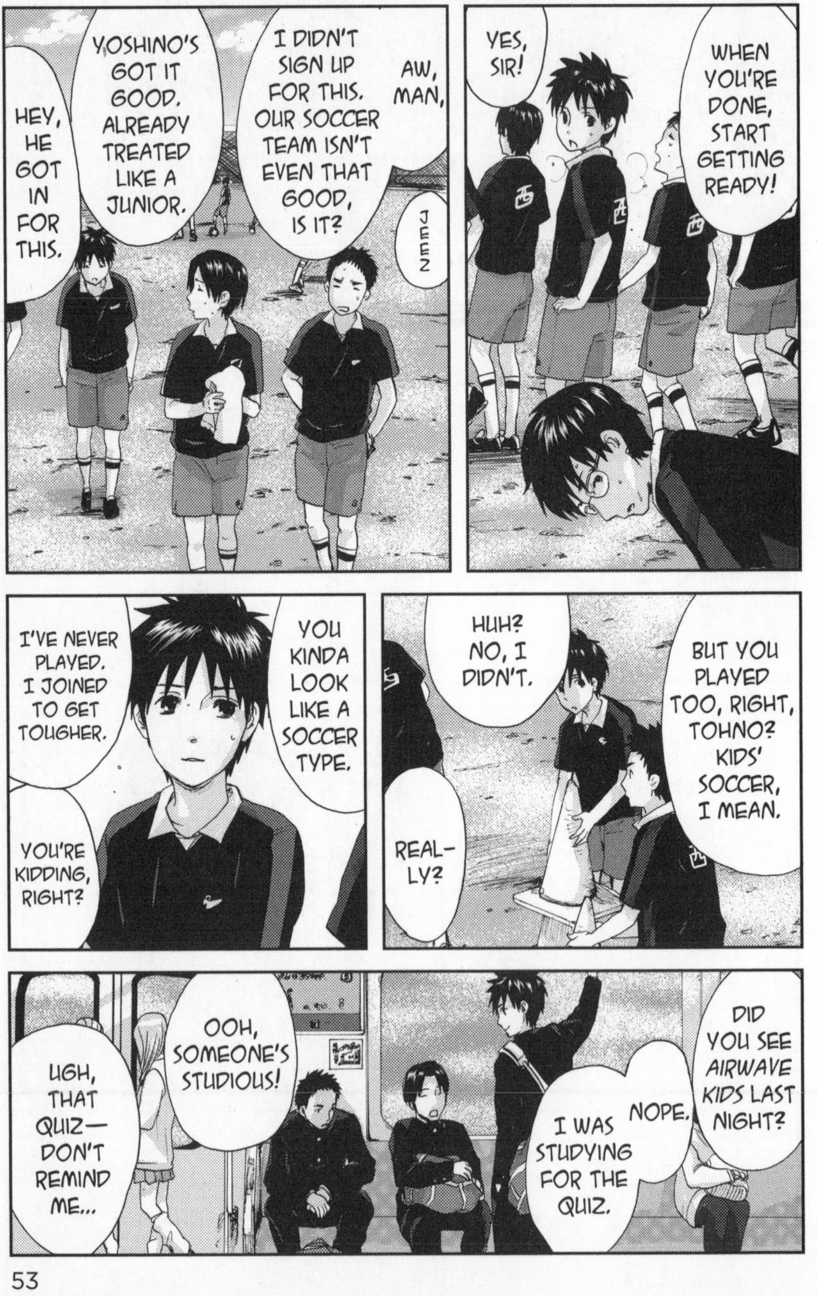
WHEN YOU'RE DONE, START GETTING READY!
YES, SIR!
AW, MAN,
I DIDN'T SIGN UP FOR THIS. OUR SOCCER TEAM ISN'T EVEN THAT GOOD, IS IT?
JEEZ
YOSHINO'S GOT IT GOOD. ALREADY TREATED LIKE A JUNIOR.
HEY, HE GOT IN FOR THIS.
BUT YOU PLAYED TOO, RIGHT, TOHNO? KIDS' SOCCER, I MEAN.
HUH? NO, I DIDN'T.
REAL-LY?
YOU KINDA LOOK LIKE A SOCCER TYPE.
I'VE NEVER PLAYED. I JOINED TO GET TOUGHER.
YOU'RE KIDDING, RIGHT?
DID YOU SEE AIRWAVE KIDS LAST NIGHT?
NOPE.
I WAS STUDYING FOR THE QUIZ.
OOH, SOMEONE'S STUDIOUS!
UGH, THAT QUIZ— DON'T REMIND ME...

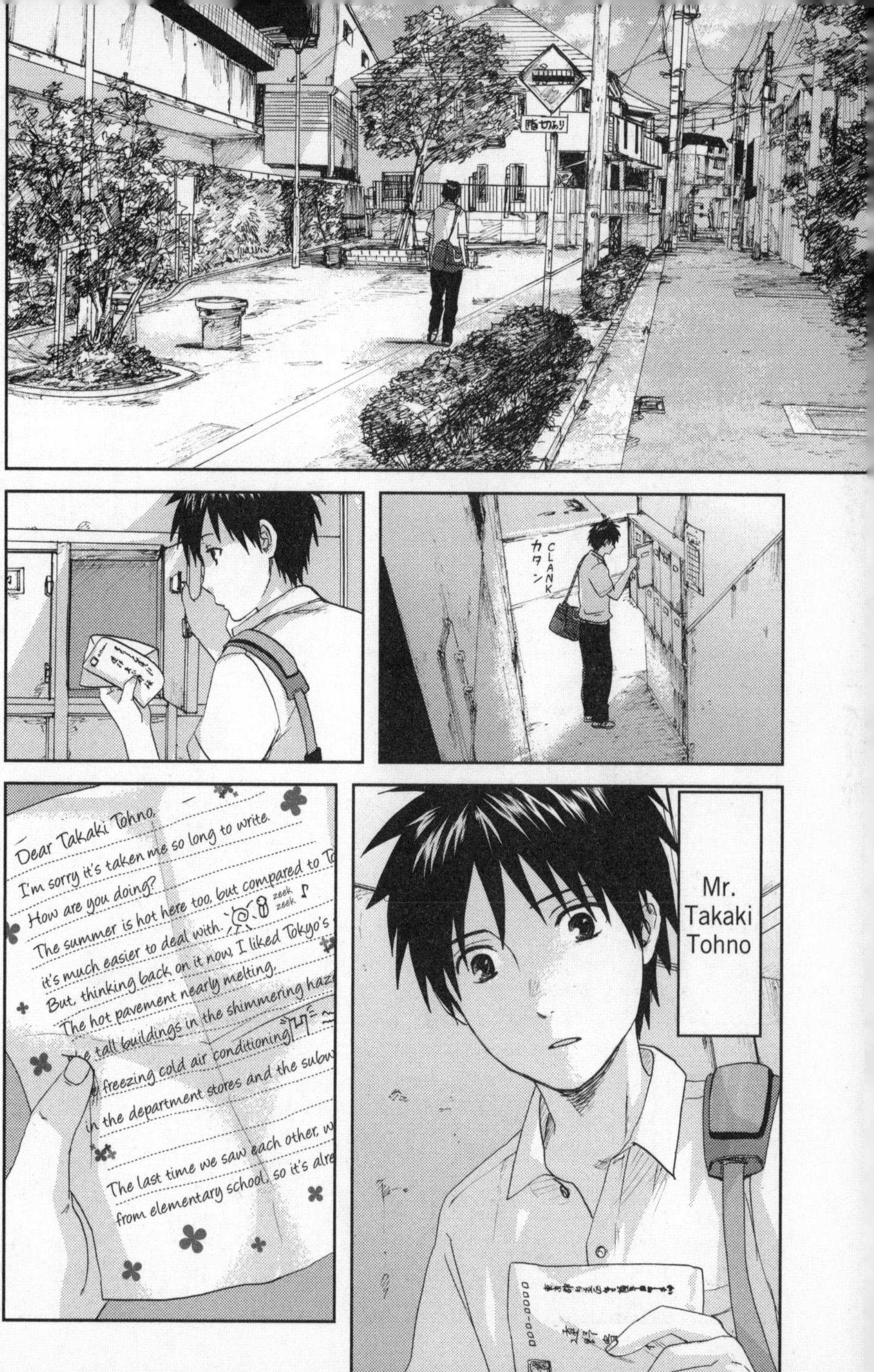
踏切あり
カタン CLANK
Mr. Takaki Tohno
Dear Takaki Tohno,
I'm sorry it's taken me so long to write.
How are you doing?
The summer is hot here too, but compared to To
it's much easier to deal with.
zeek zeek
But, thinking back on it now, I liked Tokyo's
The hot pavement nearly melting.
The tall buildings in the shimmering haz
freezing cold air conditioning
in the department stores and the subw
The last time we saw each other, w
from elementary school, so it's alre

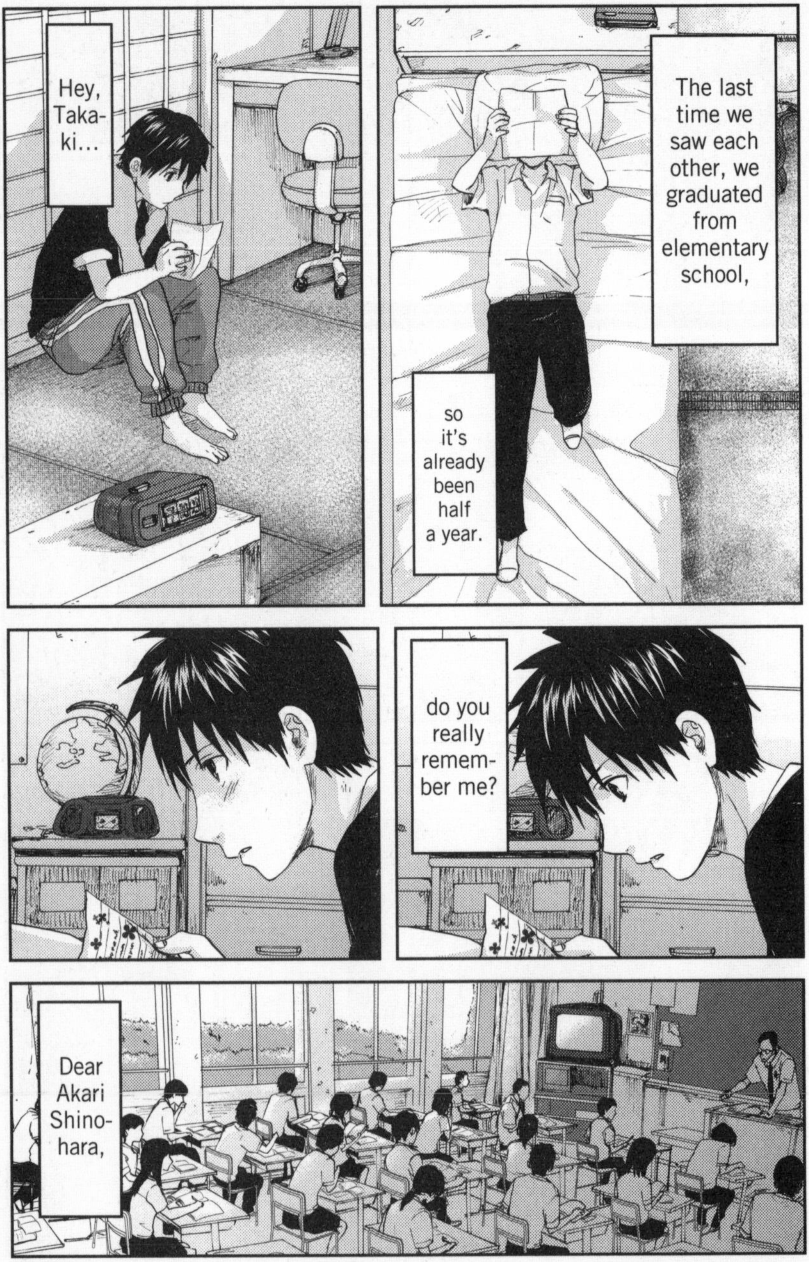
The last time we saw each other, we graduated from elementary school,
so it's already been half a year.
Hey, Taka-ki...
do you really remem-ber me?
Dear Akari Shino-hara,

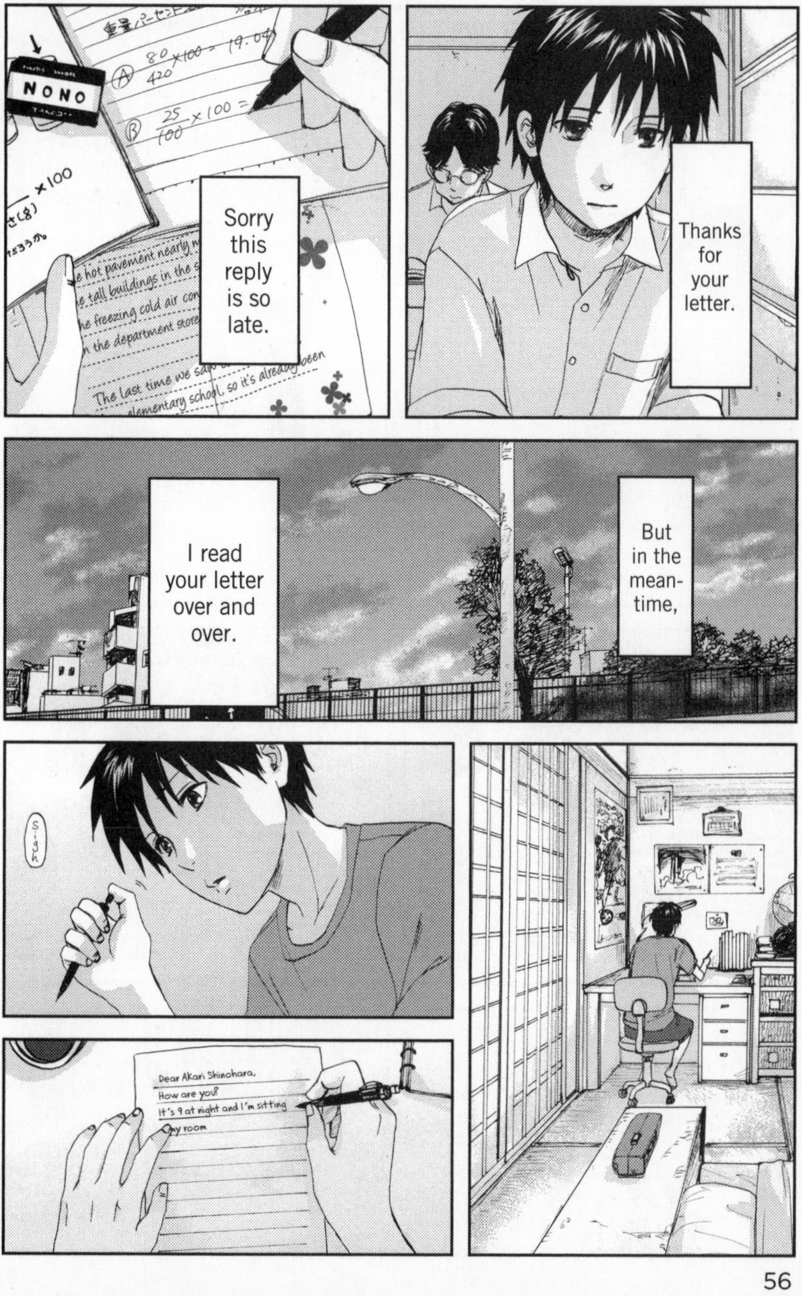
Thanks for your letter.
NONO
Sorry this reply is so late.
But in the mean-time,
I read your letter over and over.
Sigh
Dear Akari Shinohara,
How are you?
It's 9 at night and I'm sitting
my room

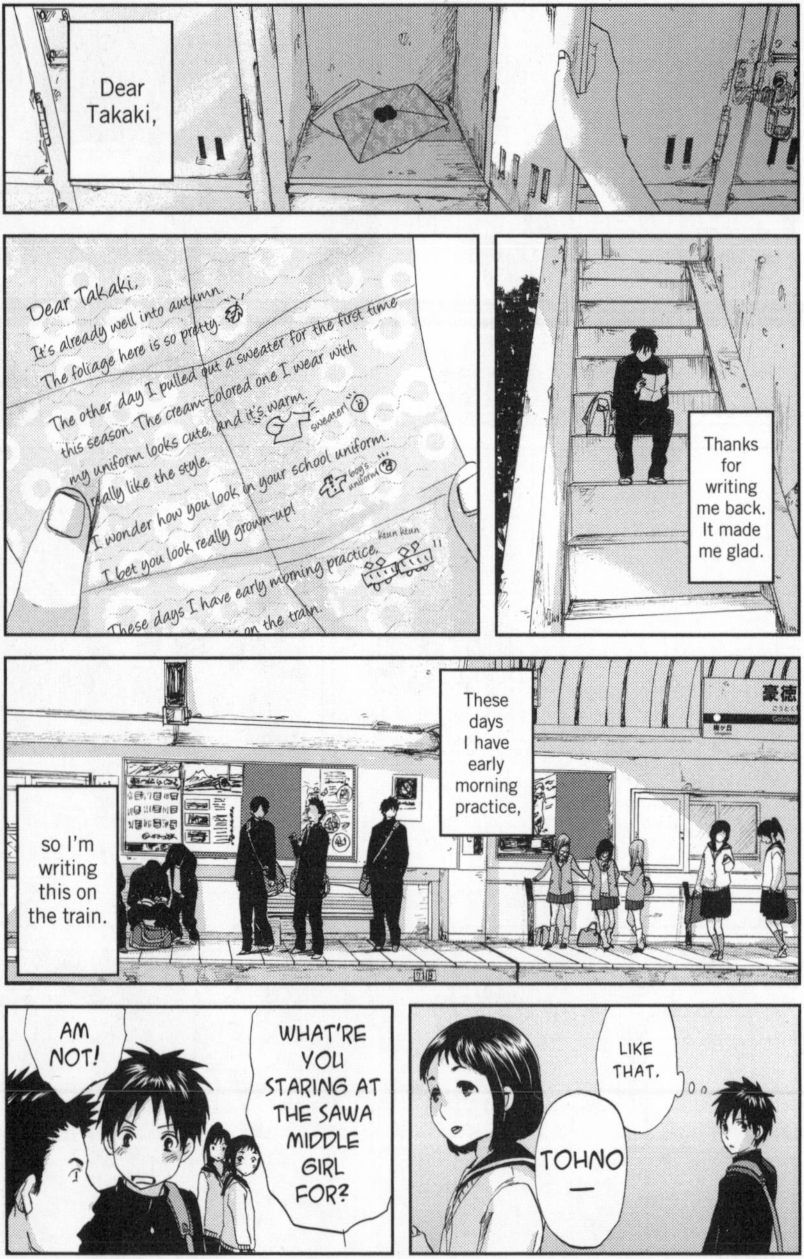
Dear Takaki,
Thanks for writing me back. It made me glad.
Dear Takaki,
It's already well into autumn.
The foliage here is so pretty.
The other day I pulled out a sweater for the first time this season. The cream-colored one I wear with my uniform looks cute, and it's warm.
sweater!
I really like the style.
I wonder how you look in your school uniform.
boy's uniform
I bet you look really grown-up!
ktun ktun
These days I have early morning practice,
on the train.
豪徳
Gotokuji
These days I have early morning practice,
so I'm writing this on the train.
LIKE THAT.
TOHNO—
WHAT'RE YOU STARING AT THE SAWA MIDDLE GIRL FOR?
AM NOT!

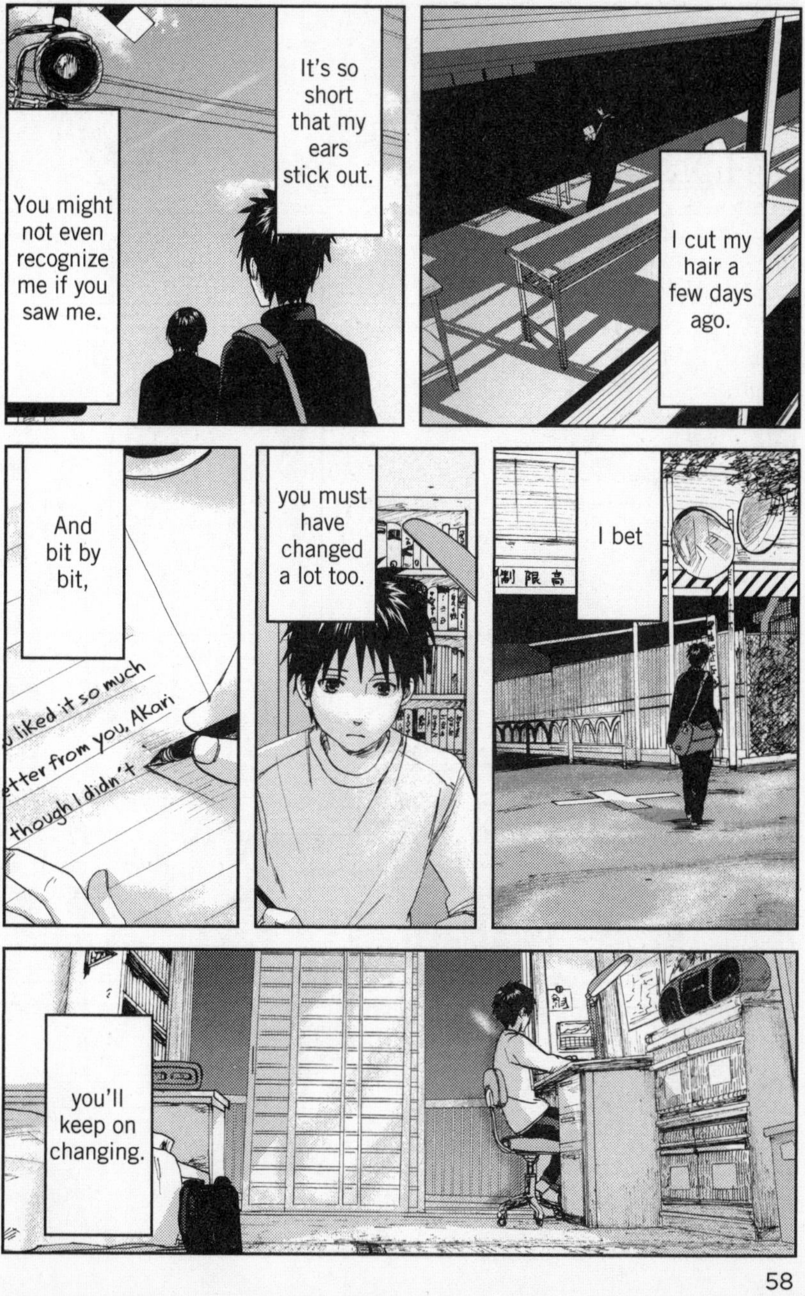
I cut my hair a few days ago.
It's so short that my ears stick out.
You might not even recognize me if you saw me.
I bet
you must have changed a lot too.
And bit by bit,
u liked it so much
etter from you, Akari
though I didn't
you'll keep on changing.

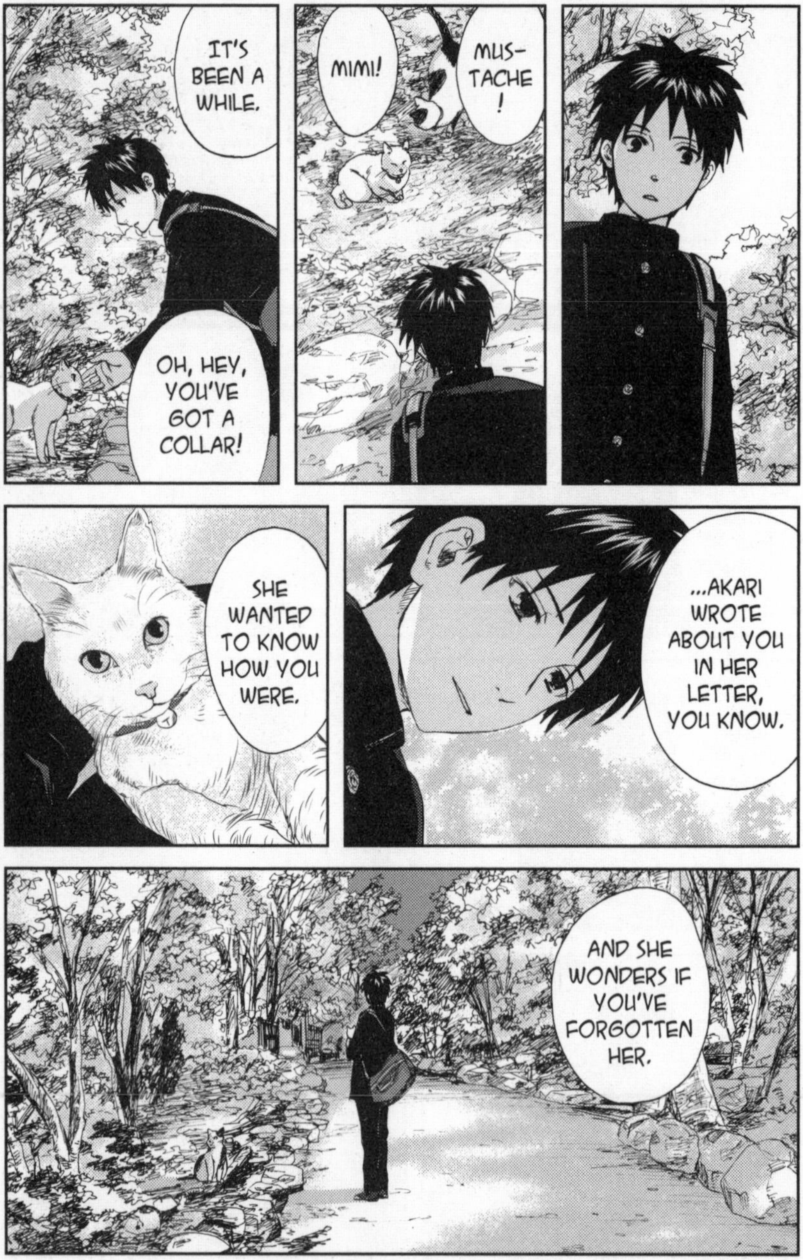
MUS-TACHE!
MIMI!
IT'S BEEN A WHILE.
OH, HEY, YOU'VE GOT A COLLAR!
...AKARI WROTE ABOUT YOU IN HER LETTER, YOU KNOW.
SHE WANTED TO KNOW HOW YOU WERE.
AND SHE WONDERS IF YOU'VE FORGOTTEN HER.

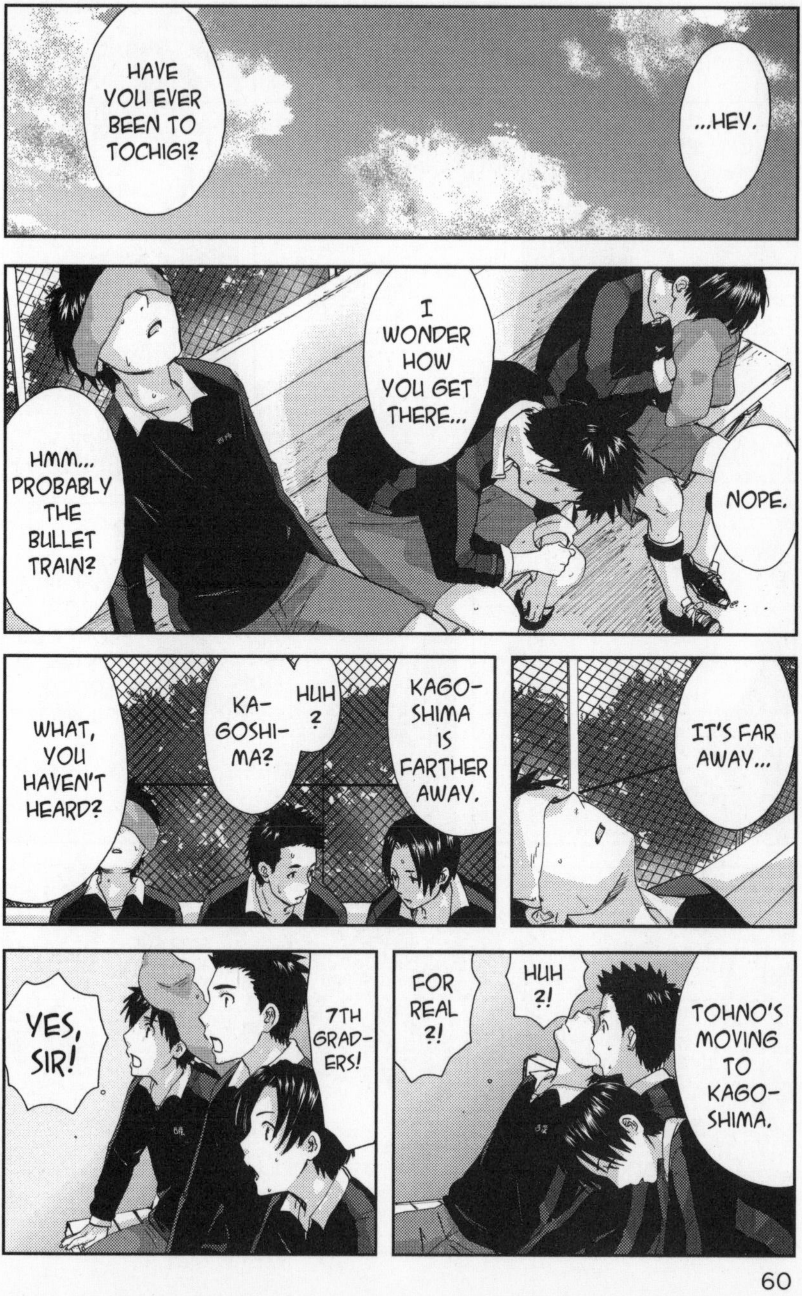
...HEY.
HAVE YOU EVER BEEN TO TOCHIGI?
NOPE.
I WONDER HOW YOU GET THERE...
HMM... PROBABLY THE BULLET TRAIN?
IT'S FAR AWAY...
KAGO-SHIMA IS FARTHER AWAY.
HUH?
KA-GOSHIMA?
WHAT, YOU HAVEN'T HEARD?
TOHNO'S MOVING TO KAGO-SHIMA.
HUH?!
FOR REAL?!
7TH GRAD-ERS!
YES, SIR!

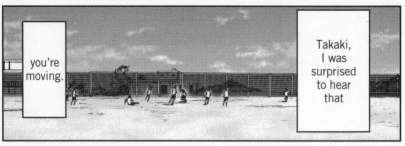

Takaki, I was surprised to hear that
you're moving.
Even though we're both used to the idea of transferring by now...
Kago-shima is pretty far.
冬の日本海を行く
1995 2
To think we might be so far apart that we couldn't even get to one another by train...
That really is
just a little bit lonely.
Dear Akari Shino-hara,
I found out that you can get from Shinjuku to Iwafune with just two transfers.

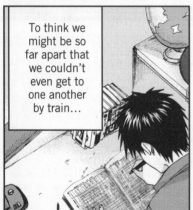

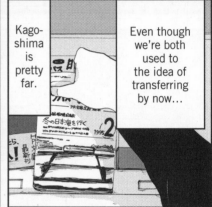

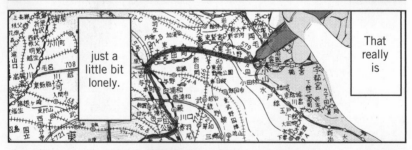

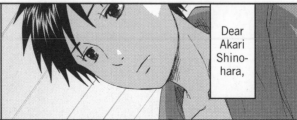

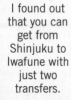

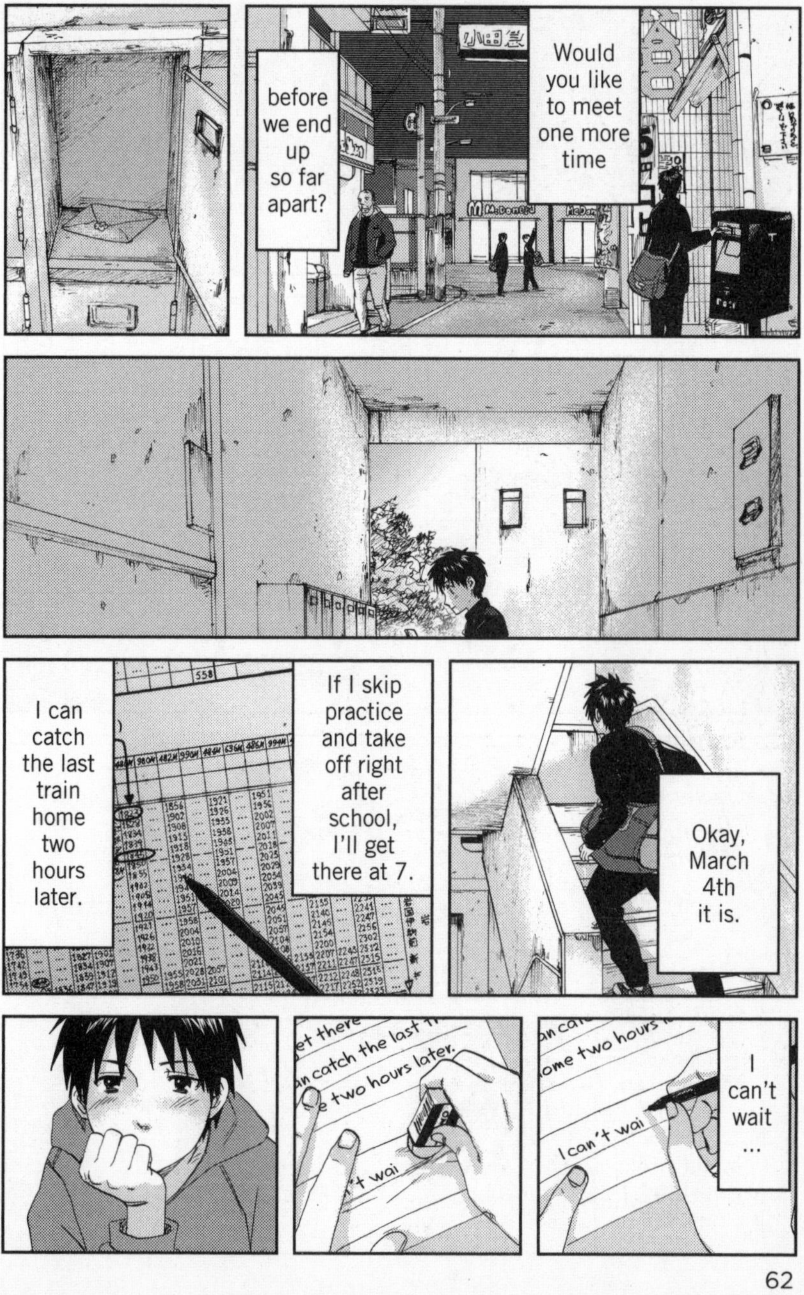
Would you like to meet one more time
before we end up so far apart?
Okay, March 4th it is.
If I skip practice and take off right after school, I'll get there at 7.
I can catch the last train home two hours later.
I can't wait ...

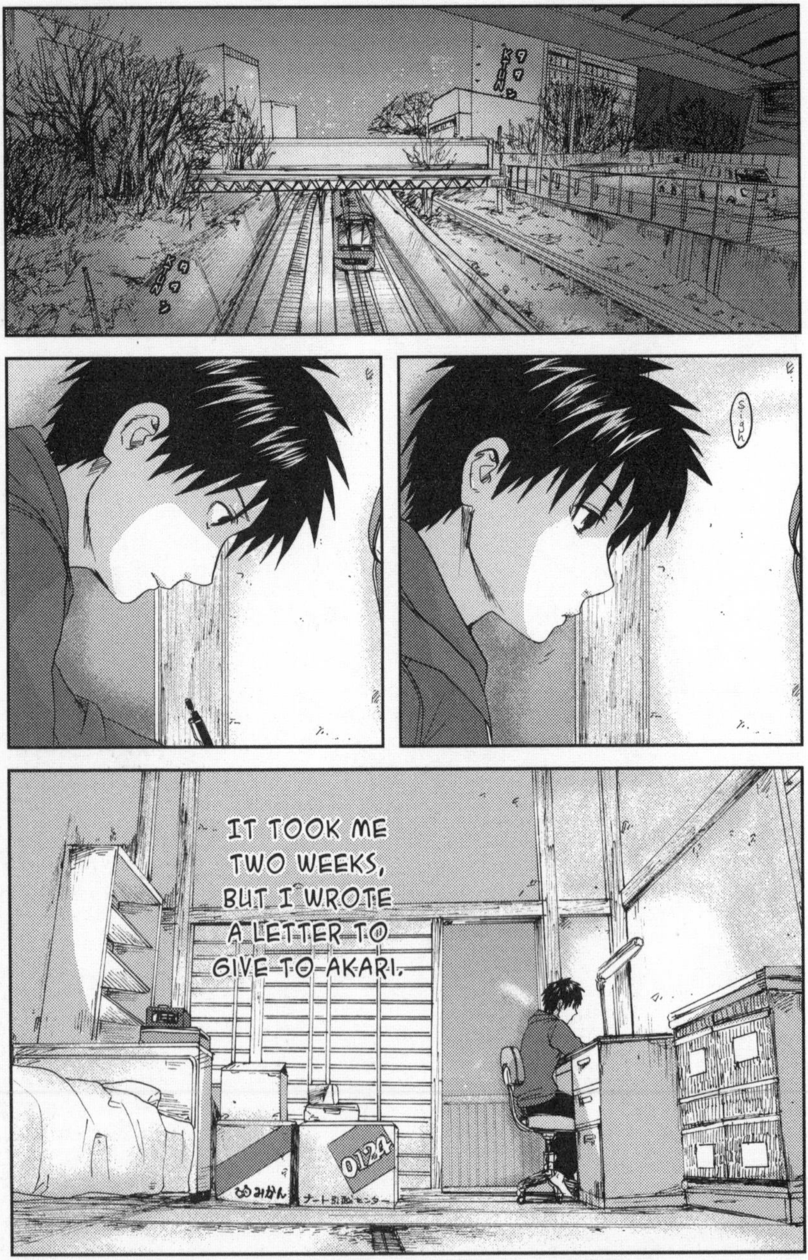
タタン
KTUN
タタン
KTUN
Sigh
IT TOOK ME TWO WEEKS, BUT I WROTE A LETTER TO GIVE TO AKARI.

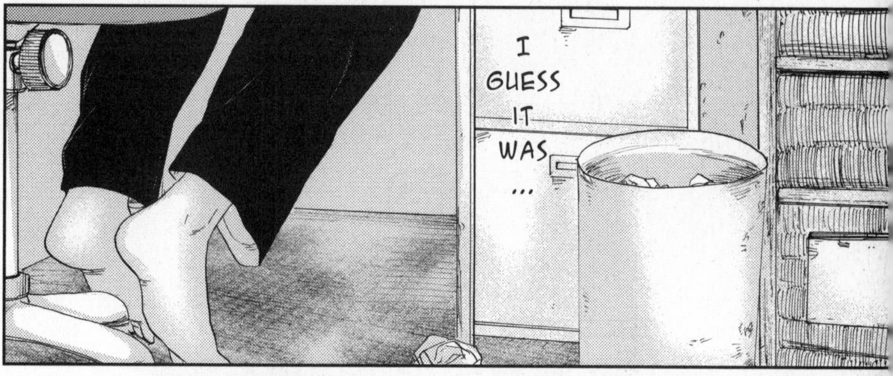
I GUESS IT WAS ...
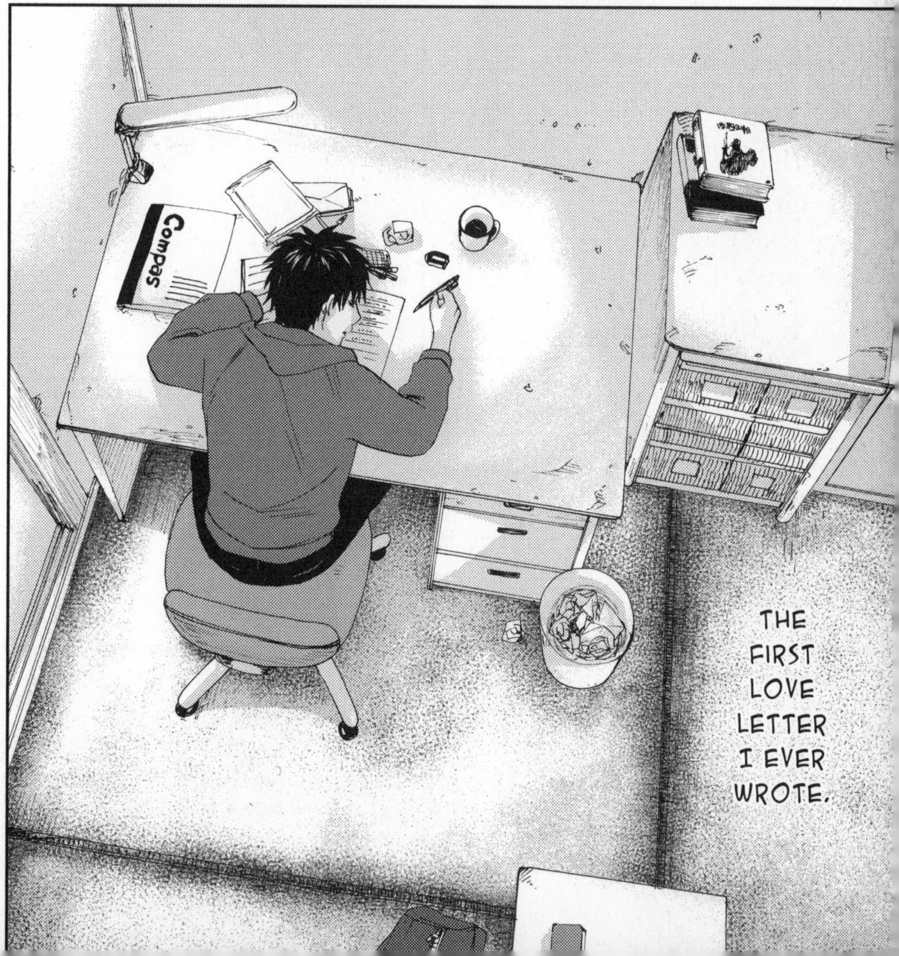
Compas
THE FIRST LOVE LETTER I EVER WROTE.

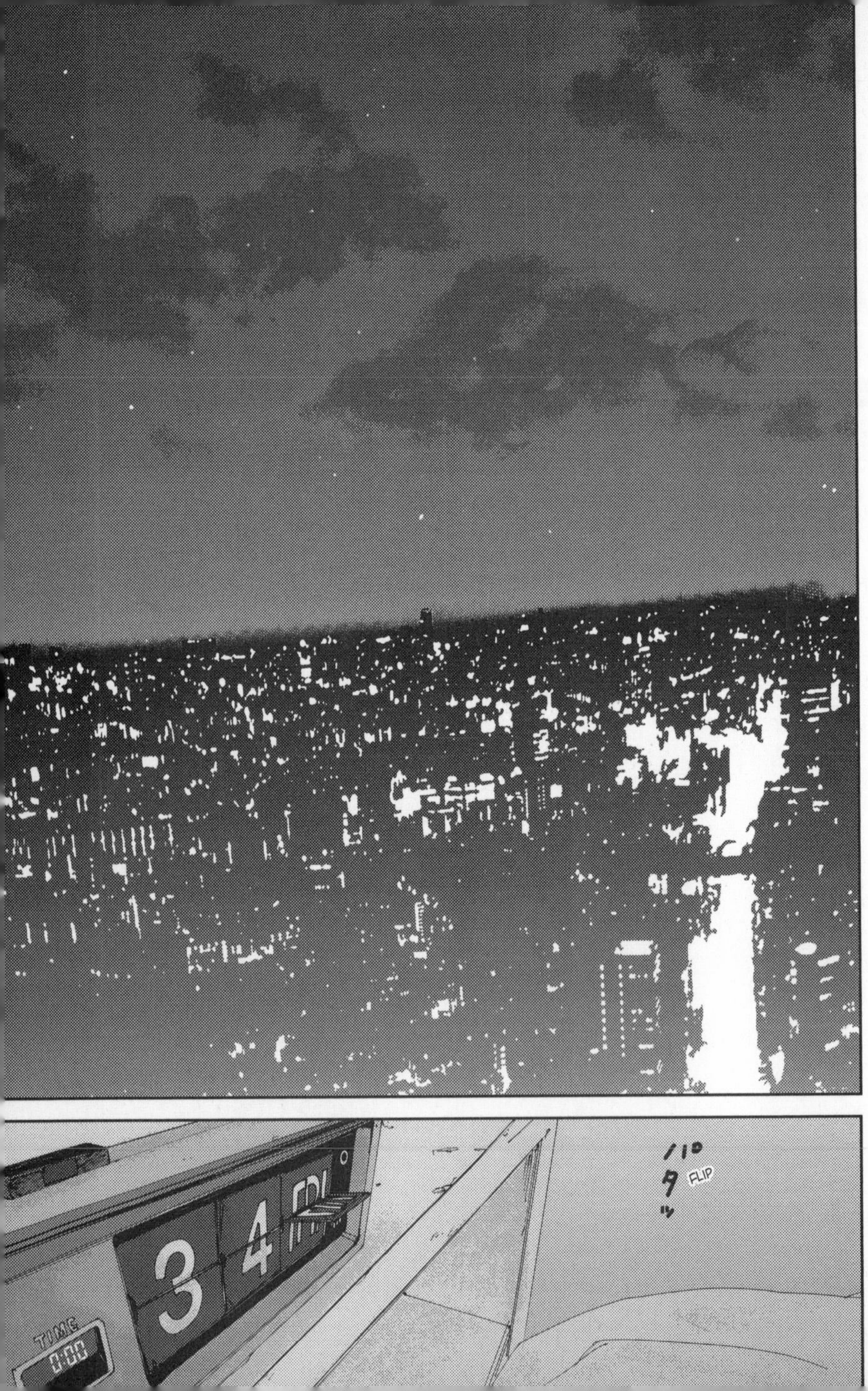
パタッ
FLIP
3 4
TIME
0:00

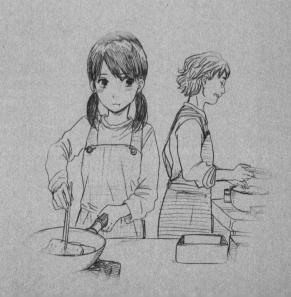

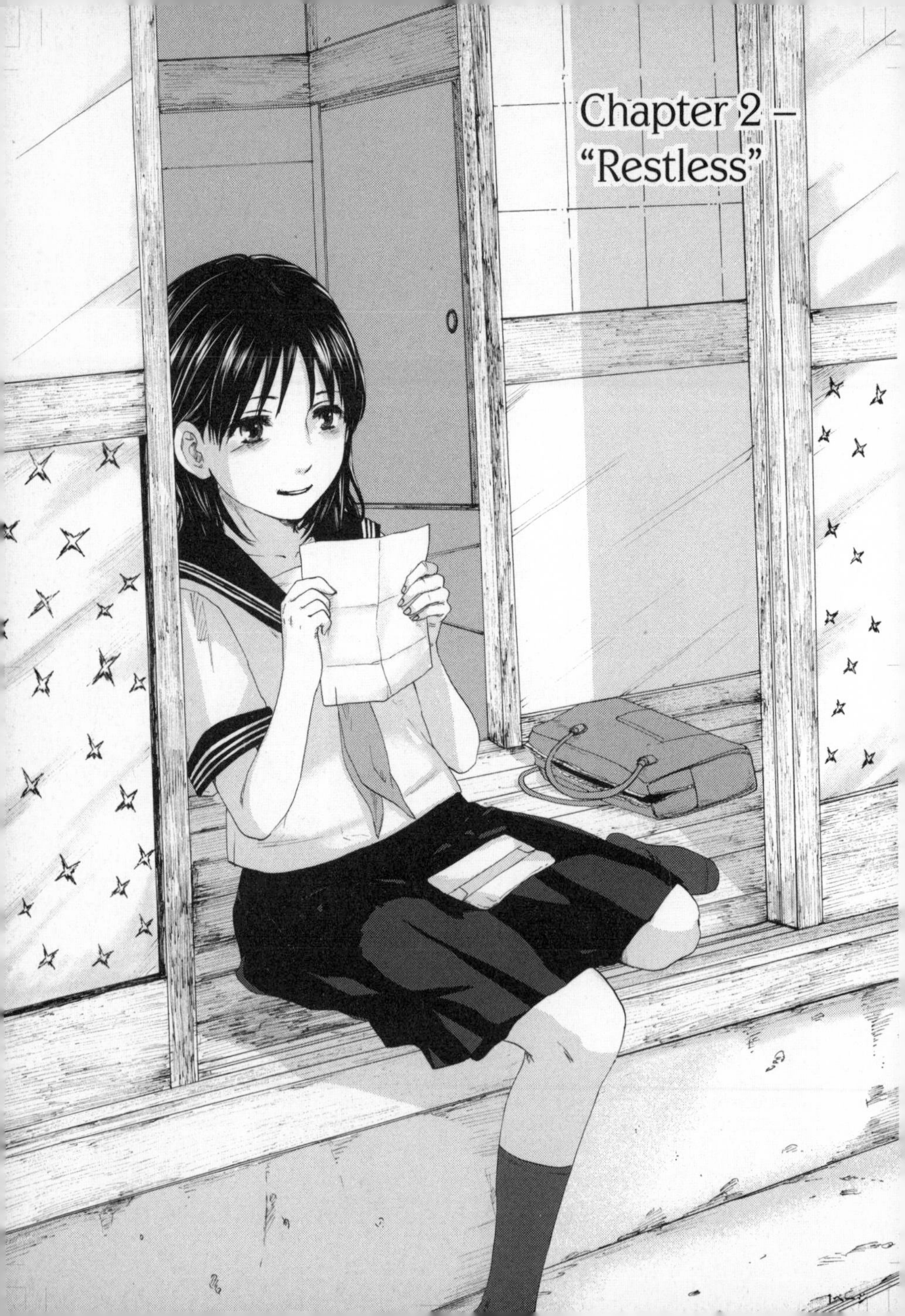
Chapter 2 –
"Restless"

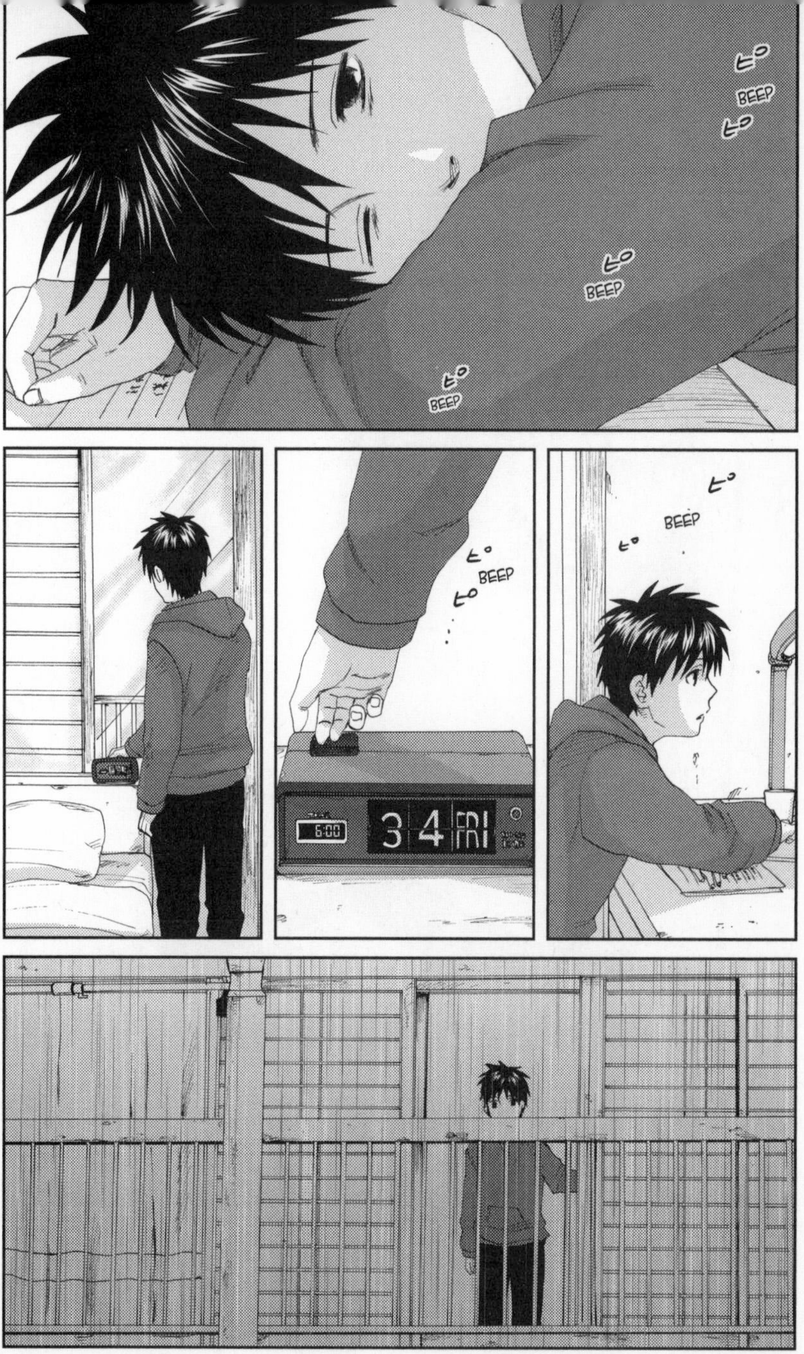
ピ
BEEP
ピ
ピ
BEEP
ピ
BEEP
ピ
BEEP
ピ
ピ
BEEP
ピ
6:00
3 4 FRI

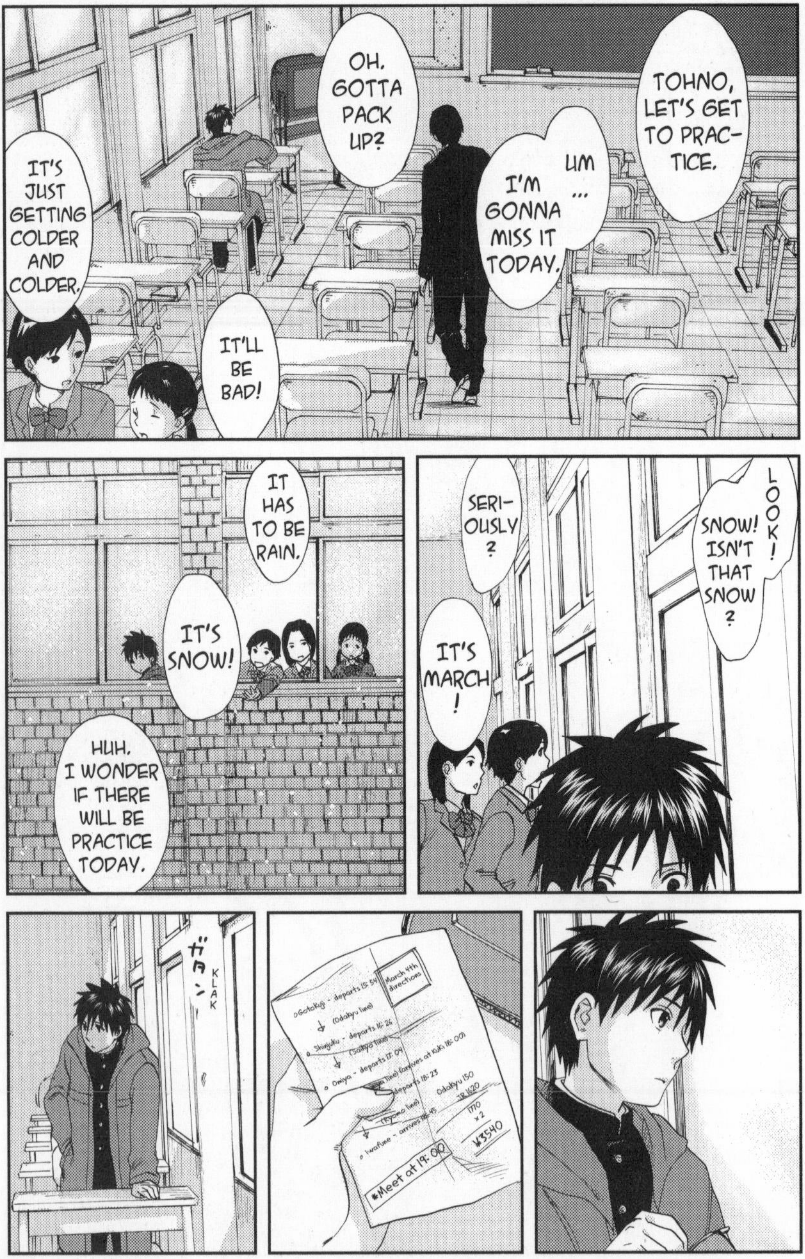
TOHNO, LET'S GET TO PRAC-TICE.
UM ... I'M GONNA MISS IT TODAY.
OH, GOTTA PACK UP?
IT'S JUST GETTING COLDER AND COLDER.
IT'LL BE BAD!
LOOK! SNOW! ISN'T THAT SNOW?
SERI-OUSLY?
IT'S MARCH!
IT HAS TO BE RAIN.
IT'S SNOW!
HUH, I WONDER IF THERE WILL BE PRACTICE TODAY.
March 4th directions
o Gotokuji - departs 15:54
(Odakyu line)
o Shinjuku - departs 16:26
(Saikyo line)
o Omiya - departs 17:04
line) (arrives at Kuki 18:00)
departs 18:23
(Ryomo line)
o Iwafune - arrives 18:45
Odakyu 150
JR 1620
1770
x 2
¥3540
*Meet at 19:00
ガタン
KLAK

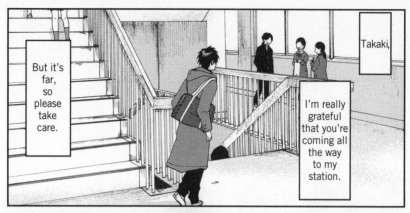

Takaki,
I'm really grateful that you're coming all the way to my station.
But it's far, so please take care.
I'll be there at 7 PM
in the waiting area.
I can't wait
GOTO-KUJI, 15:54.
SHIN-JUKU, 16:26 ON THE SAIKYO LINE.
to see you.

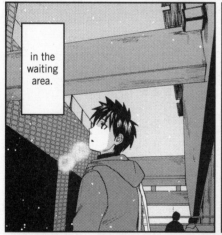

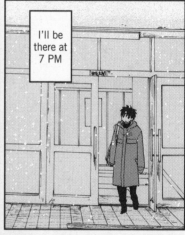

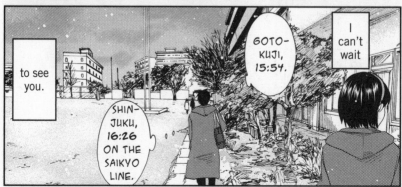

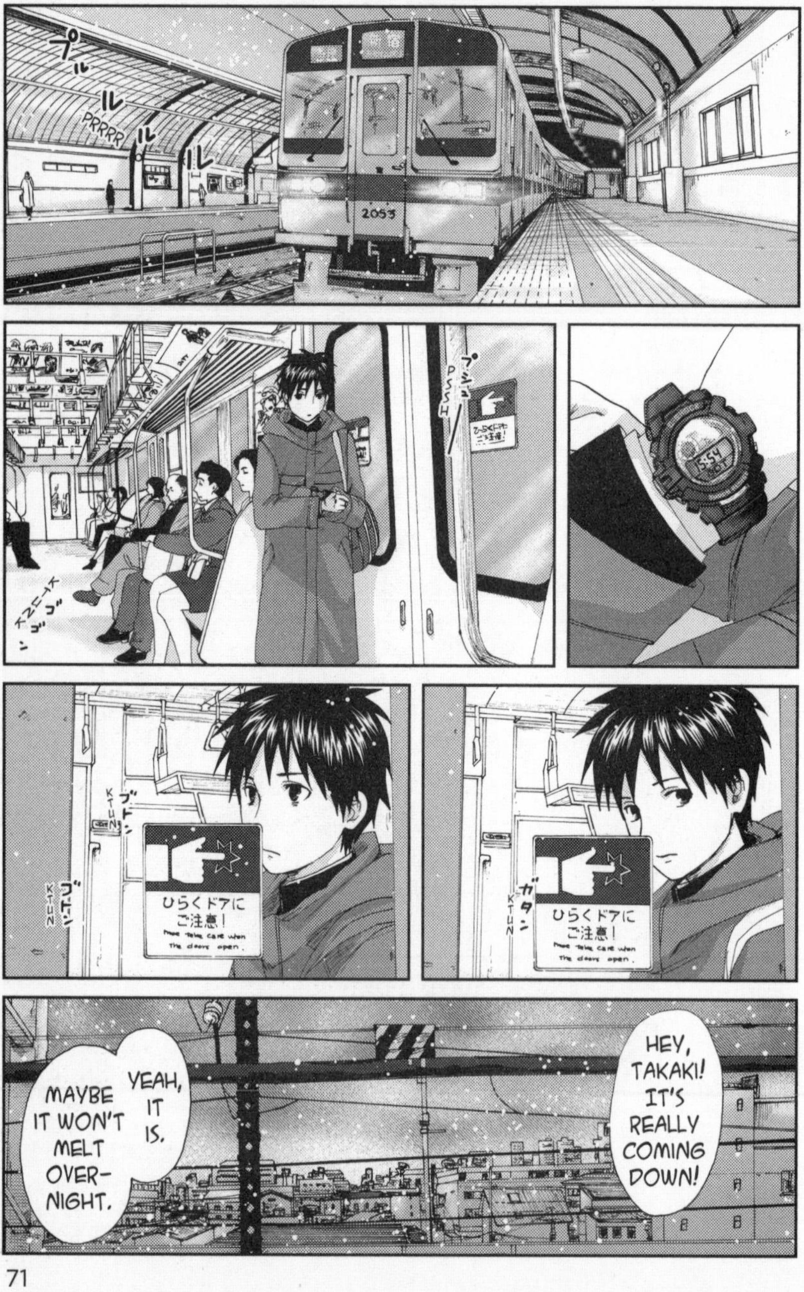
プルルル
PRRRR
プシュ
PSSH
ひらくドアにご注意!
ガタン
KTUN
ひらくドアに
ご注意!
KTUN
KTUN
ひらくドアに
ご注意!
HEY, TAKAKI! IT'S REALLY COMING DOWN!
YEAH, IT IS.
MAYBE IT WON'T MELT OVER-NIGHT.

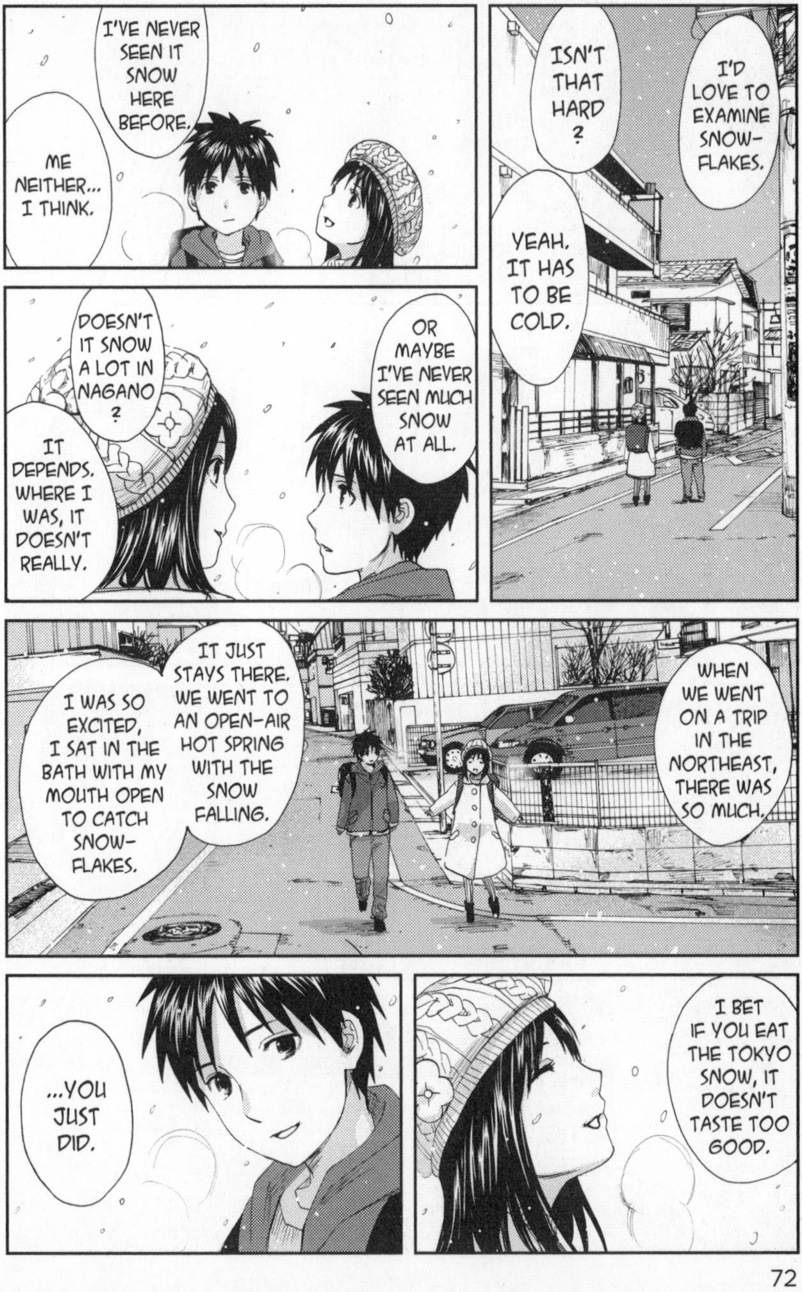
I'D LOVE TO EXAMINE SNOW-FLAKES.
ISN'T THAT HARD?
YEAH. IT HAS TO BE COLD.
I'VE NEVER SEEN IT SNOW HERE BEFORE.
ME NEITHER... I THINK.
OR MAYBE I'VE NEVER SEEN MUCH SNOW AT ALL.
DOESN'T IT SNOW A LOT IN NAGANO?
IT DEPENDS. WHERE I WAS, IT DOESN'T REALLY.
WHEN WE WENT ON A TRIP IN THE NORTHEAST, THERE WAS SO MUCH.
IT JUST STAYS THERE. WE WENT TO AN OPEN-AIR HOT SPRING WITH THE SNOW FALLING.
I WAS SO EXCITED, I SAT IN THE BATH WITH MY MOUTH OPEN TO CATCH SNOW-FLAKES.
I BET IF YOU EAT THE TOKYO SNOW, IT DOESN'T TASTE TOO GOOD.
...YOU JUST DID.

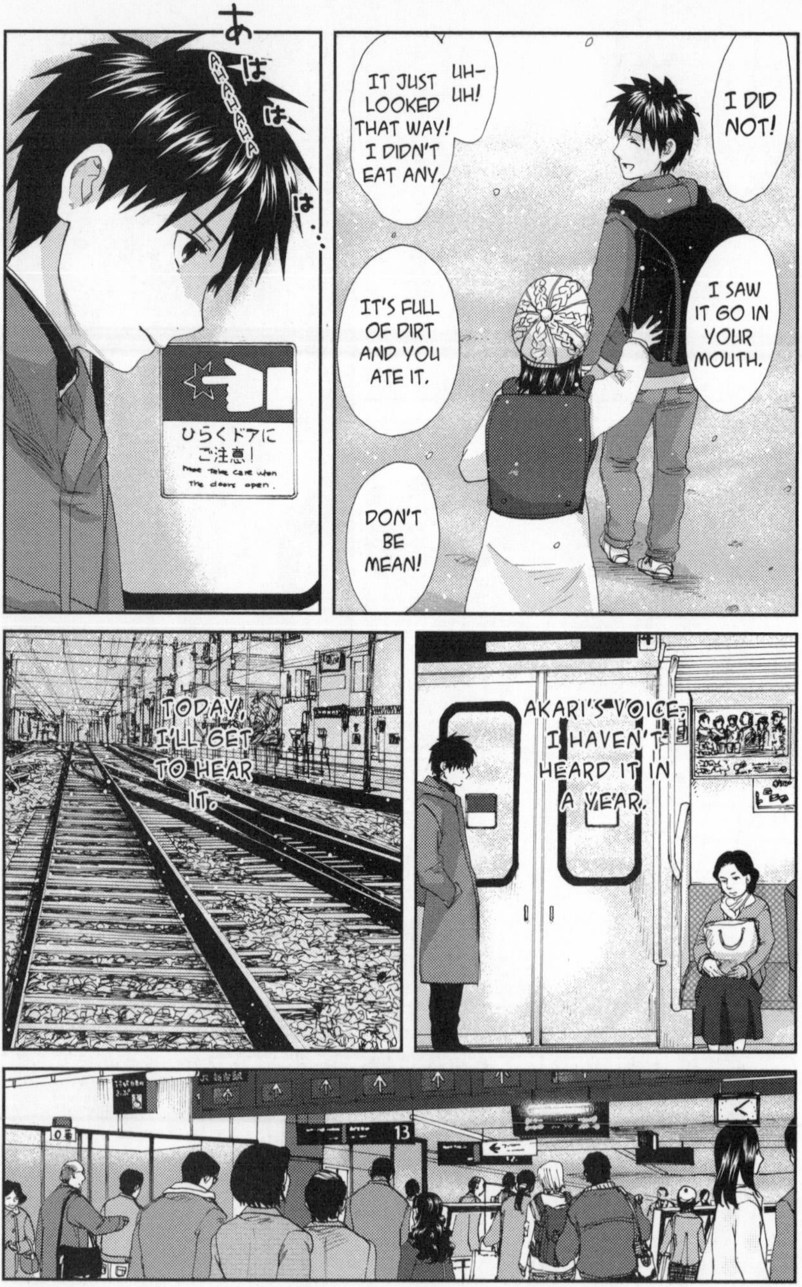
I DID NOT!
UH-UH!
IT JUST LOOKED THAT WAY! I DIDN'T EAT ANY.
I SAW IT GO IN YOUR MOUTH.
IT'S FULL OF DIRT AND YOU ATE IT.
DON'T BE MEAN!
あははは
AHAHAHA
ひらくドアに
ご注意!
Please take care when the doors open.
AKARI'S VOICE. I HAVEN'T HEARD IT IN A YEAR.
TODAY, I'LL GET TO HEAR IT.
13

?
?
JR線
120円~1,620円
6
1000円
120円~1,620円
ご案内
7
8
ザァァァ

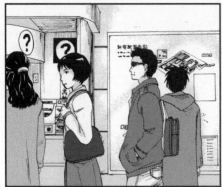

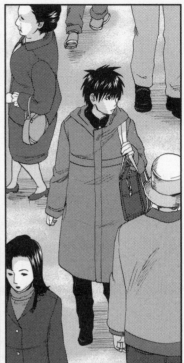

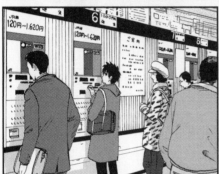

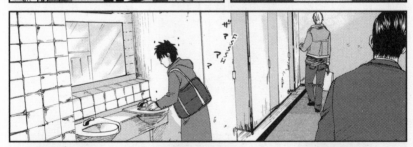

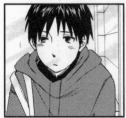

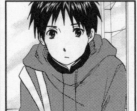

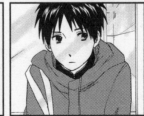

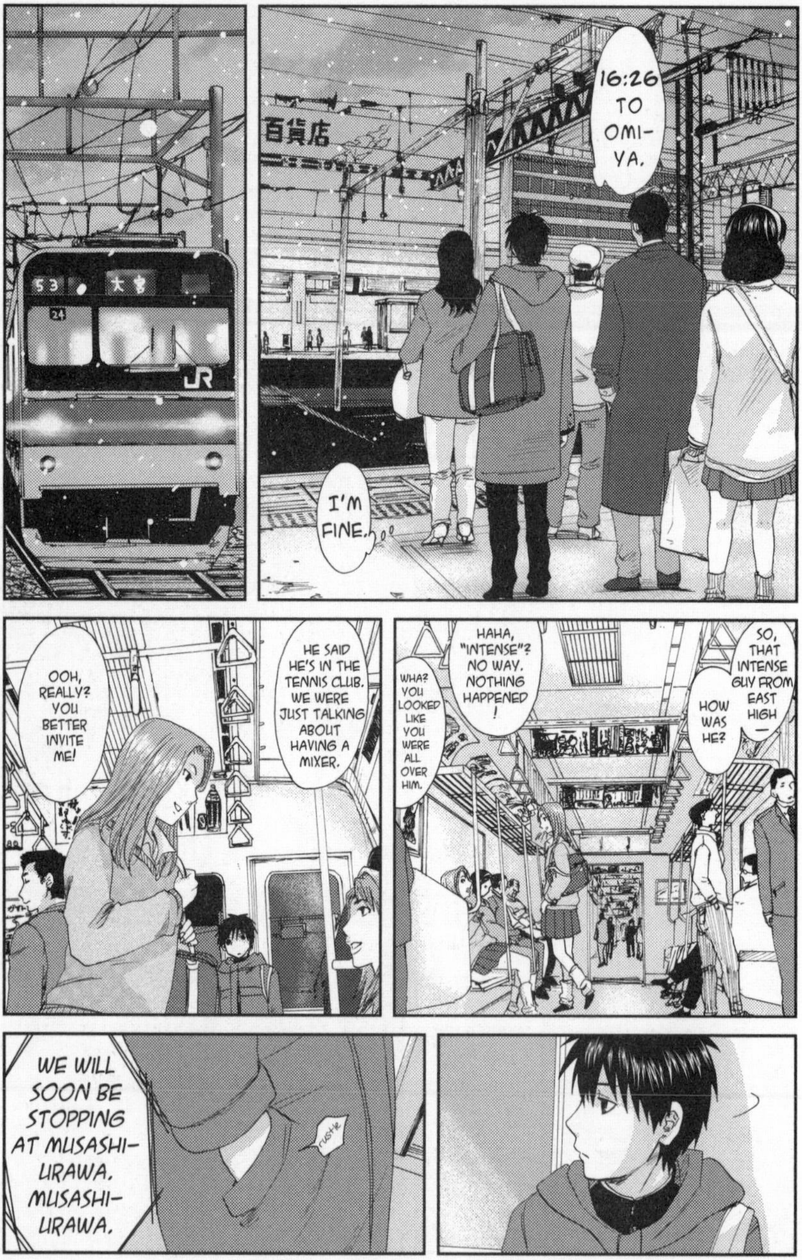
16:26 TO OMI-YA.
百貨店
I'M FINE.
53 大宮
SO, THAT INTENSE GUY FROM EAST HIGH—
HOW WAS HE?
HAHA, "INTENSE"? NO WAY. NOTHING HAPPENED!
WHA? YOU LOOKED LIKE YOU WERE ALL OVER HIM.
HE SAID HE'S IN THE TENNIS CLUB. WE WERE JUST TALKING ABOUT HAVING A MIXER.
OOH, REALLY? YOU BETTER INVITE ME!
WE WILL SOON BE STOPPING AT MUSASHI-URAWA. MUSASHI-URAWA.
rustle

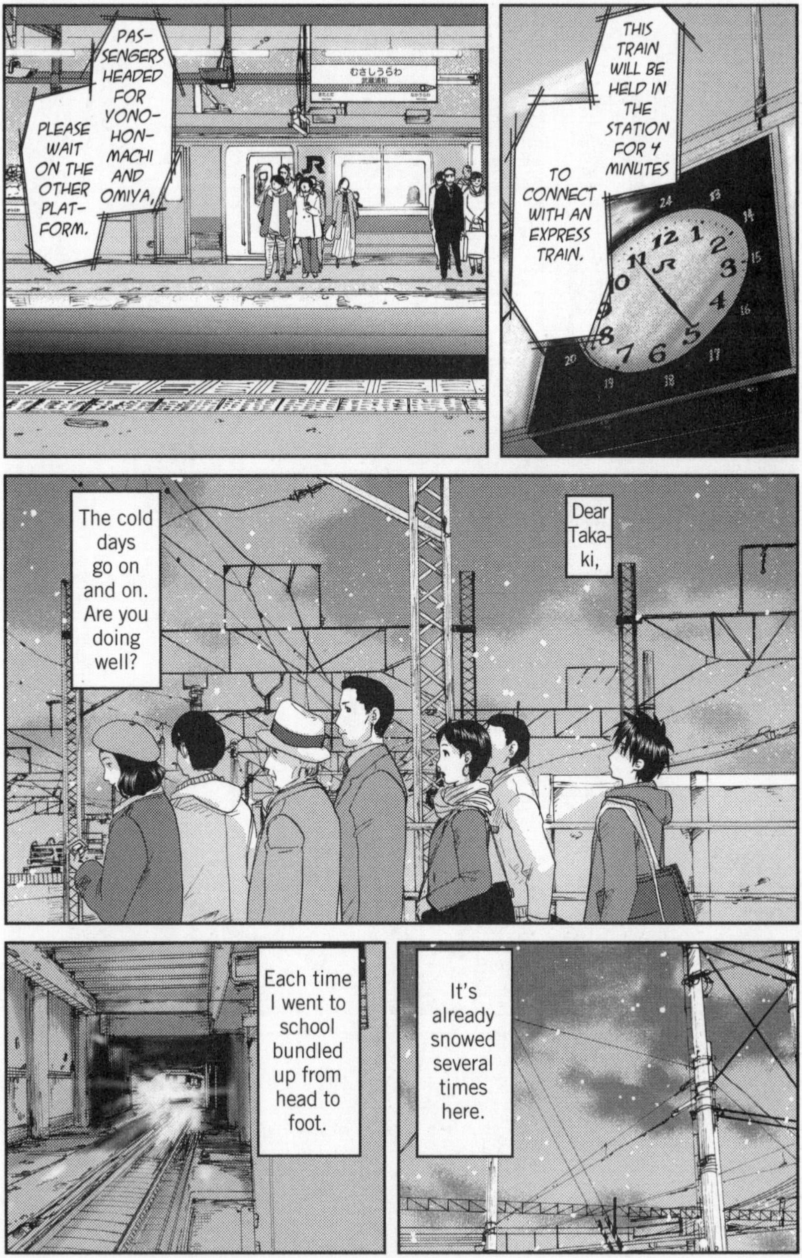
THIS TRAIN WILL BE HELD IN THE STATION FOR 4 MINUTES
TO CONNECT WITH AN EXPRESS TRAIN.
むさしうらわ
PASSENGERS HEADED FOR YONO-HONMACHI AND OMIYA,
PLEASE WAIT ON THE OTHER PLATFORM.
Dear Takaki,
The cold days go on and on. Are you doing well?
It's already snowed several times here.
Each time I went to school bundled up from head to foot.

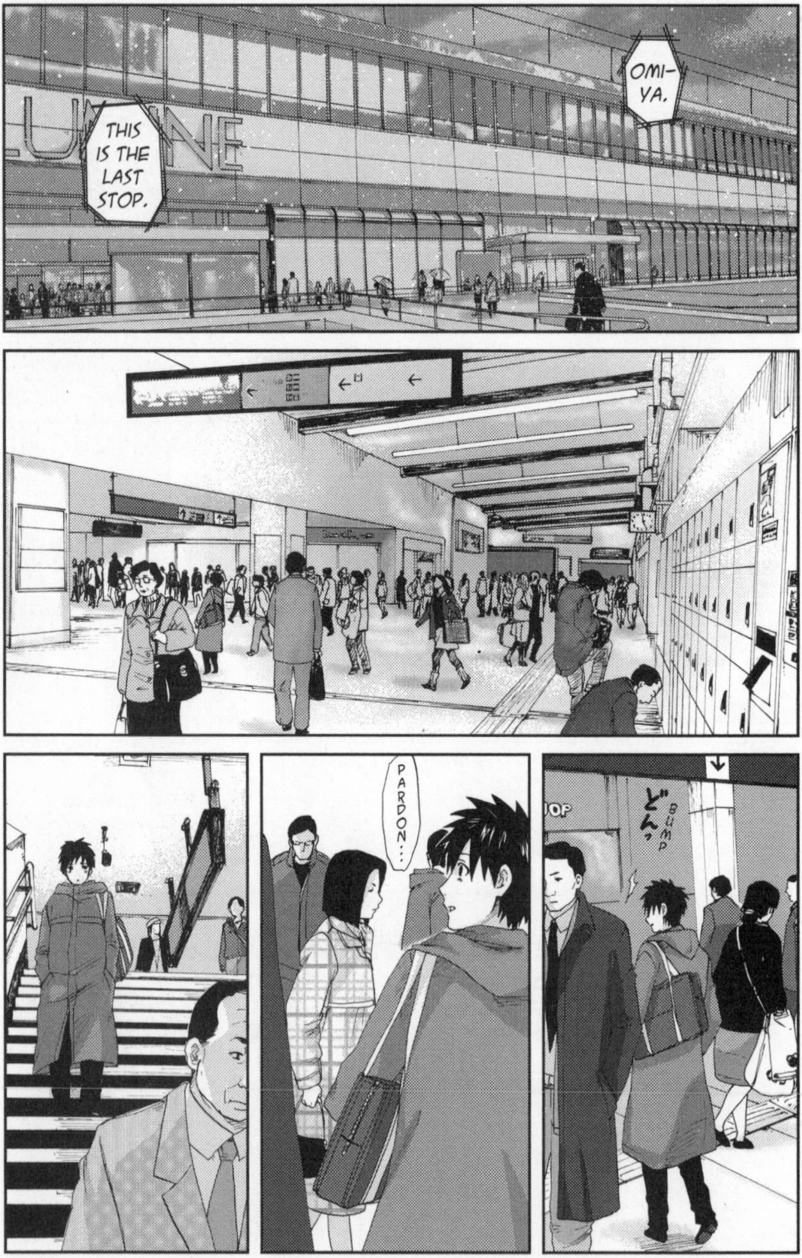
OMI-YA.
THIS IS THE LAST STOP.
どんっ
BUMP
PARDON...

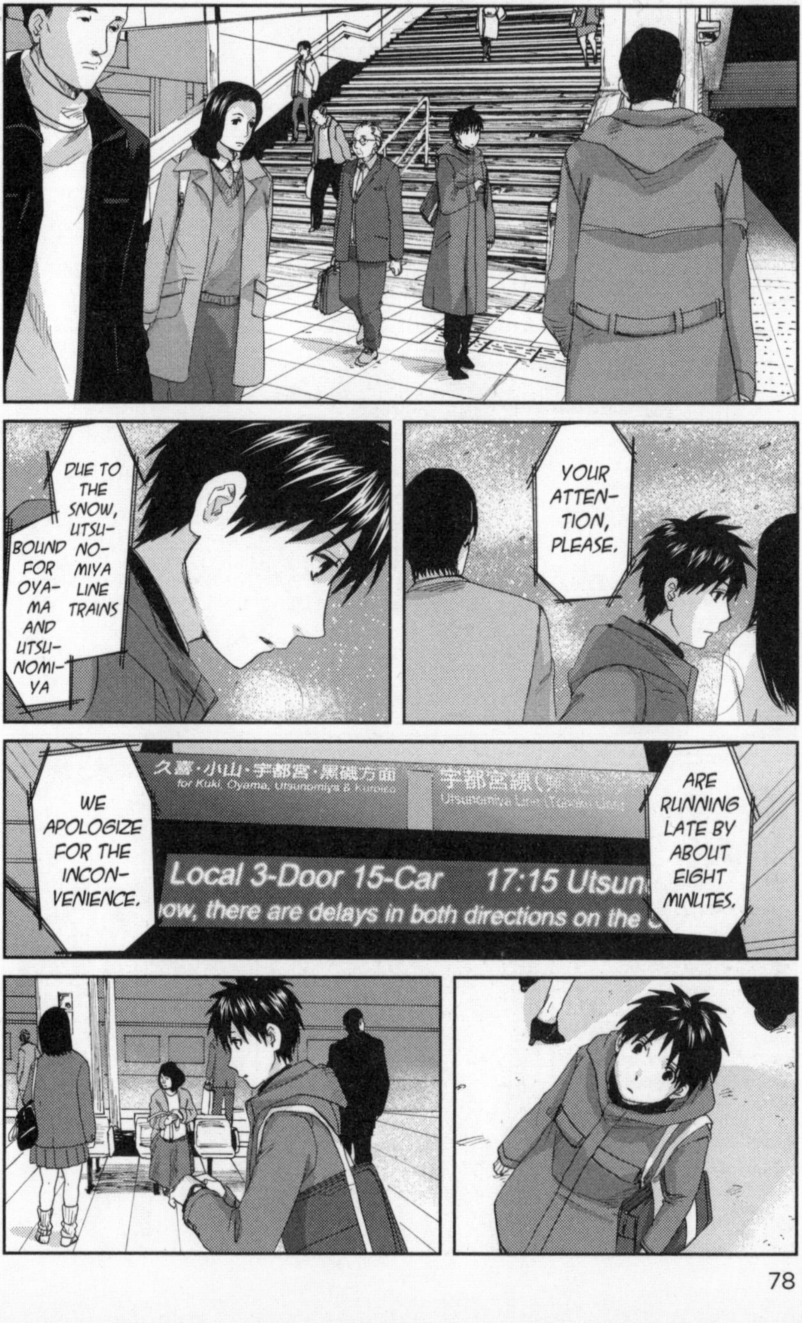
YOUR ATTEN-TION, PLEASE.
DUE TO THE SNOW, UTSU-NO-MIYA LINE TRAINS BOUND FOR OYA-MA AND UTSU-NOMI-YA
ARE RUNNING LATE BY ABOUT EIGHT MINUTES.
久喜・小山・宇都宮・黒磯方面
宇都宮線
Local 3-Door 15-Car 17:15 Utsun
ow, there are delays in both directions on the
WE APOLOGIZE FOR THE INCON-VENIENCE.

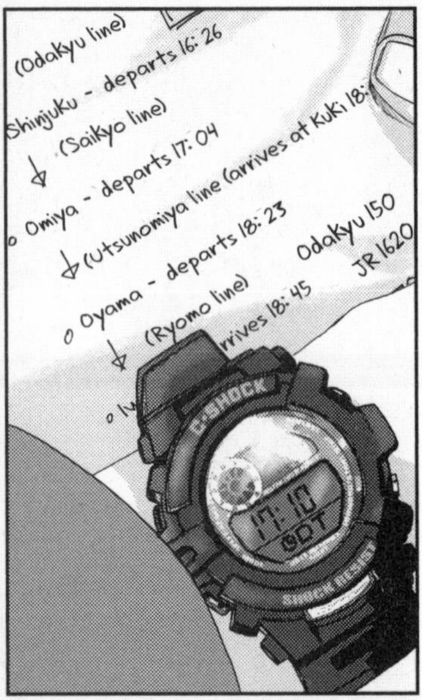

(Odakyu line)
Shinjuku - departs 16:26
↓ (Saikyo line)
o Omiya - departs 17:04
Utsunomiya line (arrives at Kuki 18:
↓ (Utsunomiya line
o Oyama - departs 18:23
↓ (Ryomo line)
arrives 18:45
Odakyu 150
JR 1620
G-SHOCK
17:10

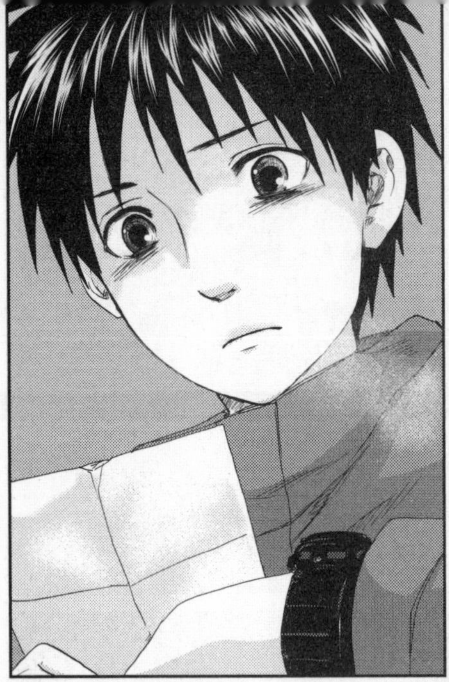

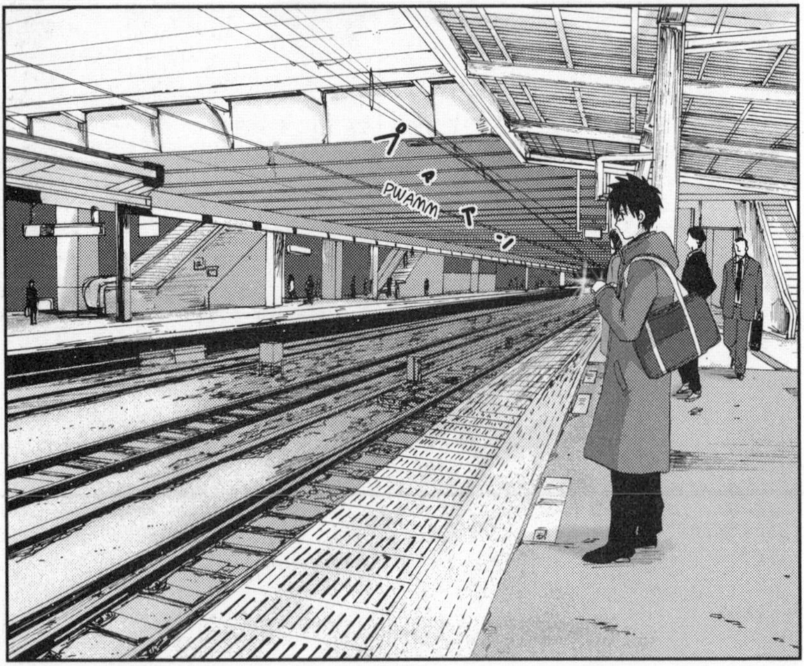

PWAMM

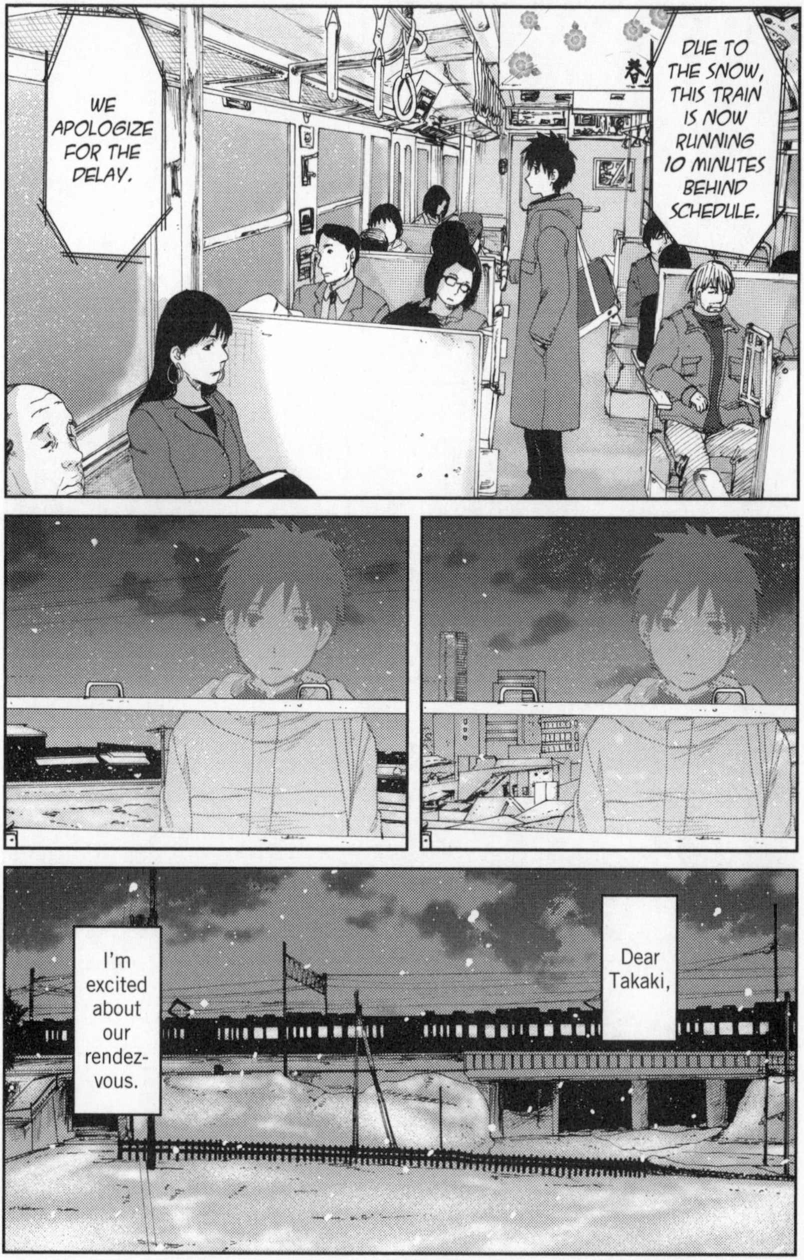
DUE TO THE SNOW, THIS TRAIN IS NOW RUNNING 10 MINUTES BEHIND SCHEDULE.
WE APOLOGIZE FOR THE DELAY.
Dear Takaki,
I'm excited about our rendez-vous.

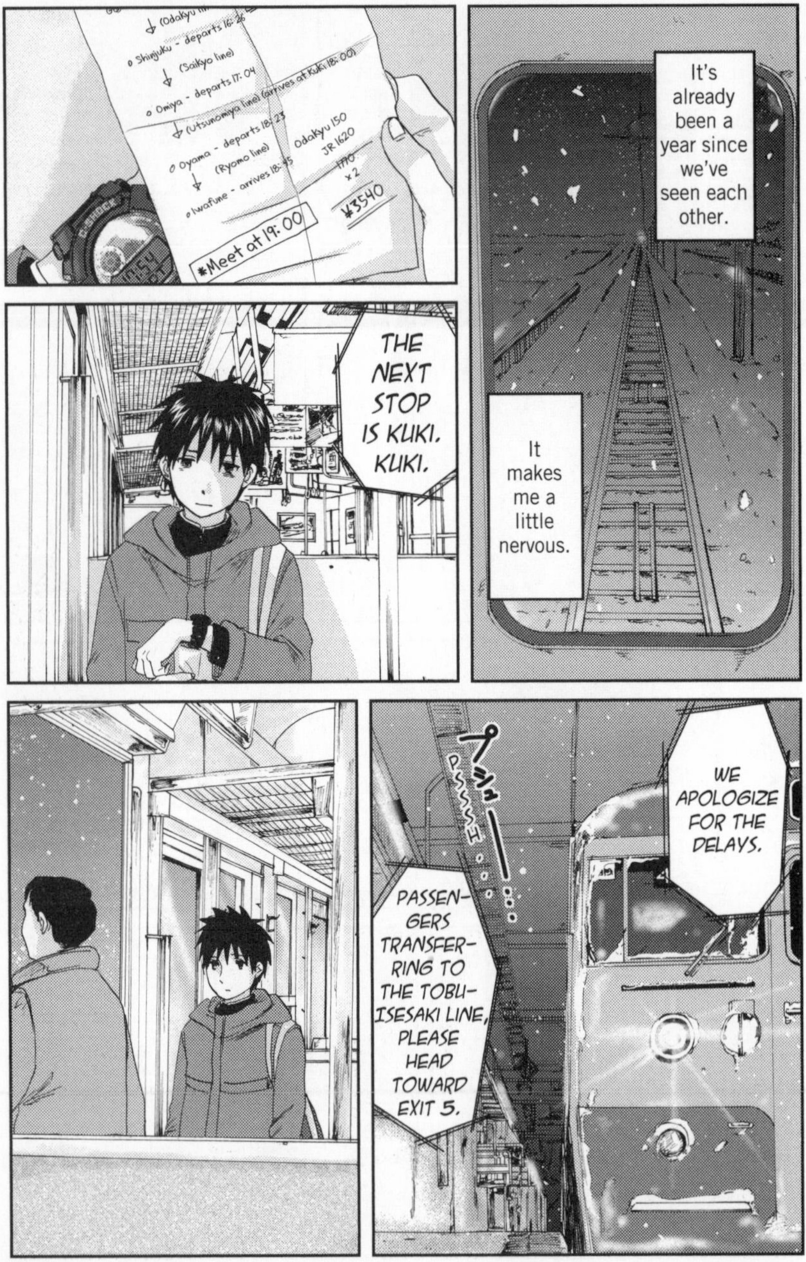
It's already been a year since we've seen each other.
It makes me a little nervous.
↓ (Odakyu line)
o Shinjuku - departs 16:26
↓ (Saikyo line)
o Omiya - departs 17:04
↓ (Utsunomiya line) (arrives at Kuki 18:00)
o Oyama - departs 18:23
↓ (Ryomo line)
o Iwafune - arrives 18:45
Odakyu 150
JR 1620
1770
×2
¥3540
*Meet at 19:00
THE NEXT STOP IS KUKI. KUKI.
WE APOLOGIZE FOR THE DELAYS.
プシュー…
PSSSSH
PASSENGERS TRANSFERRING TO THE TOBU-ISESAKI LINE, PLEASE HEAD TOWARD EXIT 5.

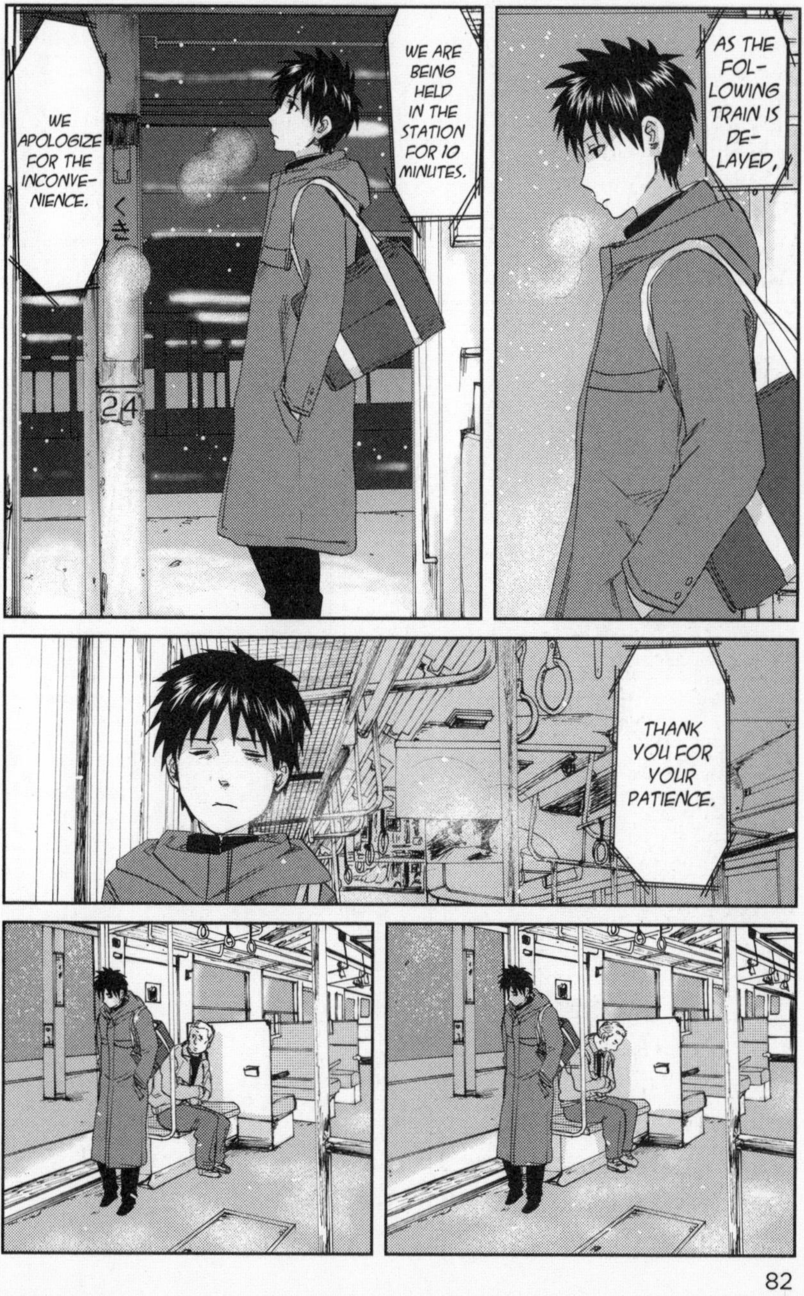
AS THE FOL-LOWING TRAIN IS DE-LAYED,
WE ARE BEING HELD IN THE STATION FOR 10 MINUTES.
WE APOLOGIZE FOR THE INCONVE-NIENCE.
THANK YOU FOR YOUR PATIENCE.

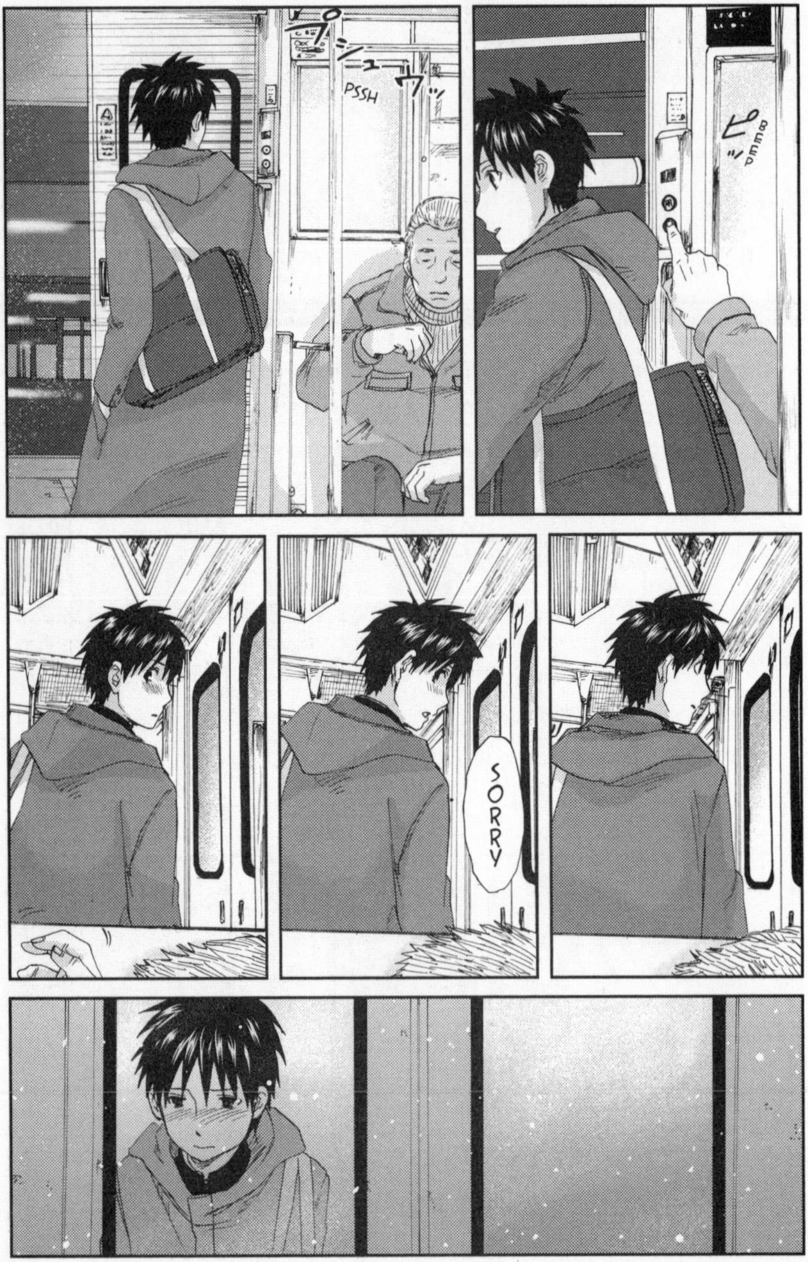
ピッ
BEEP
プシュウッ
PSSH
SORRY

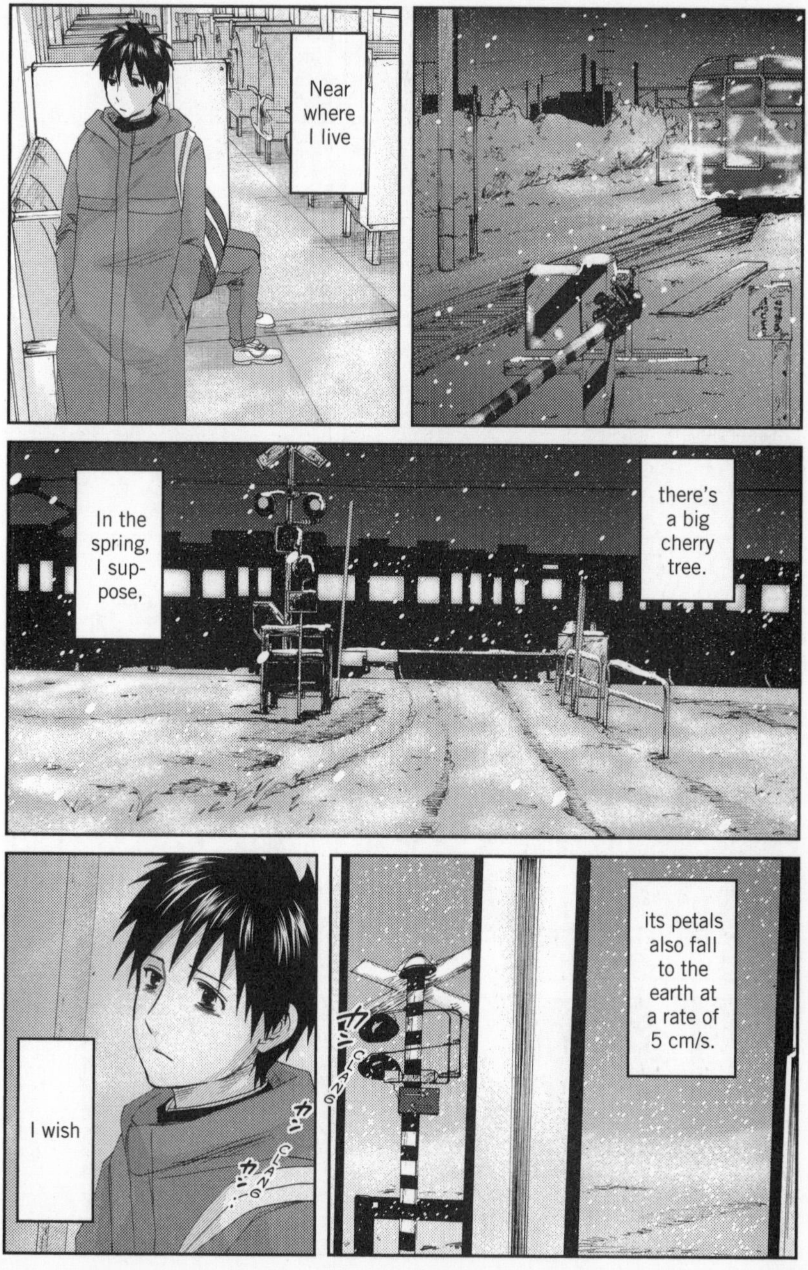
Near where I live
there's a big cherry tree.
In the spring, I suppose,
its petals also fall to the earth at a rate of 5 cm/s.
カン
CLANG
I wish
カン
CLANG
カン…

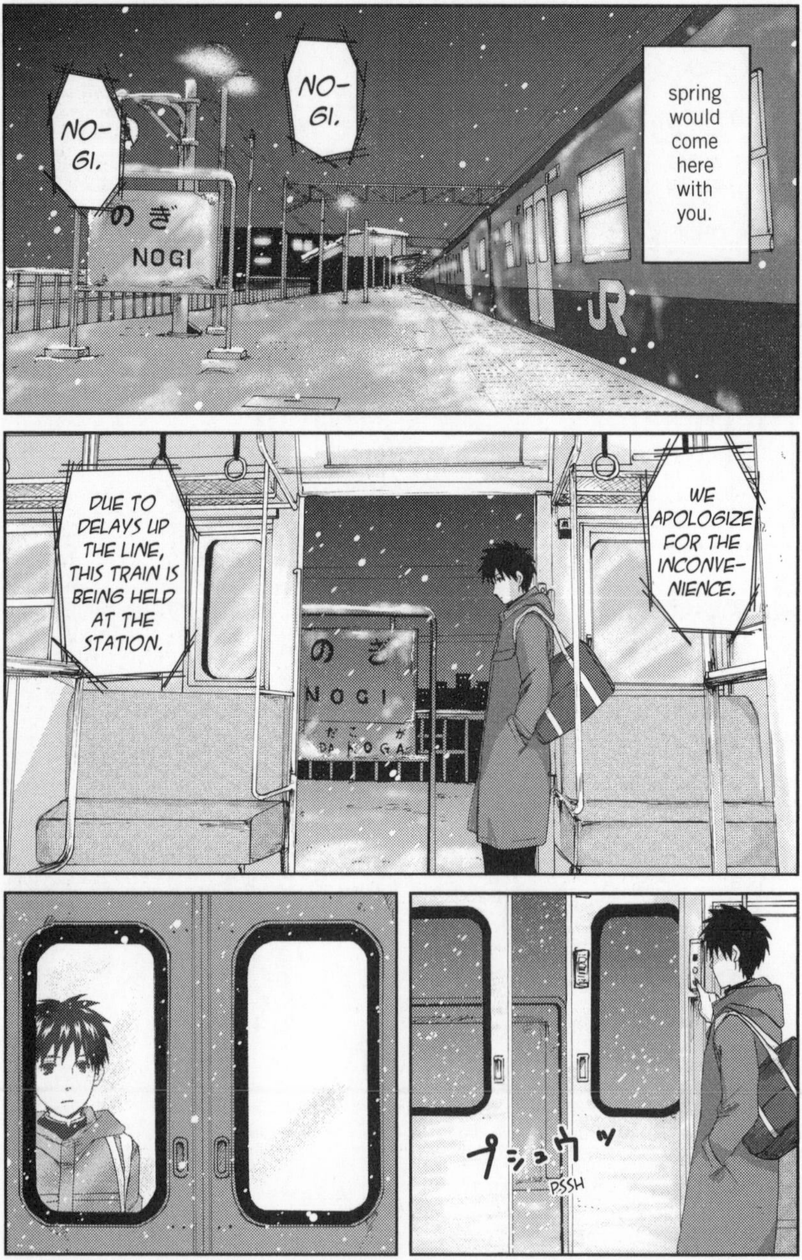
spring would come here with you.
NO-GI.
NO-GI.
のぎ
NOGI
WE APOLOGIZE FOR THE INCONVENIENCE.
DUE TO DELAYS UP THE LINE, THIS TRAIN IS BEING HELD AT THE STATION.
のぎ
NOGI
プシュウッ
PSSH

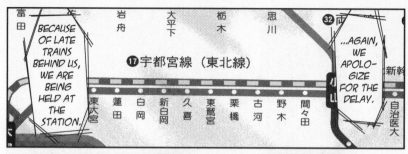

...AGAIN, WE APOLOGIZE FOR THE DELAY.
BECAUSE OF LATE TRAINS BEHIND US, WE ARE BEING HELD AT THE STATION.
⑰宇都宮線（東北線）
思川
栃木
大平下
岩舟
富田
新幹
自治医大
間々田
野木
古河
栗橋
東鷲宮
久喜
新白岡
白岡
蓮田
東大宮
18:59
19:00
ドサッ
THUMP

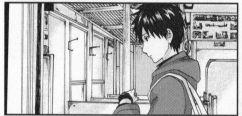

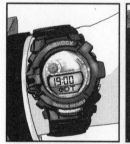

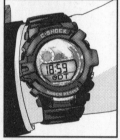

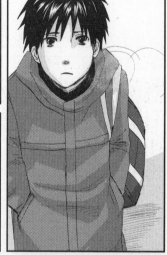

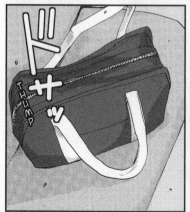

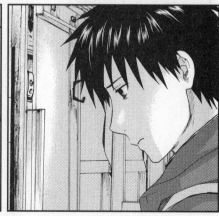

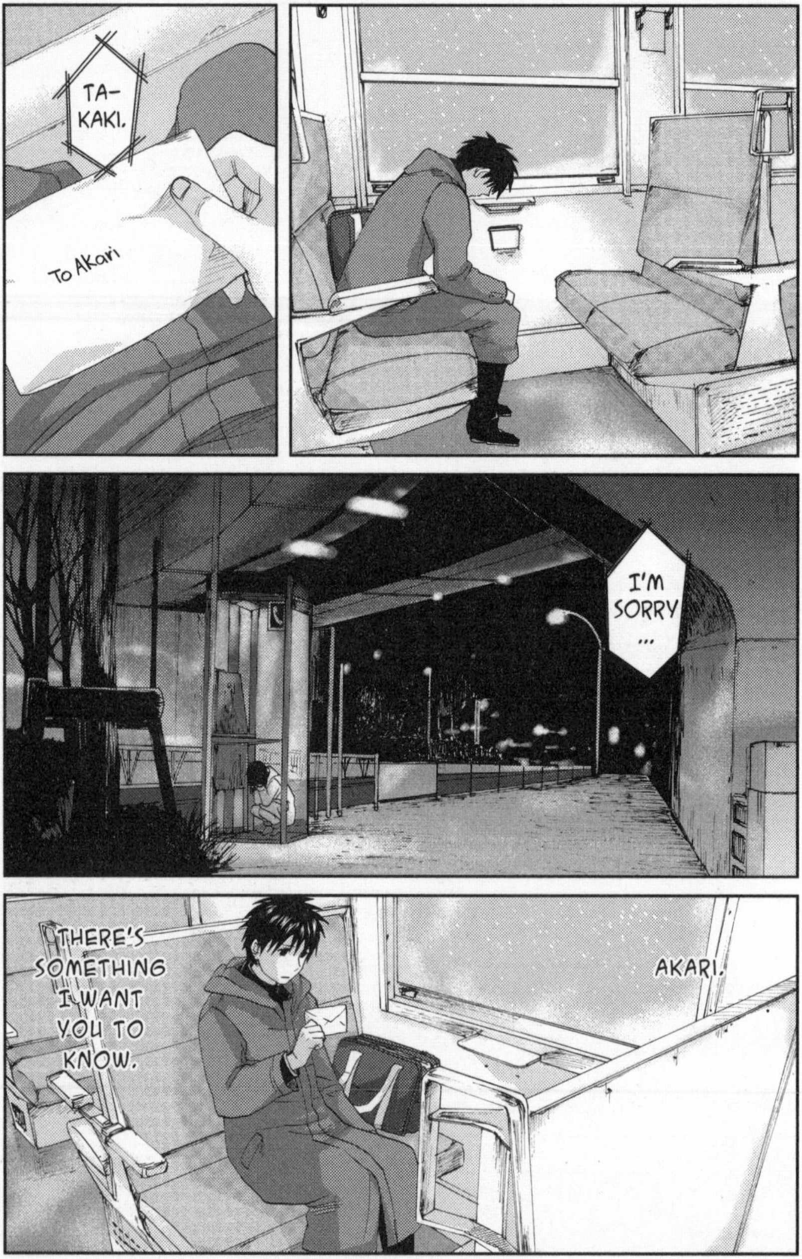
TA-KAKI.
To Akari
I'M SORRY ...
AKARI.
THERE'S SOMETHING I WANT YOU TO KNOW.

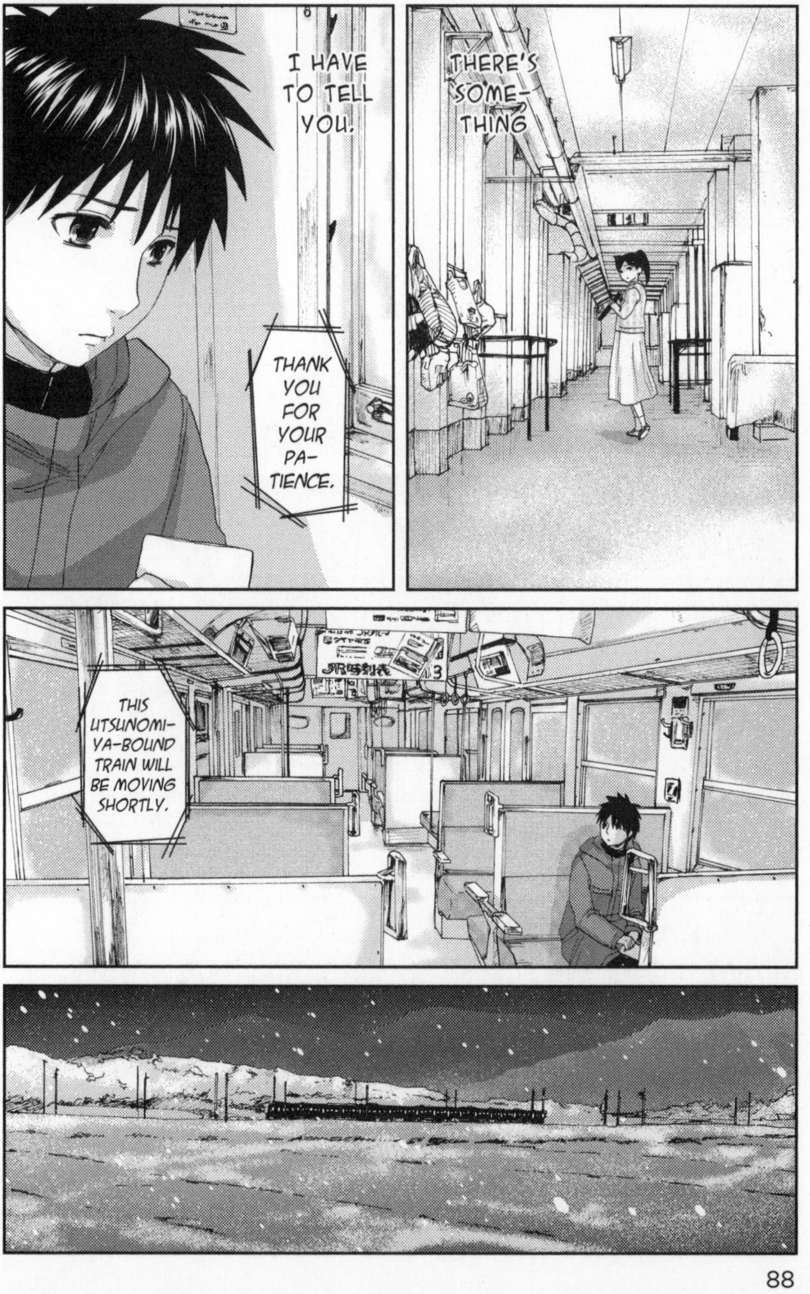
THERE'S SOME-THING
I HAVE TO TELL YOU.
THANK YOU FOR YOUR PA-TIENCE.
THIS UTSUNOMI-YA-BOUND TRAIN WILL BE MOVING SHORTLY.

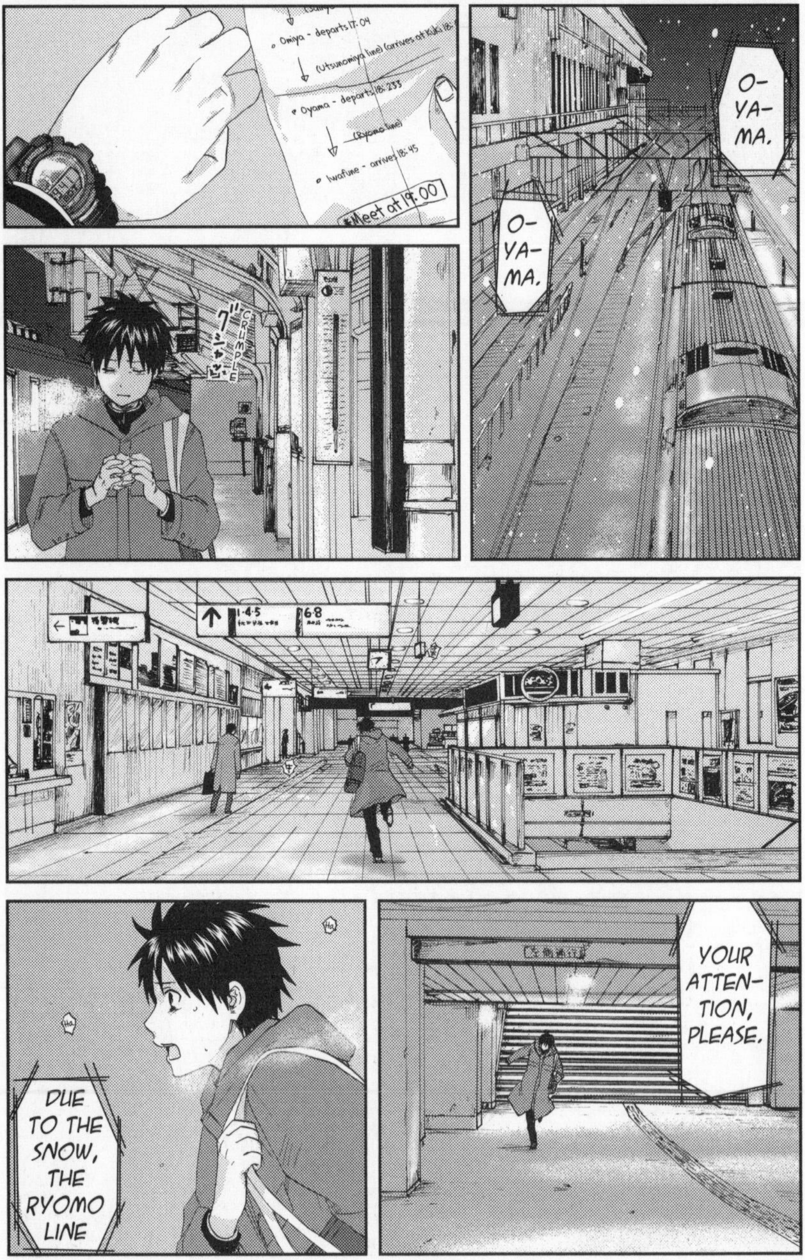
O-YA-MA.
O-YA-MA.
Omiya - departs 17:04
(Utsunomiya line) (arrives at Kuki 18:
Oyama - departs 18:233
(Ryomo line)
Iwafune - arrives 18:45
*Meet at 19:00
CRUMPLE
YOUR ATTEN-TION, PLEASE.
DUE TO THE SNOW, THE RYOMO LINE

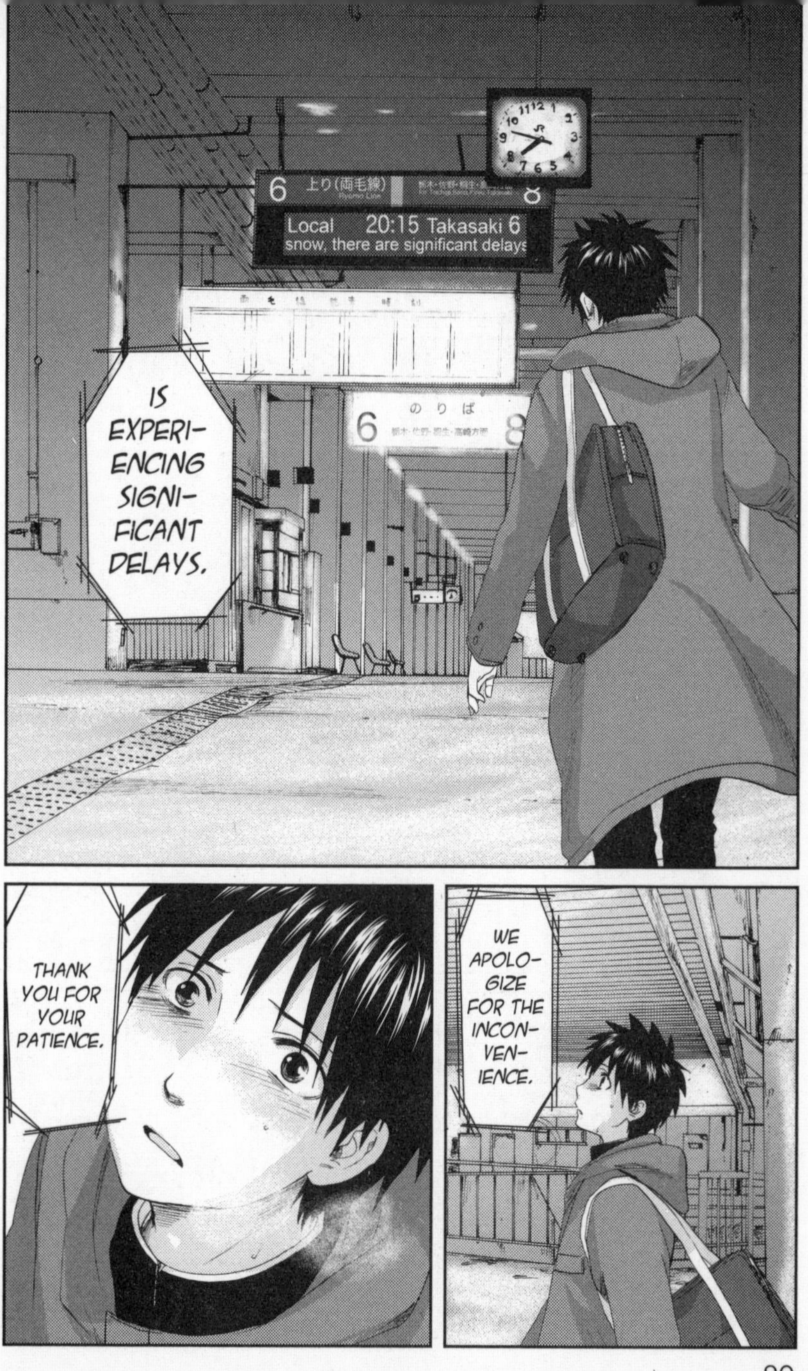
6 上り(両毛線)
Local 20:15 Takasaki 6
snow, there are significant delays
6 のりば 8
IS EXPERIENCING SIGNIFICANT DELAYS.
WE APOLOGIZE FOR THE INCONVENIENCE.
THANK YOU FOR YOUR PATIENCE.

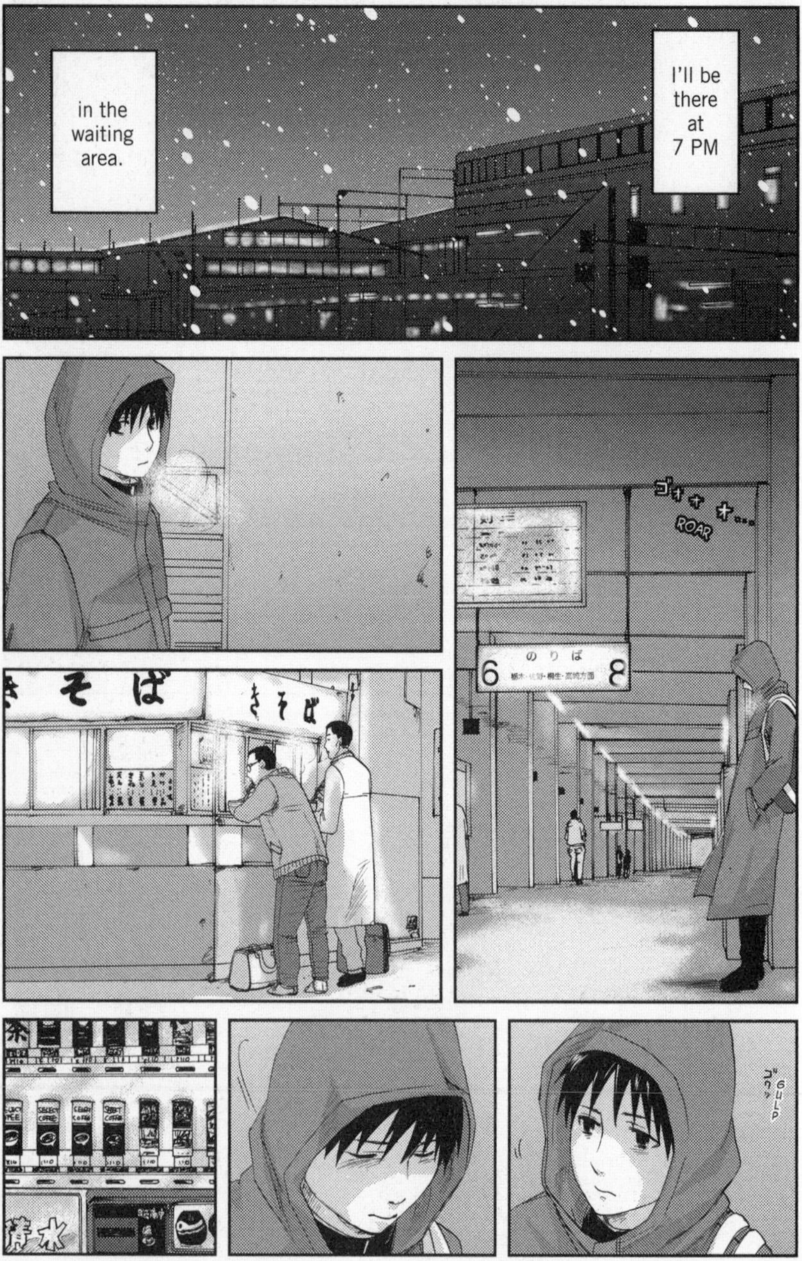
I'll be there at 7 PM
in the waiting area.
ゴォォオ…
ROAR
のりば
6
8
きそば
ゴクッ
GULP

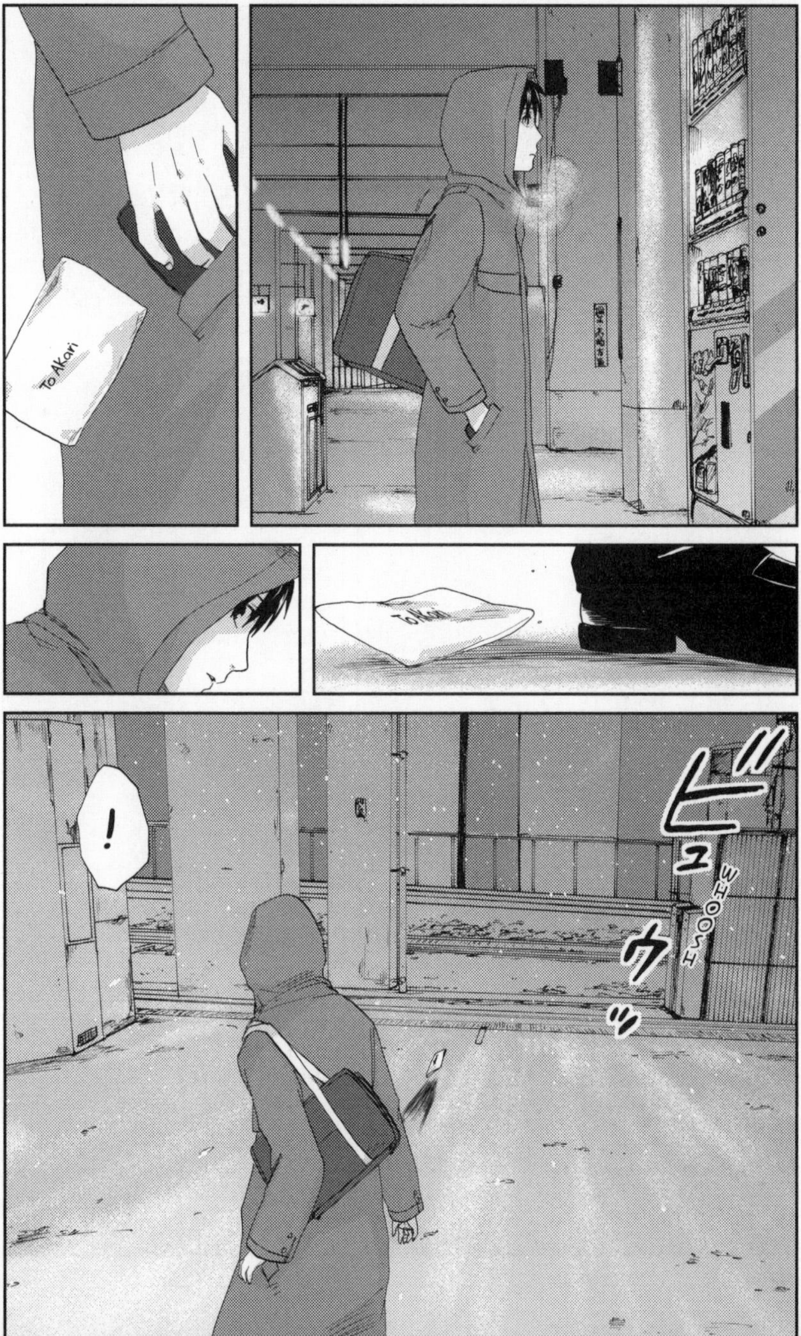
To Akari
To Akari
!
ビュゥッ
WHOOSH

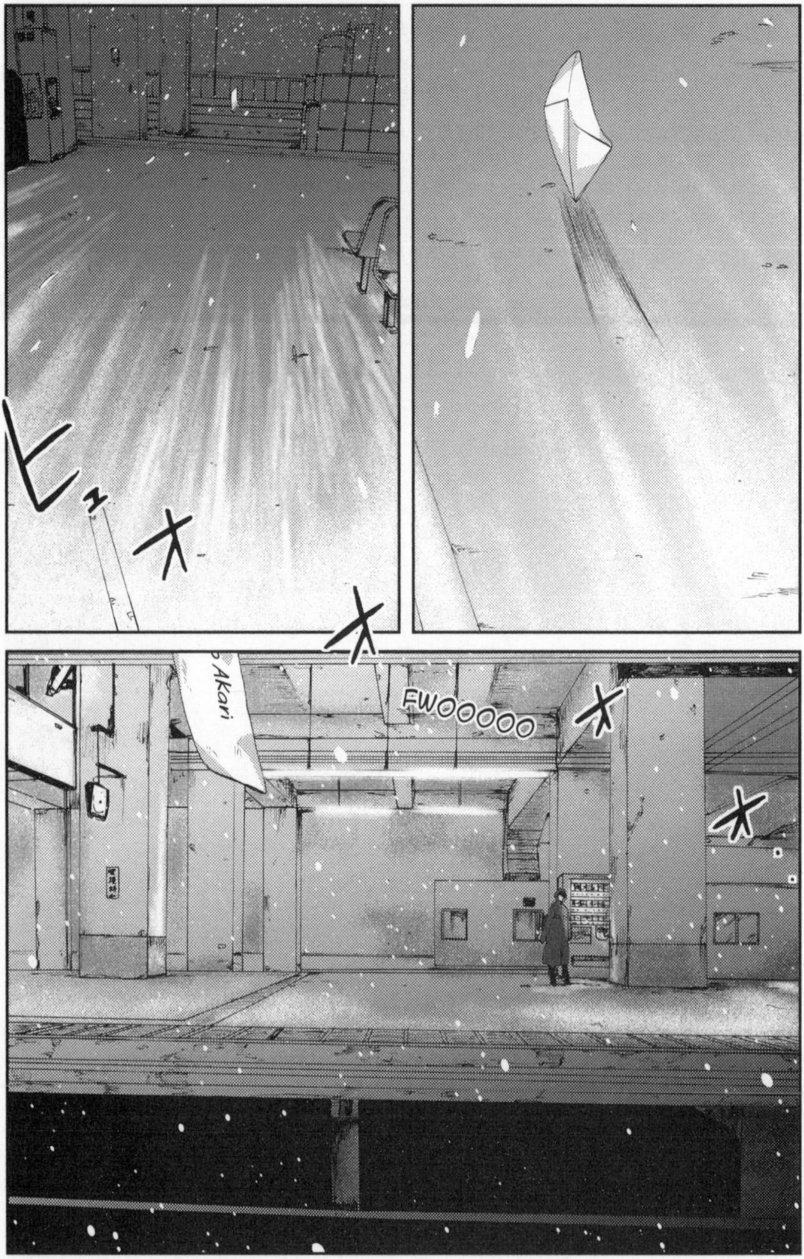
ヒュオオオオ
FWOOOOO
Akari

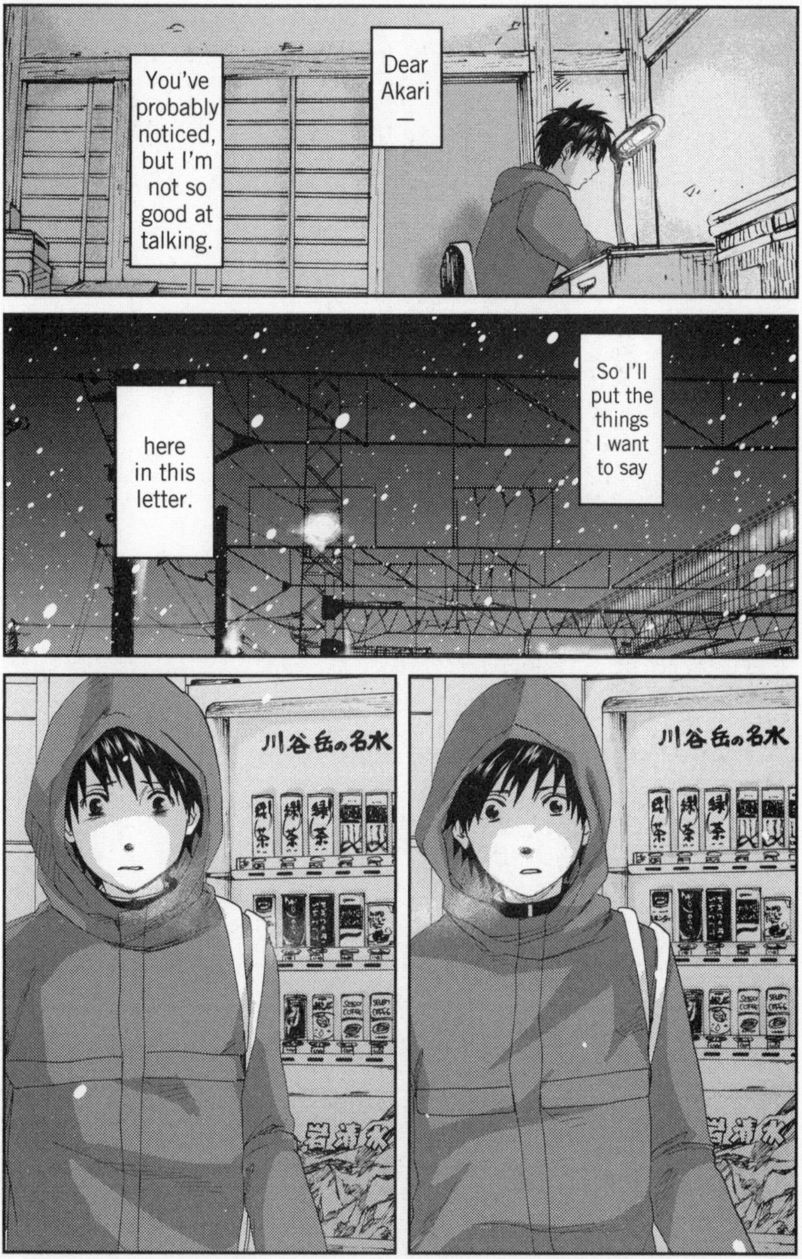
Dear Akari —
You've probably noticed, but I'm not so good at talking.
So I'll put the things I want to say
here in this letter.
川谷岳の名水
川谷岳の名水

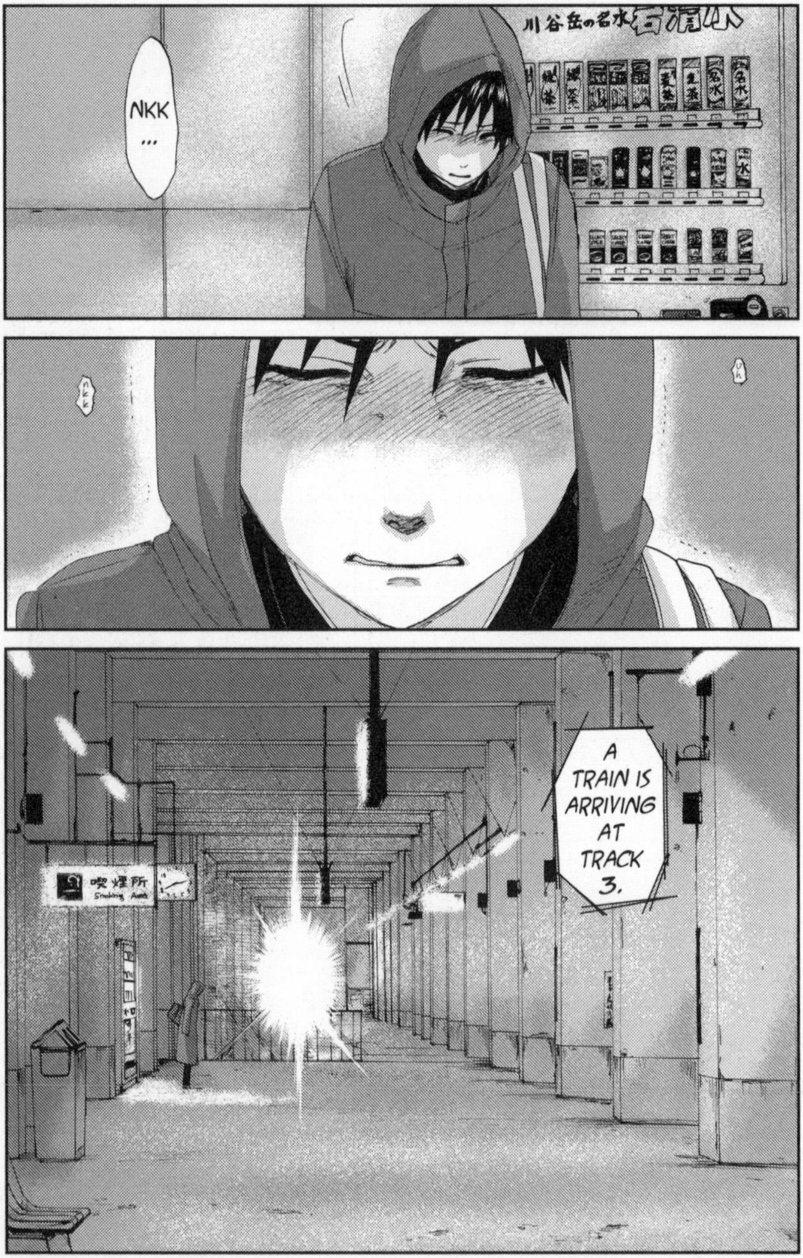

川谷岳の名水
NKK ...
uh
nkk
A TRAIN IS ARRIVING AT TRACK 3.
喫煙所
Smoking Area

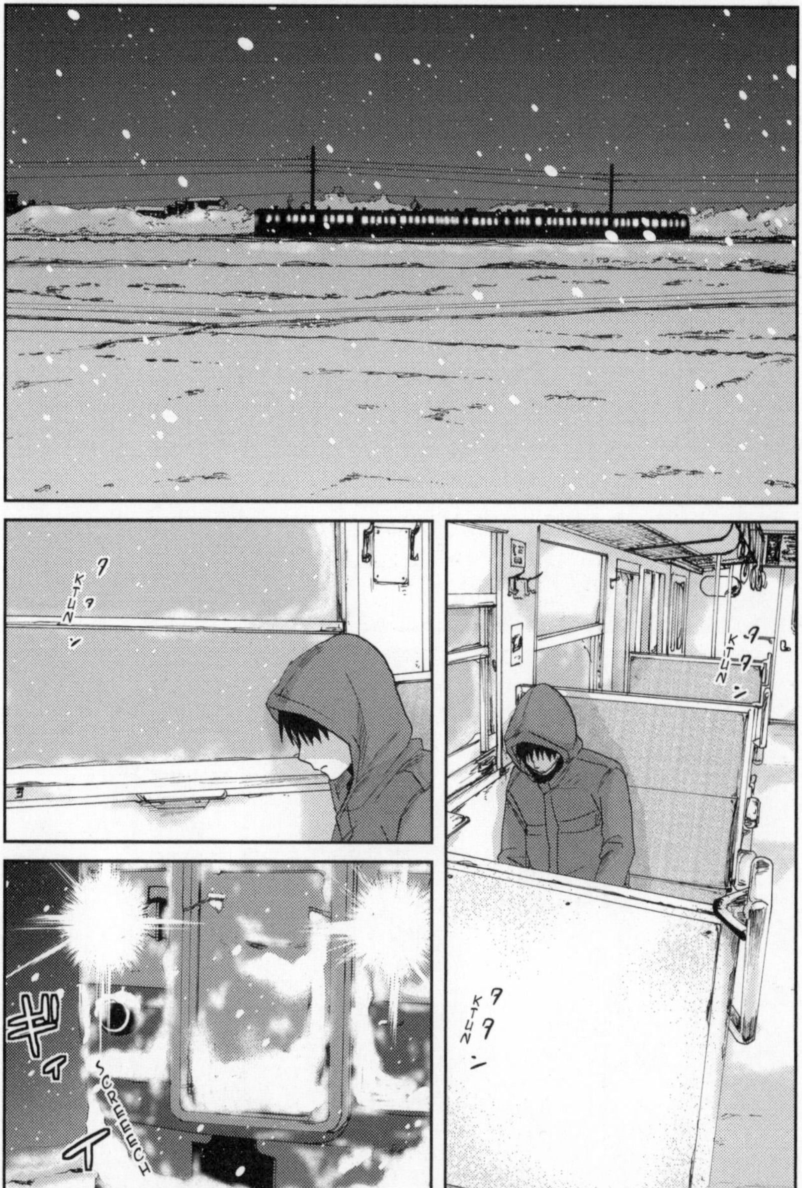
タタン
KTUN
タタン
KTUN
タタン
KTUN
ギィイイ
SCREEECH

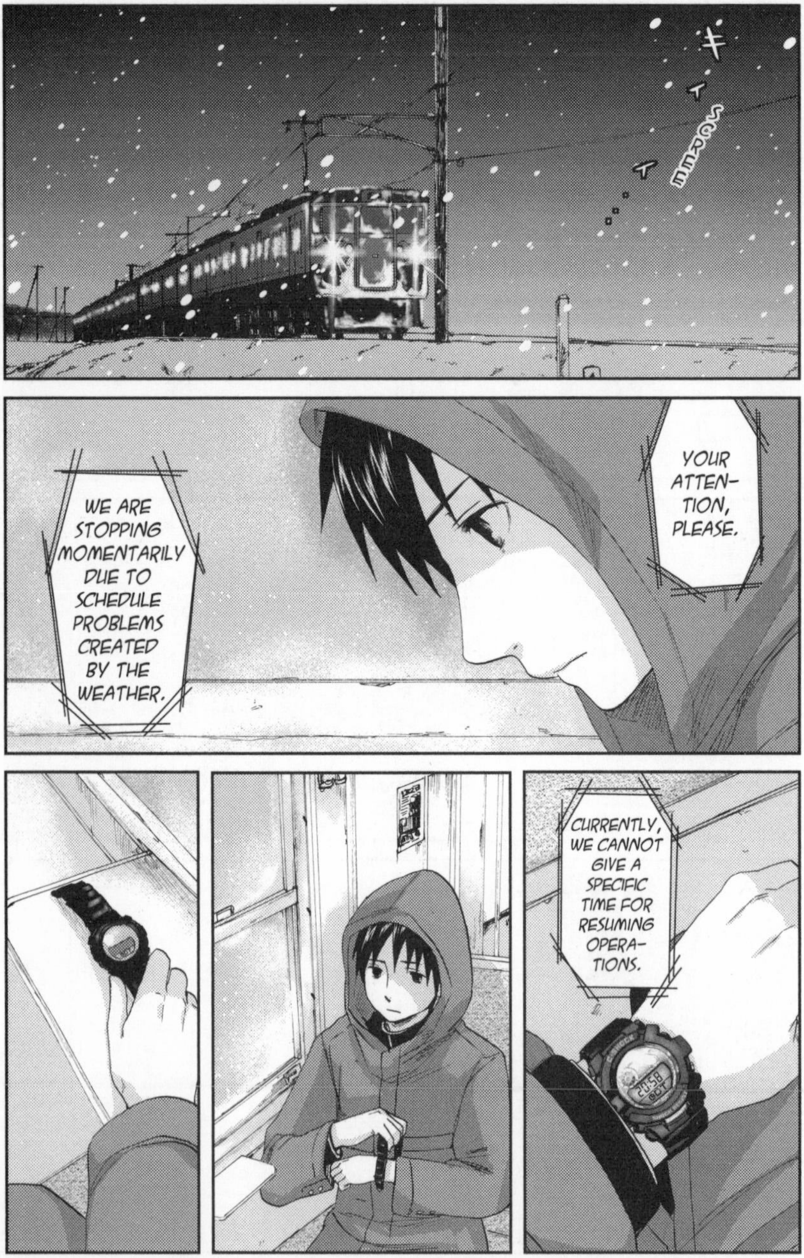
SCREEE
YOUR ATTEN- TION, PLEASE.
WE ARE STOPPING MOMENTARILY DUE TO SCHEDULE PROBLEMS CREATED BY THE WEATHER.
CURRENTLY, WE CANNOT GIVE A SPECIFIC TIME FOR RESUMING OPERA- TIONS.

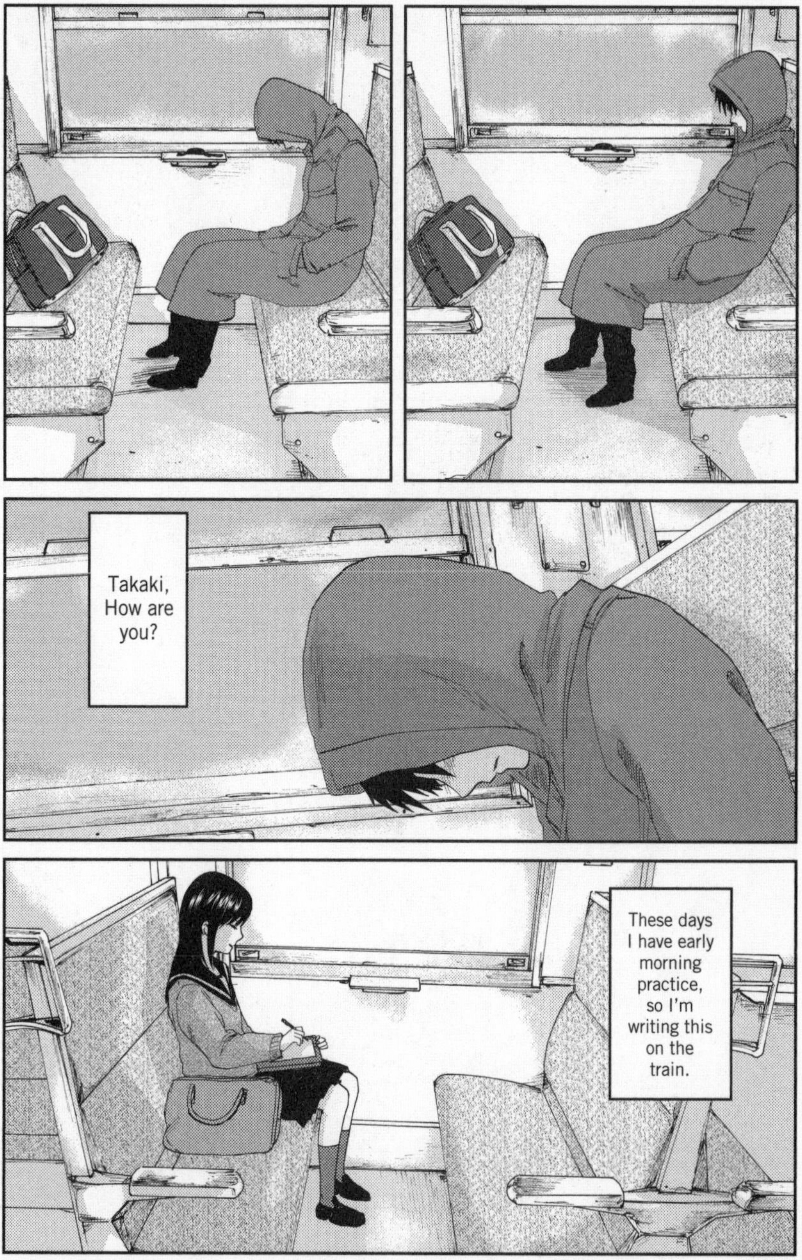
Takaki, How are you?
These days I have early morning practice, so I'm writing this on the train.

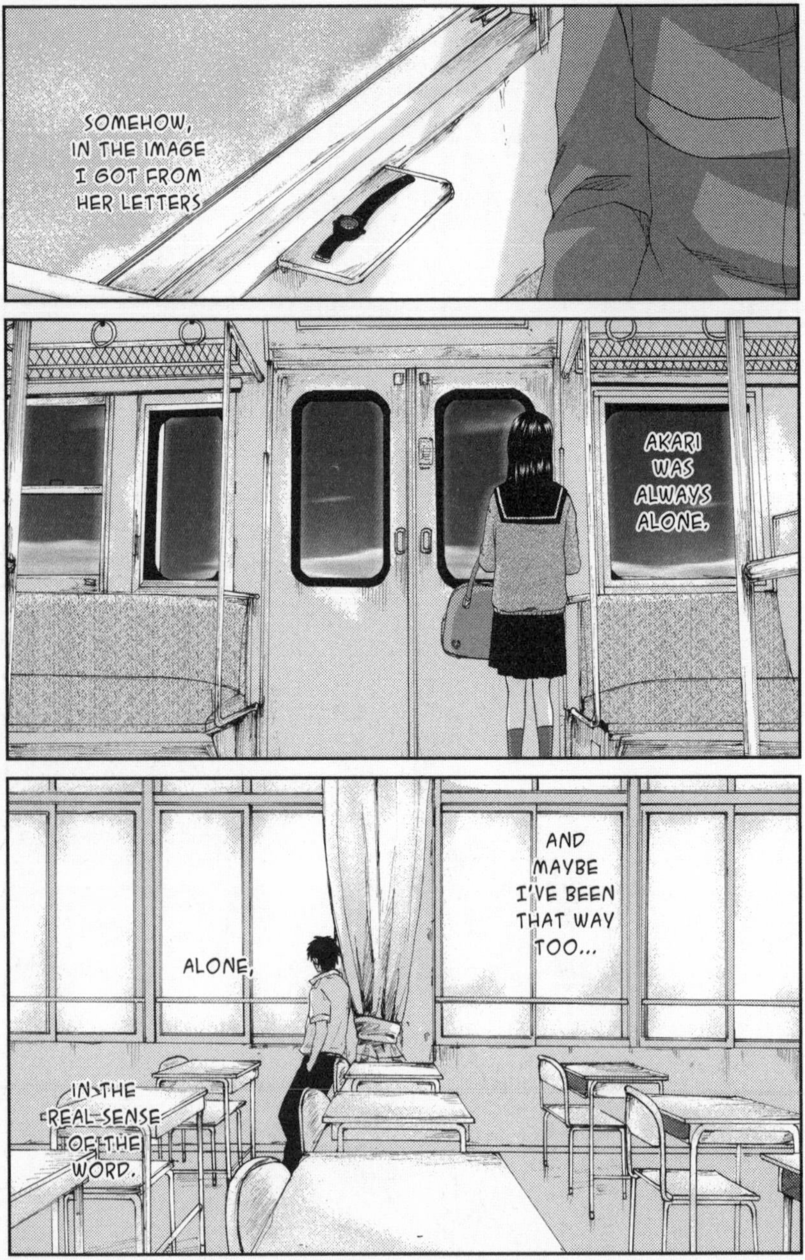
SOMEHOW, IN THE IMAGE I GOT FROM HER LETTERS
AKARI WAS ALWAYS ALONE.
AND MAYBE I'VE BEEN THAT WAY TOO...
ALONE,
IN THE REAL SENSE OF THE WORD.

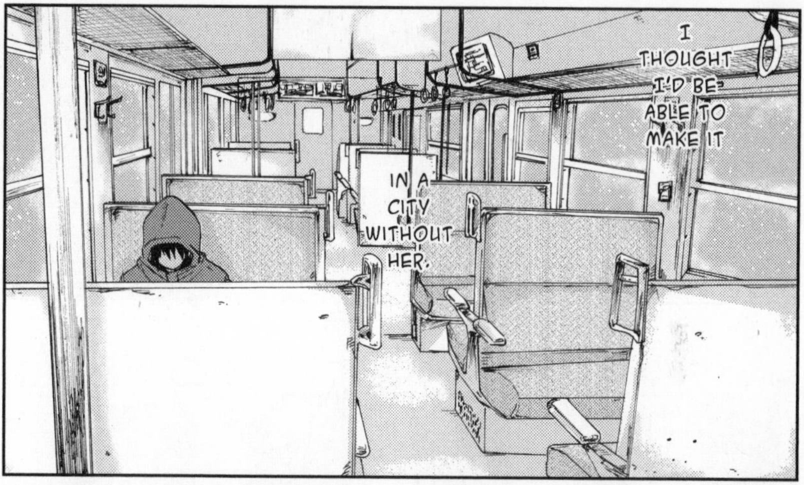
I THOUGHT I'D BE ABLE TO MAKE IT
IN A CITY WITHOUT HER.

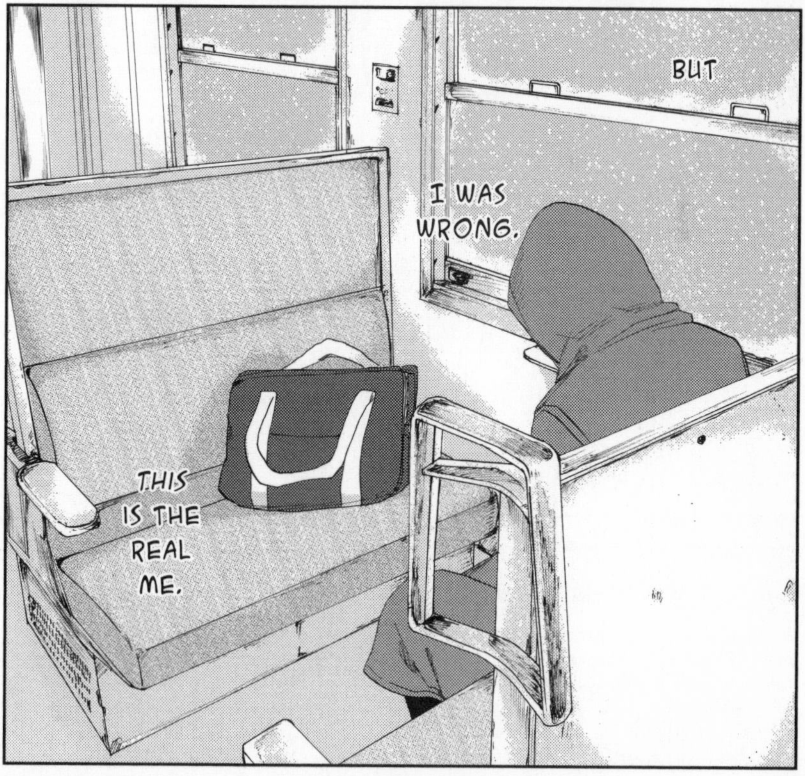
BUT
I WAS WRONG.
THIS IS THE REAL ME.

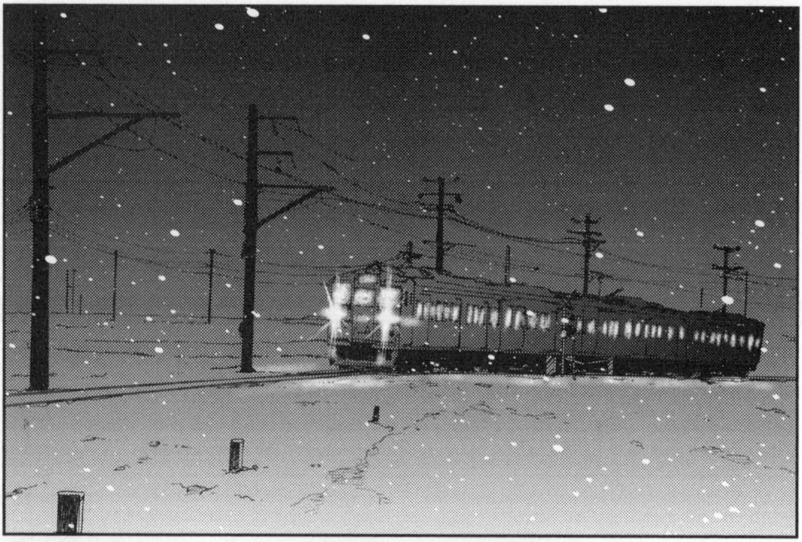

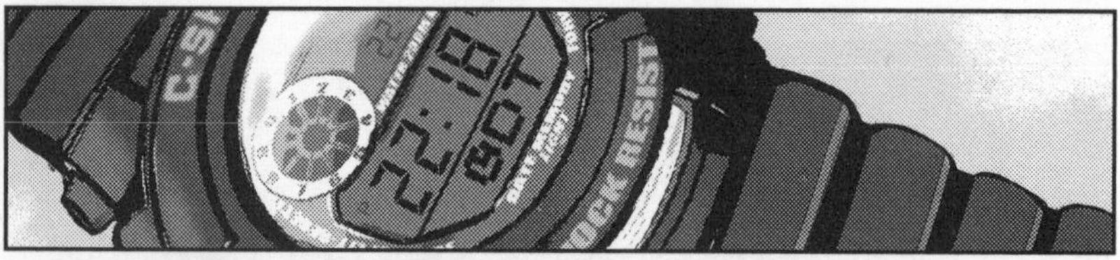

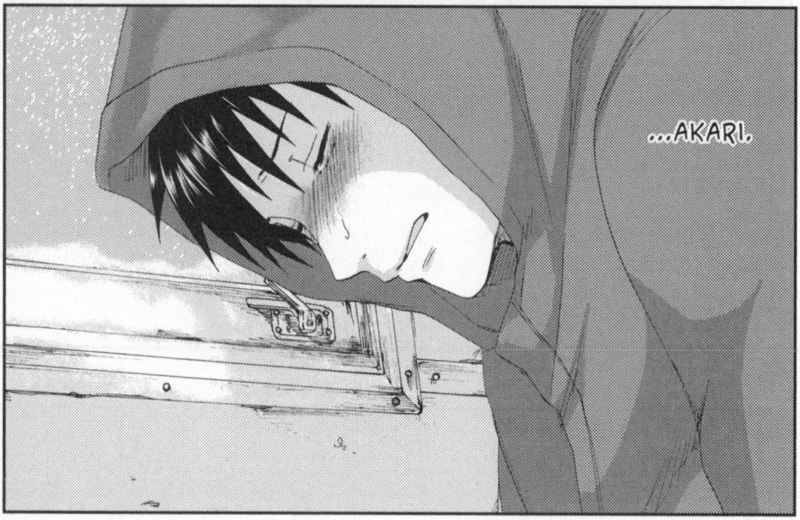

...AKARI.

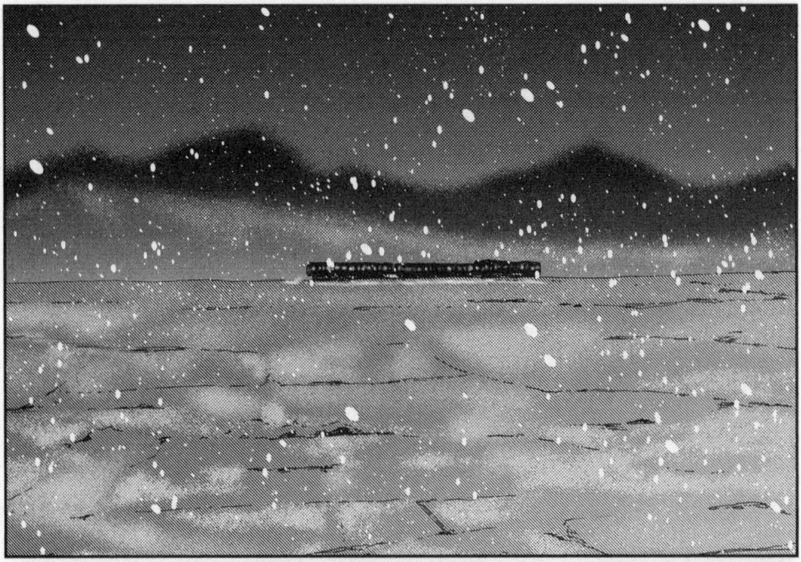

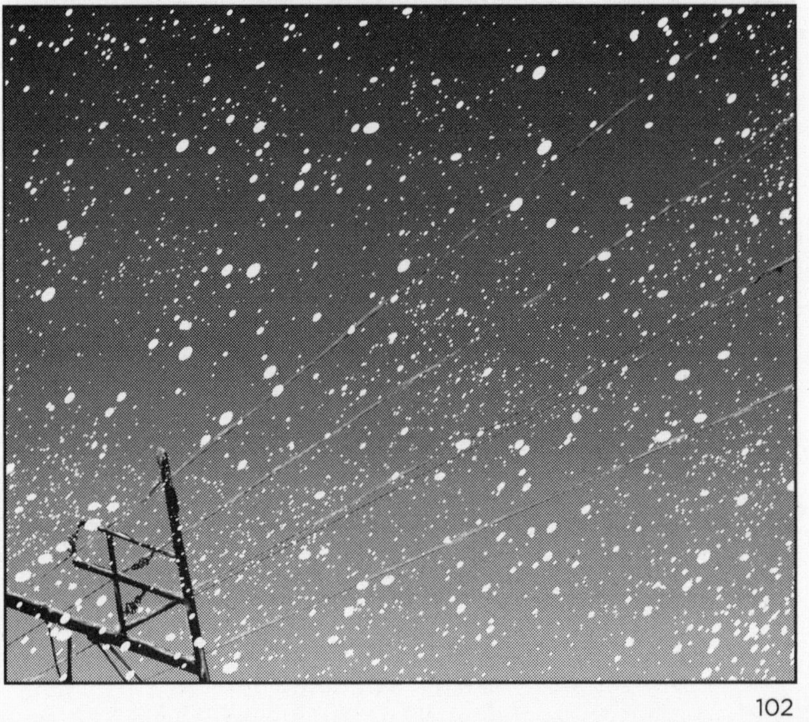

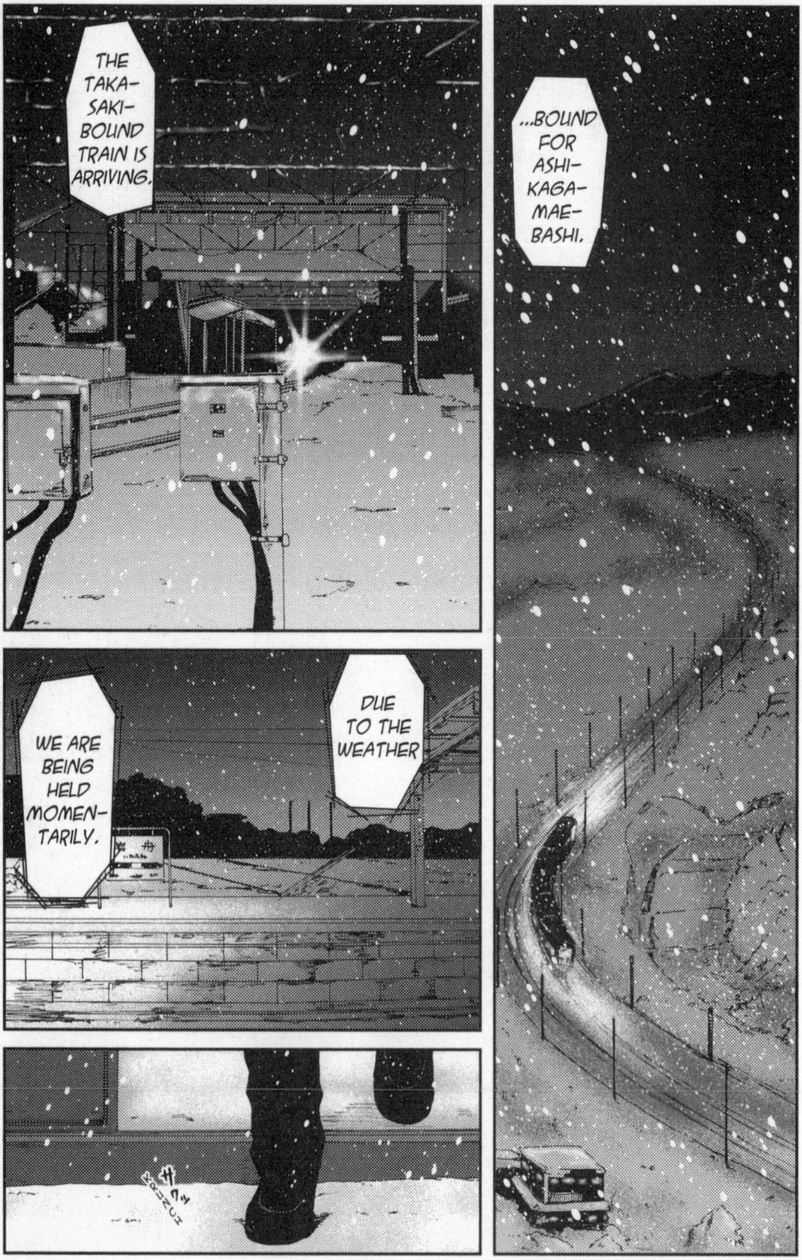
...BOUND FOR ASHI-KAGA-MAE-BASHI.
THE TAKA-SAKI-BOUND TRAIN IS ARRIVING.
DUE TO THE WEATHER
WE ARE BEING HELD MOMEN-TARILY.
岩舟
ザクッ
KRUNCH

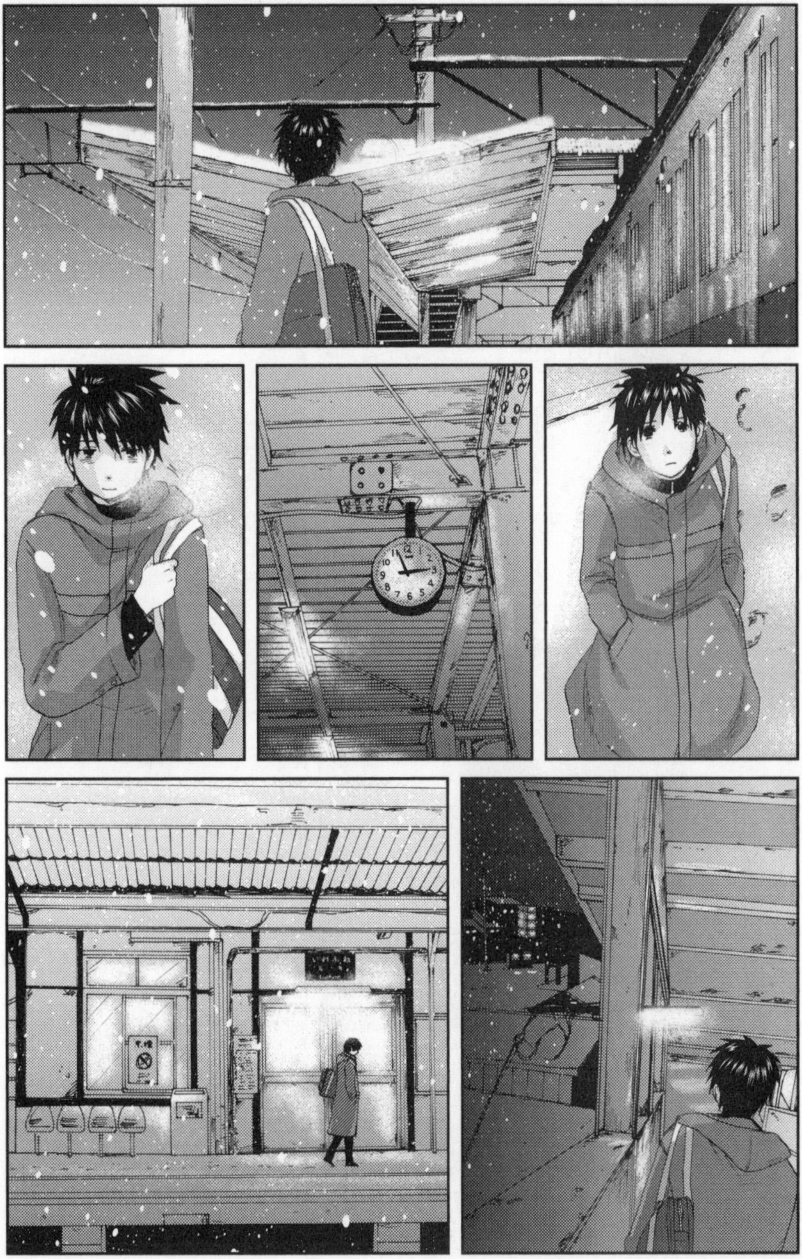

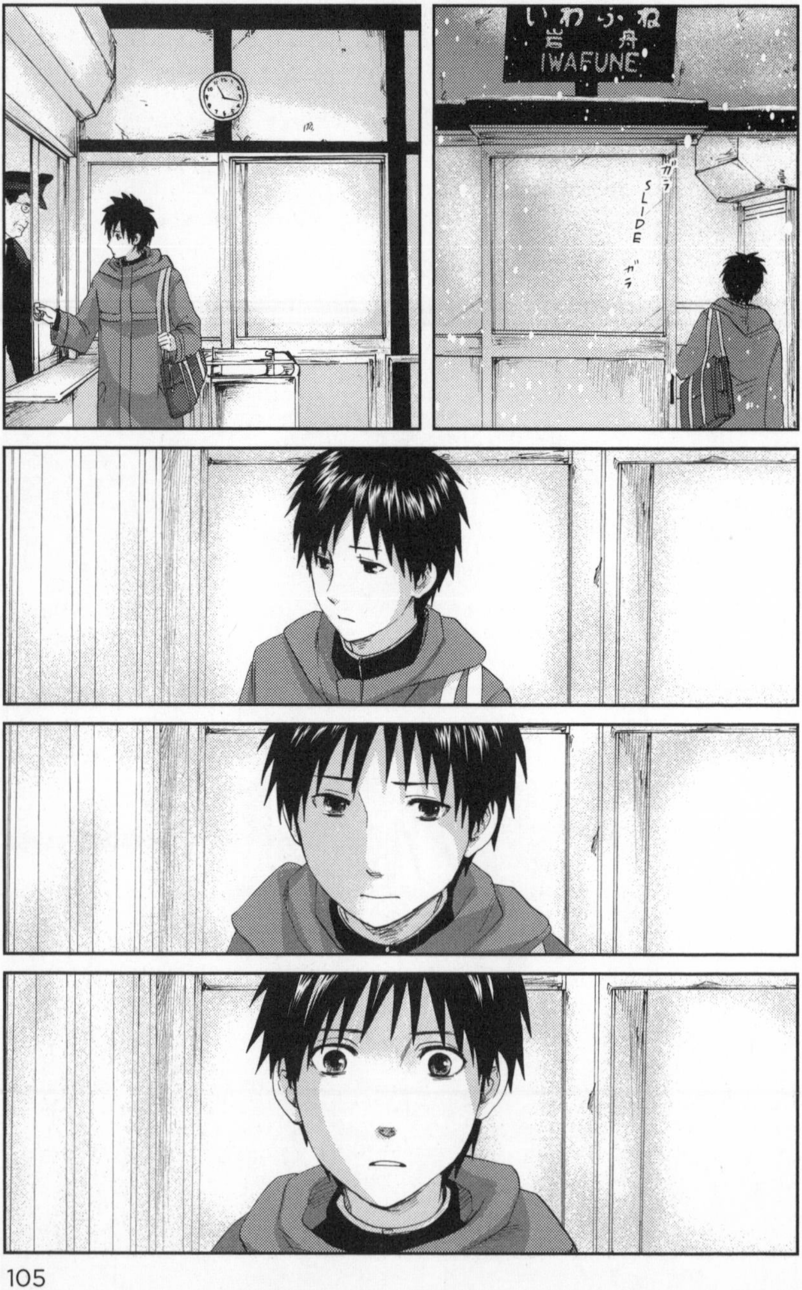
いわふね
岩舟
IWAFUNE
ガラ
SLIDE
ガラ

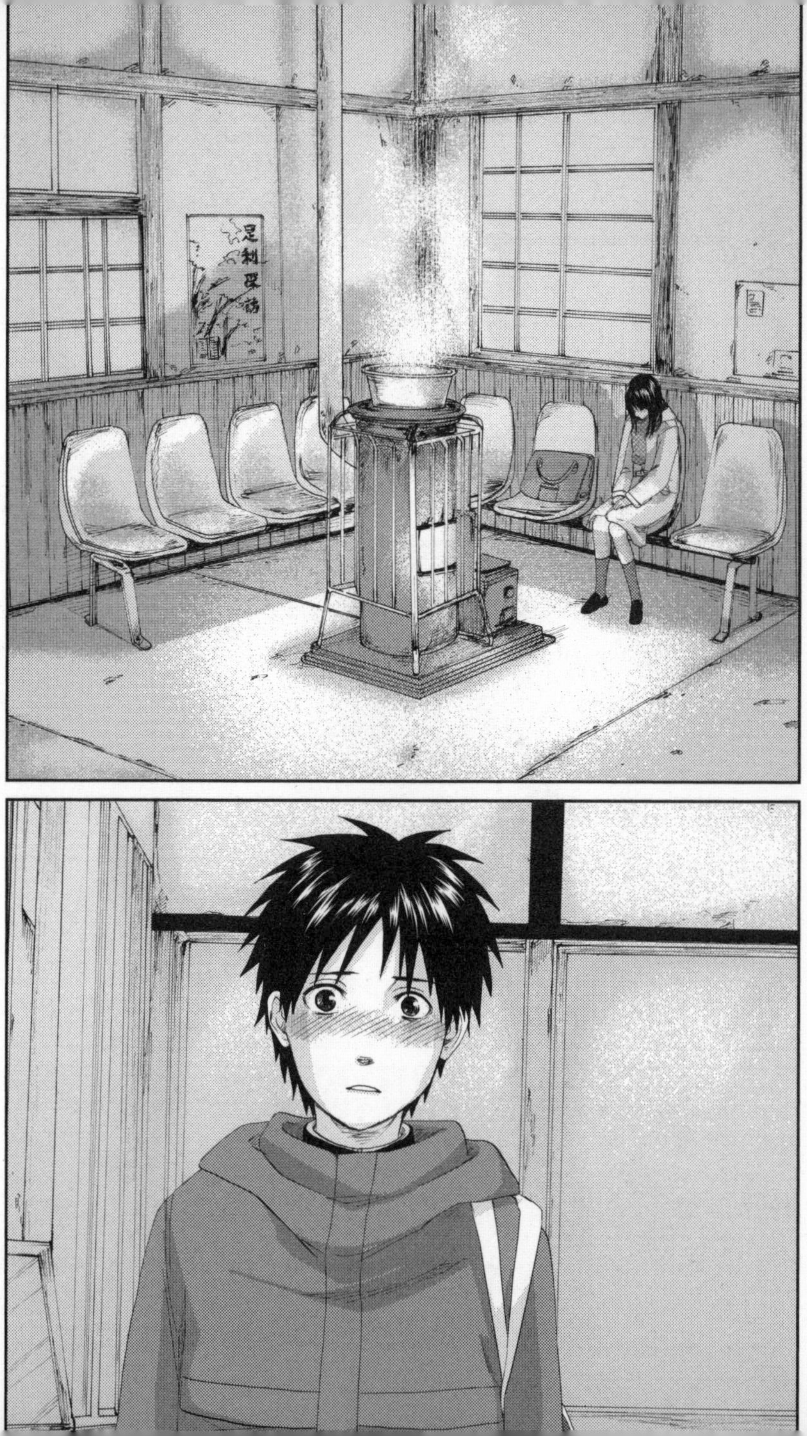
足利探訪

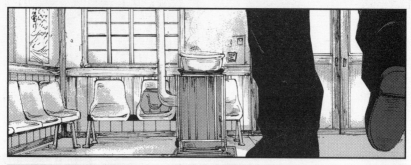

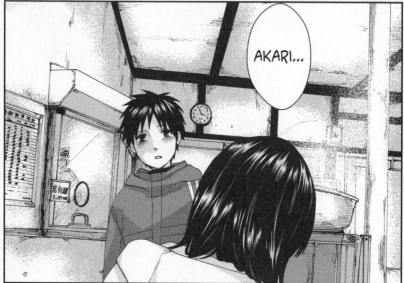

AKARI...

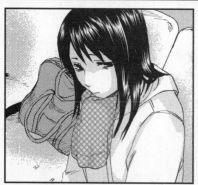

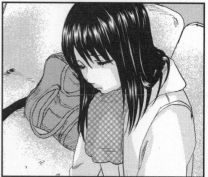

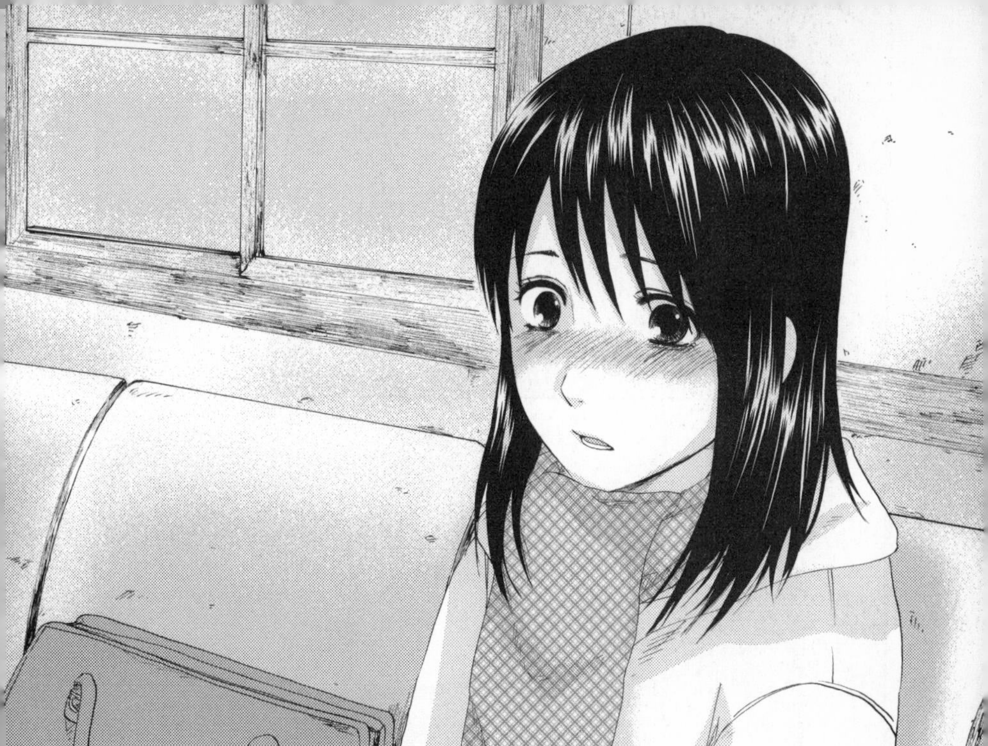

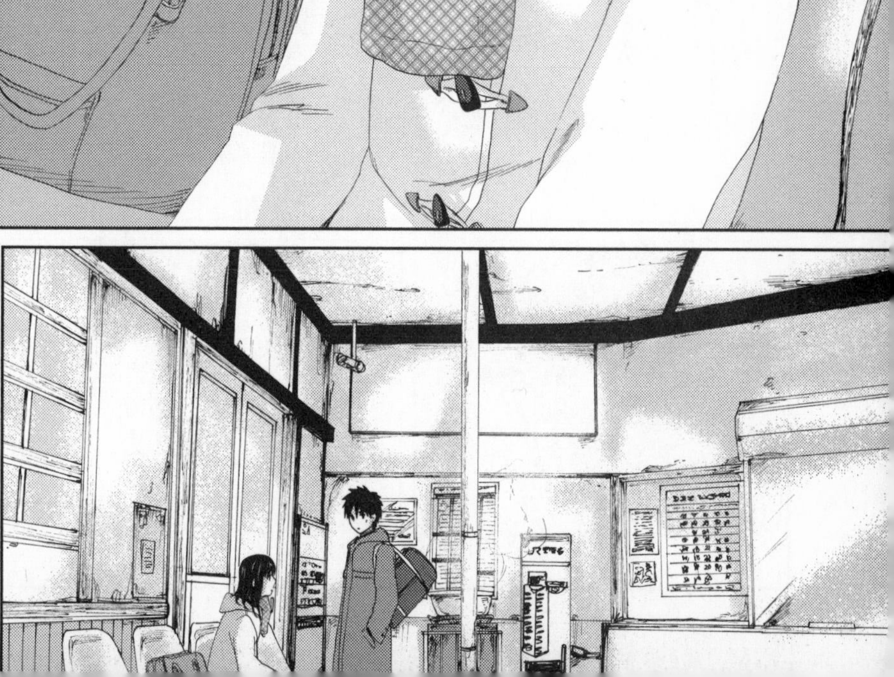

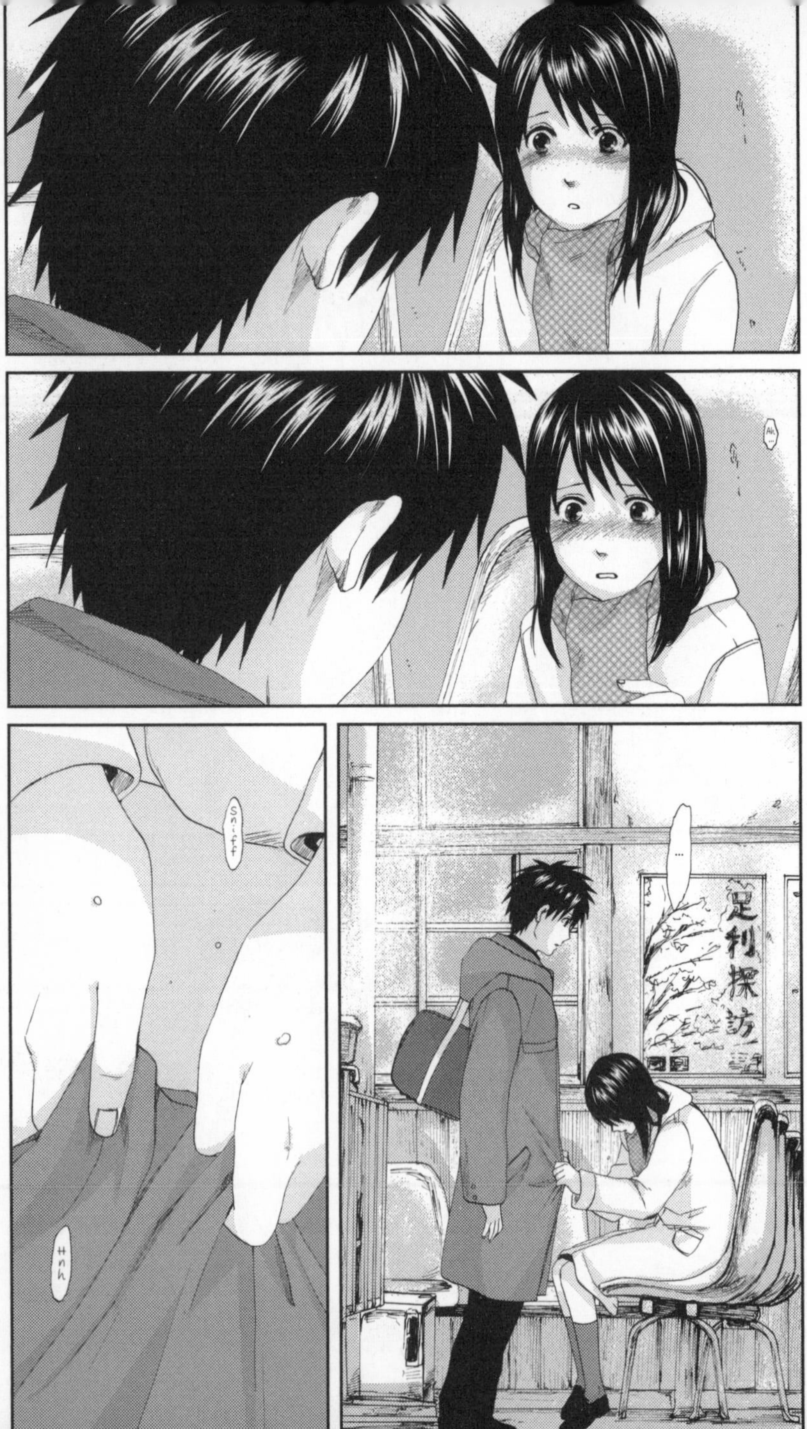
Ah...
...
足利探訪
Sniff
Hnh

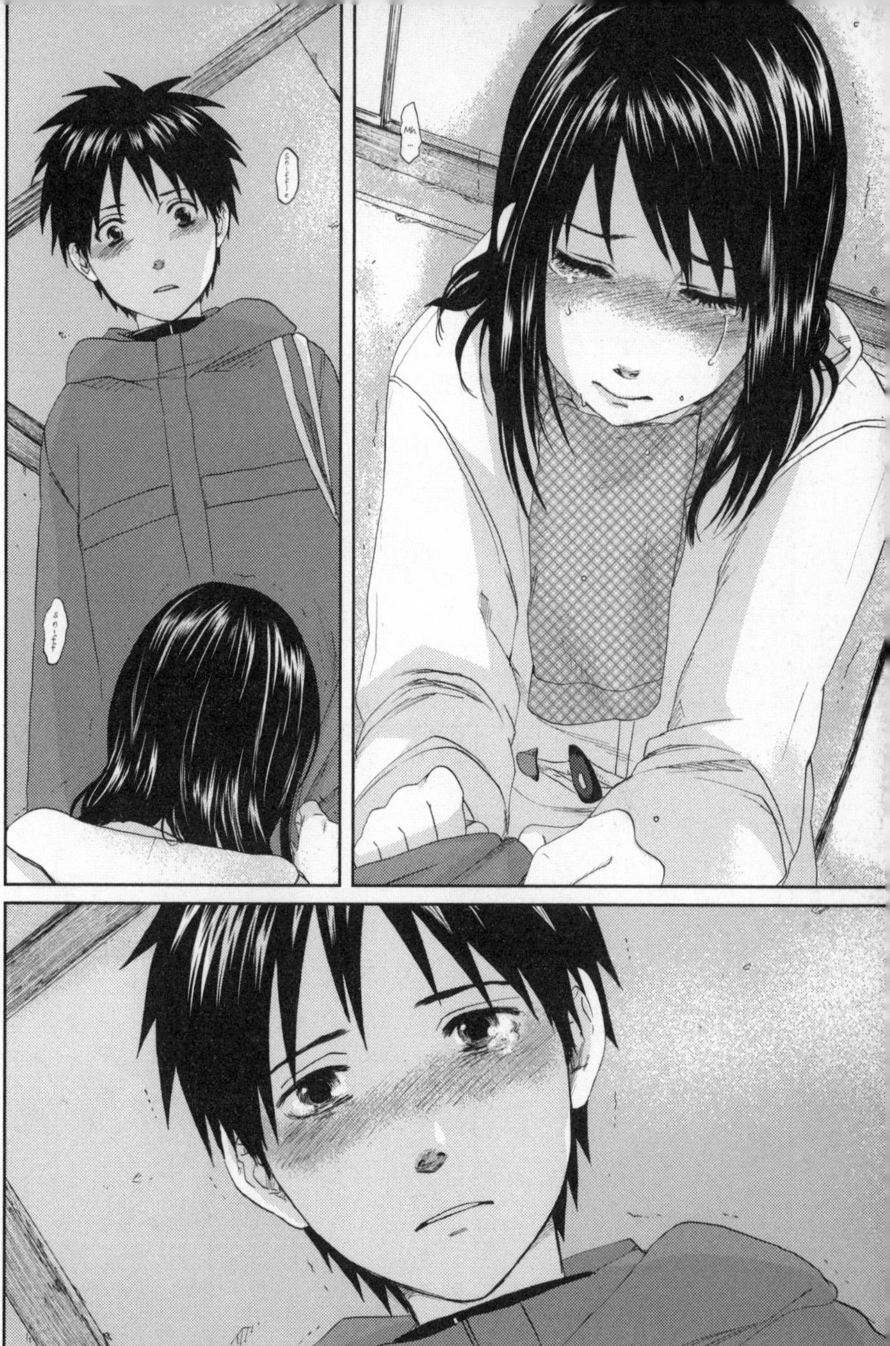
Mh...
sniffle
sniff

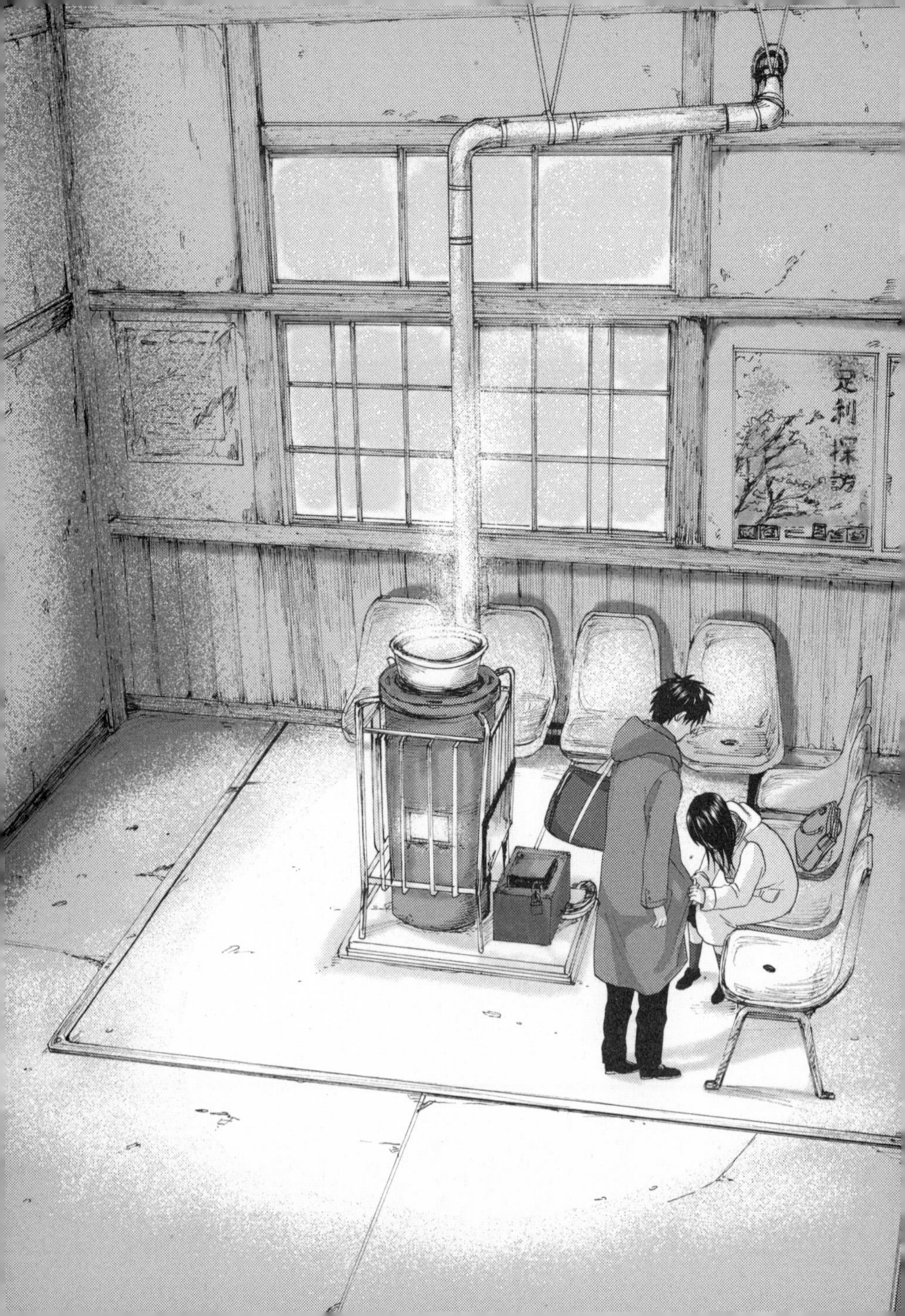
足利探訪

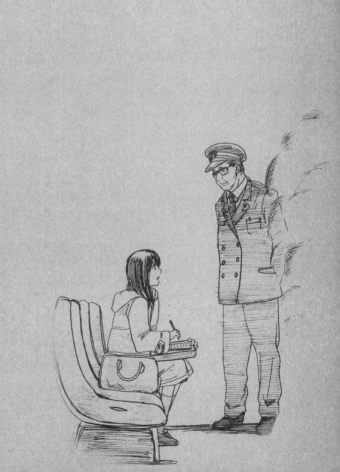

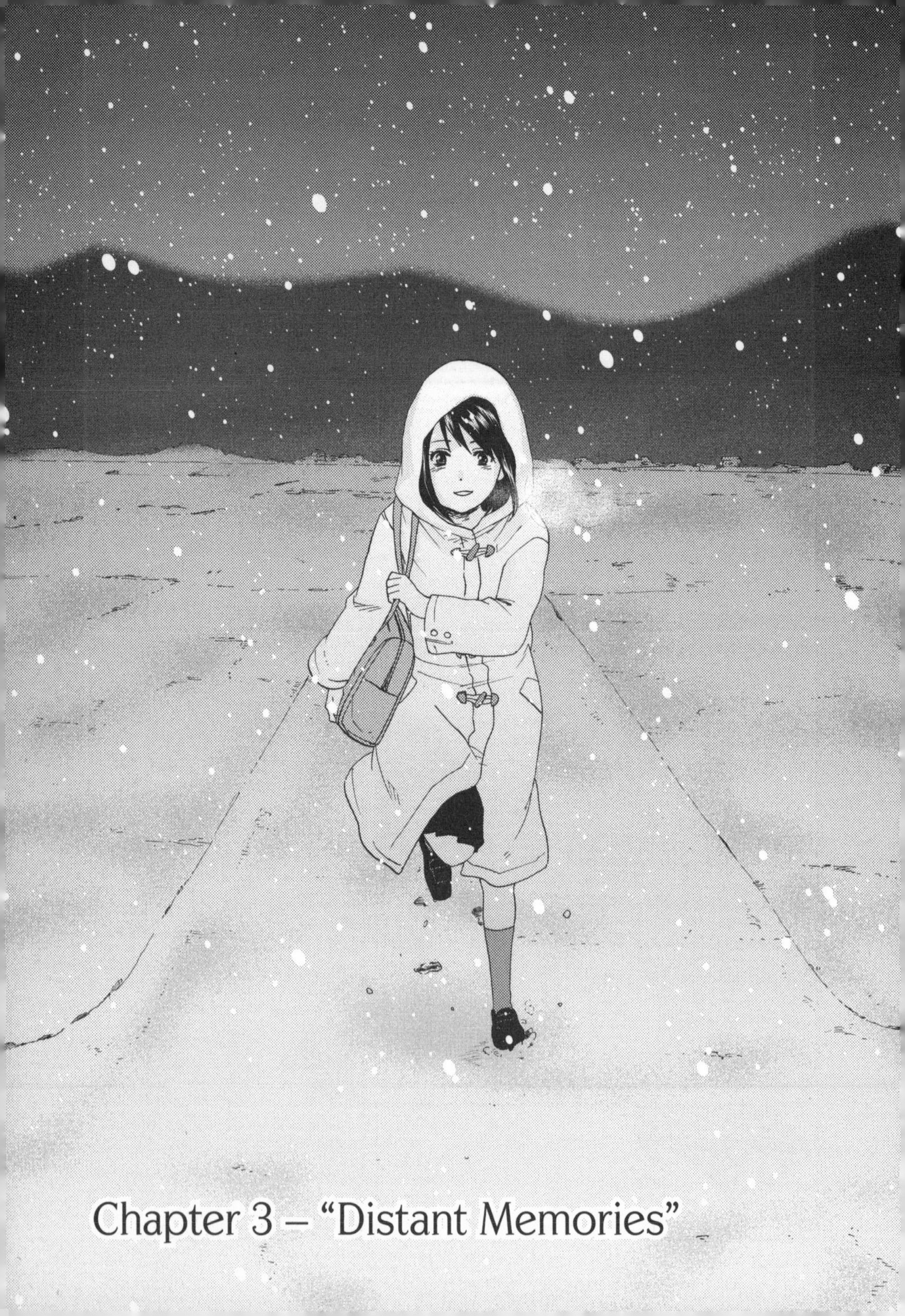

Chapter 3 – “Distant Memories”

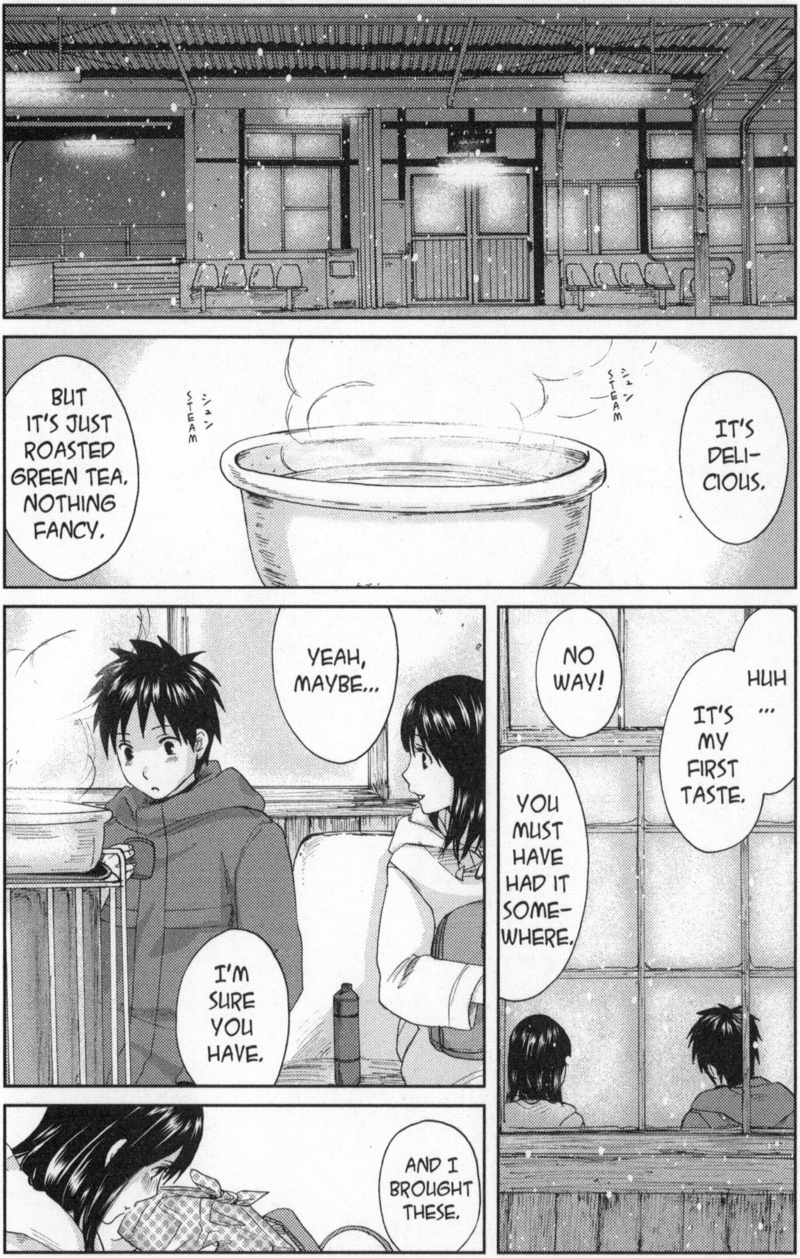
IT'S DELI-CIOUS.
STEAM
STEAM
BUT IT'S JUST ROASTED GREEN TEA. NOTHING FANCY.
HUH ...
IT'S MY FIRST TASTE.
NO WAY!
YOU MUST HAVE HAD IT SOME-WHERE.
YEAH, MAYBE...
I'M SURE YOU HAVE.
AND I BROUGHT THESE.

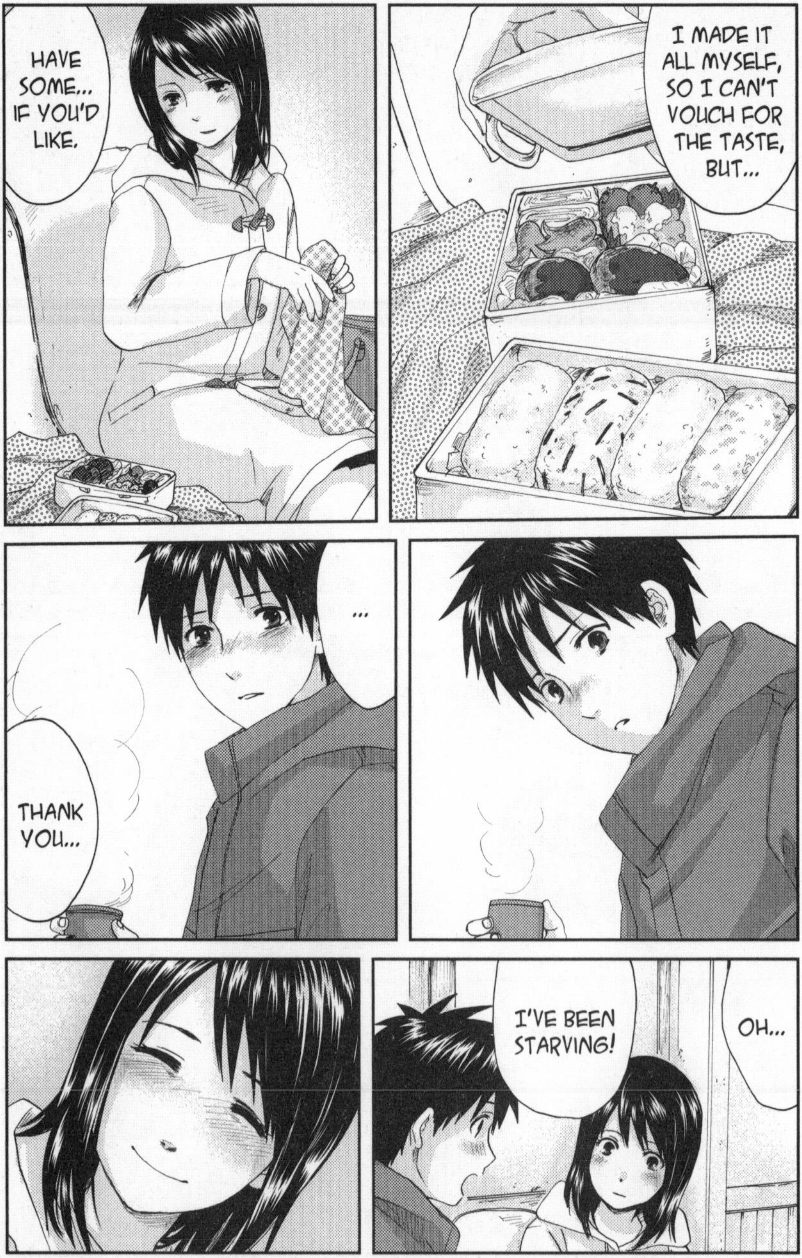
I MADE IT ALL MYSELF, SO I CAN'T VOUCH FOR THE TASTE, BUT...
HAVE SOME... IF YOU'D LIKE.
...
THANK YOU...
OH...
I'VE BEEN STARVING!

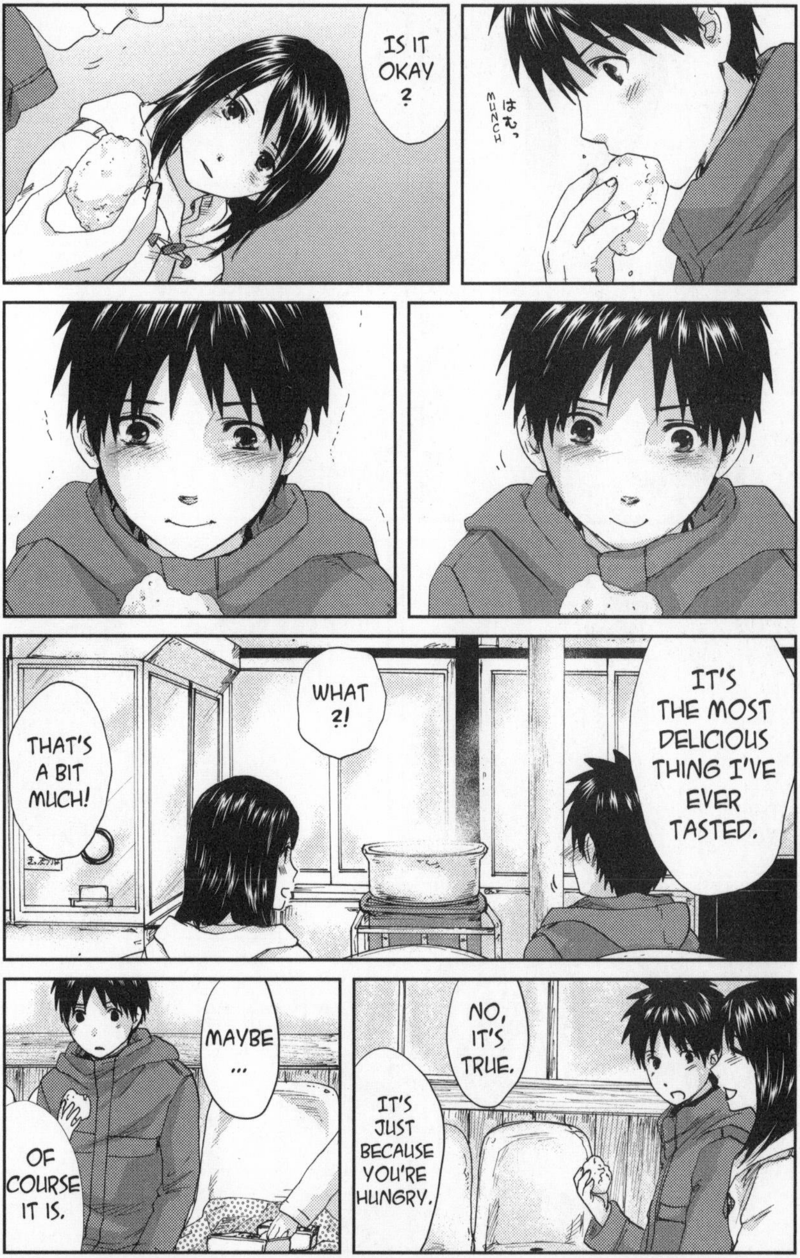
はむっ
MUNCH
IS IT OKAY?
IT'S THE MOST DELICIOUS THING I'VE EVER TASTED.
WHAT?!
THAT'S A BIT MUCH!
NO, IT'S TRUE.
IT'S JUST BECAUSE YOU'RE HUNGRY.
MAYBE...
OF COURSE IT IS.

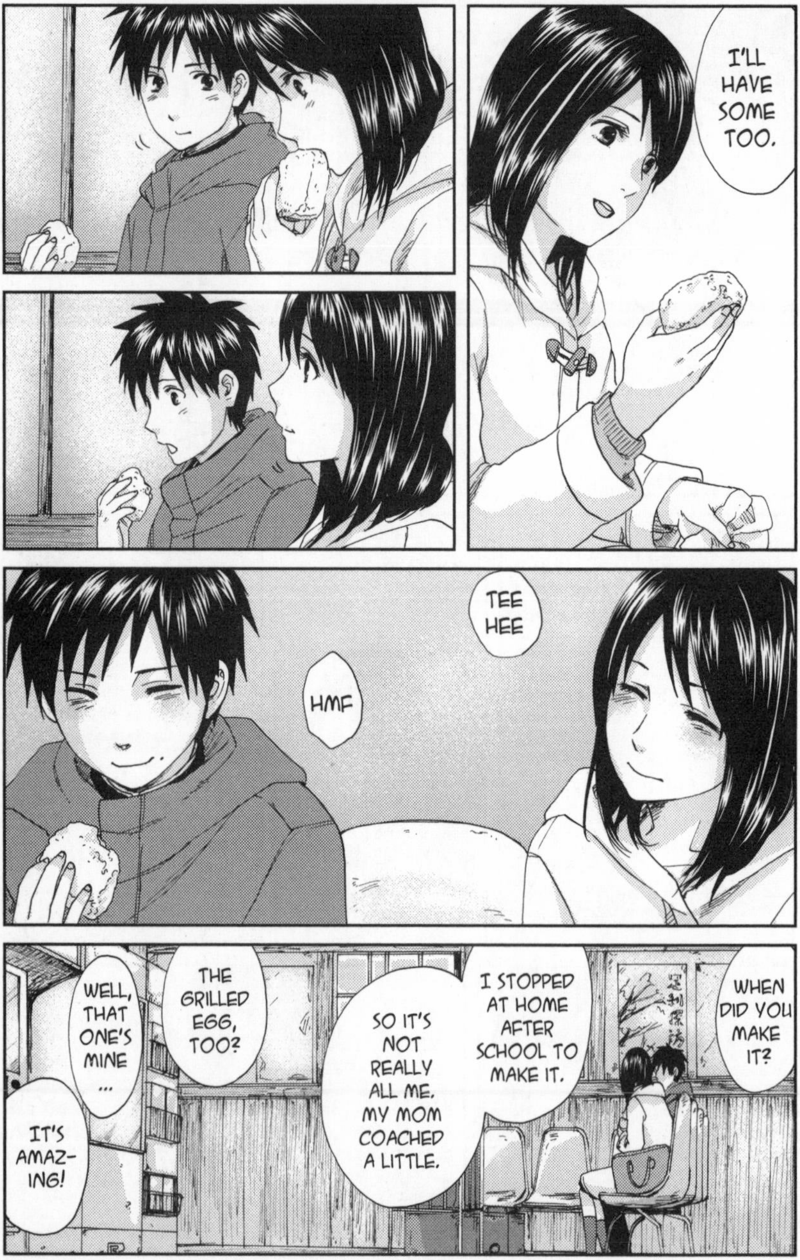
I'LL HAVE SOME TOO.
TEE HEE
HMF
WHEN DID YOU MAKE IT?
I STOPPED AT HOME AFTER SCHOOL TO MAKE IT.
SO IT'S NOT REALLY ALL ME. MY MOM COACHED A LITTLE.
THE GRILLED EGG, TOO?
WELL, THAT ONE'S MINE ...
IT'S AMAZ-ING!

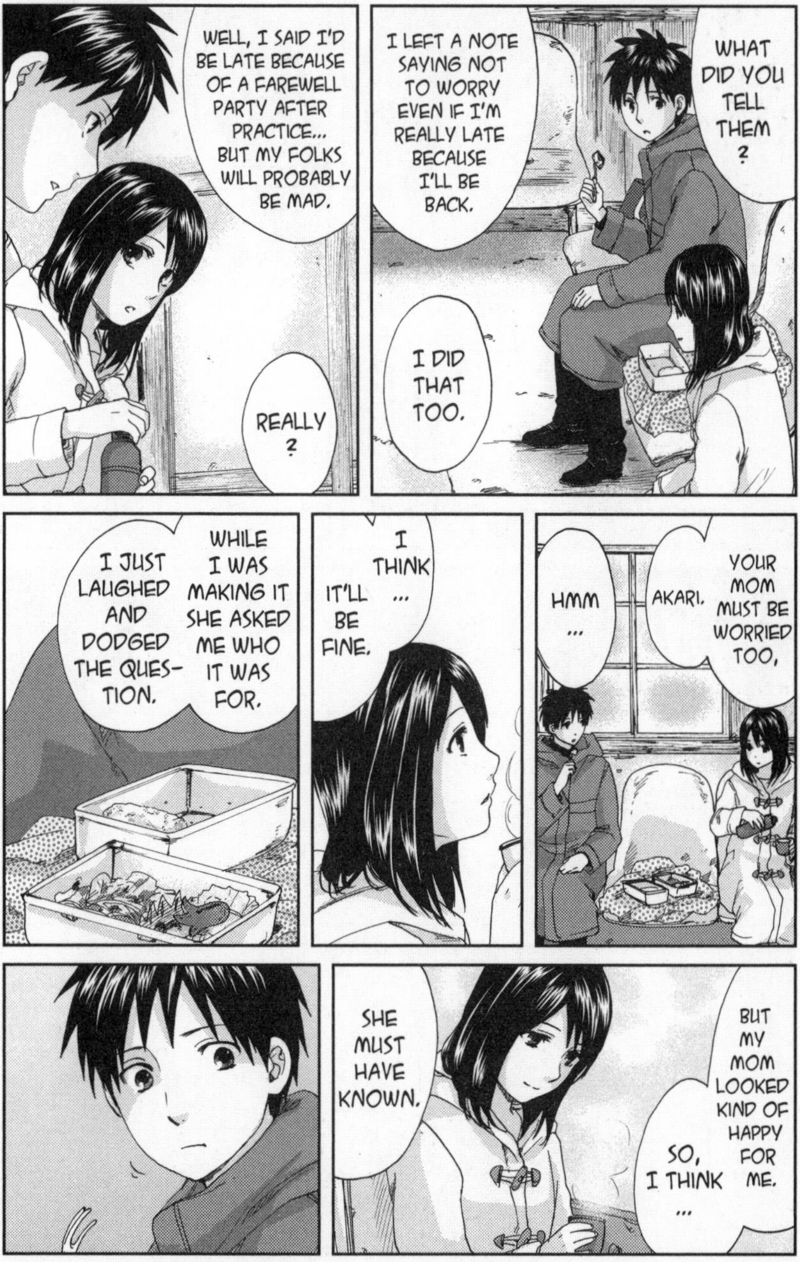
WHAT DID YOU TELL THEM?
I LEFT A NOTE SAYING NOT TO WORRY EVEN IF I'M REALLY LATE BECAUSE I'LL BE BACK.
I DID THAT TOO.
WELL, I SAID I'D BE LATE BECAUSE OF A FAREWELL PARTY AFTER PRACTICE... BUT MY FOLKS WILL PROBABLY BE MAD.
REALLY?
YOUR MOM MUST BE WORRIED TOO,
AKARI.
HMM ...
I THINK ...
IT'LL BE FINE.
WHILE I WAS MAKING IT SHE ASKED ME WHO IT WAS FOR.
I JUST LAUGHED AND DODGED THE QUES-TION.
BUT MY MOM LOOKED KIND OF HAPPY FOR ME.
SO, I THINK ...
SHE MUST HAVE KNOWN.

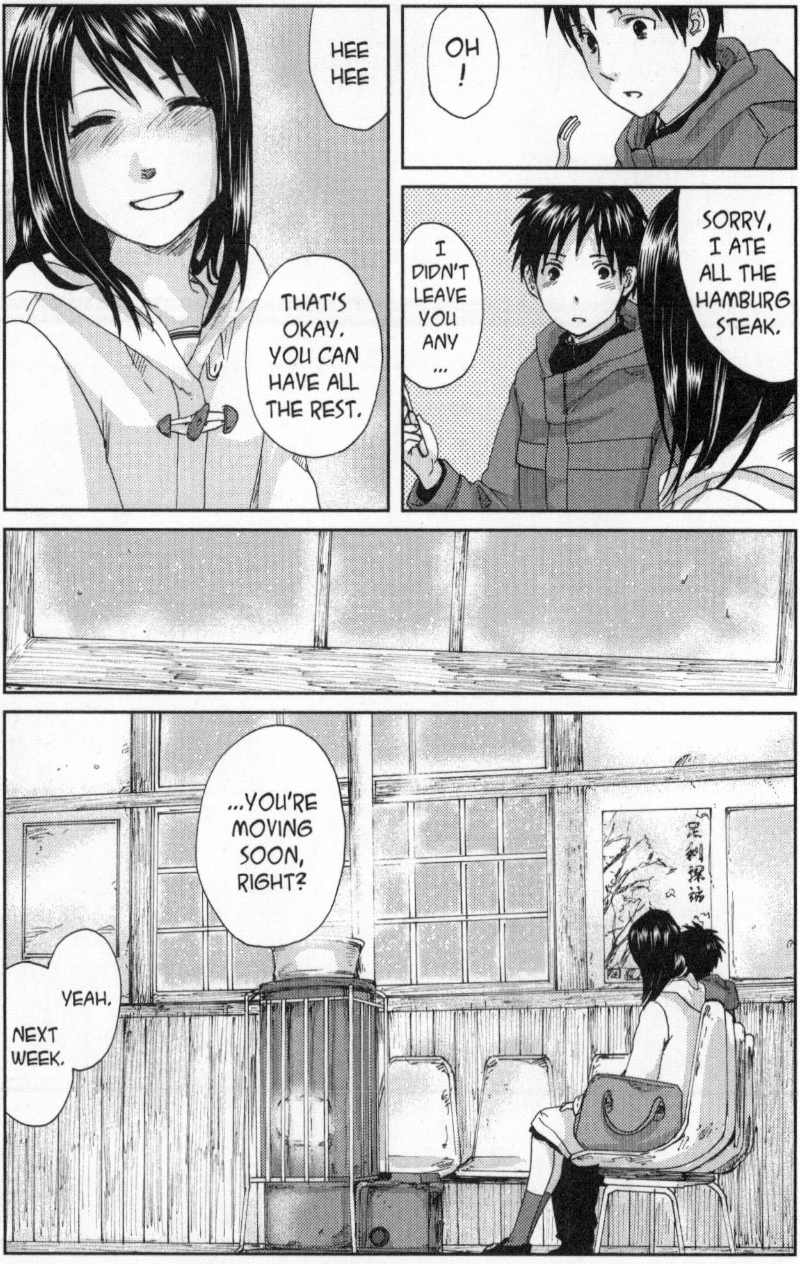
OH!
SORRY, I ATE ALL THE HAMBURG STEAK.
I DIDN'T LEAVE YOU ANY ...
HEE HEE
THAT'S OKAY. YOU CAN HAVE ALL THE REST.
...YOU'RE MOVING SOON, RIGHT?
YEAH.
NEXT WEEK.

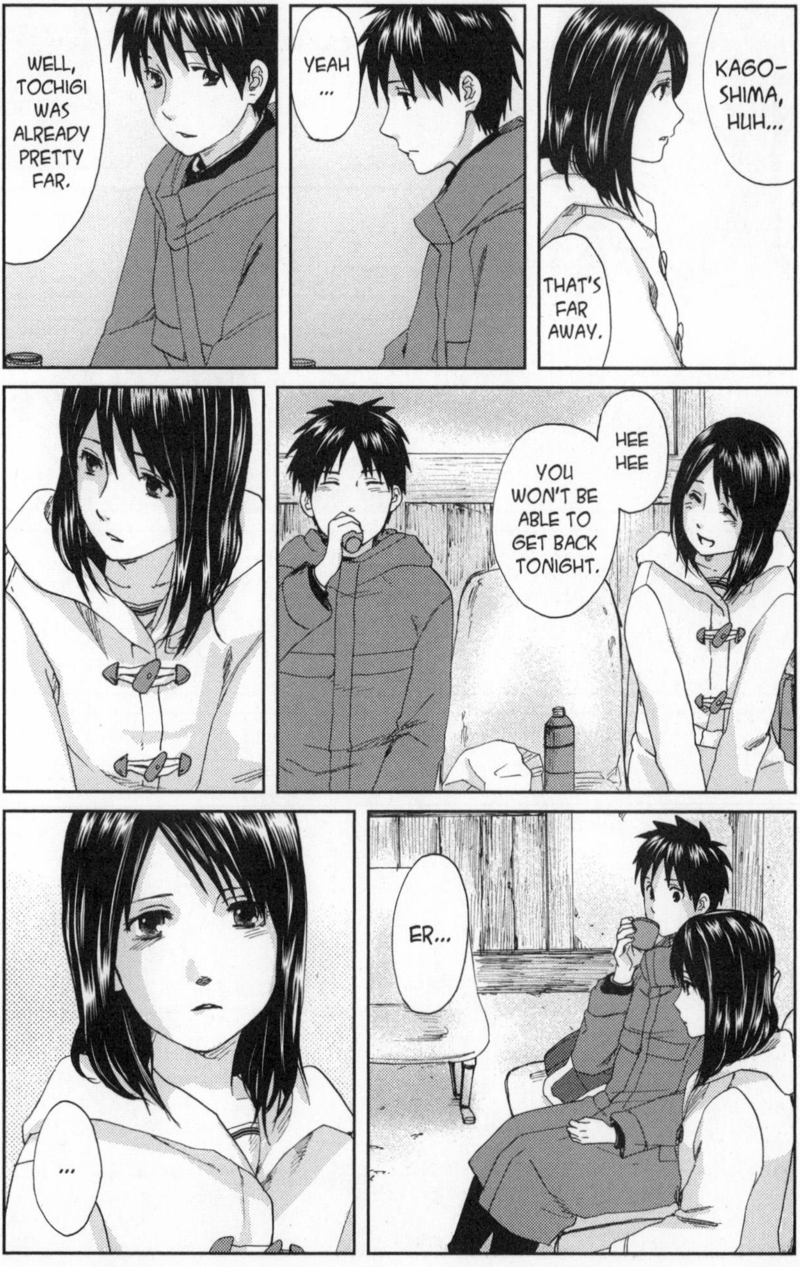
KAGO-SHIMA, HUH...
THAT'S FAR AWAY.
YEAH ...
WELL, TOCHIGI WAS ALREADY PRETTY FAR.
HEE HEE
YOU WON'T BE ABLE TO GET BACK TONIGHT.
ER...
...

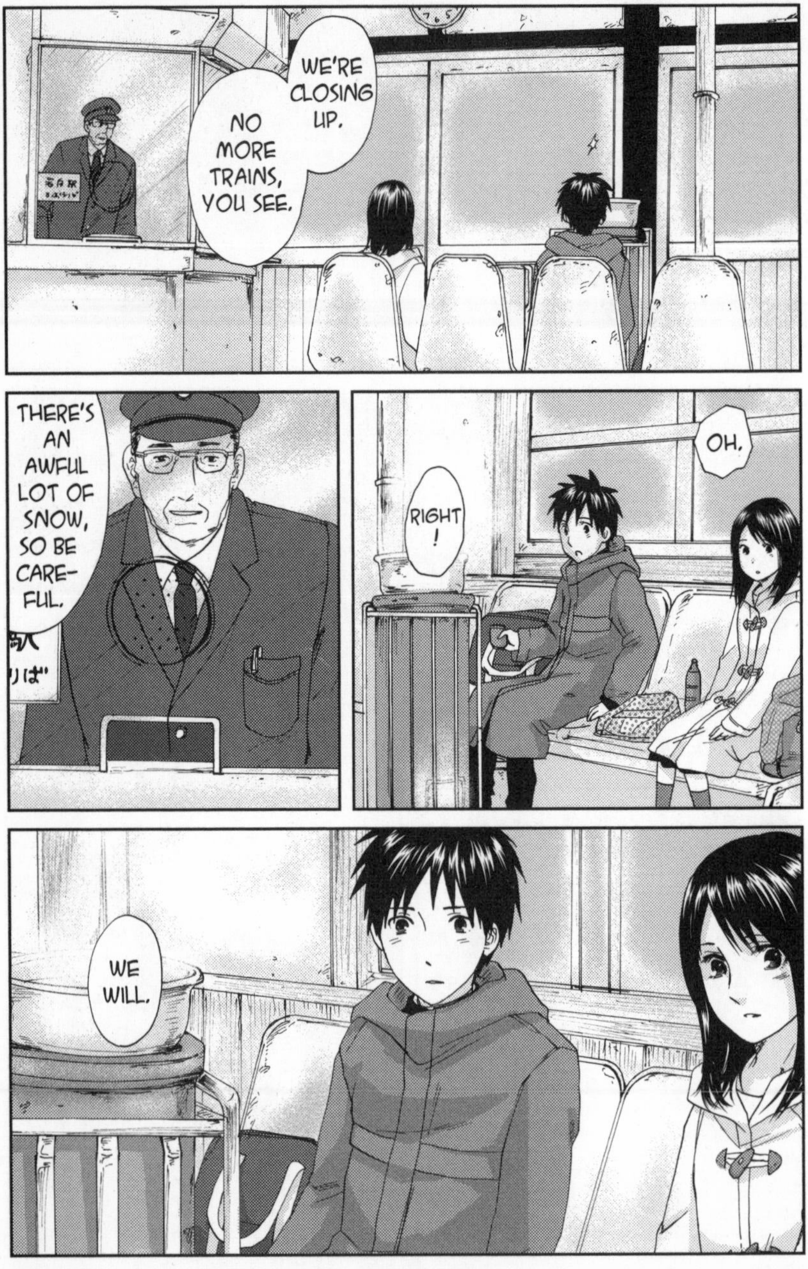
WE'RE CLOSING UP.
NO MORE TRAINS, YOU SEE.
OH.
RIGHT!
THERE'S AN AWFUL LOT OF SNOW, SO BE CARE-FUL.
WE WILL.

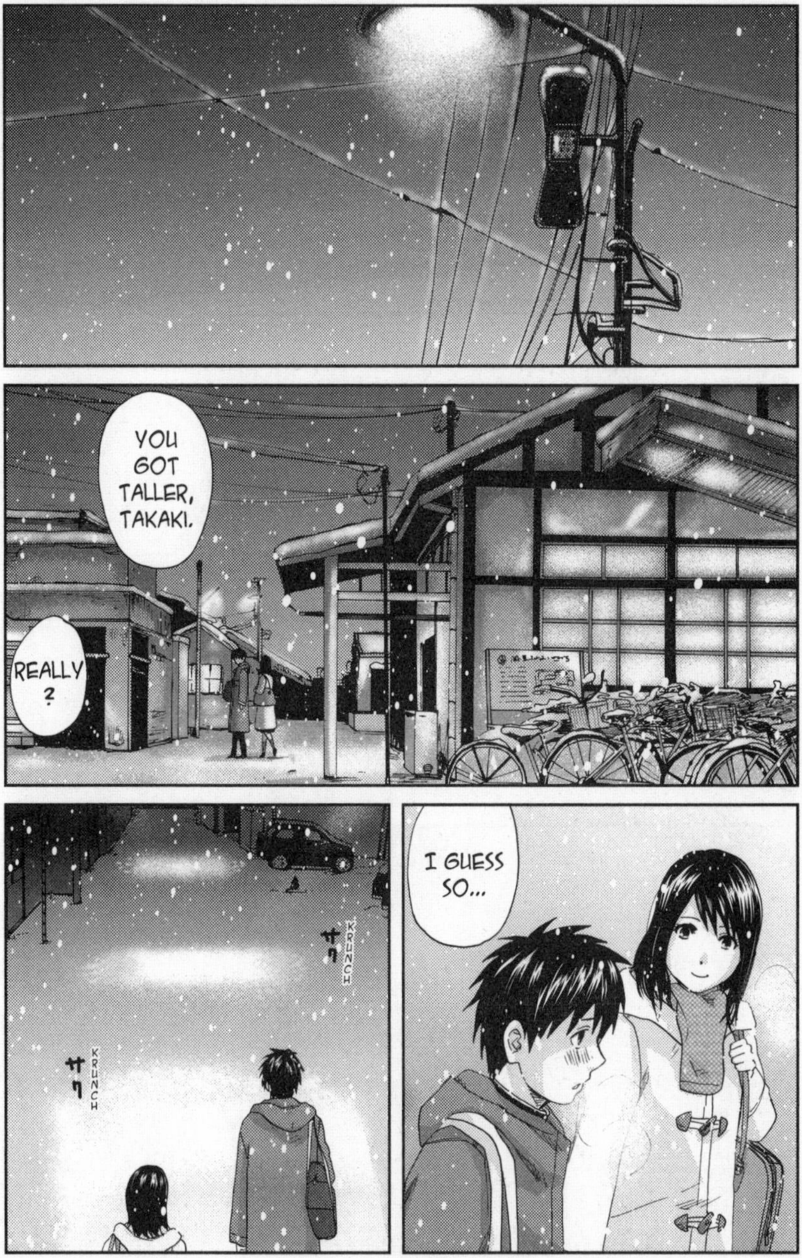
YOU GOT TALLER, TAKAKI.
REALLY?
I GUESS SO...
サク KRUNCH
サク KRUNCH

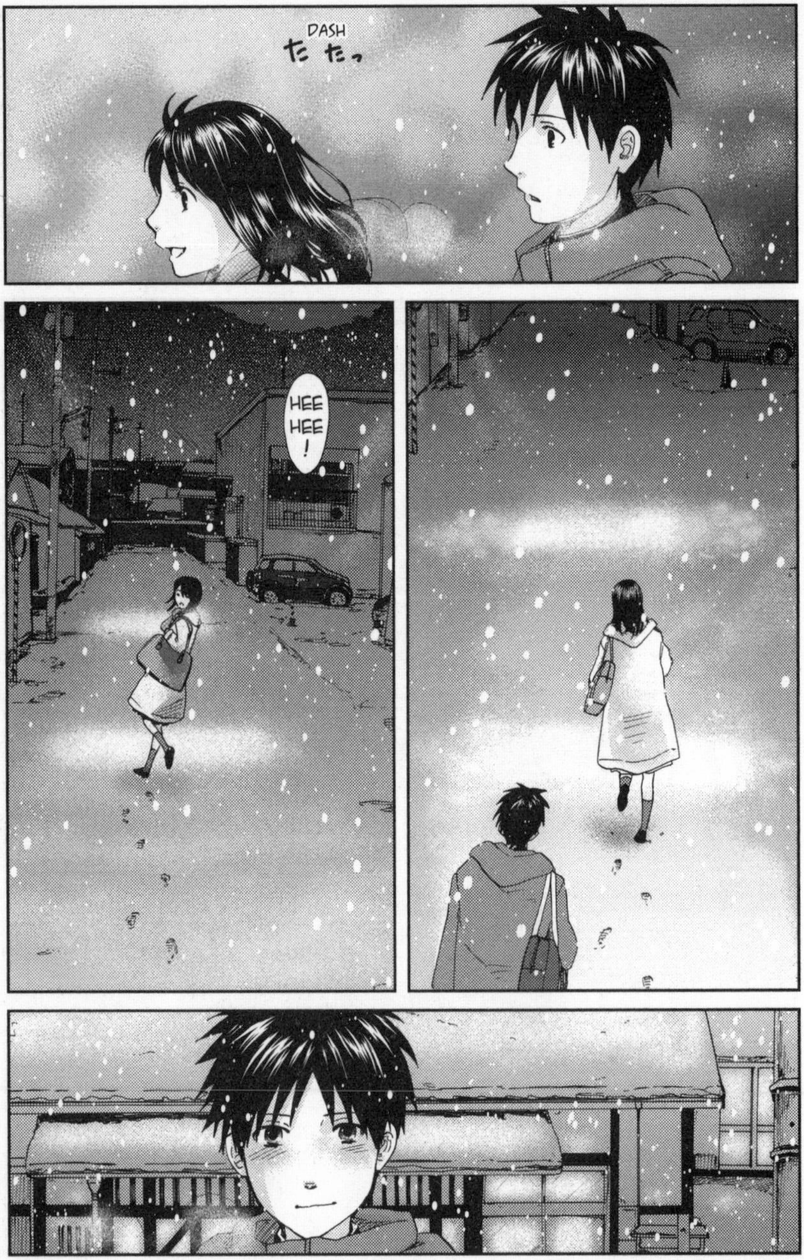
DASH
たたっ
HEE HEE !

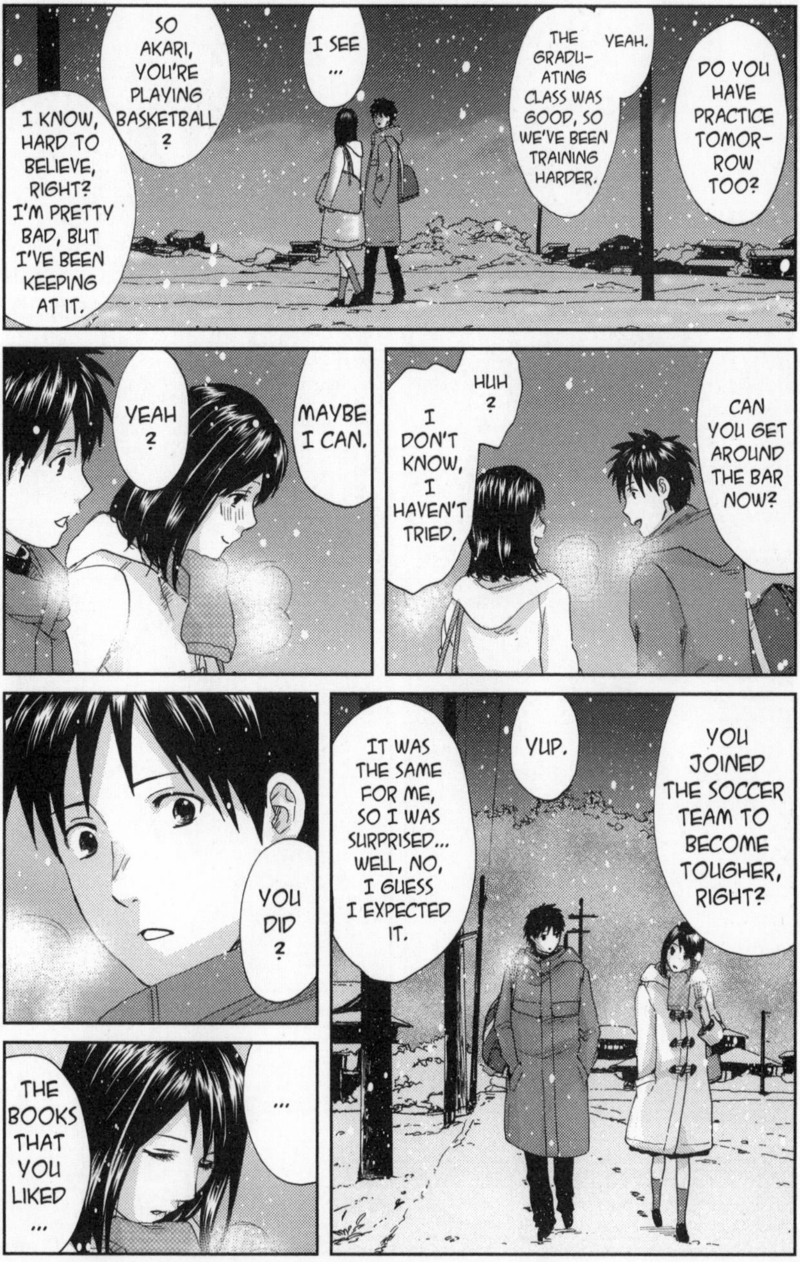
DO YOU HAVE PRACTICE TOMORROW TOO?
YEAH.
THE GRADUATING CLASS WAS GOOD, SO WE'VE BEEN TRAINING HARDER.
I SEE ...
SO AKARI, YOU'RE PLAYING BASKETBALL?
I KNOW, HARD TO BELIEVE, RIGHT? I'M PRETTY BAD, BUT I'VE BEEN KEEPING AT IT.
CAN YOU GET AROUND THE BAR NOW?
HUH?
I DON'T KNOW, I HAVEN'T TRIED.
MAYBE I CAN.
YEAH?
YOU JOINED THE SOCCER TEAM TO BECOME TOUGHER, RIGHT?
YUP.
IT WAS THE SAME FOR ME, SO I WAS SURPRISED... WELL, NO, I GUESS I EXPECTED IT.
YOU DID?
...
THE BOOKS THAT YOU LIKED ...

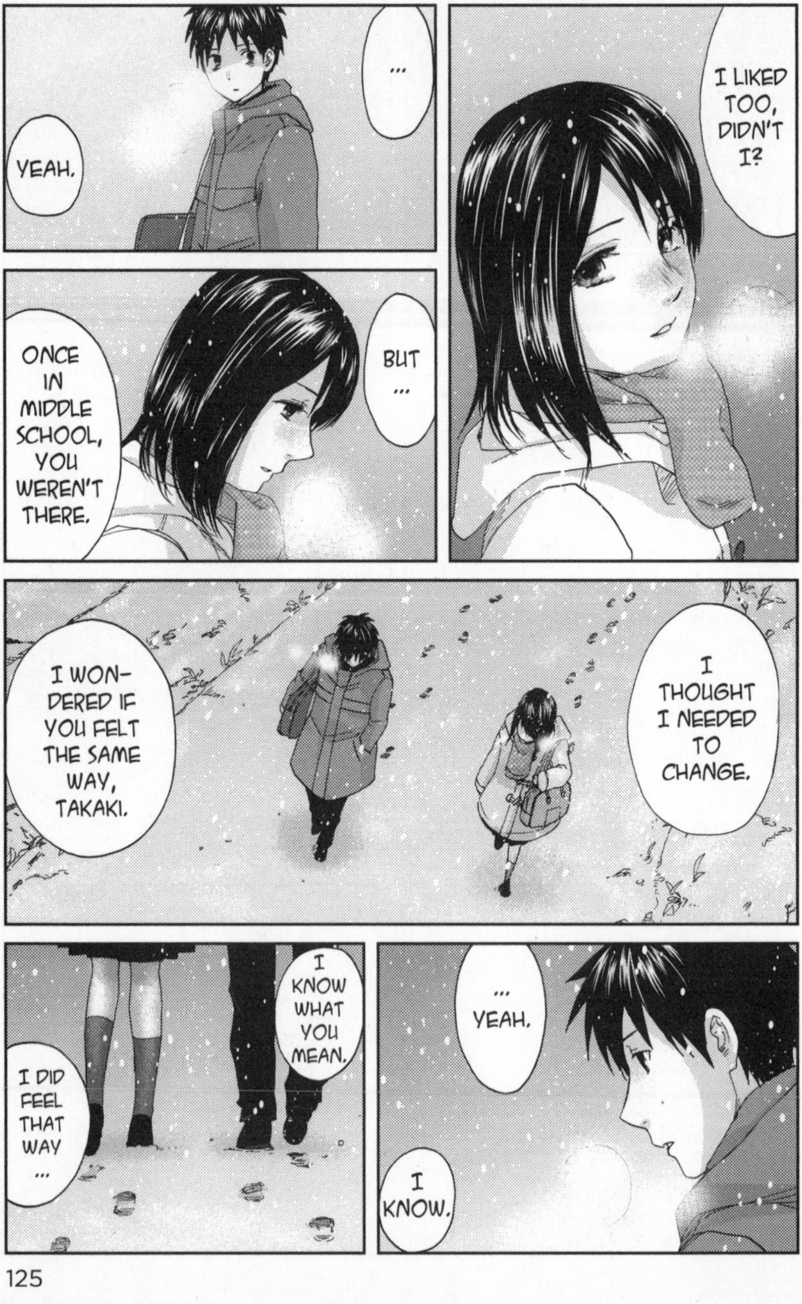
I LIKED TOO, DIDN'T I?
...
YEAH.
BUT ...
ONCE IN MIDDLE SCHOOL, YOU WEREN'T THERE.
I THOUGHT I NEEDED TO CHANGE.
I WONDERED IF YOU FELT THE SAME WAY, TAKAKI.
... YEAH.
I KNOW.
I KNOW WHAT YOU MEAN.
I DID FEEL THAT WAY ...

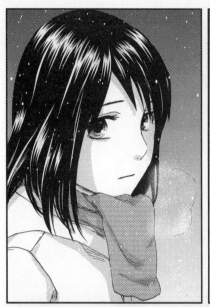

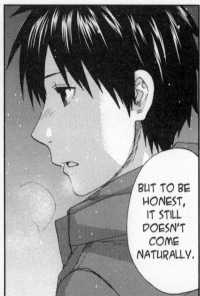

BUT TO BE HONEST, IT STILL DOESN'T COME NATURALLY.

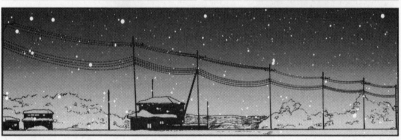

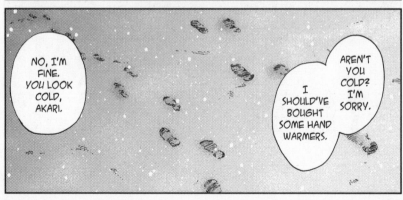

NO, I'M FINE. YOU LOOK COLD, AKARI.

I SHOULD'VE BOUGHT SOME HAND WARMERS.

AREN'T YOU COLD? I'M SORRY.

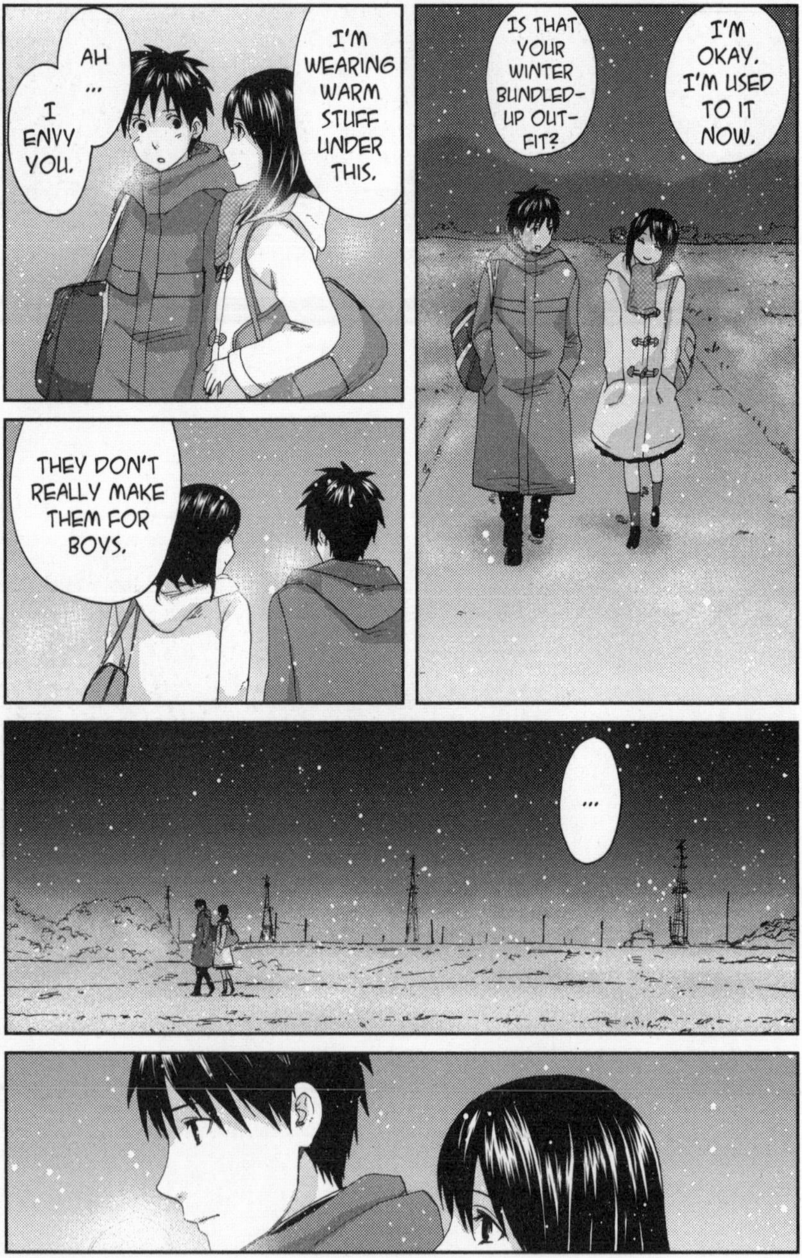
I'M OKAY. I'M USED TO IT NOW.
IS THAT YOUR WINTER BUNDLED-UP OUT-FIT?
I'M WEARING WARM STUFF UNDER THIS.
AH ... I ENVY YOU.
THEY DON'T REALLY MAKE THEM FOR BOYS.
...

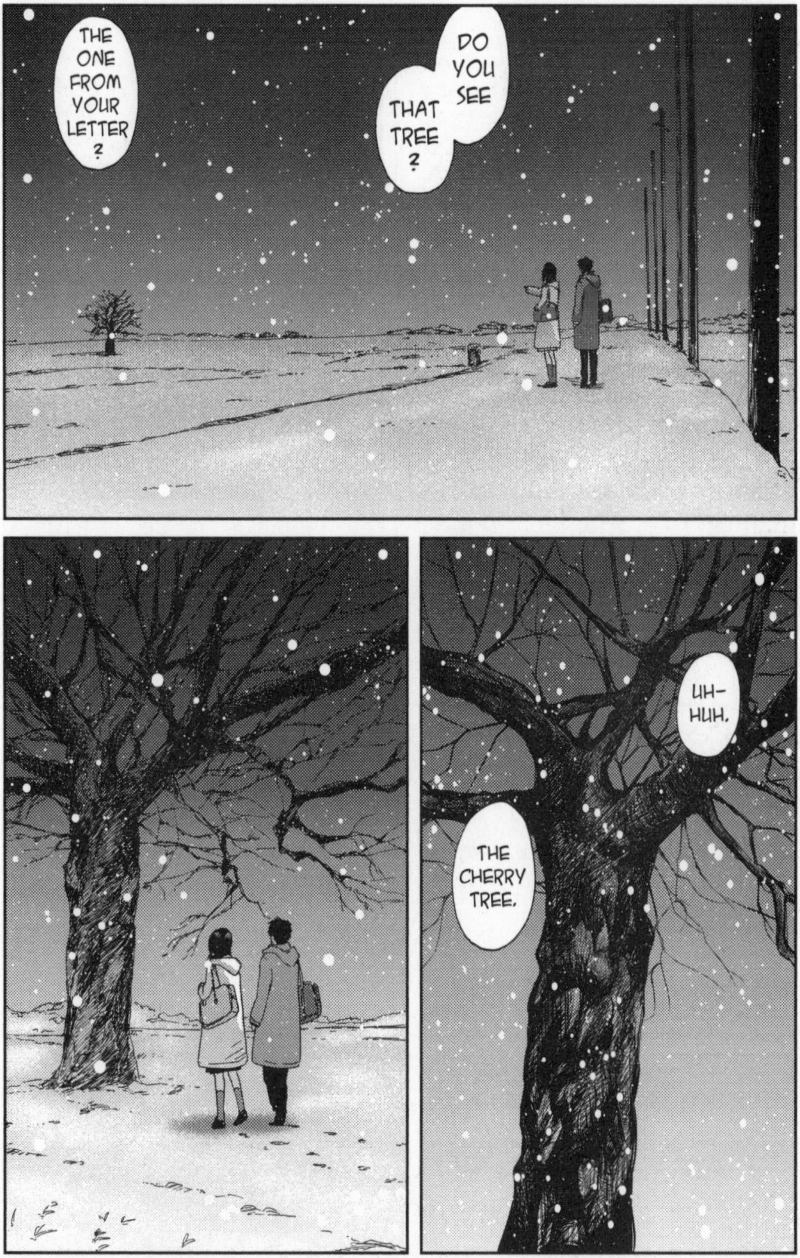
DO YOU SEE THAT TREE?
THE ONE FROM YOUR LETTER?
UH-HUH.
THE CHERRY TREE.

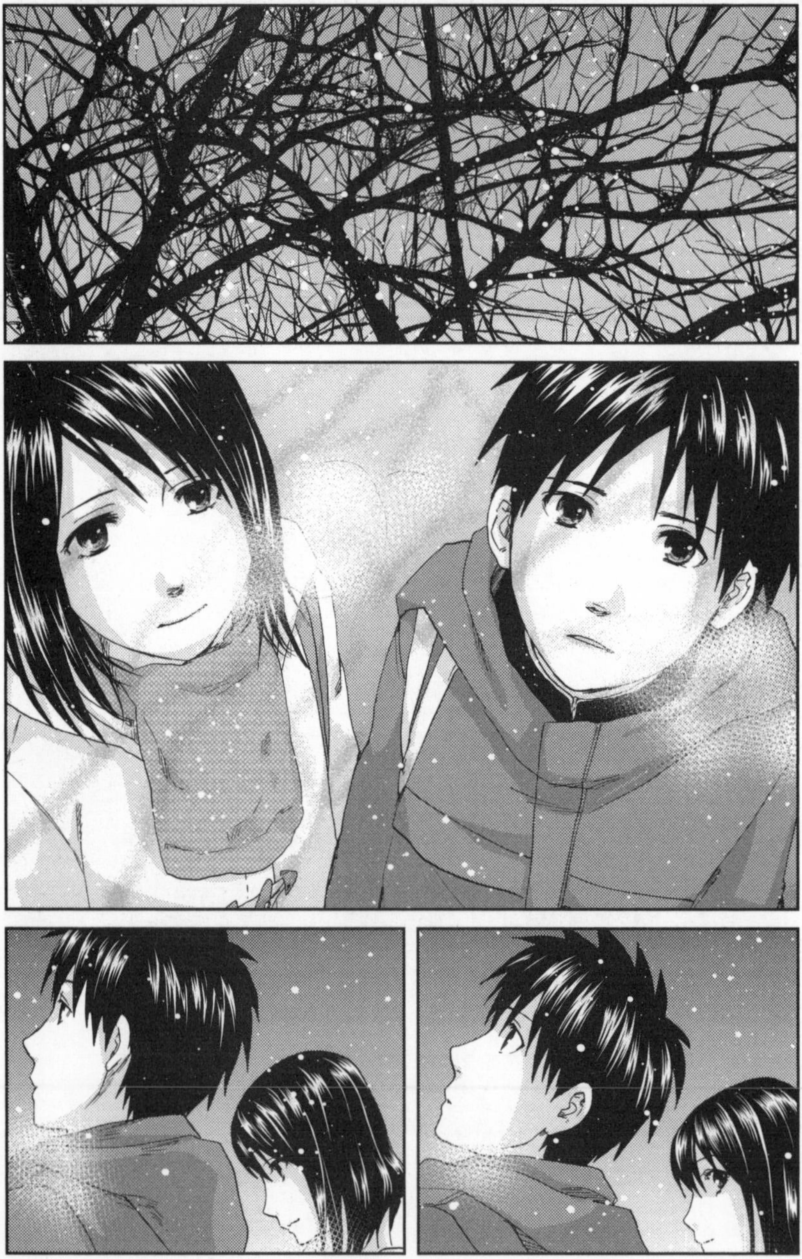

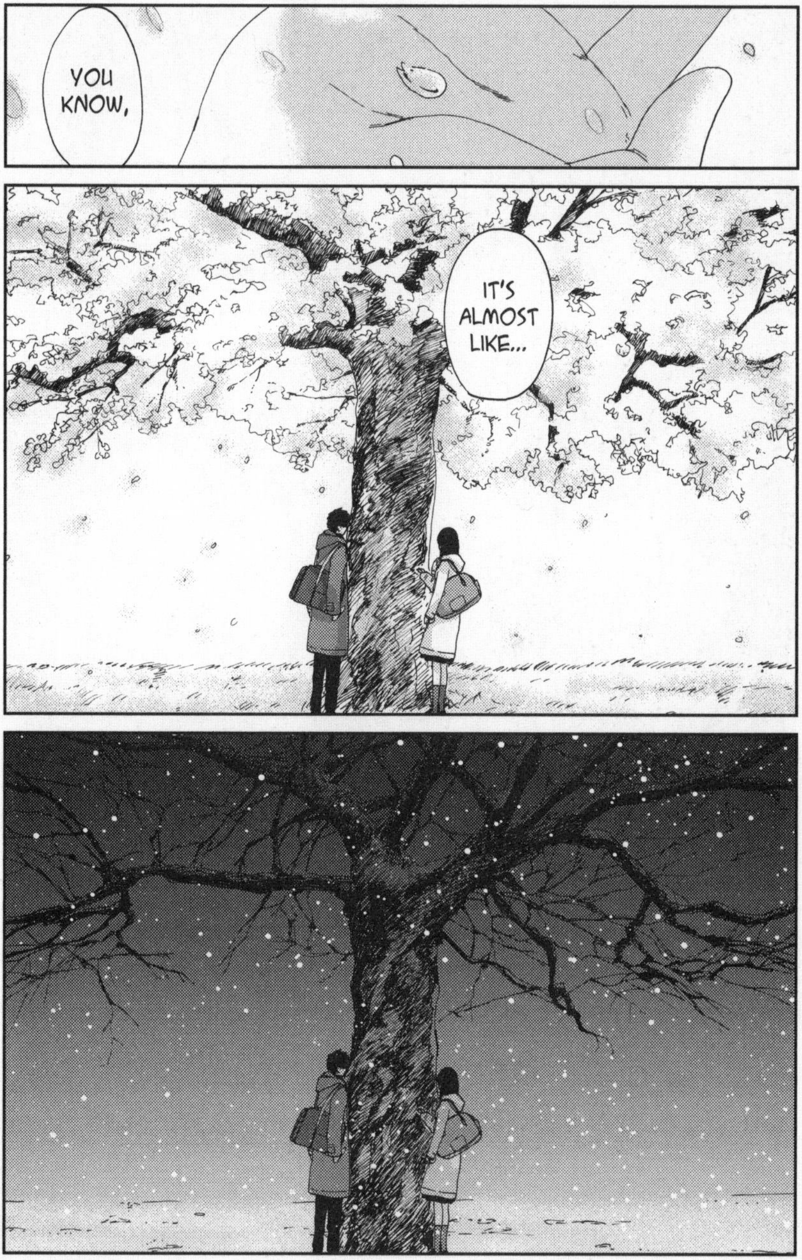
YOU KNOW,
IT'S ALMOST LIKE...

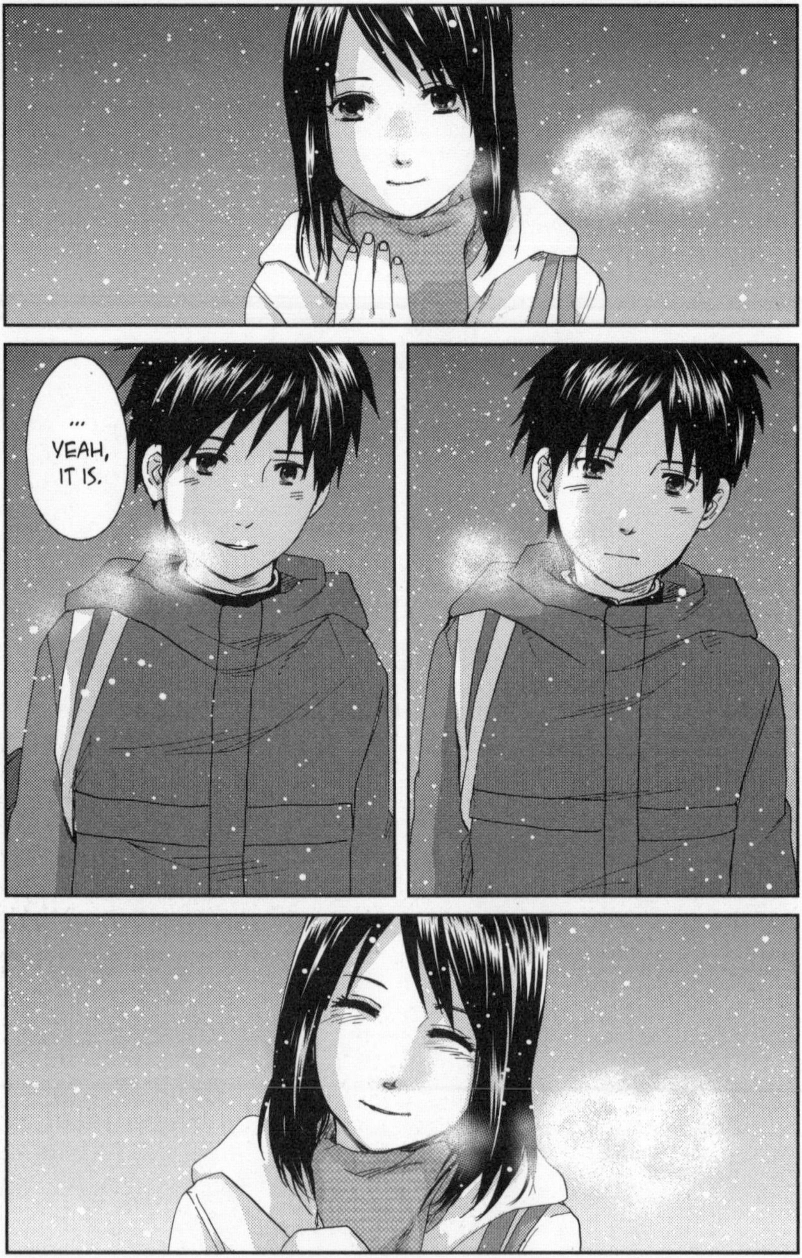
... YEAH, IT IS.

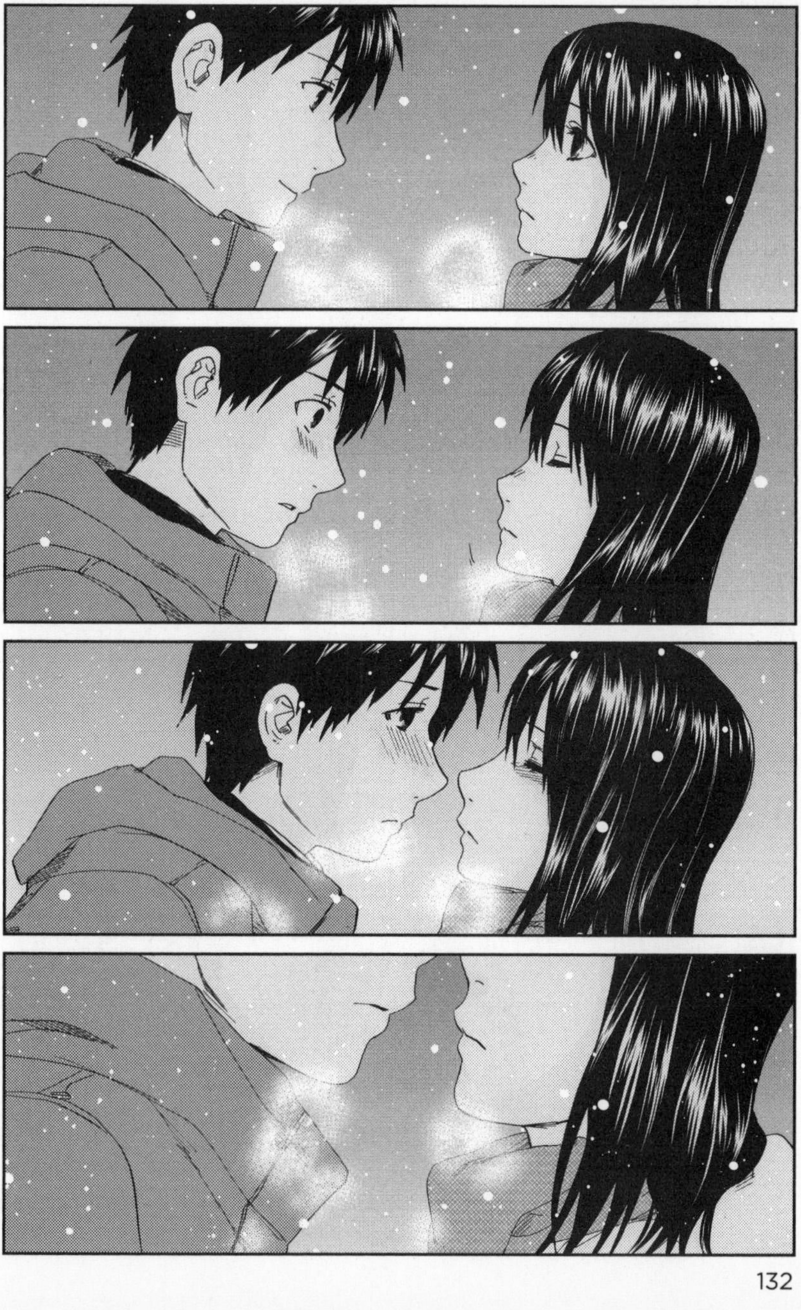

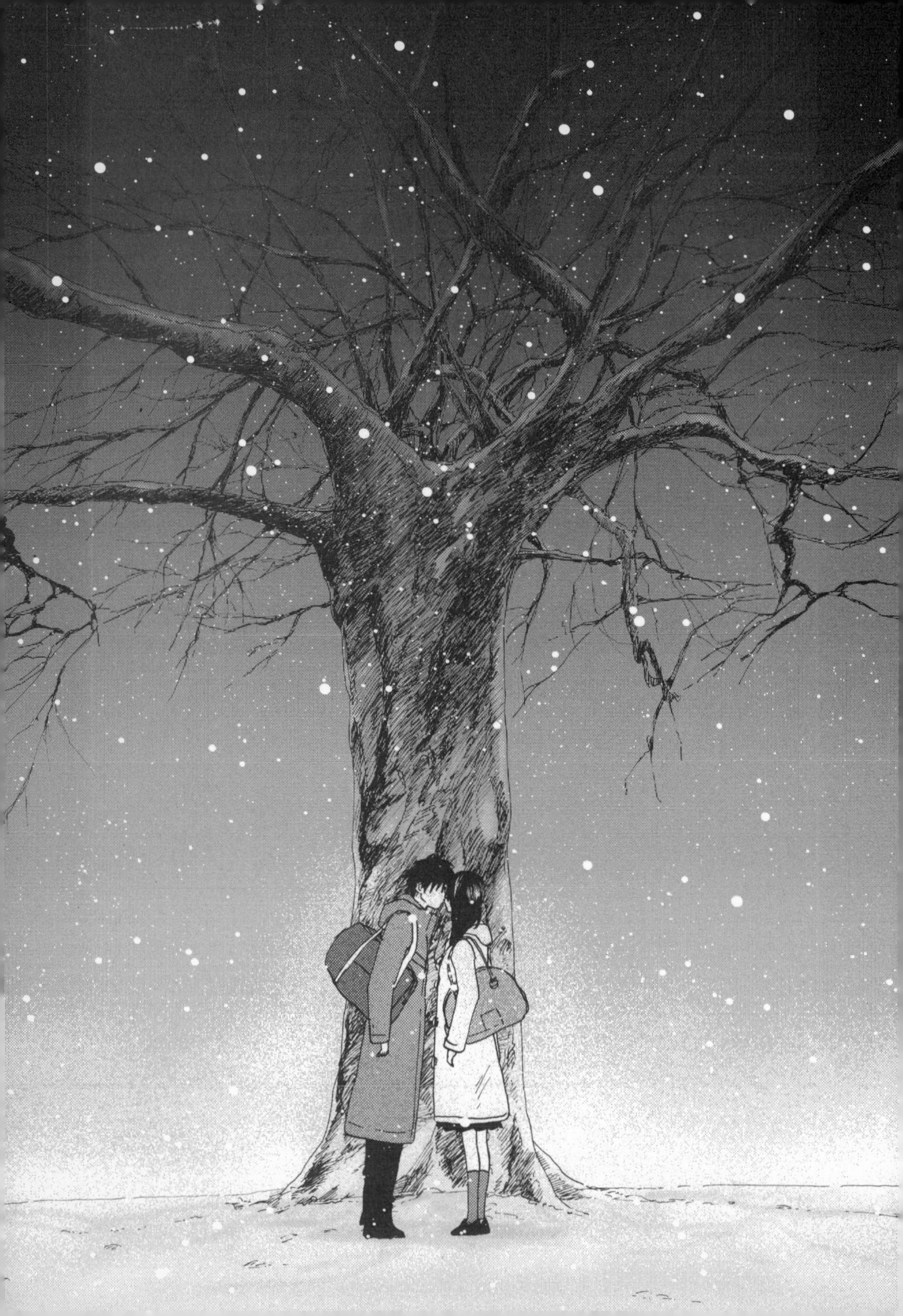

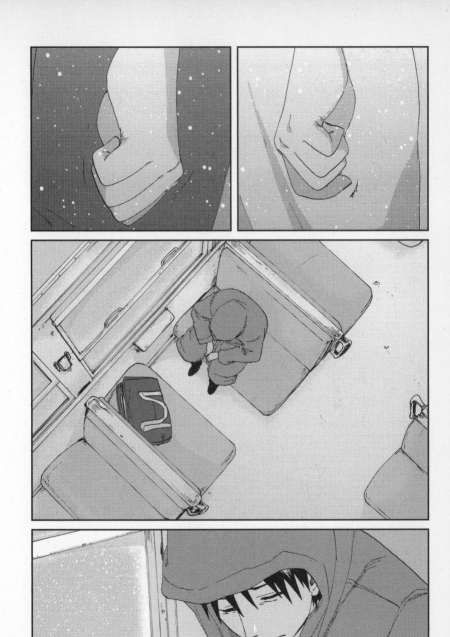

134

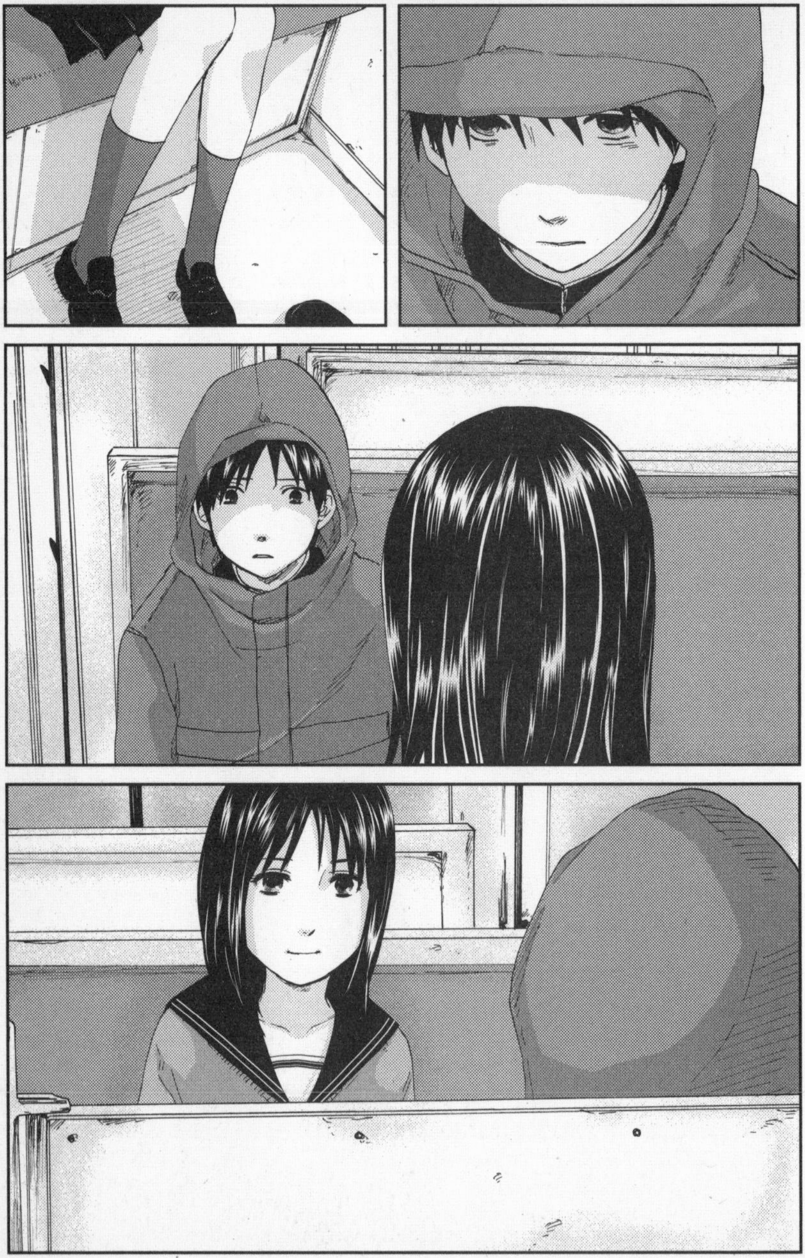

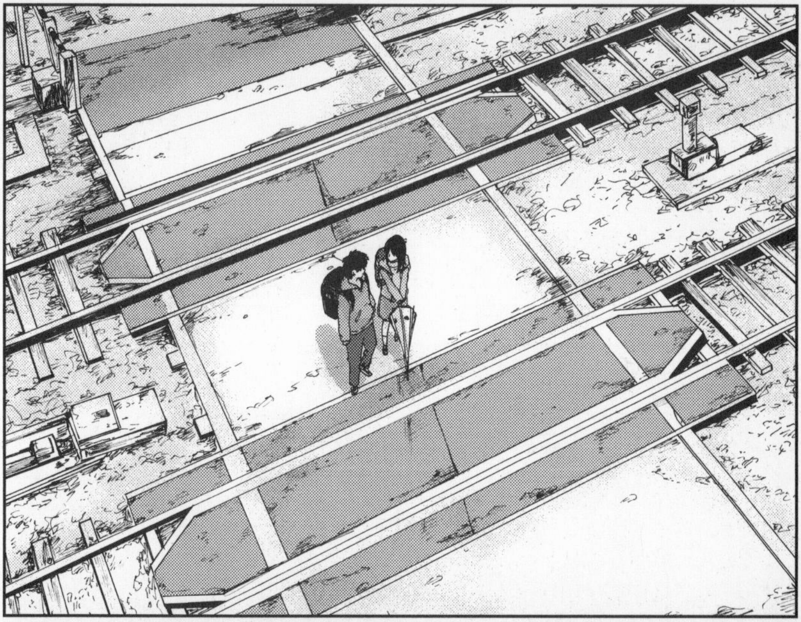
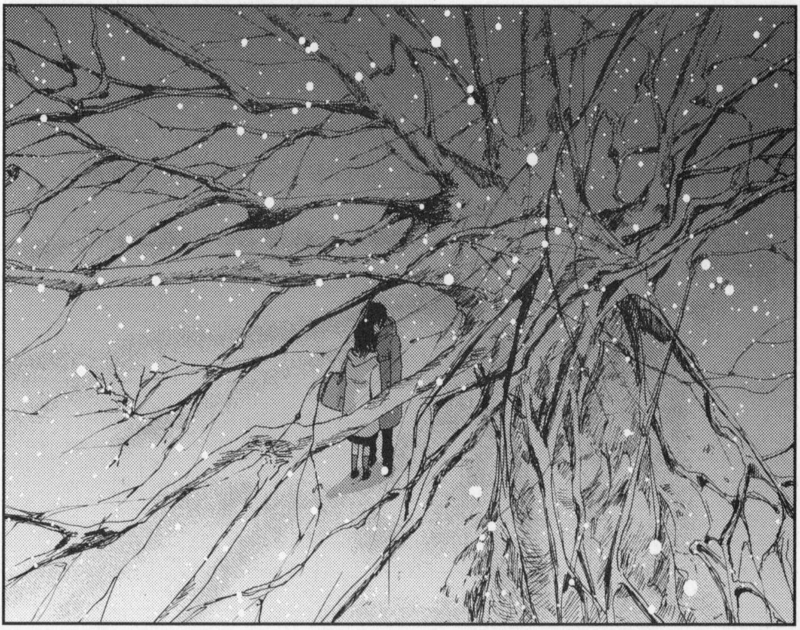

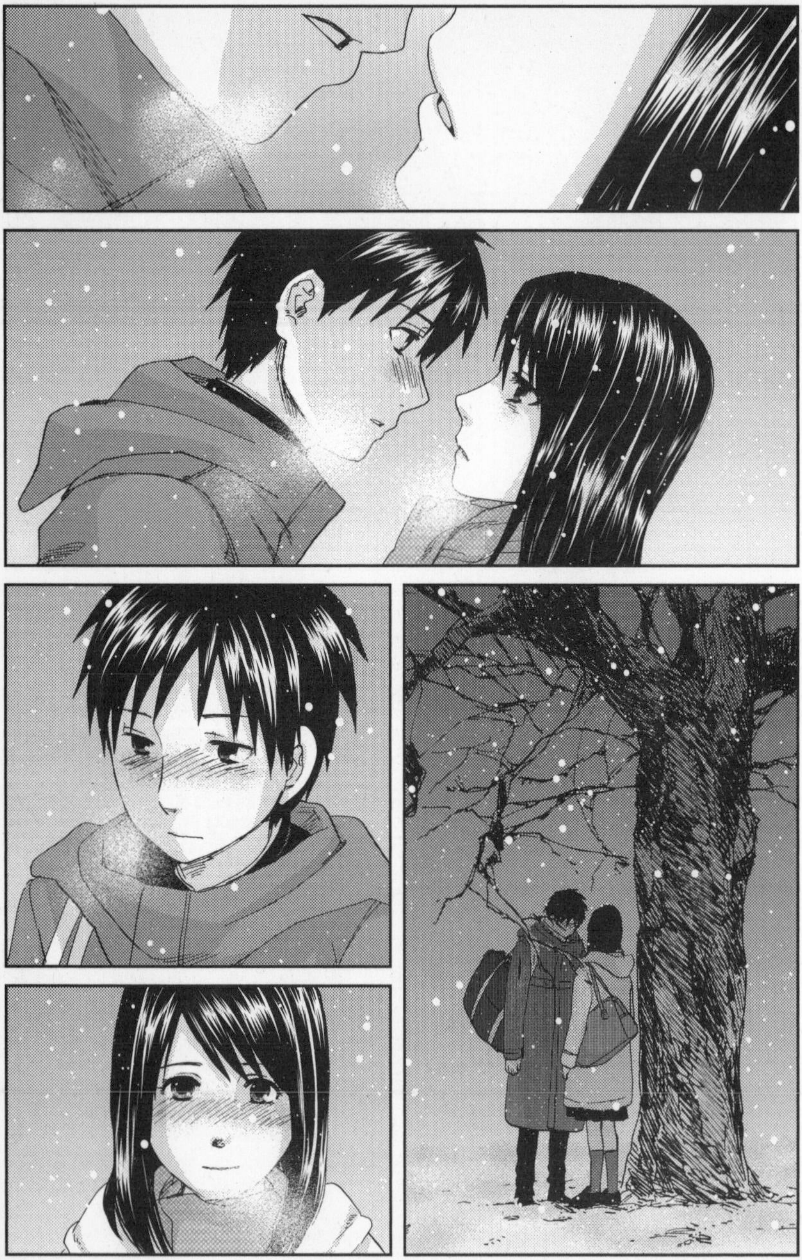

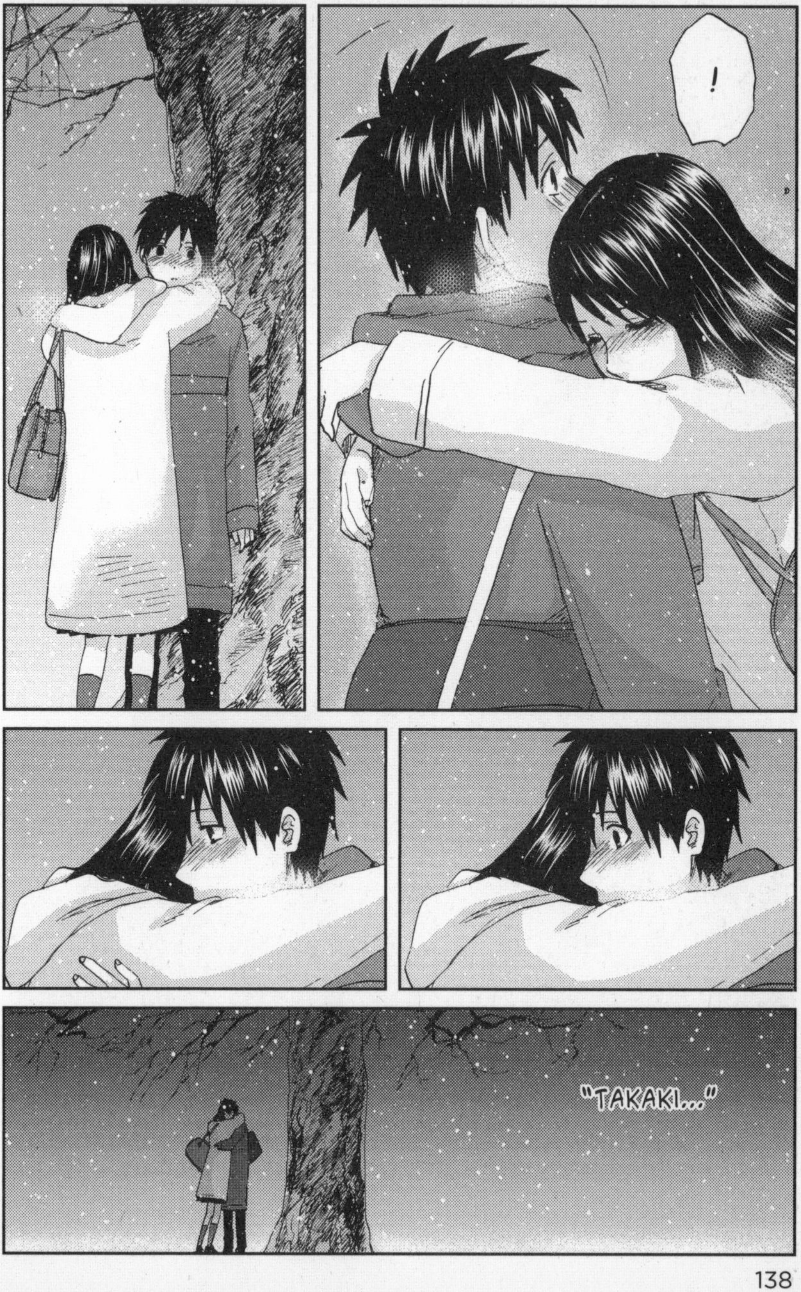
!
"TAKAKI..."

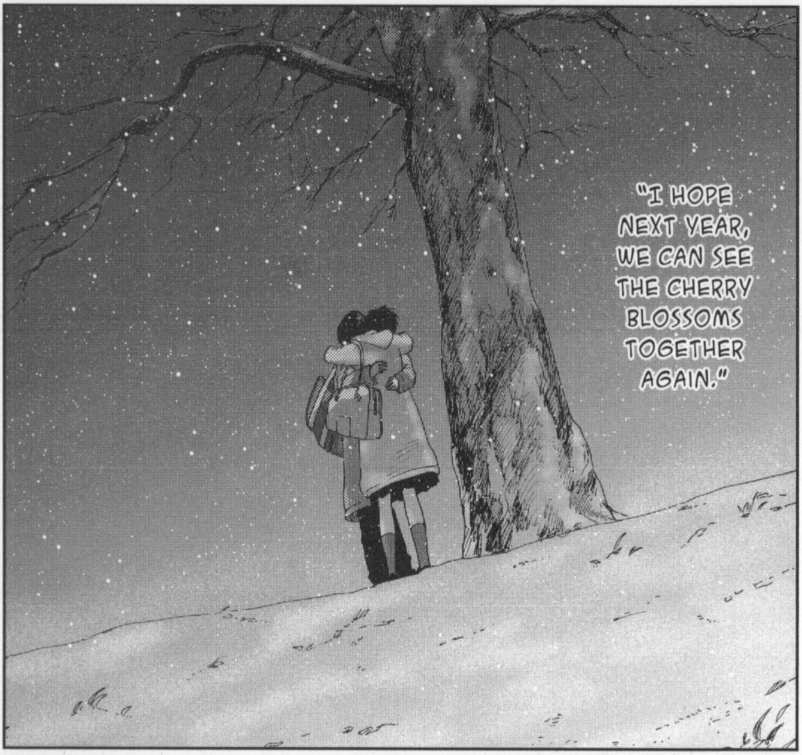
"I HOPE NEXT YEAR, WE CAN SEE THE CHERRY BLOSSOMS TOGETHER AGAIN."

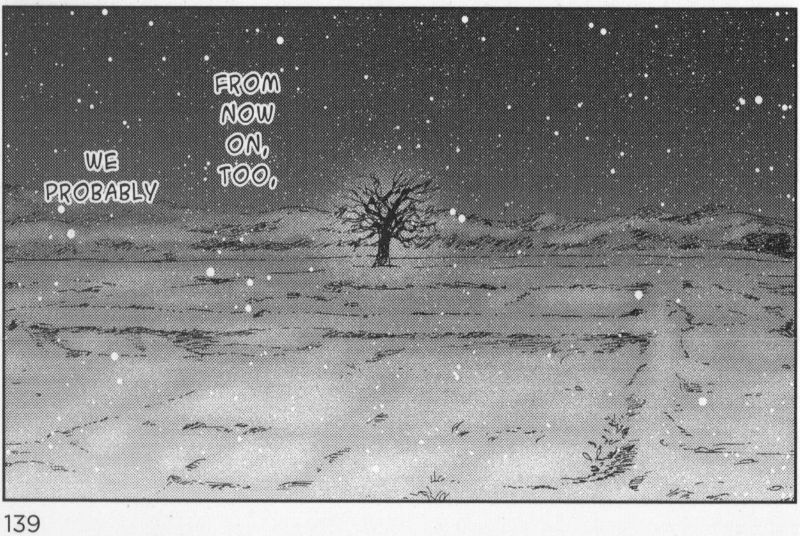
FROM NOW ON, TOO,
WE PROBABLY

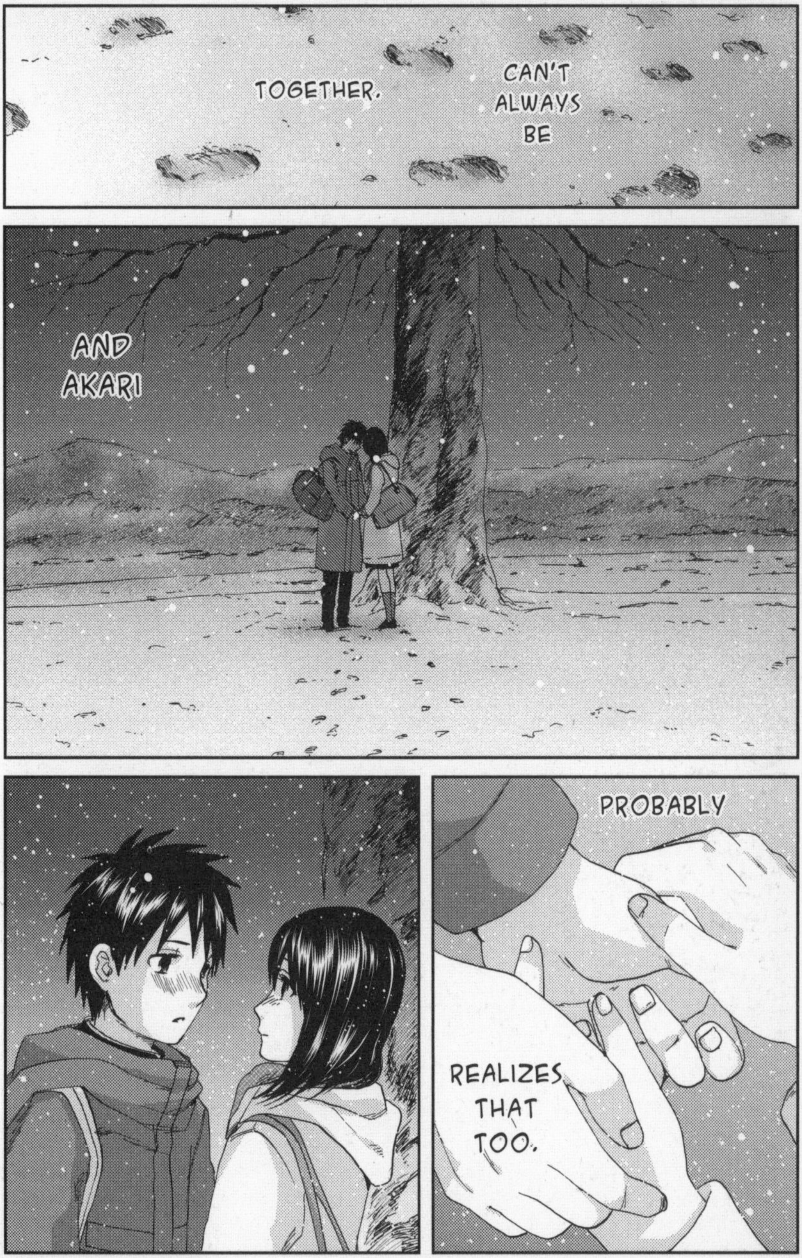
CAN'T ALWAYS BE
TOGETHER.
AND AKARI
PROBABLY
REALIZES THAT TOO.

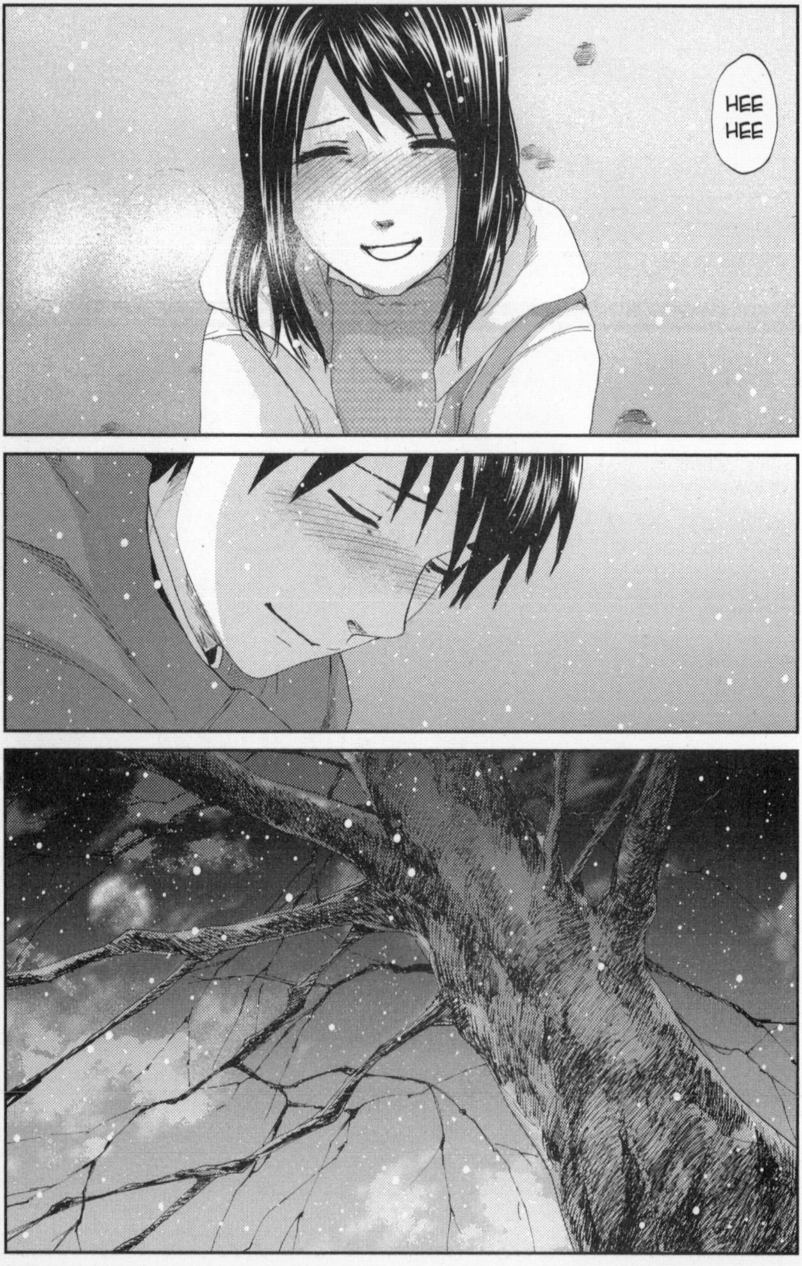
HEE HEE

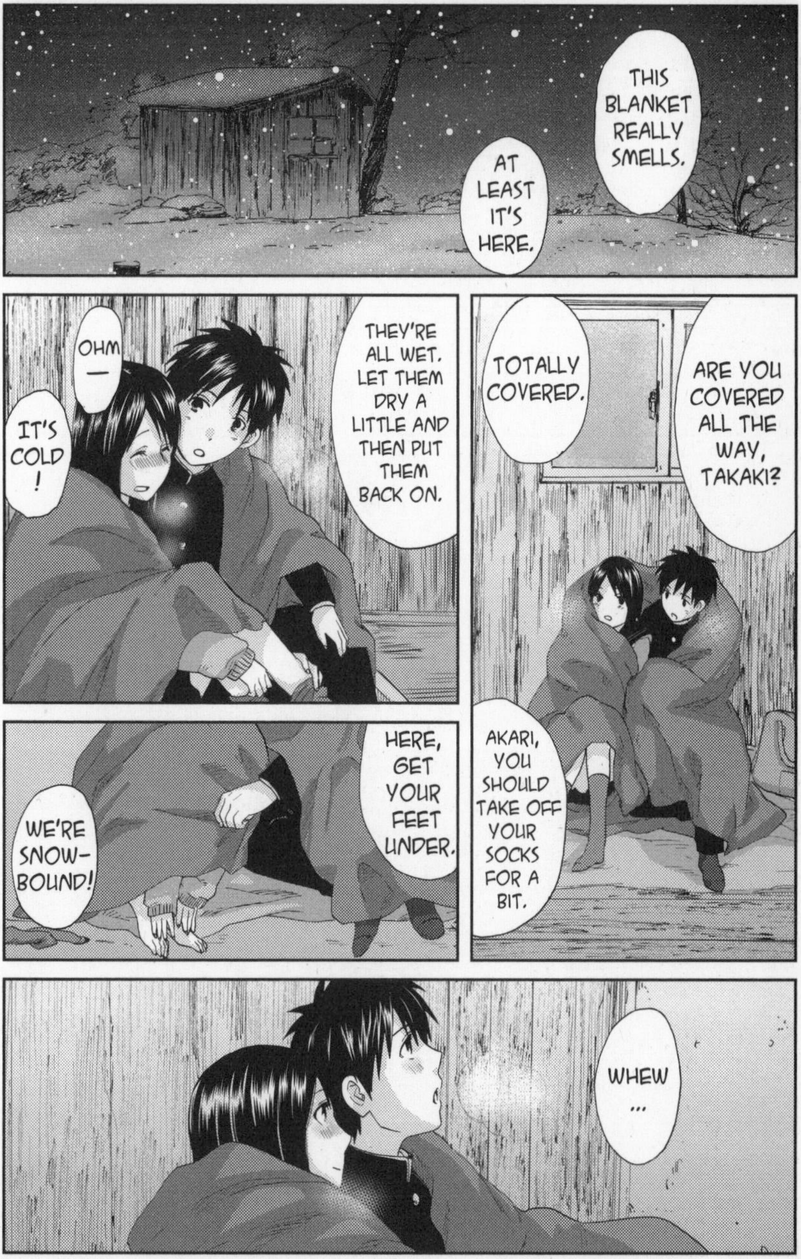
THIS BLANKET REALLY SMELLS.
AT LEAST IT'S HERE.
ARE YOU COVERED ALL THE WAY, TAKAKI?
TOTALLY COVERED.
AKARI, YOU SHOULD TAKE OFF YOUR SOCKS FOR A BIT.
THEY'RE ALL WET. LET THEM DRY A LITTLE AND THEN PUT THEM BACK ON.
OHM —
IT'S COLD!
HERE, GET YOUR FEET UNDER.
WE'RE SNOW-BOUND!
WHEW ...

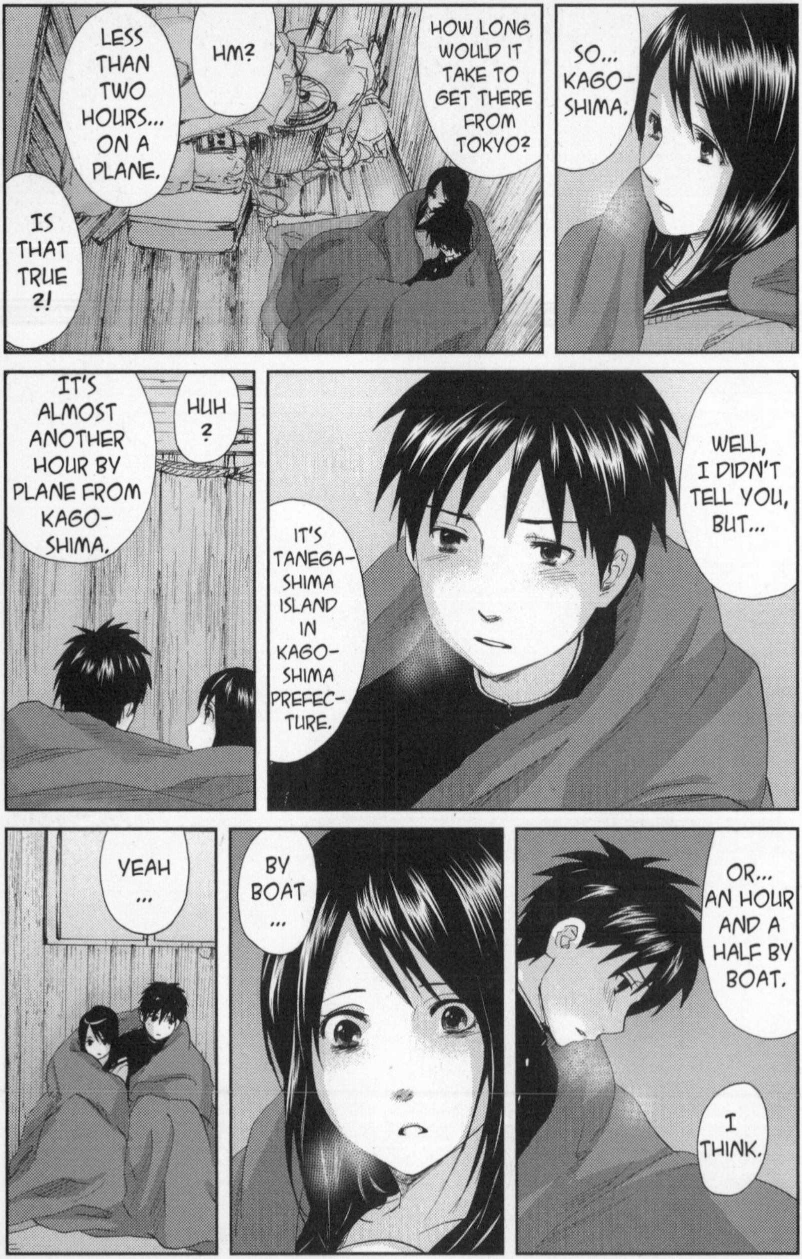
SO... KAGO-SHIMA.
HOW LONG WOULD IT TAKE TO GET THERE FROM TOKYO?
HM?
LESS THAN TWO HOURS... ON A PLANE.
IS THAT TRUE?!
WELL, I DIDN'T TELL YOU, BUT...
IT'S TANEGA-SHIMA ISLAND IN KAGO-SHIMA PREFEC-TURE.
HUH?
IT'S ALMOST ANOTHER HOUR BY PLANE FROM KAGO-SHIMA.
OR... AN HOUR AND A HALF BY BOAT.
I THINK.
BY BOAT...
YEAH...

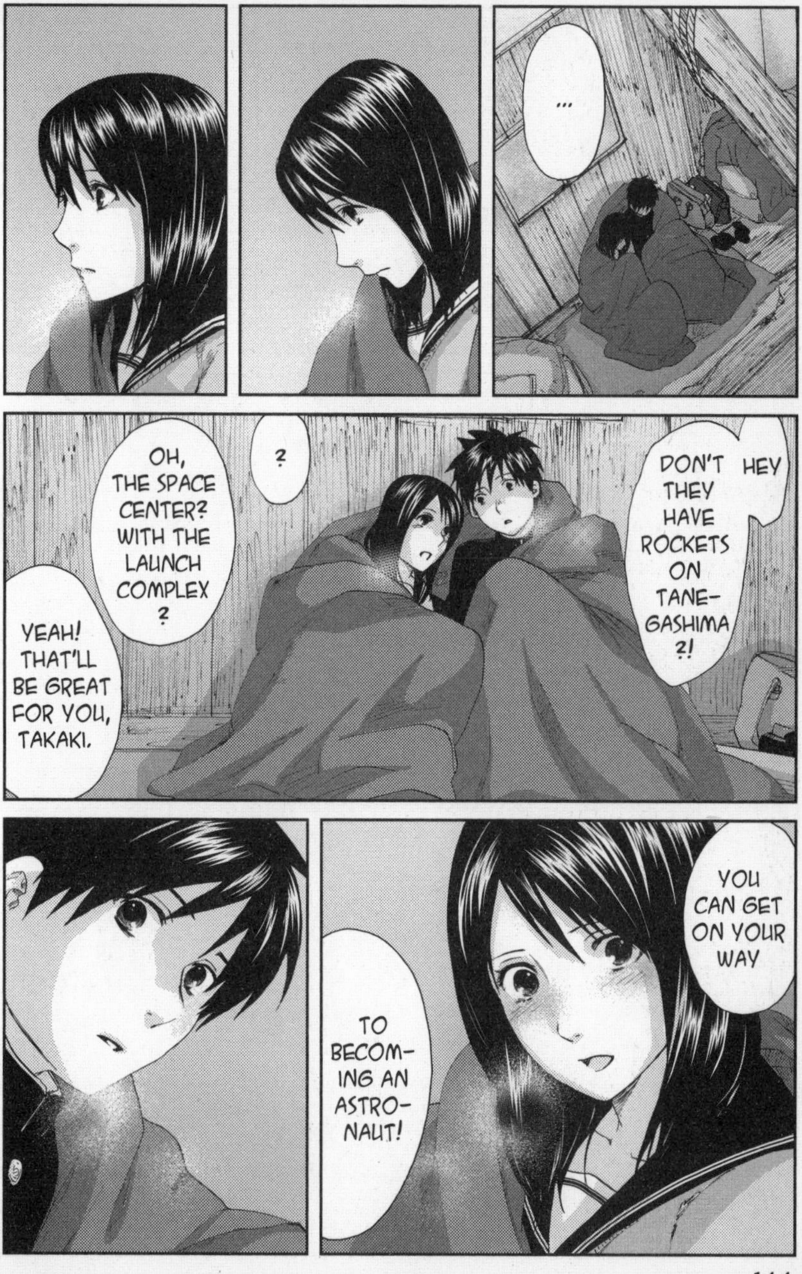
...
HEY
DON'T THEY HAVE ROCKETS ON TANE-GASHIMA?!
?
OH, THE SPACE CENTER? WITH THE LAUNCH COMPLEX?
YEAH! THAT'LL BE GREAT FOR YOU, TAKAKI.
YOU CAN GET ON YOUR WAY
TO BECOMING AN ASTRONAUT!

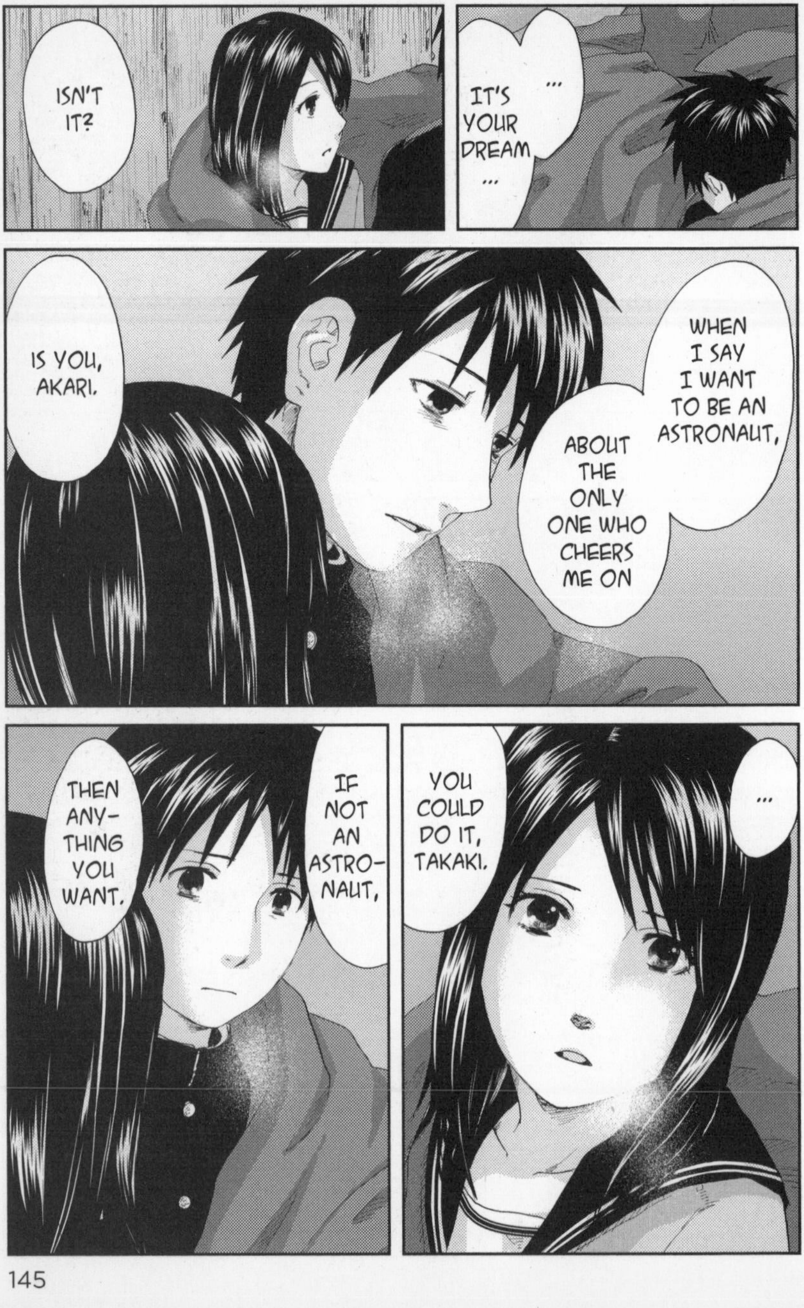
... IT'S YOUR DREAM ...
ISN'T IT?
WHEN I SAY I WANT TO BE AN ASTRONAUT,
ABOUT THE ONLY ONE WHO CHEERS ME ON
IS YOU, AKARI.
...
YOU COULD DO IT, TAKAKI.
IF NOT AN ASTRO-NAUT,
THEN ANY-THING YOU WANT.

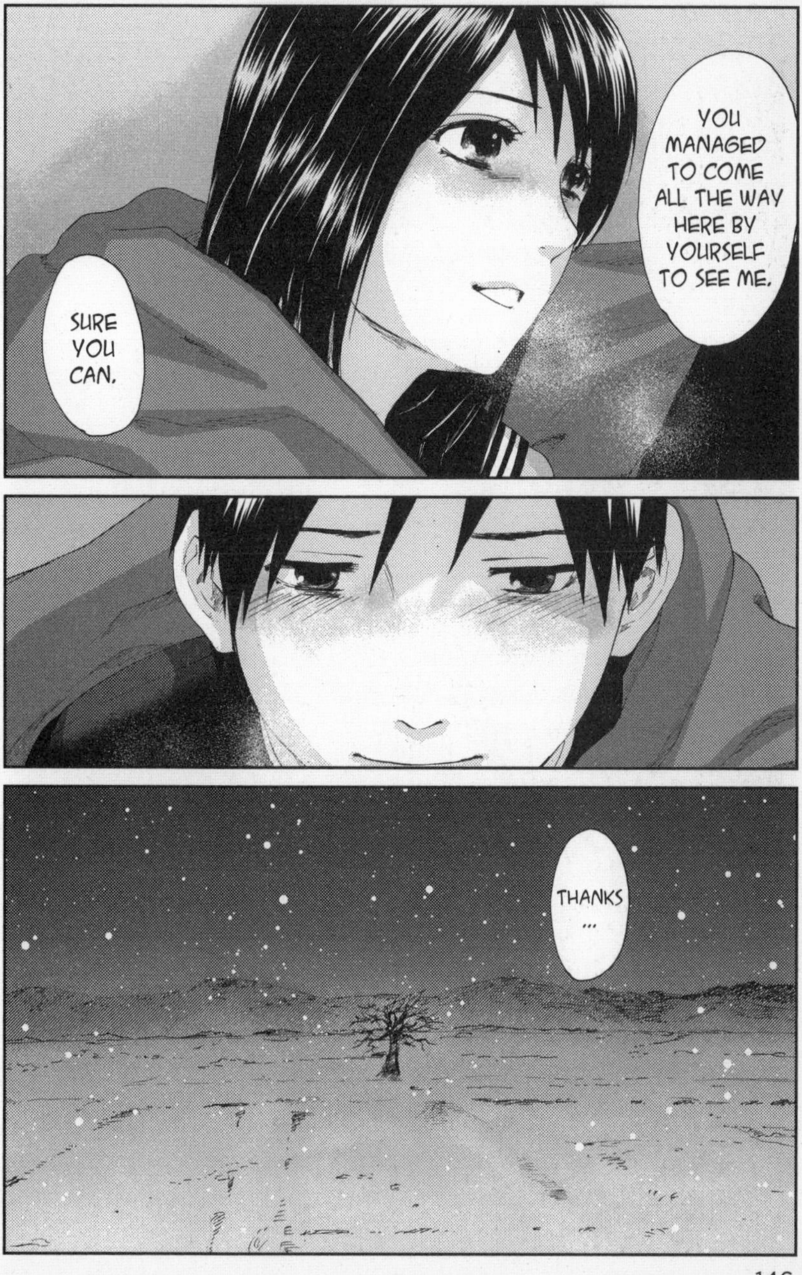
YOU MANAGED TO COME ALL THE WAY HERE BY YOURSELF TO SEE ME.
SURE YOU CAN.
THANKS ...

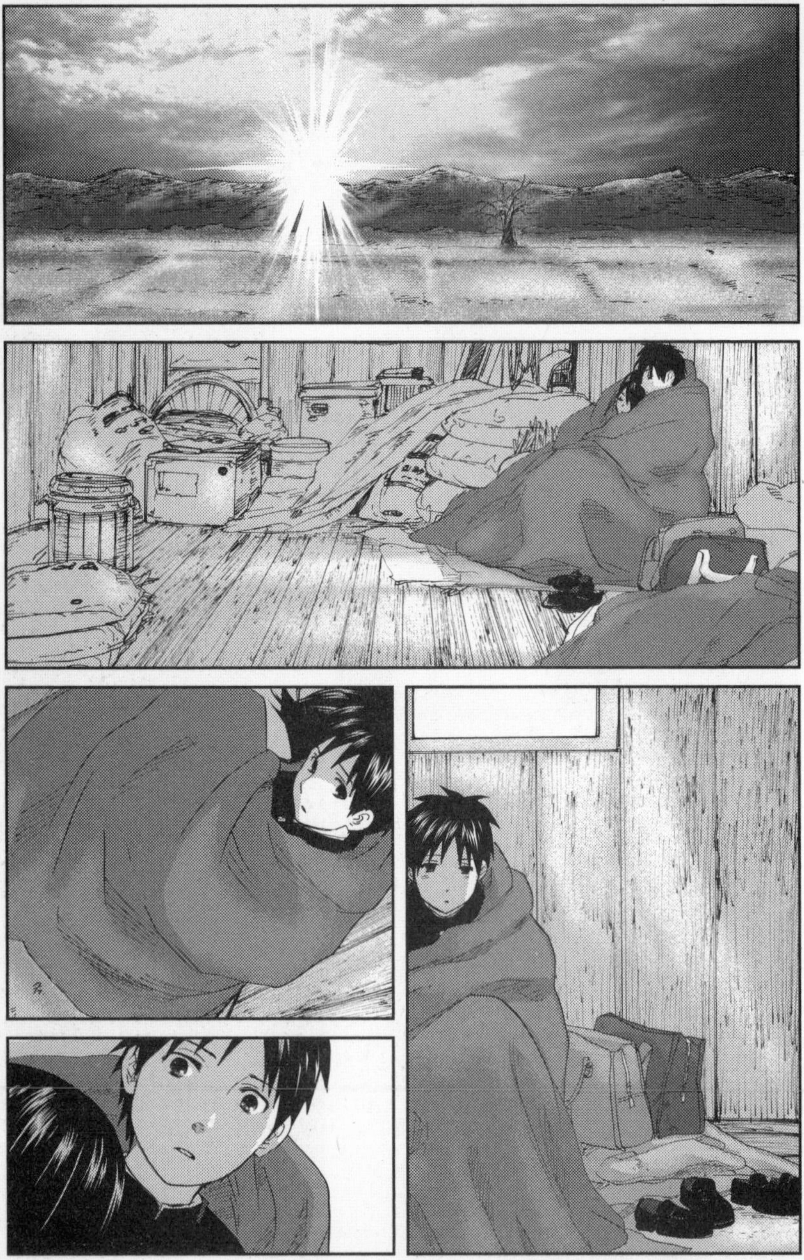

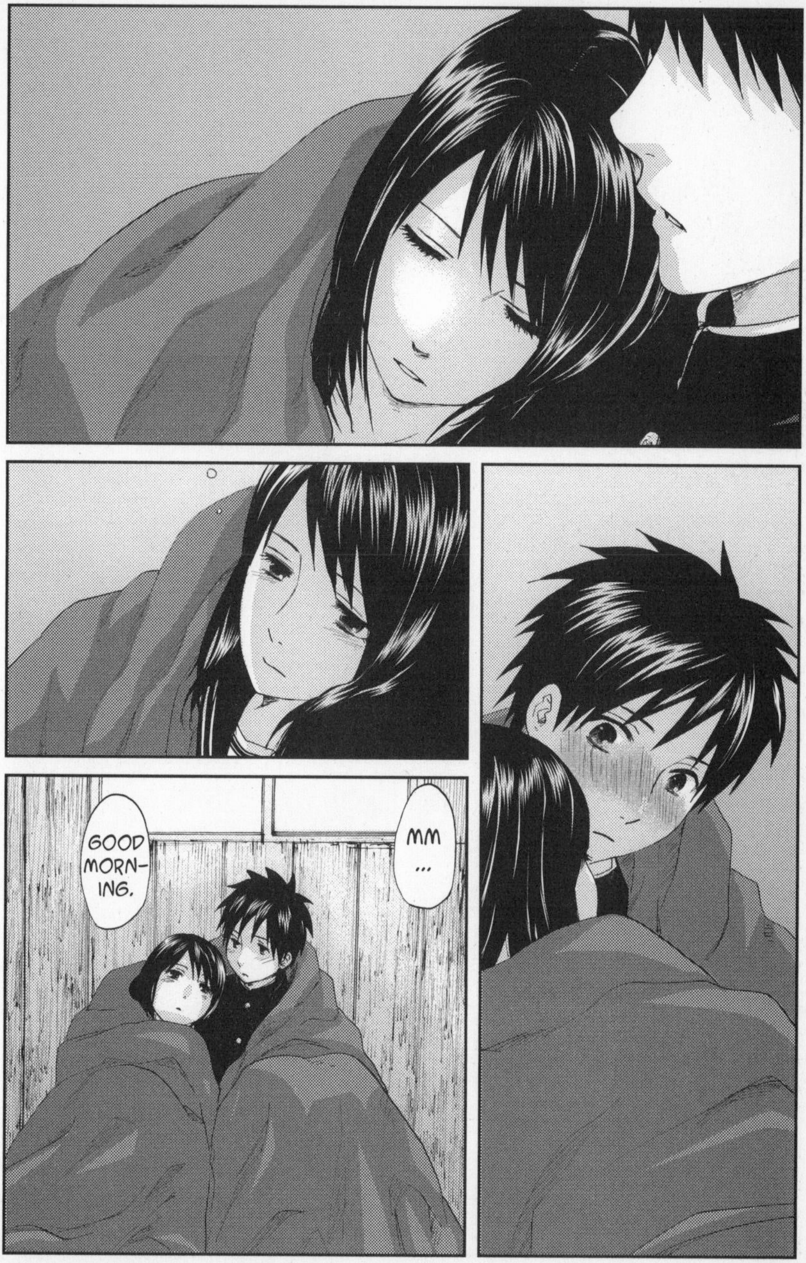
MM ...
GOOD MORN-ING.

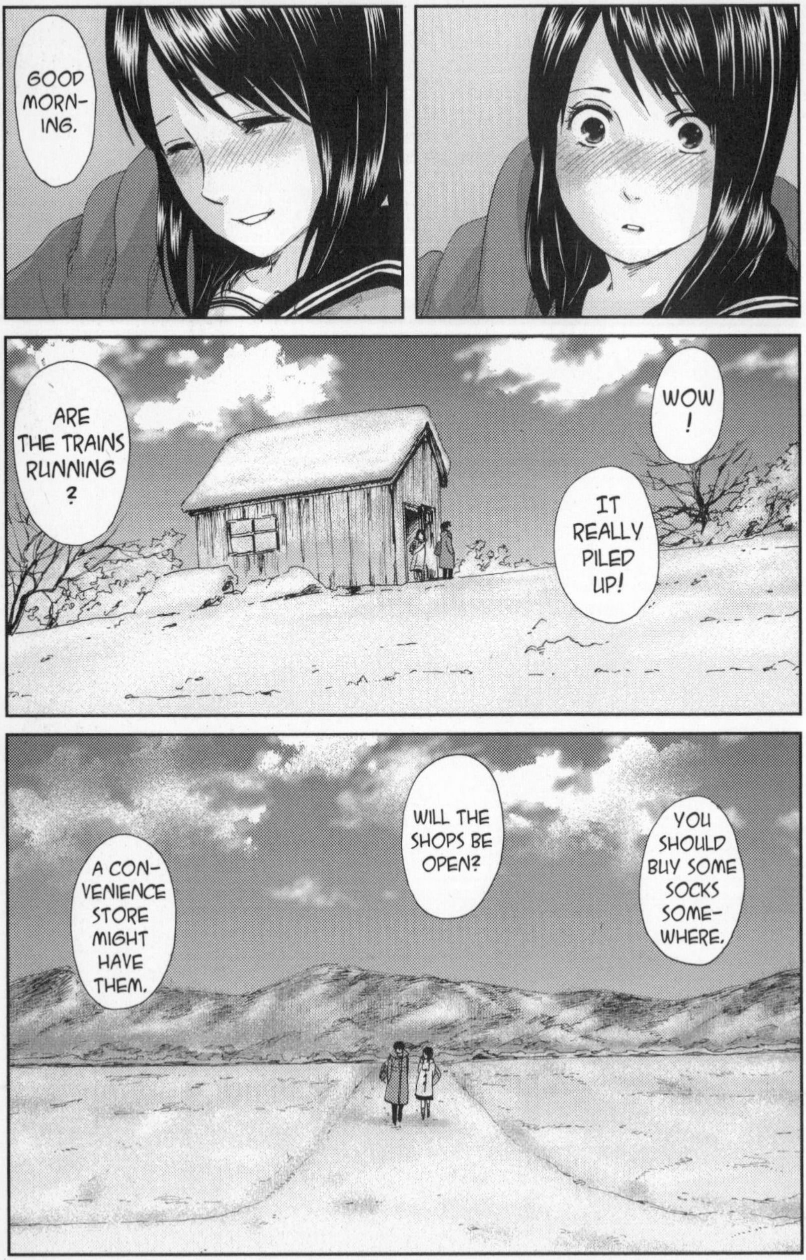
GOOD MORN-ING.
WOW!
IT REALLY PILED UP!
ARE THE TRAINS RUNNING?
YOU SHOULD BUY SOME SOCKS SOME-WHERE.
WILL THE SHOPS BE OPEN?
A CON-VENIENCE STORE MIGHT HAVE THEM.

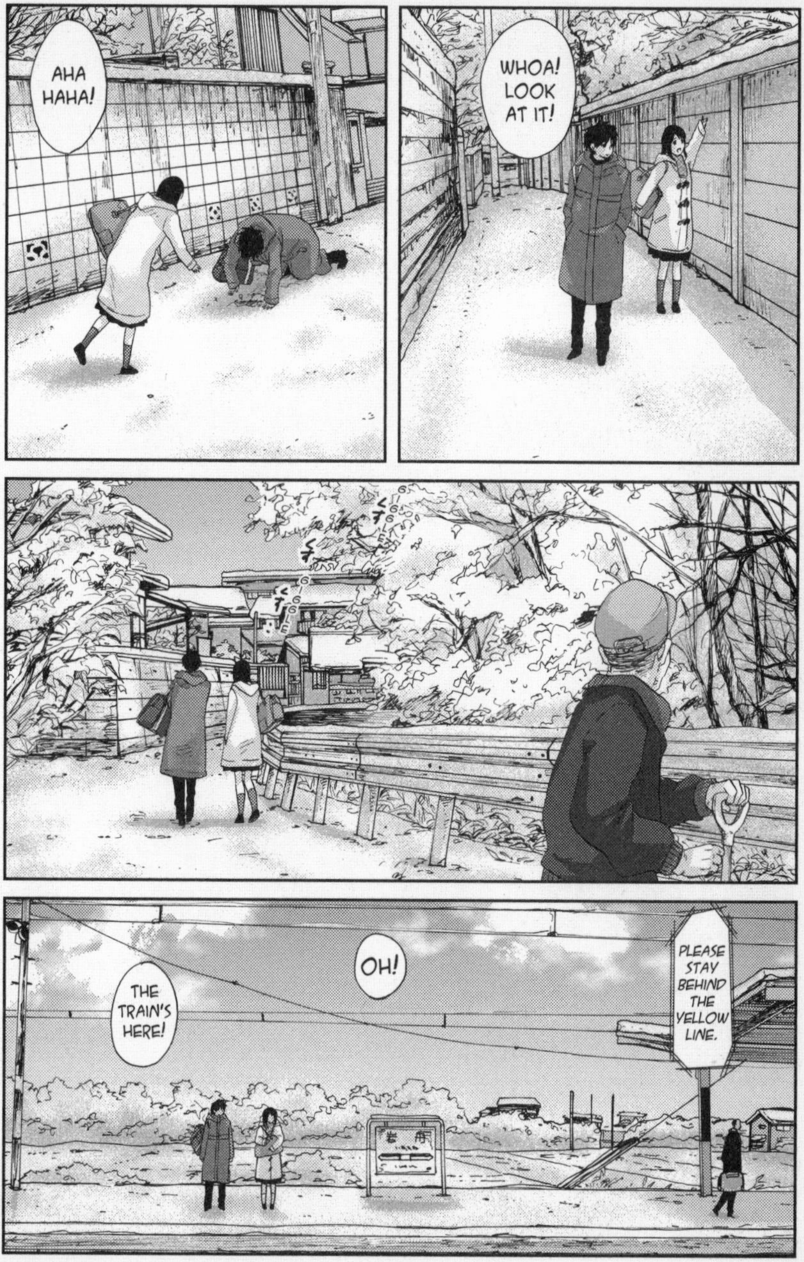
WHOA! LOOK AT IT!
AHA HAHA!
くす
GIGGLE
くす
くす
GIGGLE
PLEASE STAY BEHIND THE YELLOW LINE.
OH!
THE TRAIN'S HERE!

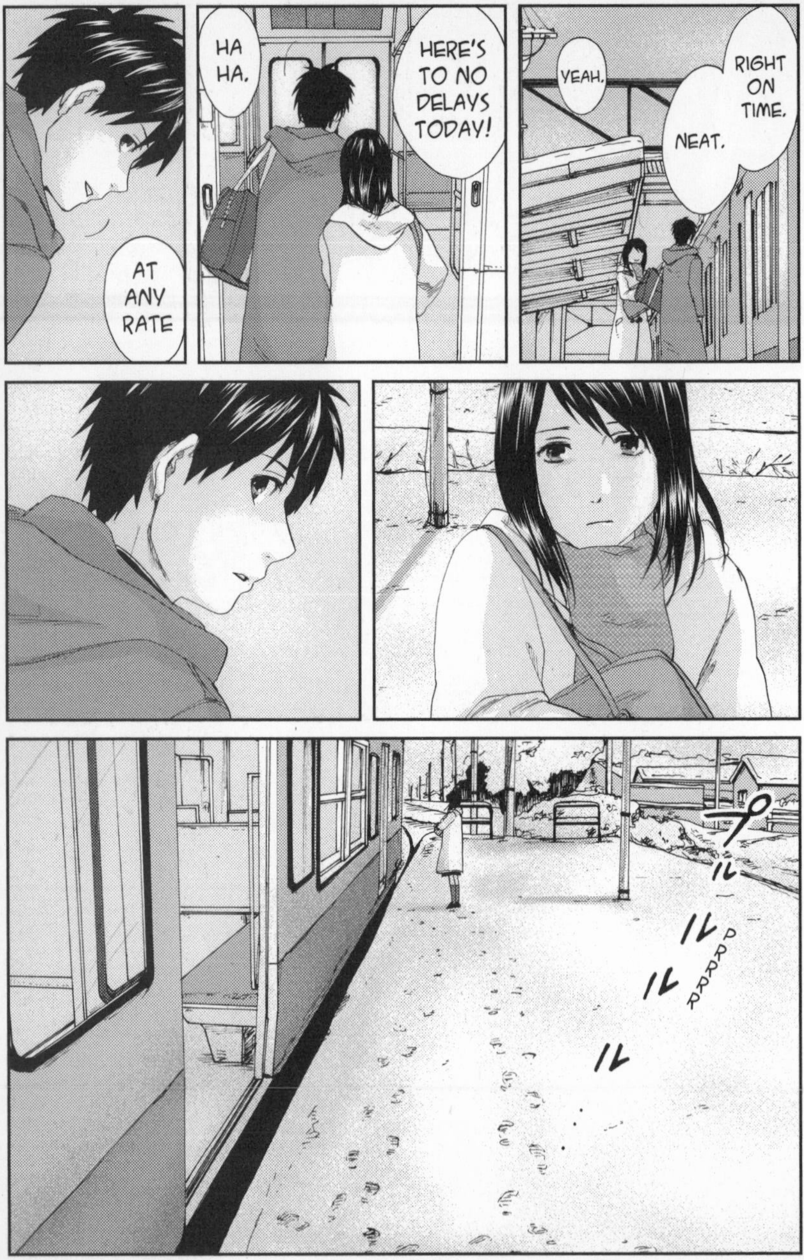
RIGHT ON TIME.
NEAT.
YEAH.
HERE'S TO NO DELAYS TODAY!
HA HA.
AT ANY RATE
プルルルル
PRRRR

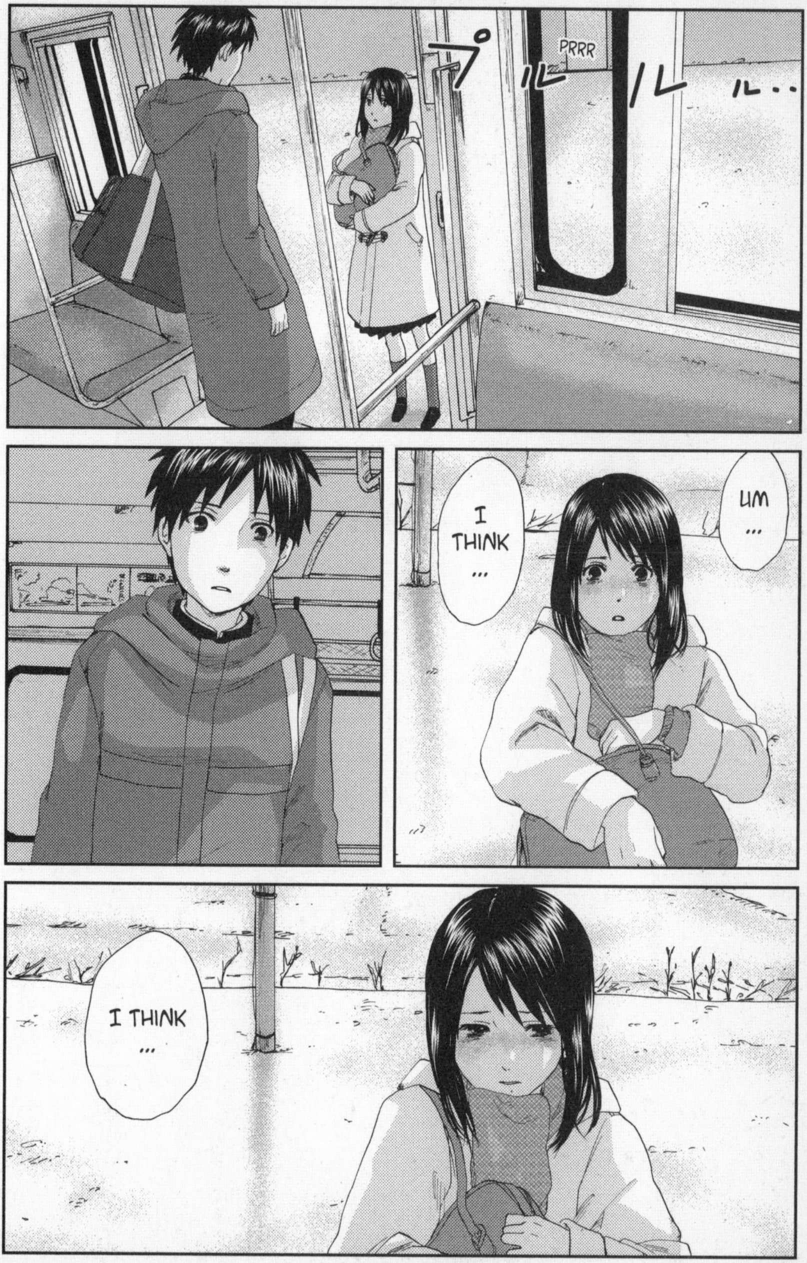
プルルル..
PRRR
UM ...
I THINK ...
I THINK ...

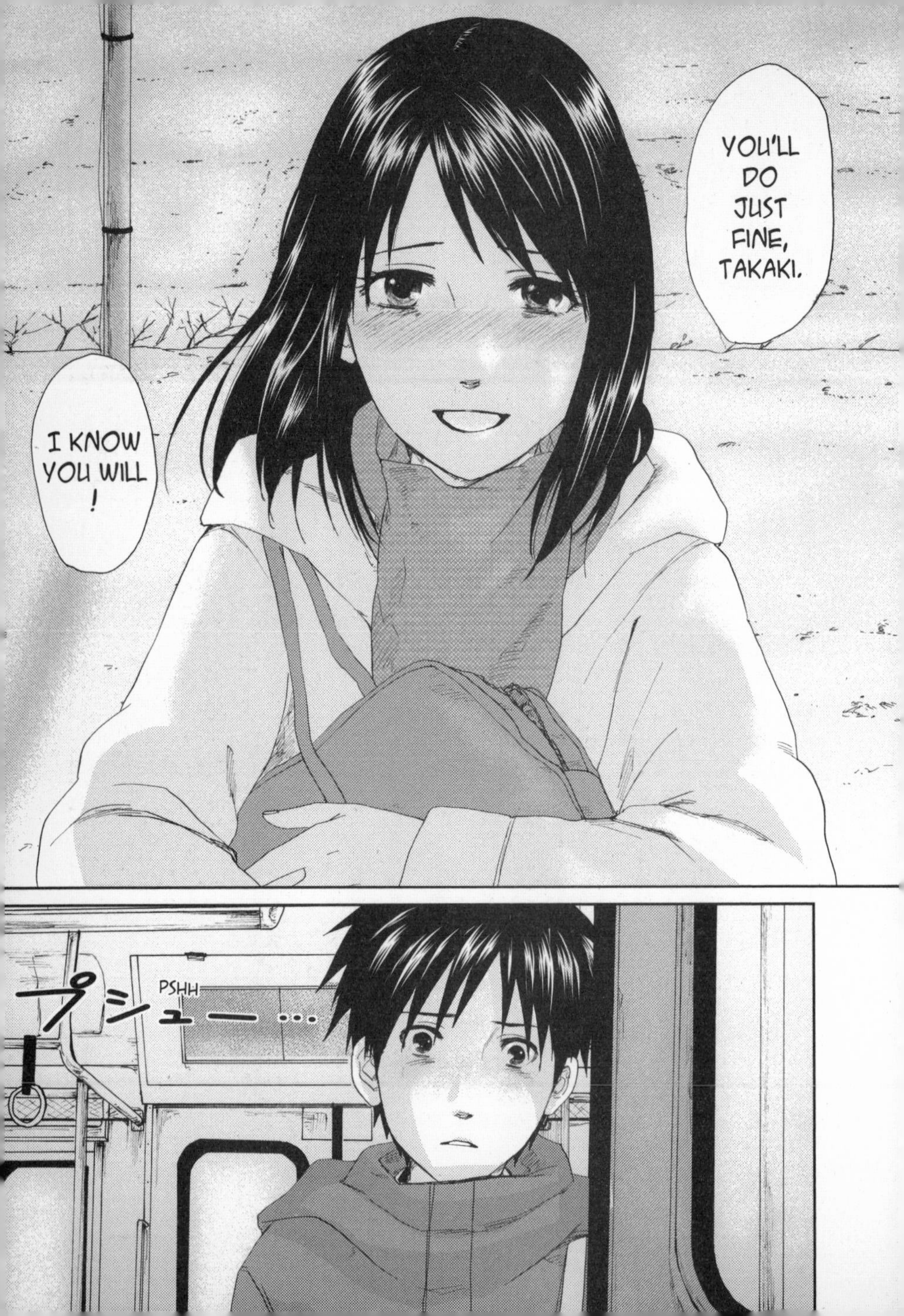
YOU'LL DO JUST FINE, TAKAKI.
I KNOW YOU WILL!
プシュー…
PSHH

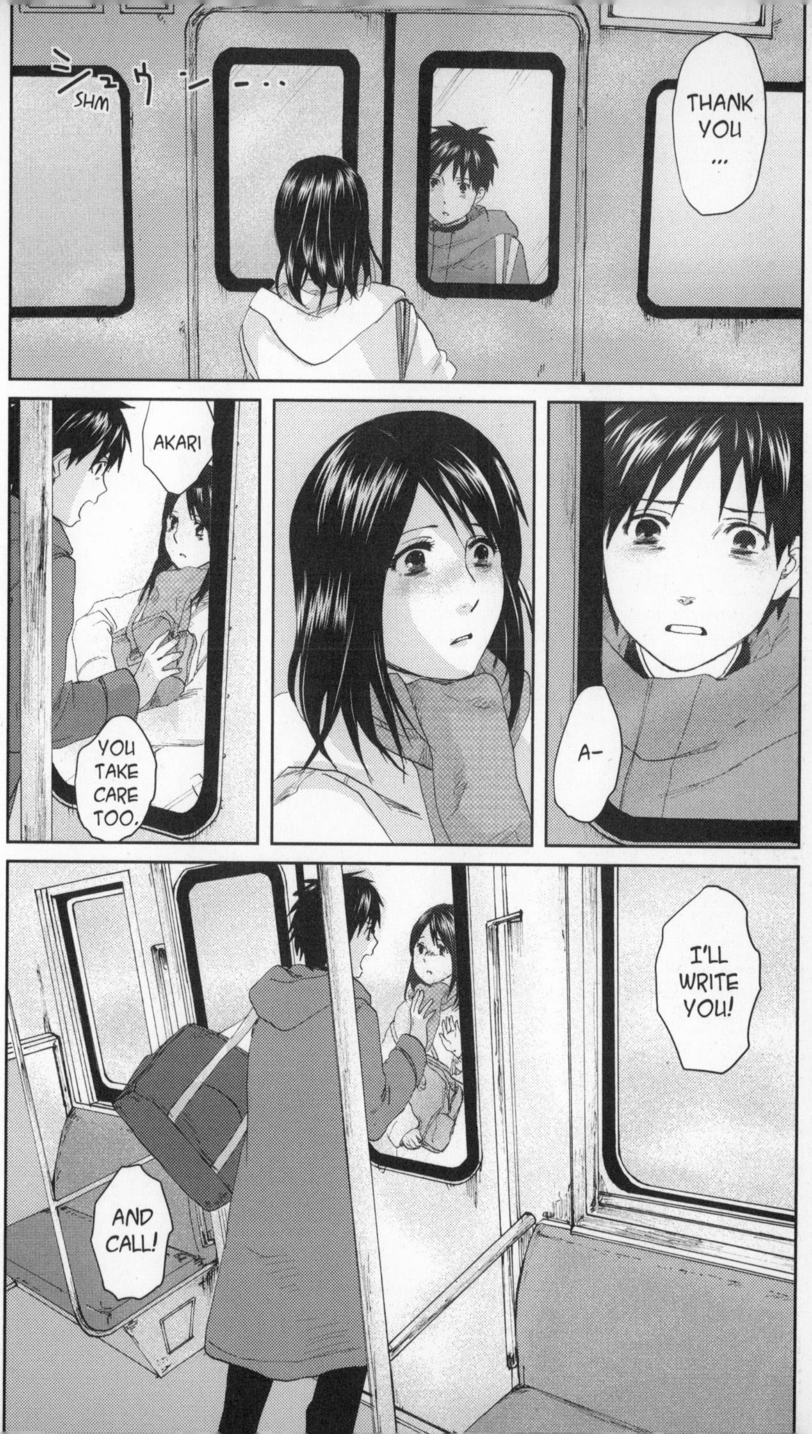
THANK YOU ...
SHM
A-
AKARI
YOU TAKE CARE TOO.
I'LL WRITE YOU!
AND CALL!

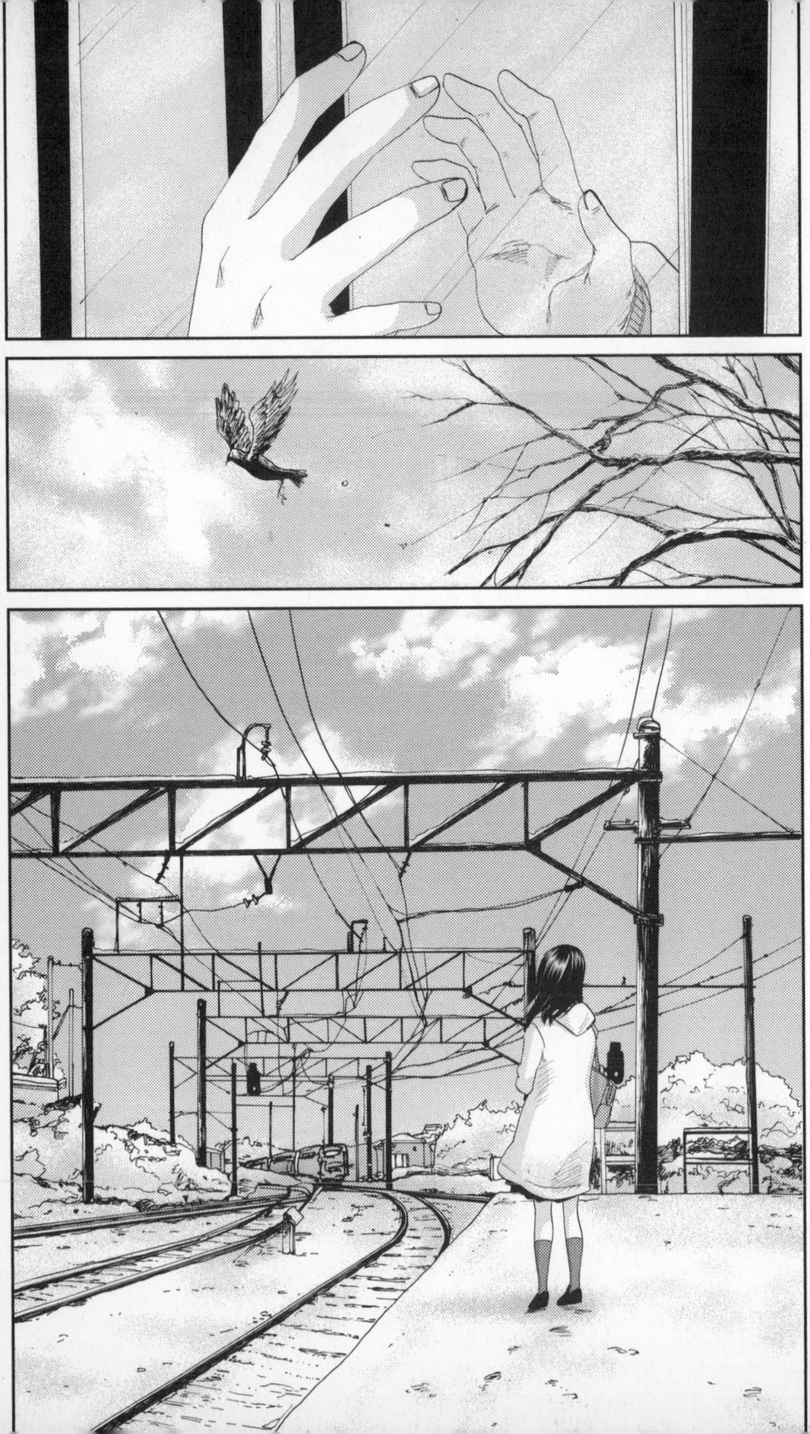

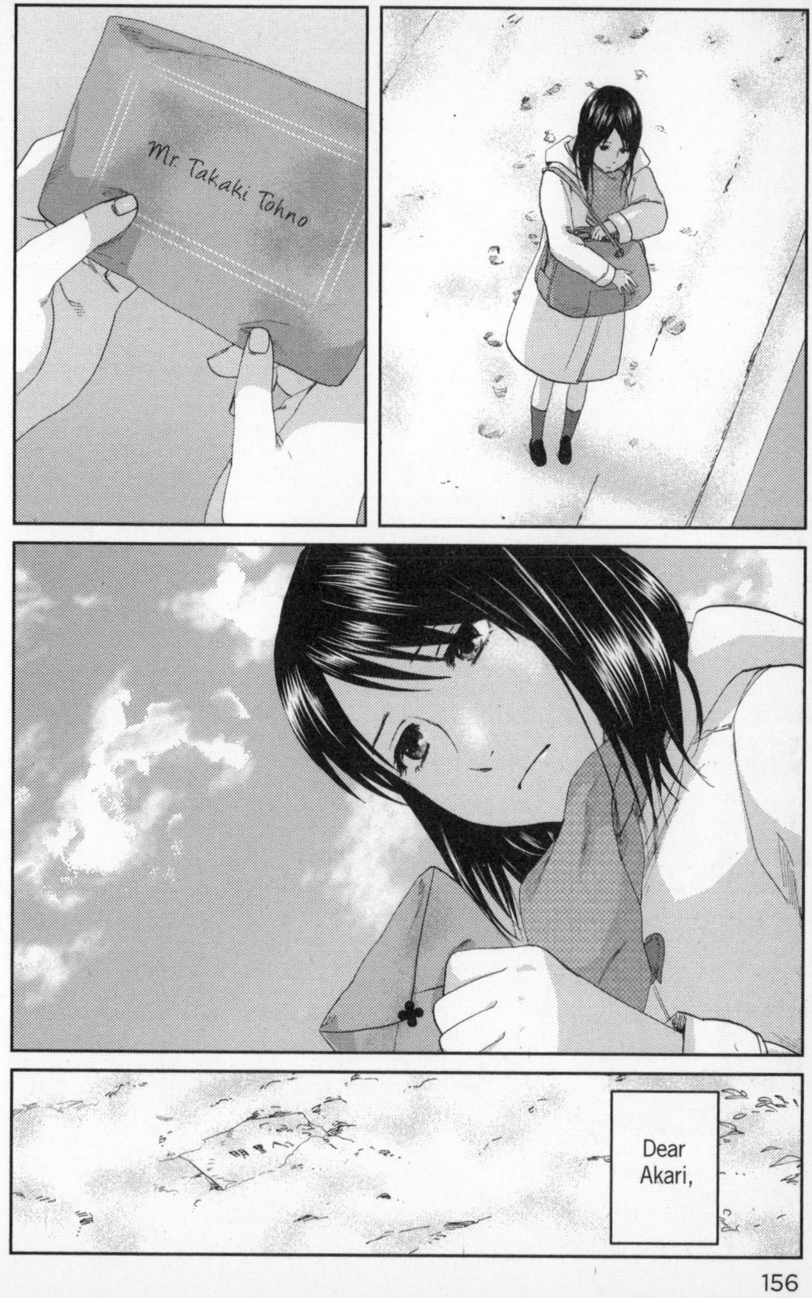
Mr. Takaki Tohno
Dear Akari,

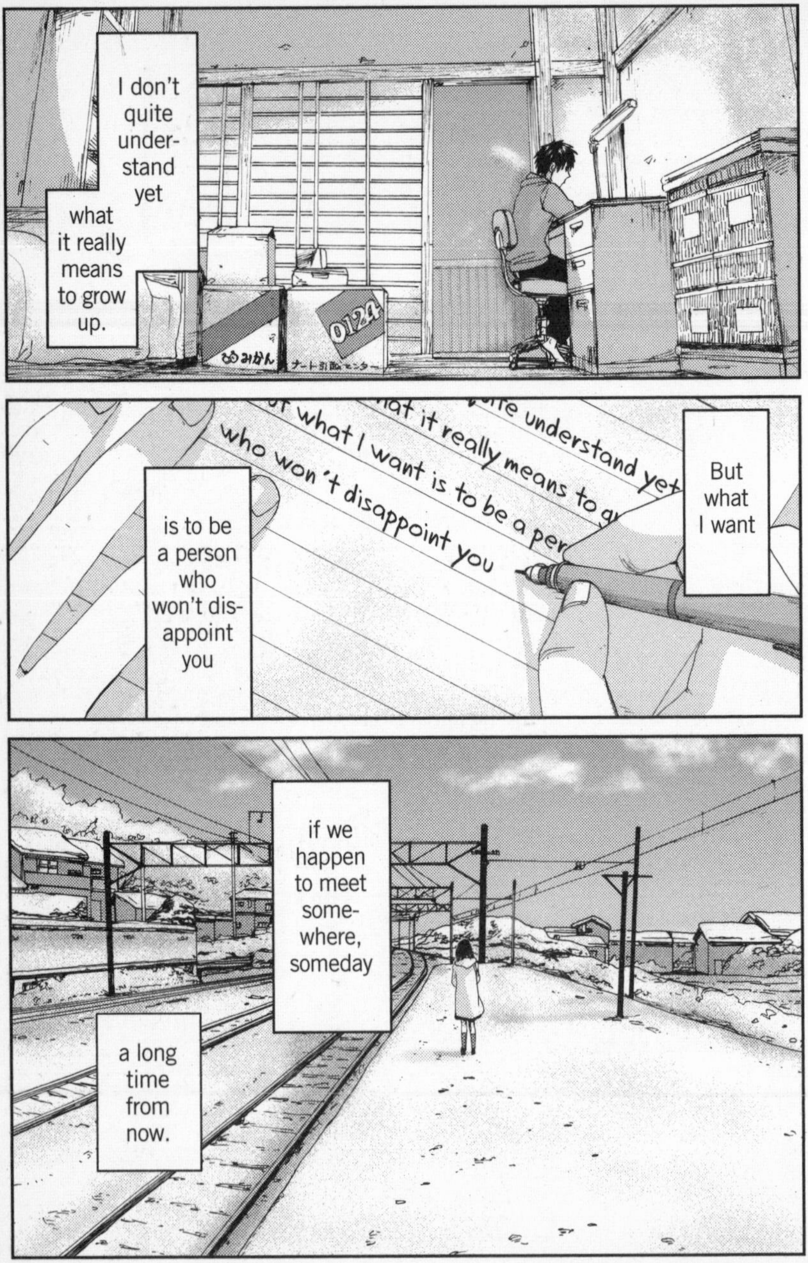
I don't quite under-stand yet
what it really means to grow up.
But what I want
uite understand yet
what it really means to g
what I want is to be a per
who won't disappoint you
is to be a person who won't dis-appoint you
if we happen to meet some-where, someday
a long time from now.

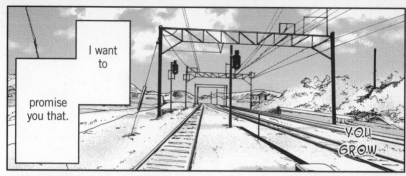

I want to

promise you that.

YOU GROW

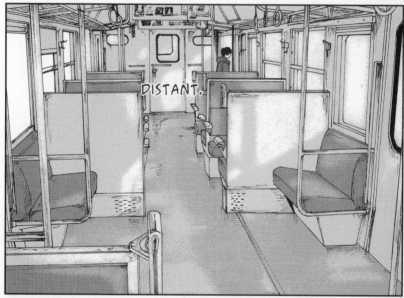

DISTANT.

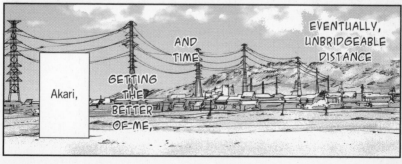

EVENTUALLY, UNBRIDGEABLE DISTANCE

AND TIME

GETTING THE BETTER OF ME,

Akari,

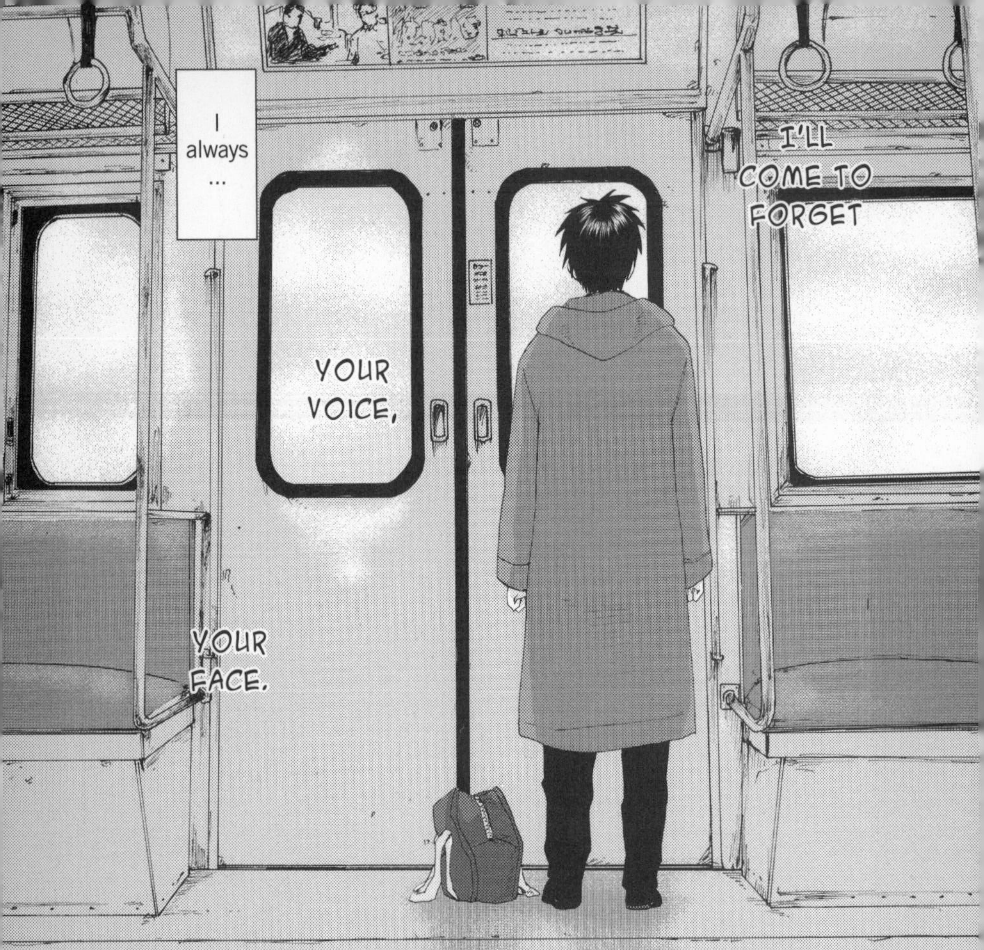
I'LL COME TO FORGET
I always ...
YOUR VOICE,
YOUR FACE.

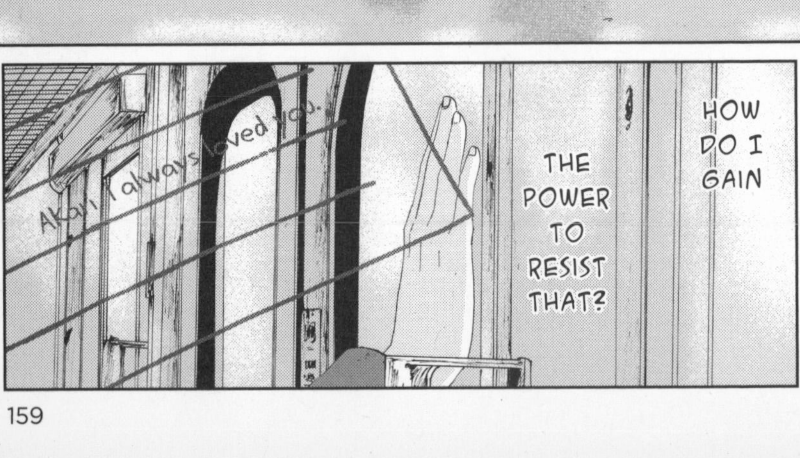
HOW DO I GAIN
THE POWER TO RESIST THAT?
Akari, I always loved you.

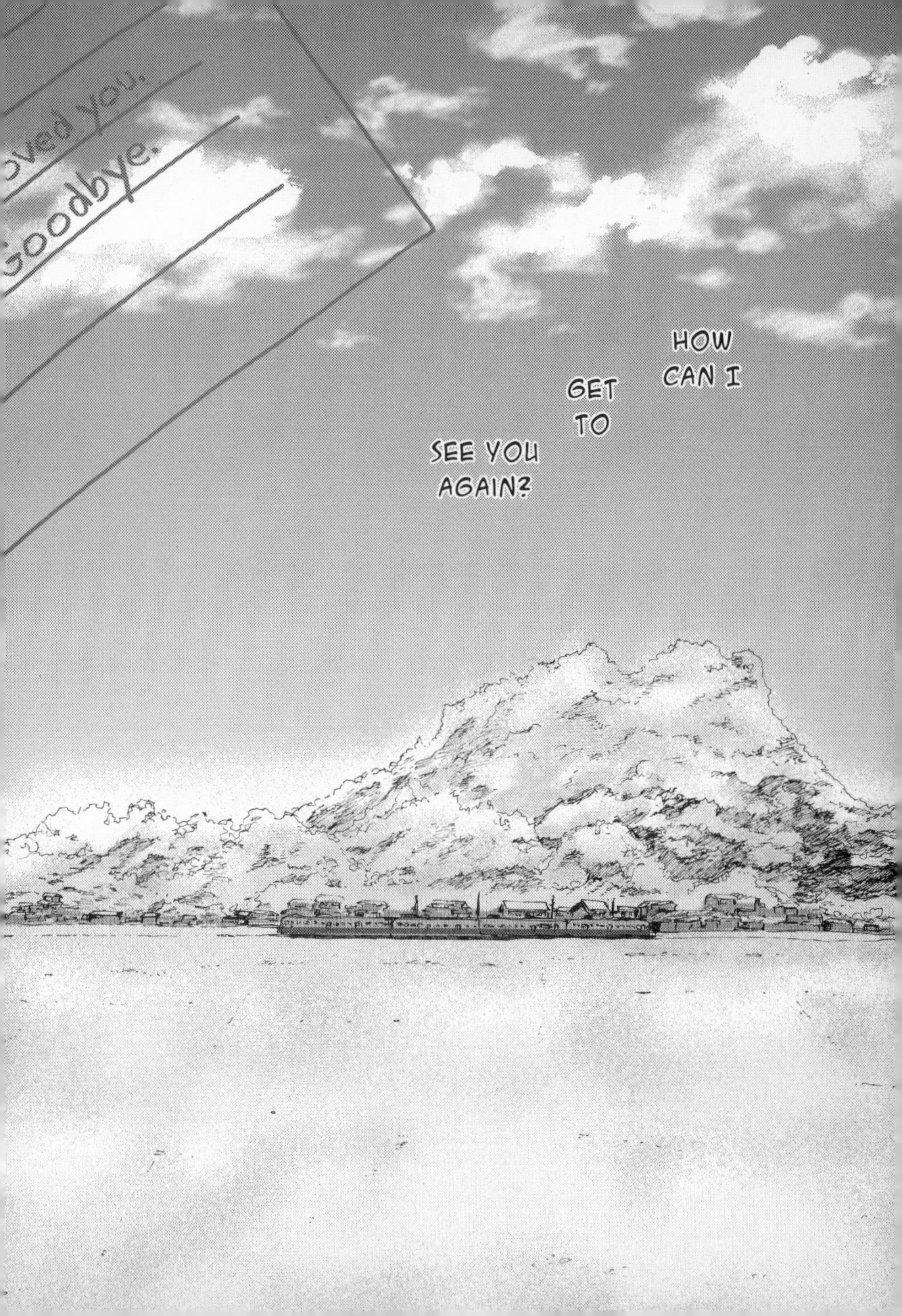
oved you.
Goodbye.
HOW CAN I
GET TO
SEE YOU AGAIN?

Chapter 4 – "Kanae's Feelings"

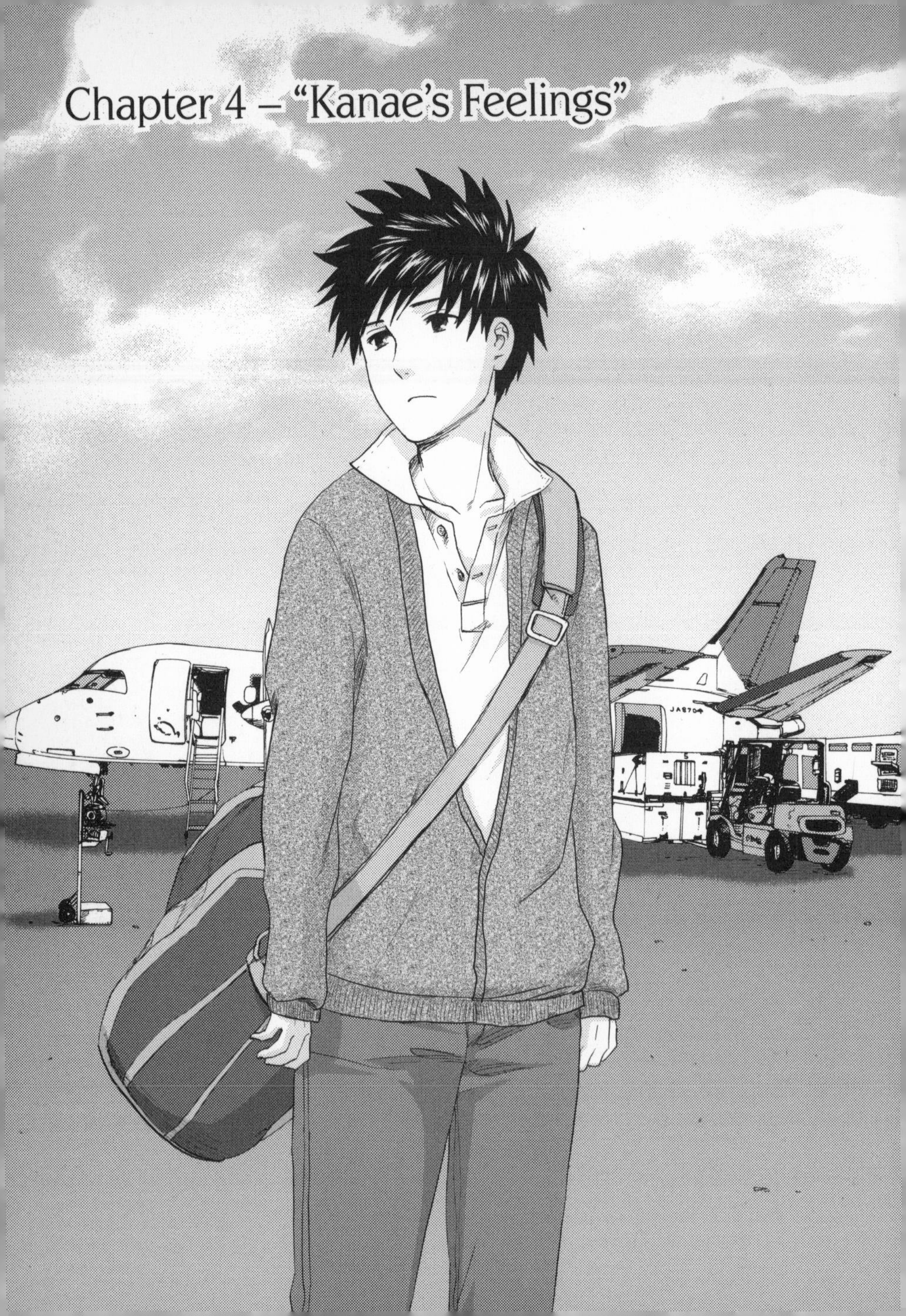

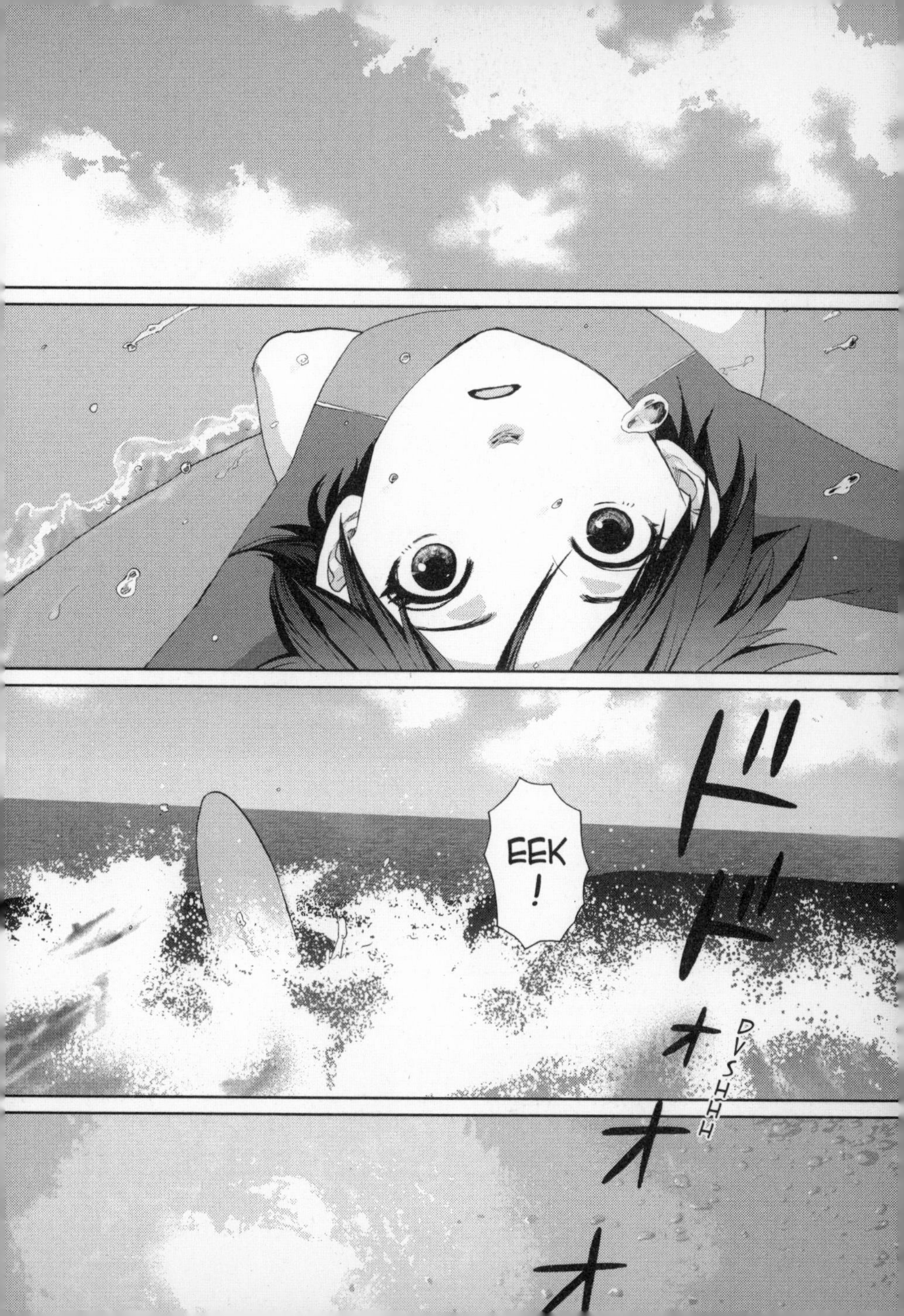
EEK
!
ドドオオオオ
DVSHHHH

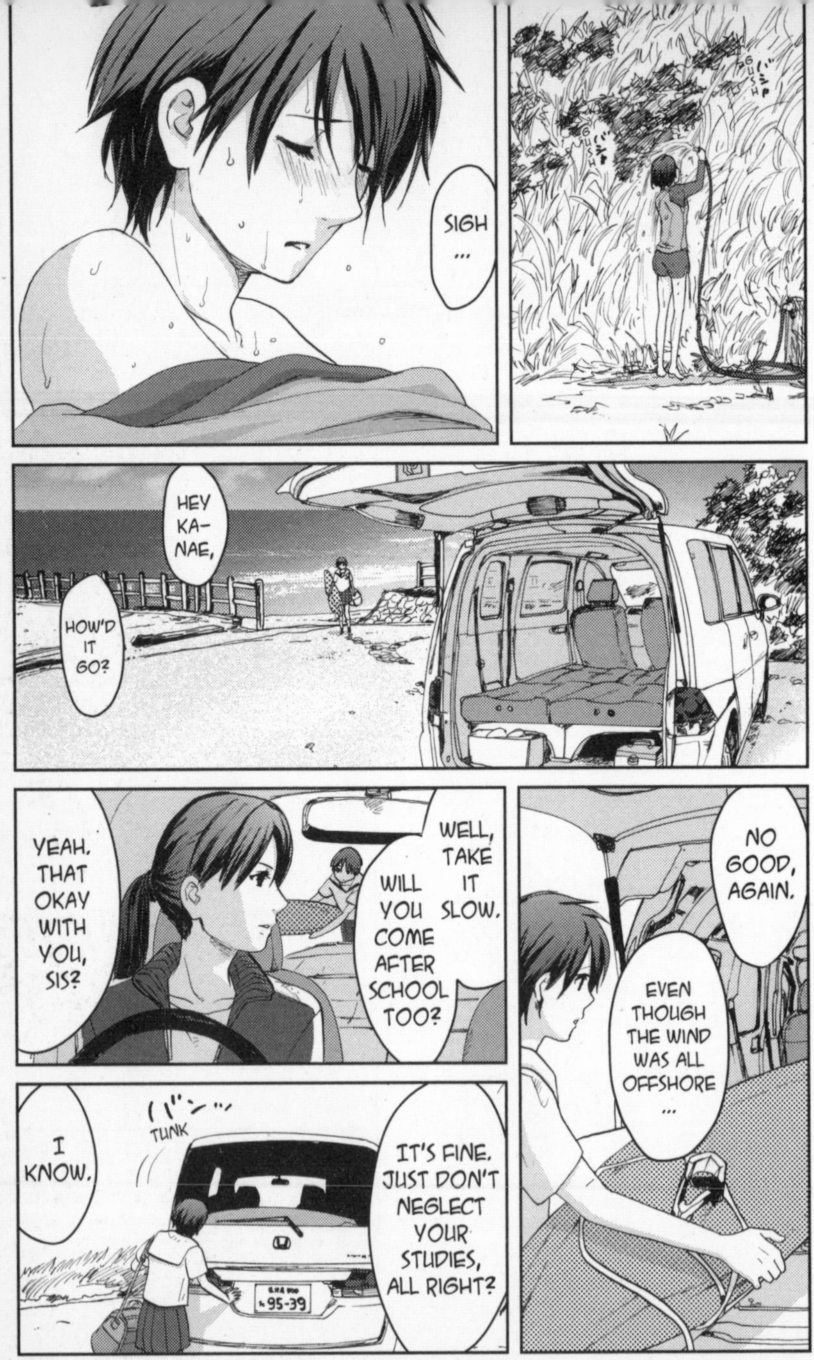

GUSH
GUSH
SIGH ...
HEY KA-NAE,
HOW'D IT GO?
NO GOOD, AGAIN.
EVEN THOUGH THE WIND WAS ALL OFFSHORE ...
WELL, TAKE IT SLOW.
WILL YOU COME AFTER SCHOOL TOO?
YEAH. THAT OKAY WITH YOU, SIS?
IT'S FINE. JUST DON'T NEGLECT YOUR STUDIES, ALL RIGHT?
TUNK
I KNOW.

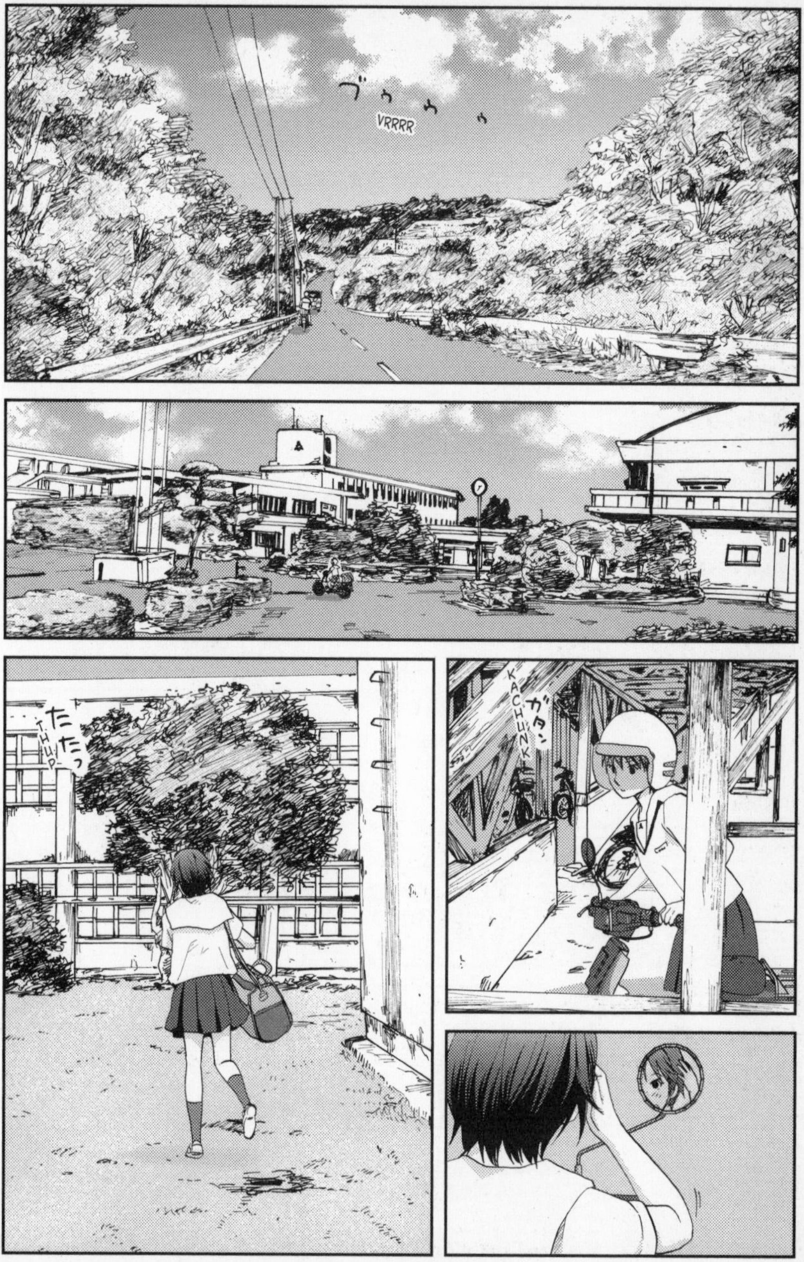
ヴぅぅぅ
VRRRR
ガタン
KACHUNK
たたっ
THUP

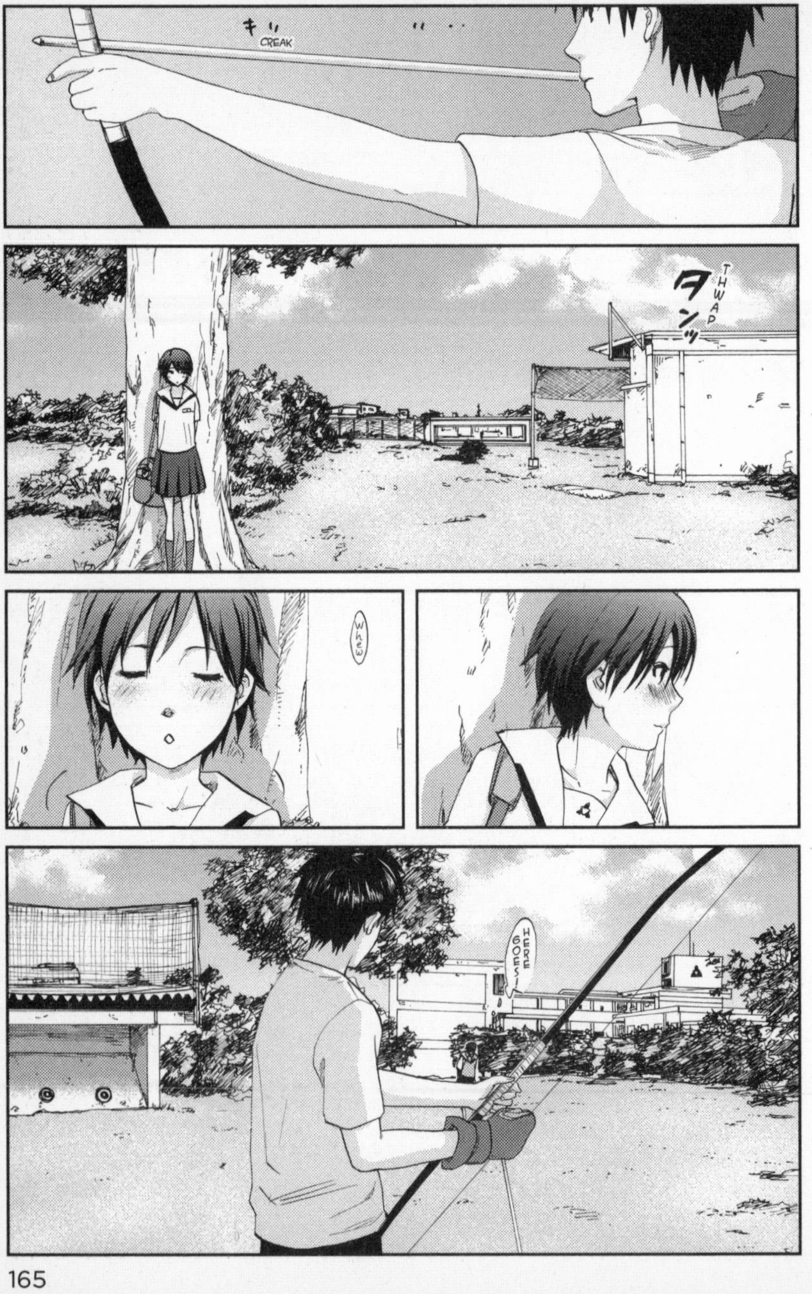
キリ
CREAK
タンッ
THWAP
whew
HERE GOES!

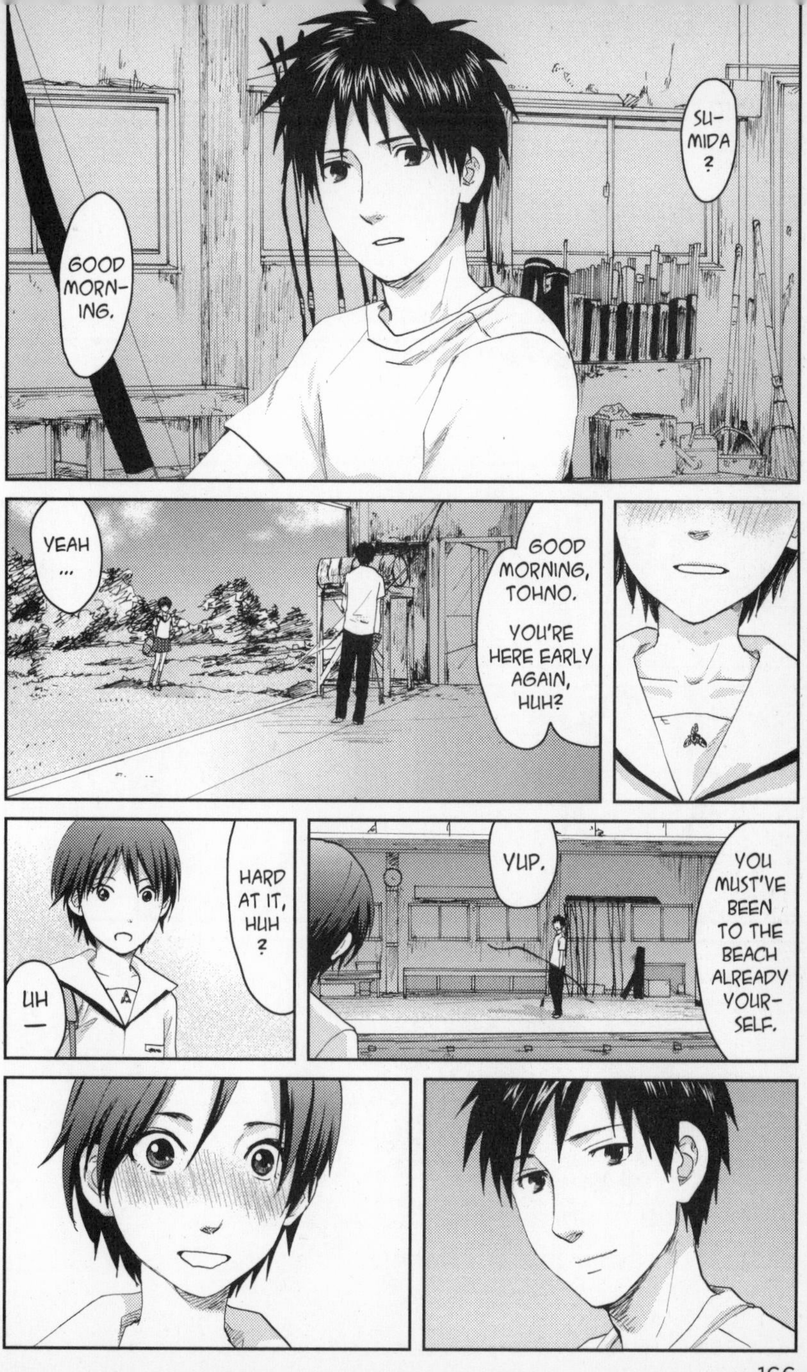
SU-MIDA?
GOOD MORNING.
GOOD MORNING, TOHNO.
YOU'RE HERE EARLY AGAIN, HUH?
YEAH ...
YOU MUST'VE BEEN TO THE BEACH ALREADY YOURSELF.
YUP.
HARD AT IT, HUH?
UH —

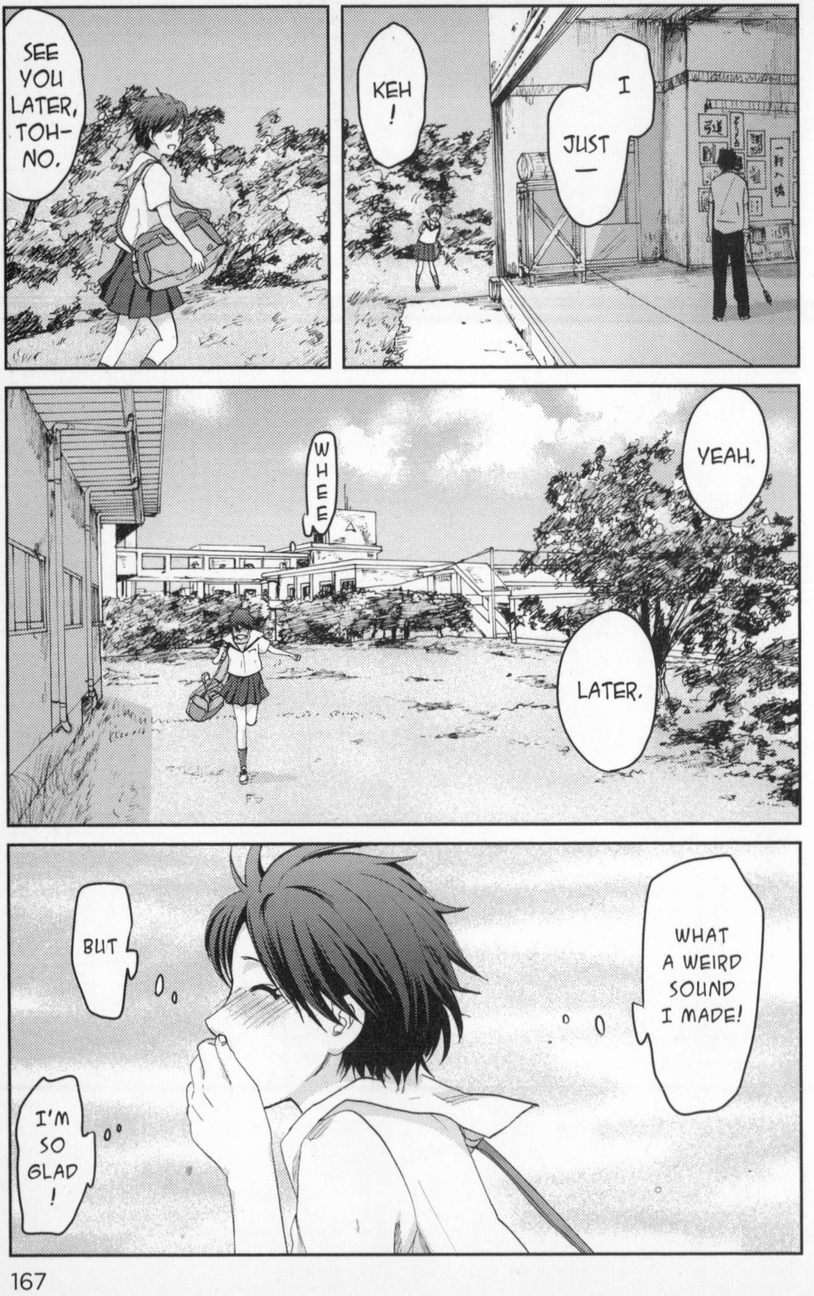
I JUST —
KEH!
SEE YOU LATER, TOH-NO.
YEAH.
LATER.
WHEE
WHAT A WEIRD SOUND I MADE!
BUT
I'M SO GLAD!

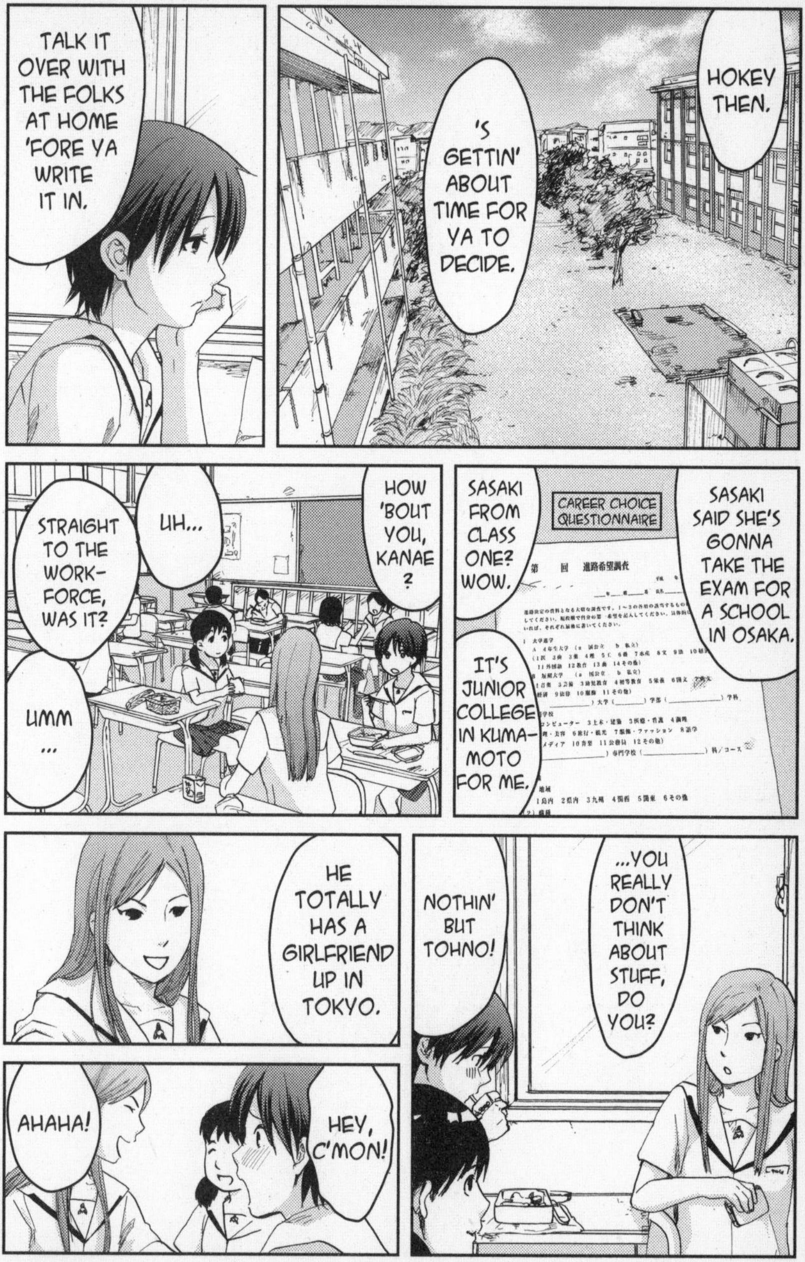
HOKEY THEN.
'S GETTIN' ABOUT TIME FOR YA TO DECIDE.
TALK IT OVER WITH THE FOLKS AT HOME 'FORE YA WRITE IT IN.
SASAKI SAID SHE'S GONNA TAKE THE EXAM FOR A SCHOOL IN OSAKA.
CAREER CHOICE QUESTIONNAIRE
第 回 進路希望調査
SASAKI FROM CLASS ONE? WOW.
IT'S JUNIOR COLLEGE IN KUMAMOTO FOR ME.
HOW 'BOUT YOU, KANAE?
UH...
STRAIGHT TO THE WORK-FORCE, WAS IT?
UMM ...
...YOU REALLY DON'T THINK ABOUT STUFF, DO YOU?
NOTHIN' BUT TOHNO!
HE TOTALLY HAS A GIRLFRIEND UP IN TOKYO.
HEY, C'MON!
AHAHA!

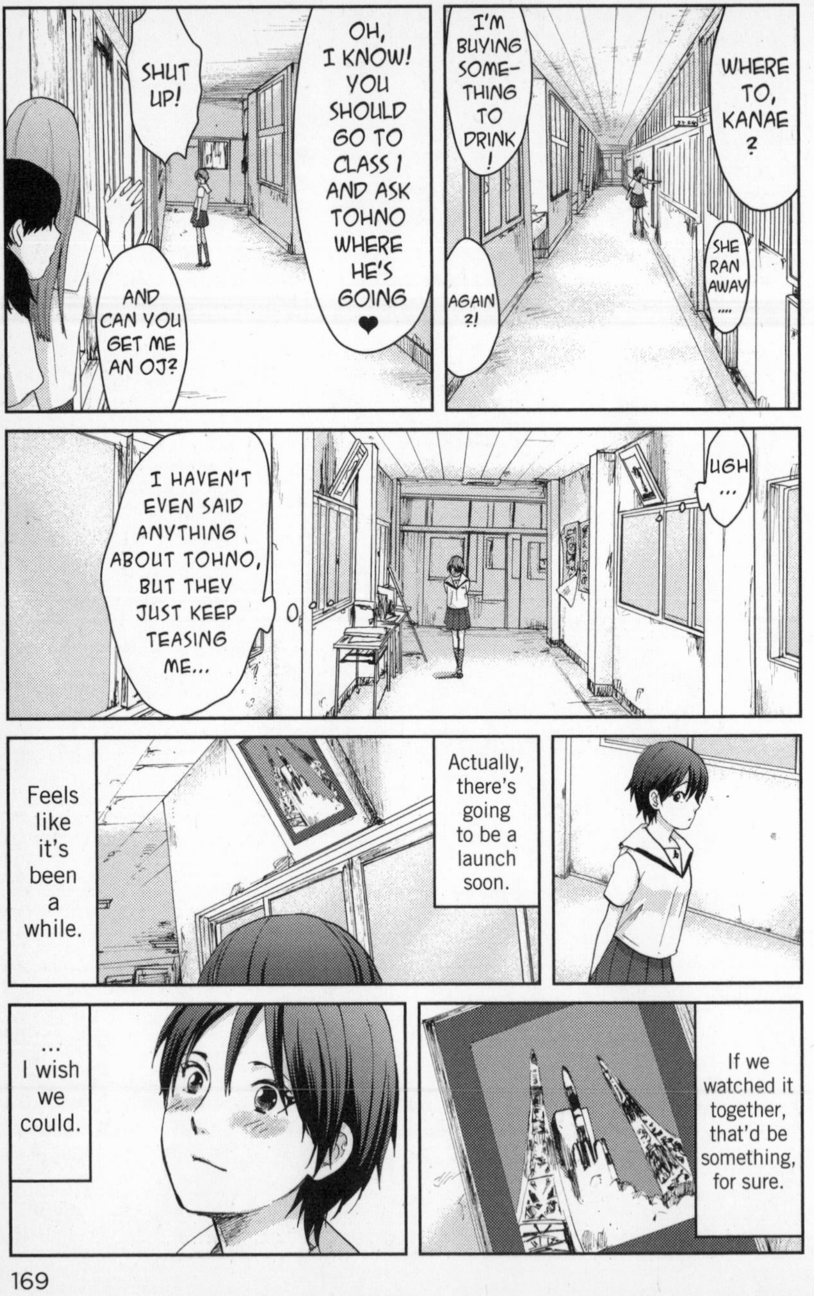
WHERE TO, KANAE?
I'M BUYING SOMETHING TO DRINK!
SHE RAN AWAY....
AGAIN?!
OH, I KNOW! YOU SHOULD GO TO CLASS 1 AND ASK TOHNO WHERE HE'S GOING ❤
SHUT UP!
AND CAN YOU GET ME AN OJ?
UGH...
I HAVEN'T EVEN SAID ANYTHING ABOUT TOHNO, BUT THEY JUST KEEP TEASING ME...
Actually, there's going to be a launch soon.
Feels like it's been a while.
If we watched it together, that'd be something, for sure.
... I wish we could.

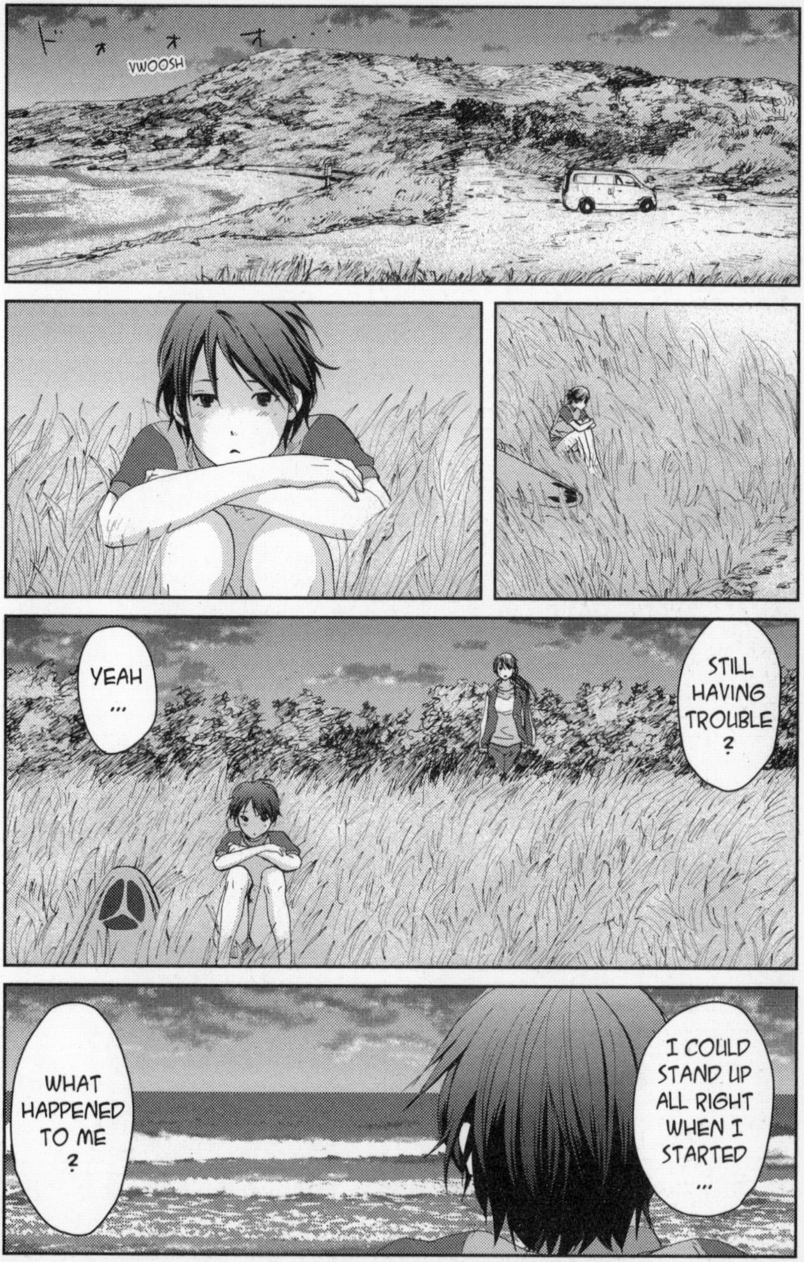
ドォオオ…
VWOOSH
STILL HAVING TROUBLE?
YEAH ...
I COULD STAND UP ALL RIGHT WHEN I STARTED ...
WHAT HAPPENED TO ME?

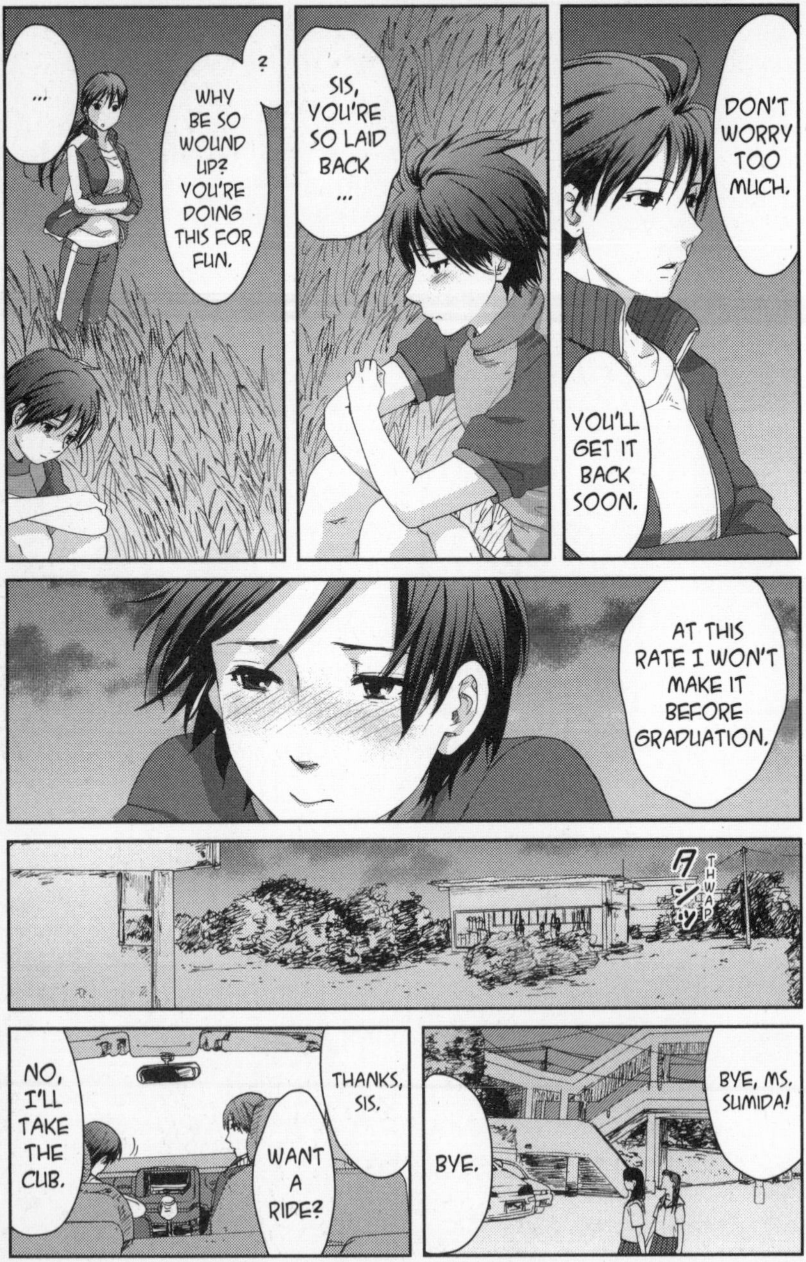
DON'T WORRY TOO MUCH.
YOU'LL GET IT BACK SOON.
SIS, YOU'RE SO LAID BACK ...
?
WHY BE SO WOUND UP? YOU'RE DOING THIS FOR FUN.
...
AT THIS RATE I WON'T MAKE IT BEFORE GRADUATION.
THWAP
BYE, MS. SUMIDA!
BYE.
THANKS, SIS.
WANT A RIDE?
NO, I'LL TAKE THE CUB.

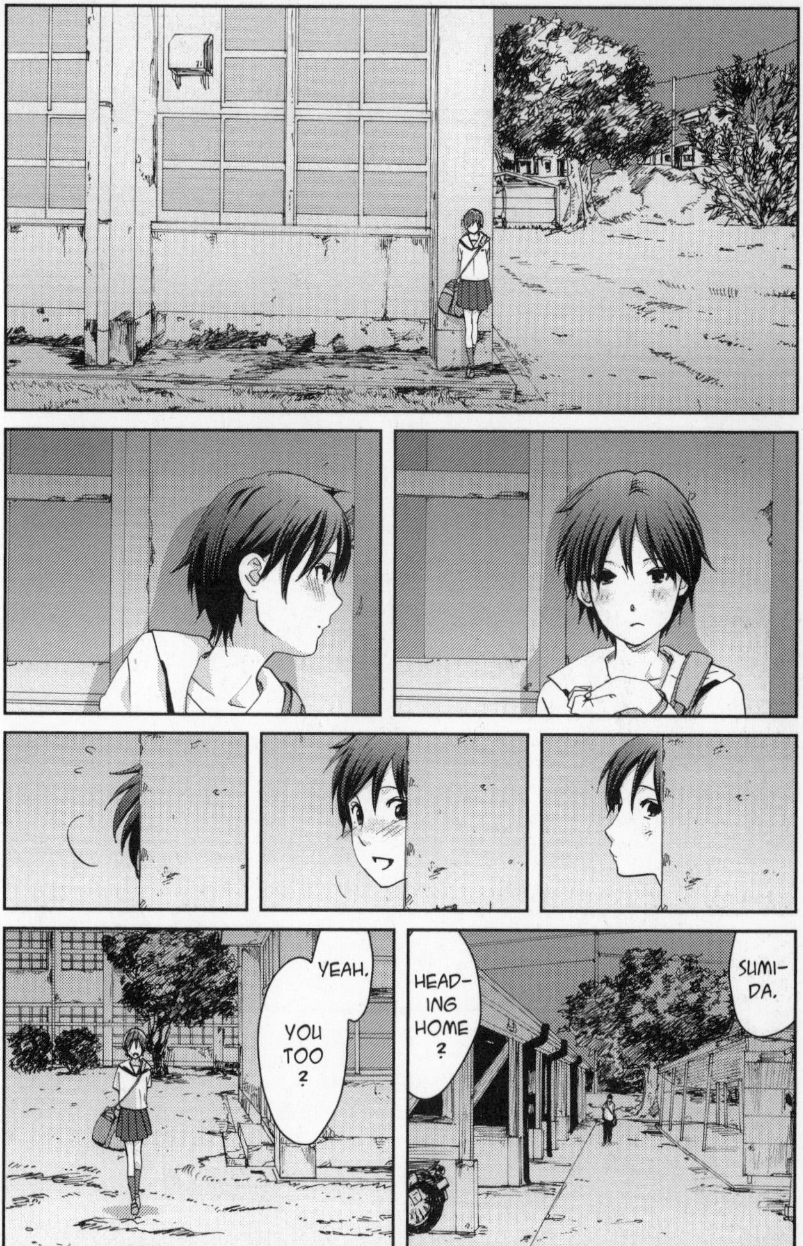
SUMI-DA.
HEAD-ING HOME?
YEAH.
YOU TOO?

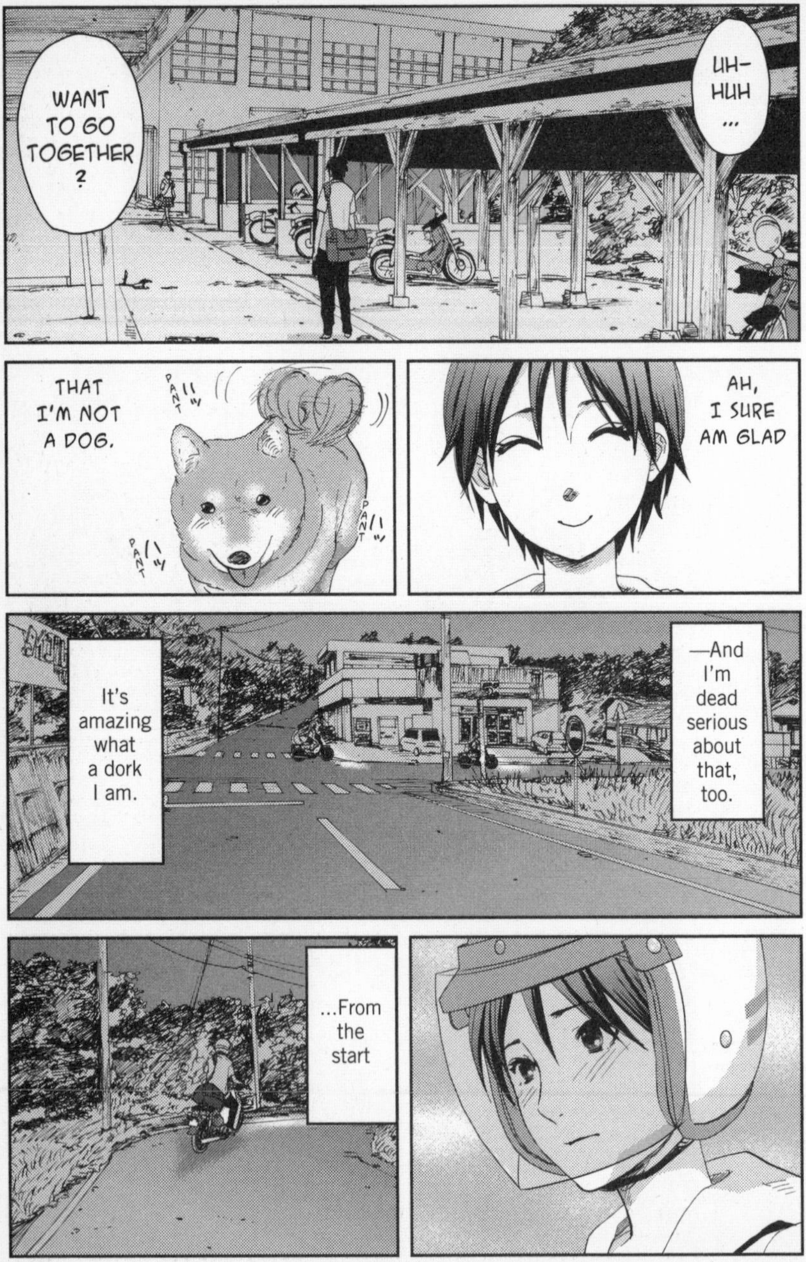
UH-HUH ...
WANT TO GO TOGETHER ?
AH, I SURE AM GLAD
THAT I'M NOT A DOG.
PANT PANT PANT
—And I'm dead serious about that, too.
It's amazing what a dork I am.
...From the start

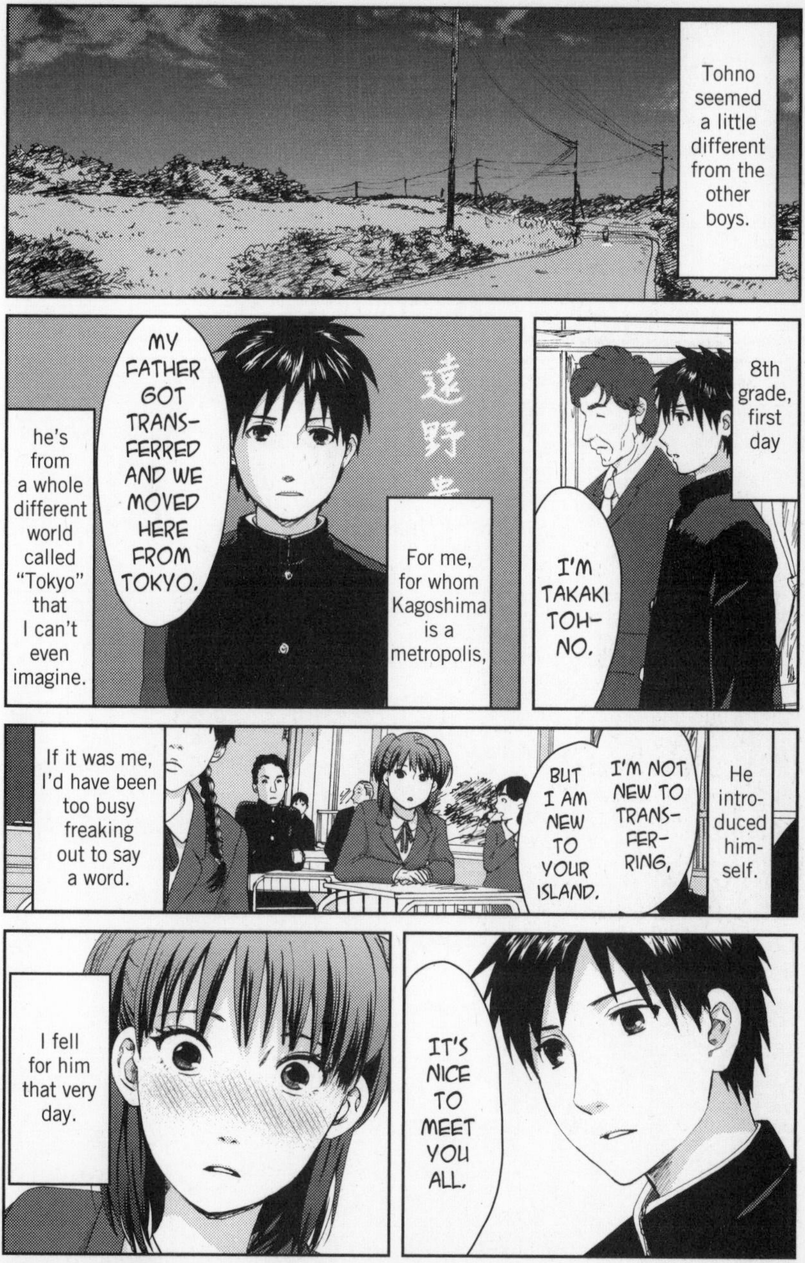
Tohno seemed a little different from the other boys.
8th grade, first day
I'M TAKAKI TOH-NO.
遠野
MY FATHER GOT TRANS-FERRED AND WE MOVED HERE FROM TOKYO.
For me, for whom Kagoshima is a metropolis,
he's from a whole different world called "Tokyo" that I can't even imagine.
He intro-duced him-self.
I'M NOT NEW TO TRANS-FER-RING,
BUT I AM NEW TO YOUR ISLAND.
If it was me, I'd have been too busy freaking out to say a word.
IT'S NICE TO MEET YOU ALL.
I fell for him that very day.

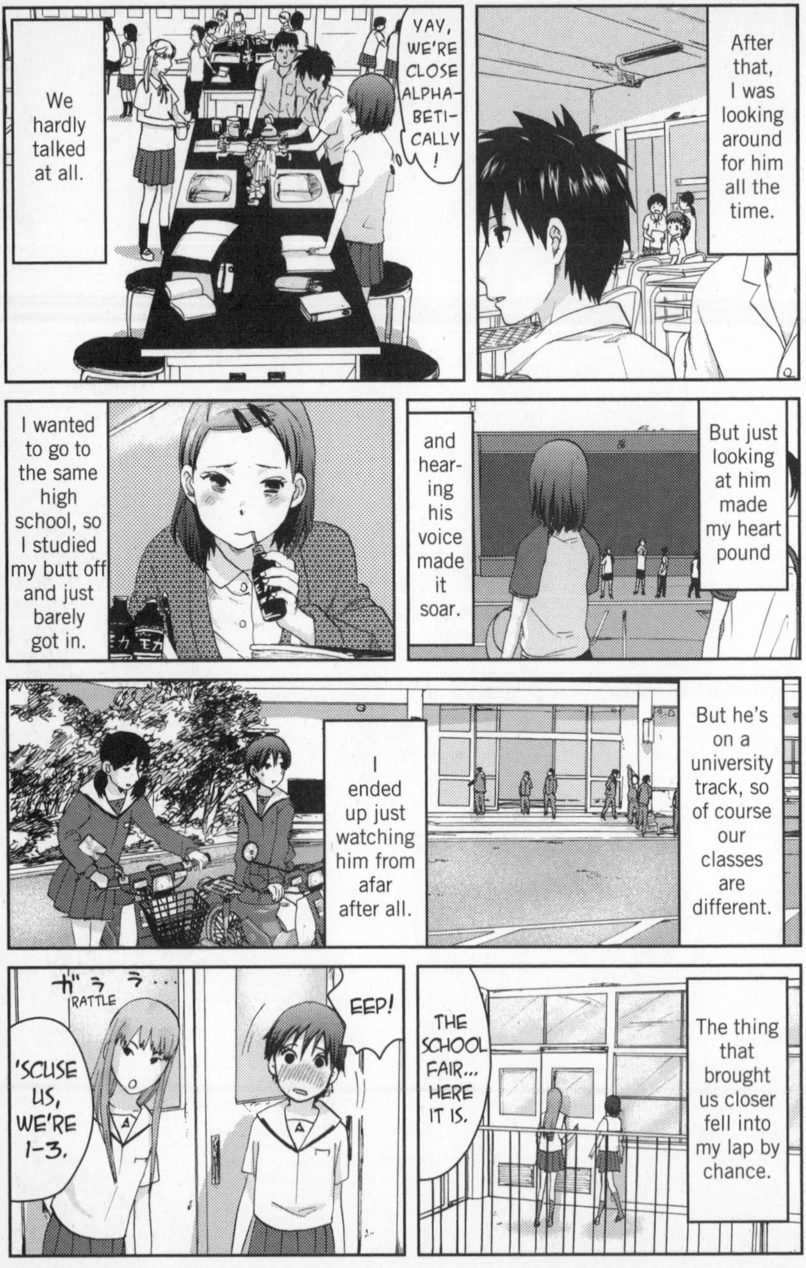
After that, I was looking around for him all the time.
YAY, WE'RE CLOSE ALPHABETICALLY!
We hardly talked at all.
But just looking at him made my heart pound
and hearing his voice made it soar.
I wanted to go to the same high school, so I studied my butt off and just barely got in.
But he's on a university track, so of course our classes are different.
I ended up just watching him from afar after all.
The thing that brought us closer fell into my lap by chance.
THE SCHOOL FAIR... HERE IT IS.
EEP!
ガラ ラ... RATTLE
'SCUSE US, WE'RE 1-3.

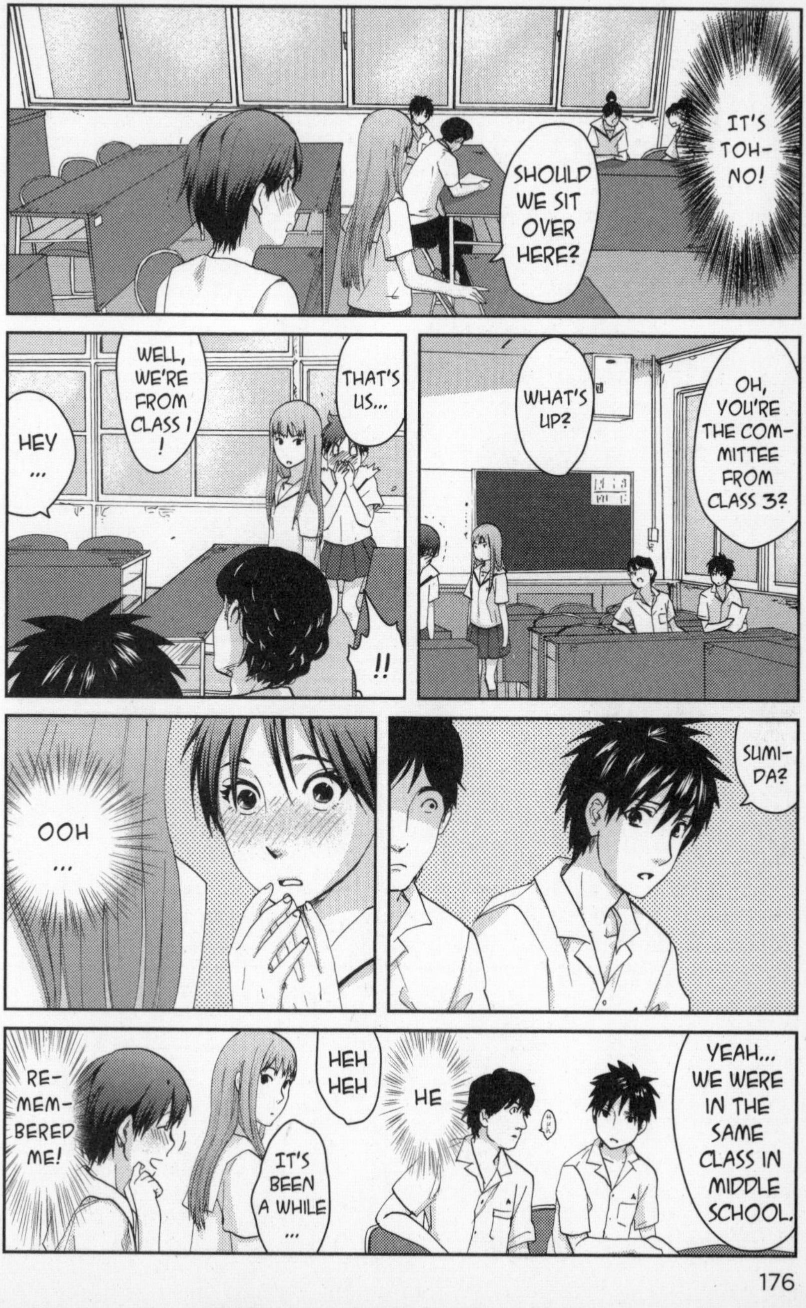
IT'S TOH-NO!
SHOULD WE SIT OVER HERE?
OH, YOU'RE THE COM-MITTEE FROM CLASS 3?
WHAT'S UP?
THAT'S US...
WELL, WE'RE FROM CLASS 1 !
HEY ...
!!
SUMI-DA?
OOH ...
YEAH... WE WERE IN THE SAME CLASS IN MIDDLE SCHOOL.
HE
HEH HEH
IT'S BEEN A WHILE ...
RE-MEM-BERED ME!

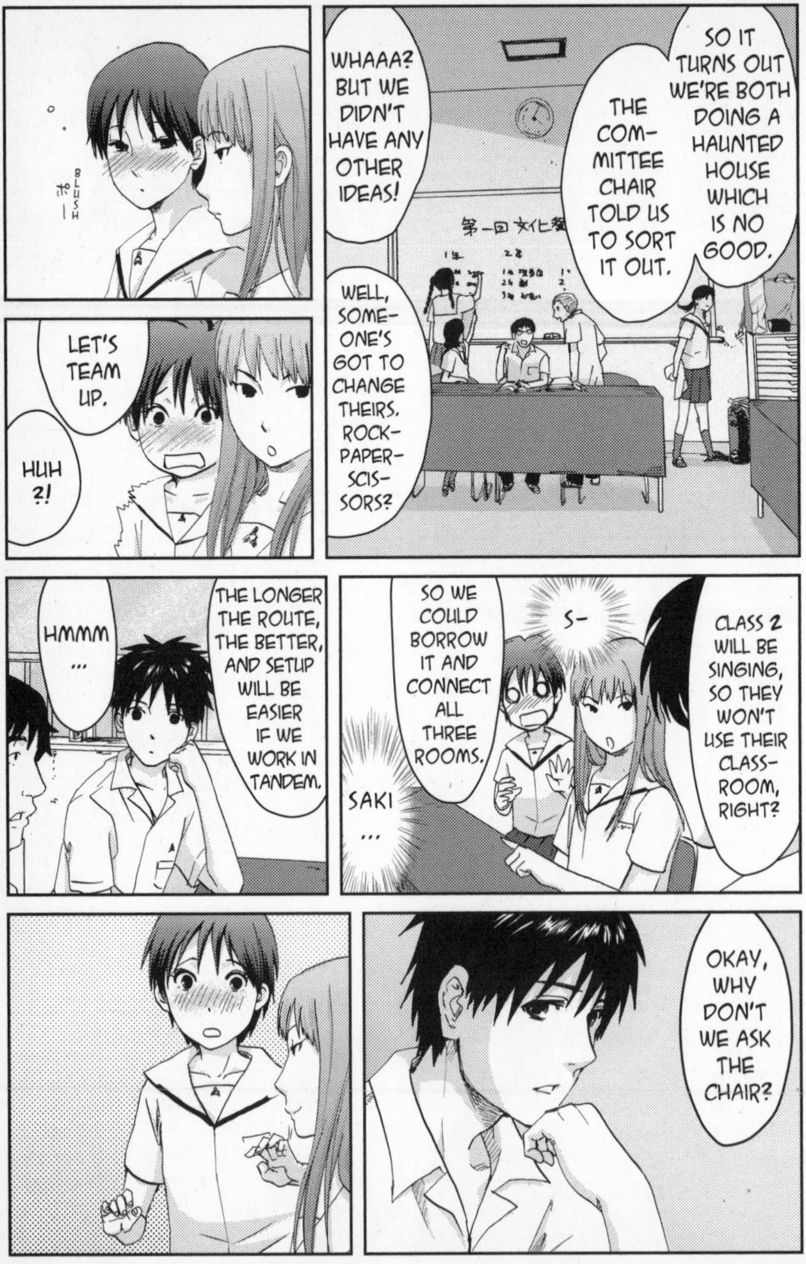
SO IT TURNS OUT WE'RE BOTH DOING A HAUNTED HOUSE WHICH IS NO GOOD.
THE COMMITTEE CHAIR TOLD US TO SORT IT OUT.
WHAAA? BUT WE DIDN'T HAVE ANY OTHER IDEAS!
WELL, SOMEONE'S GOT TO CHANGE THEIRS. ROCK-PAPER-SCISSORS?
BLUSH ポー
LET'S TEAM UP.
HUH?!
CLASS 2 WILL BE SINGING, SO THEY WON'T USE THEIR CLASSROOM, RIGHT?
S-
SO WE COULD BORROW IT AND CONNECT ALL THREE ROOMS.
SAKI...
THE LONGER THE ROUTE, THE BETTER, AND SETUP WILL BE EASIER IF WE WORK IN TANDEM.
HMMM...
OKAY, WHY DON'T WE ASK THE CHAIR?

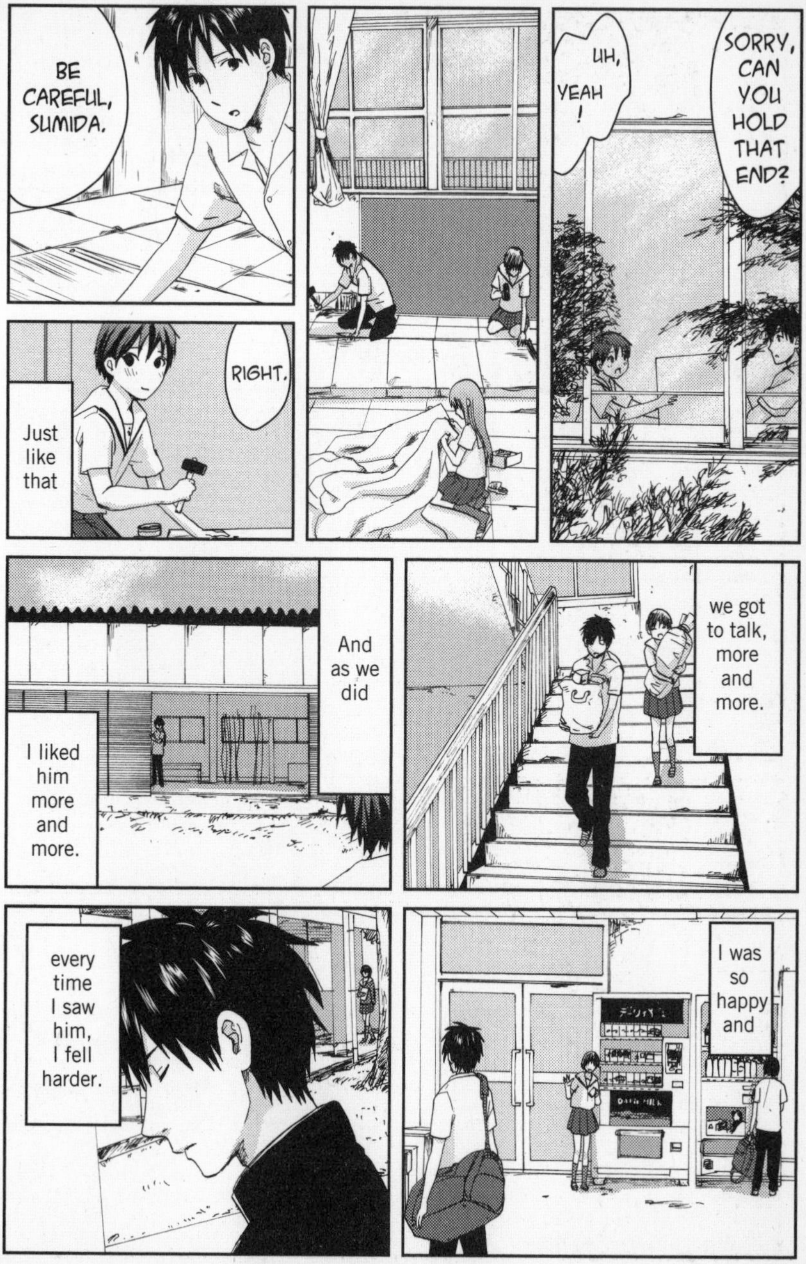
SORRY, CAN YOU HOLD THAT END?
UH, YEAH!
BE CAREFUL, SUMIDA.
RIGHT.
Just like that
we got to talk, more and more.
And as we did
I liked him more and more.
I was so happy and
every time I saw him, I fell harder.

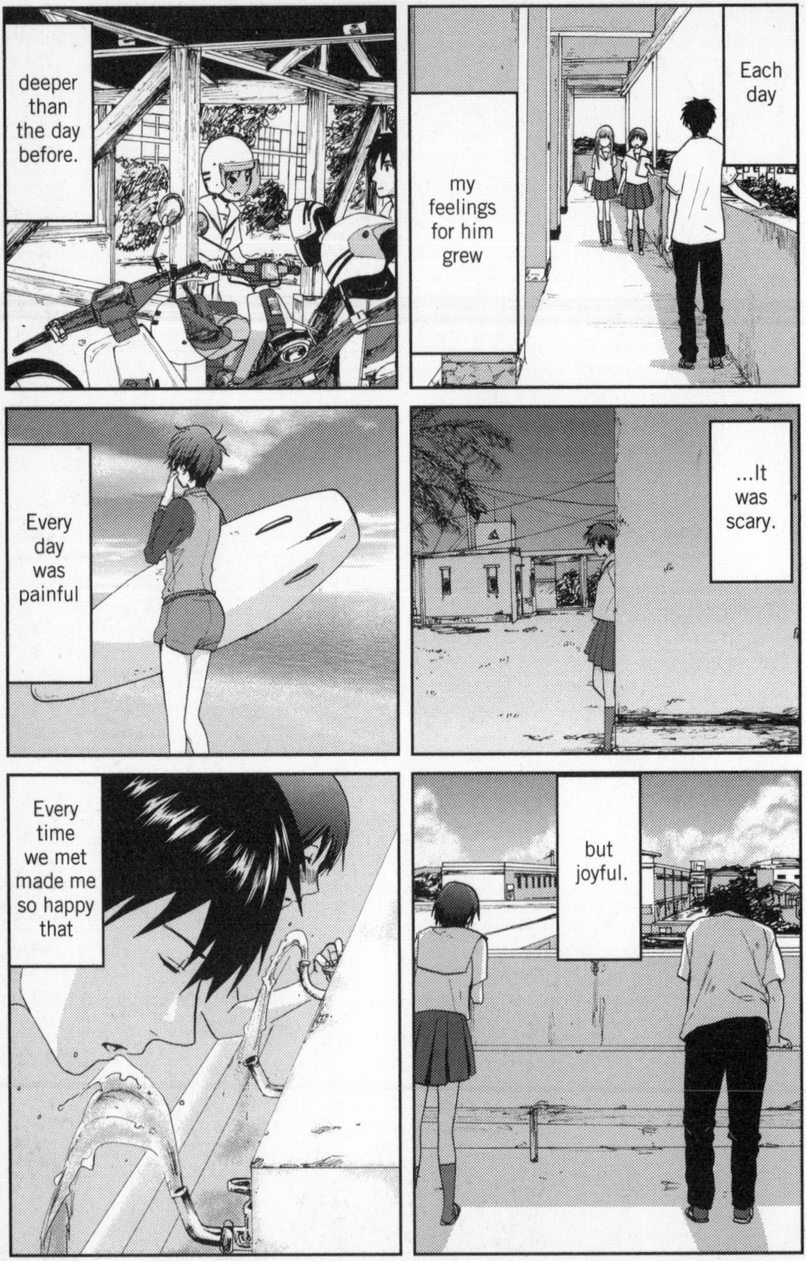
Each day
my feelings for him grew
deeper than the day before.
...It was scary.
Every day was painful
but joyful.
Every time we met made me so happy that

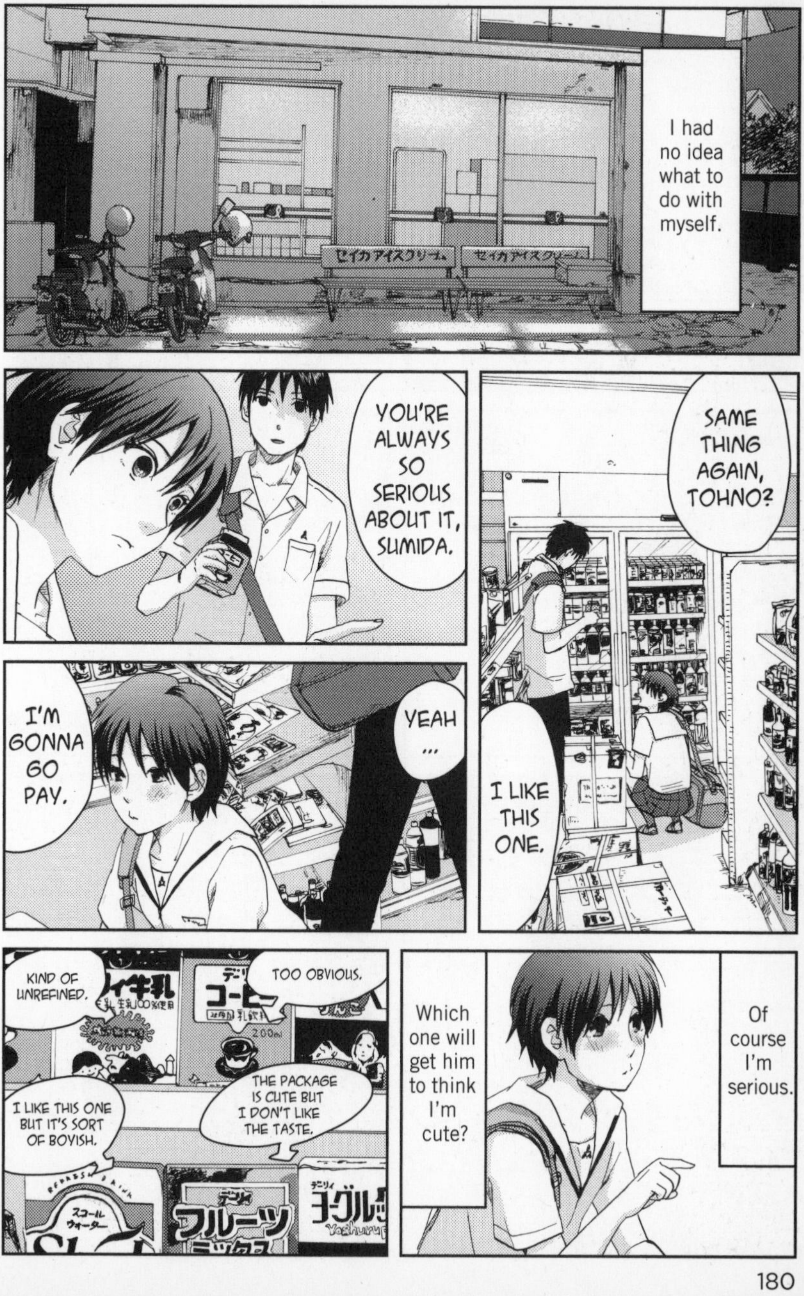
I had no idea what to do with myself.
SAME THING AGAIN, TOHNO?
I LIKE THIS ONE.
YOU'RE ALWAYS SO SERIOUS ABOUT IT, SUMIDA.
YEAH ...
I'M GONNA GO PAY.
Of course I'm serious.
Which one will get him to think I'm cute?
TOO OBVIOUS.
KIND OF UNREFINED.
THE PACKAGE IS CUTE BUT I DON'T LIKE THE TASTE.
I LIKE THIS ONE BUT IT'S SORT OF BOYISH.

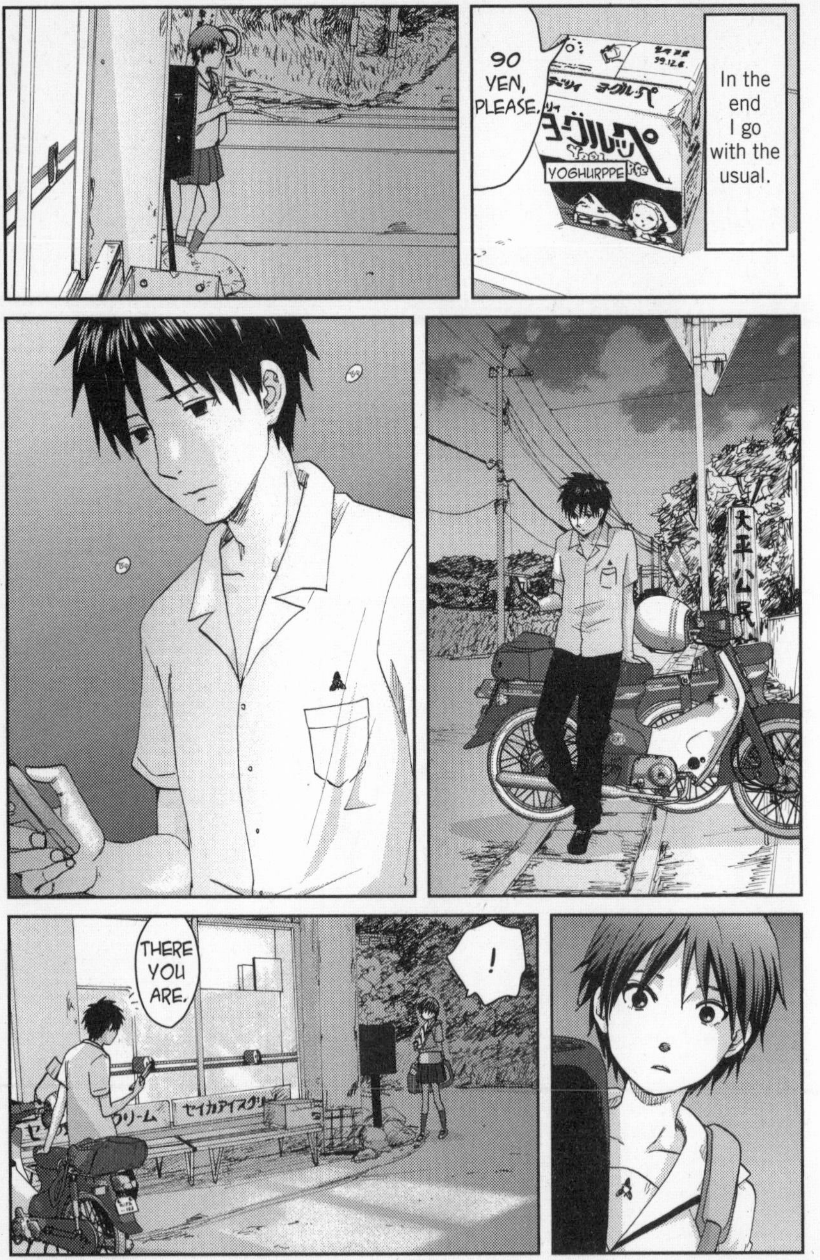
In the end I go with the usual.
90 YEN, PLEASE.
YOGHURPPE
!
THERE YOU ARE.

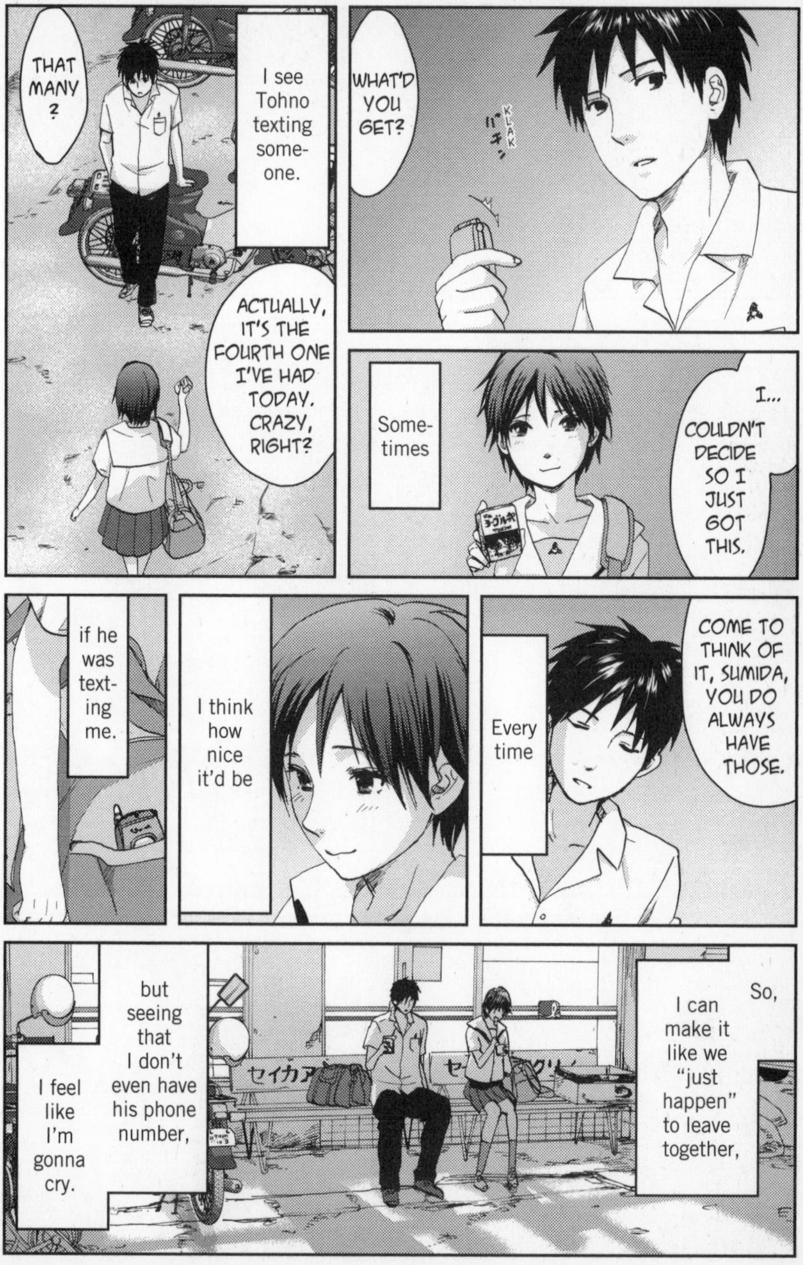
WHAT'D YOU GET?
KLAK
I... COULDN'T DECIDE SO I JUST GOT THIS.
Sometimes
I see Tohno texting someone.
THAT MANY?
ACTUALLY, IT'S THE FOURTH ONE I'VE HAD TODAY. CRAZY, RIGHT?
COME TO THINK OF IT, SUMIDA, YOU DO ALWAYS HAVE THOSE.
Every time
I think how nice it'd be
if he was texting me.
So,
I can make it like we "just happen" to leave together,
but seeing that I don't even have his phone number,
I feel like I'm gonna cry.

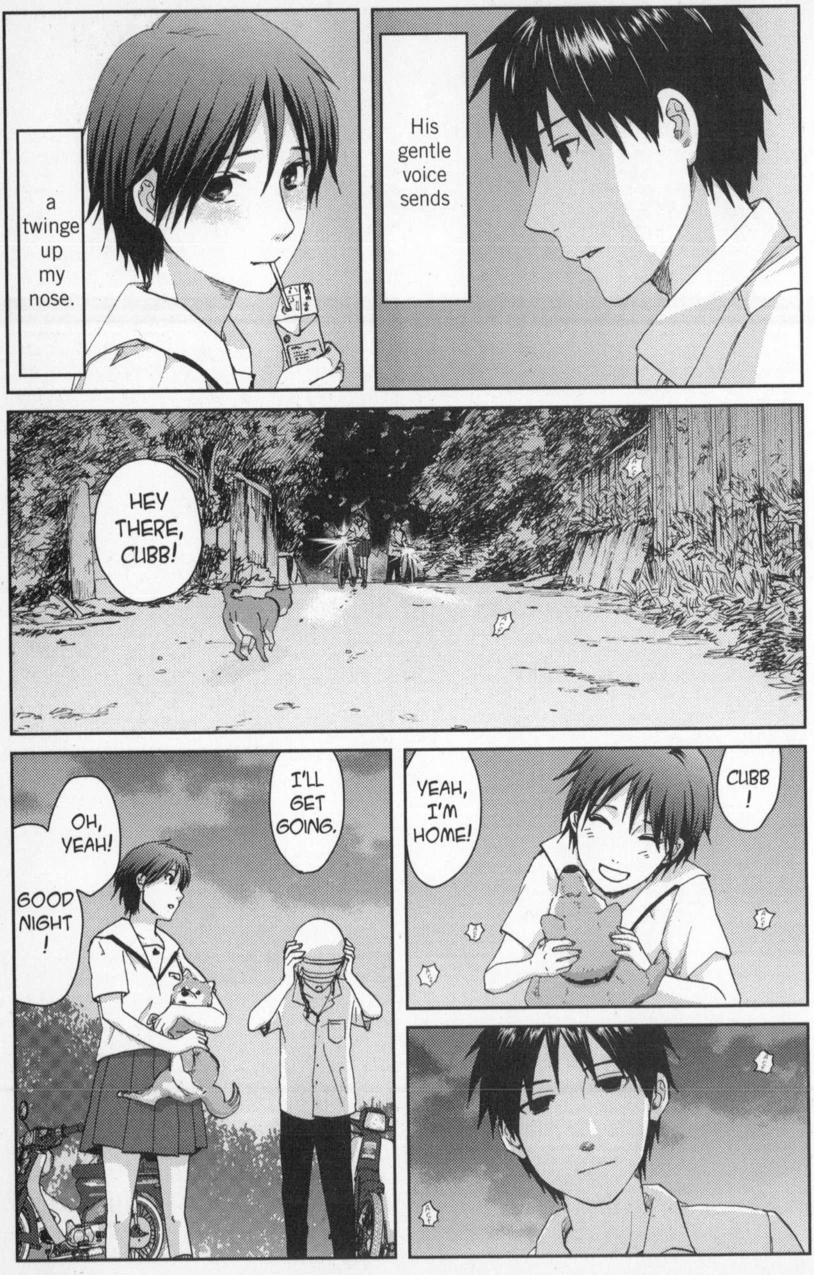
His gentle voice sends
a twinge up my nose.
HEY THERE, CUBB!
CUBB!
YEAH, I'M HOME!
I'LL GET GOING.
OH, YEAH!
GOOD NIGHT!

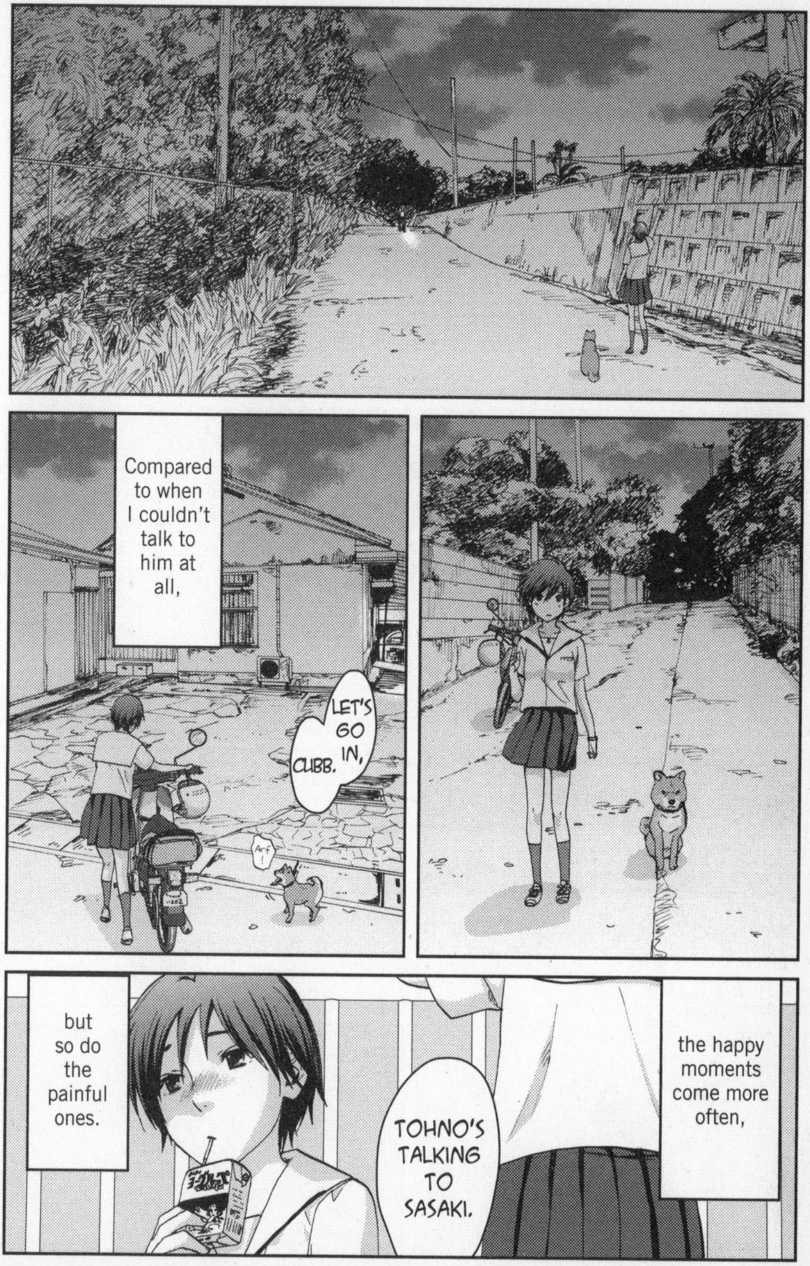
Compared to when I couldn't talk to him at all,
LET'S GO IN, CUBB.
Arf!
the happy moments come more often,
TOHNO'S TALKING TO SASAKI.
but so do the painful ones.

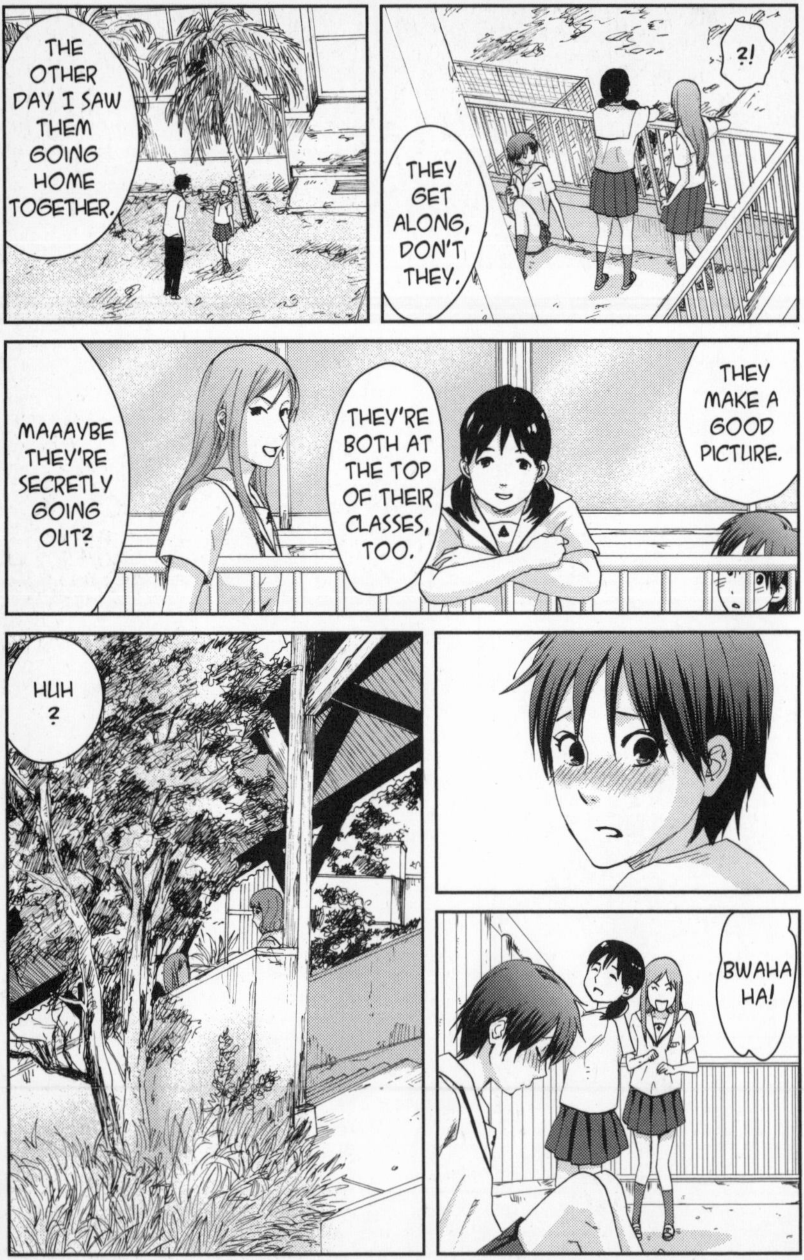
?!
THEY GET ALONG, DON'T THEY.
THE OTHER DAY I SAW THEM GOING HOME TOGETHER.
THEY MAKE A GOOD PICTURE.
THEY'RE BOTH AT THE TOP OF THEIR CLASSES, TOO.
MAAAYBE THEY'RE SECRETLY GOING OUT?
BWAHAHA!
HUH?

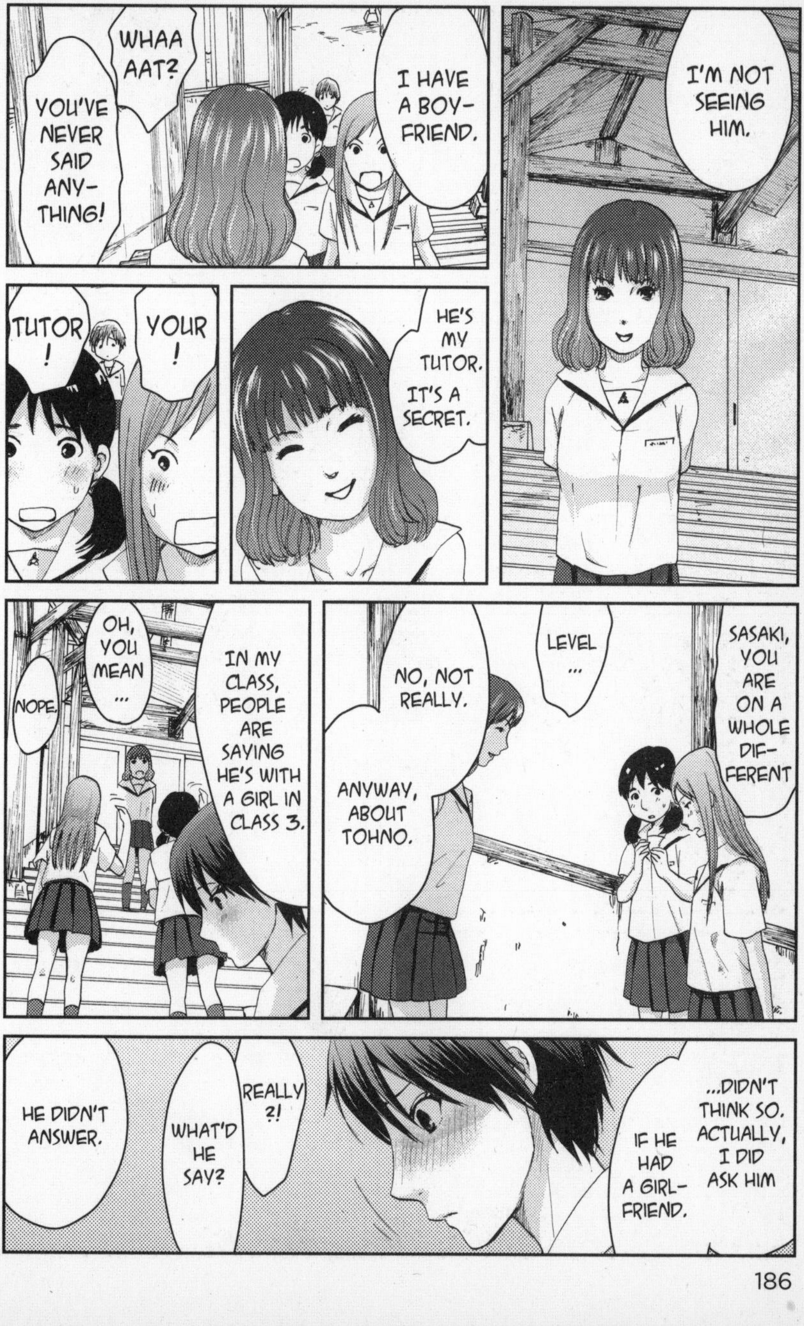
I'M NOT SEEING HIM.
I HAVE A BOY-FRIEND.
WHAA AAT?
YOU'VE NEVER SAID ANY-THING!
HE'S MY TUTOR.
IT'S A SECRET.
YOUR!
TUTOR!
SASAKI, YOU ARE ON A WHOLE DIF-FERENT
LEVEL...
NO, NOT REALLY.
ANYWAY, ABOUT TOHNO.
IN MY CLASS, PEOPLE ARE SAYING HE'S WITH A GIRL IN CLASS 3.
OH, YOU MEAN...
NOPE.
...DIDN'T THINK SO. ACTUALLY, I DID ASK HIM
IF HE HAD A GIRL-FRIEND.
REALLY?!
WHAT'D HE SAY?
HE DIDN'T ANSWER.

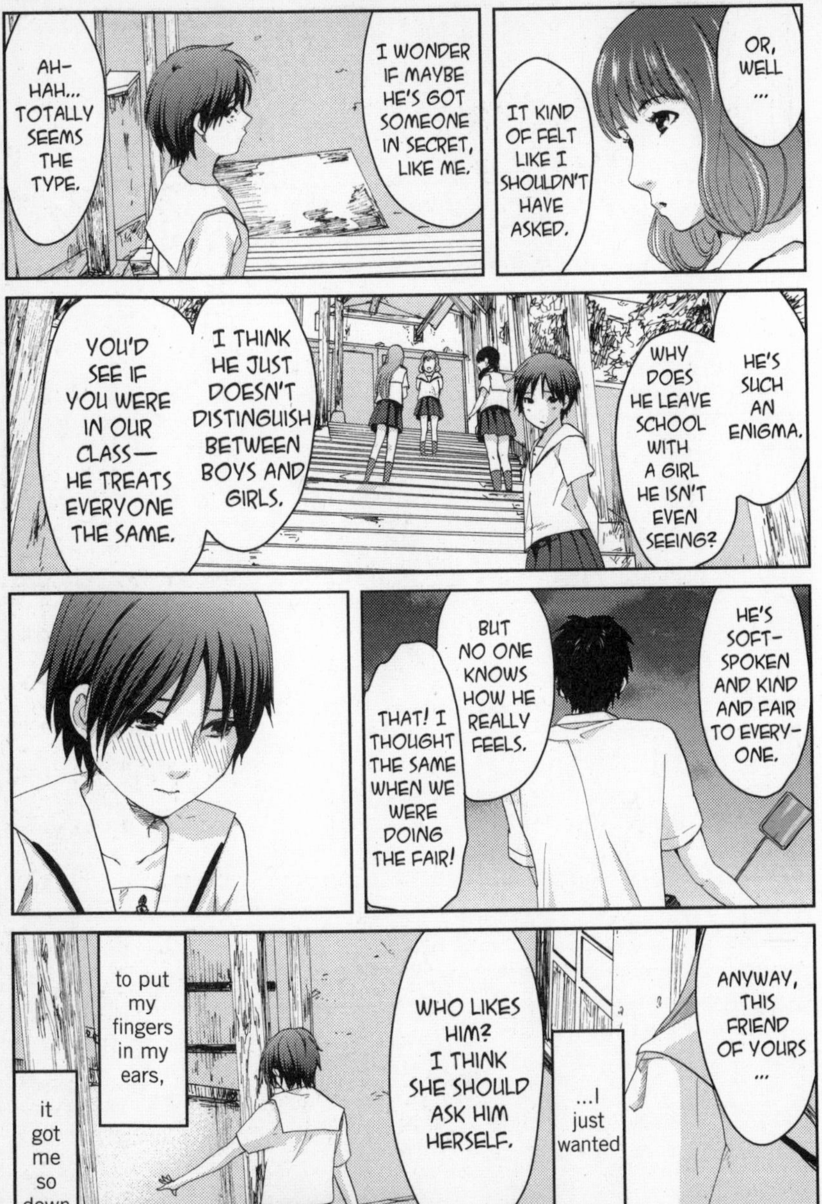
OR, WELL ...
IT KIND OF FELT LIKE I SHOULDN'T HAVE ASKED.
I WONDER IF MAYBE HE'S GOT SOMEONE IN SECRET, LIKE ME.
AH-HAH... TOTALLY SEEMS THE TYPE.
HE'S SUCH AN ENIGMA.
WHY DOES HE LEAVE SCHOOL WITH A GIRL HE ISN'T EVEN SEEING?
I THINK HE JUST DOESN'T DISTINGUISH BETWEEN BOYS AND GIRLS.
YOU'D SEE IF YOU WERE IN OUR CLASS— HE TREATS EVERYONE THE SAME.
HE'S SOFT-SPOKEN AND KIND AND FAIR TO EVERY-ONE.
BUT NO ONE KNOWS HOW HE REALLY FEELS.
THAT! I THOUGHT THE SAME WHEN WE WERE DOING THE FAIR!
ANYWAY, THIS FRIEND OF YOURS ...
WHO LIKES HIM? I THINK SHE SHOULD ASK HIM HERSELF.
...I just wanted
to put my fingers in my ears,
it got me so down.

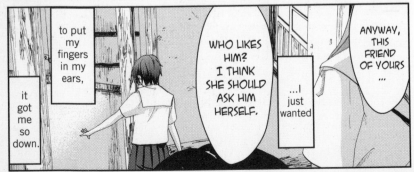

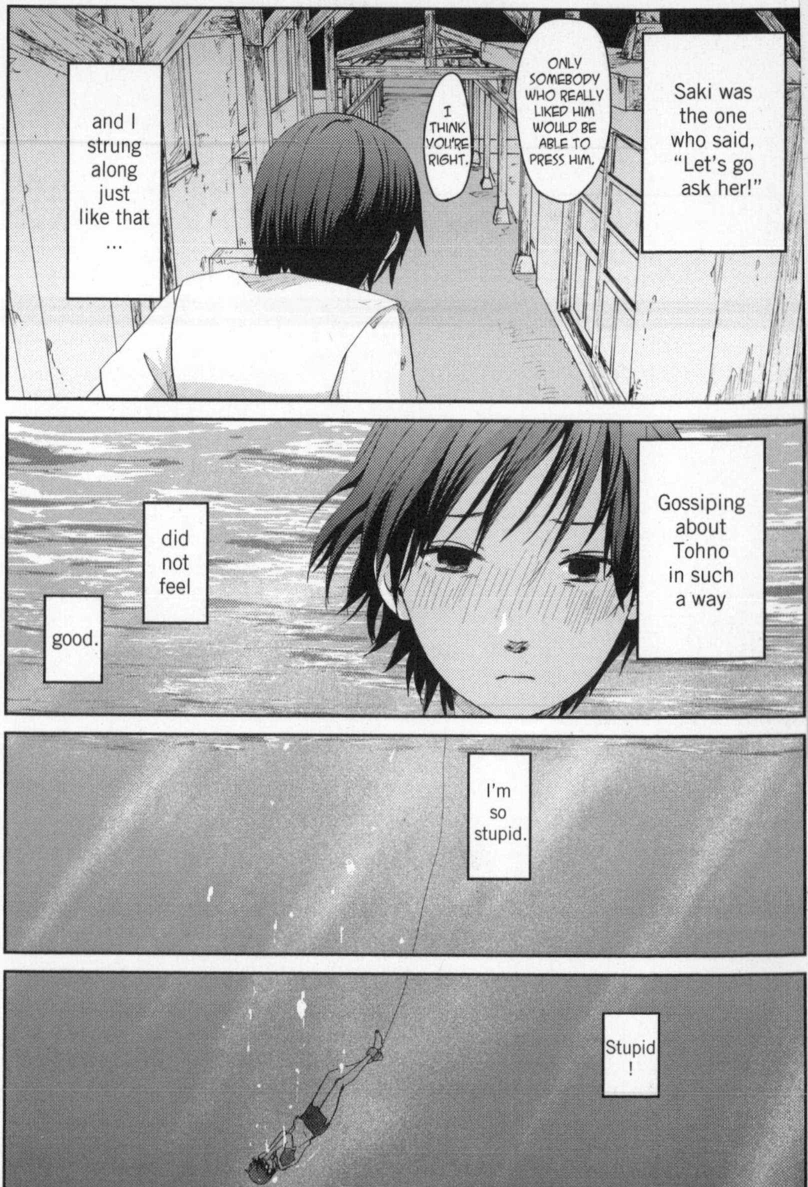
Saki was the one who said, "Let's go ask her!"
ONLY SOMEBODY WHO REALLY LIKED HIM WOULD BE ABLE TO PRESS HIM.
I THINK YOU'RE RIGHT.
and I strung along just like that ...
Gossiping about Tohno in such a way
did not feel
good.
I'm so stupid.
Stupid!

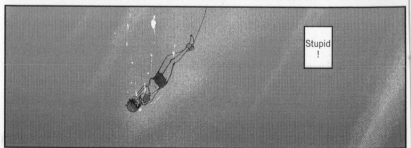

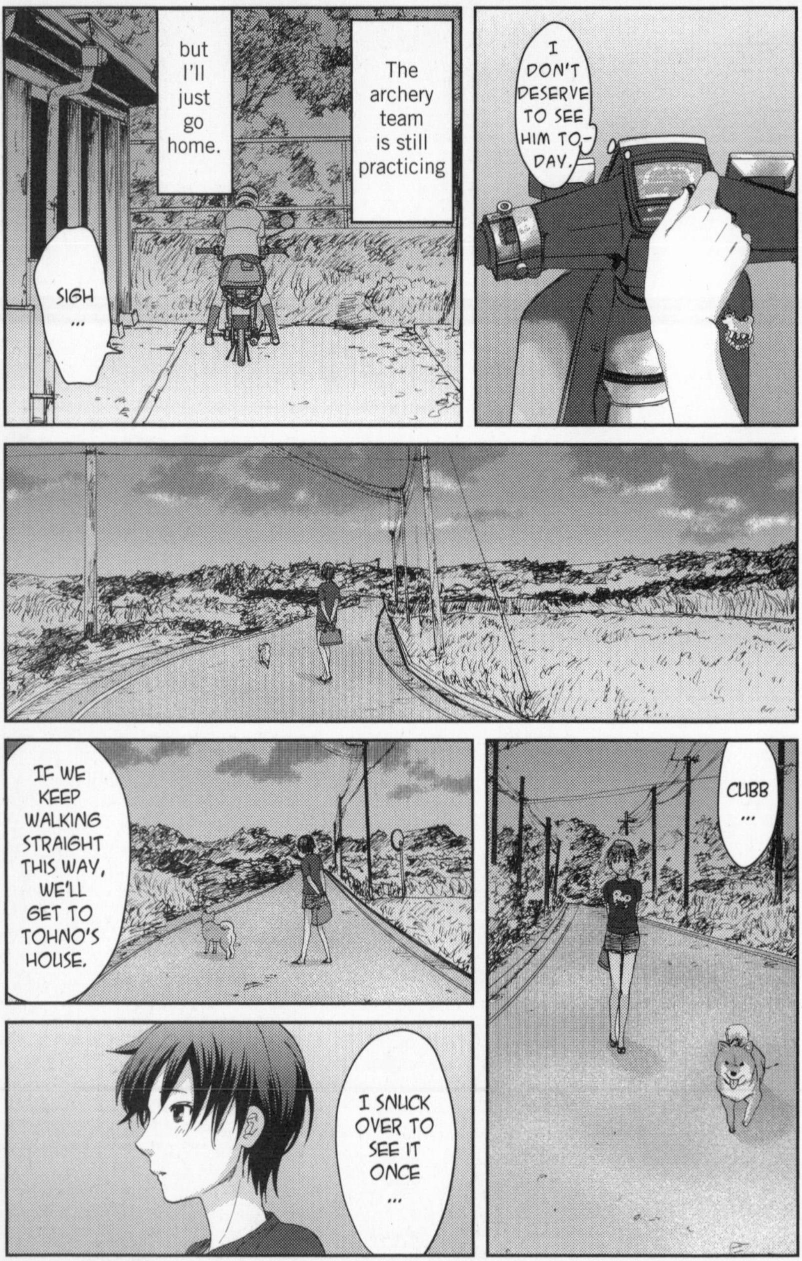
I DON'T DESERVE TO SEE HIM TO-DAY.
The archery team is still practicing
but I'll just go home.
SIGH ...
CUBB ...
IF WE KEEP WALKING STRAIGHT THIS WAY, WE'LL GET TO TOHNO'S HOUSE.
I SNUCK OVER TO SEE IT ONCE ...

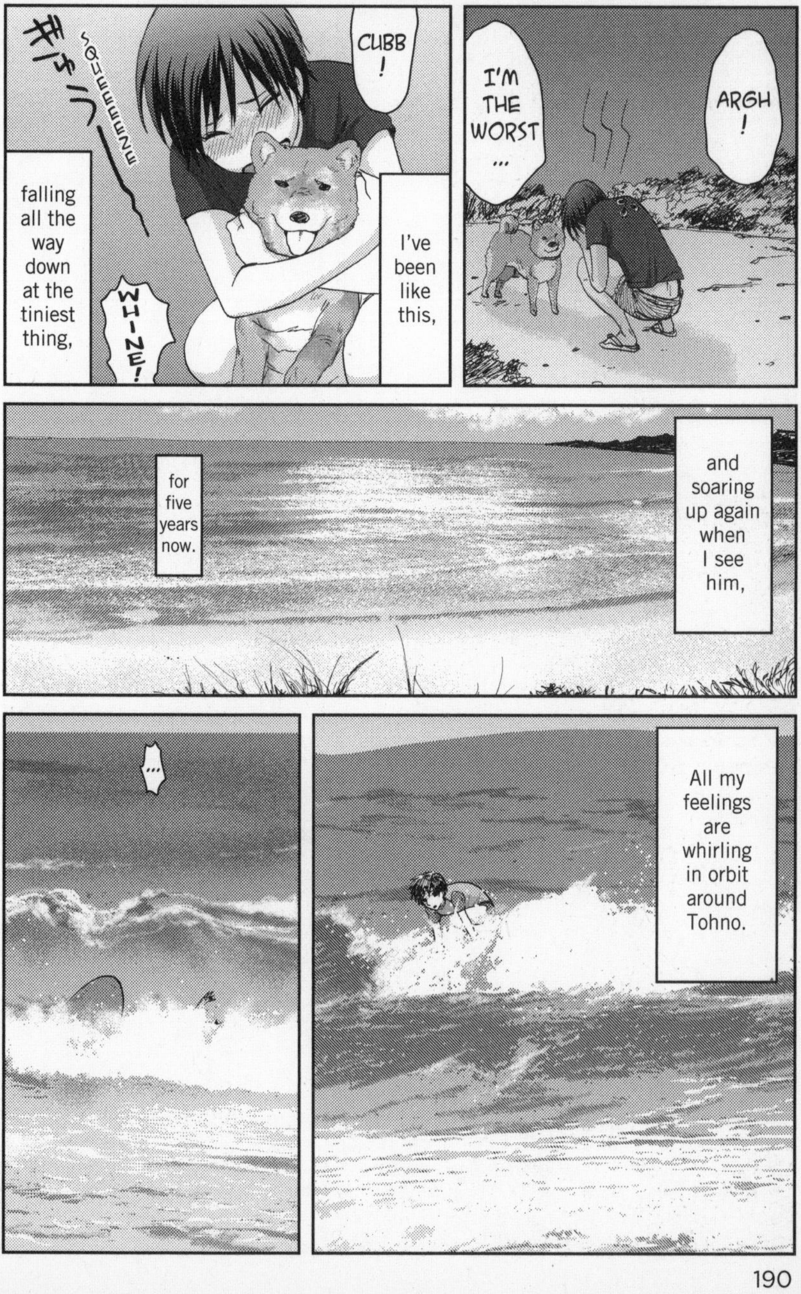

ARGH!
I'M THE WORST...
CUBB!
I've been like this,
ぎゅう
SQUEEEEEZE
falling all the way down at the tiniest thing,
WHINE!
and soaring up again when I see him,
for five years now.
All my feelings are whirling in orbit around Tohno.
...

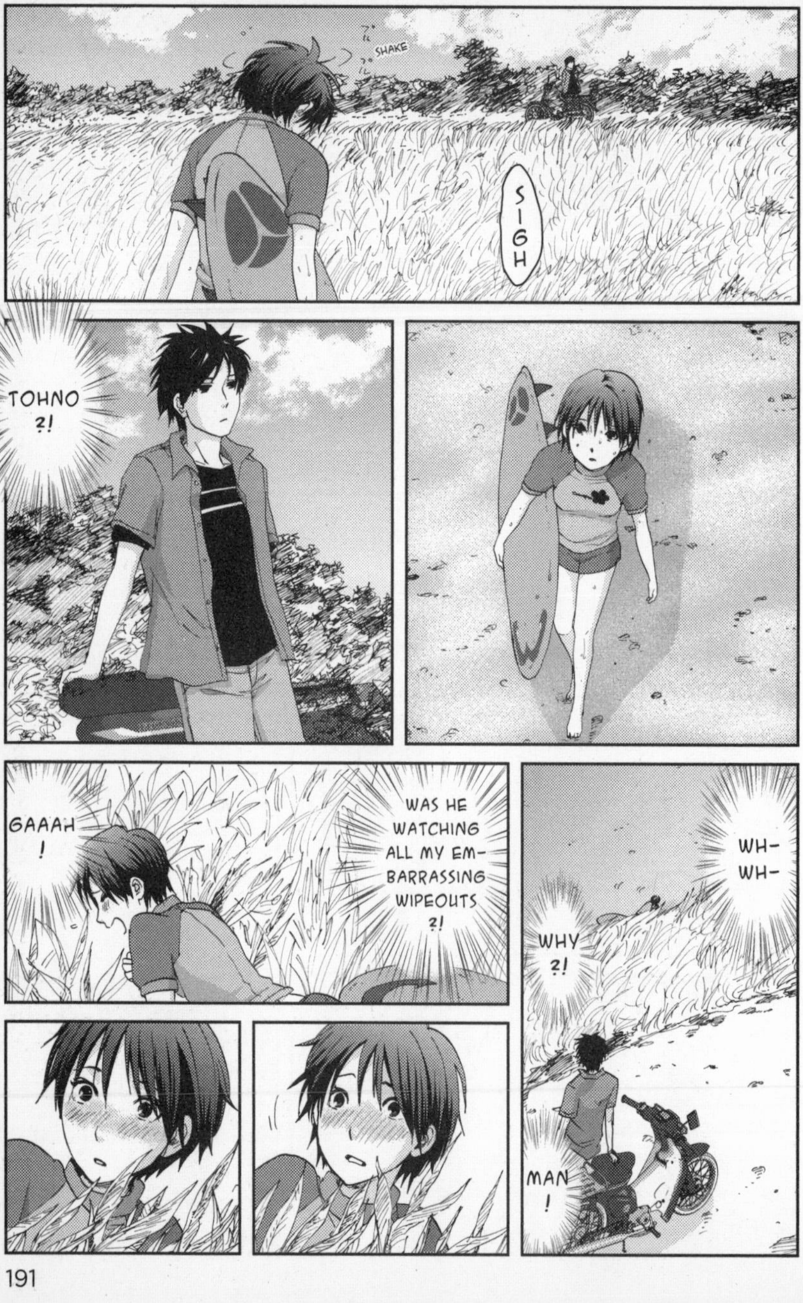
SHAKE
SIGH
TOHNO ?!
WH- WH-
WHY ?!
MAN !
WAS HE WATCHING ALL MY EM- BARRASSING WIPEOUTS ?!
GAAAH !

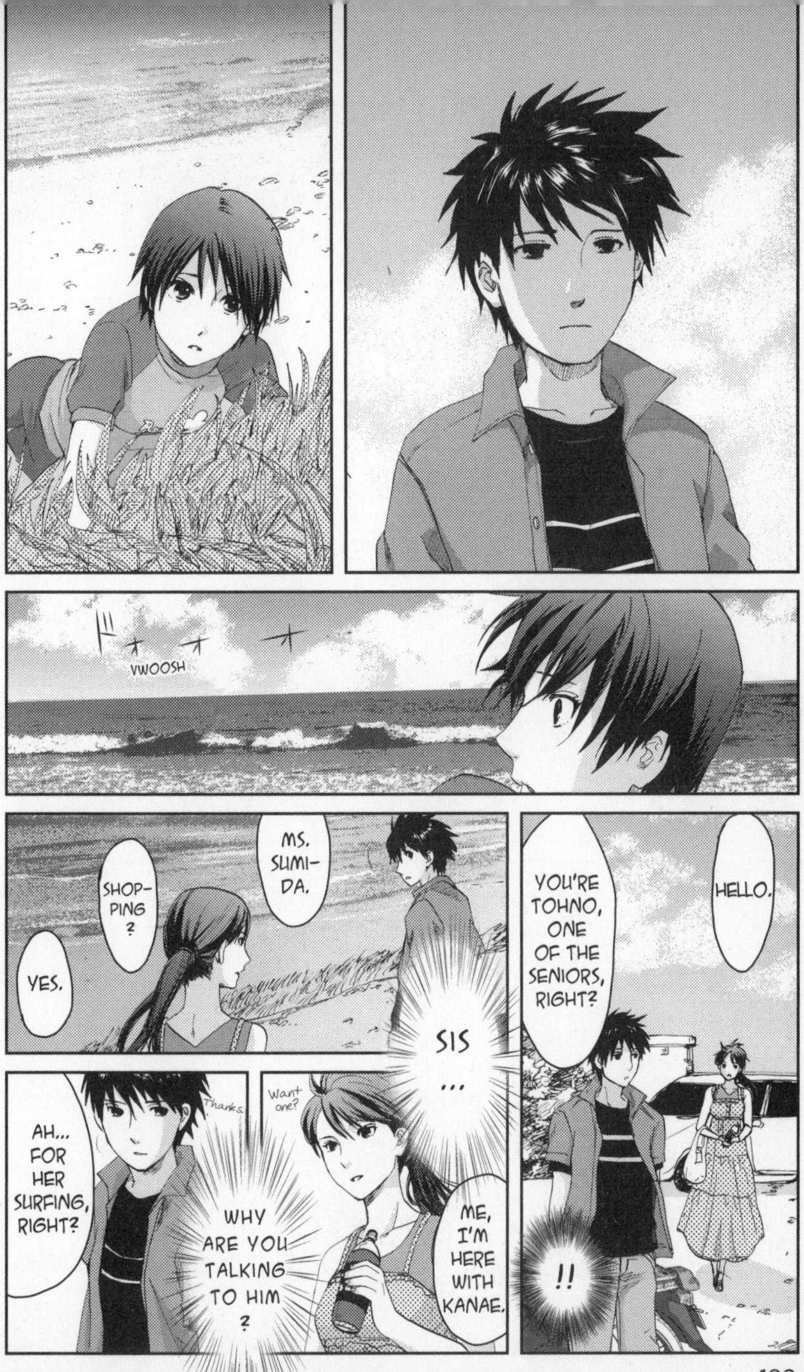
ドォォーオ
VWOOSH
HELLO.
YOU'RE TOHNO, ONE OF THE SENIORS, RIGHT?
!!
MS. SUMIDA.
SHOPPING?
YES.
SIS...
Want one?
ME, I'M HERE WITH KANAE.
WHY ARE YOU TALKING TO HIM?
Thanks.
AH... FOR HER SURFING, RIGHT?

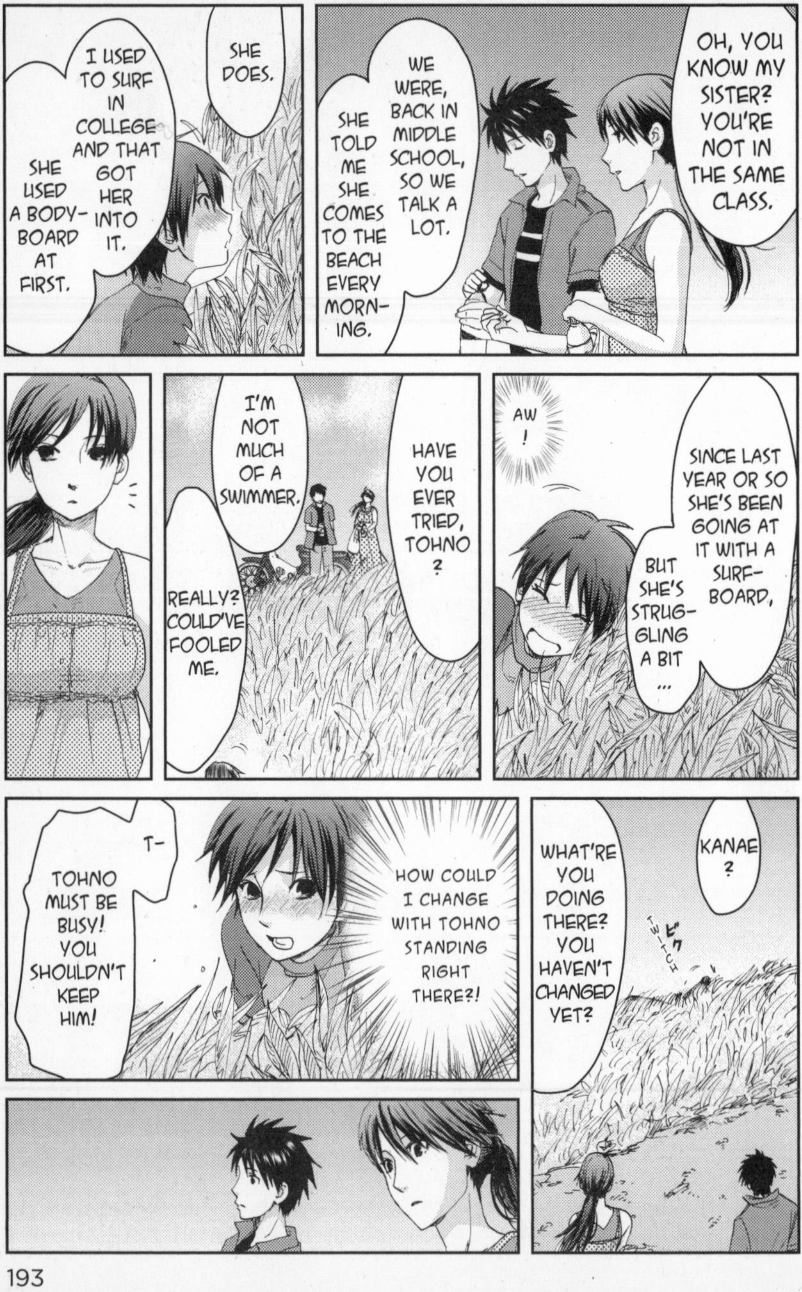
OH, YOU KNOW MY SISTER? YOU'RE NOT IN THE SAME CLASS.
WE WERE, BACK IN MIDDLE SCHOOL, SO WE TALK A LOT.
SHE TOLD ME SHE COMES TO THE BEACH EVERY MORNING.
SHE DOES.
I USED TO SURF IN COLLEGE AND THAT GOT HER INTO IT.
SHE USED A BODY-BOARD AT FIRST.
SINCE LAST YEAR OR SO SHE'S BEEN GOING AT IT WITH A SURF-BOARD,
BUT SHE'S STRUGGLING A BIT ...
AW!
HAVE YOU EVER TRIED, TOHNO?
I'M NOT MUCH OF A SWIMMER.
REALLY? COULD'VE FOOLED ME.
KANAE?
WHAT'RE YOU DOING THERE? YOU HAVEN'T CHANGED YET?
ビク
TWITCH
HOW COULD I CHANGE WITH TOHNO STANDING RIGHT THERE?!
T-
TOHNO MUST BE BUSY! YOU SHOULDN'T KEEP HIM!

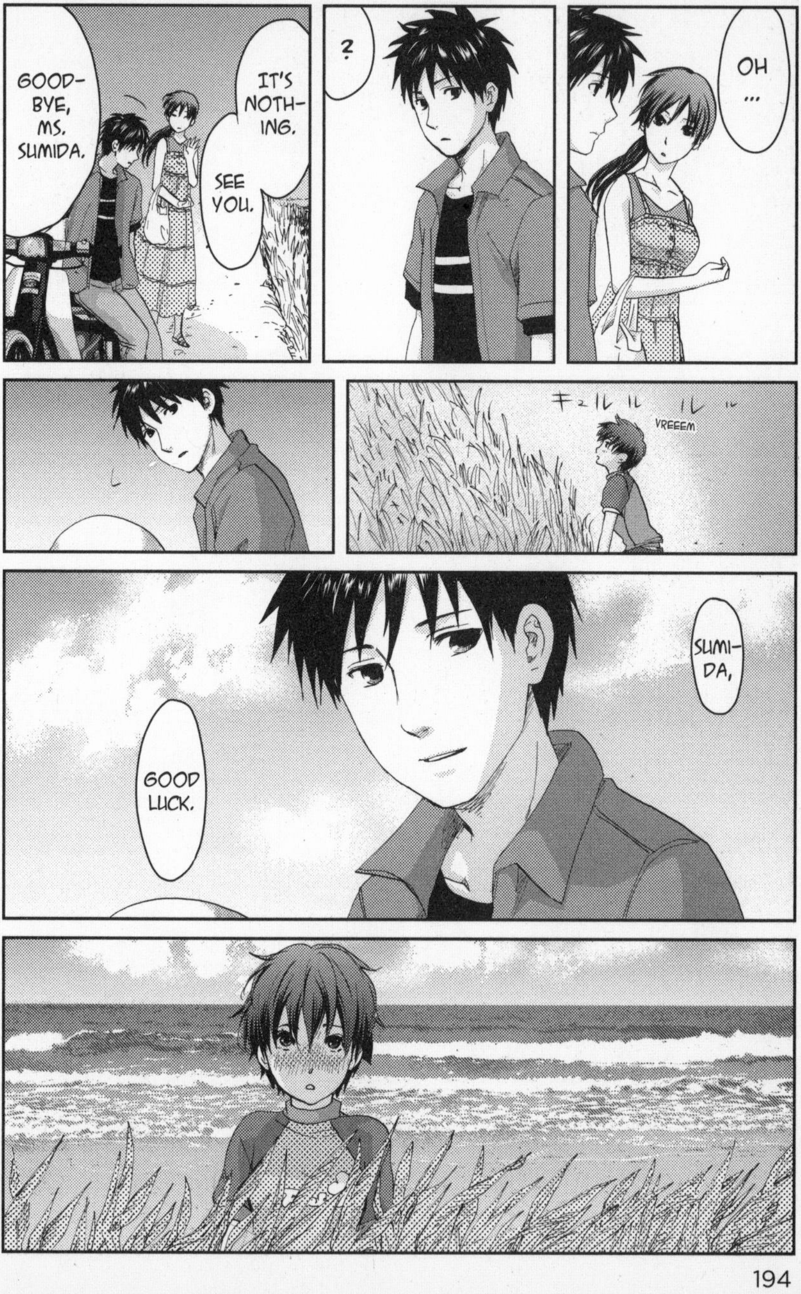
OH ...
?
IT'S NOTHING.
SEE YOU.
GOOD-BYE, MS. SUMIDA.
キュルル ル ル
VREEEM
SUMIDA,
GOOD LUCK.

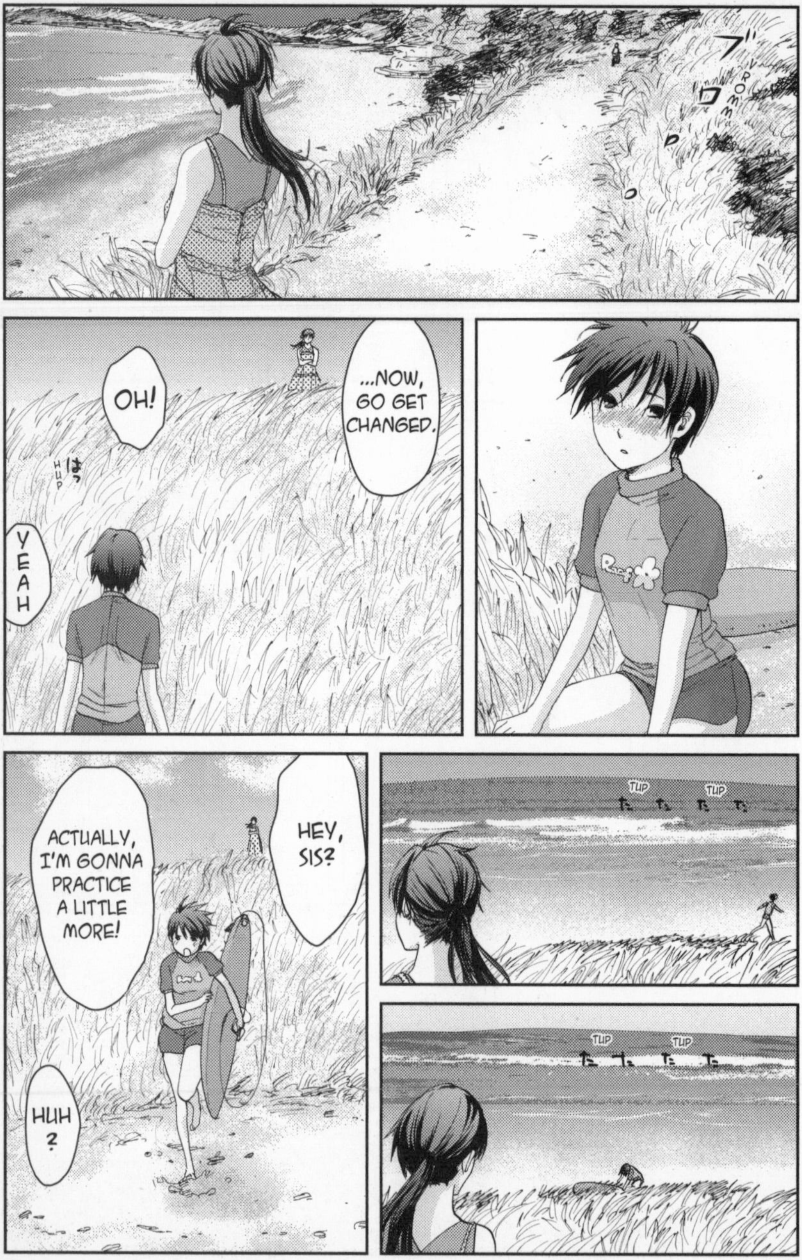
VROOM
...NOW, GO GET CHANGED.
OH!
HUP
YEAH
TUP TUP
TUP TUP
HEY, SIS?
ACTUALLY, I'M GONNA PRACTICE A LITTLE MORE!
HUH?

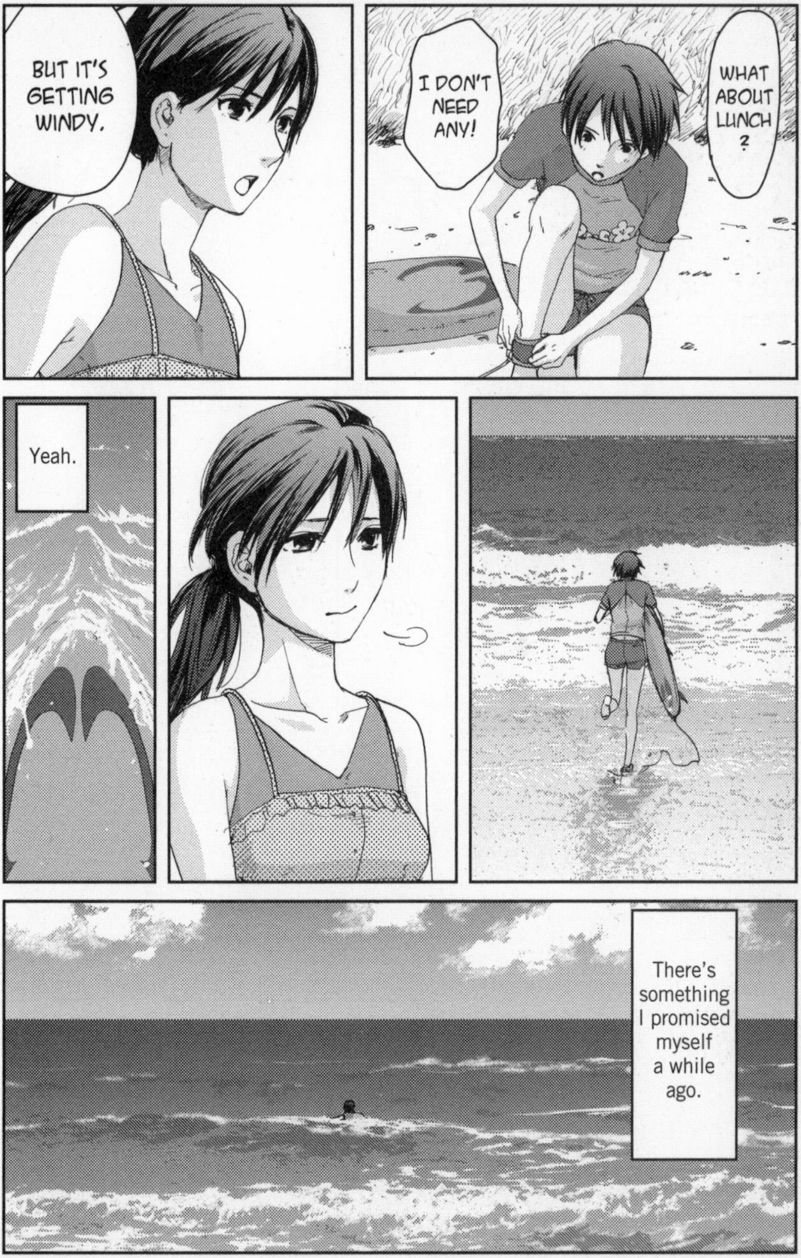
WHAT ABOUT LUNCH?
I DON'T NEED ANY!
BUT IT'S GETTING WINDY.
Yeah.
There's something I promised myself a while ago.

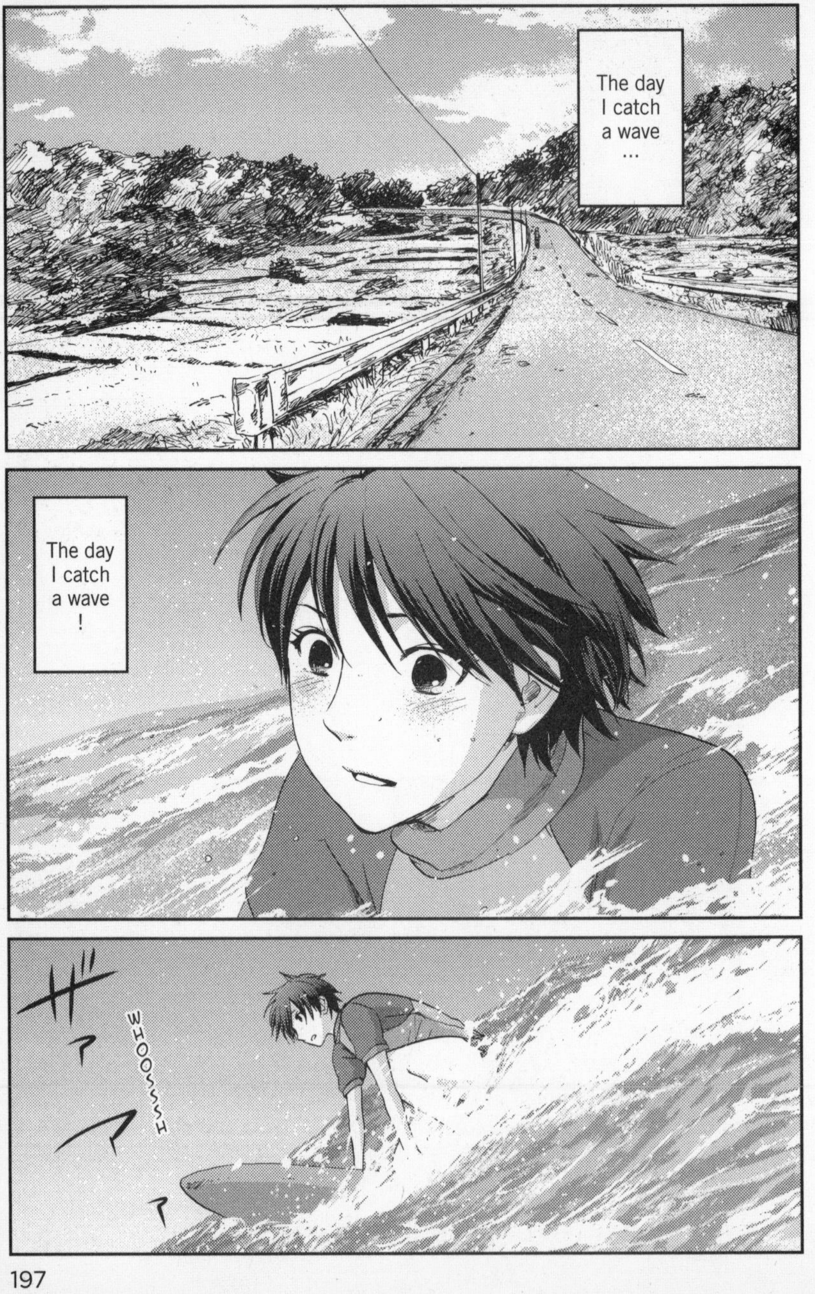
The day I catch a wave ...
The day I catch a wave !
ザァアァ
WHOOSSSH

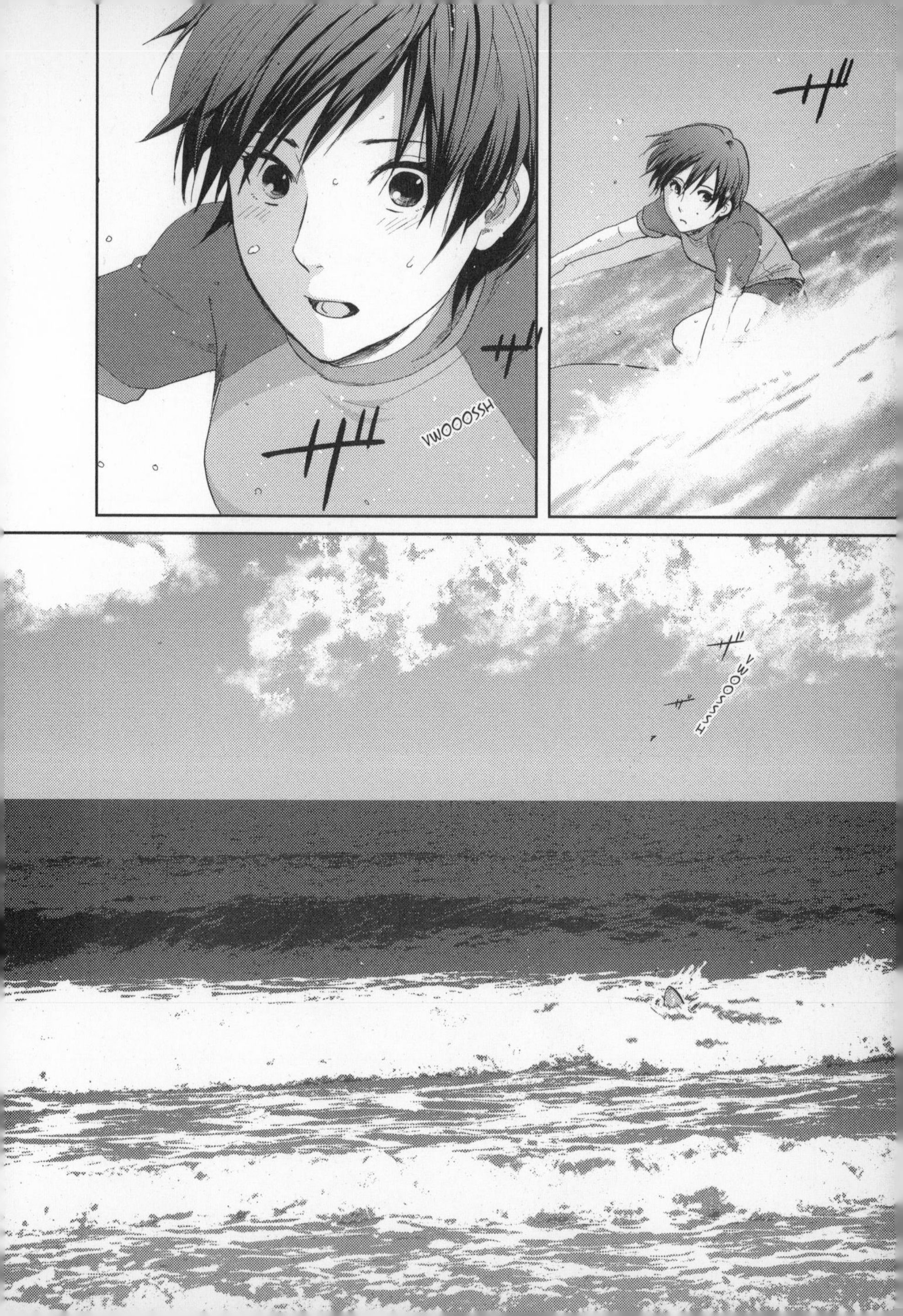
VWOOOSSH

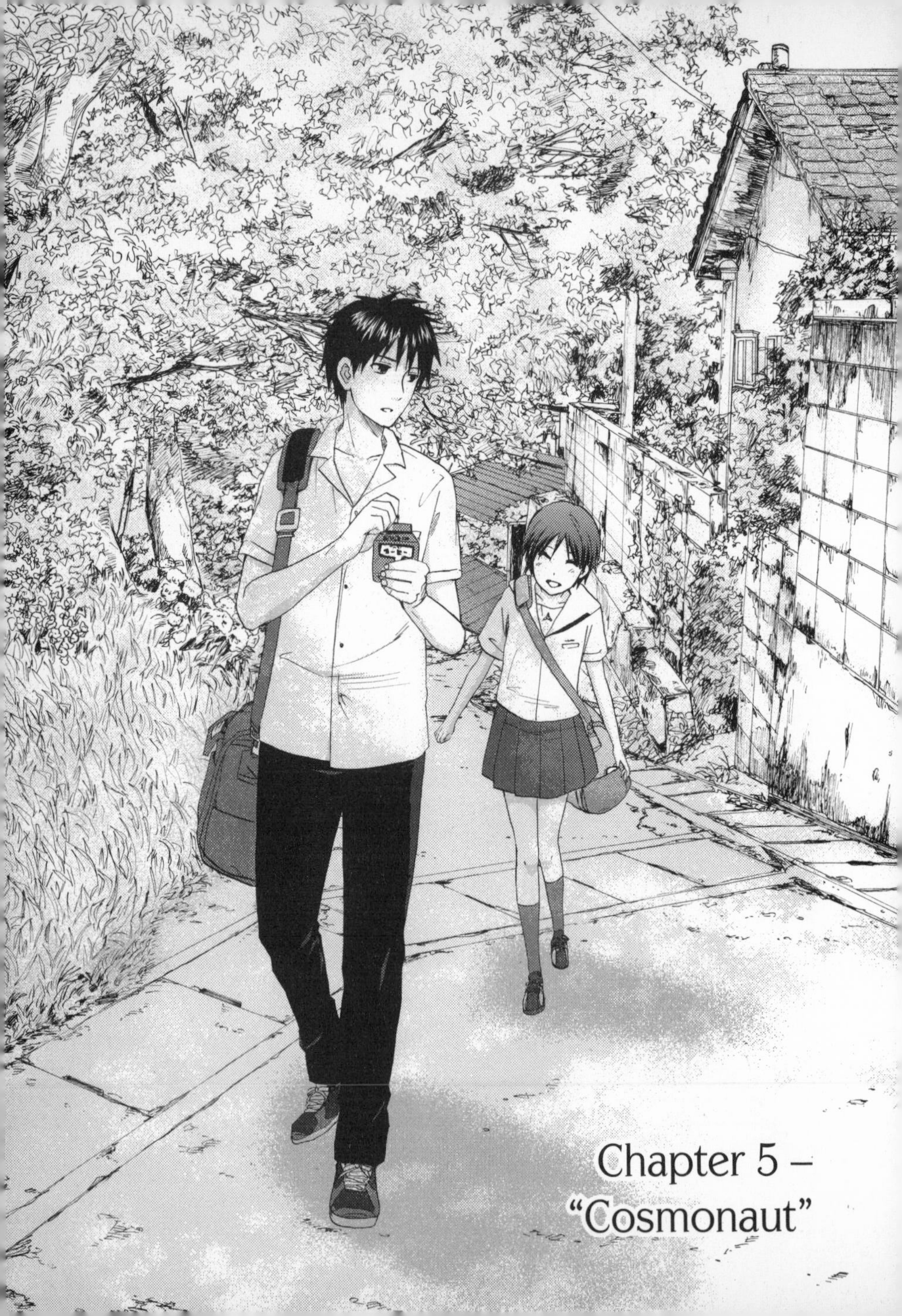

Chapter 5 –
"Cosmonaut"

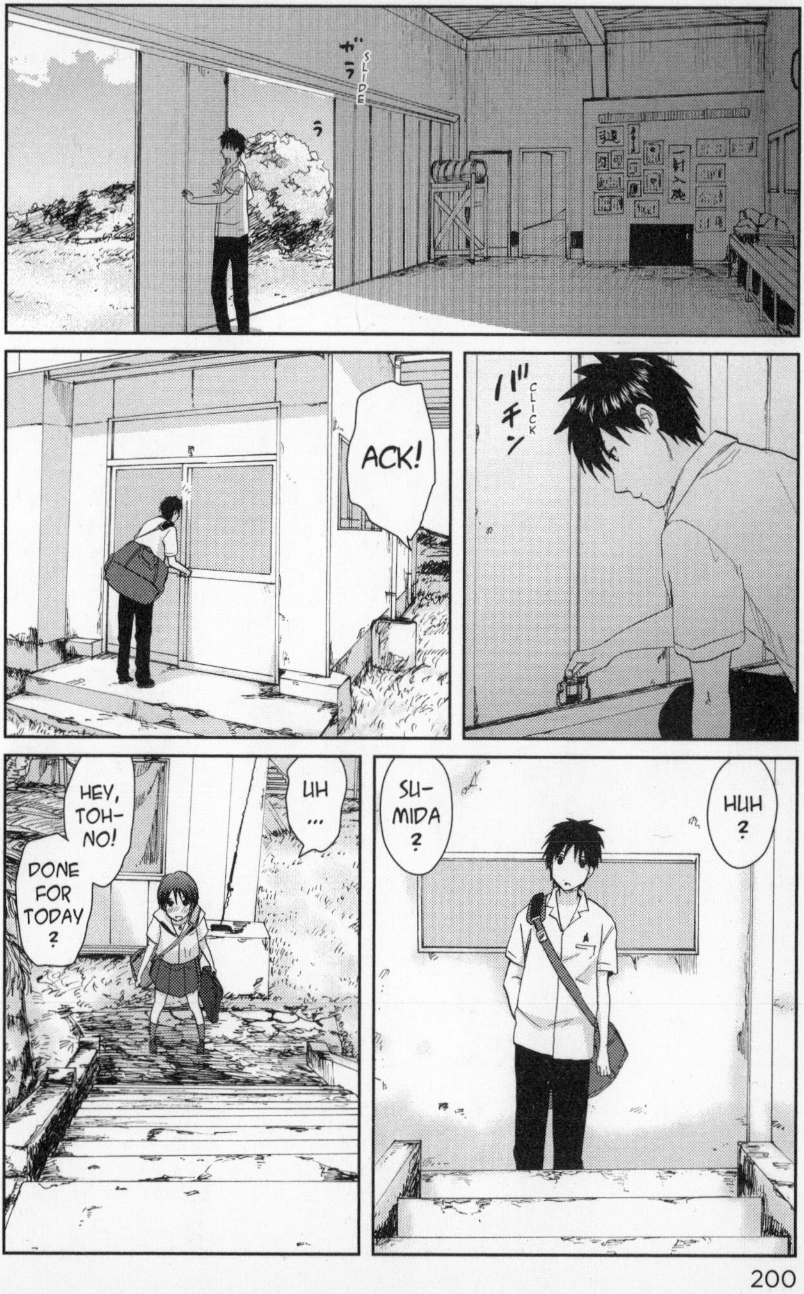
ガラ
SLIDE
ラ
バチン
CLICK
ACK!
HUH?
SU-MIDA?
UH...
HEY, TOH-NO!
DONE FOR TODAY?

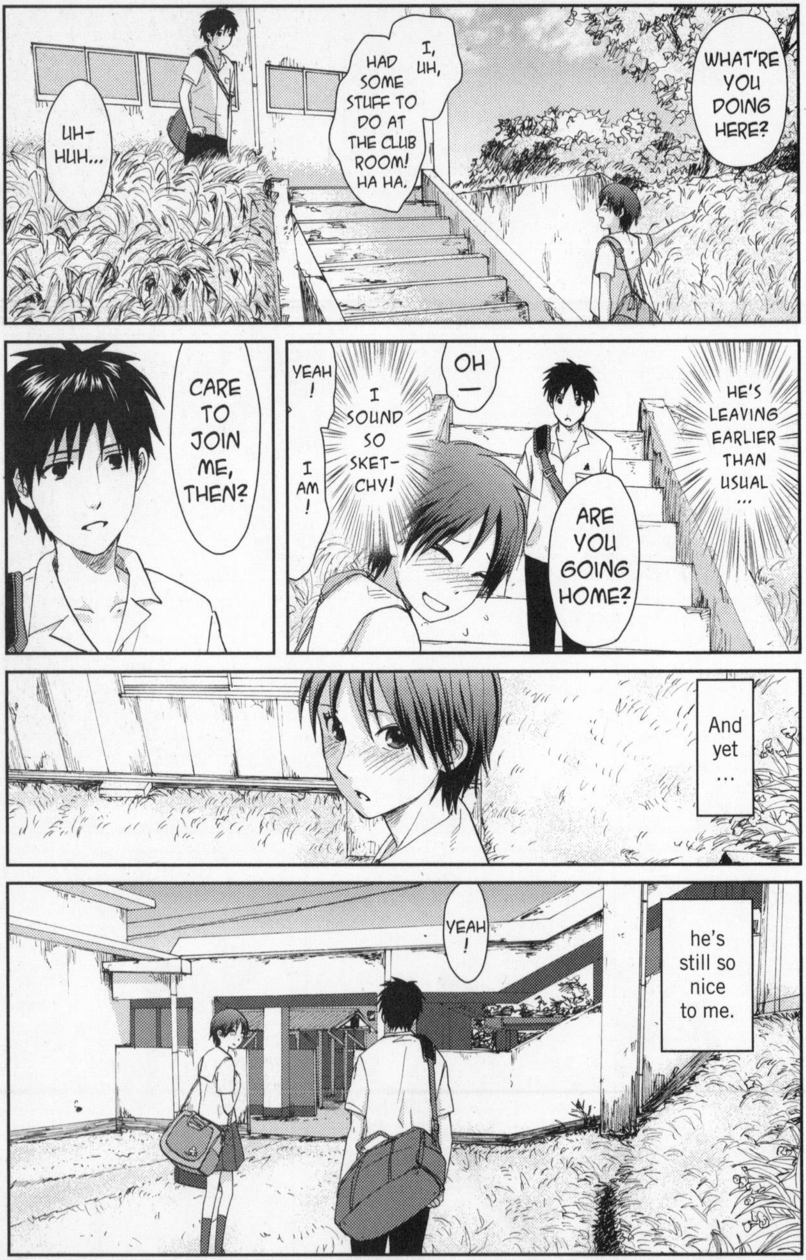
WHAT'RE YOU DOING HERE?
I, UH, HAD SOME STUFF TO DO AT THE CLUB ROOM! HA HA.
UH-HUH...
HE'S LEAVING EARLIER THAN USUAL...
OH—
ARE YOU GOING HOME?
I SOUND SO SKETCHY!
YEAH! I AM!
CARE TO JOIN ME, THEN?
And yet...
he's still so nice to me.
YEAH!

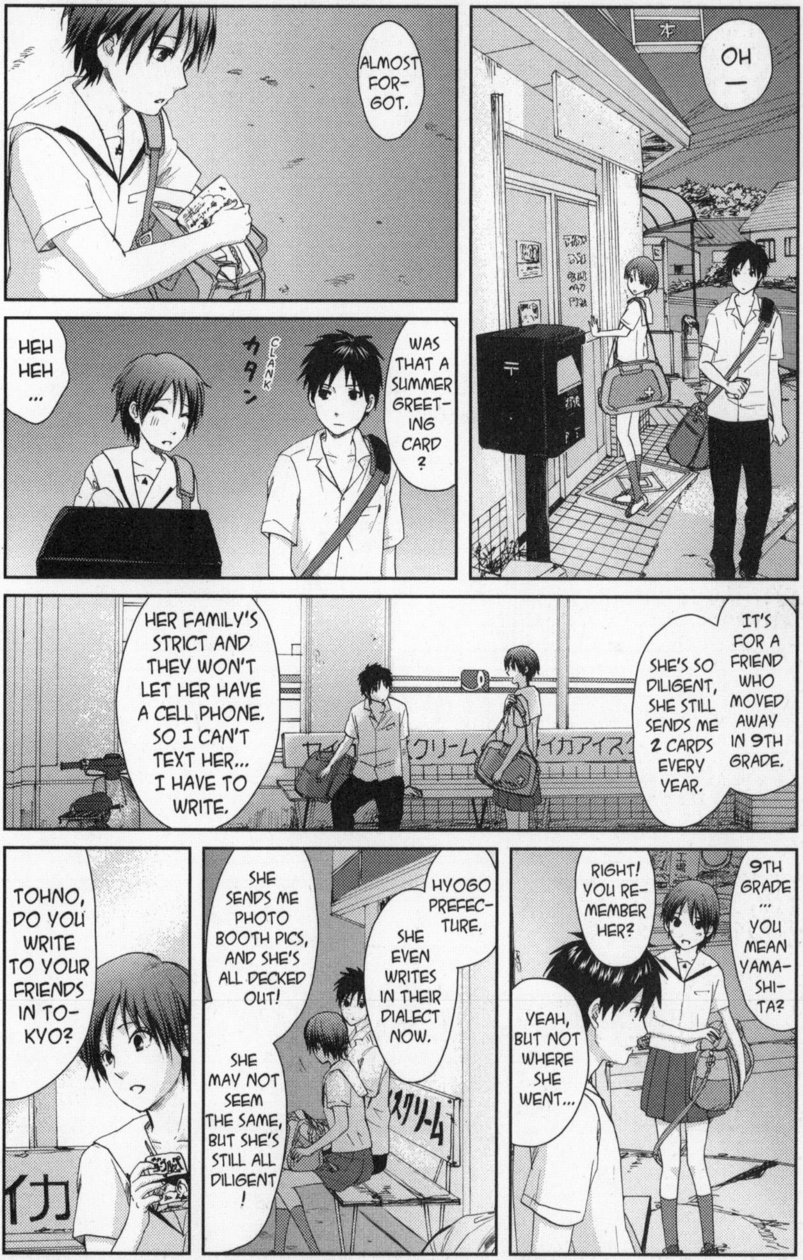
OH —
ALMOST FORGOT.
WAS THAT A SUMMER GREETING CARD?
CLANK
カタン
HEH HEH ...
IT'S FOR A FRIEND WHO MOVED AWAY IN 9TH GRADE.
SHE'S SO DILIGENT, SHE STILL SENDS ME 2 CARDS EVERY YEAR.
HER FAMILY'S STRICT AND THEY WON'T LET HER HAVE A CELL PHONE. SO I CAN'T TEXT HER... I HAVE TO WRITE.
9TH GRADE... YOU MEAN YAMASHITA?
RIGHT! YOU REMEMBER HER?
YEAH, BUT NOT WHERE SHE WENT...
HYOGO PREFECTURE.
SHE EVEN WRITES IN THEIR DIALECT NOW.
SHE SENDS ME PHOTO BOOTH PICS, AND SHE'S ALL DECKED OUT!
SHE MAY NOT SEEM THE SAME, BUT SHE'S STILL ALL DILIGENT!
TOHNO, DO YOU WRITE TO YOUR FRIENDS IN TOKYO?

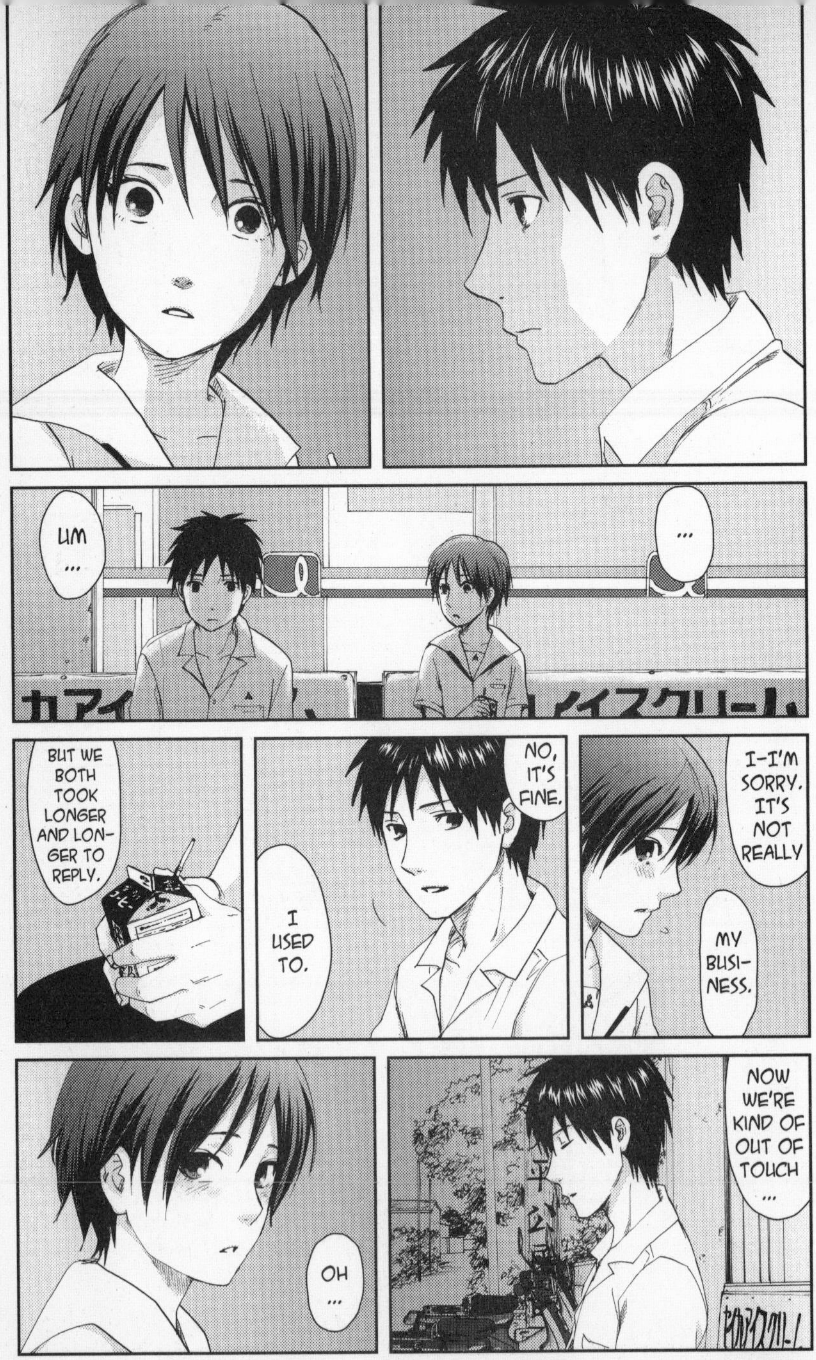
...
UM ...
I-I'M SORRY. IT'S NOT REALLY
MY BUSINESS.
NO, IT'S FINE.
I USED TO.
BUT WE BOTH TOOK LONGER AND LONGER TO REPLY.
NOW WE'RE KIND OF OUT OF TOUCH ...
OH ...

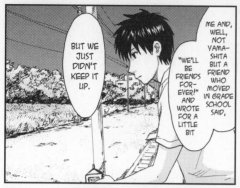

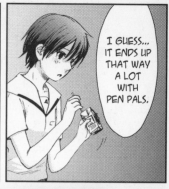

I GUESS... IT ENDS UP THAT WAY A LOT WITH PEN PALS.
ME AND, WELL, NOT YAMA-SHITA BUT A FRIEND WHO MOVED IN GRADE SCHOOL SAID,
"WE'LL BE FRIENDS FOR-EVER!" AND WROTE FOR A LITTLE BIT
BUT WE JUST DIDN'T KEEP IT UP.
IT FEELS AWKWARD TALKING ABOUT PEOPLE THE OTHER PERSON DOESN'T KNOW,
AND THEN AFTER A WHILE THERE'S NOTHING TO SAY.
I'LL NEVER SEE HER AGAIN, SO I'M BEING A BURDEN,
YOU START THINKING...
BUT HEY!
A NEW YEAR'S CARD ISN'T SO HARD, RIGHT?
I SEND ONE TO YAMA BECAUSE I KNOW SHE'LL SEND ME ONE.
WE DON'T TALK ON THE PHONE, AND SHE'S FAR AWAY...

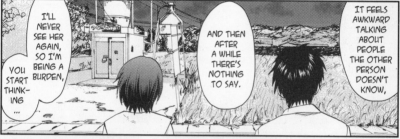

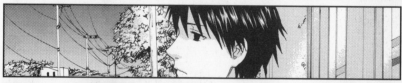

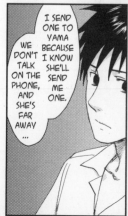

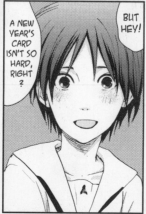

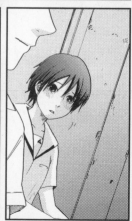

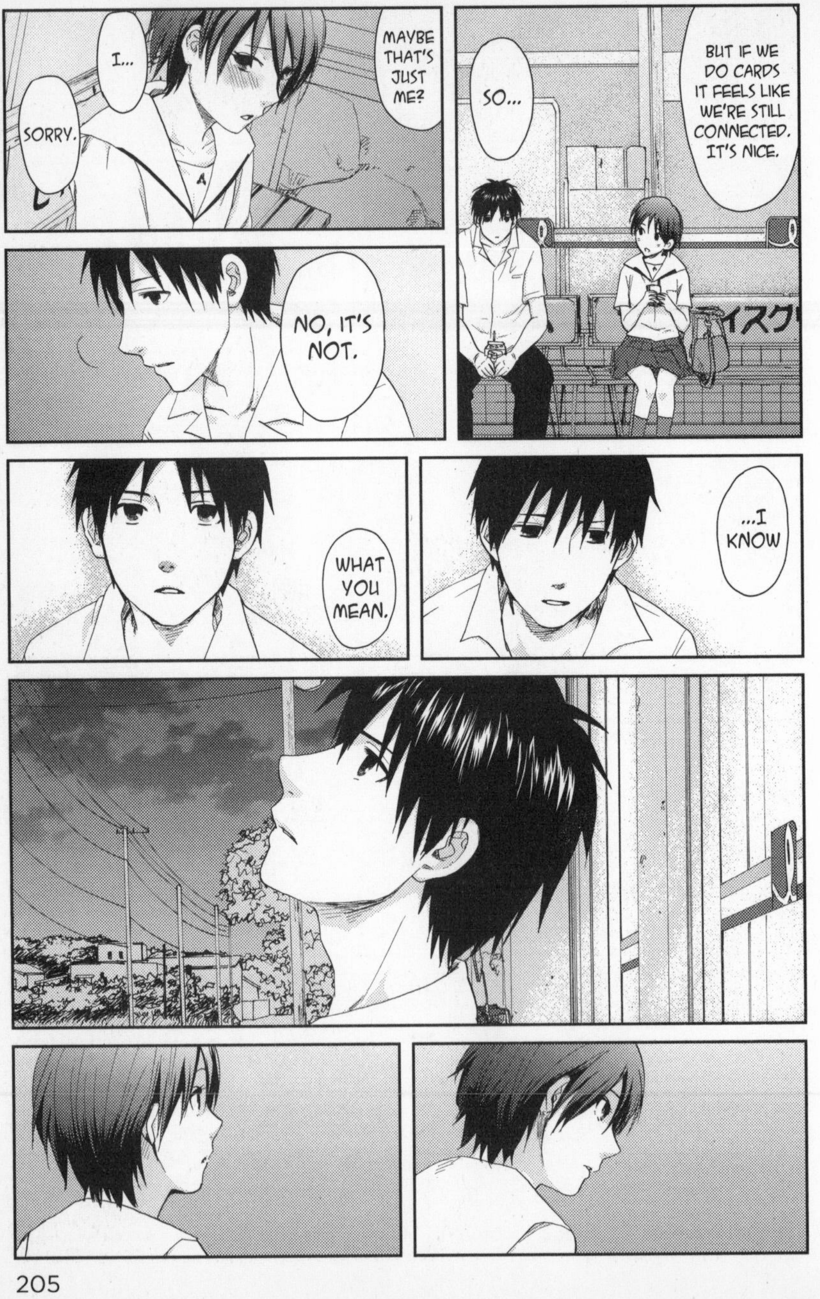
BUT IF WE DO CARDS IT FEELS LIKE WE'RE STILL CONNECTED. IT'S NICE.
SO...
MAYBE THAT'S JUST ME?
I...
SORRY.
NO, IT'S NOT.
...I KNOW
WHAT YOU MEAN.

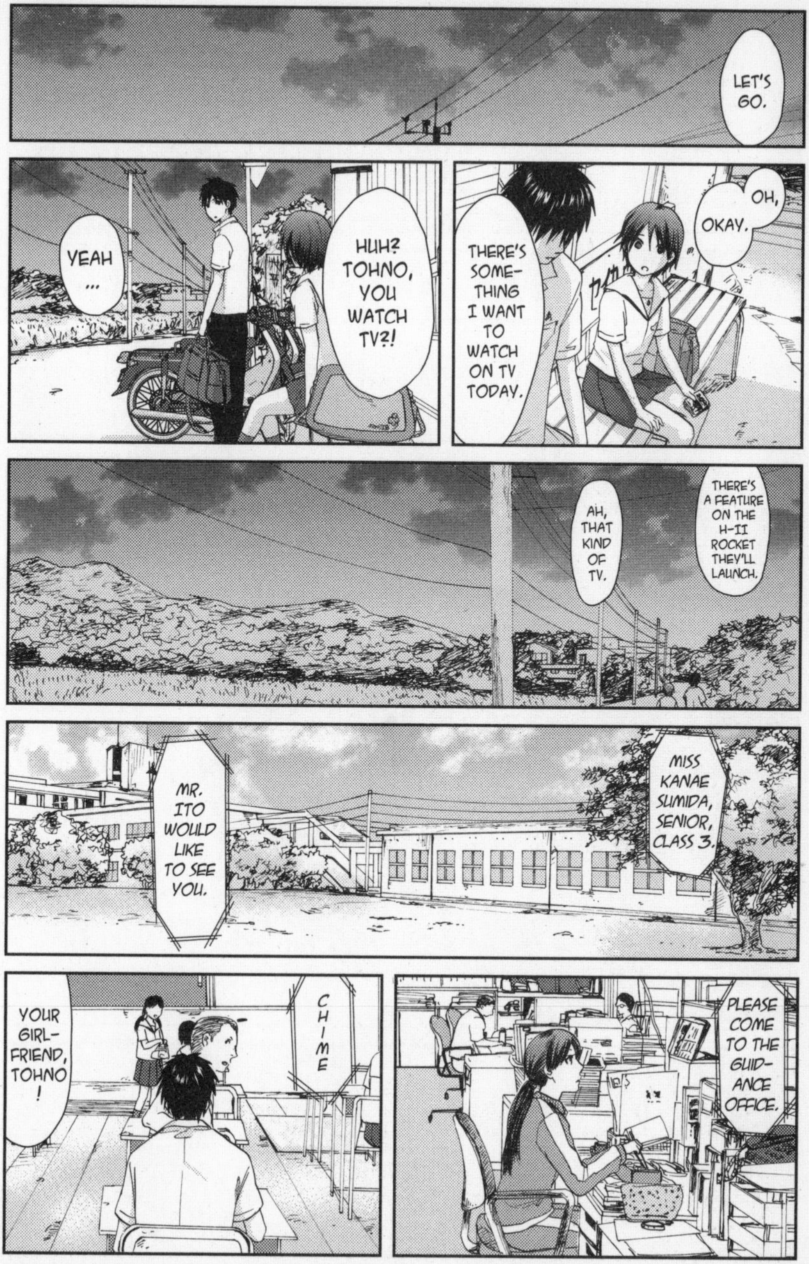
LET'S GO.
OH, OKAY.
THERE'S SOME-THING I WANT TO WATCH ON TV TODAY.
HUH? TOHNO, YOU WATCH TV?!
YEAH ...
THERE'S A FEATURE ON THE H-II ROCKET THEY'LL LAUNCH.
AH, THAT KIND OF TV.
MISS KANAE SUMIDA, SENIOR, CLASS 3.
MR. ITO WOULD LIKE TO SEE YOU.
PLEASE COME TO THE GUID-ANCE OFFICE.
CHIME
YOUR GIRL-FRIEND, TOHNO!

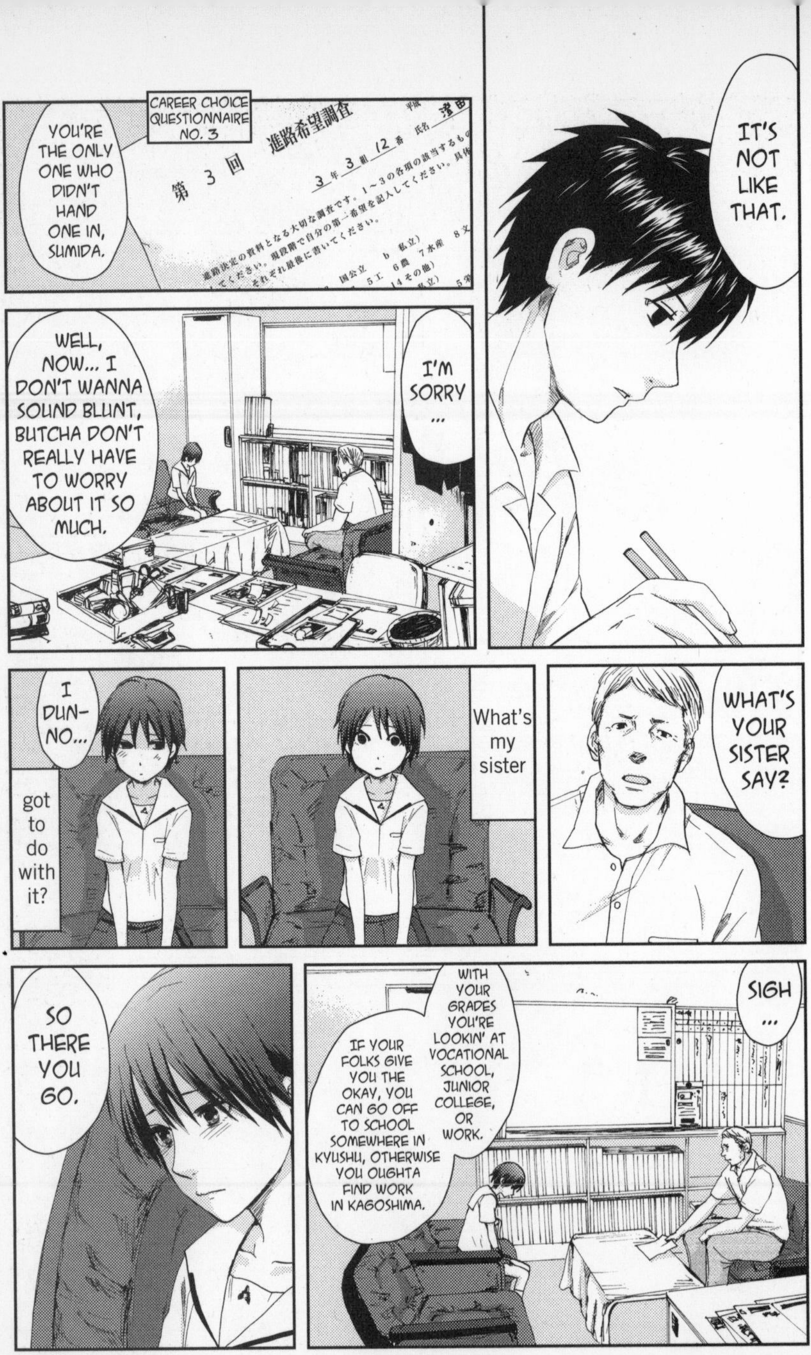
IT'S NOT LIKE THAT.
CAREER CHOICE QUESTIONNAIRE NO. 3
YOU'RE THE ONLY ONE WHO DIDN'T HAND ONE IN, SUMIDA.
I'M SORRY...
WELL, NOW... I DON'T WANNA SOUND BLUNT, BUTCHA DON'T REALLY HAVE TO WORRY ABOUT IT SO MUCH.
WHAT'S YOUR SISTER SAY?
What's my sister
I DUN-NO...
got to do with it?
SIGH...
WITH YOUR GRADES YOU'RE LOOKIN' AT VOCATIONAL SCHOOL, JUNIOR COLLEGE, OR WORK.
IF YOUR FOLKS GIVE YOU THE OKAY, YOU CAN GO OFF TO SCHOOL SOMEWHERE IN KYUSHU, OTHERWISE YOU OUGHTA FIND WORK IN KAGOSHIMA.
SO THERE YOU GO.

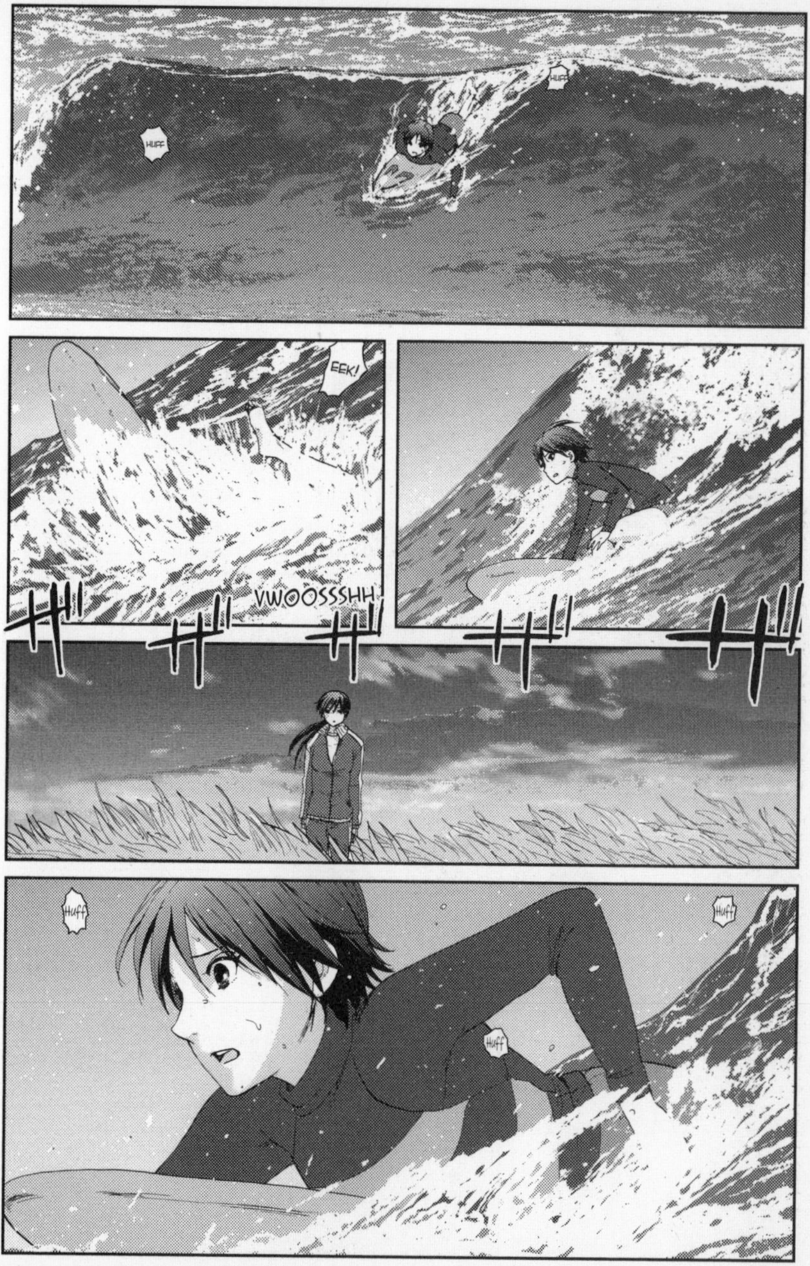
HUFF
HUFF
EEK!
VWOOSSSHH
Huff
Huff
Huff

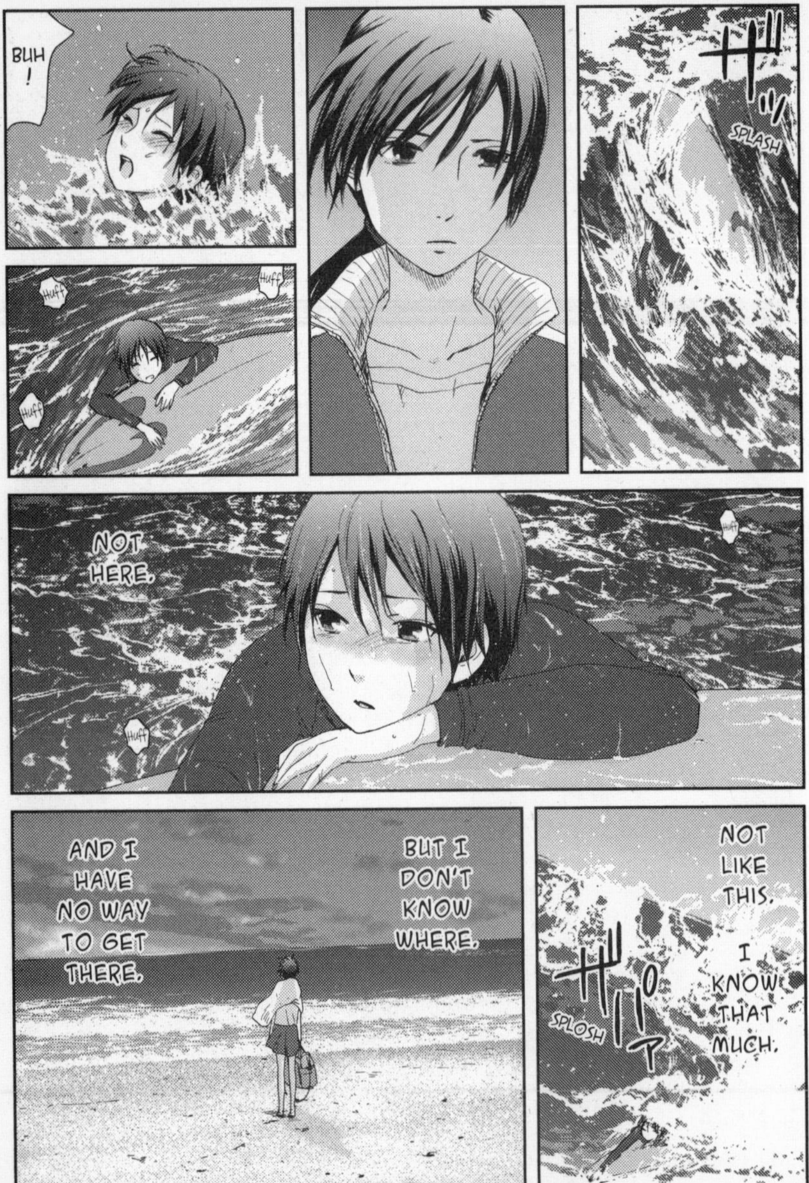
SPLASH
BUH!
Huff
Huff
Huff
Huff
NOT HERE.
Huff
NOT LIKE THIS.
I KNOW THAT MUCH.
SPLOSH
BUT I DON'T KNOW WHERE.
AND I HAVE NO WAY TO GET THERE.

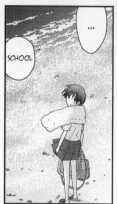

KA-NAE!
プァン
HONK
NOT THE WAY I AM NOW ...
HOME? SCHOOL?
...
SCHOOL
"Talk it over with your sister, okay?"
"I'll be lettin' her know, too."
WHY ISN'T SHE SAYING ANYTHING?
HAVING PEOPLE TIPTOE AROUND ME
IS JUST KIND OF
PAINFUL.

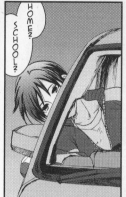

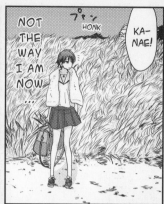

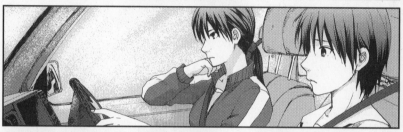

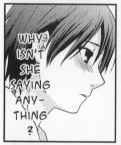

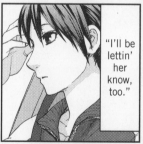

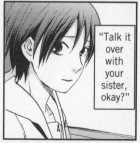

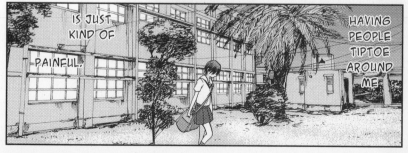

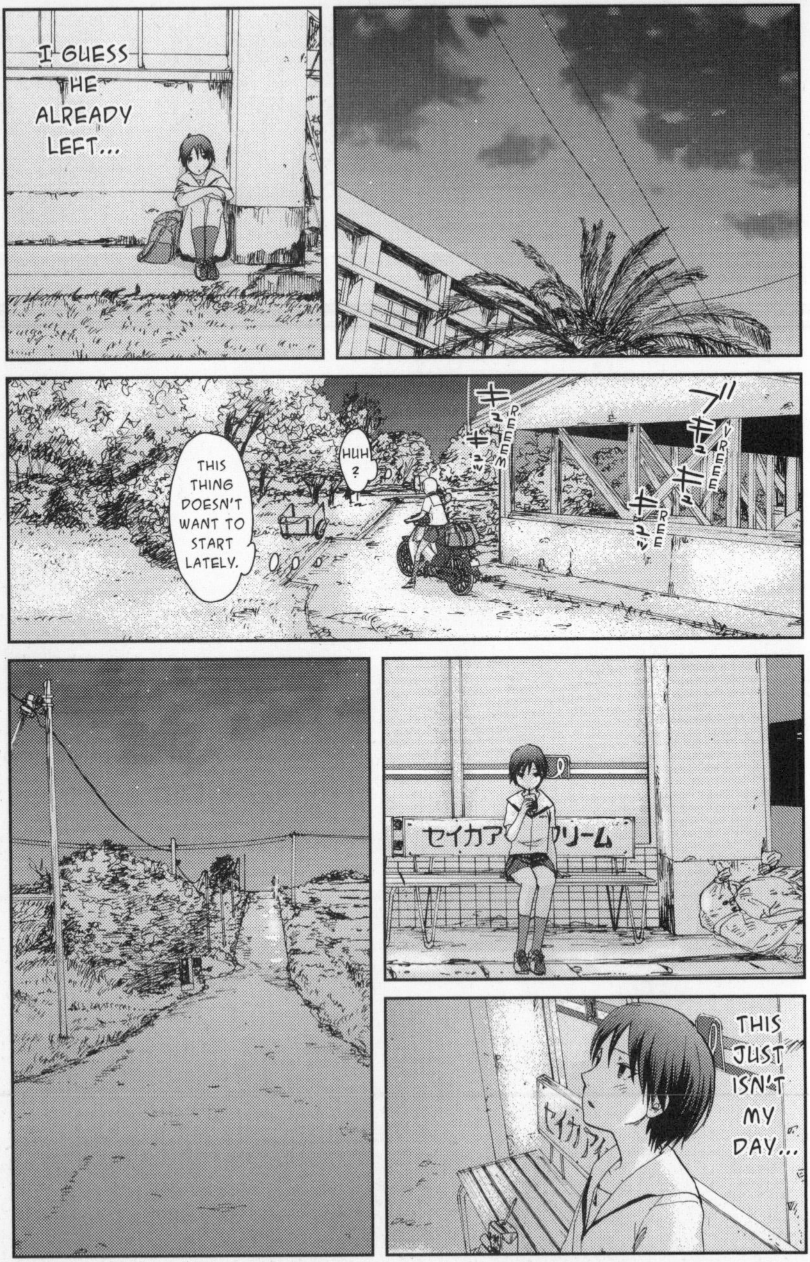
I GUESS HE ALREADY LEFT...
ブキュキュキュッ
VREEE
REE
キュキュッ
REEEM
HUH?
THIS THING DOESN'T WANT TO START LATELY.
セイカア
リーム
THIS JUST ISN'T MY DAY...
セイカアイ

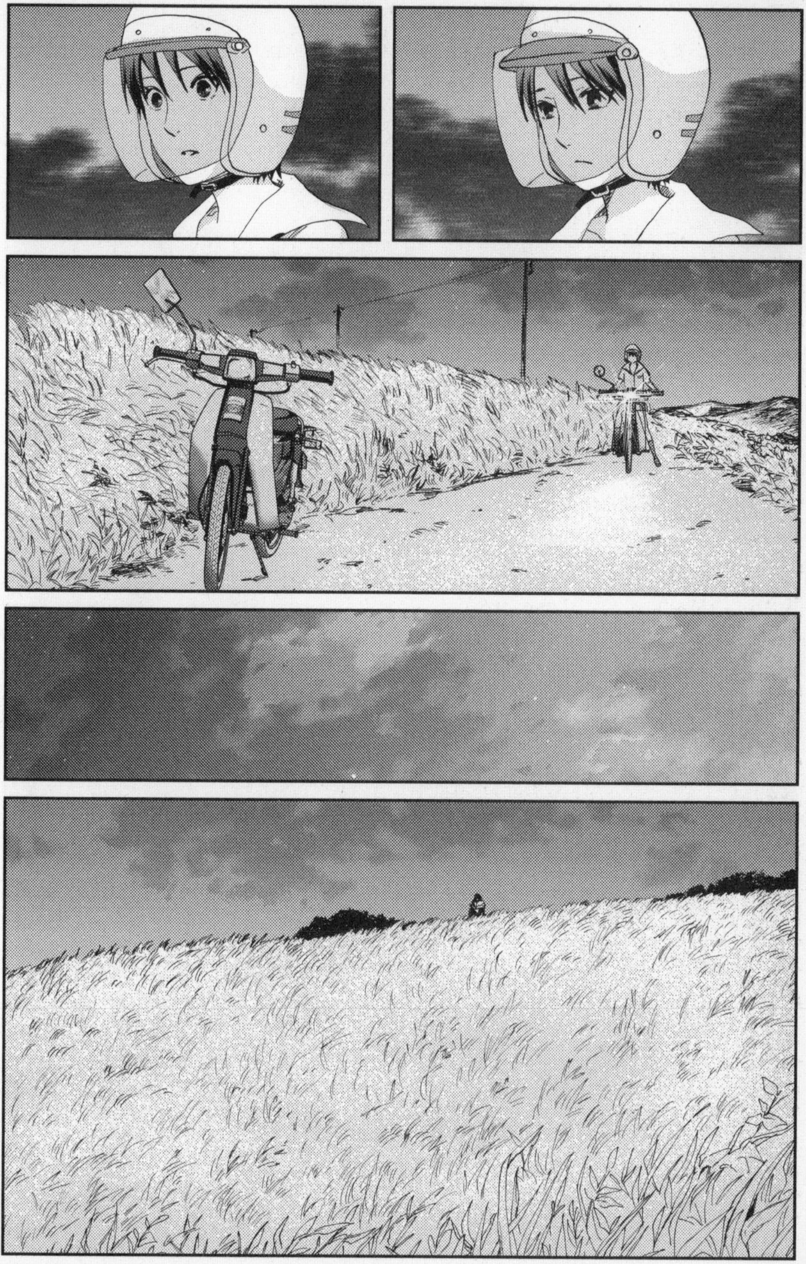

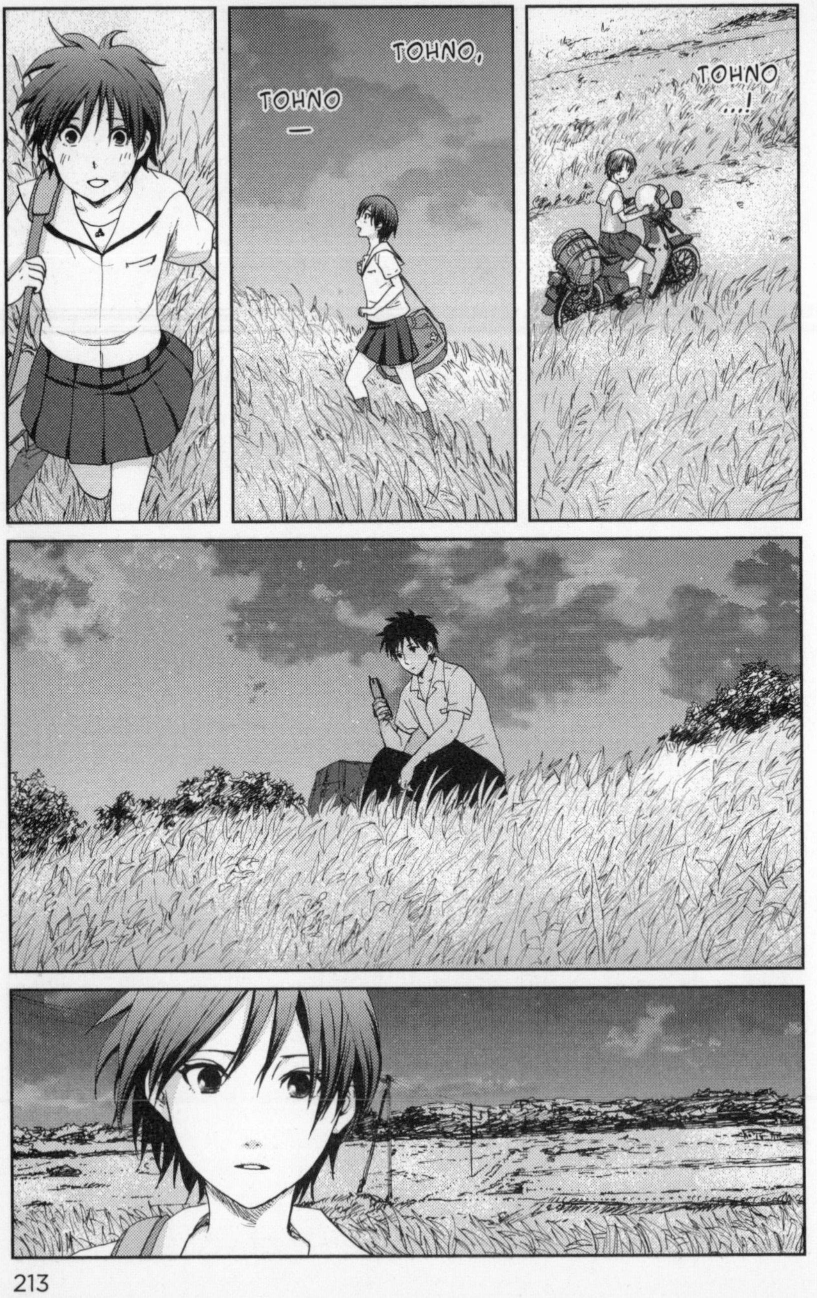
TOHNO ...!
TOHNO,
TOHNO —

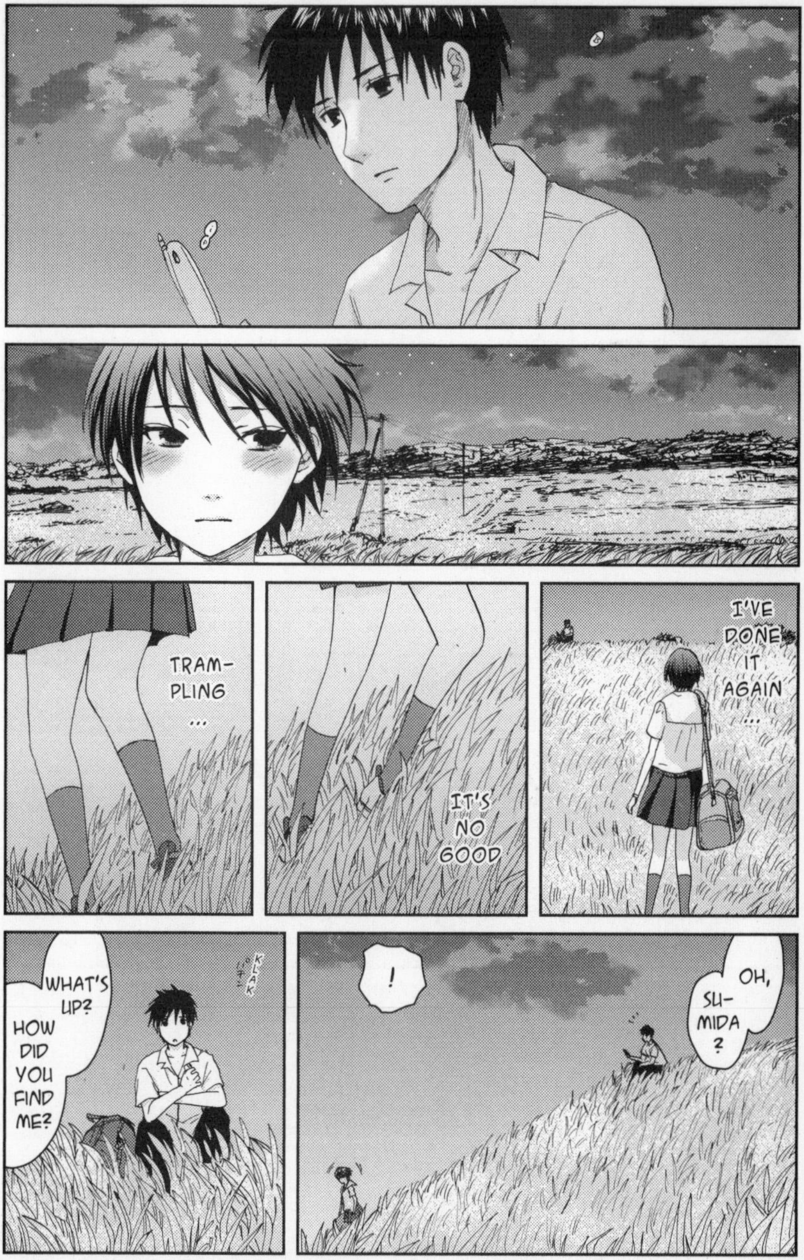
I'VE DONE IT AGAIN ...
IT'S NO GOOD
TRAM-PLING ...
OH, SU-MIDA?
!
KLAK
WHAT'S UP? HOW DID YOU FIND ME?

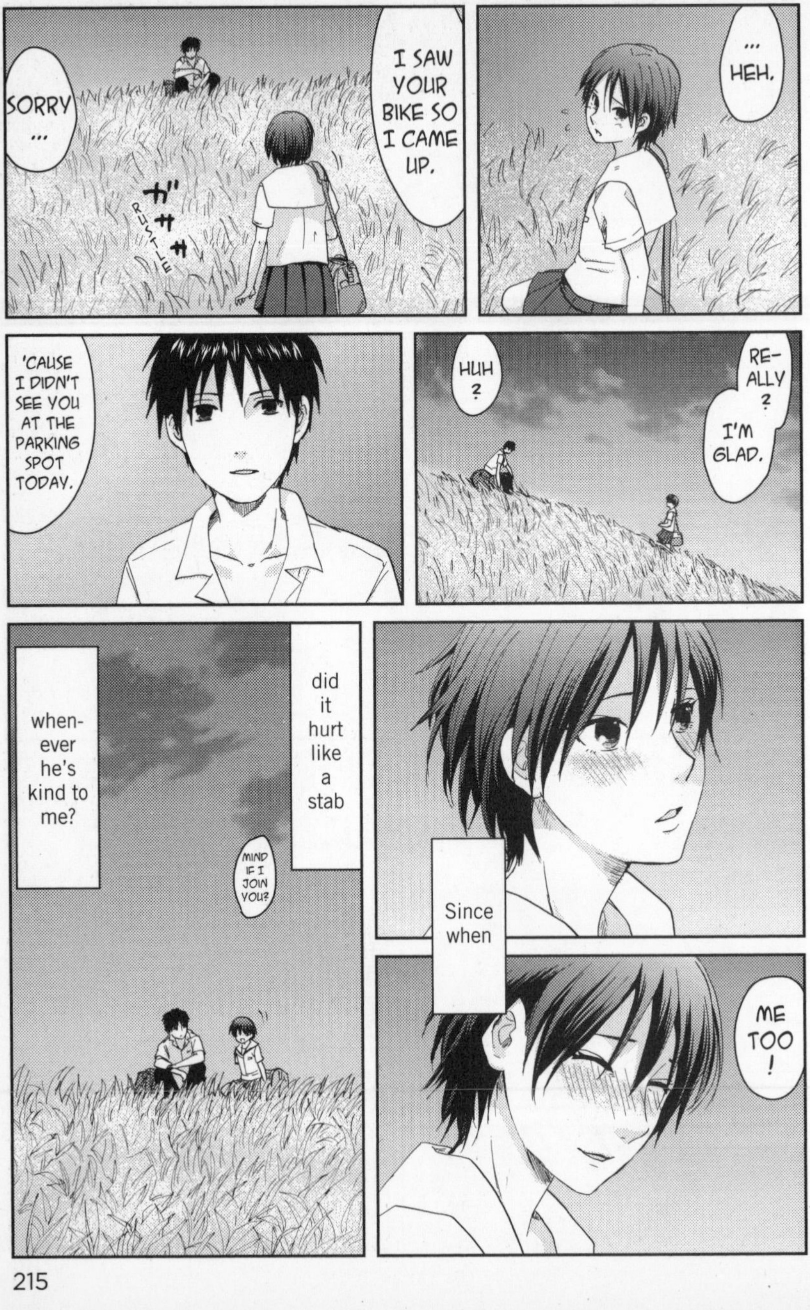

... HEH.
I SAW YOUR BIKE SO I CAME UP.
ガサササ
RUSTLE
SORRY ...
RE-ALLY? I'M GLAD.
HUH?
'CAUSE I DIDN'T SEE YOU AT THE PARKING SPOT TODAY.
Since when
ME TOO!
did it hurt like a stab
when-ever he's kind to me?
MIND IF I JOIN YOU?

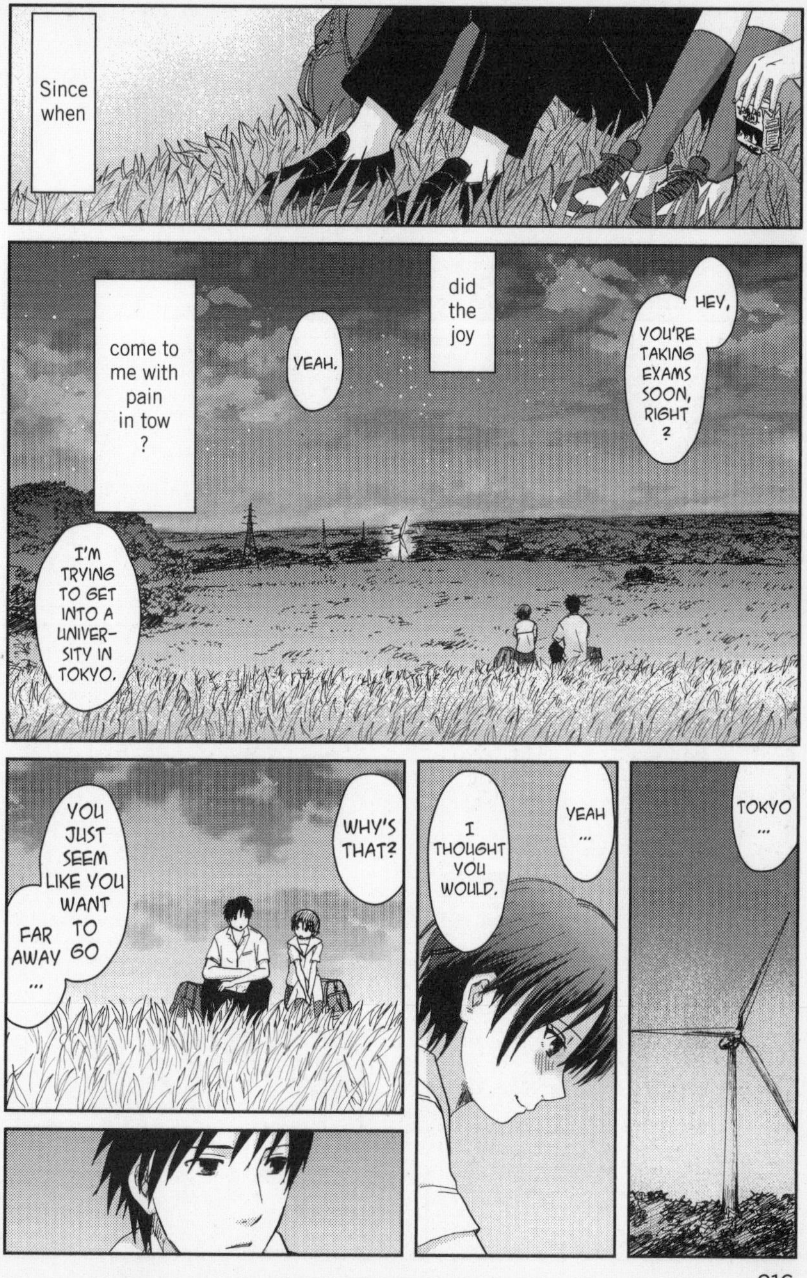
Since when
HEY, YOU'RE TAKING EXAMS SOON, RIGHT?
did the joy
YEAH.
come to me with pain in tow ?
I'M TRYING TO GET INTO A UNIVER-SITY IN TOKYO.
TOKYO ...
YEAH ...
I THOUGHT YOU WOULD.
WHY'S THAT?
YOU JUST SEEM LIKE YOU WANT TO GO
FAR AWAY ...

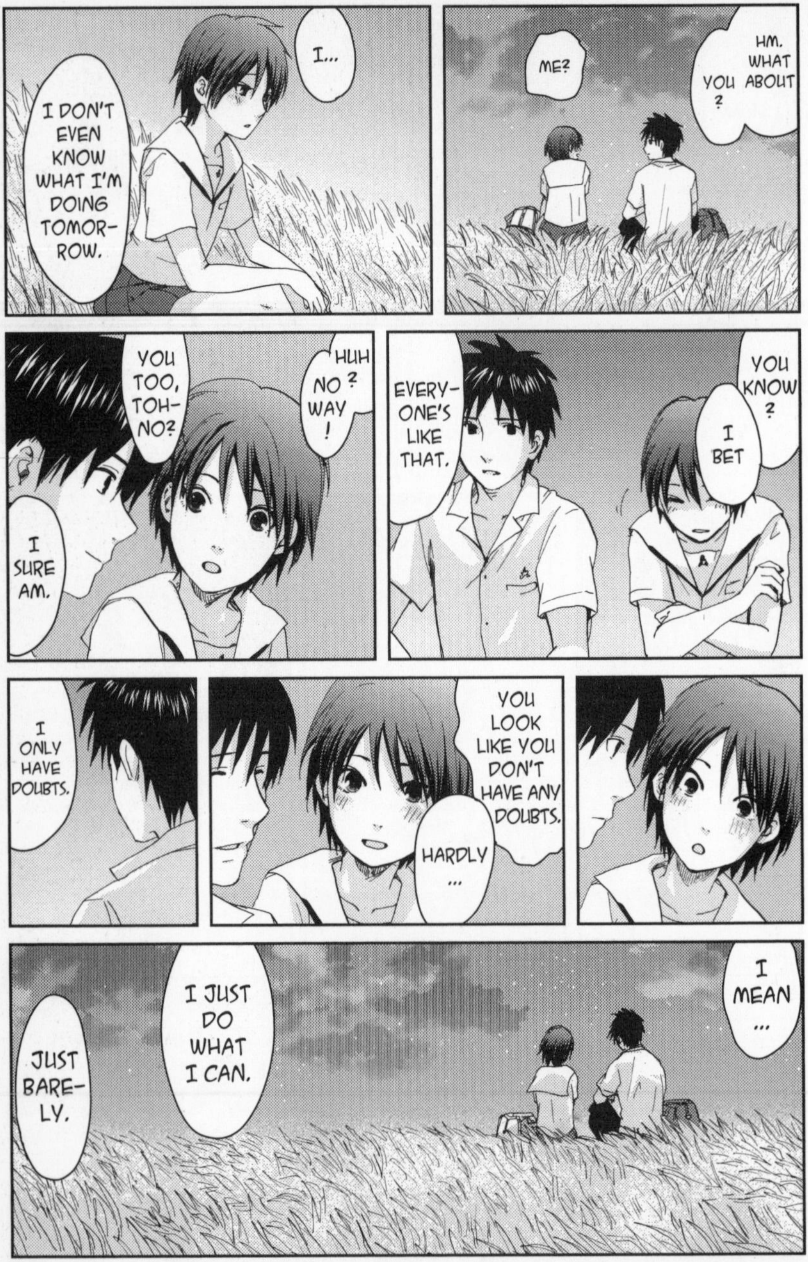
HM. WHAT ABOUT YOU?
ME?
I...
I DON'T EVEN KNOW WHAT I'M DOING TOMORROW.
YOU KNOW?
I BET
EVERYONE'S LIKE THAT.
HUH? NO WAY!
YOU TOO, TOHNO?
I SURE AM.
YOU LOOK LIKE YOU DON'T HAVE ANY DOUBTS.
HARDLY...
I ONLY HAVE DOUBTS.
I MEAN...
I JUST DO WHAT I CAN.
JUST BARELY.

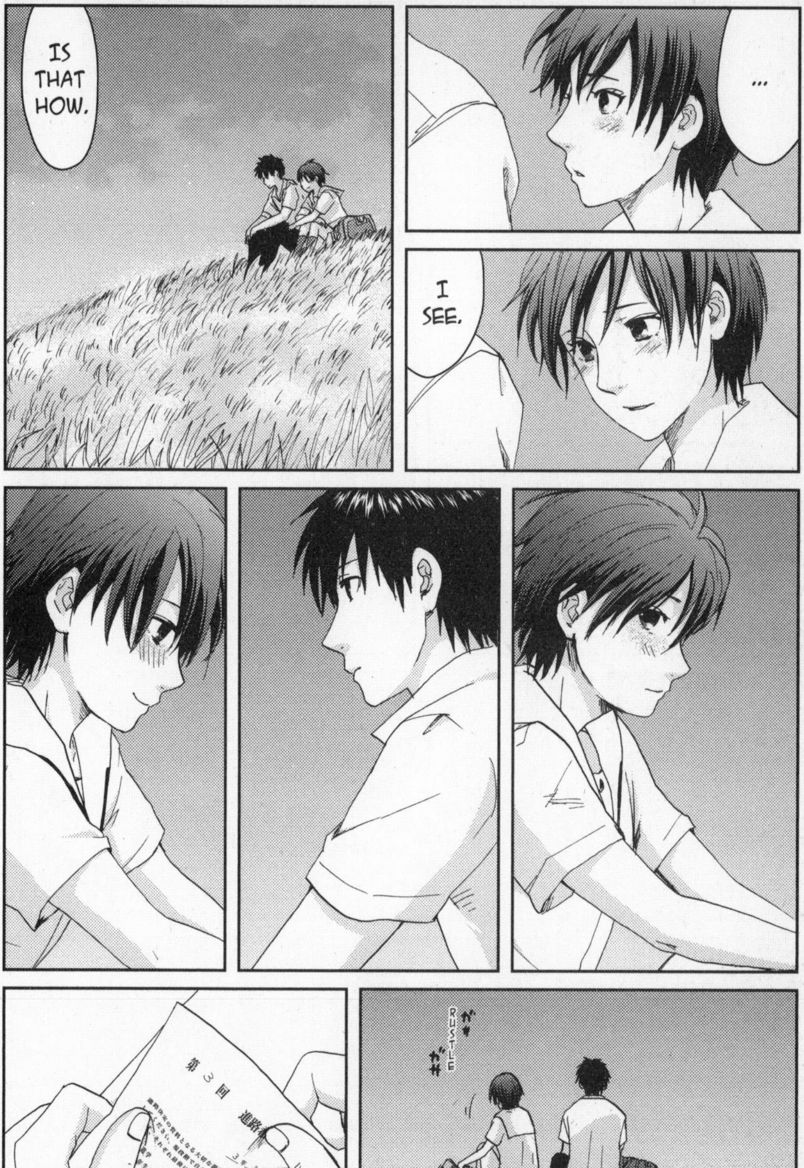
...
I SEE.
IS THAT HOW.
ガサ
ガサ
RUSTLE

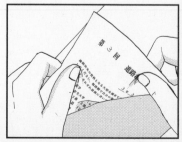

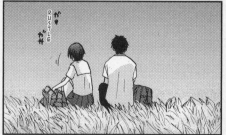

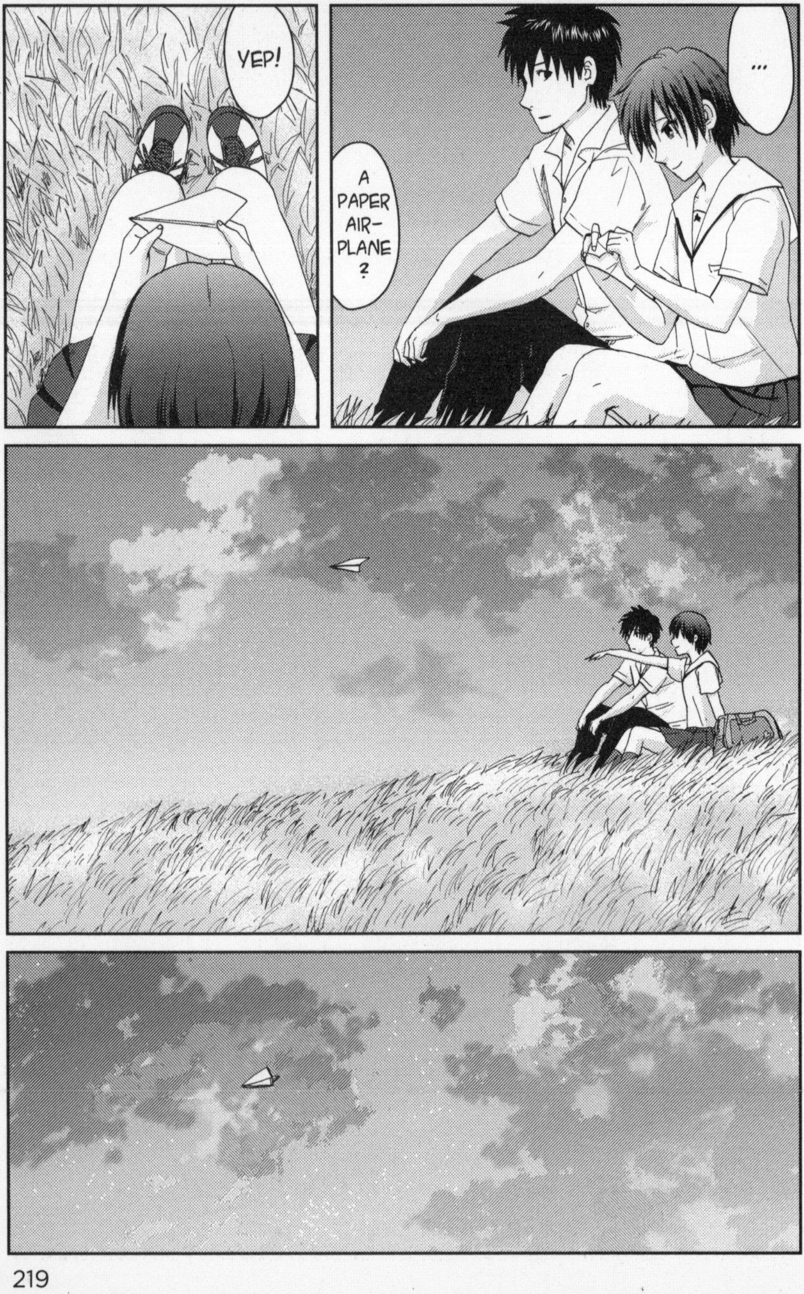
...
A PAPER AIR-PLANE?
YEP!

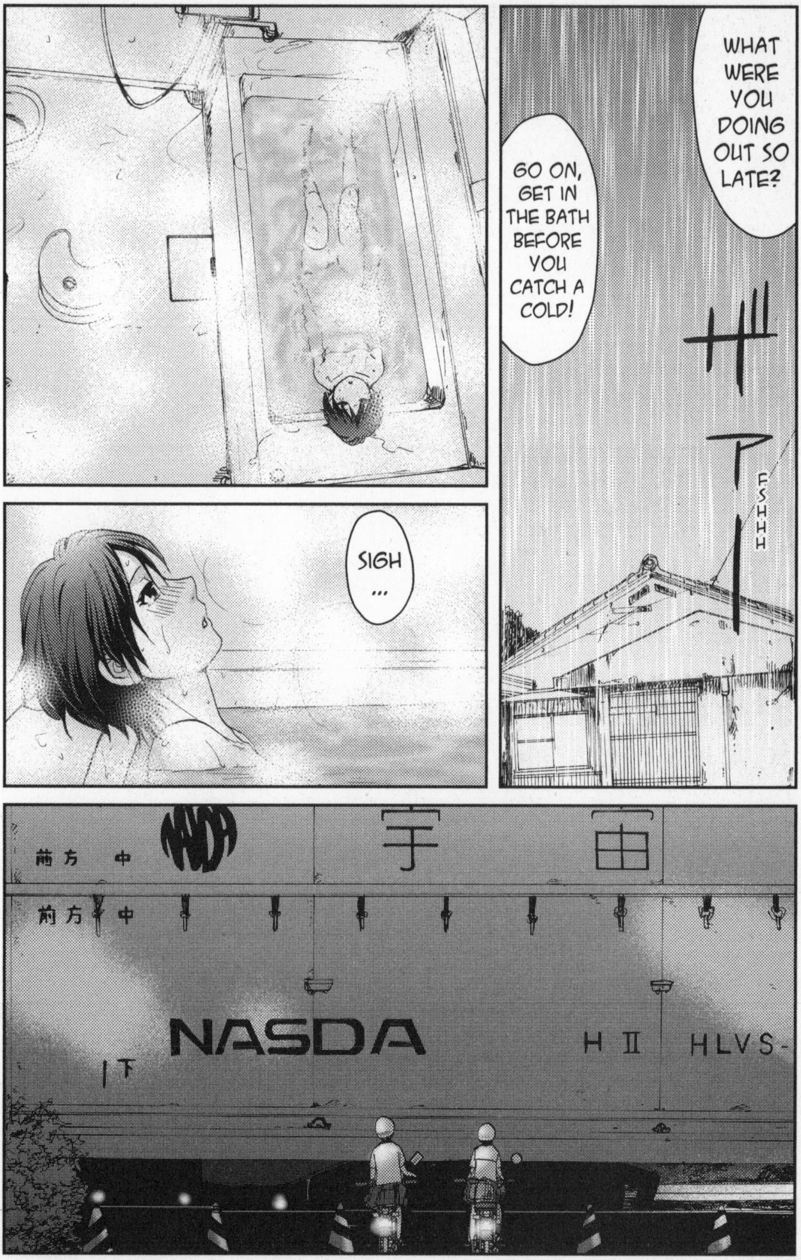

WHAT WERE YOU DOING OUT SO LATE?
GO ON, GET IN THE BATH BEFORE YOU CATCH A COLD!
ザァー
FSHHH
SIGH ...
前方 中
宇宙
前方 中
NASDA
H II
HLVS-

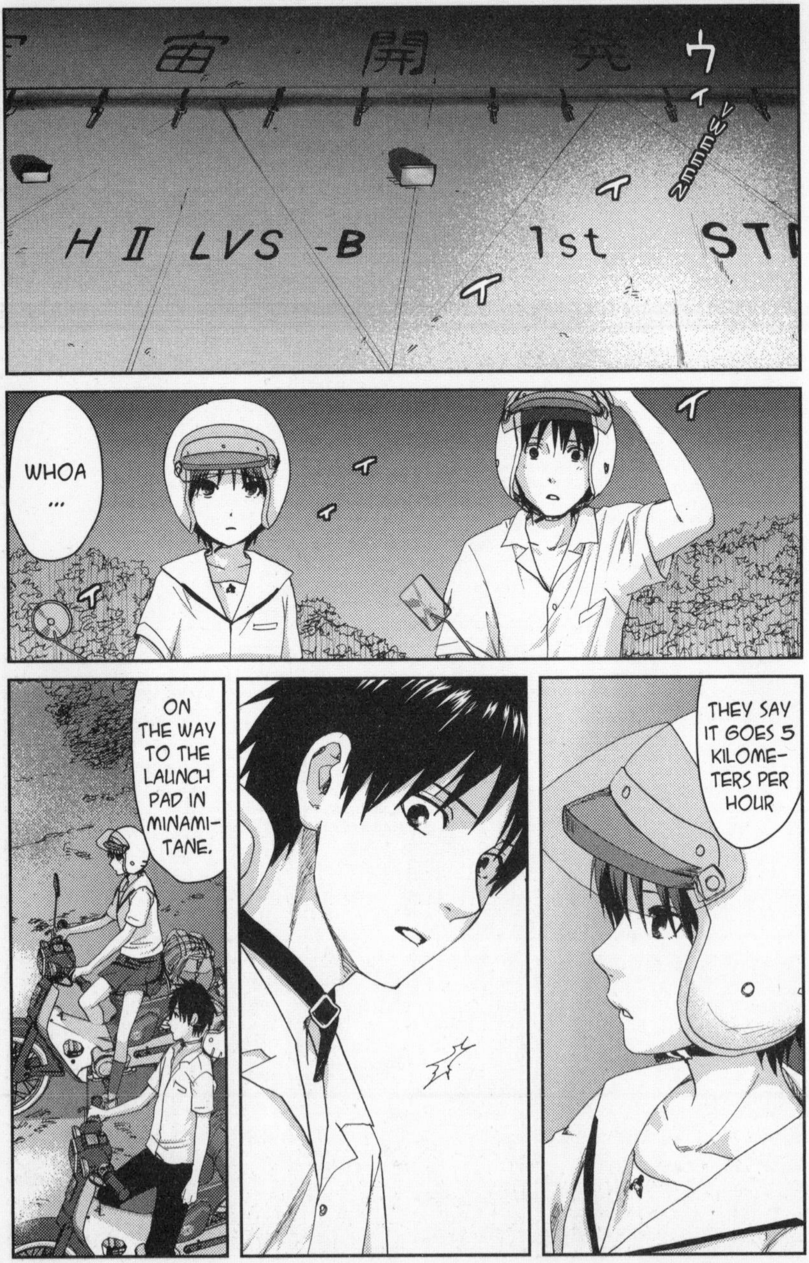
宙開発
ウィ
zmmmm
H II LVS -B 1st ST
WHOA ...
THEY SAY IT GOES 5 KILOME-TERS PER HOUR
ON THE WAY TO THE LAUNCH PAD IN MINAMI-TANE.

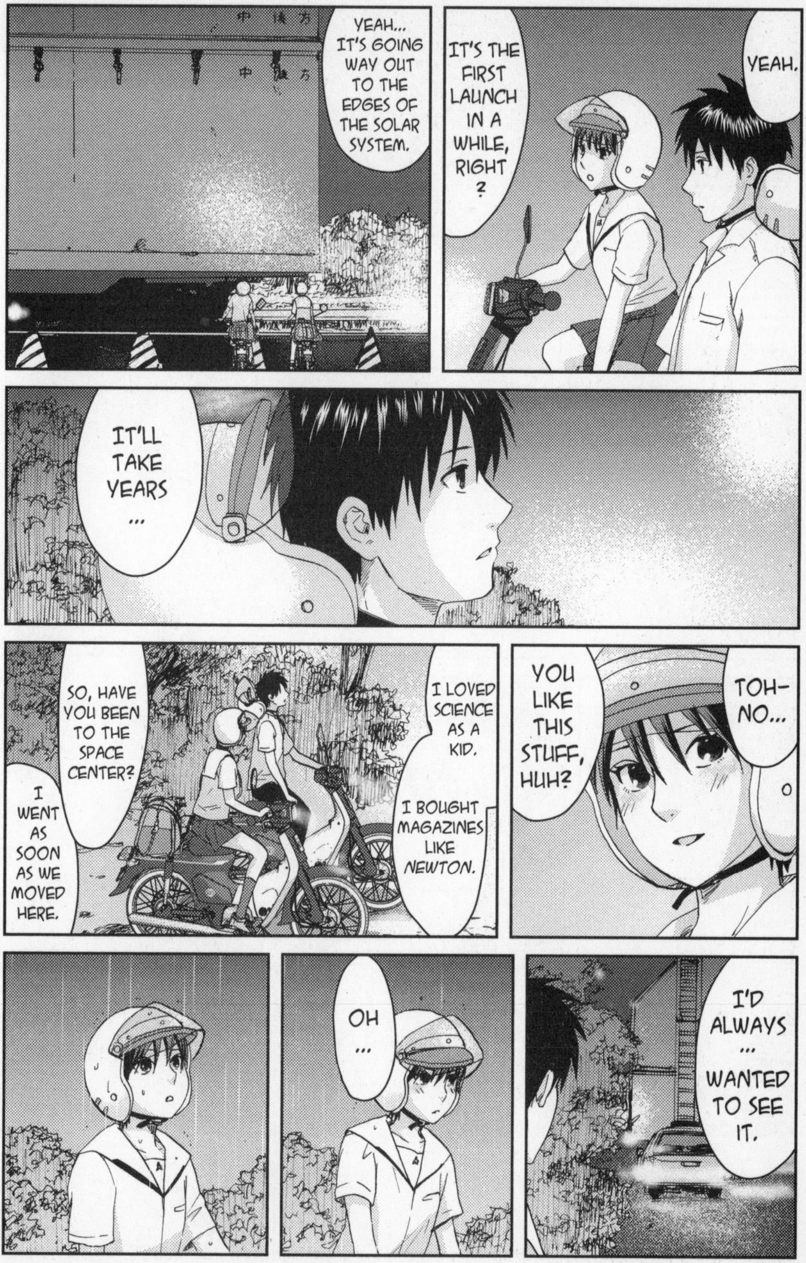
YEAH.
IT'S THE FIRST LAUNCH IN A WHILE, RIGHT?
YEAH... IT'S GOING WAY OUT TO THE EDGES OF THE SOLAR SYSTEM.
IT'LL TAKE YEARS...
TOH-NO...
YOU LIKE THIS STUFF, HUH?
I LOVED SCIENCE AS A KID.
I BOUGHT MAGAZINES LIKE NEWTON.
SO, HAVE YOU BEEN TO THE SPACE CENTER?
I WENT AS SOON AS WE MOVED HERE.
I'D ALWAYS... WANTED TO SEE IT.
OH...

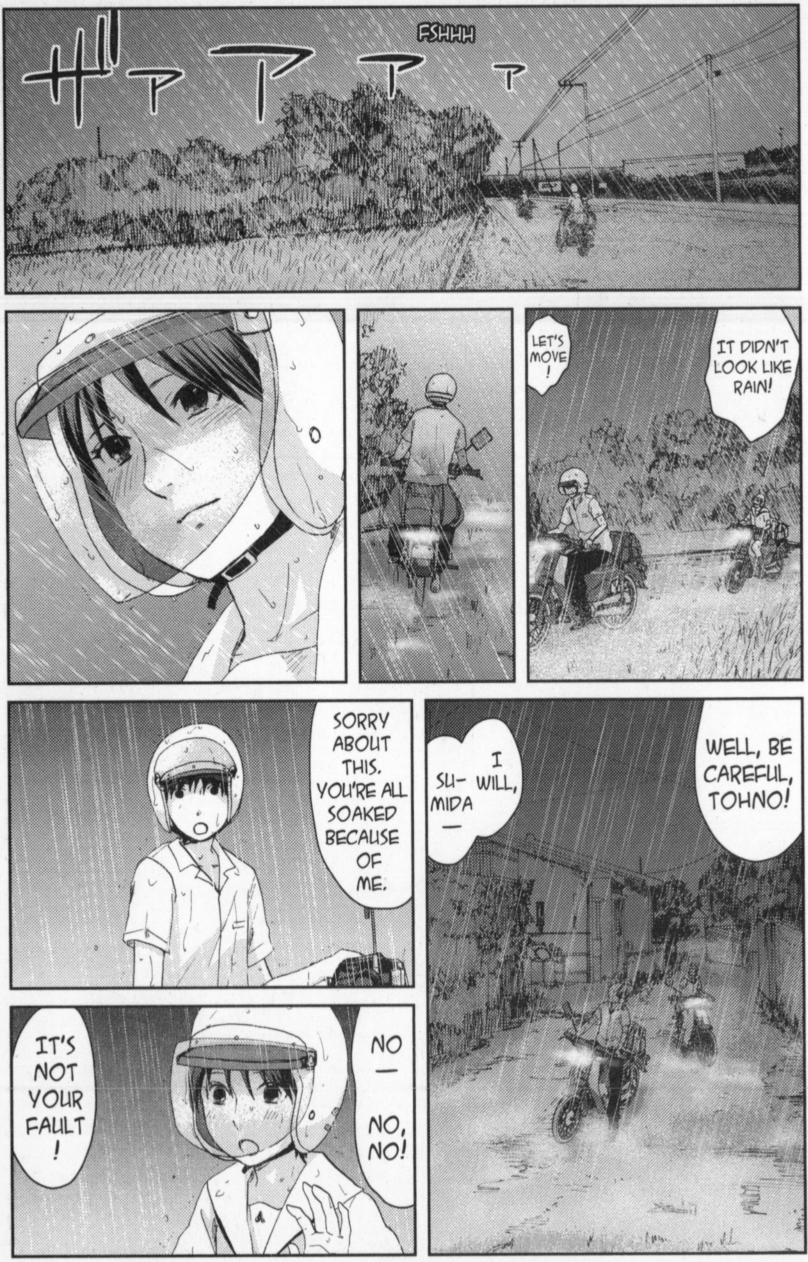
ザァアアァ
FSHHH
IT DIDN'T LOOK LIKE RAIN!
LET'S MOVE!
WELL, BE CAREFUL, TOHNO!
I WILL, SUMIDA—
SORRY ABOUT THIS. YOU'RE ALL SOAKED BECAUSE OF ME.
NO— NO, NO!
IT'S NOT YOUR FAULT!

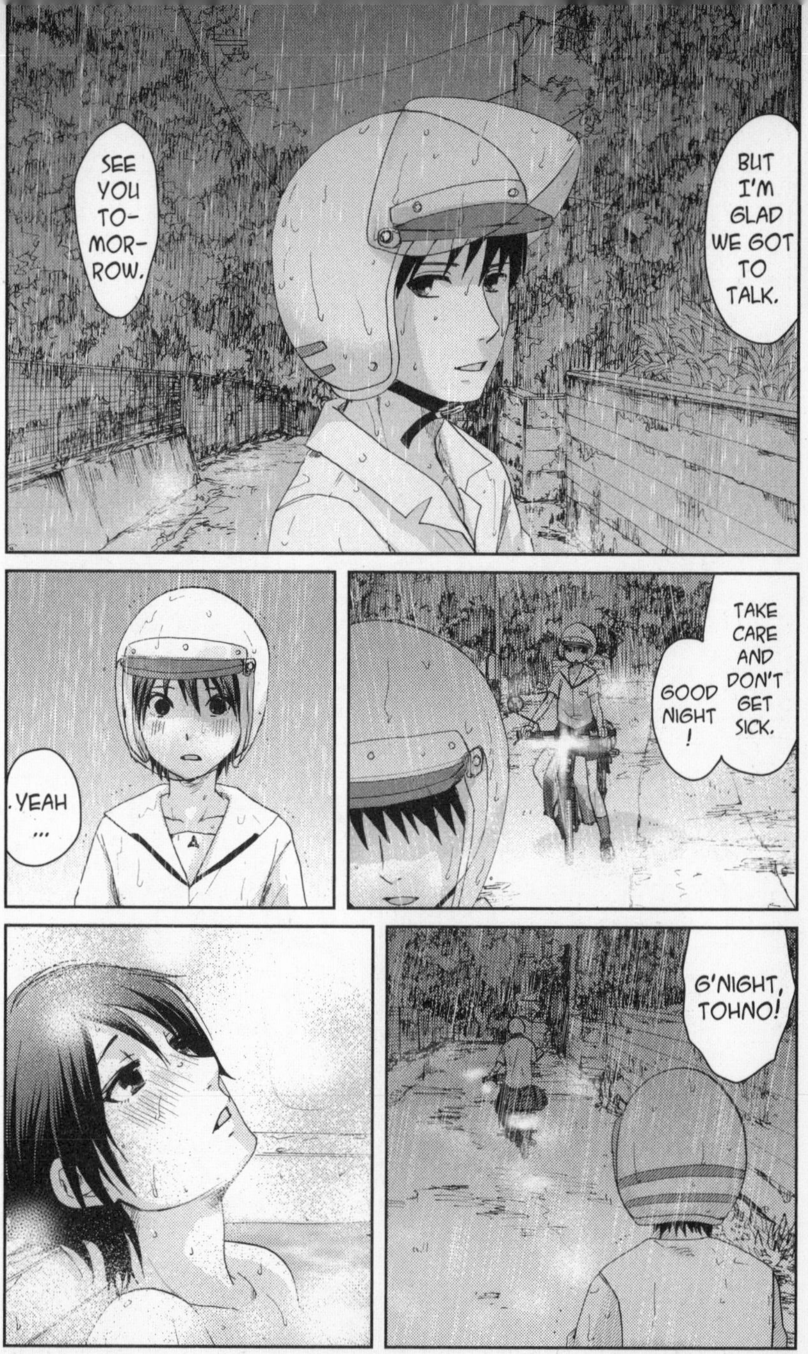
BUT I'M GLAD WE GOT TO TALK.
SEE YOU TO-MOR-ROW.
TAKE CARE AND DON'T GET SICK.
GOOD NIGHT!
. YEAH ...
G'NIGHT, TOHNO!

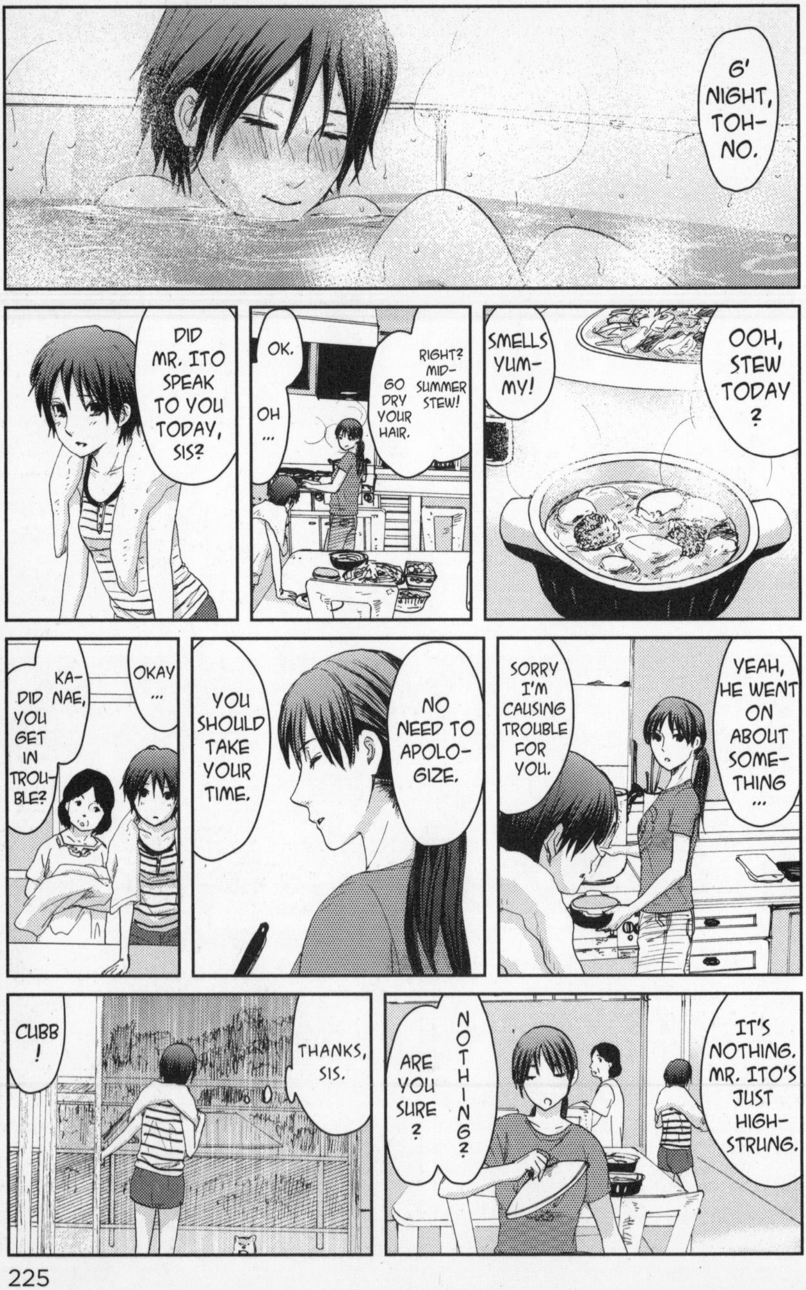
G' NIGHT, TOH-NO.
OOH, STEW TODAY ?
SMELLS YUM-MY!
RIGHT? MID-SUMMER STEW!
GO DRY YOUR HAIR.
OK.
OH ...
DID MR. ITO SPEAK TO YOU TODAY, SIS?
YEAH, HE WENT ON ABOUT SOME-THING ...
SORRY I'M CAUSING TROUBLE FOR YOU.
NO NEED TO APOLO-GIZE.
YOU SHOULD TAKE YOUR TIME.
OKAY ...
KA-NAE, DID YOU GET IN TROU-BLE?
IT'S NOTHING. MR. ITO'S JUST HIGH-STRUNG.
NOTHING?
ARE YOU SURE ?
THANKS, SIS.
CUBB !

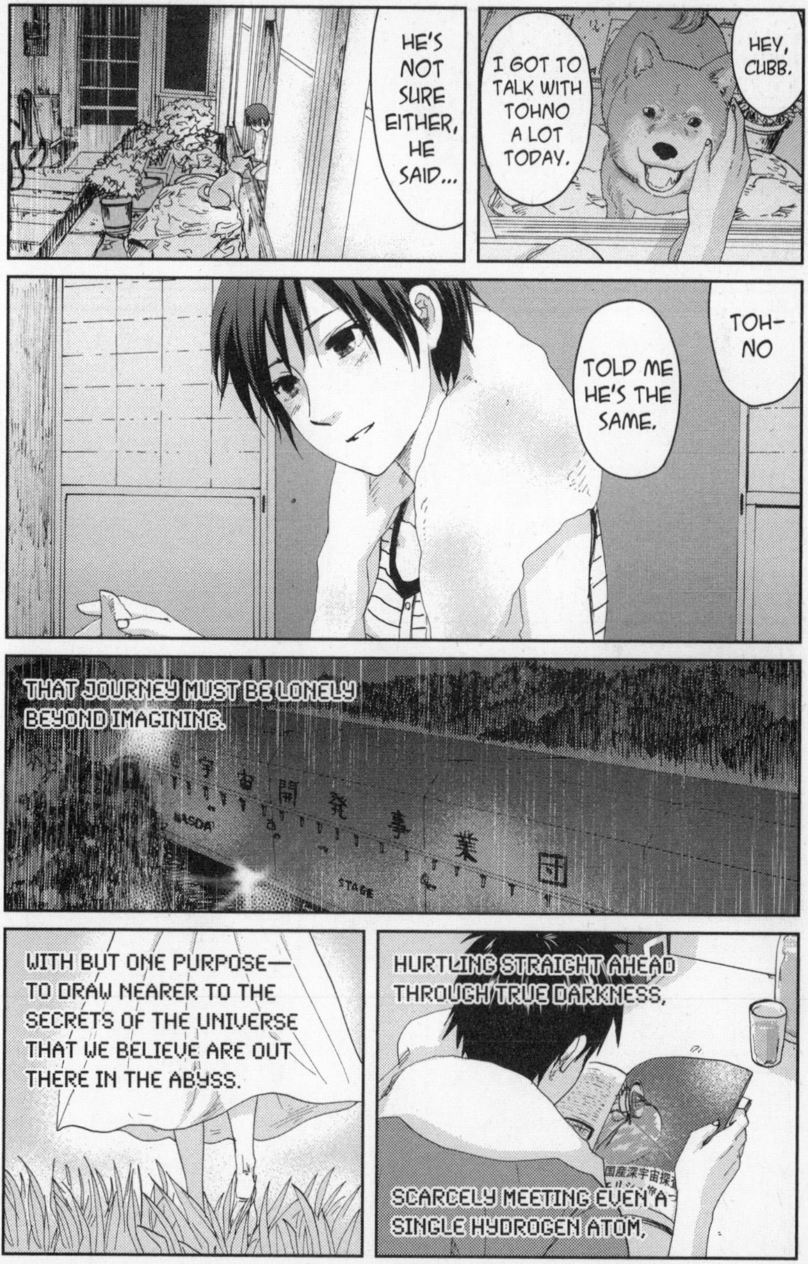
HEY, CUBB.
I GOT TO TALK WITH TOHNO A LOT TODAY.
HE'S NOT SURE EITHER, HE SAID...
TOH-NO
TOLD ME HE'S THE SAME.
THAT JOURNEY MUST BE LONELY BEYOND IMAGINING.
宇宙開発事業団
NASDA
STAGE
HURTLING STRAIGHT AHEAD THROUGH TRUE DARKNESS,
SCARCELY MEETING EVEN A SINGLE HYDROGEN ATOM,
WITH BUT ONE PURPOSE— TO DRAW NEARER TO THE SECRETS OF THE UNIVERSE THAT WE BELIEVE ARE OUT THERE IN THE ABYSS.

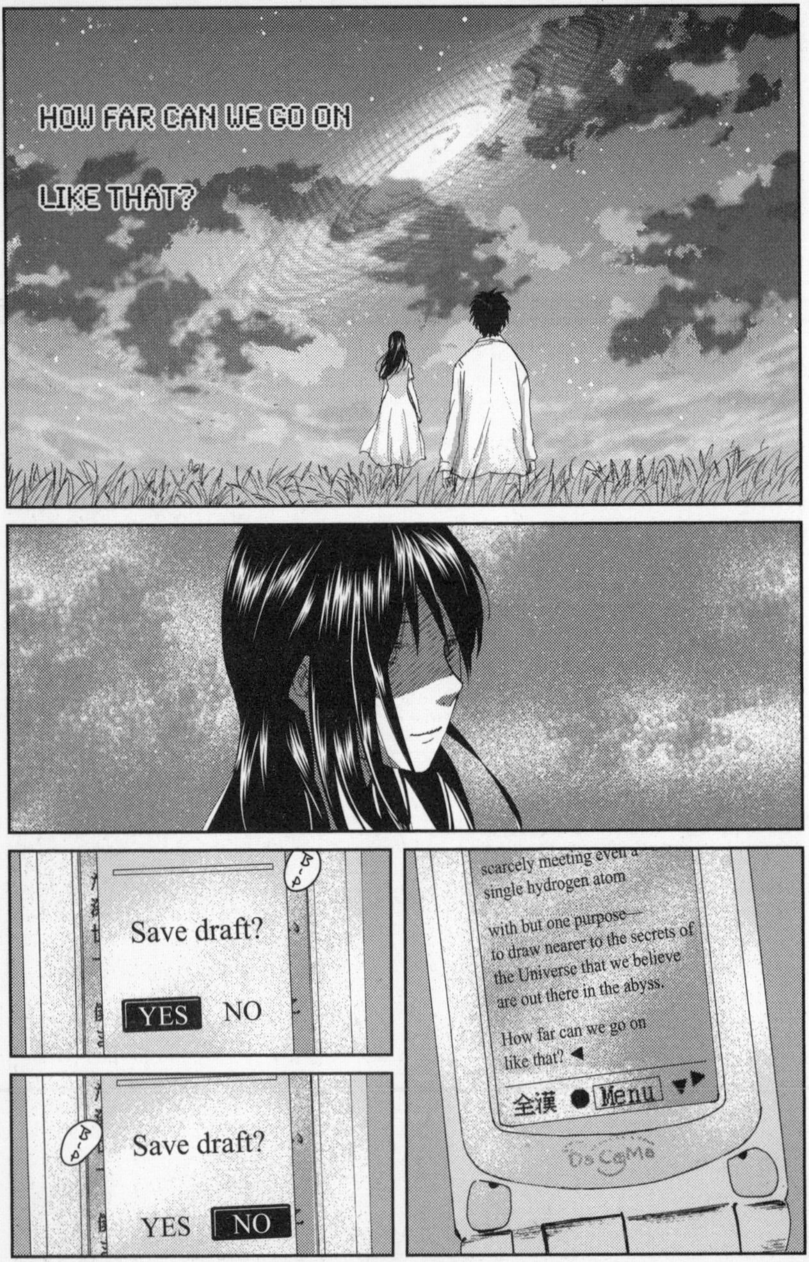
HOW FAR CAN WE GO ON
LIKE THAT?
scarcely meeting even a single hydrogen atom
with but one purpose—to draw nearer to the secrets of the Universe that we believe are out there in the abyss.
How far can we go on like that?
全漢
Menu
Save draft?
YES
NO
Save draft?
YES
NO

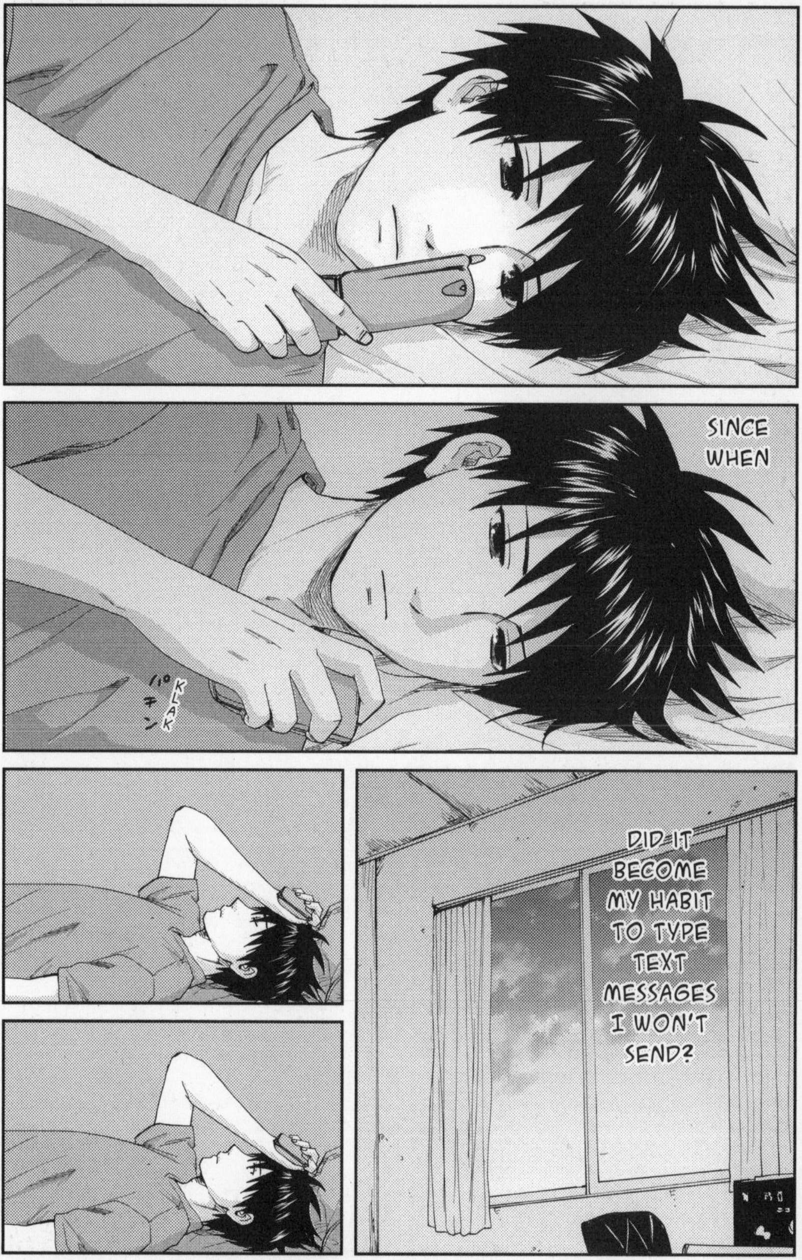
SINCE WHEN
KLAK
DID IT BECOME MY HABIT TO TYPE TEXT MESSAGES I WON'T SEND?

TOHNO
Mr. Takaki Tohno

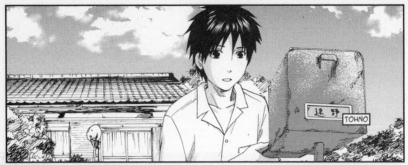

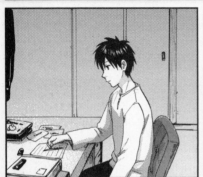

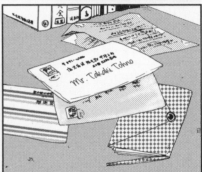

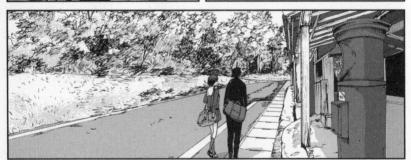

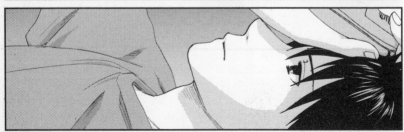

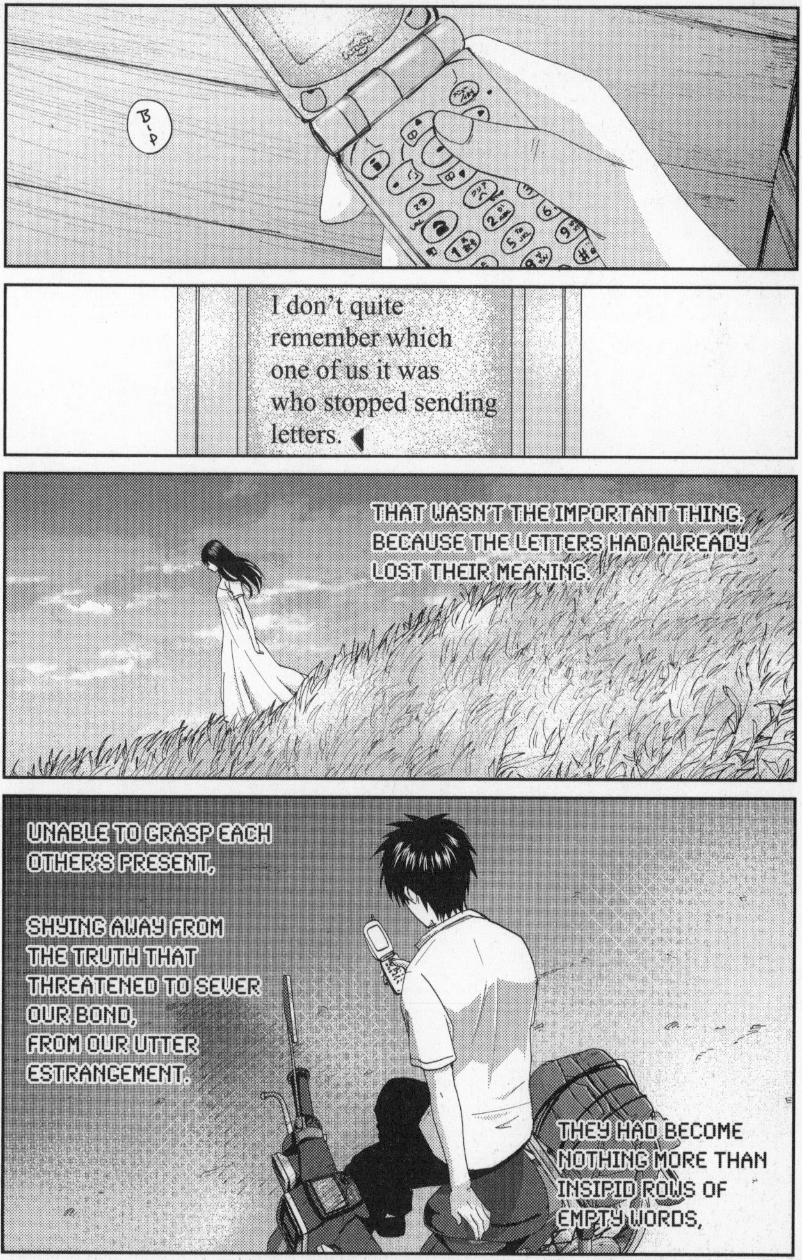

BIP
I don't quite remember which one of us it was who stopped sending letters.
THAT WASN'T THE IMPORTANT THING. BECAUSE THE LETTERS HAD ALREADY LOST THEIR MEANING.
UNABLE TO GRASP EACH OTHER'S PRESENT,
SHYING AWAY FROM THE TRUTH THAT THREATENED TO SEVER OUR BOND, FROM OUR UTTER ESTRANGEMENT.
THEY HAD BECOME NOTHING MORE THAN INSIPID ROWS OF EMPTY WORDS,

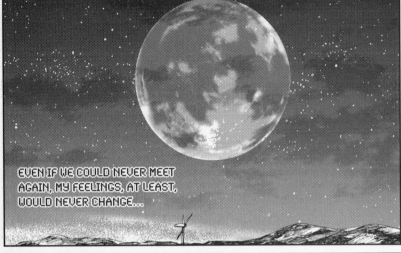

I THOUGHT WE WOULD ALWAYS BE TOGETHER—

EVEN IF WE COULD NEVER MEET AGAIN, MY FEELINGS, AT LEAST, WOULD NEVER CHANGE...

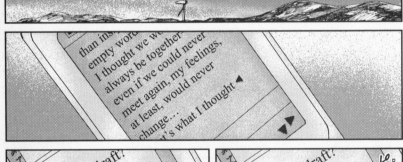

than ins...
empty word...
I thought we wo...
always be together
even if we could never
meet again, my feelings,
at least, would never
change...
...t's what I thought

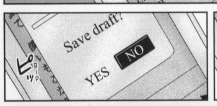

Save draft!

YES   NO

BIP

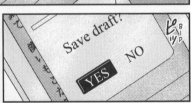

Save draft!

YES   NO

BIP

BIP

another side

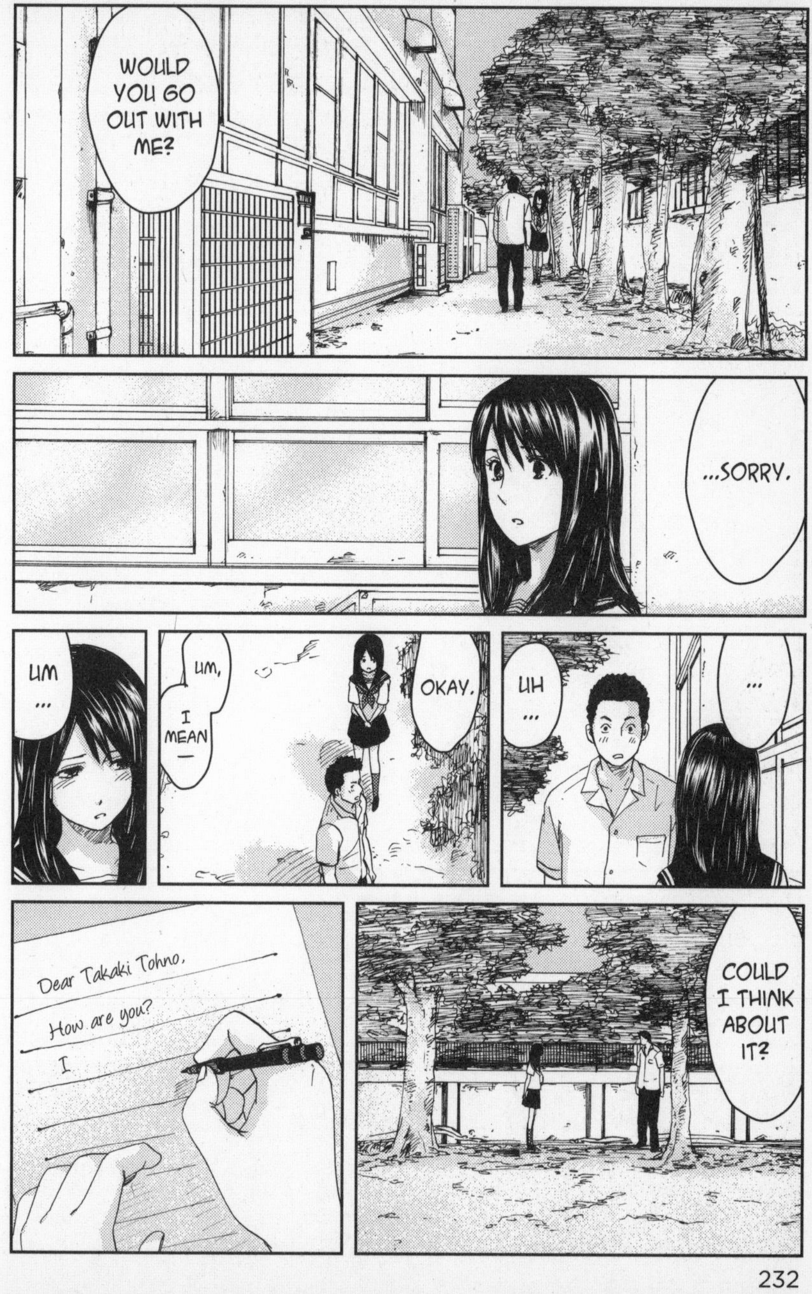
WOULD YOU GO OUT WITH ME?
...SORRY.
...
UH ...
OKAY.
UM, I MEAN —
UM ...
COULD I THINK ABOUT IT?
Dear Takaki Tohno,
How are you?
I

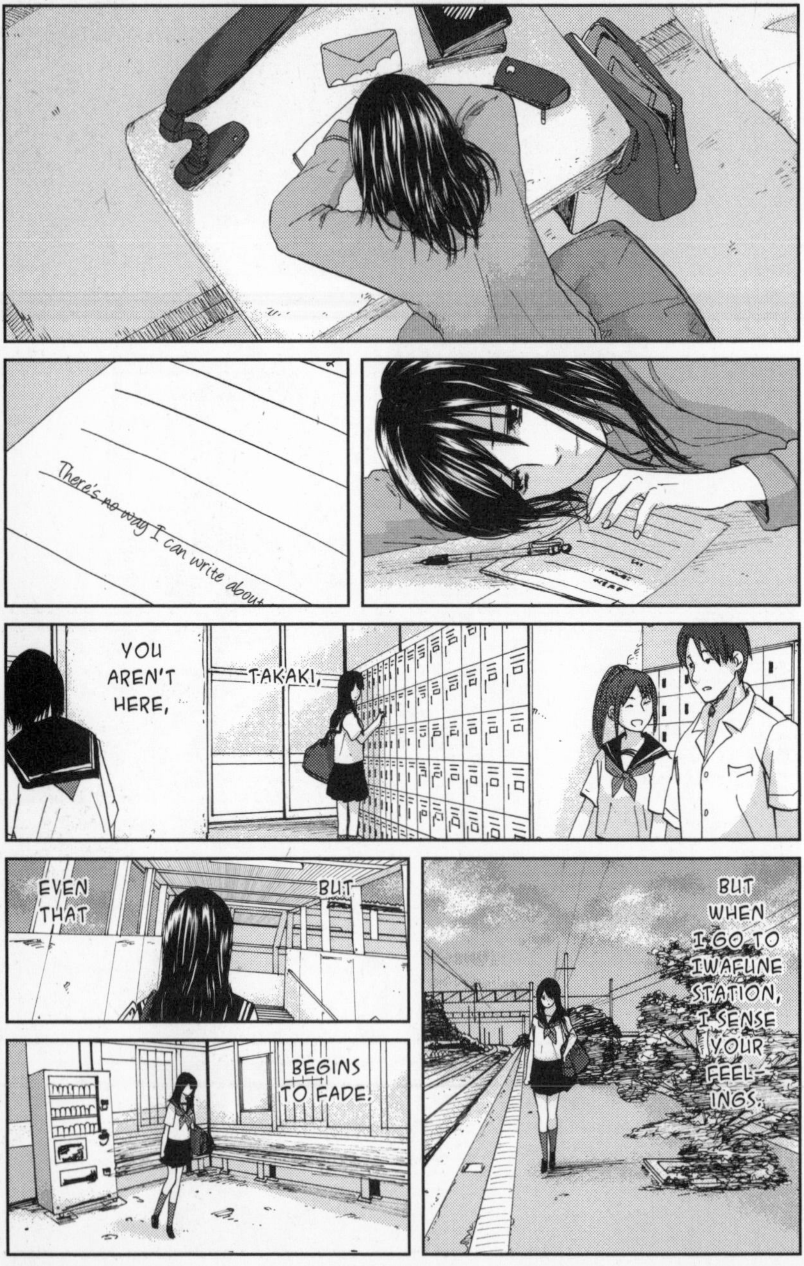
There's no way I can write about
TAKAKI,
YOU AREN'T HERE,
BUT WHEN I GO TO IWAFUNE STATION, I SENSE YOUR FEEL-INGS.
BUT
EVEN THAT
BEGINS TO FADE.

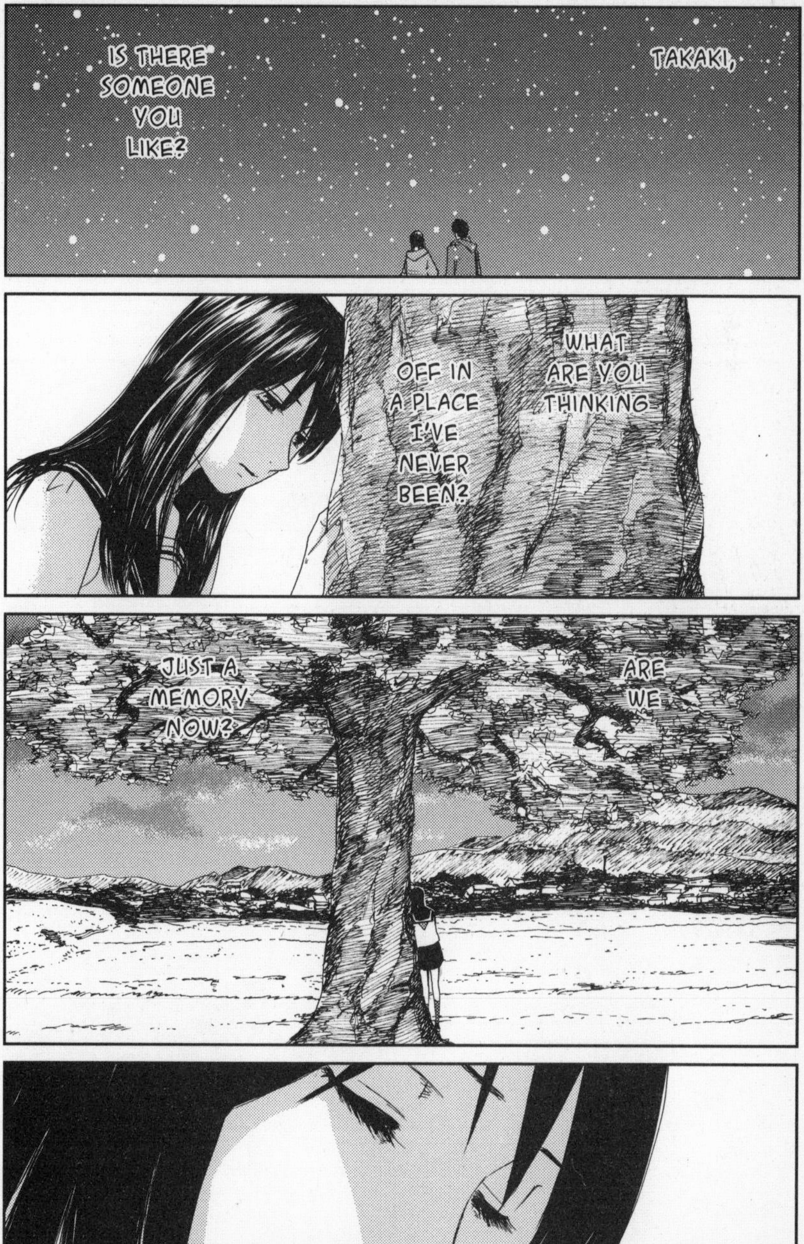
TAKAKI,
IS THERE SOMEONE YOU LIKE?
WHAT ARE YOU THINKING
OFF IN A PLACE I'VE NEVER BEEN?
ARE WE
JUST A MEMORY NOW?

Chapter 6 – "To Be Your Number One..."

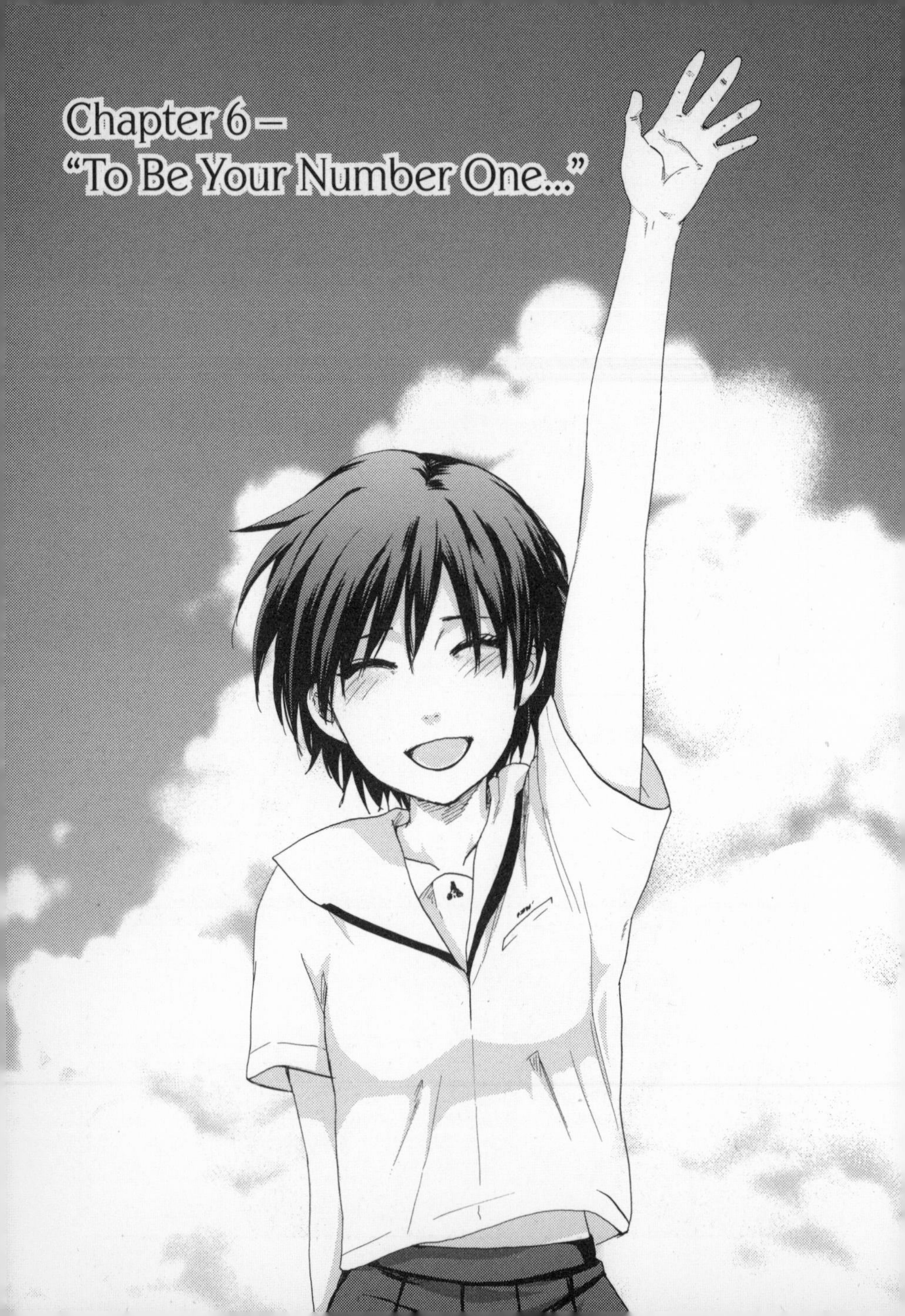

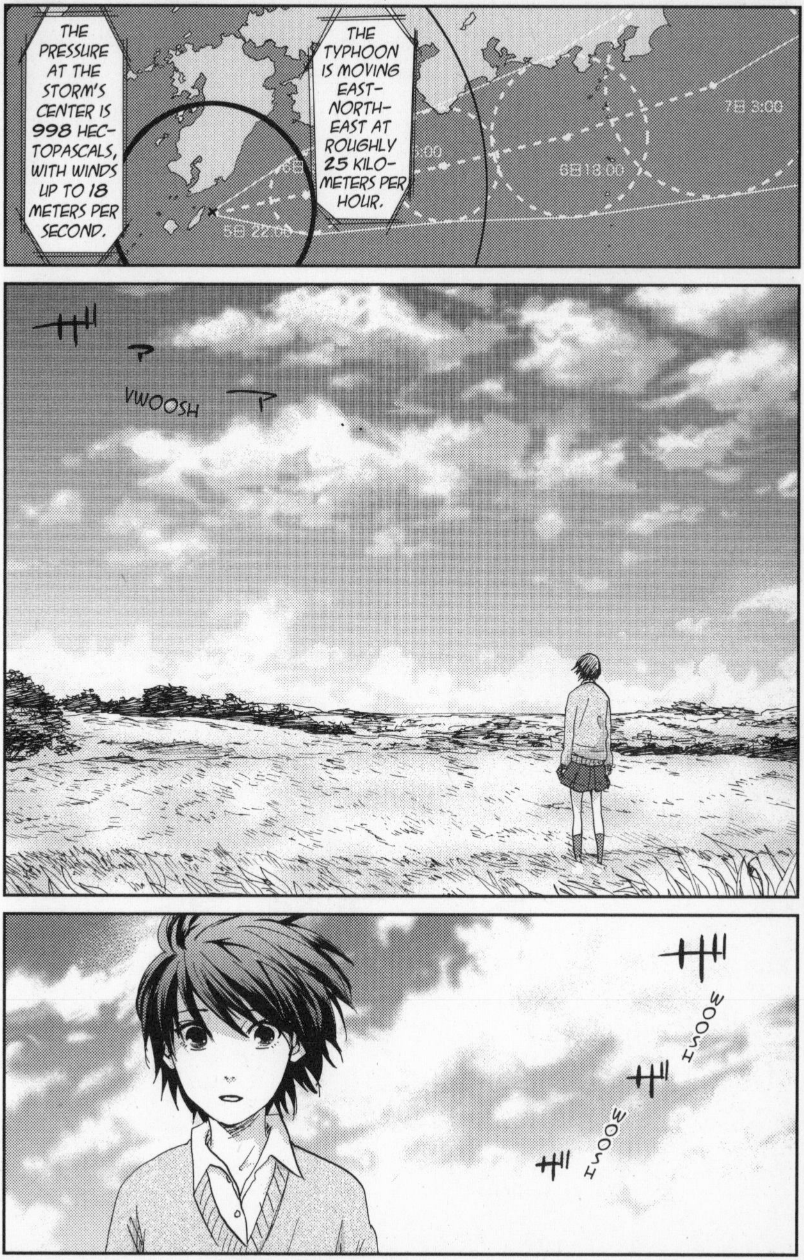
THE TYPHOON IS MOVING EAST-NORTH-EAST AT ROUGHLY 25 KILOMETERS PER HOUR.
THE PRESSURE AT THE STORM'S CENTER IS 998 HECTOPASCALS, WITH WINDS UP TO 18 METERS PER SECOND.
7日 3:00
6日 18:00
5日 22:00
VWOOSH
WOOSH
WOOSH

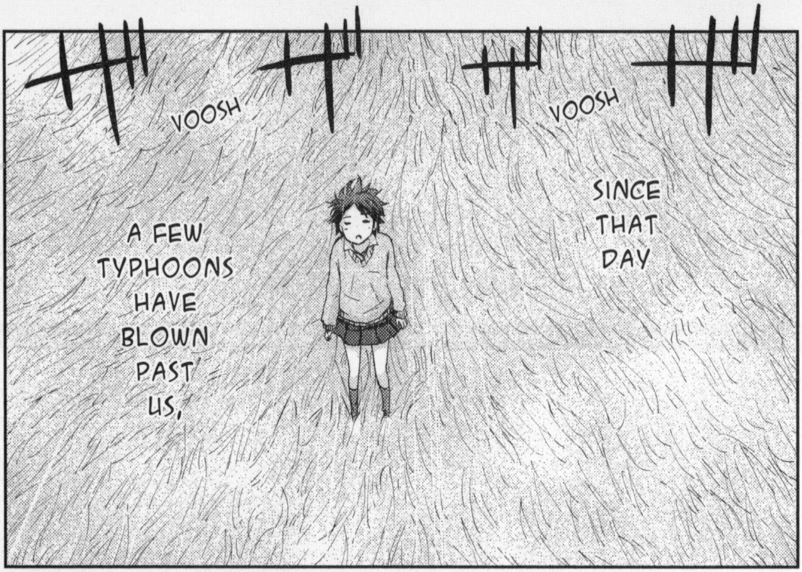
VOOSH
VOOSH
SINCE THAT DAY
A FEW TYPHOONS HAVE BLOWN PAST US,

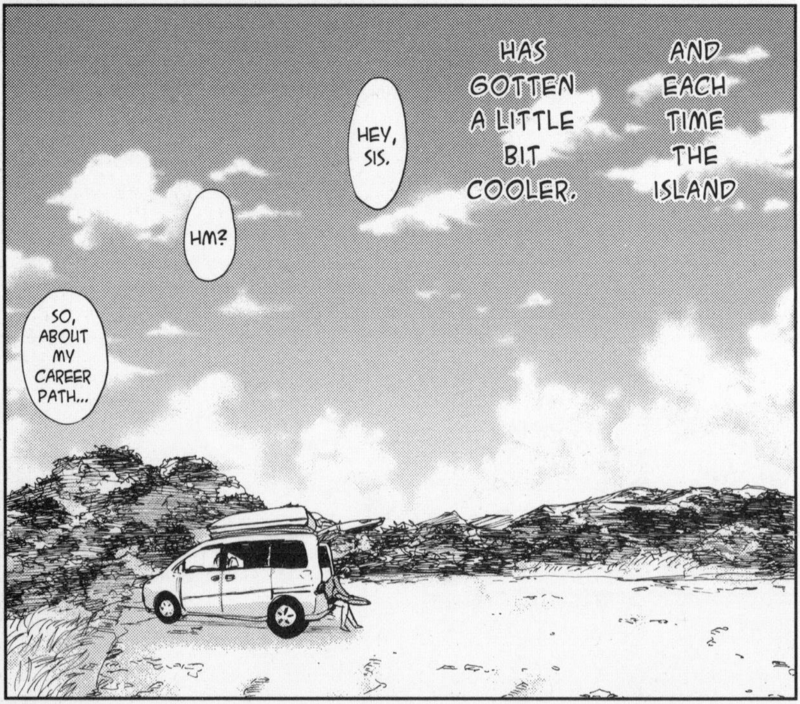
AND EACH TIME THE ISLAND
HAS GOTTEN A LITTLE BIT COOLER.
HEY, SIS.
HM?
SO, ABOUT MY CAREER PATH...

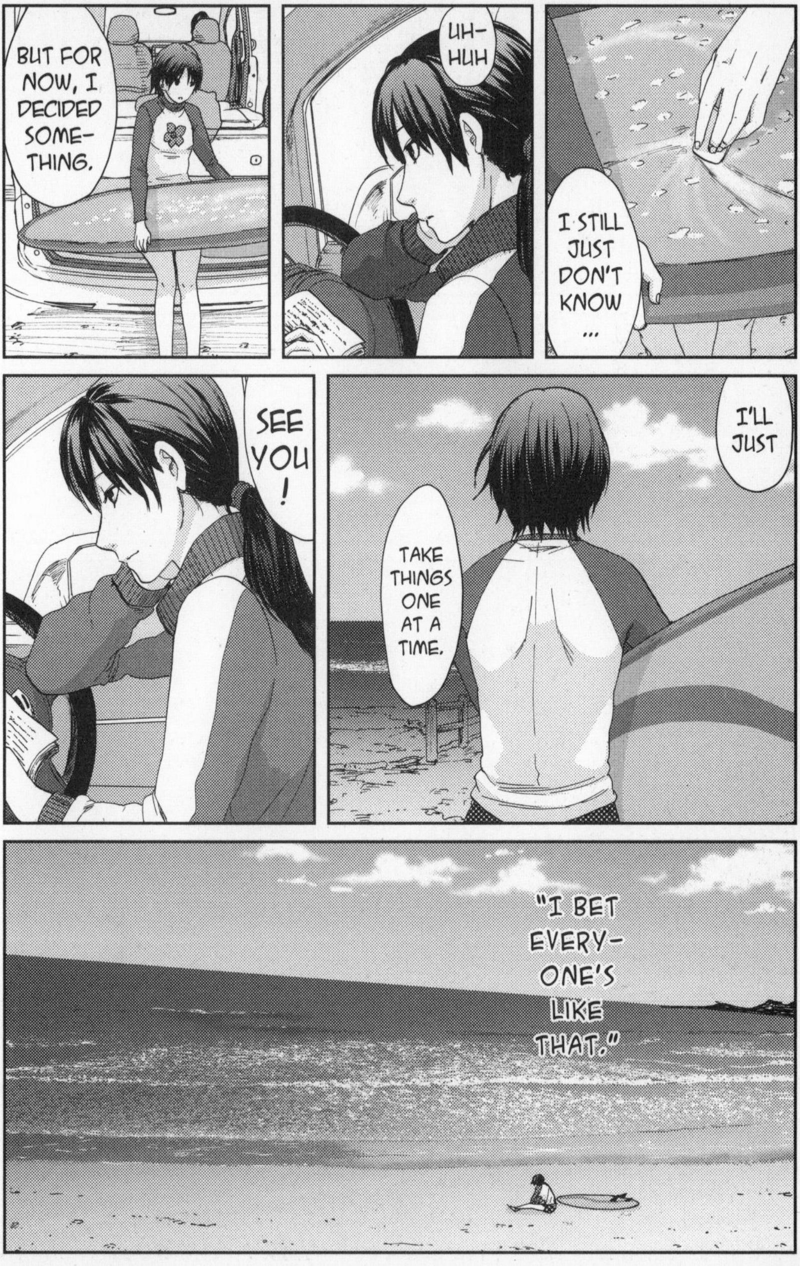
I STILL JUST DON'T KNOW ...
UH-HUH
BUT FOR NOW, I DECIDED SOMETHING.
I'LL JUST
TAKE THINGS ONE AT A TIME.
SEE YOU!
"I BET EVERYONE'S LIKE THAT."

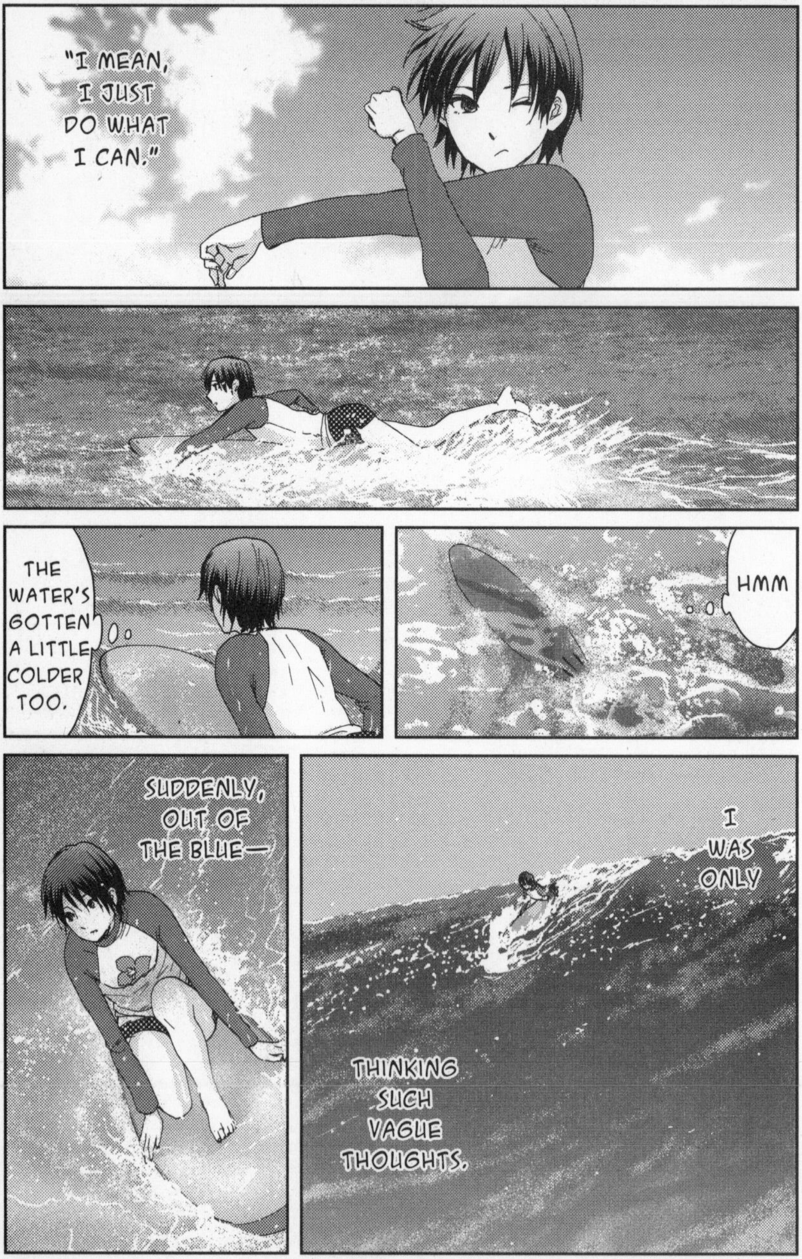
"I MEAN, I JUST DO WHAT I CAN."
HMM
THE WATER'S GOTTEN A LITTLE COLDER TOO.
I WAS ONLY
THINKING SUCH VAGUE THOUGHTS.
SUDDENLY, OUT OF THE BLUE—

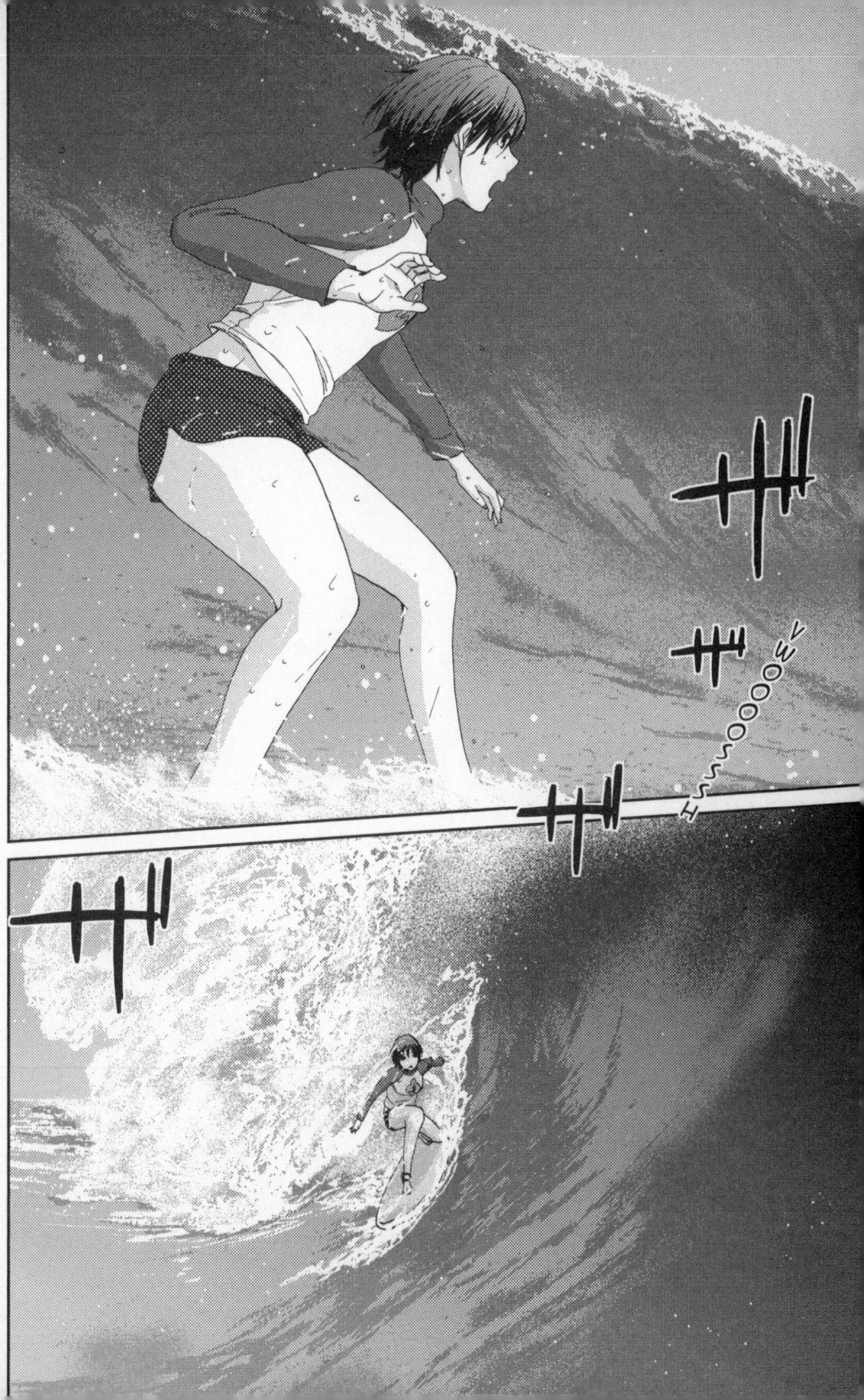

ザザ
ザザ
VWOOOOOOMMMH
ザザ
ザザ

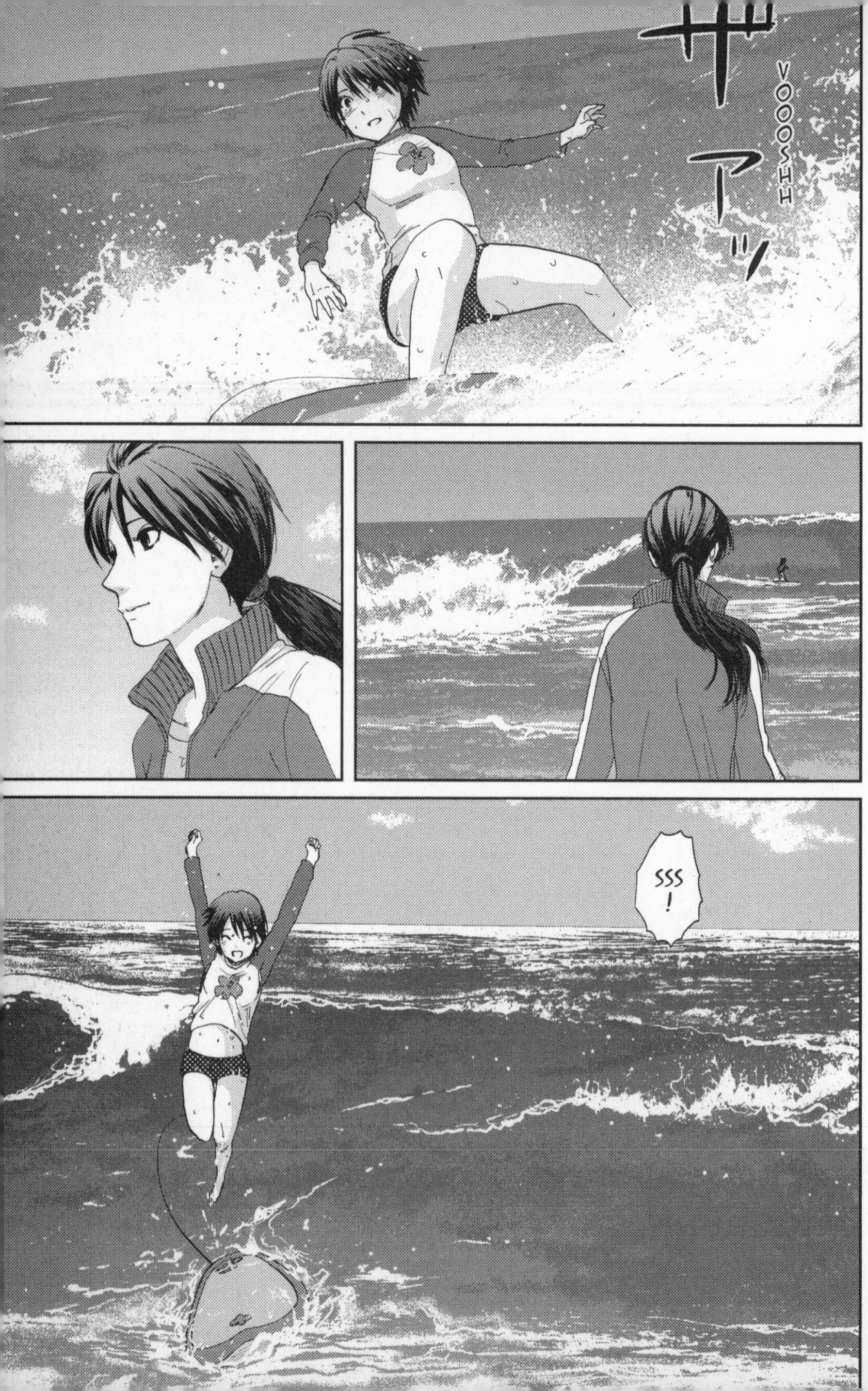
ザアッ
VOOOSHH
SSS!

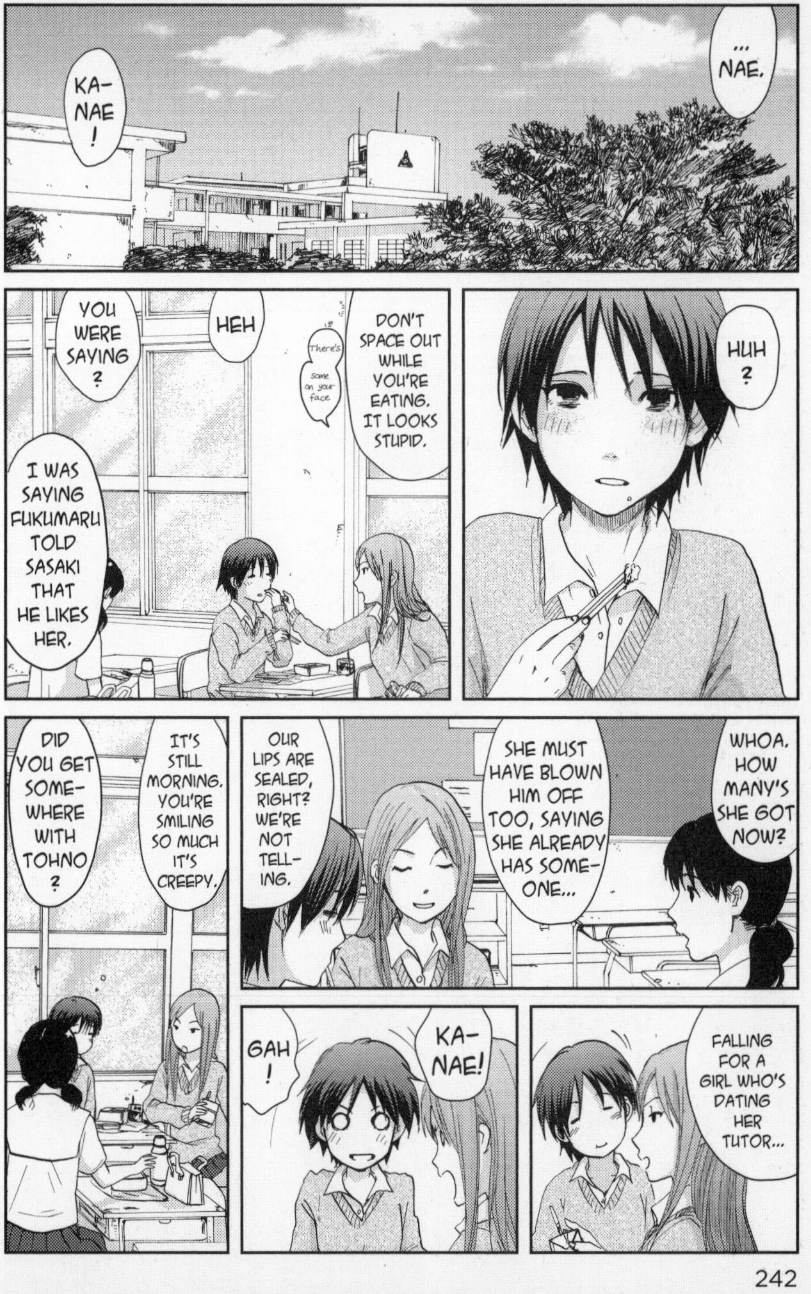
... NAE.
KA-NAE!
HUH?
DON'T SPACE OUT WHILE YOU'RE EATING. IT LOOKS STUPID.
There's some on your face
HEH
YOU WERE SAYING?
I WAS SAYING FUKUMARU TOLD SASAKI THAT HE LIKES HER.
WHOA. HOW MANY'S SHE GOT NOW?
SHE MUST HAVE BLOWN HIM OFF TOO, SAYING SHE ALREADY HAS SOME-ONE...
OUR LIPS ARE SEALED, RIGHT? WE'RE NOT TELL-ING.
FALLING FOR A GIRL WHO'S DATING HER TUTOR...
KA-NAE!
GAH!
IT'S STILL MORNING. YOU'RE SMILING SO MUCH IT'S CREEPY.
DID YOU GET SOME-WHERE WITH TOHNO?

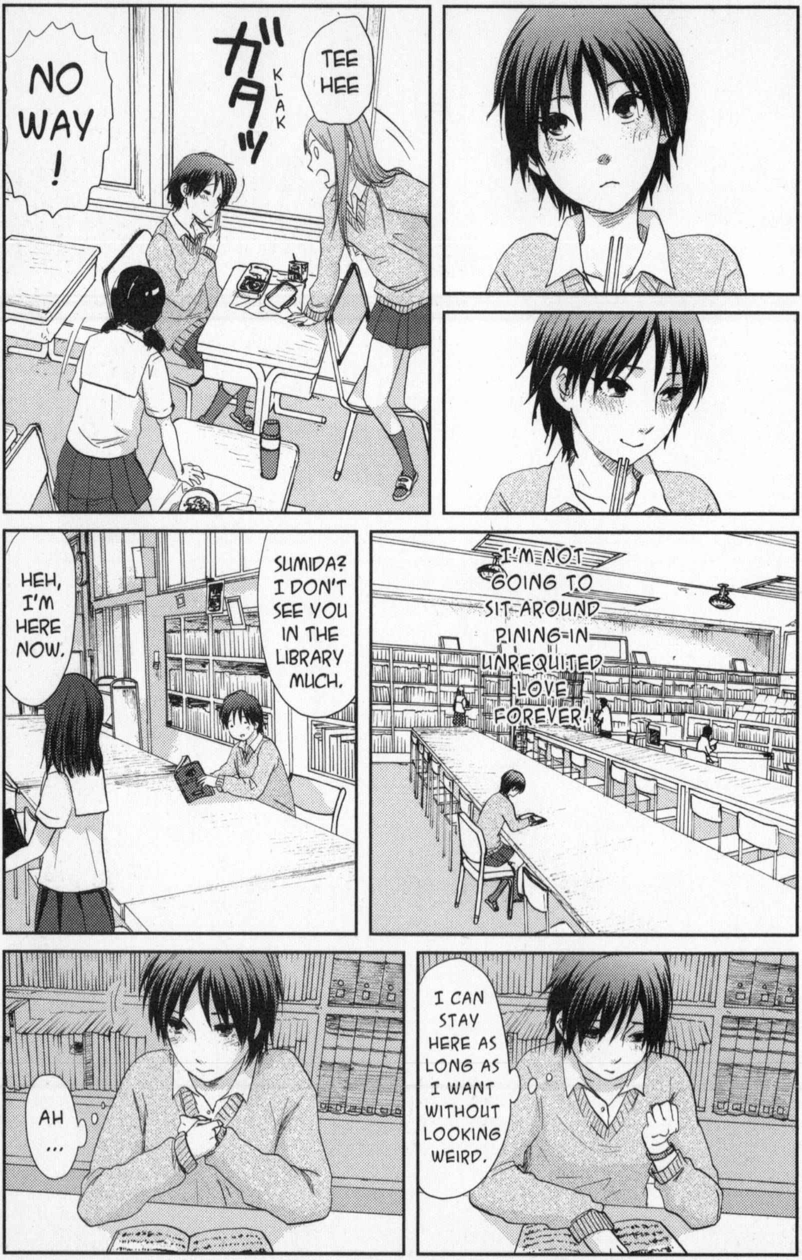
TEE HEE
ガタッ
KLAK
NO WAY!
I'M NOT GOING TO SIT AROUND PINING IN UNREQUITED LOVE FOREVER!
SUMIDA? I DON'T SEE YOU IN THE LIBRARY MUCH.
HEH, I'M HERE NOW.
I CAN STAY HERE AS LONG AS I WANT WITHOUT LOOKING WEIRD.
AH ...

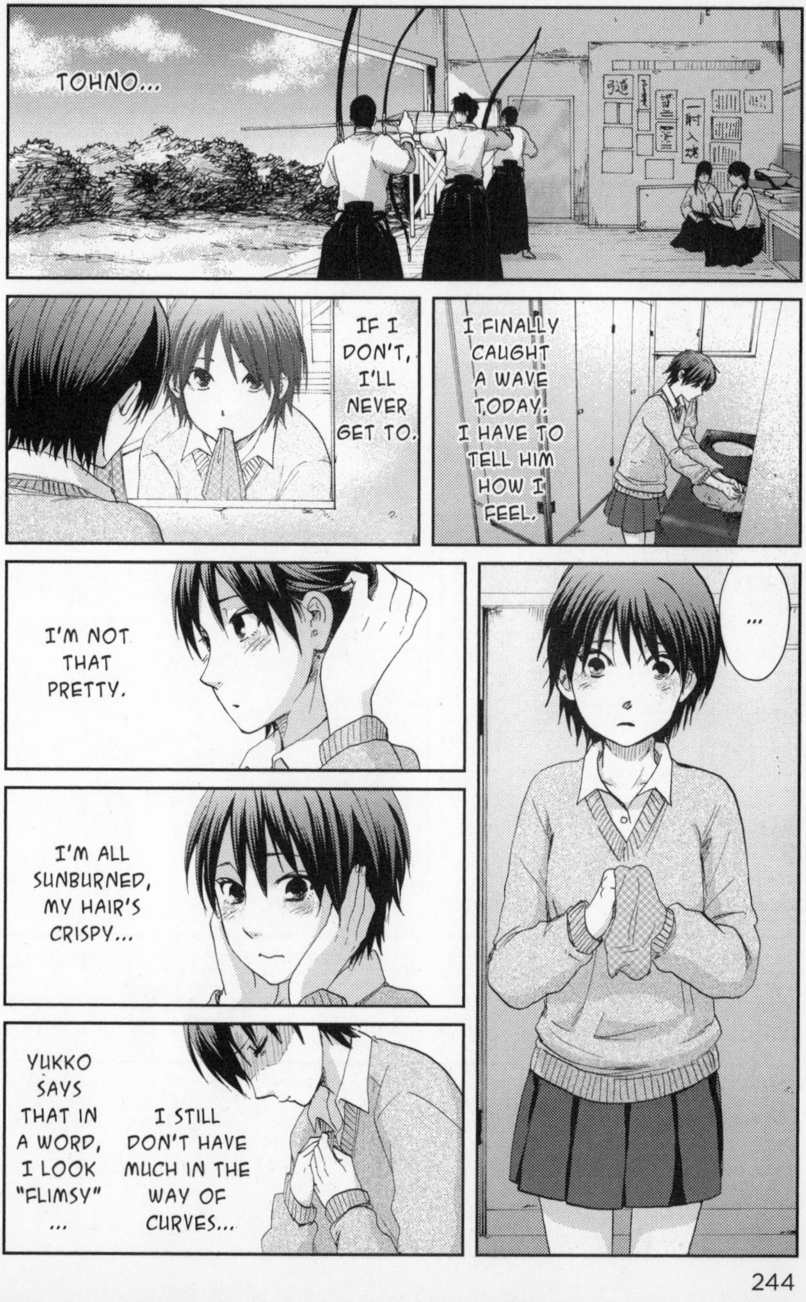

TOHNO...
I FINALLY CAUGHT A WAVE TODAY. I HAVE TO TELL HIM HOW I FEEL.
IF I DON'T, I'LL NEVER GET TO.
...
I'M NOT THAT PRETTY.
I'M ALL SUNBURNED, MY HAIR'S CRISPY...
I STILL DON'T HAVE MUCH IN THE WAY OF CURVES...
YUKKO SAYS THAT IN A WORD, I LOOK "FLIMSY" ...

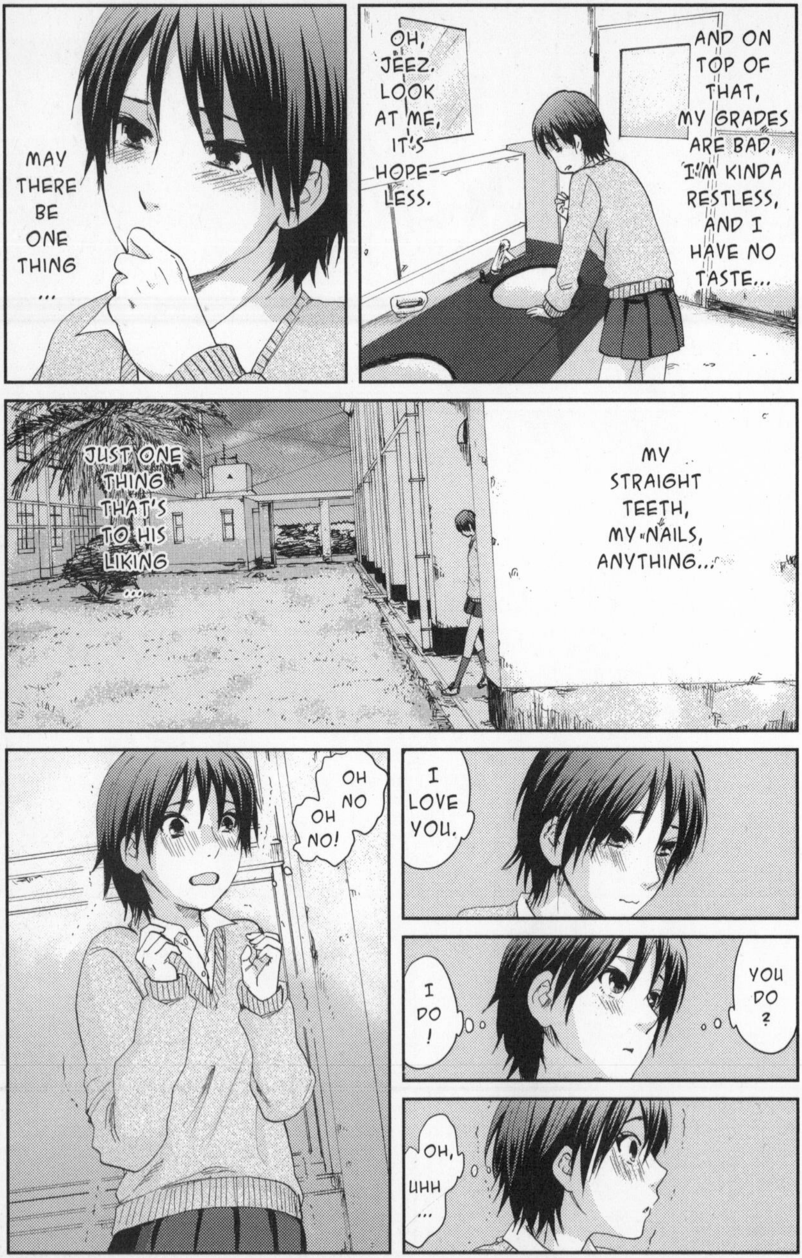
AND ON TOP OF THAT, MY GRADES ARE BAD, I'M KINDA RESTLESS, AND I HAVE NO TASTE...
OH, JEEZ. LOOK AT ME, IT'S HOPE-LESS.
MAY THERE BE ONE THING ...
MY STRAIGHT TEETH, MY NAILS, ANYTHING...
JUST ONE THING THAT'S TO HIS LIKING ...
I LOVE YOU.
YOU DO?
I DO!
OH, UHH ...
OH NO
OH NO!

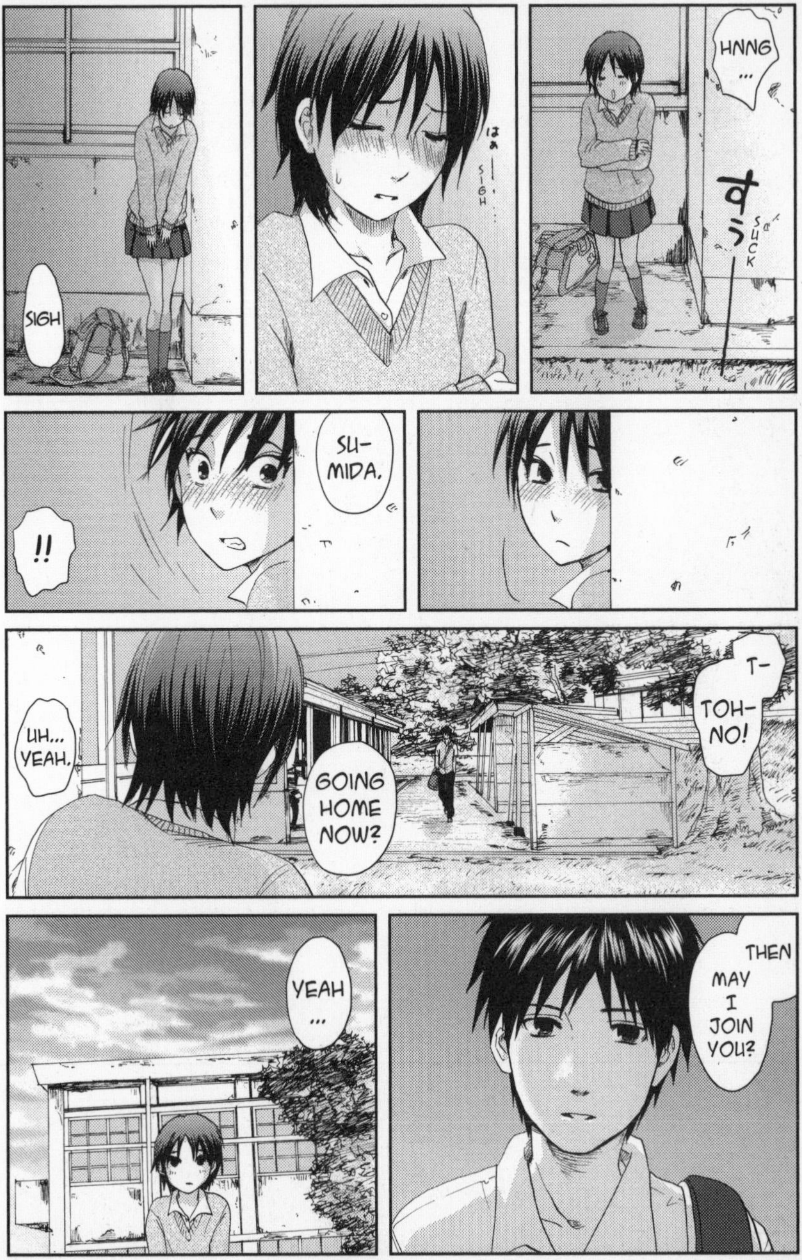
HNNG ...
すう
SUCK
はぁ──
SIGH
SIGH
SU-MIDA.
!!
T- TOH-NO!
GOING HOME NOW?
UH... YEAH.
THEN MAY I JOIN YOU?
YEAH ...

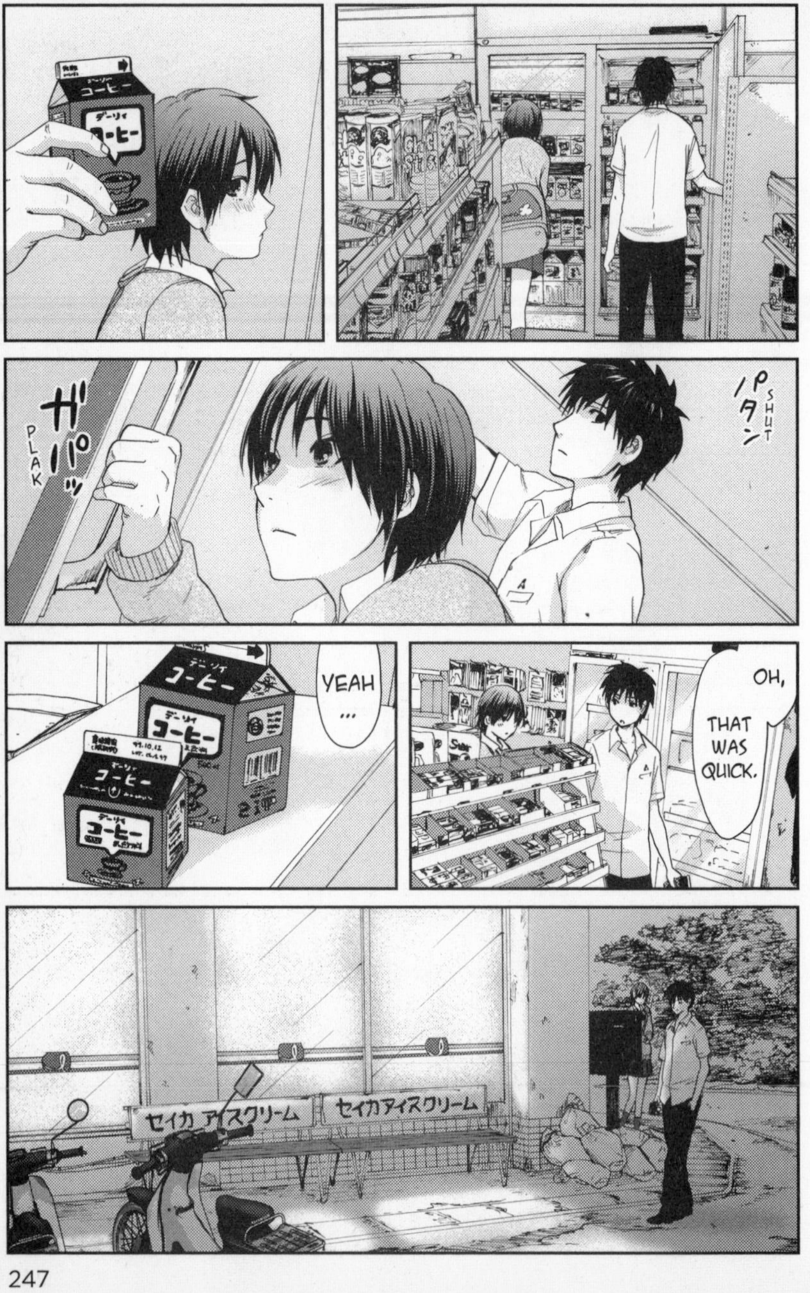
デーリィ コーヒー
パタン
SHUT
ガパッ
PLAK
OH, THAT WAS QUICK.
YEAH ...
デーリィ コーヒー
セイカアイスクリーム
セイカ アイスクリーム

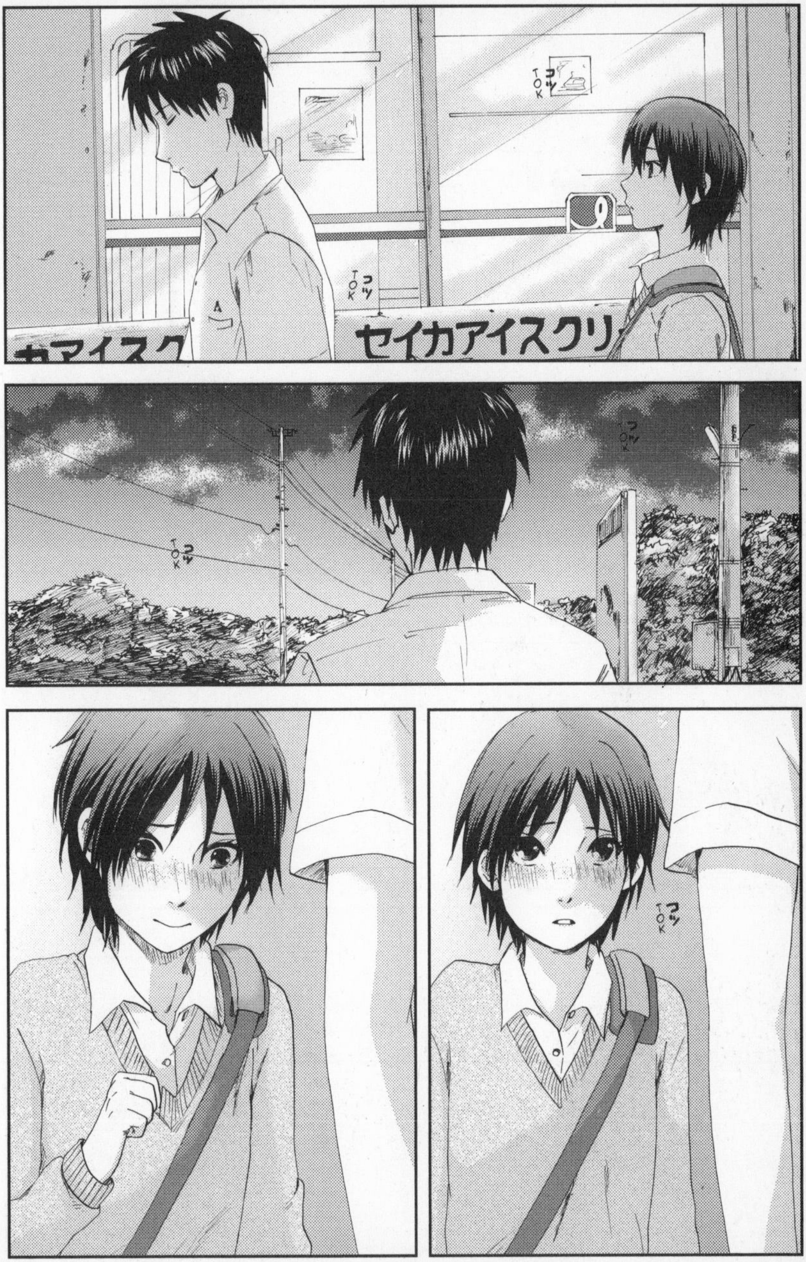
コツ TOK
コツ TOK
セイカアイスクリ
カアイスク
コツ TOK
コツ TOK
コツ TOK

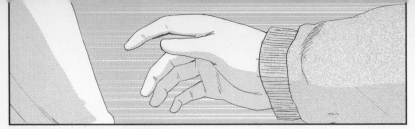

！

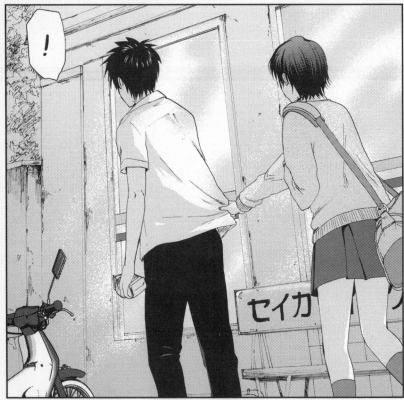

セイカ

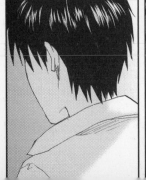
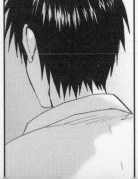
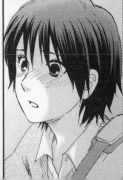

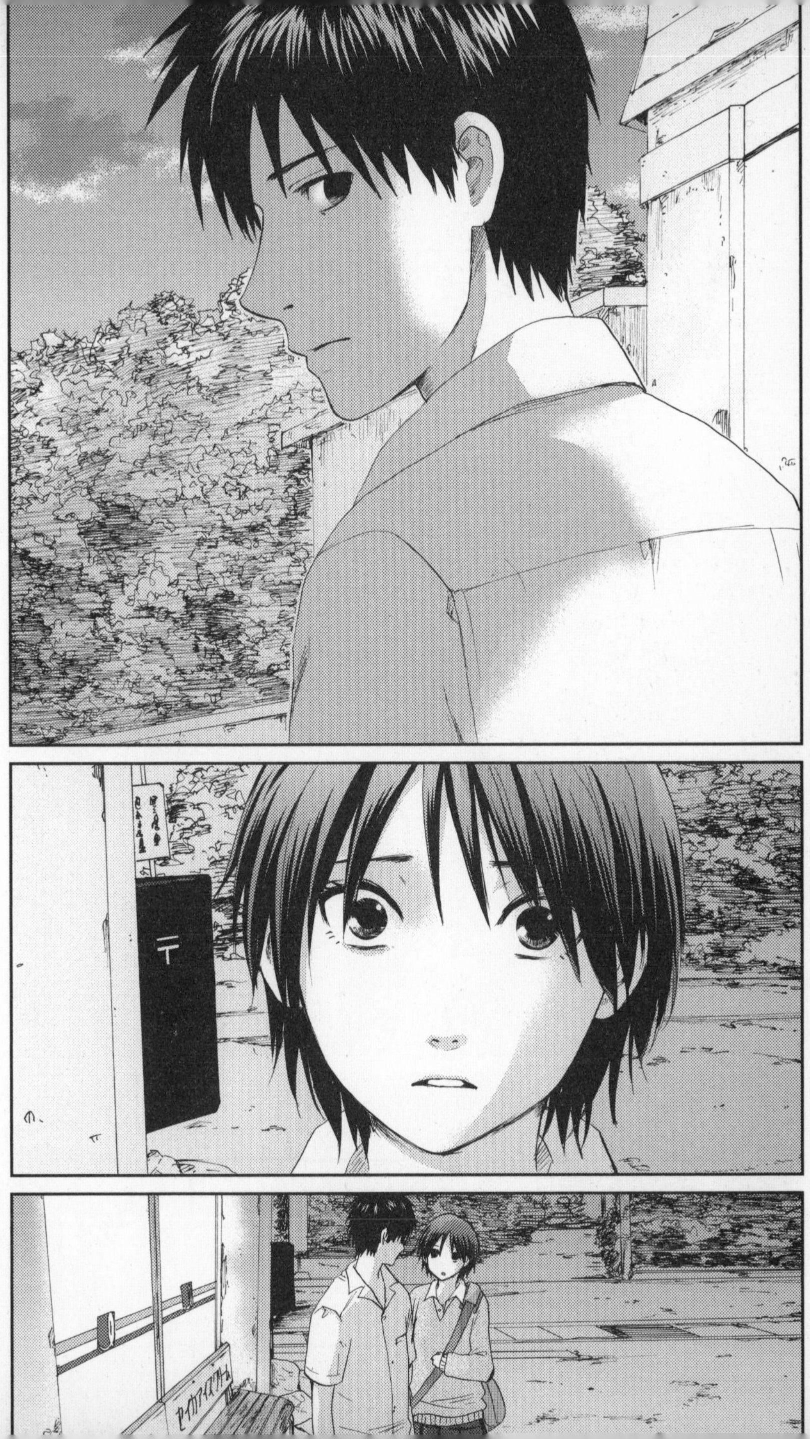
セイカアイスクリーム

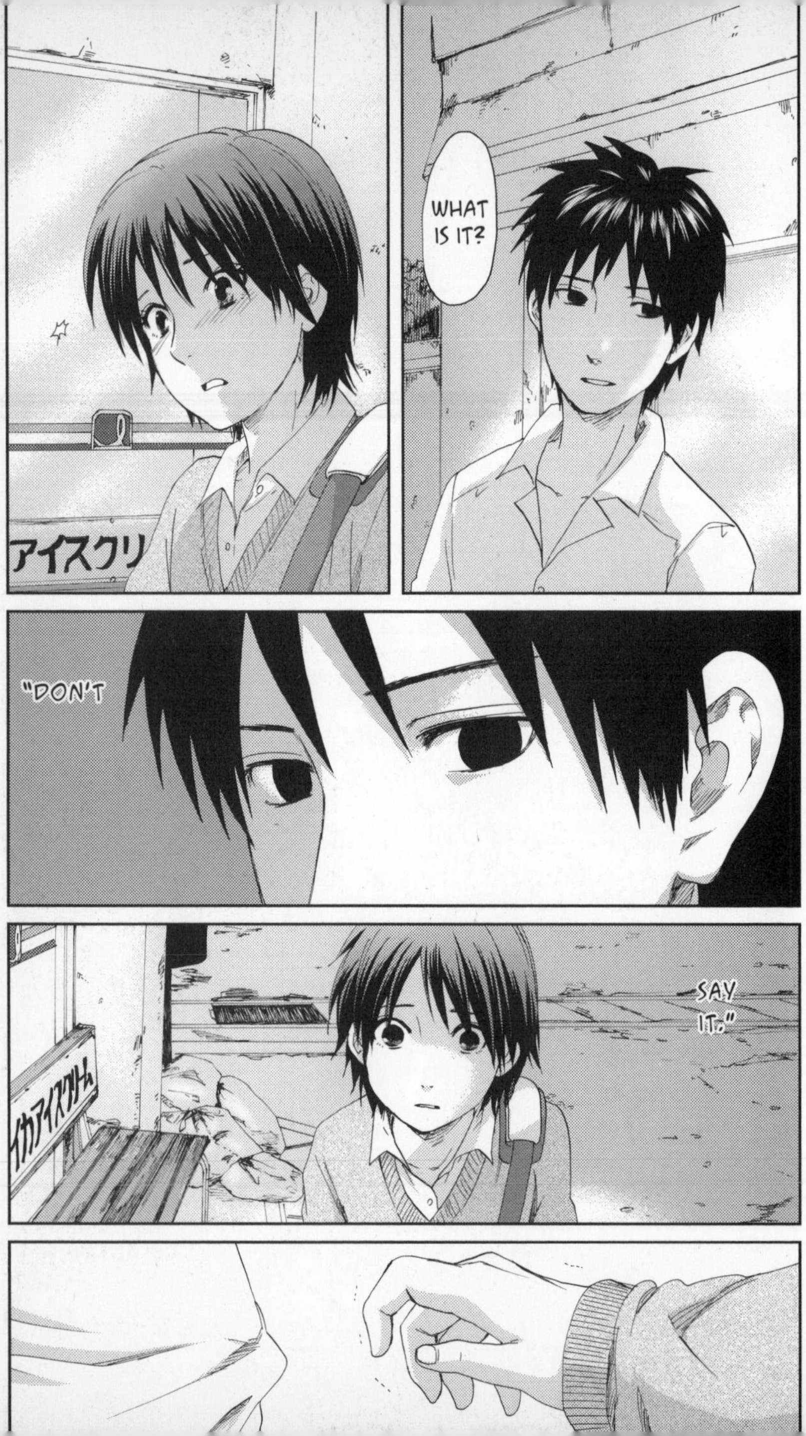
WHAT IS IT?
アイスクリ
"DON'T
SAY IT."
イカアイスクリーム

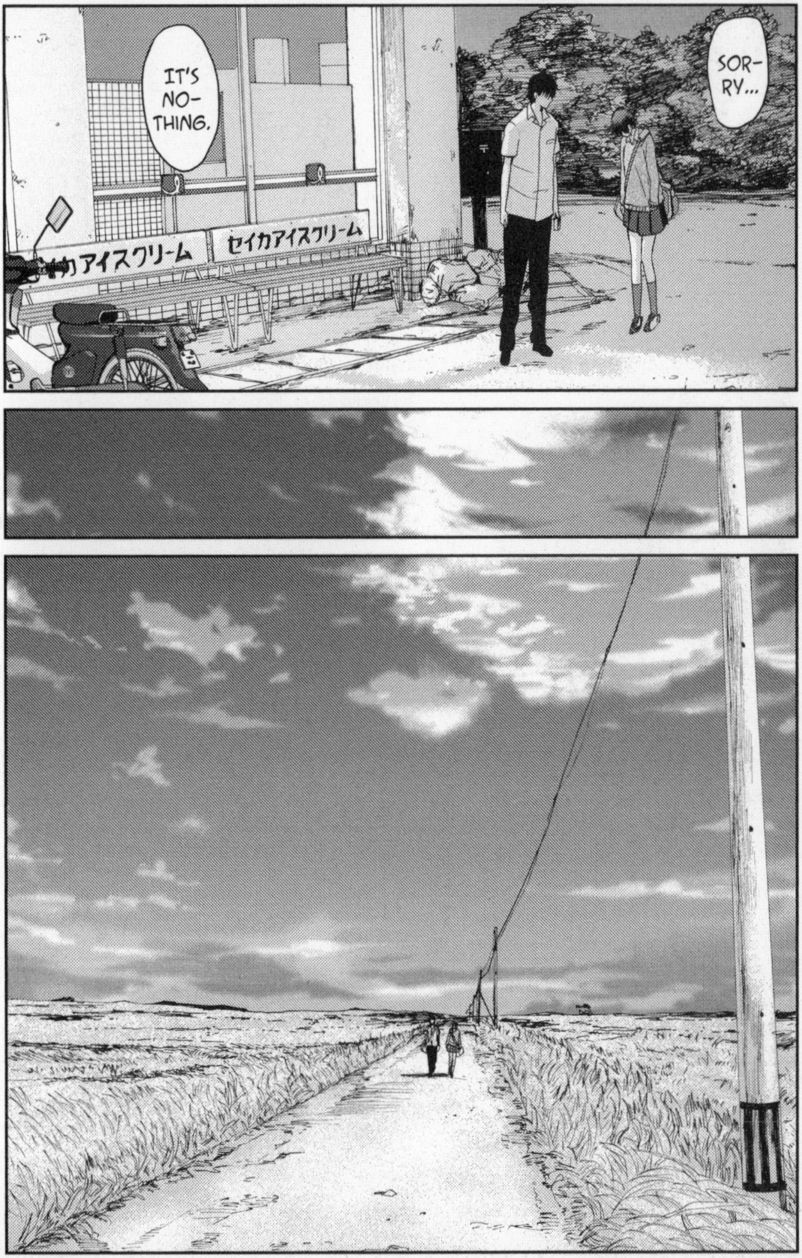
SOR-RY...
IT'S NO-THING.
セイカアイスクリーム
カアイスクリーム

TOK
TOK
TOK
TOK
TOK

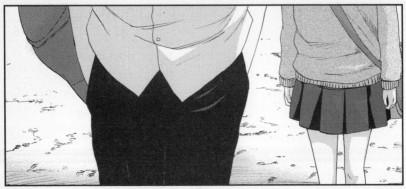

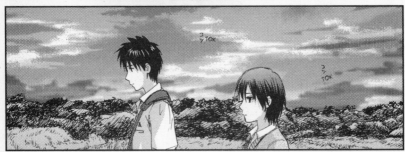

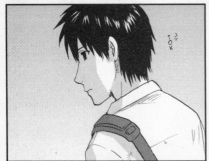

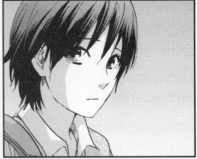

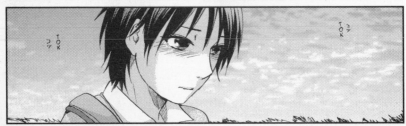

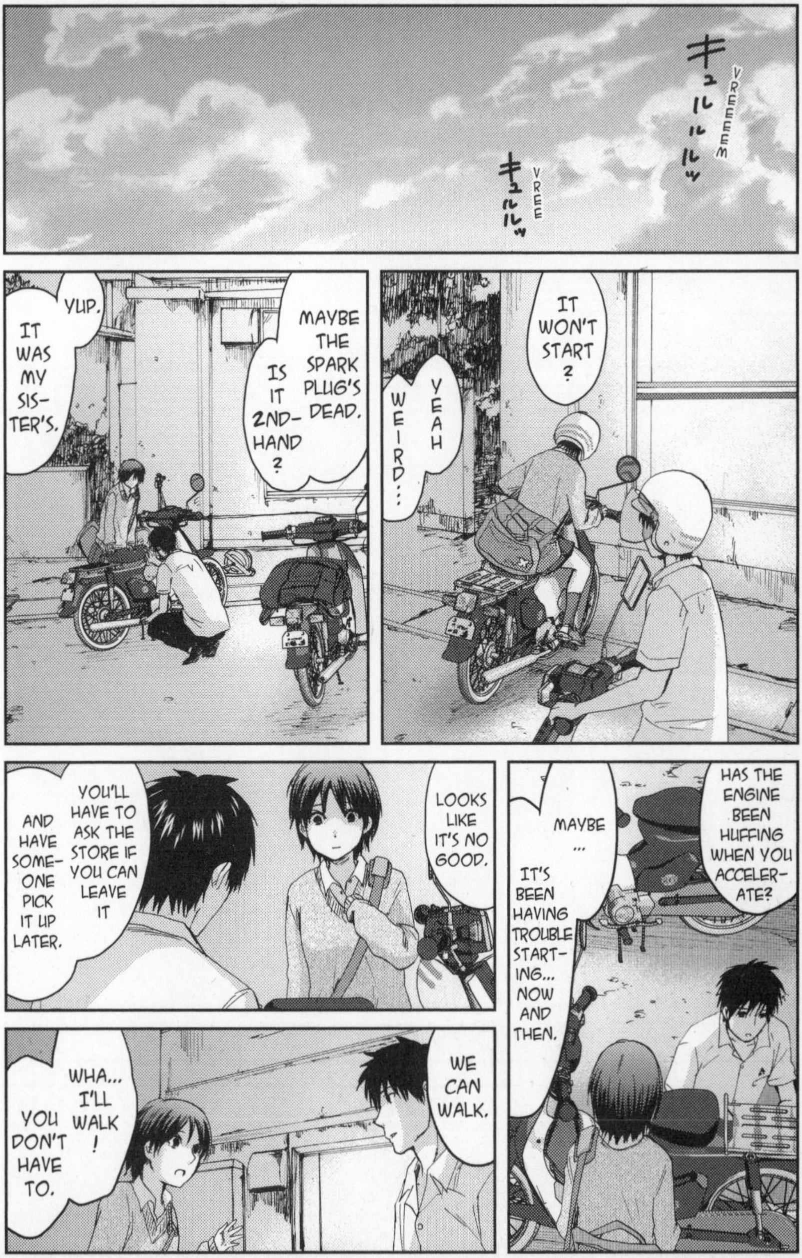
キュルルルッ
VREEEEM
キュルルッ
VREE
IT WON'T START?
YEAH WEIRD...
MAYBE THE SPARK PLUG'S DEAD.
IS IT 2ND-HAND?
YUP.
IT WAS MY SISTER'S.
HAS THE ENGINE BEEN HUFFING WHEN YOU ACCELERATE?
MAYBE ...
IT'S BEEN HAVING TROUBLE STARTING... NOW AND THEN.
LOOKS LIKE IT'S NO GOOD.
YOU'LL HAVE TO ASK THE STORE IF YOU CAN LEAVE IT
AND HAVE SOMEONE PICK IT UP LATER.
WE CAN WALK.
WHA... I'LL WALK!
YOU DON'T HAVE TO.

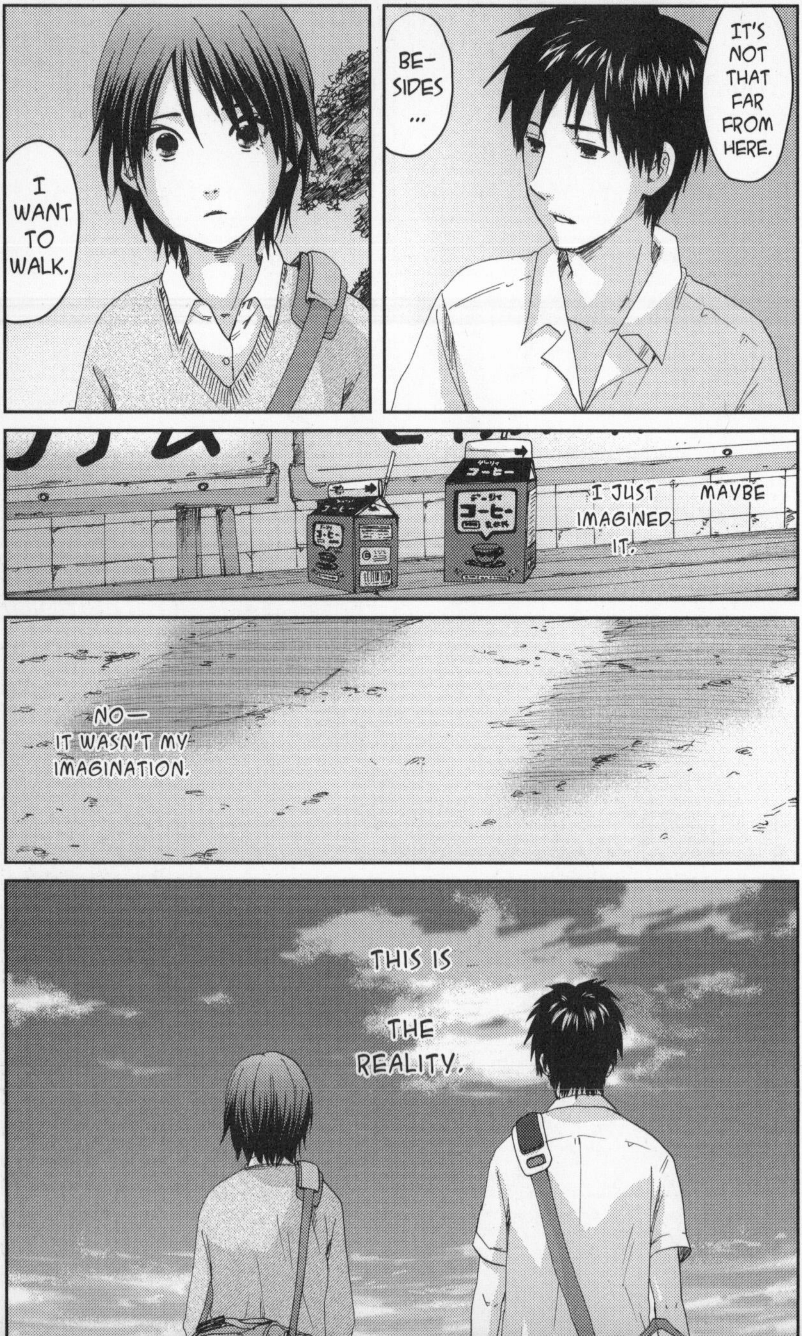
IT'S NOT THAT FAR FROM HERE.
BE-SIDES...
I WANT TO WALK.
MAYBE
I JUST IMAGINED IT.
NO—
IT WASN'T MY IMAGINATION.
THIS IS
THE REALITY.

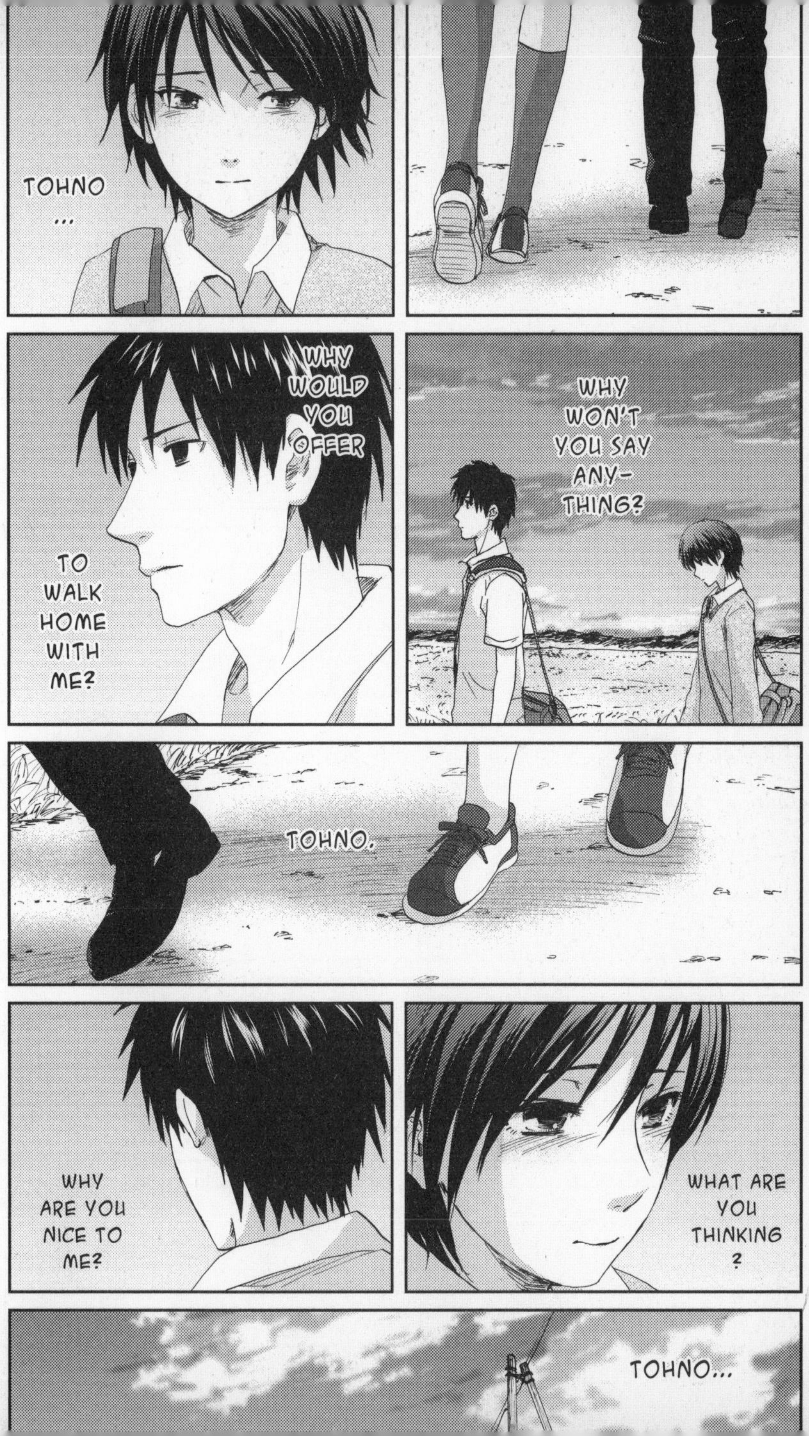
TOHNO ...
WHY WON'T YOU SAY ANY-THING?
WHY WOULD YOU OFFER
TO WALK HOME WITH ME?
TOHNO.
WHAT ARE YOU THINKING ?
WHY ARE YOU NICE TO ME?
TOHNO...

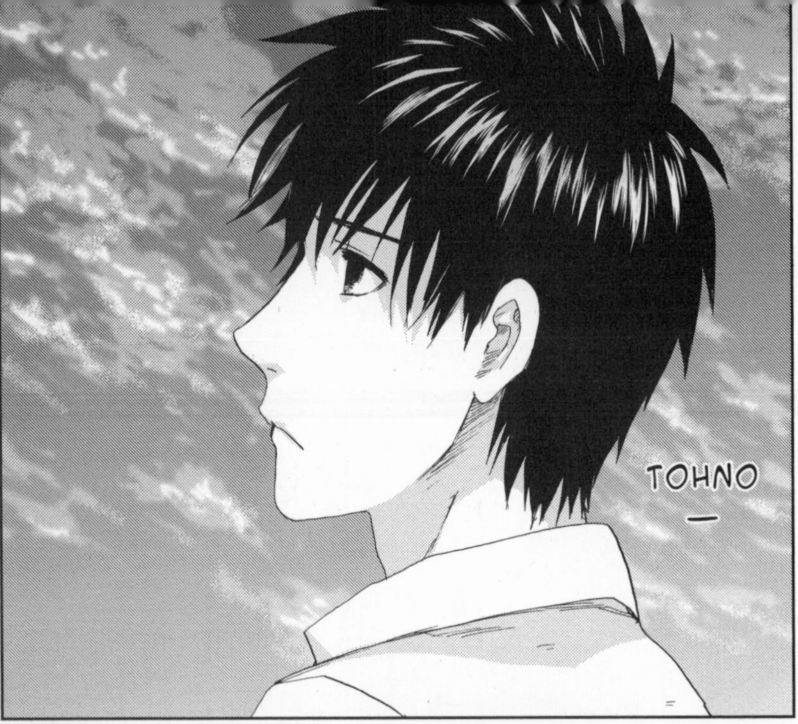
TOHNO
—
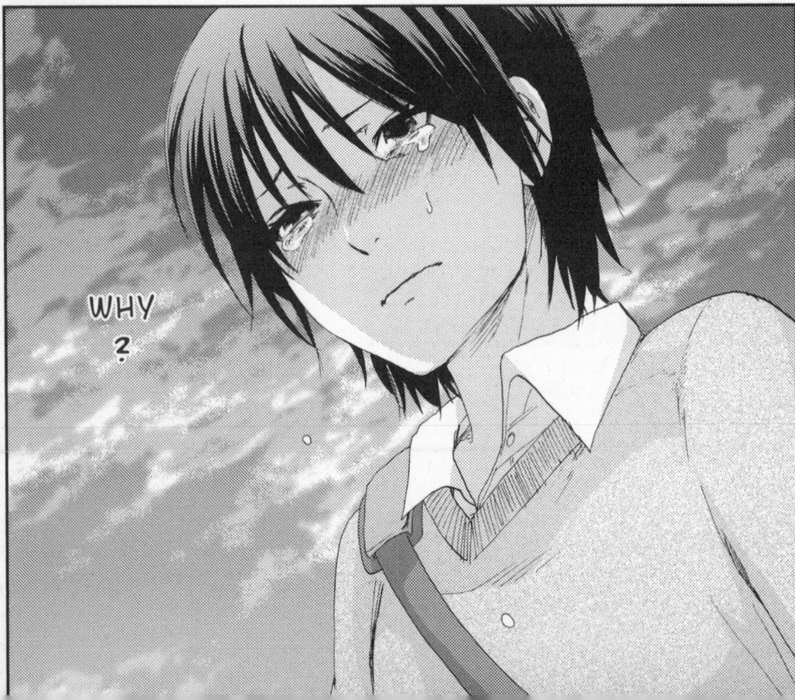
WHY
?

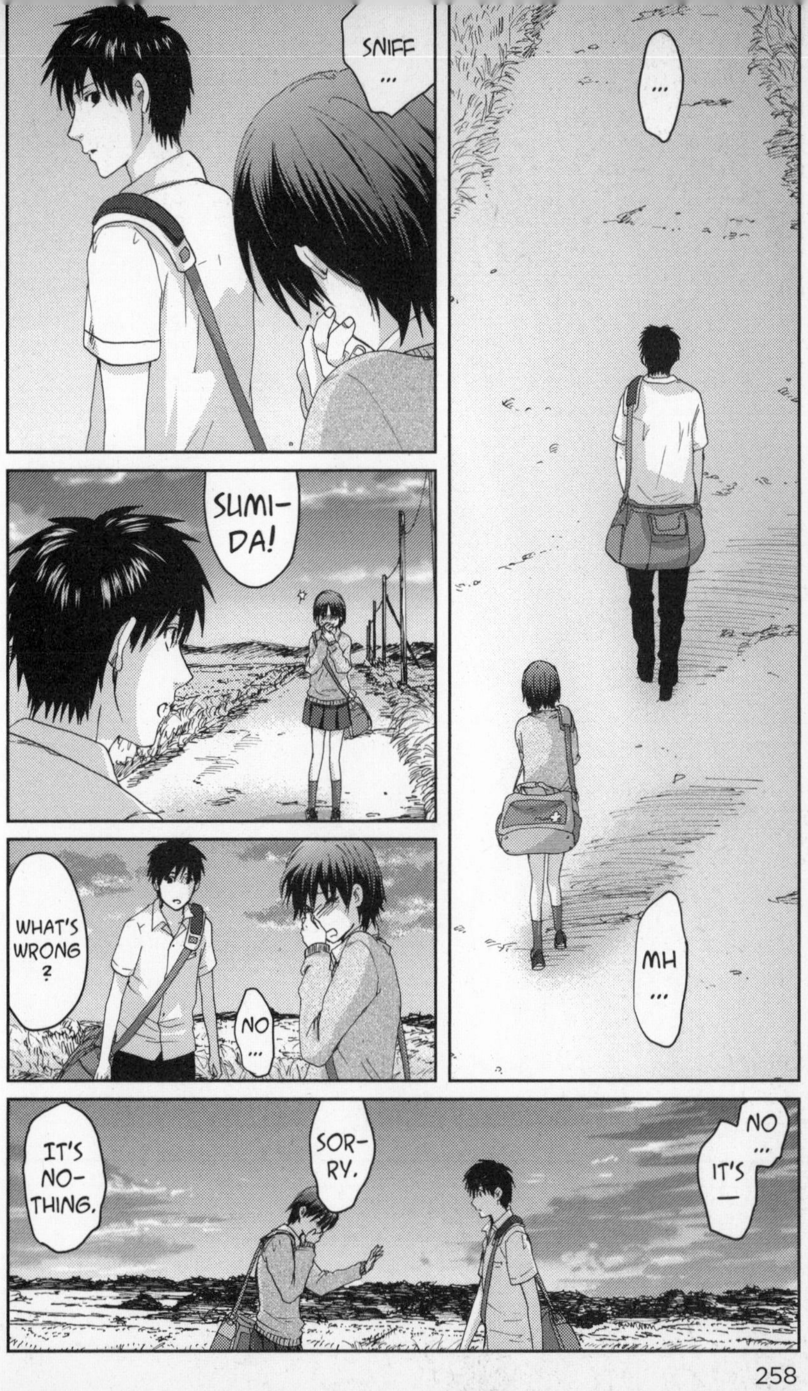
...
MH ...
SNIFF ...
SUMI-DA!
WHAT'S WRONG?
NO ...
NO ... IT'S —
SOR-RY.
IT'S NO-THING.

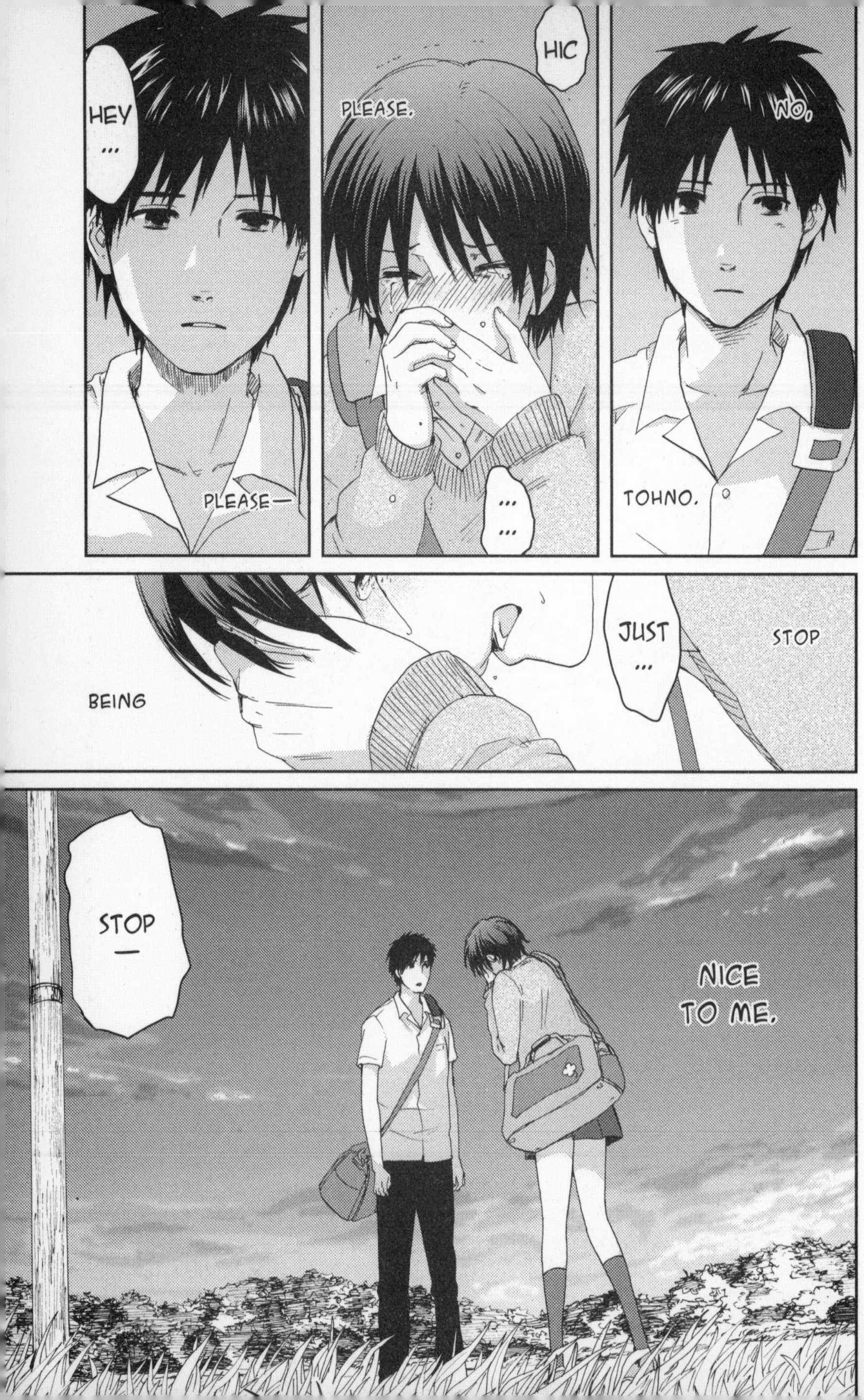
NO.
TOHNO.
HIC
PLEASE.
... ...
HEY ...
PLEASE—
STOP
JUST ...
BEING
NICE TO ME.
STOP —

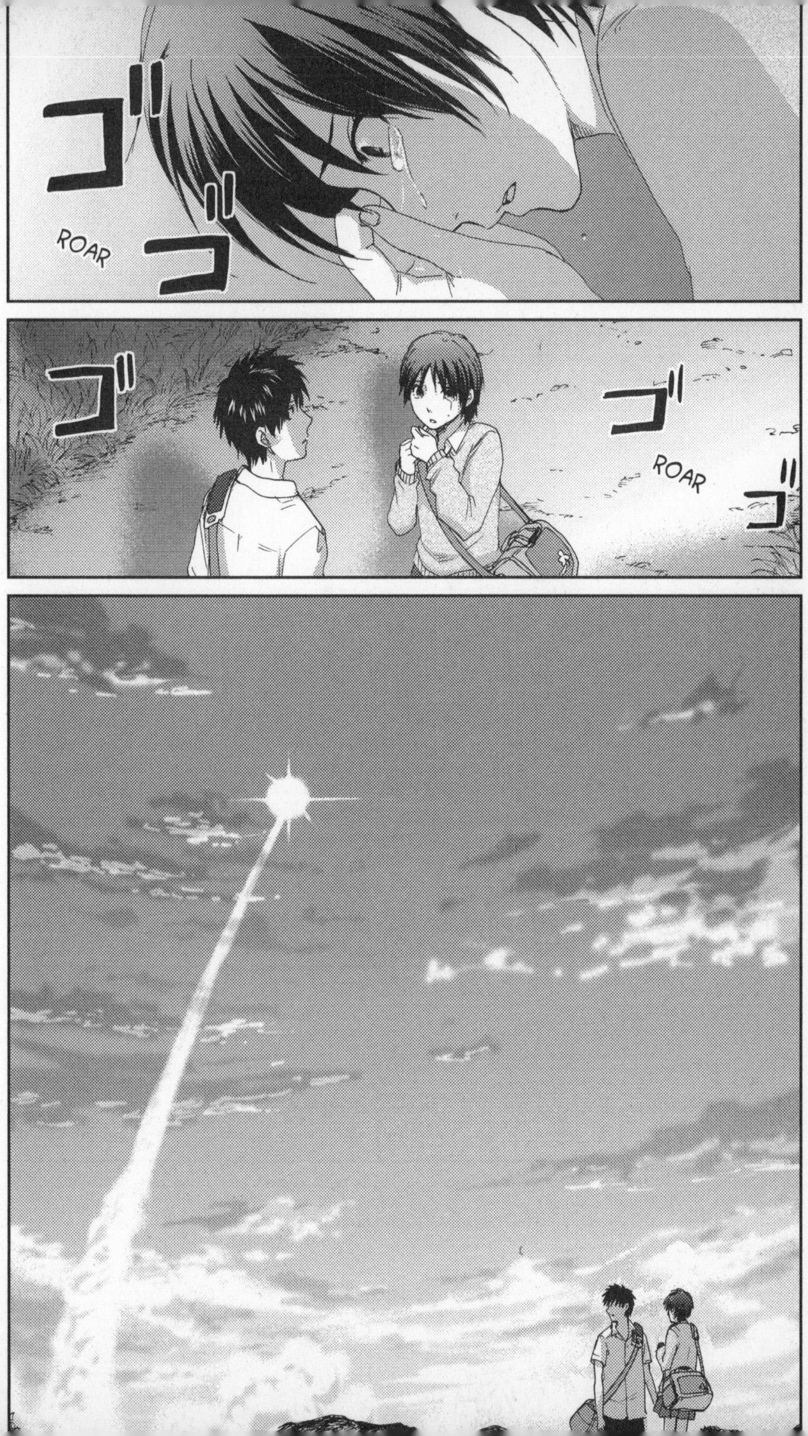
ゴゴ
ROAR
ゴゴ
ROAR
ゴ

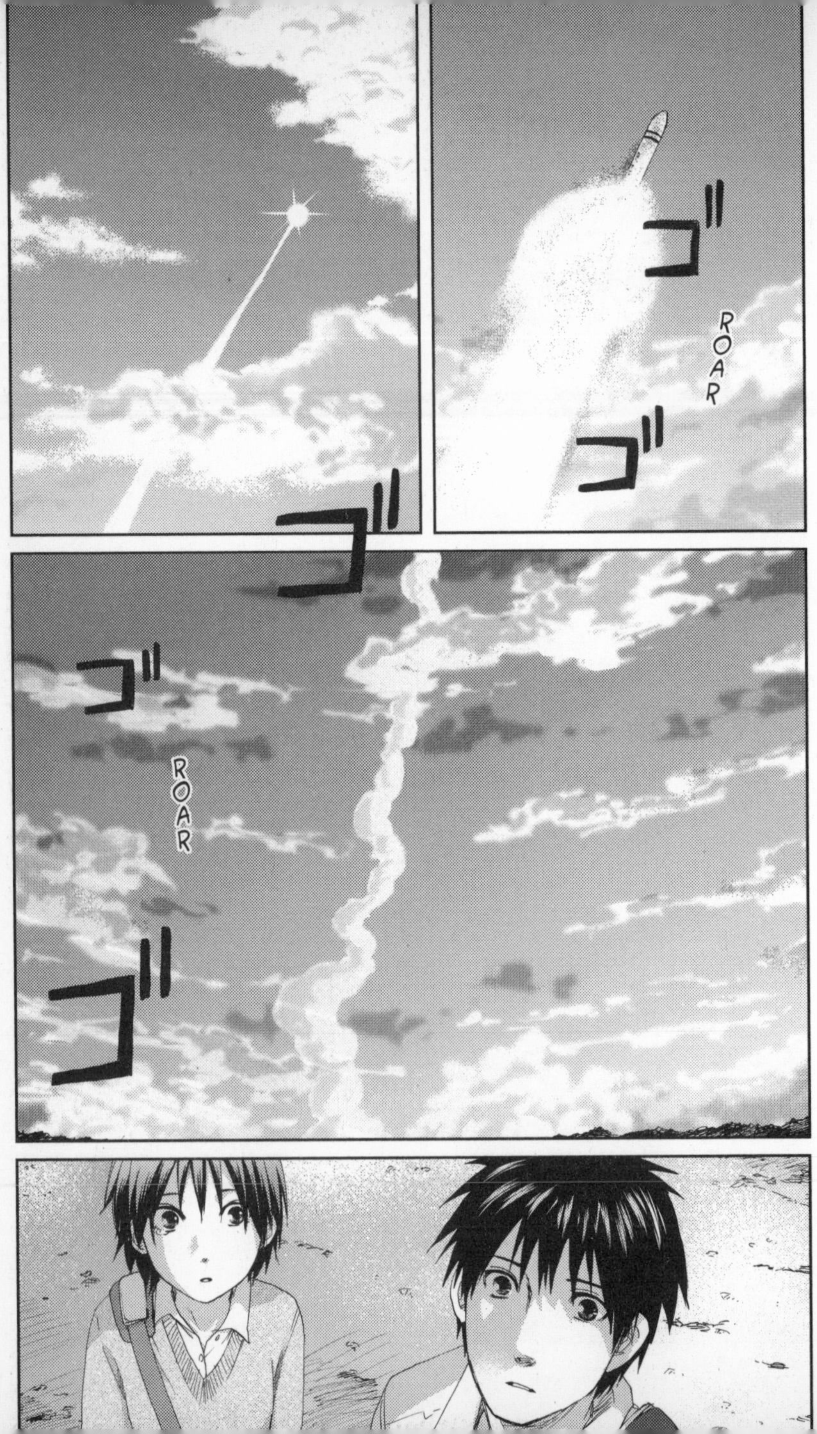
ゴ
ROAR
ゴ
ゴ
ゴ
ROAR
ゴ

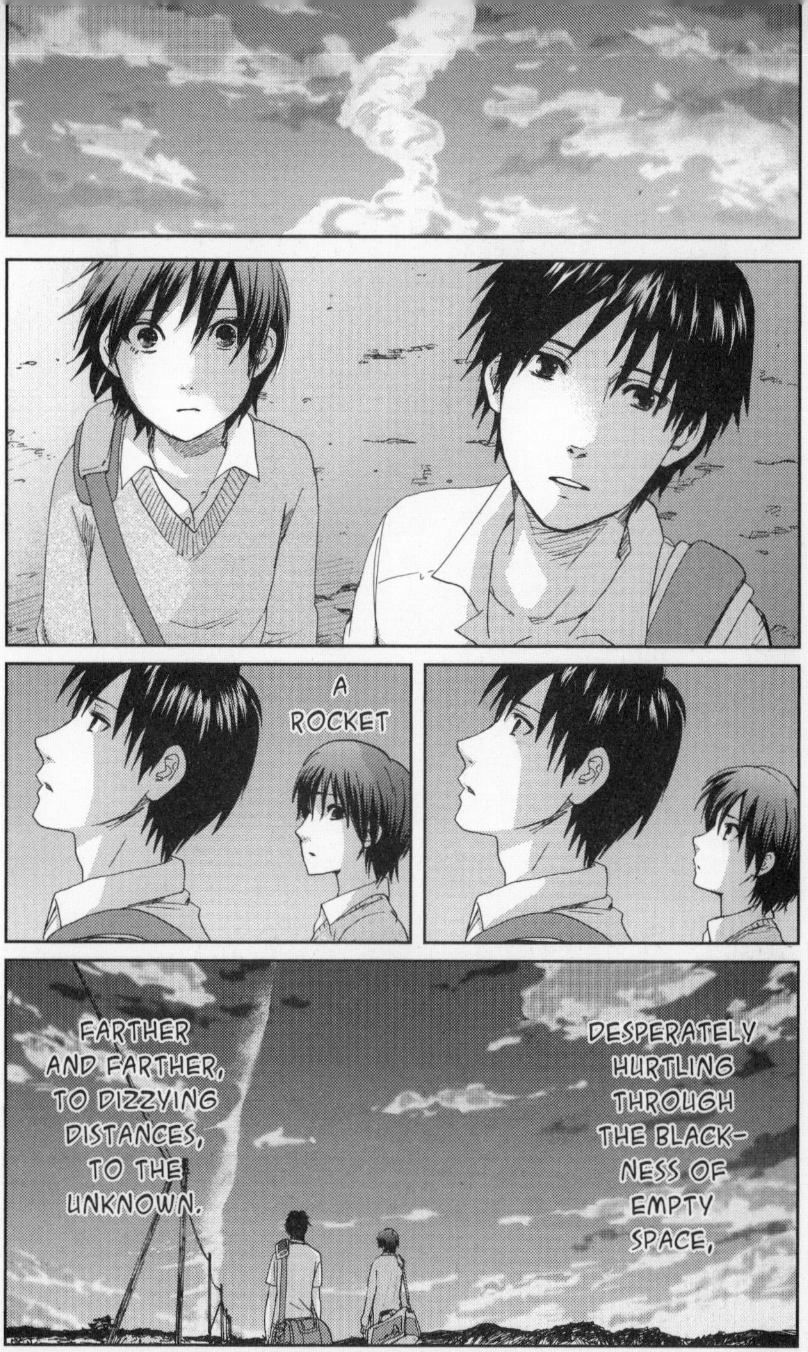
A ROCKET
DESPERATELY HURTLING THROUGH THE BLACK-NESS OF EMPTY SPACE,
FARTHER AND FARTHER, TO DIZZYING DISTANCES, TO THE UNKNOWN.

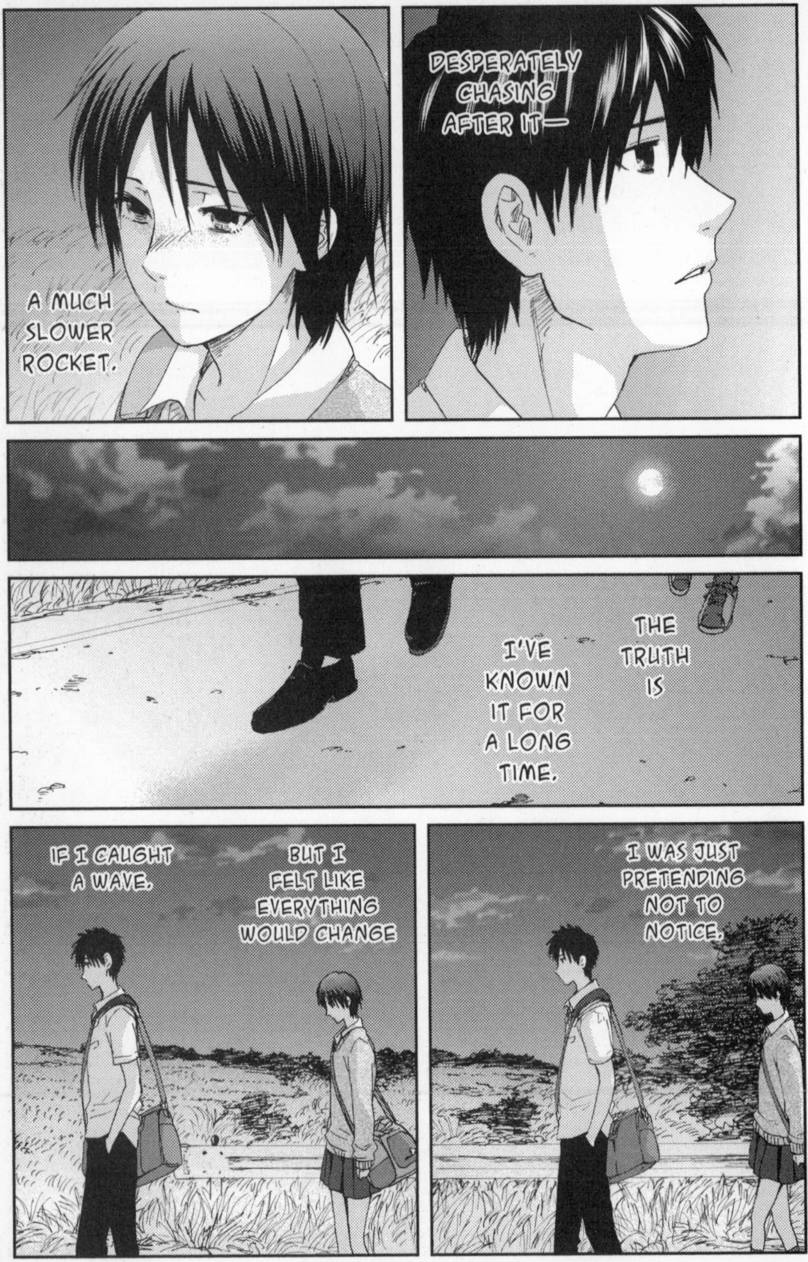
DESPERATELY CHASING AFTER IT—
A MUCH SLOWER ROCKET.
THE TRUTH IS
I'VE KNOWN IT FOR A LONG TIME.
I WAS JUST PRETENDING NOT TO NOTICE.
BUT I FELT LIKE EVERYTHING WOULD CHANGE
IF I CAUGHT A WAVE.

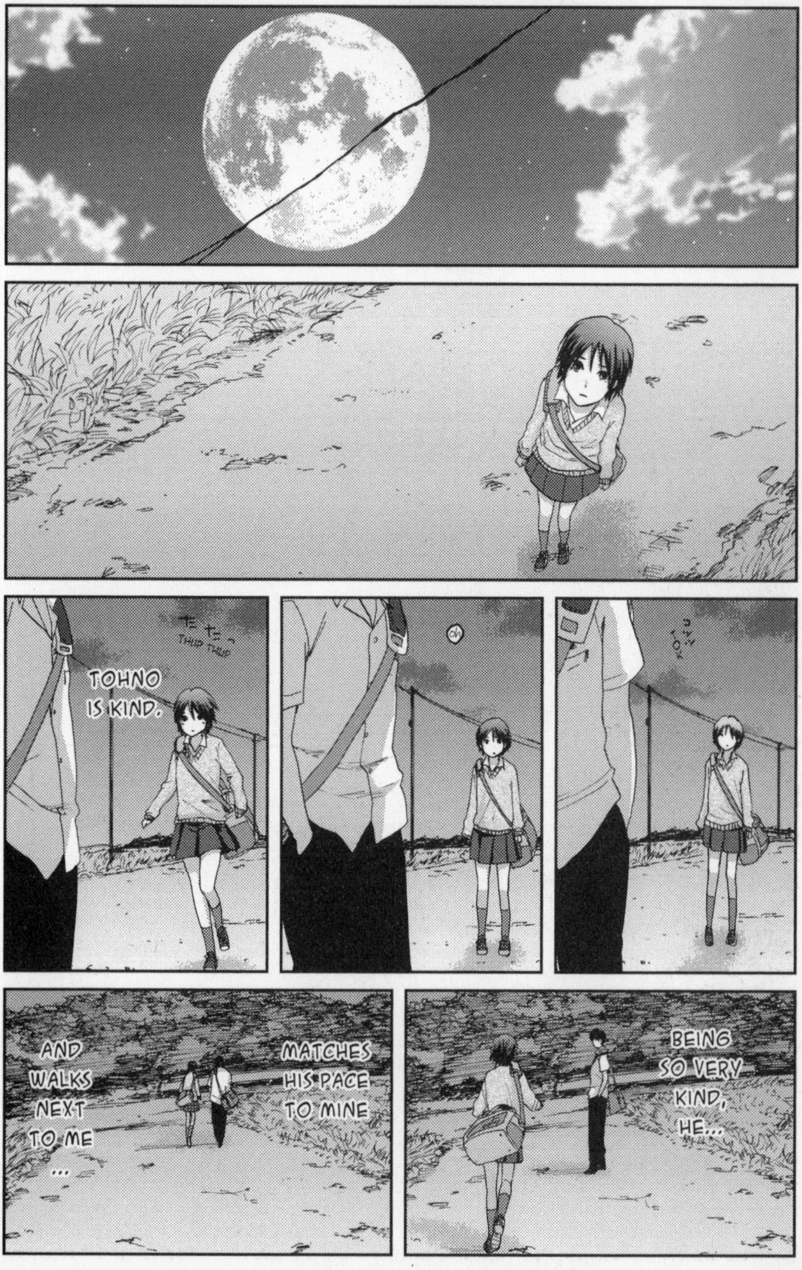
コツ
TOK
oh
たたっ
THUP THUP
TOHNO IS KIND.
BEING SO VERY KIND, HE...
MATCHES HIS PACE TO MINE
AND WALKS NEXT TO ME ...

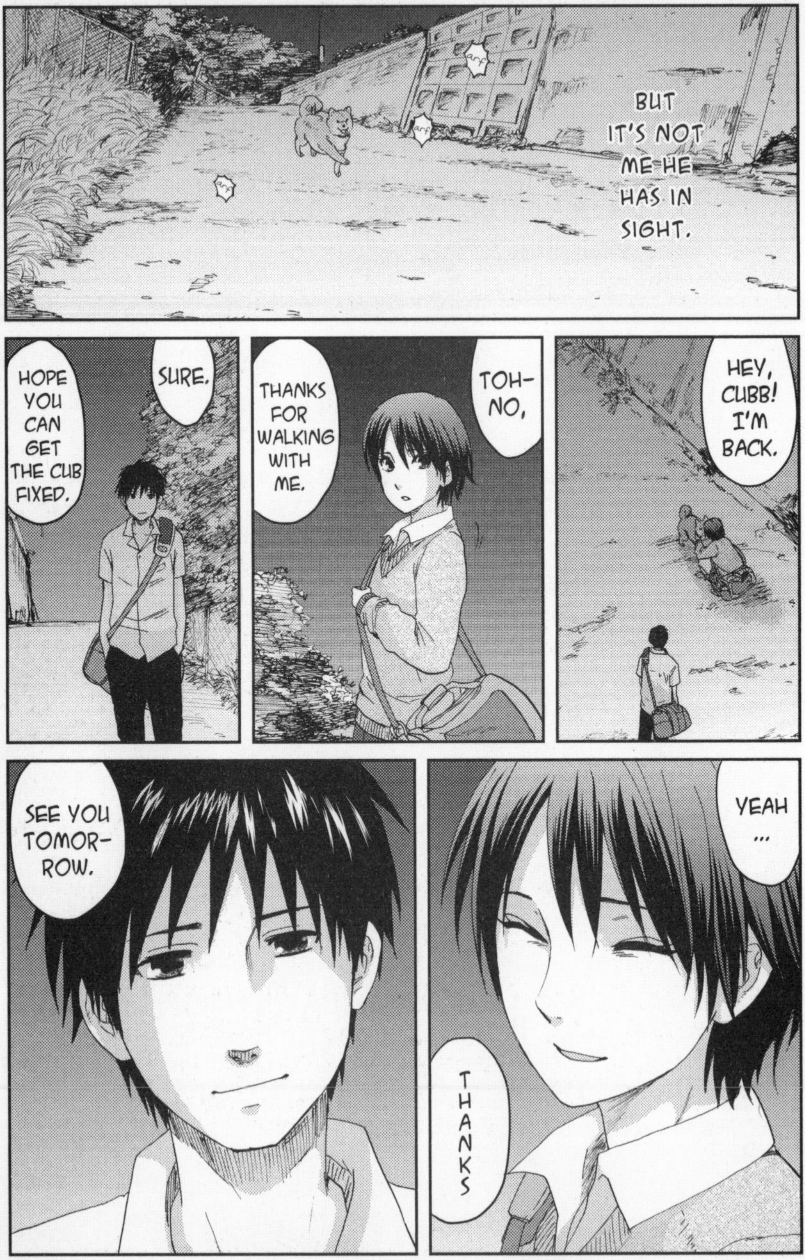
arf
arf
arf
BUT IT'S NOT ME HE HAS IN SIGHT.
HEY, CUBB! I'M BACK.
TOH-NO,
THANKS FOR WALKING WITH ME.
SURE.
HOPE YOU CAN GET THE CUB FIXED.
YEAH ...
THANKS
SEE YOU TOMOR-ROW.

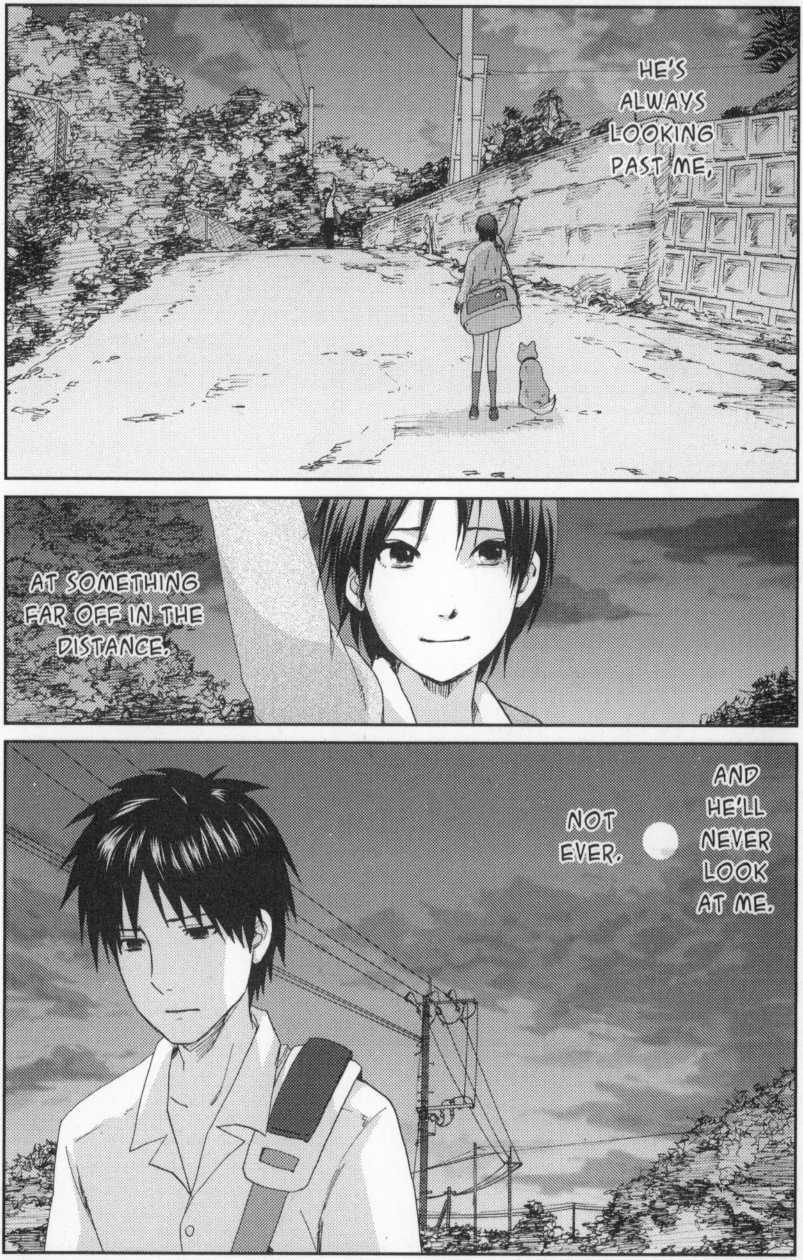
HE'S ALWAYS LOOKING PAST ME,
AT SOMETHING FAR OFF IN THE DISTANCE.
AND HE'LL NEVER LOOK AT ME.
NOT EVER.

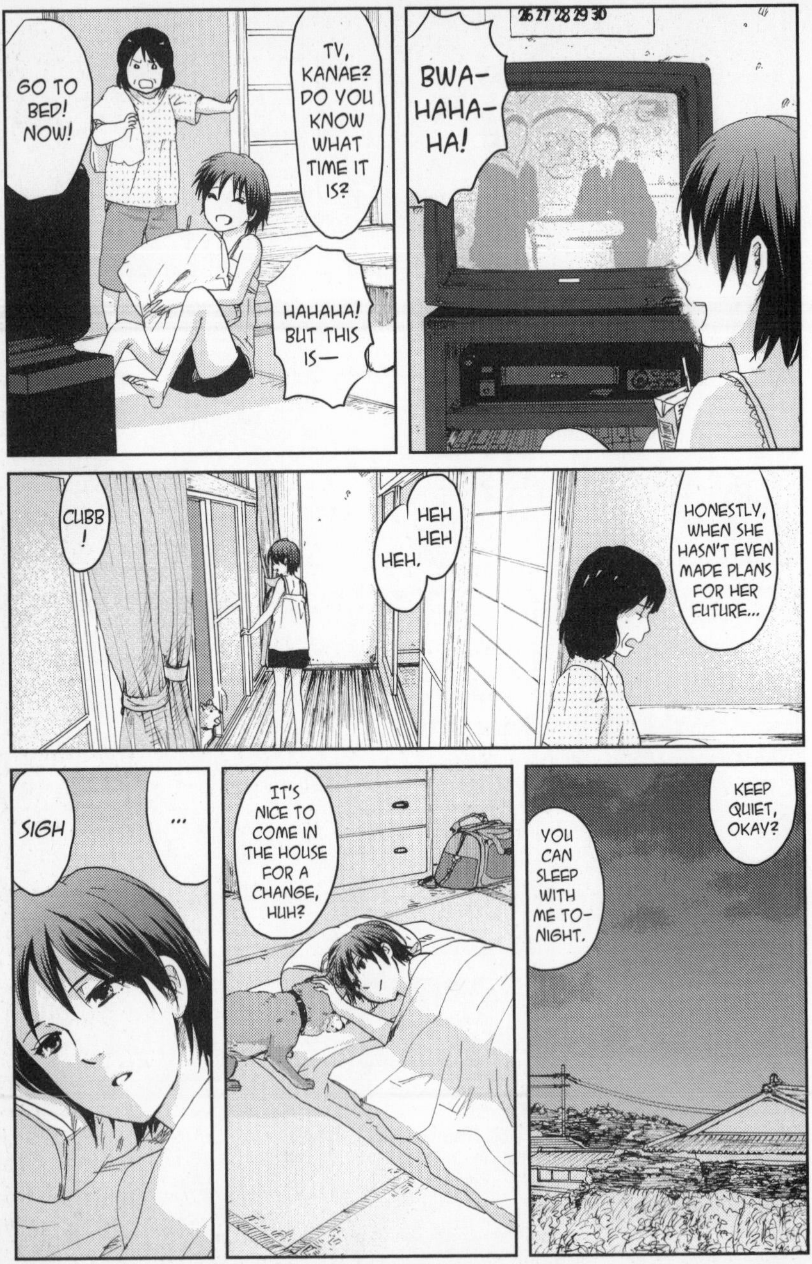
26 27 28 29 30
BWA-HAHAHA-HA!
TV, KANAE? DO YOU KNOW WHAT TIME IT IS?
HAHAHA! BUT THIS IS—
GO TO BED! NOW!
HONESTLY, WHEN SHE HASN'T EVEN MADE PLANS FOR HER FUTURE...
HEH HEH HEH.
CUBB!
KEEP QUIET, OKAY?
YOU CAN SLEEP WITH ME TO-NIGHT.
IT'S NICE TO COME IN THE HOUSE FOR A CHANGE, HUH?
...
SIGH

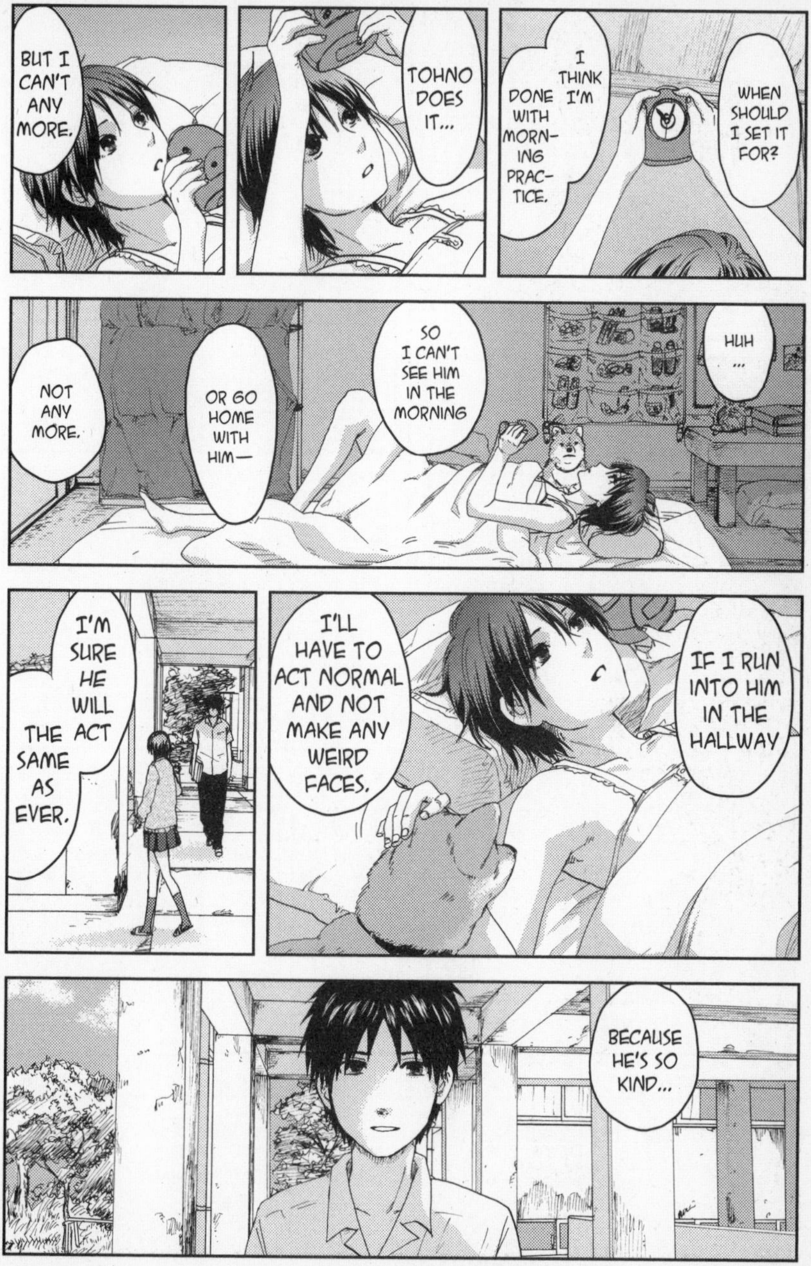
WHEN SHOULD I SET IT FOR?
I THINK I'M DONE WITH MORNING-ING PRAC-TICE.
TOHNO DOES IT...
BUT I CAN'T ANY MORE.
HUH ...
SO I CAN'T SEE HIM IN THE MORNING
OR GO HOME WITH HIM—
NOT ANY MORE.
IF I RUN INTO HIM IN THE HALLWAY
I'LL HAVE TO ACT NORMAL AND NOT MAKE ANY WEIRD FACES.
I'M SURE HE WILL ACT THE SAME AS EVER.
BECAUSE HE'S SO KIND...

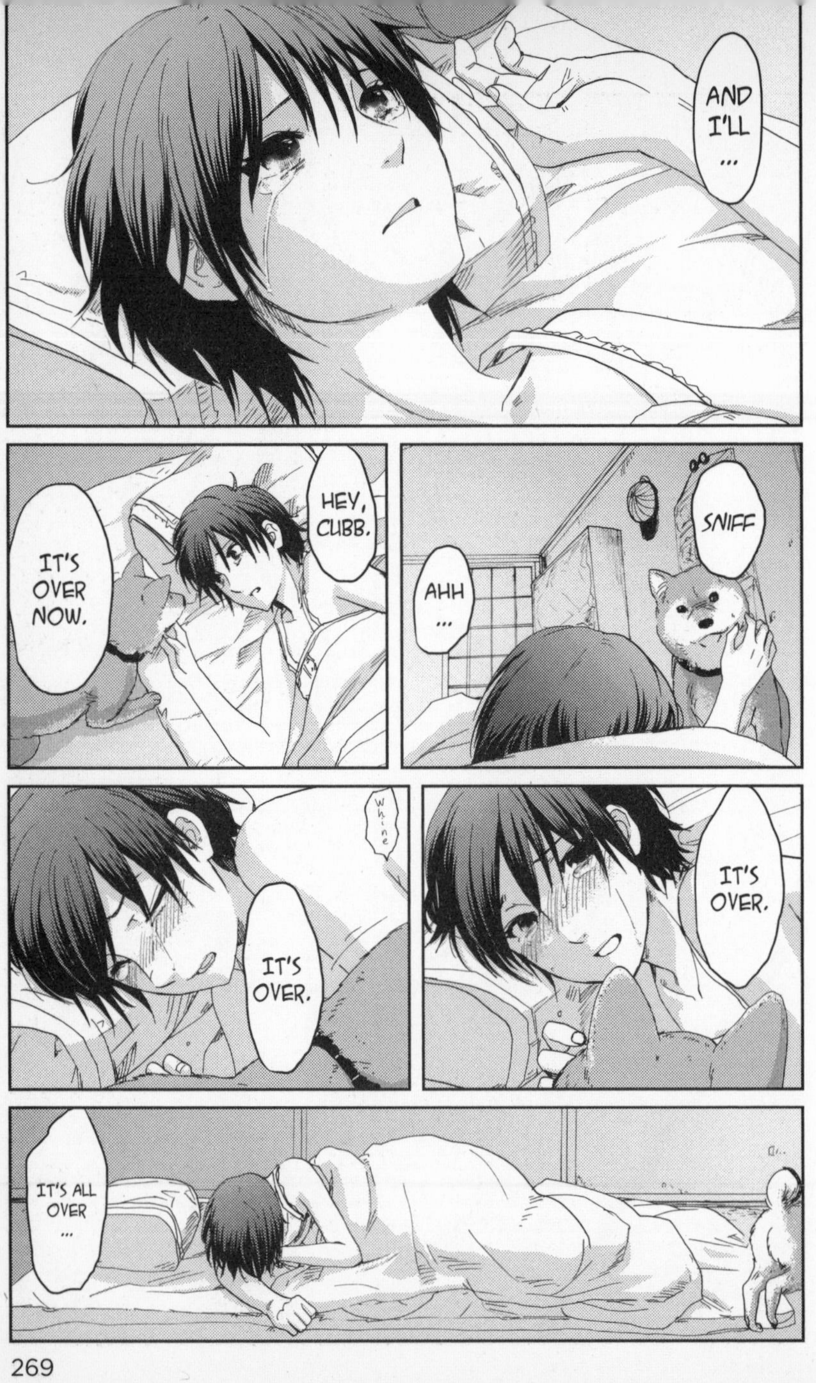
AND I'LL ...
SNIFF
AHH ...
HEY, CUBB.
IT'S OVER NOW.
IT'S OVER.
Whine
IT'S OVER.
IT'S ALL OVER ...

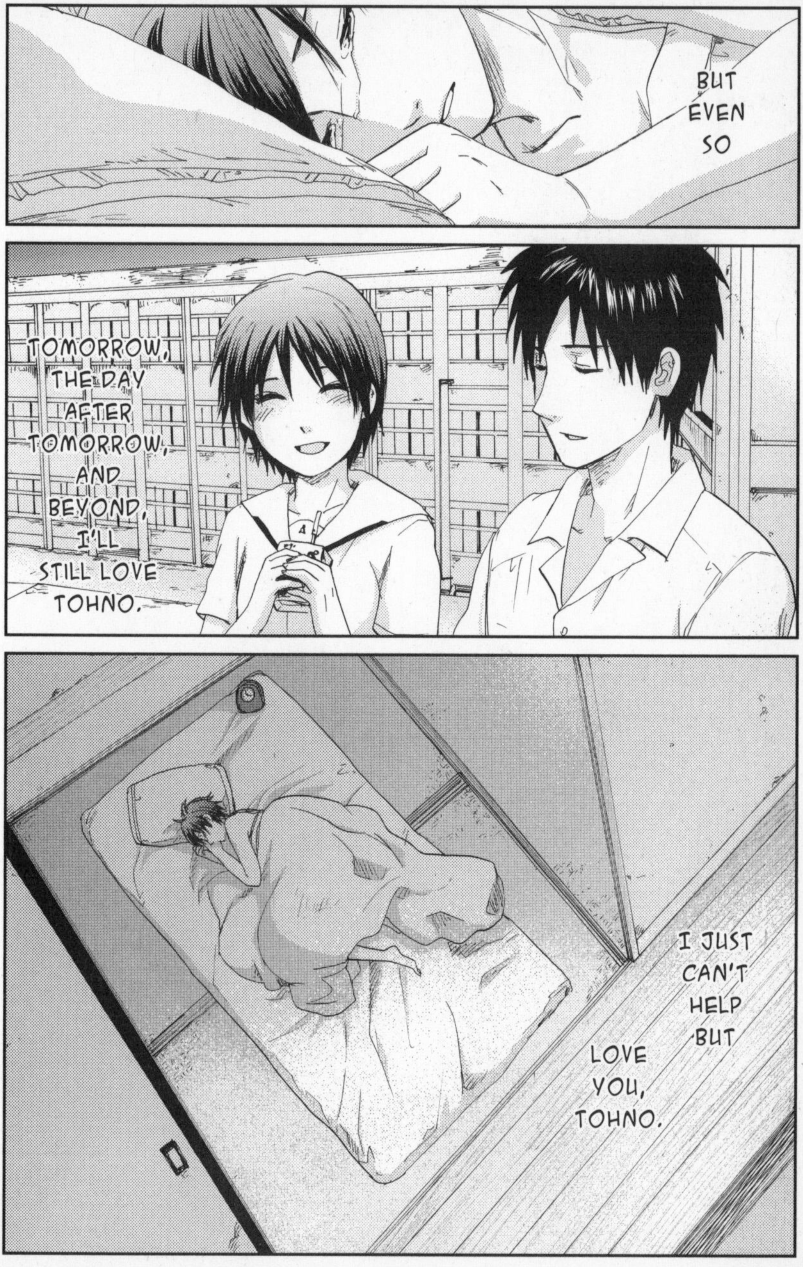
BUT EVEN SO
TOMORROW, THE DAY AFTER TOMORROW, AND BEYOND, I'LL STILL LOVE TOHNO.
I JUST CAN'T HELP BUT
LOVE YOU, TOHNO.

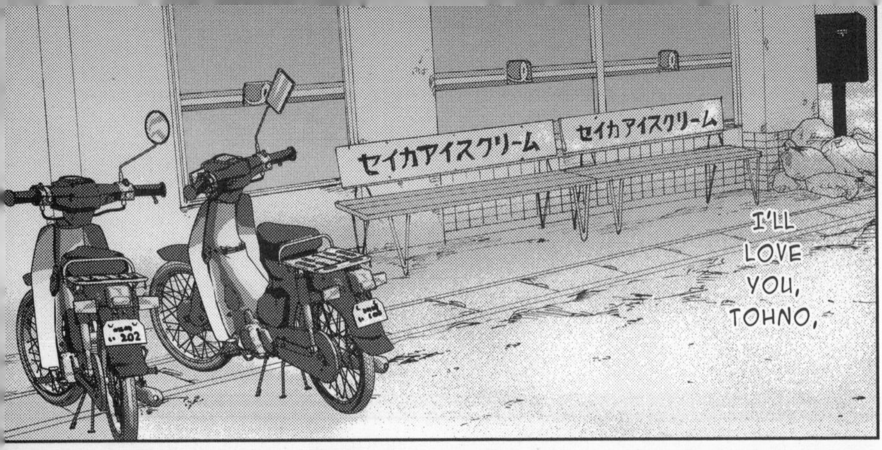
セイカアイスクリーム
セイカアイスクリーム
I'LL LOVE YOU, TOHNO,
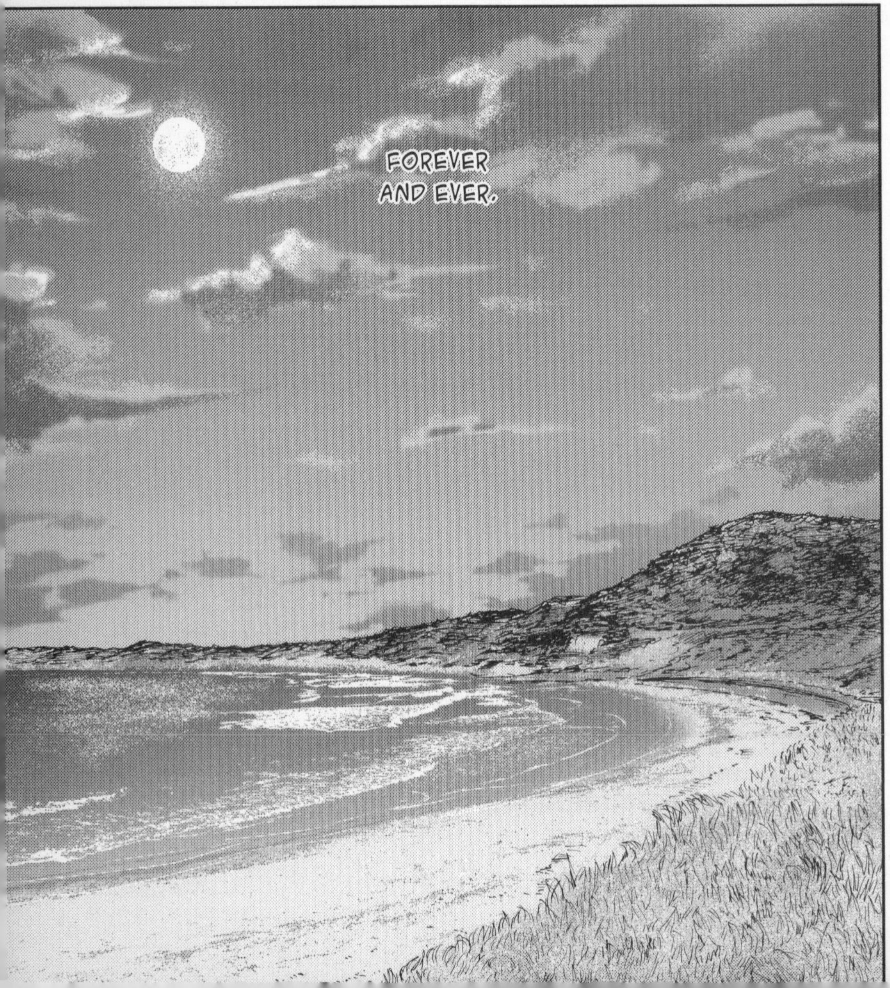
FOREVER AND EVER.

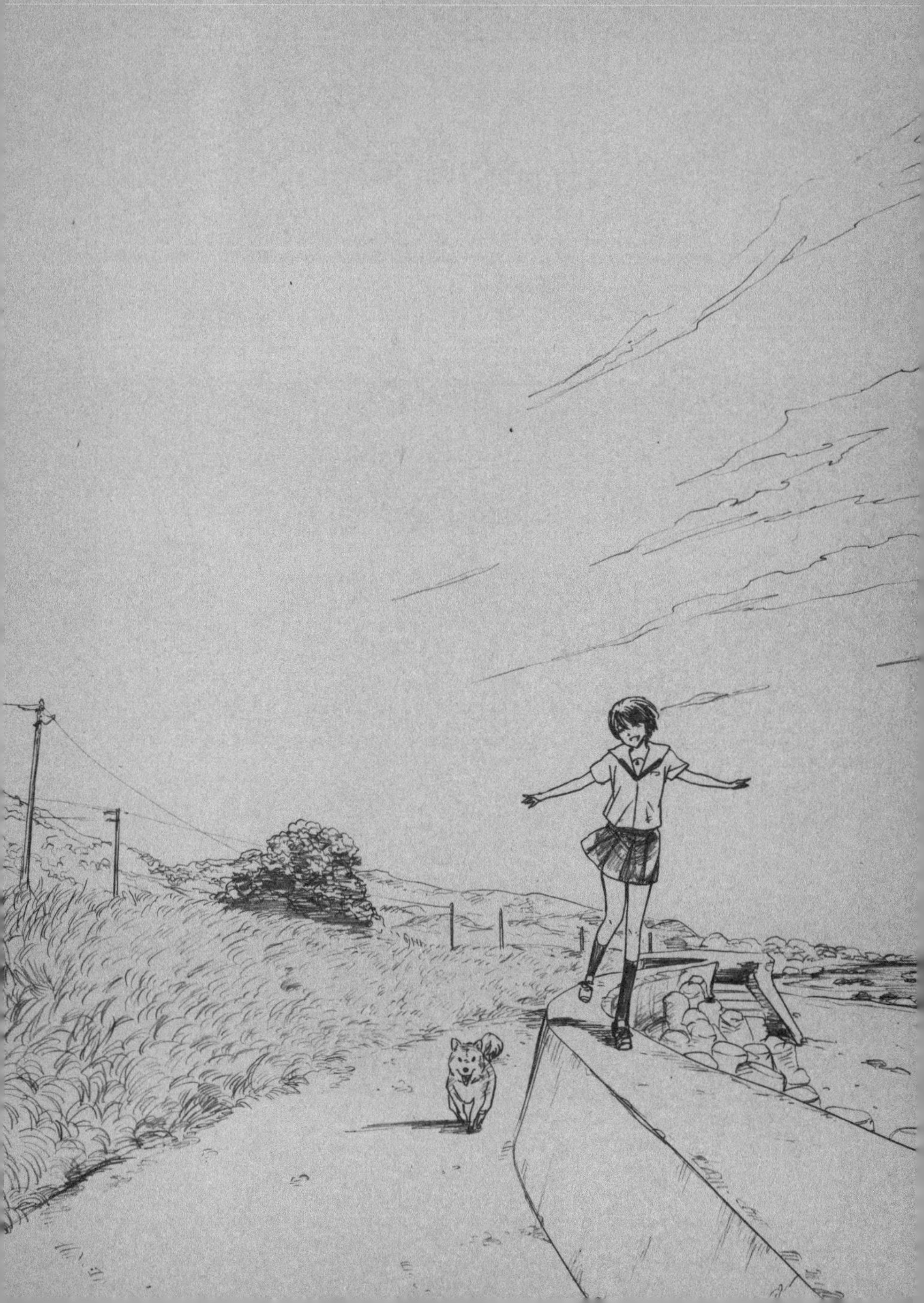

Chapter 7 – "END THEME_1"

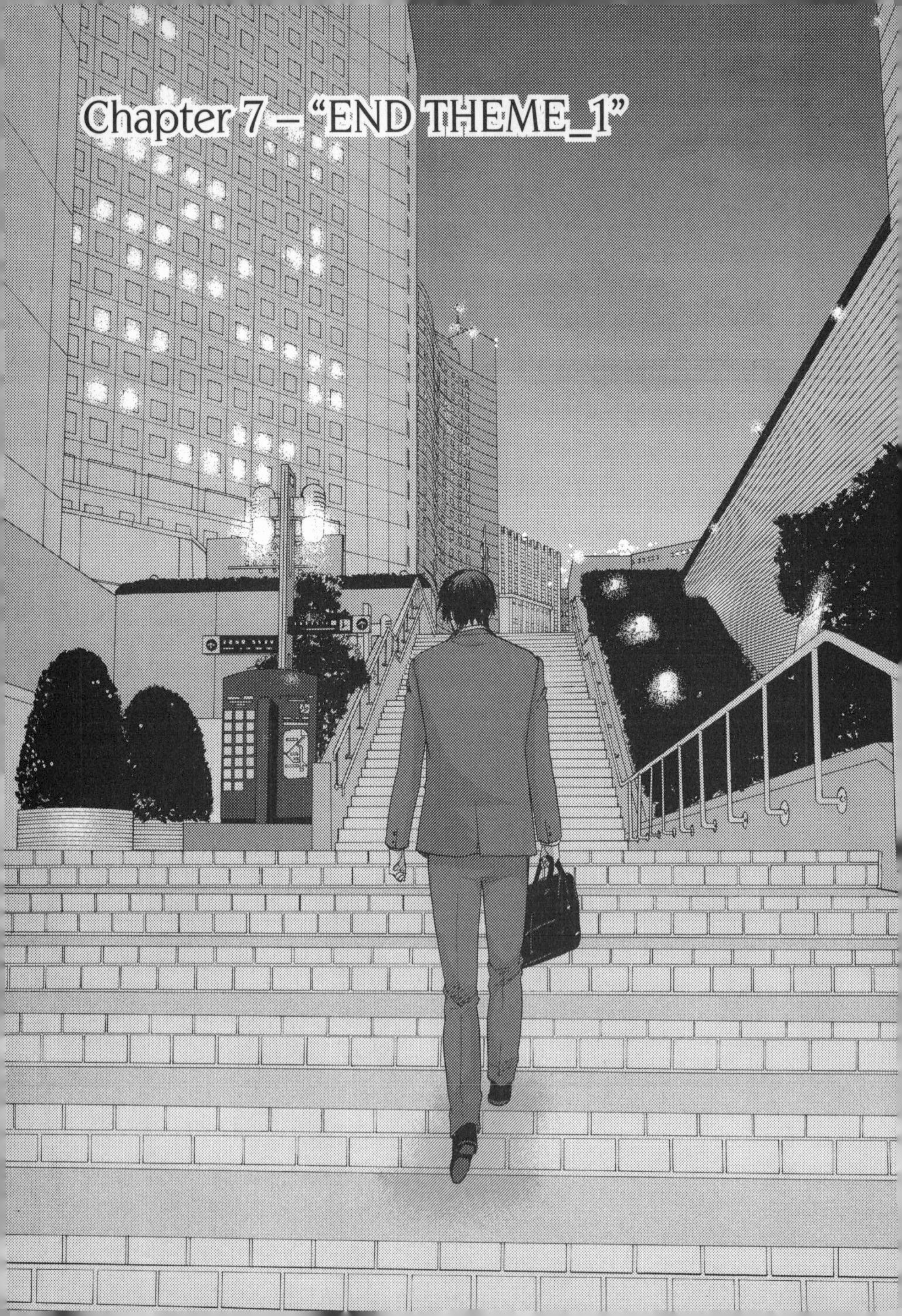

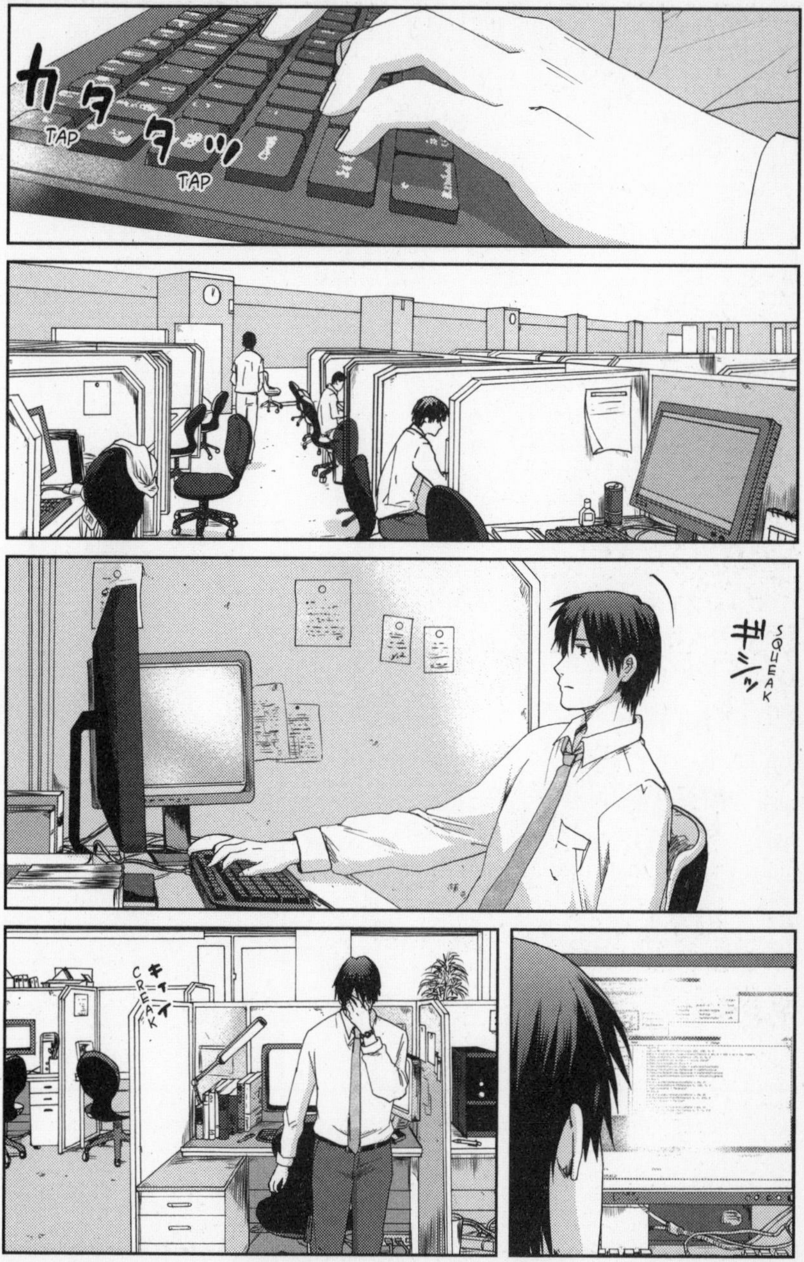
カタ
TAP
タタッ
TAP
ギシッ
SQUEAK
キィイ
CREAK

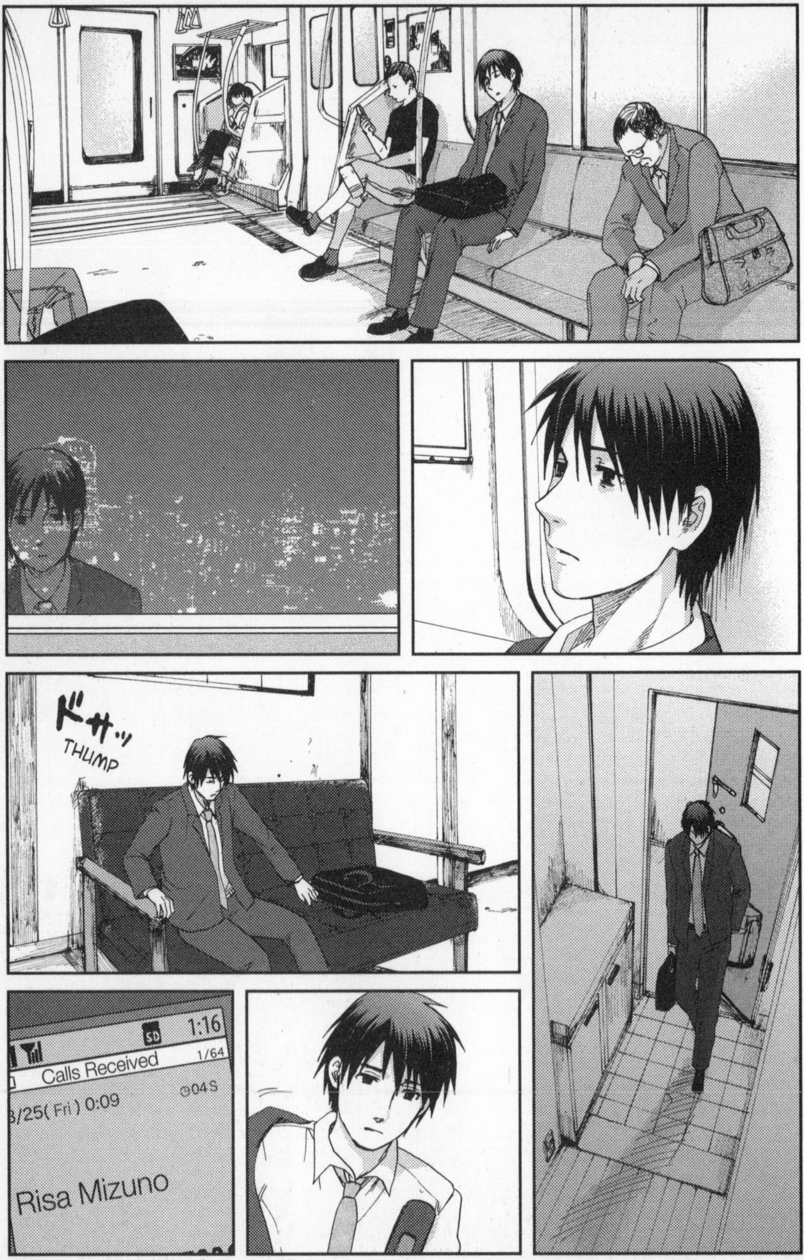
ドサッ
THUMP
1:16
SD
Calls Received
1/64
/25(Fri) 0:09
04S
Risa Mizuno

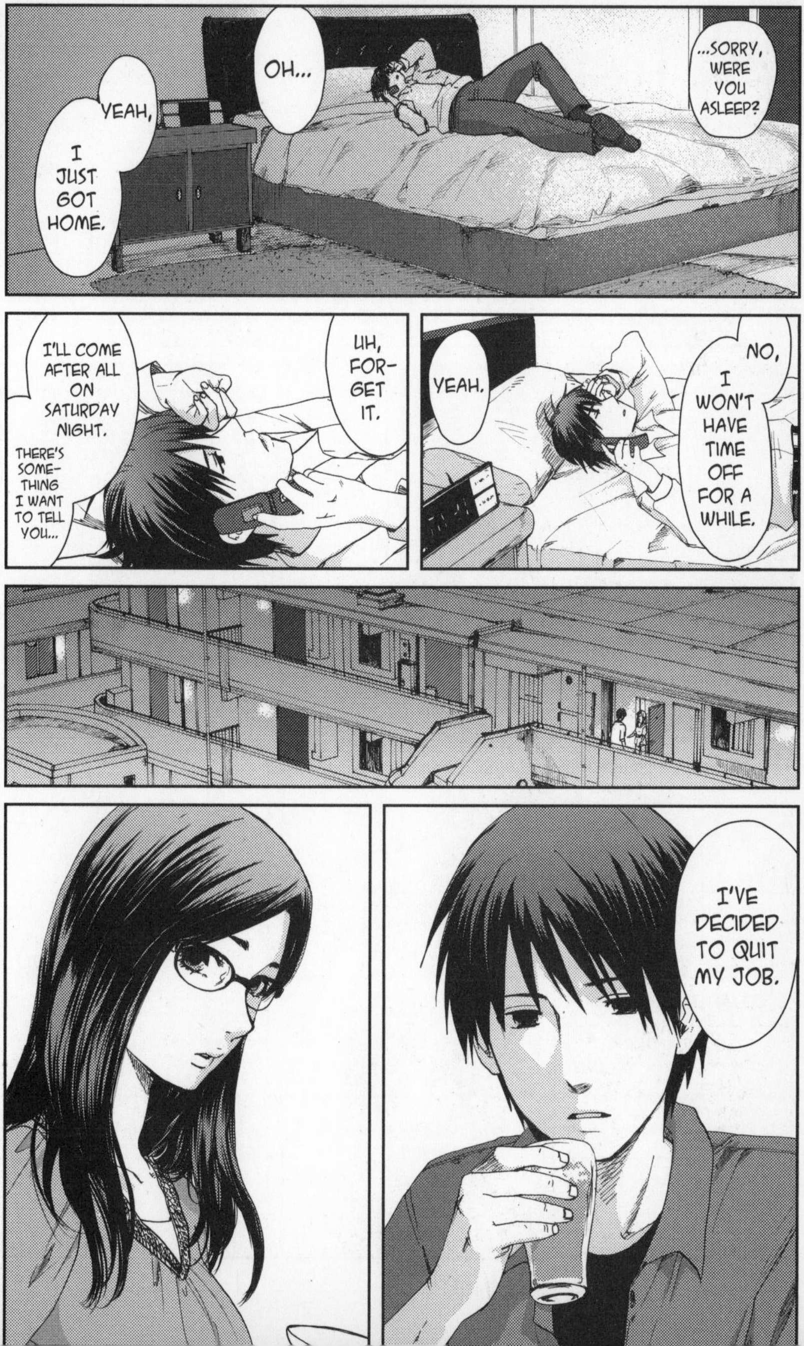
...SORRY, WERE YOU ASLEEP?
OH...
YEAH,
I JUST GOT HOME.
NO, I WON'T HAVE TIME OFF FOR A WHILE.
YEAH.
UH, FOR-GET IT.
I'LL COME AFTER ALL ON SATURDAY NIGHT.
THERE'S SOME-THING I WANT TO TELL YOU...
I'VE DECIDED TO QUIT MY JOB.

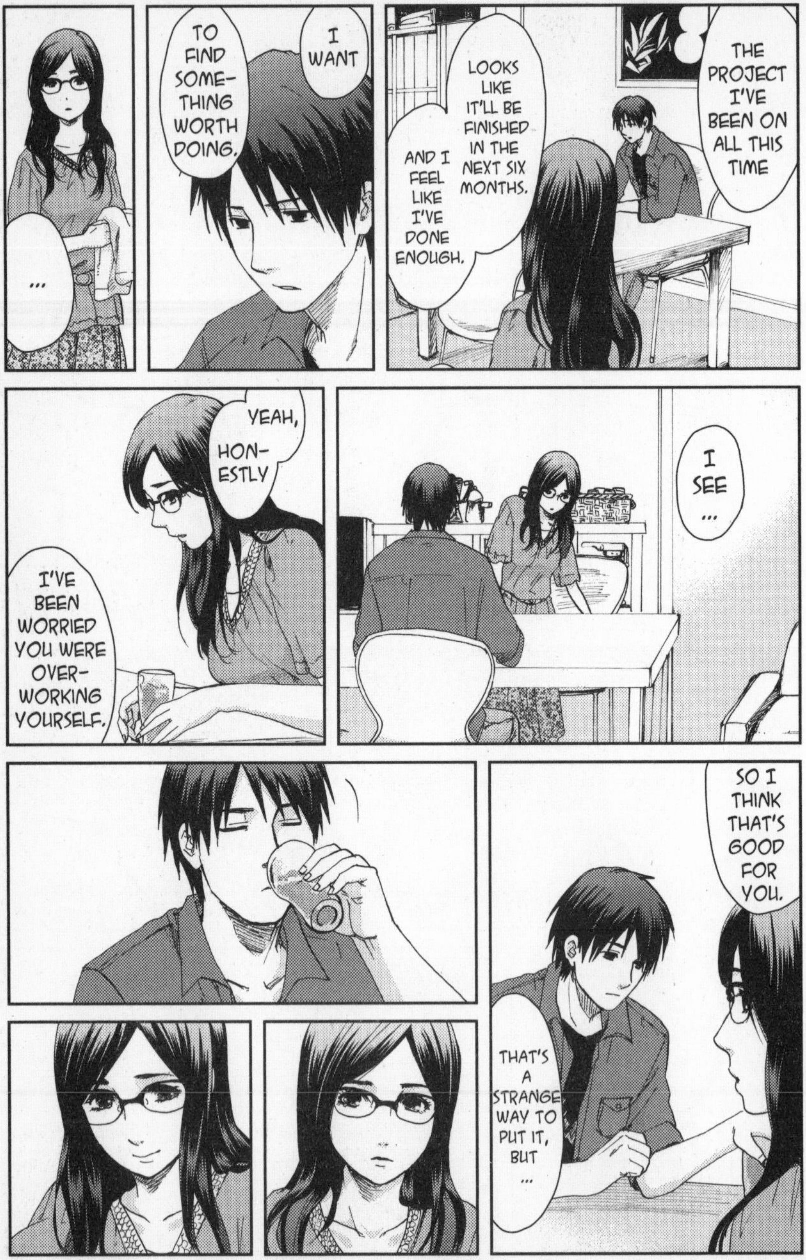
THE PROJECT I'VE BEEN ON ALL THIS TIME
LOOKS LIKE IT'LL BE FINISHED IN THE NEXT SIX MONTHS.
AND I FEEL LIKE I'VE DONE ENOUGH.
I WANT
TO FIND SOME-THING WORTH DOING.
...
I SEE ...
YEAH, HON-ESTLY
I'VE BEEN WORRIED YOU WERE OVER-WORKING YOURSELF.
SO I THINK THAT'S GOOD FOR YOU.
THAT'S A STRANGE WAY TO PUT IT, BUT ...

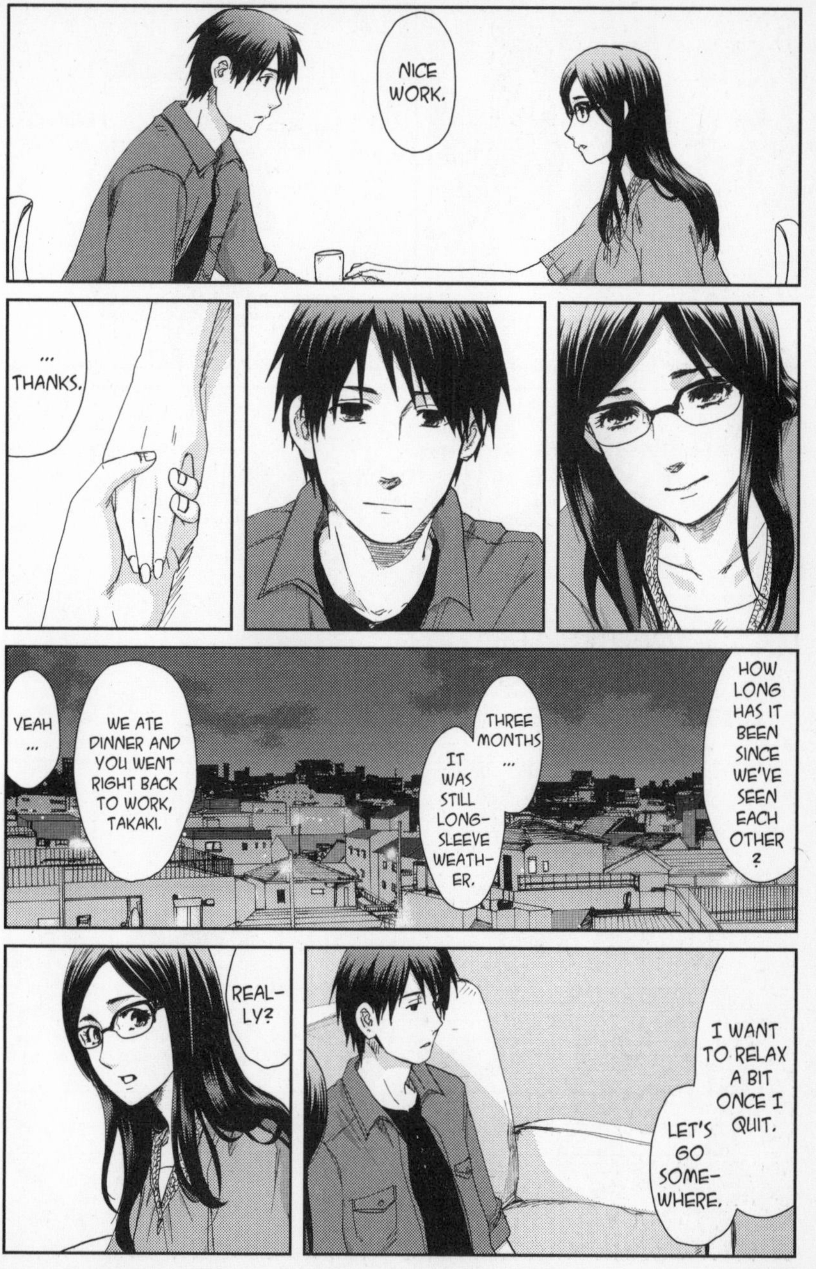
NICE WORK.
... THANKS.
HOW LONG HAS IT BEEN SINCE WE'VE SEEN EACH OTHER?
THREE MONTHS ...
IT WAS STILL LONG-SLEEVE WEATHER.
WE ATE DINNER AND YOU WENT RIGHT BACK TO WORK, TAKAKI.
YEAH ...
I WANT TO RELAX A BIT ONCE I QUIT.
LET'S GO SOME-WHERE.
REAL-LY?

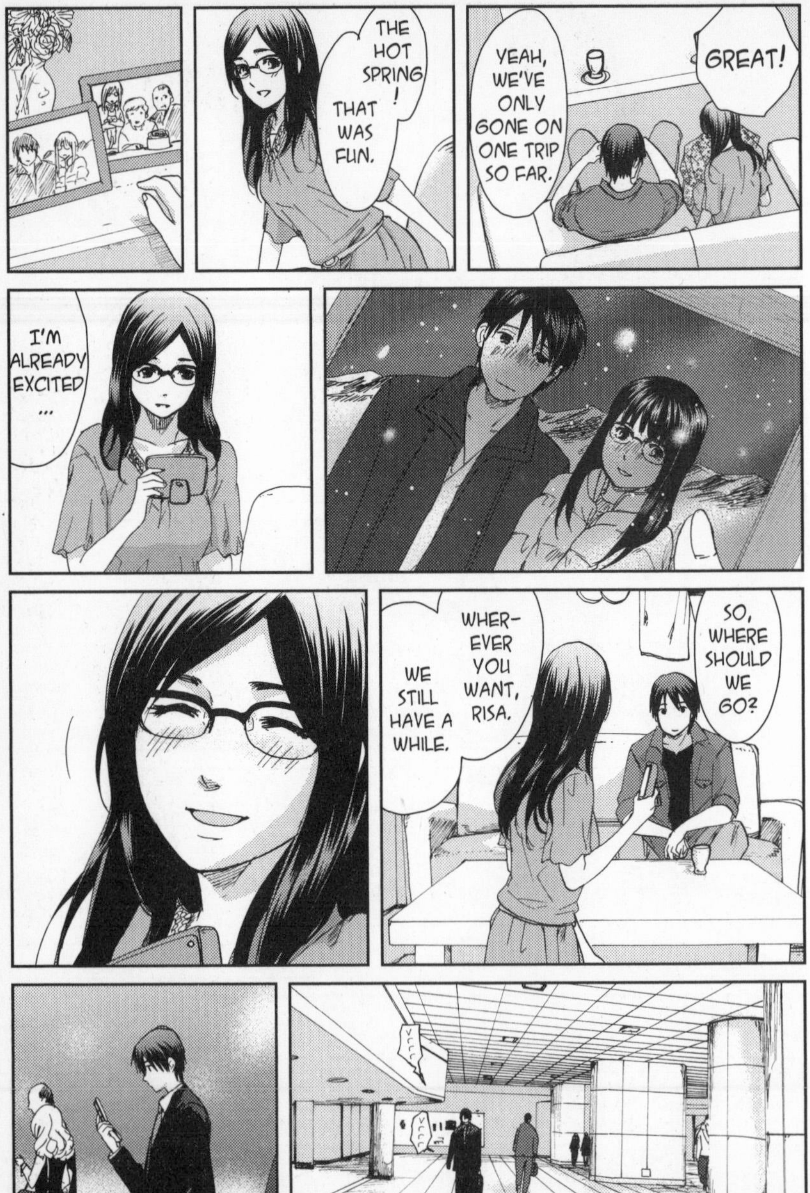
GREAT!
YEAH, WE'VE ONLY GONE ON ONE TRIP SO FAR.
THE HOT SPRING! THAT WAS FUN.
I'M ALREADY EXCITED...
SO, WHERE SHOULD WE GO?
WHEREVER YOU WANT, RISA.
WE STILL HAVE A WHILE.
VRRR
VRRR

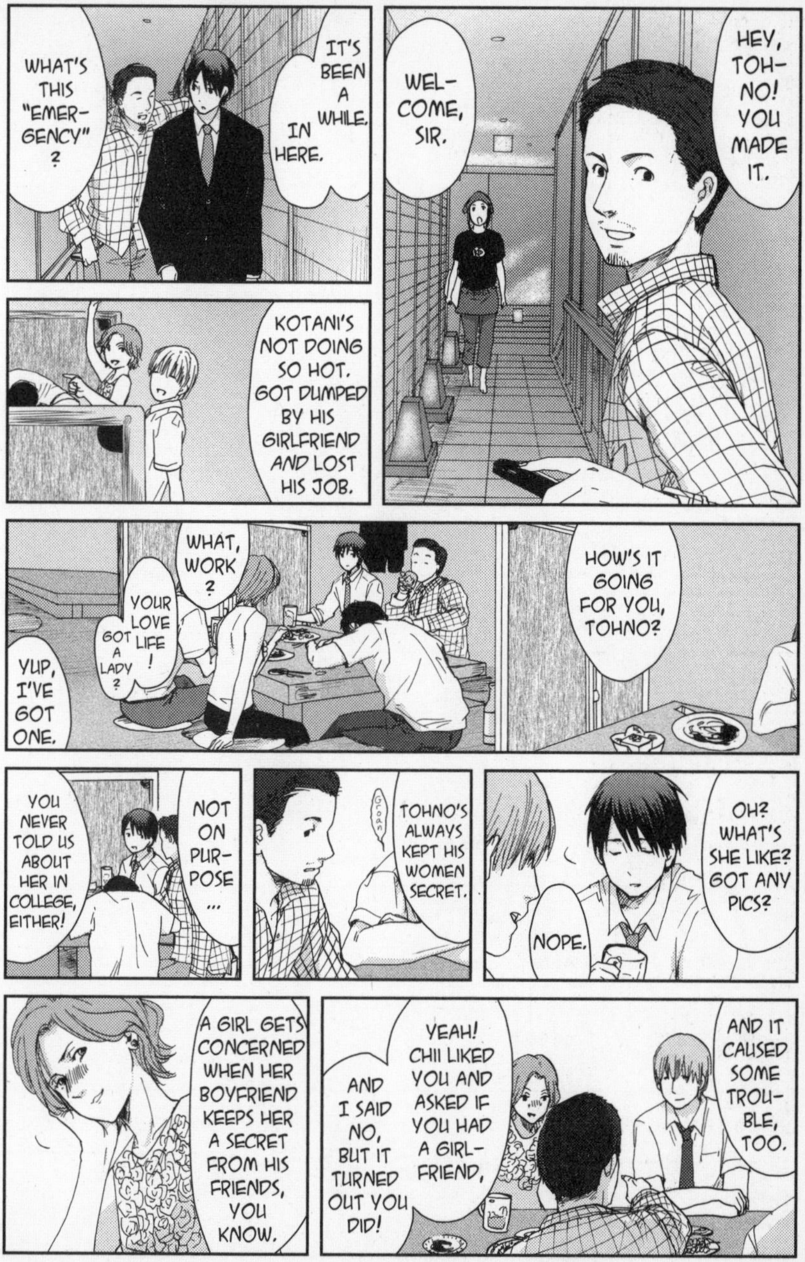
HEY, TOH-NO! YOU MADE IT.
WEL-COME, SIR.
IT'S BEEN A WHILE.
IN HERE.
WHAT'S THIS "EMER-GENCY"?
KOTANI'S NOT DOING SO HOT. GOT DUMPED BY HIS GIRLFRIEND AND LOST HIS JOB.
HOW'S IT GOING FOR YOU, TOHNO?
WHAT, WORK?
YOUR LOVE LIFE!
GOT A LADY?
YUP, I'VE GOT ONE.
OH? WHAT'S SHE LIKE? GOT ANY PICS?
NOPE.
Groan
TOHNO'S ALWAYS KEPT HIS WOMEN SECRET.
NOT ON PUR-POSE...
YOU NEVER TOLD US ABOUT HER IN COLLEGE, EITHER!
AND IT CAUSED SOME TROU-BLE, TOO.
YEAH! CHII LIKED YOU AND ASKED IF YOU HAD A GIRL-FRIEND,
AND I SAID NO, BUT IT TURNED OUT YOU DID!
A GIRL GETS CONCERNED WHEN HER BOYFRIEND KEEPS HER A SECRET FROM HIS FRIENDS, YOU KNOW.

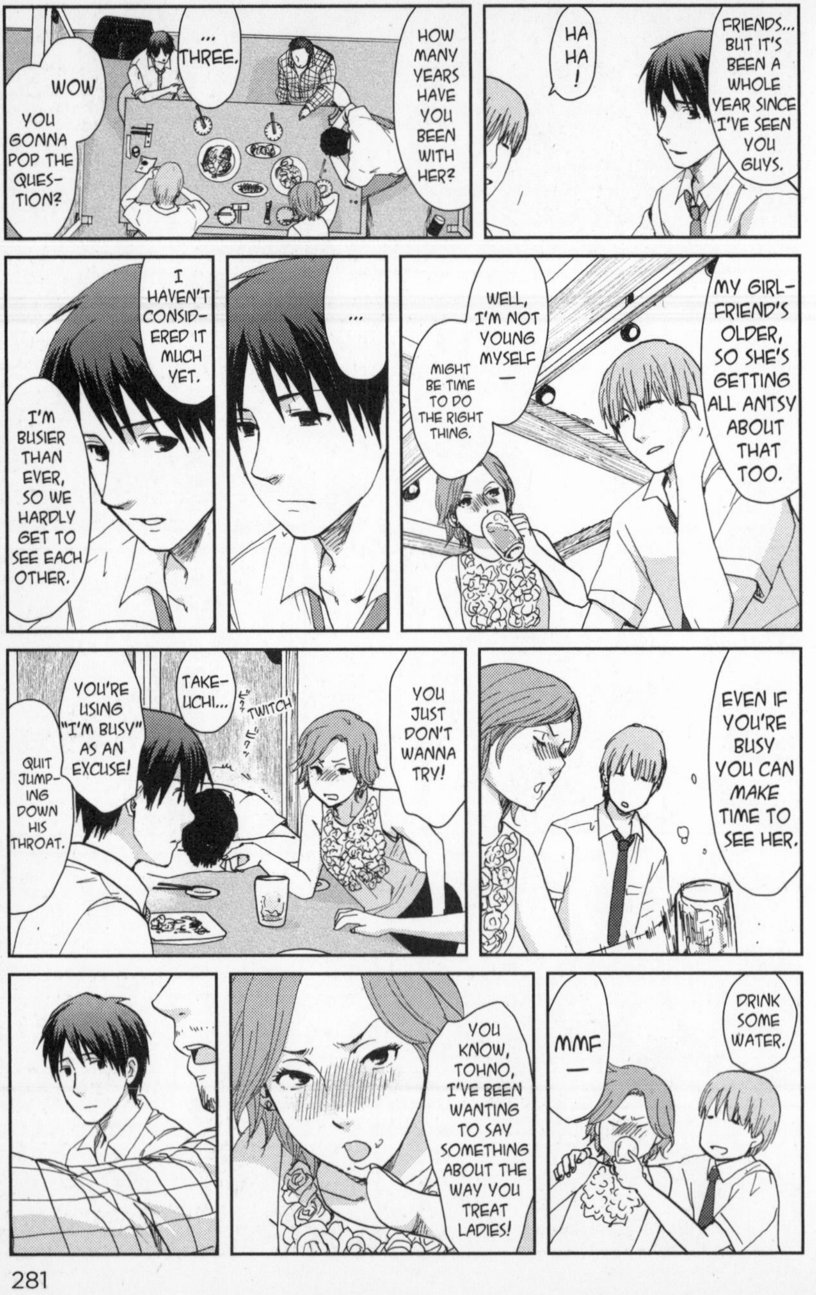
FRIENDS... BUT IT'S BEEN A WHOLE YEAR SINCE I'VE SEEN YOU GUYS.
HA HA!
HOW MANY YEARS HAVE YOU BEEN WITH HER?
... THREE.
WOW
YOU GONNA POP THE QUES-TION?
MY GIRL-FRIEND'S OLDER, SO SHE'S GETTING ALL ANTSY ABOUT THAT TOO.
WELL, I'M NOT YOUNG MYSELF—
MIGHT BE TIME TO DO THE RIGHT THING.
...
I HAVEN'T CONSID-ERED IT MUCH YET.
I'M BUSIER THAN EVER, SO WE HARDLY GET TO SEE EACH OTHER.
EVEN IF YOU'RE BUSY YOU CAN MAKE TIME TO SEE HER.
YOU JUST DON'T WANNA TRY!
TWITCH
TAKE-UCHI...
YOU'RE USING "I'M BUSY" AS AN EXCUSE!
QUIT JUMPING DOWN HIS THROAT.
DRINK SOME WATER.
MMF—
YOU KNOW, TOHNO, I'VE BEEN WANTING TO SAY SOMETHING ABOUT THE WAY YOU TREAT LADIES!

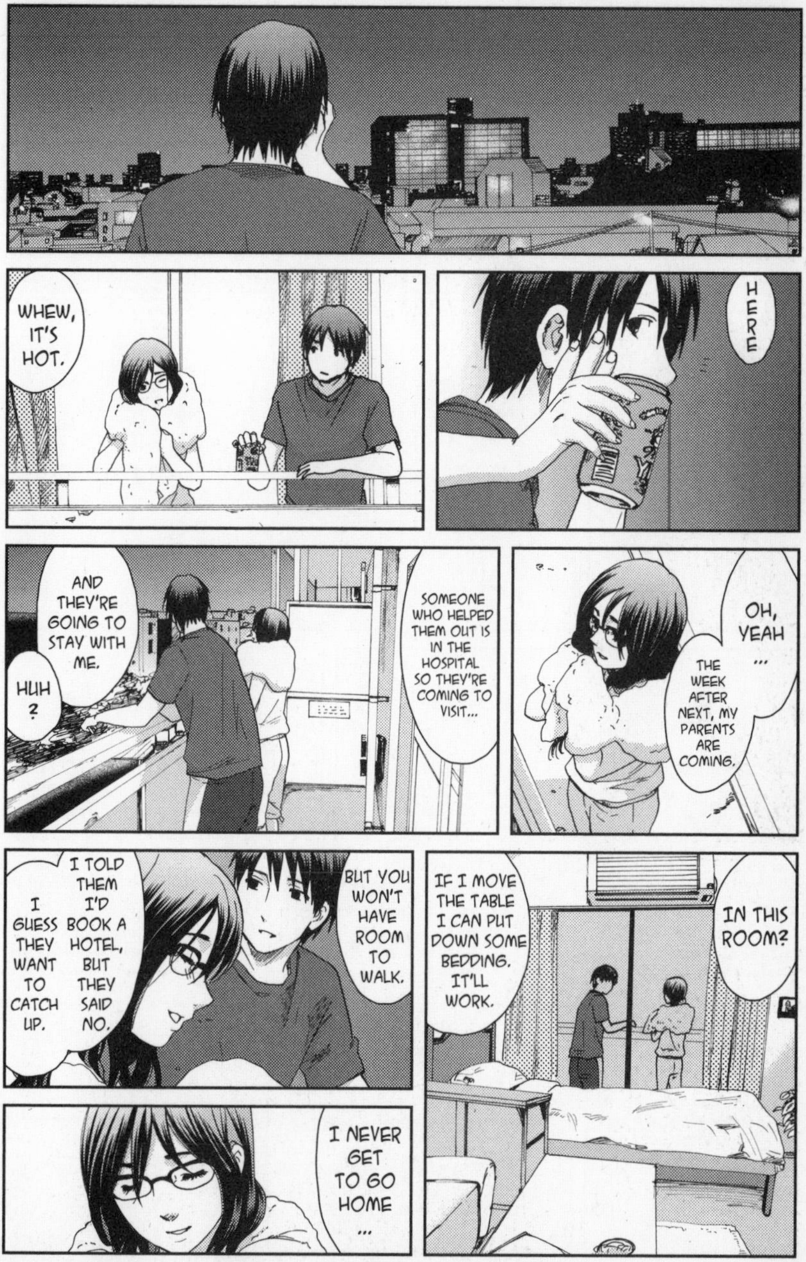
HERE
WHEW, IT'S HOT.
OH, YEAH ...
THE WEEK AFTER NEXT, MY PARENTS ARE COMING.
SOMEONE WHO HELPED THEM OUT IS IN THE HOSPITAL SO THEY'RE COMING TO VISIT...
AND THEY'RE GOING TO STAY WITH ME.
HUH?
IN THIS ROOM?
IF I MOVE THE TABLE I CAN PUT DOWN SOME BEDDING. IT'LL WORK.
BUT YOU WON'T HAVE ROOM TO WALK.
I TOLD THEM I'D BOOK A HOTEL, BUT THEY SAID NO.
I GUESS THEY WANT TO CATCH UP.
I NEVER GET TO GO HOME ...

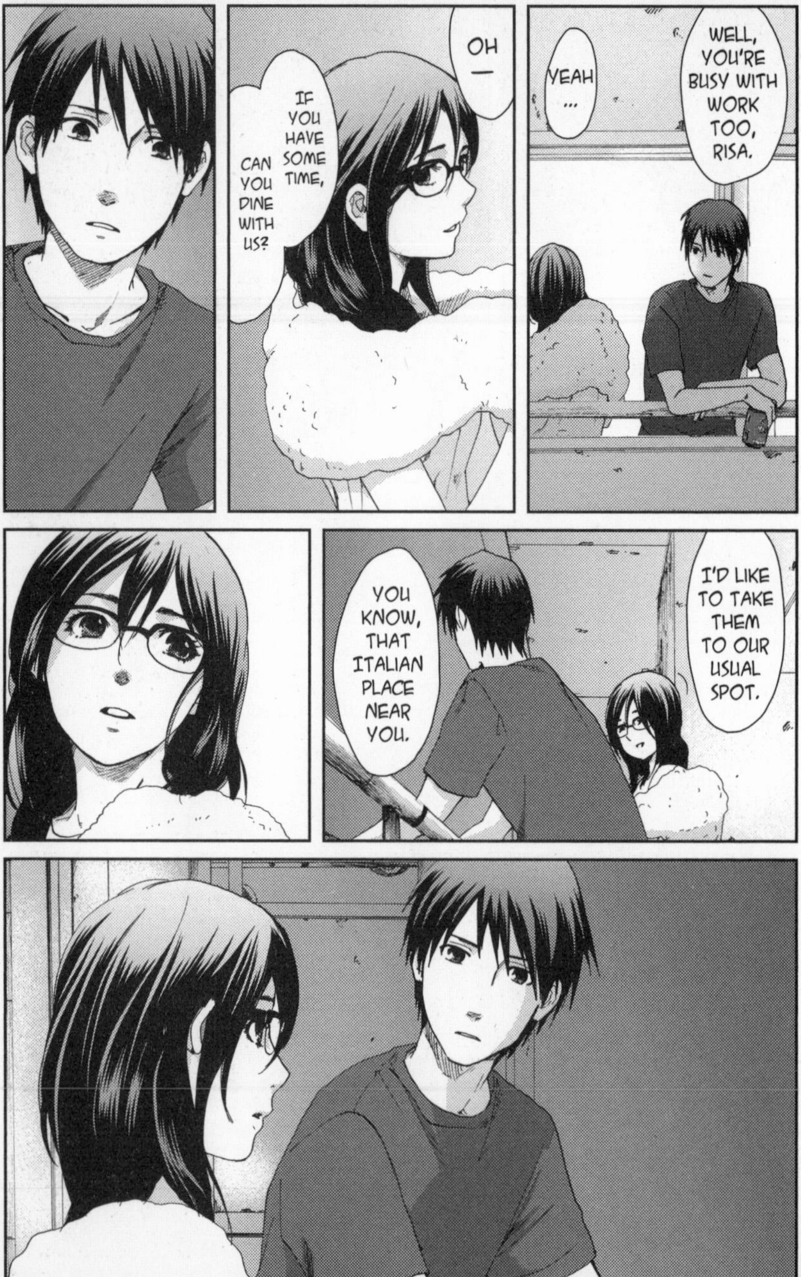
WELL, YOU'RE BUSY WITH WORK TOO, RISA.
YEAH ...
OH —
IF YOU HAVE SOME TIME, CAN YOU DINE WITH US?
I'D LIKE TO TAKE THEM TO OUR USUAL SPOT.
YOU KNOW, THAT ITALIAN PLACE NEAR YOU.

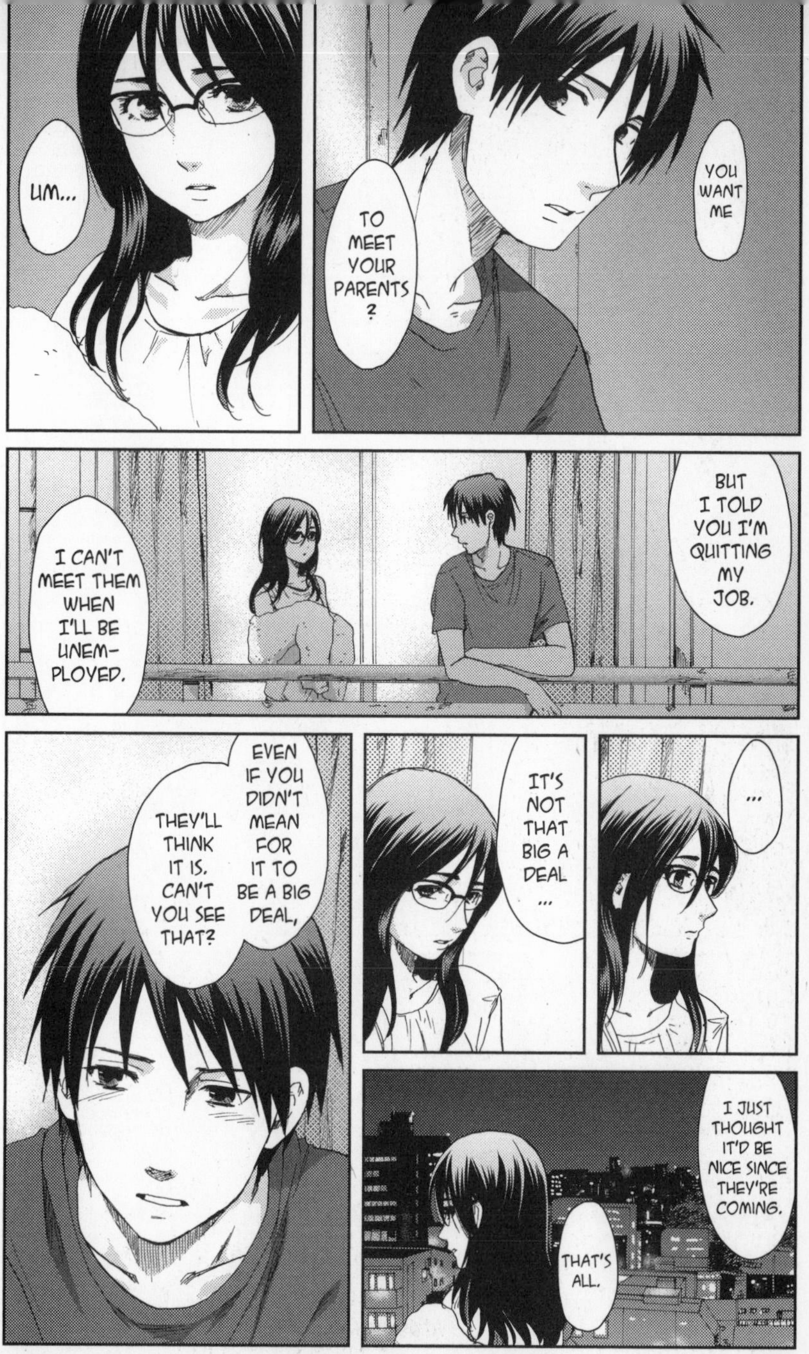
YOU WANT ME
TO MEET YOUR PARENTS?
UM...
BUT I TOLD YOU I'M QUITTING MY JOB.
I CAN'T MEET THEM WHEN I'LL BE UNEM-PLOYED.
...
IT'S NOT THAT BIG A DEAL...
I JUST THOUGHT IT'D BE NICE SINCE THEY'RE COMING.
THAT'S ALL.
EVEN IF YOU DIDN'T MEAN FOR IT TO BE A BIG DEAL,
THEY'LL THINK IT IS. CAN'T YOU SEE THAT?

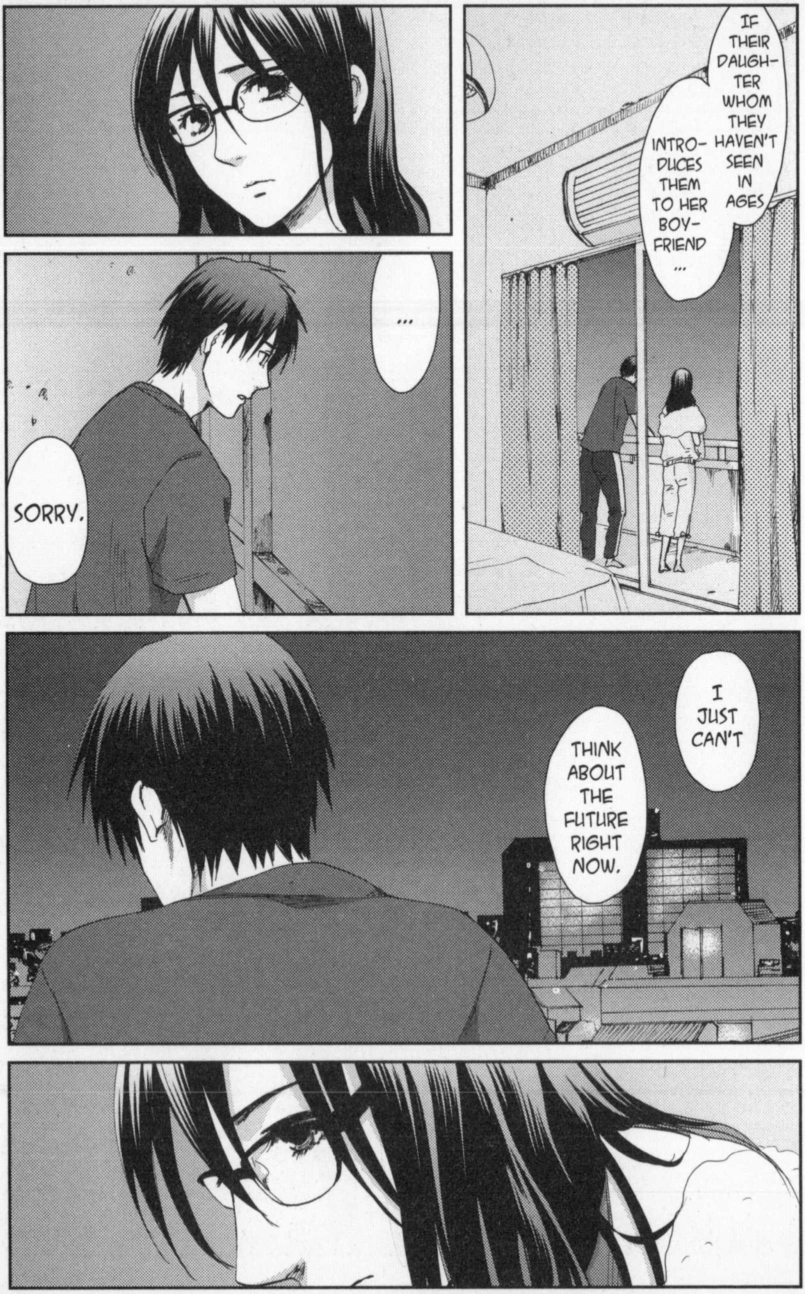
IF THEIR DAUGHTER WHOM THEY HAVEN'T SEEN IN AGES
INTRODUCES THEM TO HER BOYFRIEND ...
...
SORRY.
I JUST CAN'T
THINK ABOUT THE FUTURE RIGHT NOW.

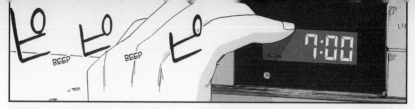

BEEP
BEEP

7:00

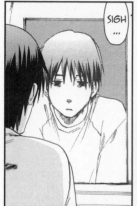

SIGH
...

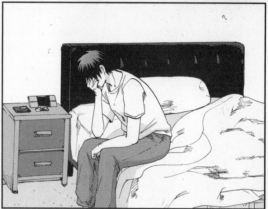

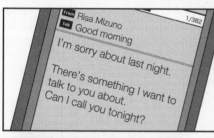

From Risa Mizuno
Sub Good morning

1/382

I'm sorry about last night.

There's something I want to talk to you about. Can I call you tonight?

Sub Re: Good morning

No, sorry.
I don't know when I'll get out of work today.
I'll let you know when I have time.

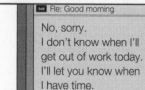

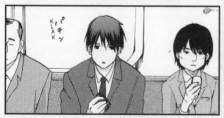

KLAK

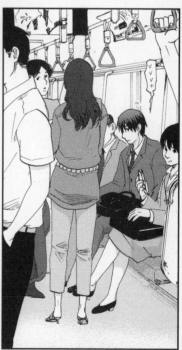

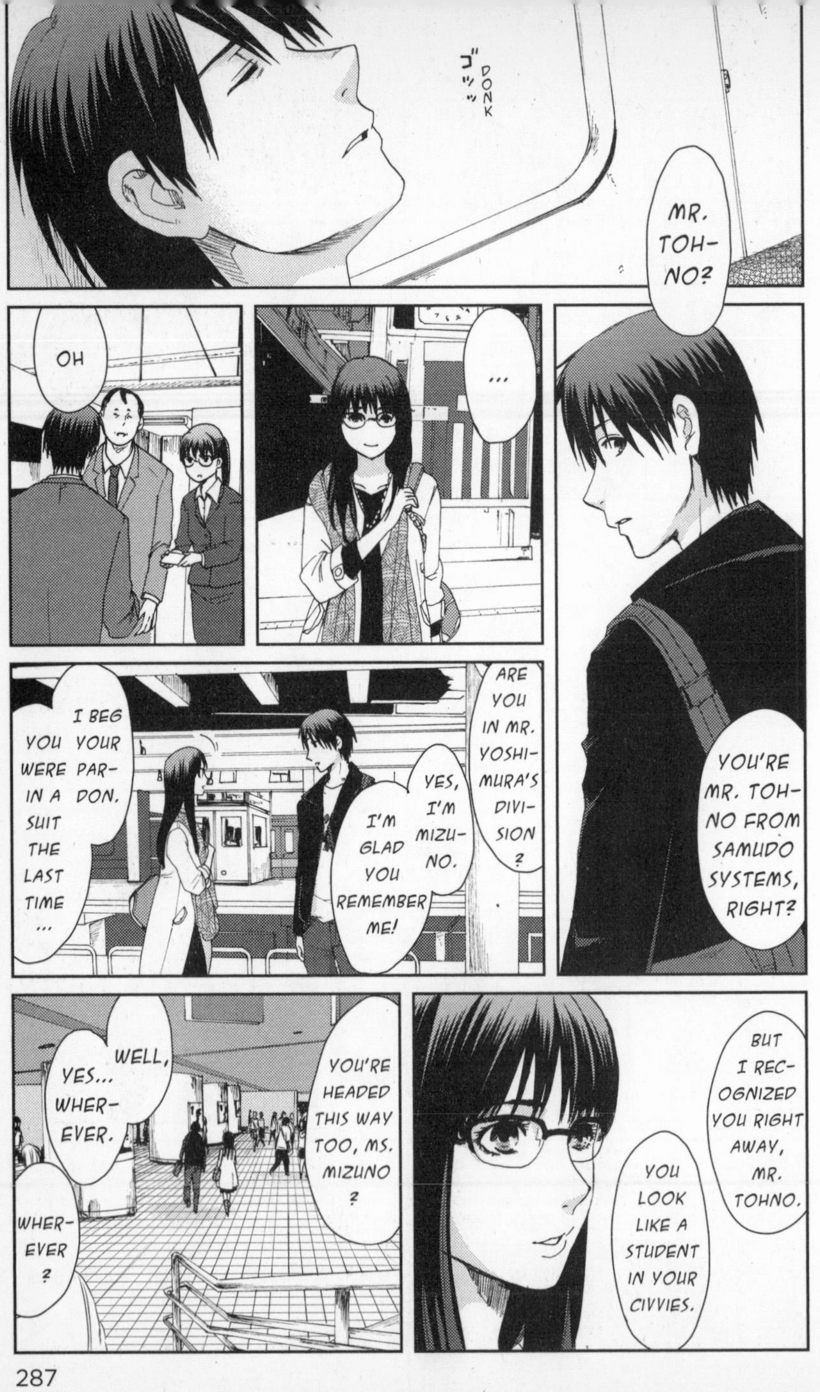
ゴッ
DONK
MR. TOH-NO?
YOU'RE MR. TOH-NO FROM SAMUDO SYSTEMS, RIGHT?
...
OH
ARE YOU IN MR. YOSHI-MURA'S DIVI-SION?
YES, I'M MIZU-NO.
I'M GLAD YOU REMEMBER ME!
I BEG YOUR PAR-DON.
YOU WERE IN A SUIT THE LAST TIME...
BUT I REC-OGNIZED YOU RIGHT AWAY, MR. TOHNO.
YOU LOOK LIKE A STUDENT IN YOUR CIVVIES.
YOU'RE HEADED THIS WAY TOO, MS. MIZUNO?
WELL, YES... WHER-EVER.
WHER-EVER?

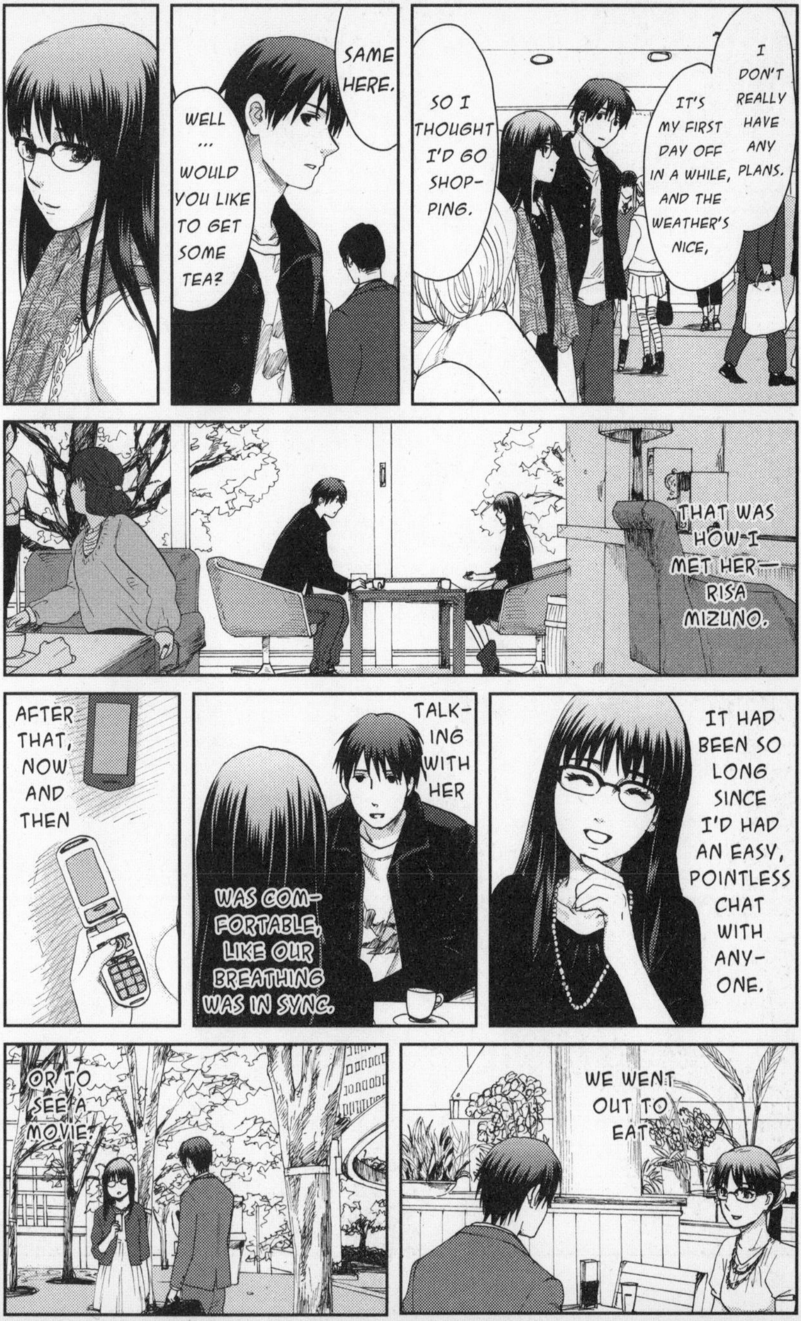
I DON'T REALLY HAVE ANY PLANS.
IT'S MY FIRST DAY OFF IN A WHILE, AND THE WEATHER'S NICE,
SO I THOUGHT I'D GO SHOP-PING.
SAME HERE.
WELL ... WOULD YOU LIKE TO GET SOME TEA?
THAT WAS HOW I MET HER— RISA MIZUNO.
IT HAD BEEN SO LONG SINCE I'D HAD AN EASY, POINTLESS CHAT WITH ANY-ONE.
TALK-ING WITH HER
WAS COM-FORTABLE, LIKE OUR BREATHING WAS IN SYNC.
AFTER THAT, NOW AND THEN
WE WENT OUT TO EAT
OR TO SEE A MOVIE.

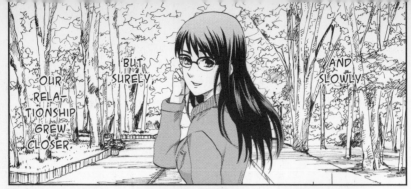

OUR RELA- TIONSHIP GREW CLOSER.

BUT SURELY,

AND SLOWLY.

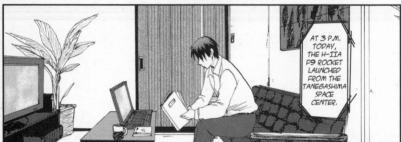

AT 3 P.M. TODAY, THE H-IIA F9 ROCKET LAUNCHED FROM THE TANEGASHIMA SPACE CENTER.

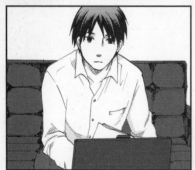

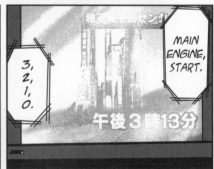

3, 2, 1, 0.

MAIN ENGINE, START.

午後3時13分

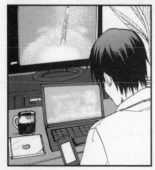

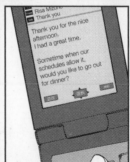

Risa Mizuno
Thank you

Thank you for the nice afternoon.
I had a great time.

Sometime when our schedules allow it, would you like to go out for dinner?

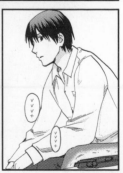

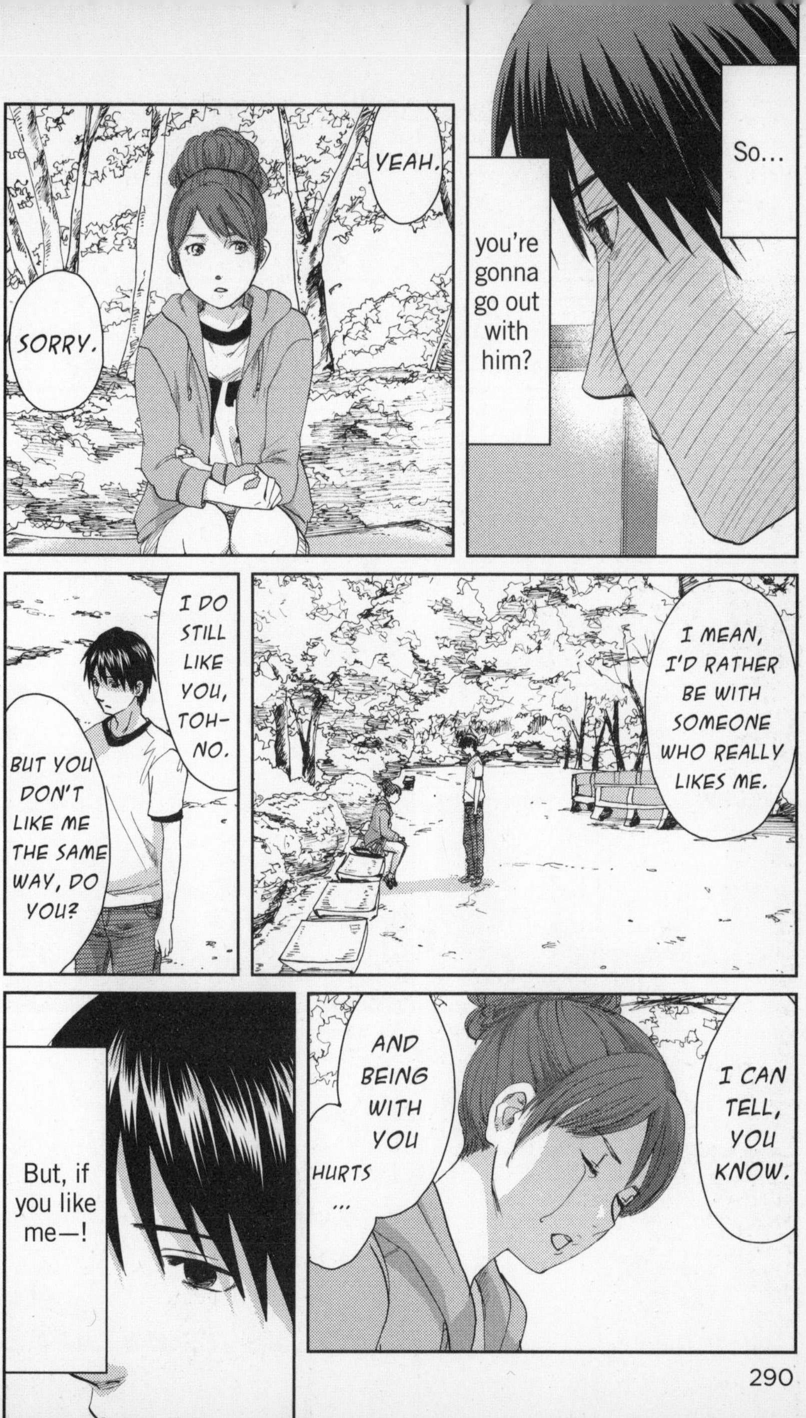
So...
you're gonna go out with him?
YEAH.
SORRY.
I MEAN, I'D RATHER BE WITH SOMEONE WHO REALLY LIKES ME.
I DO STILL LIKE YOU, TOH-NO.
BUT YOU DON'T LIKE ME THE SAME WAY, DO YOU?
I CAN TELL, YOU KNOW.
AND BEING WITH YOU HURTS...
But, if you like me—!

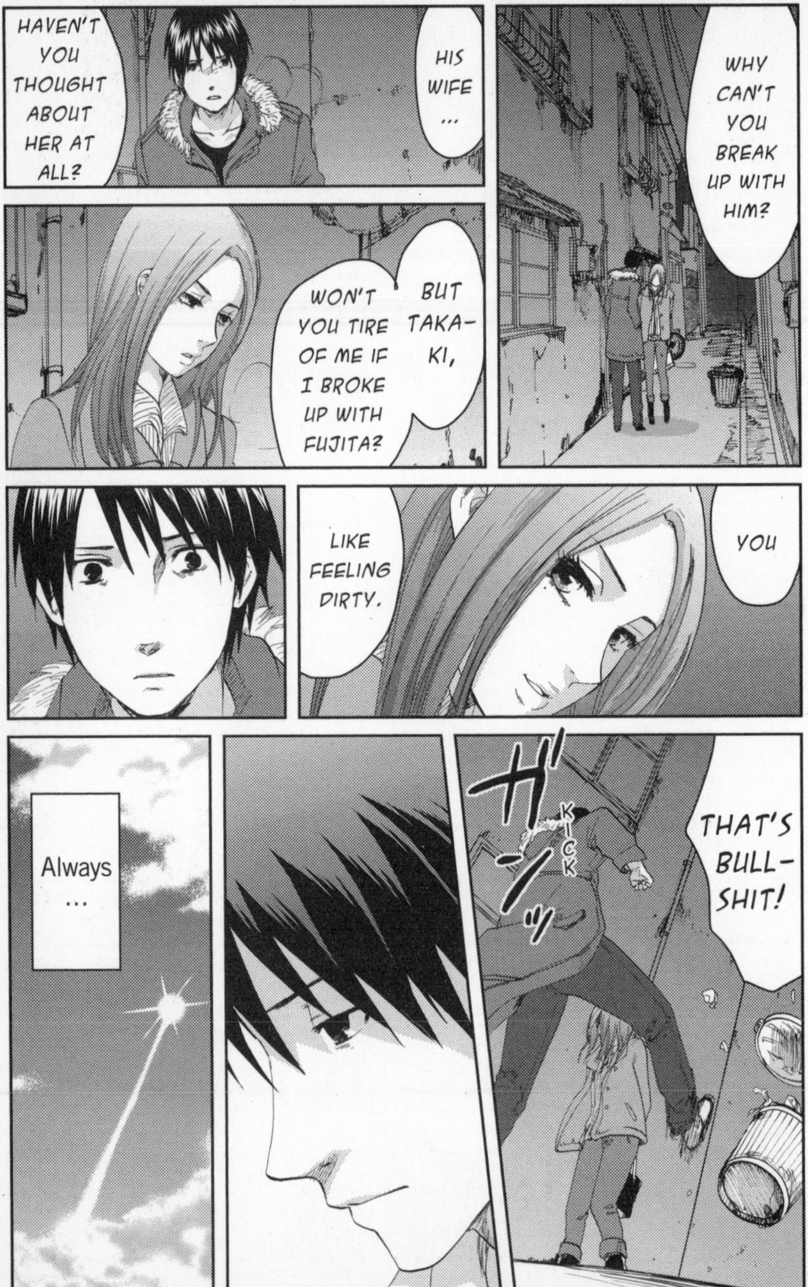
WHY CAN'T YOU BREAK UP WITH HIM?
HIS WIFE ...
HAVEN'T YOU THOUGHT ABOUT HER AT ALL?
BUT TAKA-KI,
WON'T YOU TIRE OF ME IF I BROKE UP WITH FUJITA?
YOU
LIKE FEELING DIRTY.
THAT'S BULL-SHIT!
KICK
Always ...

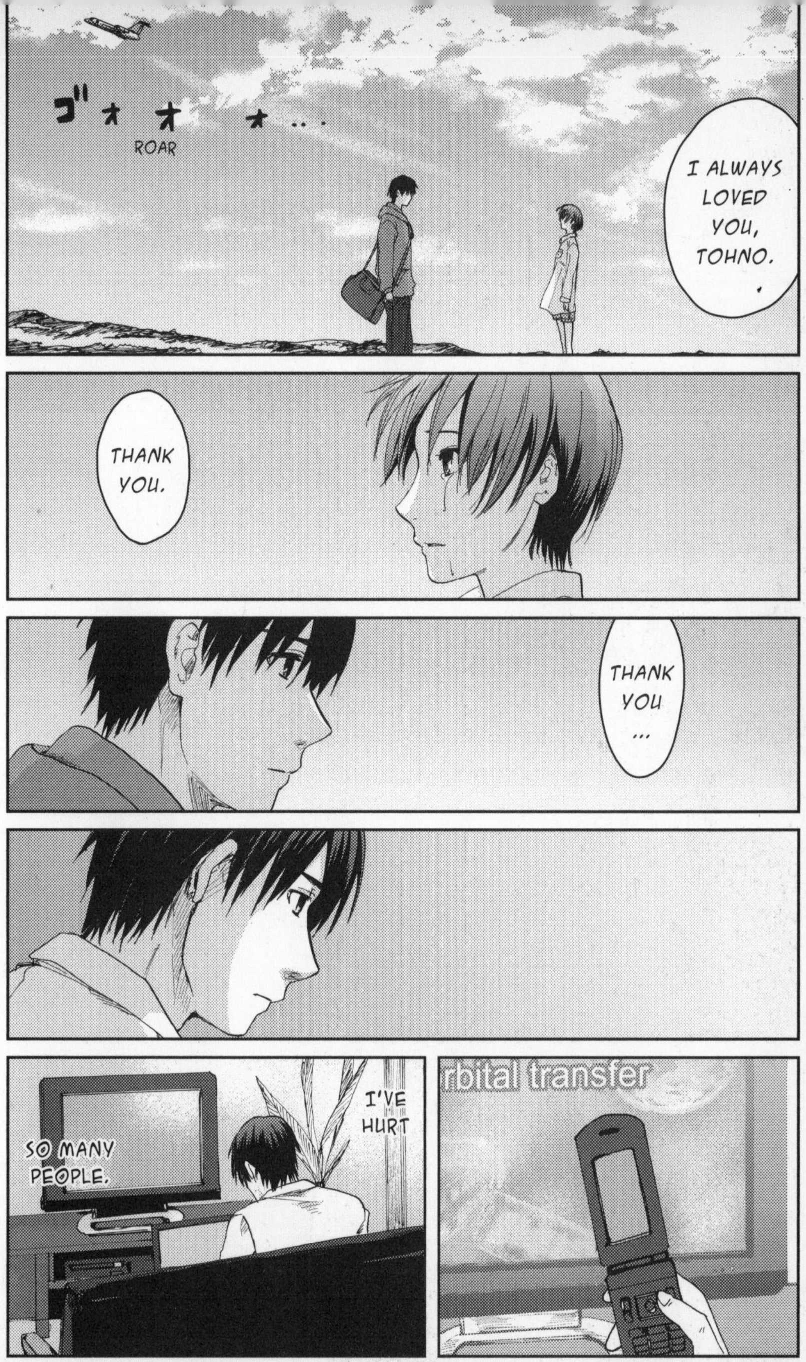
I ALWAYS LOVED YOU, TOHNO.
ゴォオォ...
ROAR
THANK YOU.
THANK YOU ...
rbital transfer
I'VE HURT
SO MANY PEOPLE.

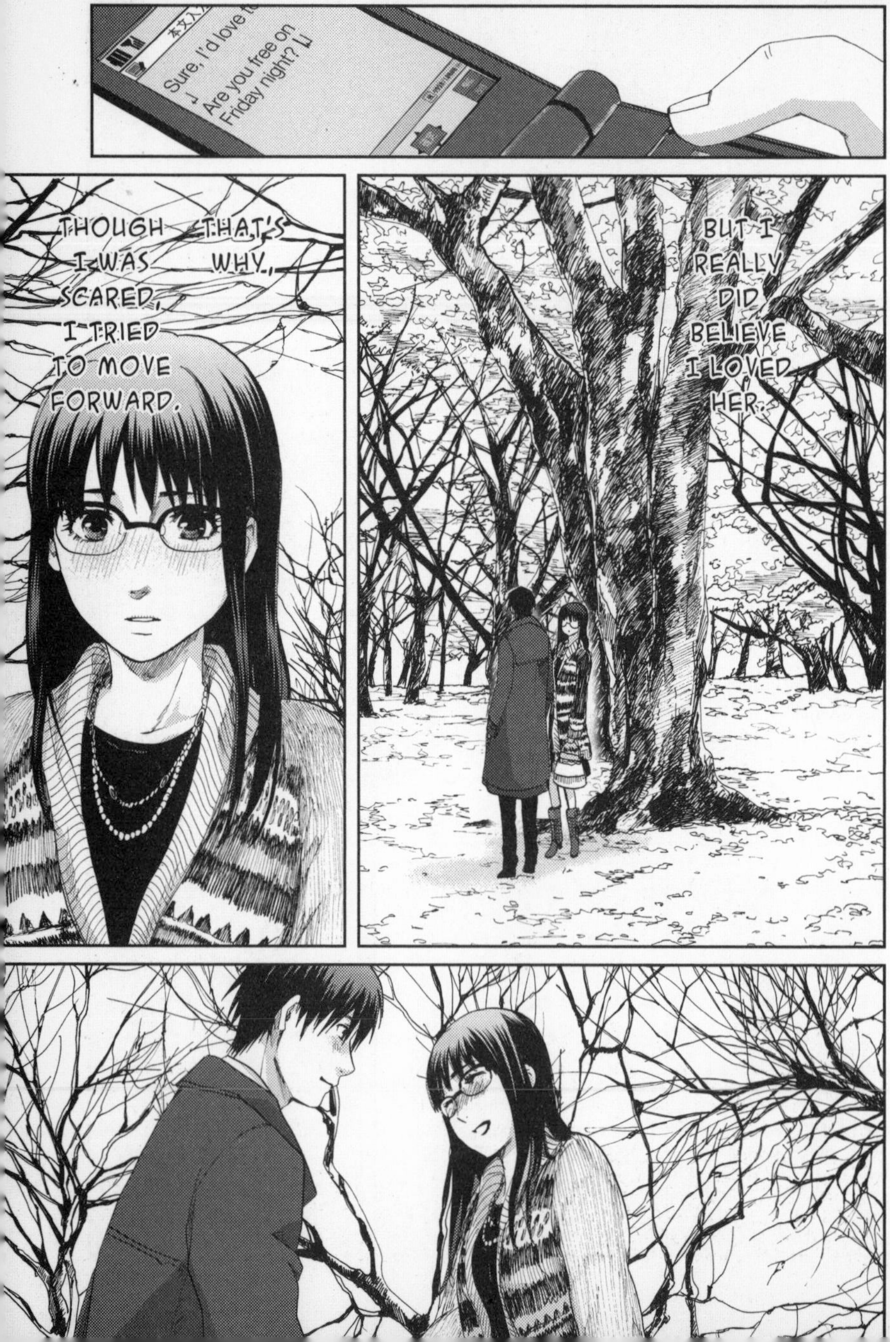

Sure, I'd love t
Are you free on Friday night?
BUT I REALLY DID BELIEVE I LOVED HER.
THAT'S WHY,
THOUGH I WAS SCARED, I TRIED TO MOVE FORWARD.

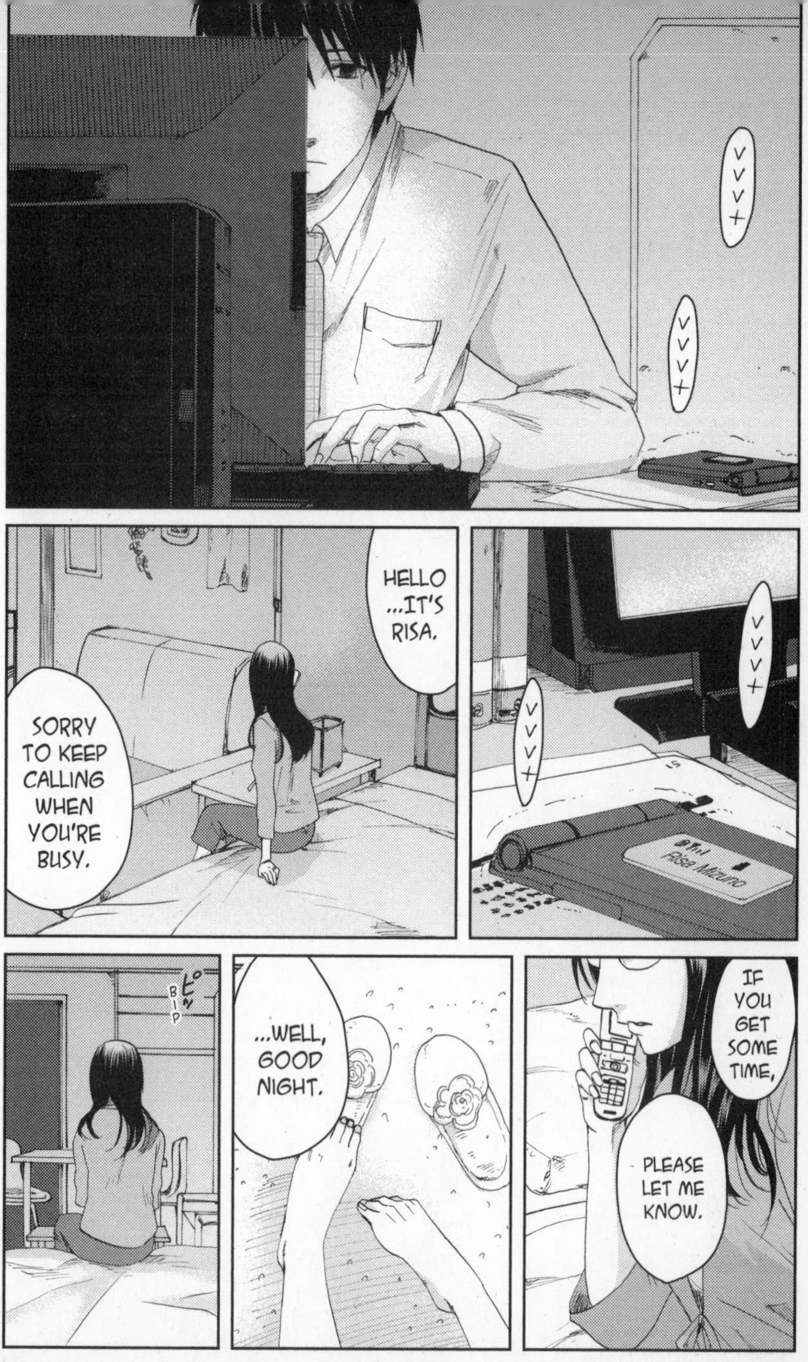
VVV+
VVV+
VVV+
VVV+
Risa Mizuno
HELLO ...IT'S RISA.
SORRY TO KEEP CALLING WHEN YOU'RE BUSY.
IF YOU GET SOME TIME,
PLEASE LET ME KNOW.
...WELL, GOOD NIGHT.
BIP

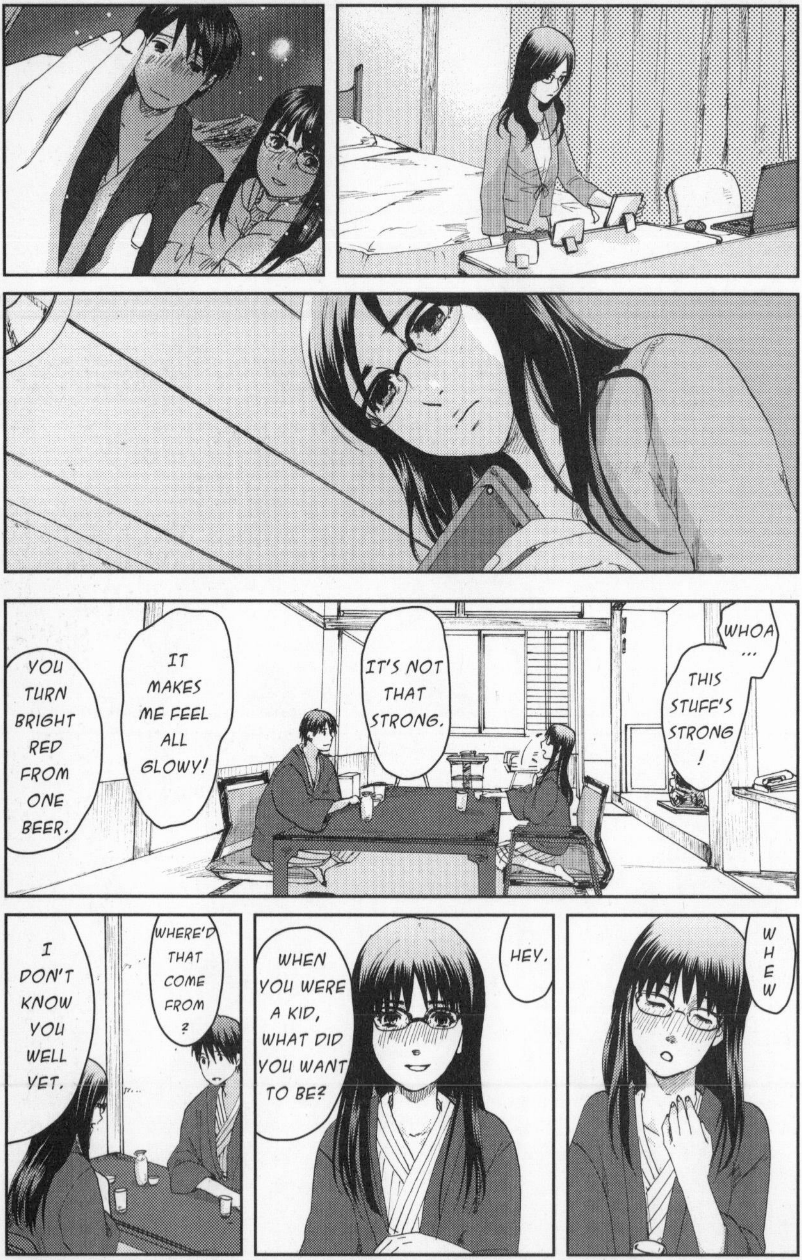
WHOA... THIS STUFF'S STRONG!
IT'S NOT THAT STRONG.
IT MAKES ME FEEL ALL GLOWY!
YOU TURN BRIGHT RED FROM ONE BEER.
WHEW
HEY.
WHEN YOU WERE A KID, WHAT DID YOU WANT TO BE?
WHERE'D THAT COME FROM?
I DON'T KNOW YOU WELL YET.

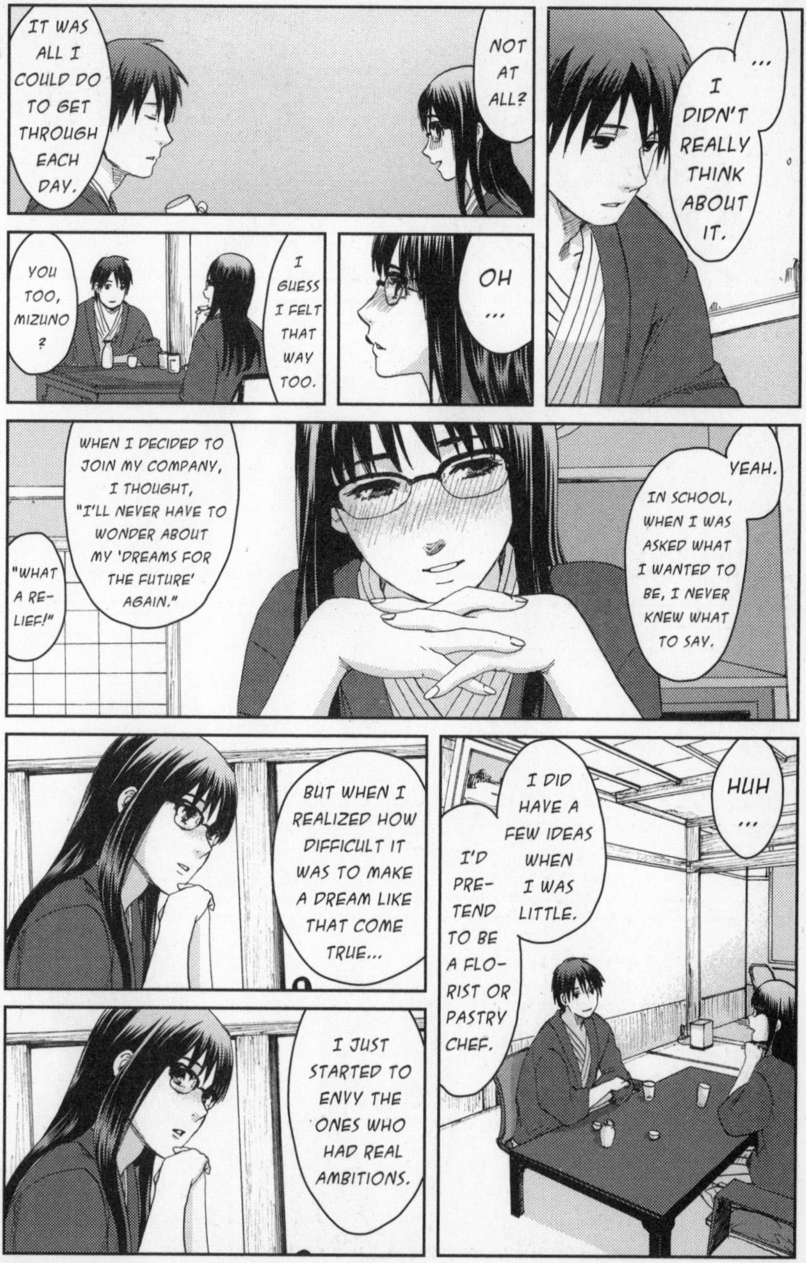
... I DIDN'T REALLY THINK ABOUT IT.
NOT AT ALL?
IT WAS ALL I COULD DO TO GET THROUGH EACH DAY.
OH ...
I GUESS I FELT THAT WAY TOO.
YOU TOO, MIZUNO?
YEAH.
IN SCHOOL, WHEN I WAS ASKED WHAT I WANTED TO BE, I NEVER KNEW WHAT TO SAY.
WHEN I DECIDED TO JOIN MY COMPANY, I THOUGHT, "I'LL NEVER HAVE TO WONDER ABOUT MY 'DREAMS FOR THE FUTURE' AGAIN."
"WHAT A RE-LIEF!"
HUH ...
I DID HAVE A FEW IDEAS WHEN I WAS LITTLE.
I'D PRE-TEND TO BE A FLO-RIST OR PASTRY CHEF.
BUT WHEN I REALIZED HOW DIFFICULT IT WAS TO MAKE A DREAM LIKE THAT COME TRUE...
I JUST STARTED TO ENVY THE ONES WHO HAD REAL AMBITIONS.

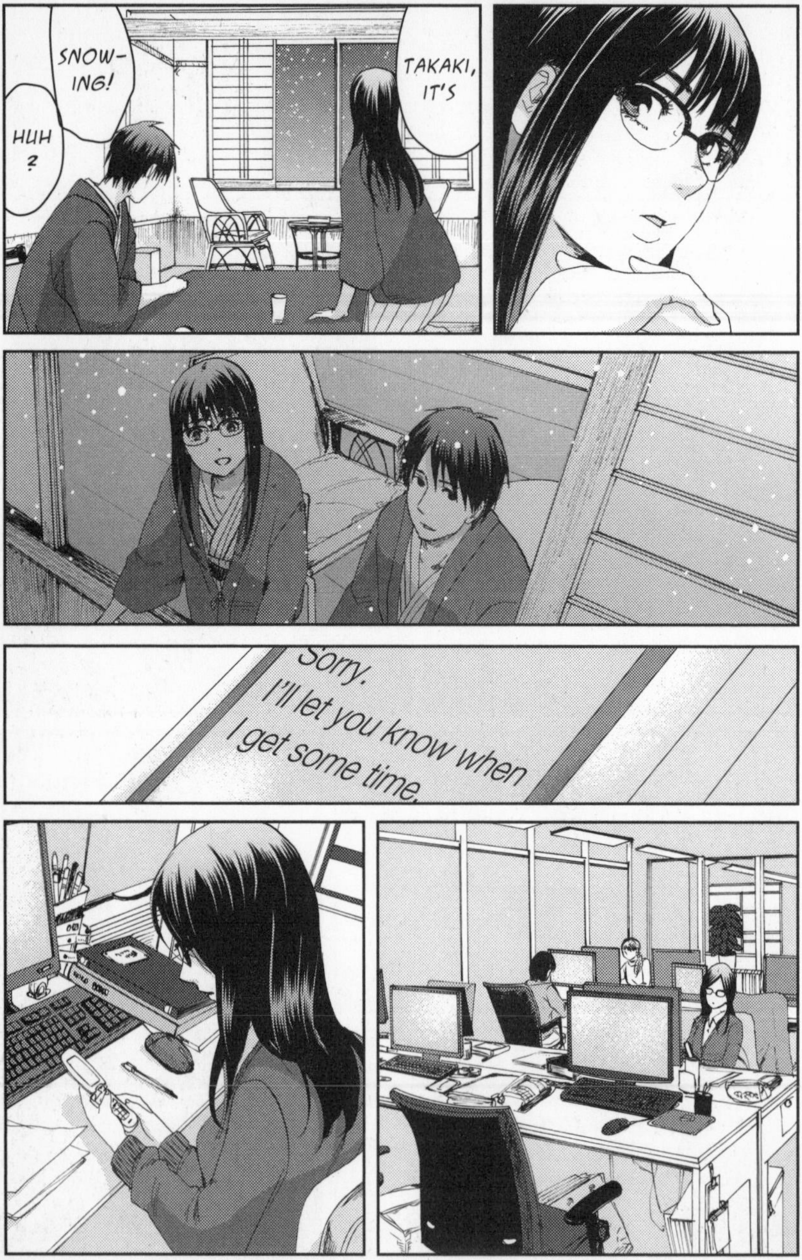
TAKAKI, IT'S
SNOWING!
HUH?
Sorry.
I'll let you know when
I get some time.

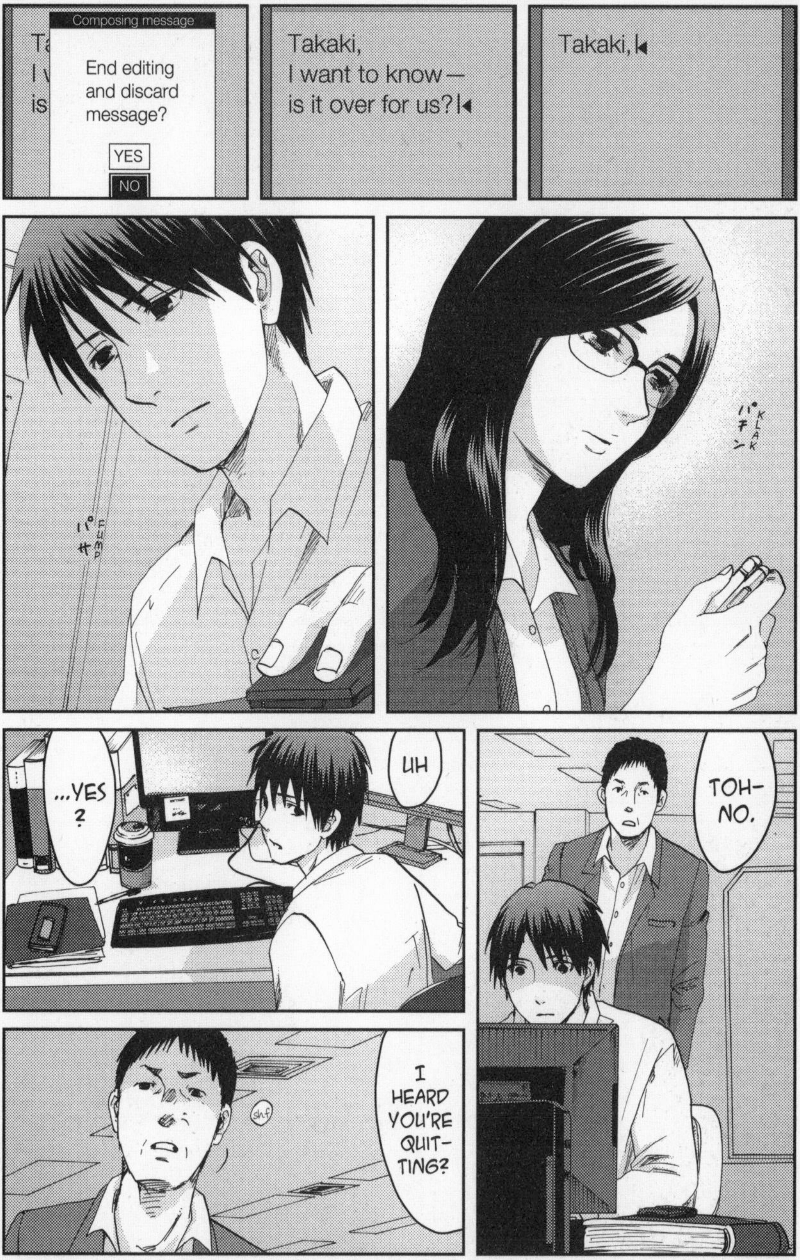
Takaki, I
Takaki,
I want to know—
is it over for us? I
Composing message
End editing
and discard
message?
YES
NO
パチン
KLAK
パサ
FUMP
TOH-NO.
UH
...YES?
I HEARD YOU'RE QUIT-TING?
shf

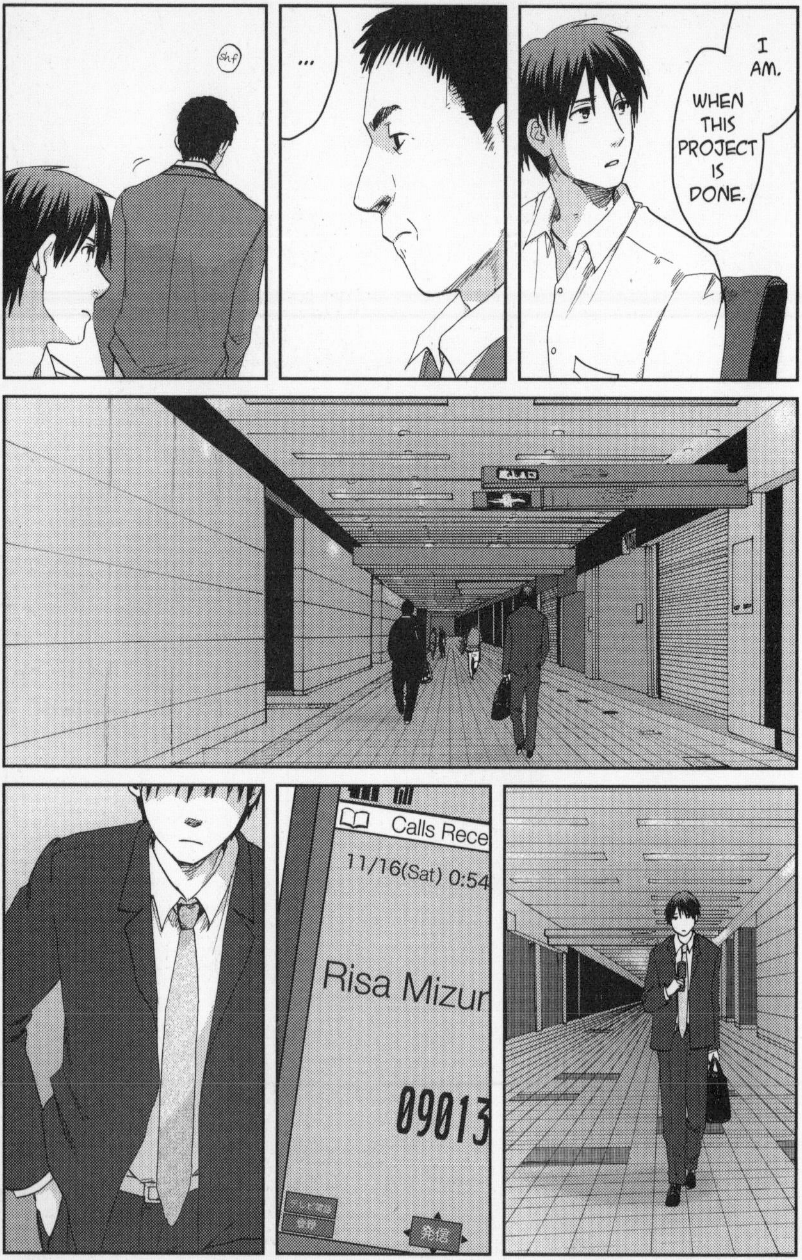
I AM. WHEN THIS PROJECT IS DONE.
...
shf
Calls Rece
11/16(Sat) 0:54
Risa Mizur
09013
発信

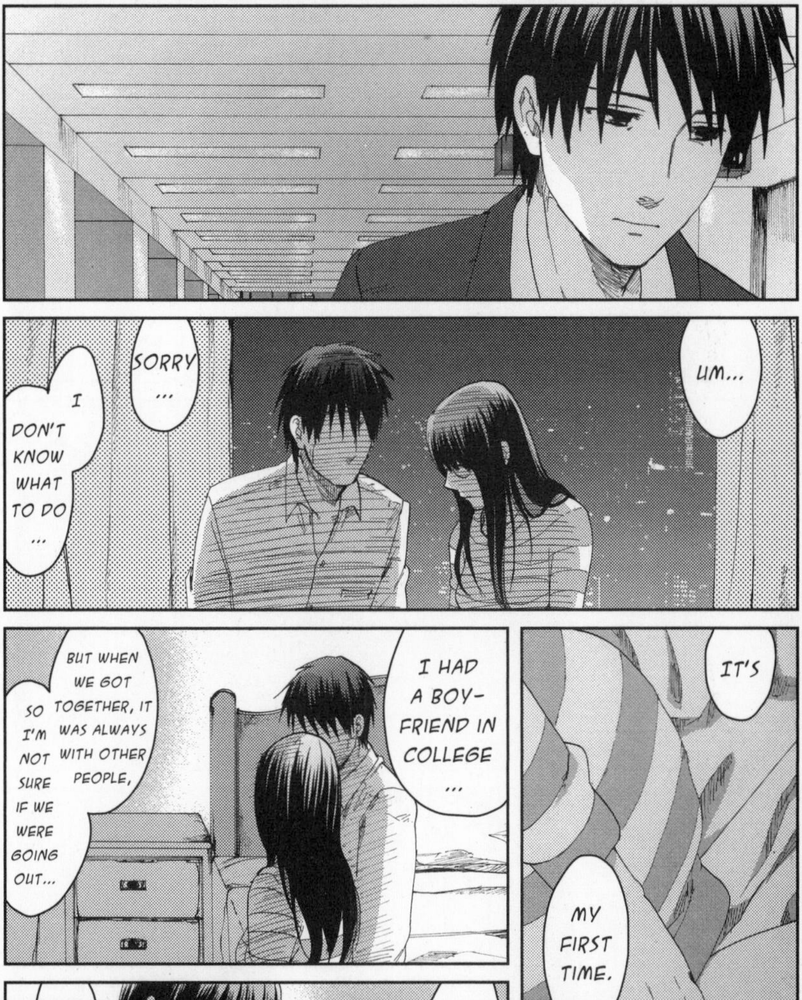
UM...
SORRY ...
I DON'T KNOW WHAT TO DO ...
IT'S
MY FIRST TIME.
I HAD A BOY-FRIEND IN COLLEGE ...
BUT WHEN WE GOT TOGETHER, IT WAS ALWAYS WITH OTHER PEOPLE,
SO I'M NOT SURE IF WE WERE GOING OUT...
AND THEN, BEFORE I KNEW IT HE GOT CLOSER TO ANOTHER GIRL, AND THAT WAS IT...
SO ...
UMM ...

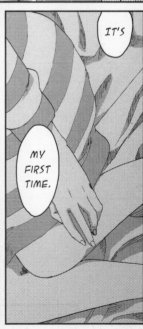

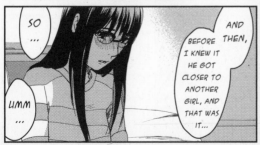

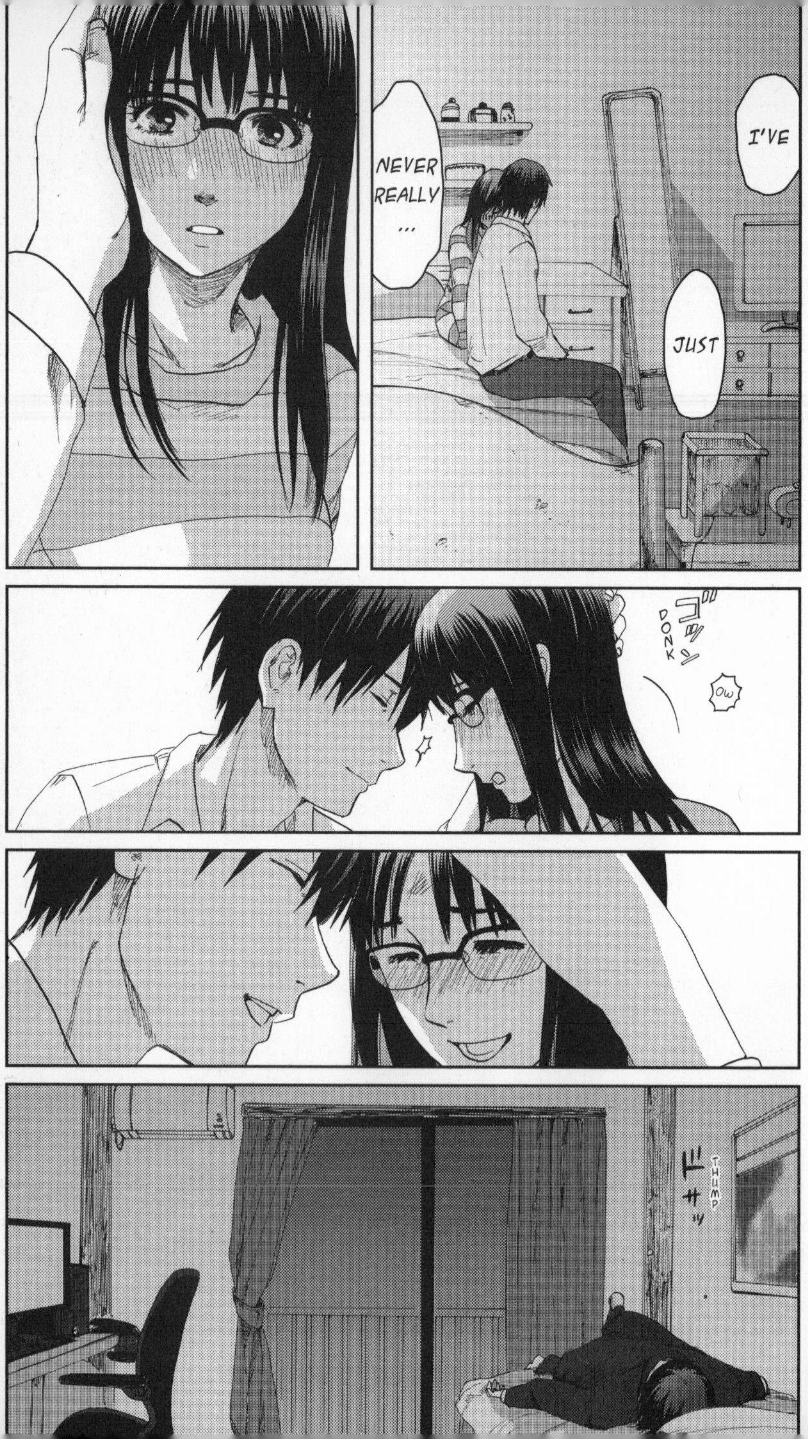
I'VE
NEVER REALLY ...
JUST
DONK
OW
THUMP

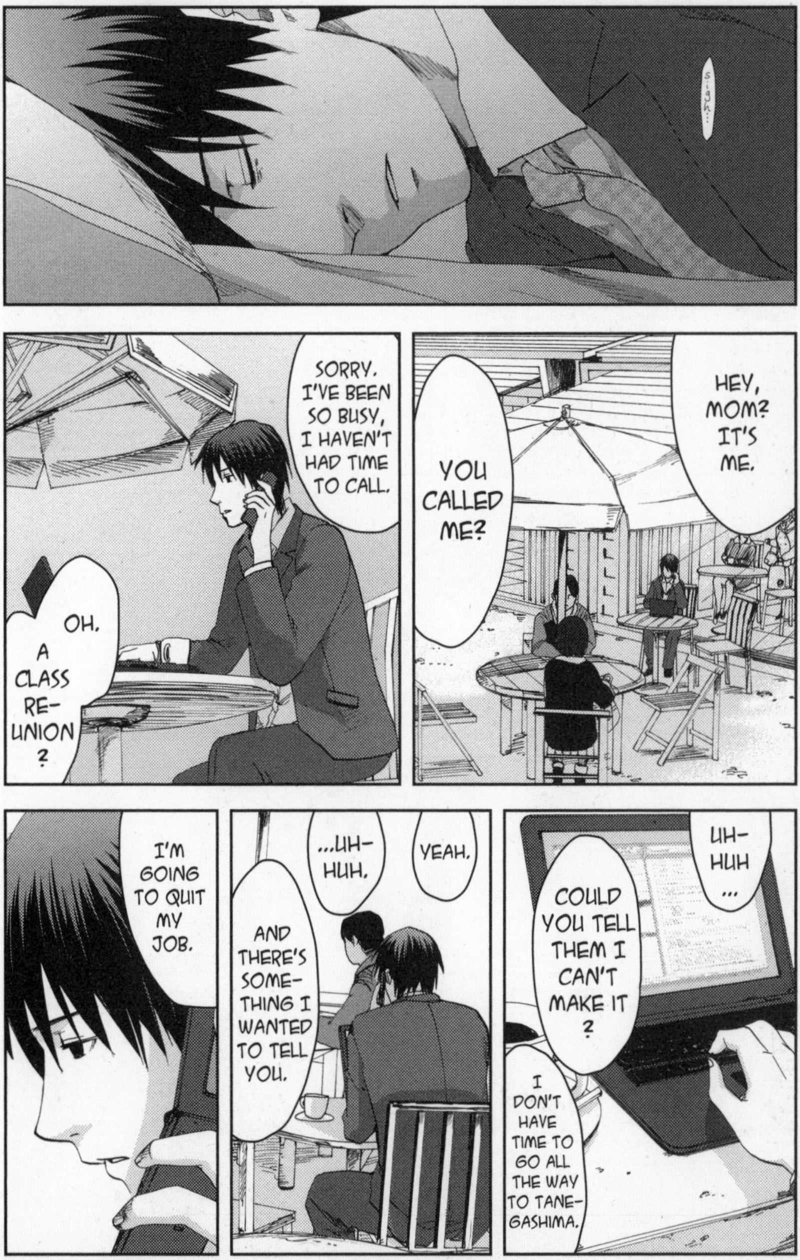
sigh...
HEY, MOM? IT'S ME.
YOU CALLED ME?
SORRY. I'VE BEEN SO BUSY, I HAVEN'T HAD TIME TO CALL.
OH. A CLASS RE-UNION?
UH-HUH ...
COULD YOU TELL THEM I CAN'T MAKE IT?
I DON'T HAVE TIME TO GO ALL THE WAY TO TANE-GASHIMA.
YEAH.
...UH-HUH.
AND THERE'S SOME-THING I WANTED TO TELL YOU.
I'M GOING TO QUIT MY JOB.

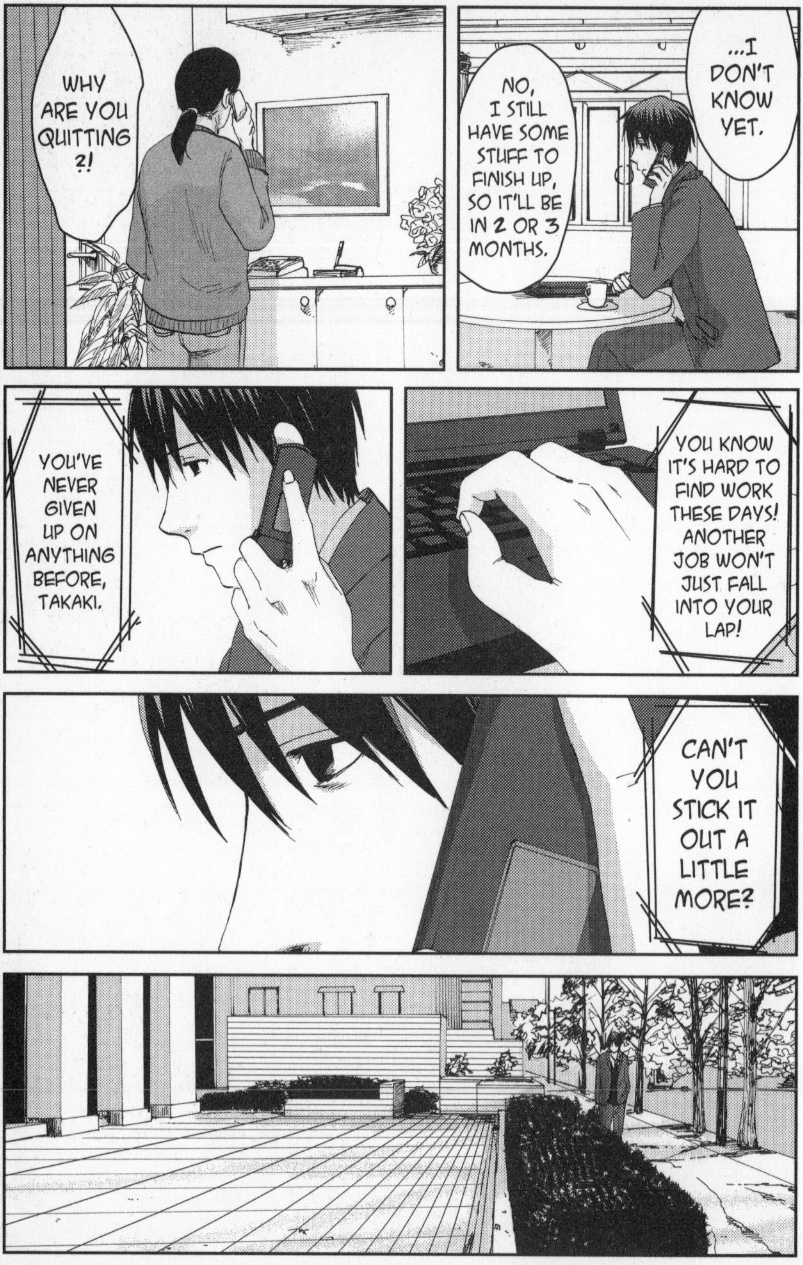
...I DON'T KNOW YET.
NO, I STILL HAVE SOME STUFF TO FINISH UP, SO IT'LL BE IN 2 OR 3 MONTHS.
WHY ARE YOU QUITTING?!
YOU KNOW IT'S HARD TO FIND WORK THESE DAYS! ANOTHER JOB WON'T JUST FALL INTO YOUR LAP!
YOU'VE NEVER GIVEN UP ON ANYTHING BEFORE, TAKAKI.
CAN'T YOU STICK IT OUT A LITTLE MORE?

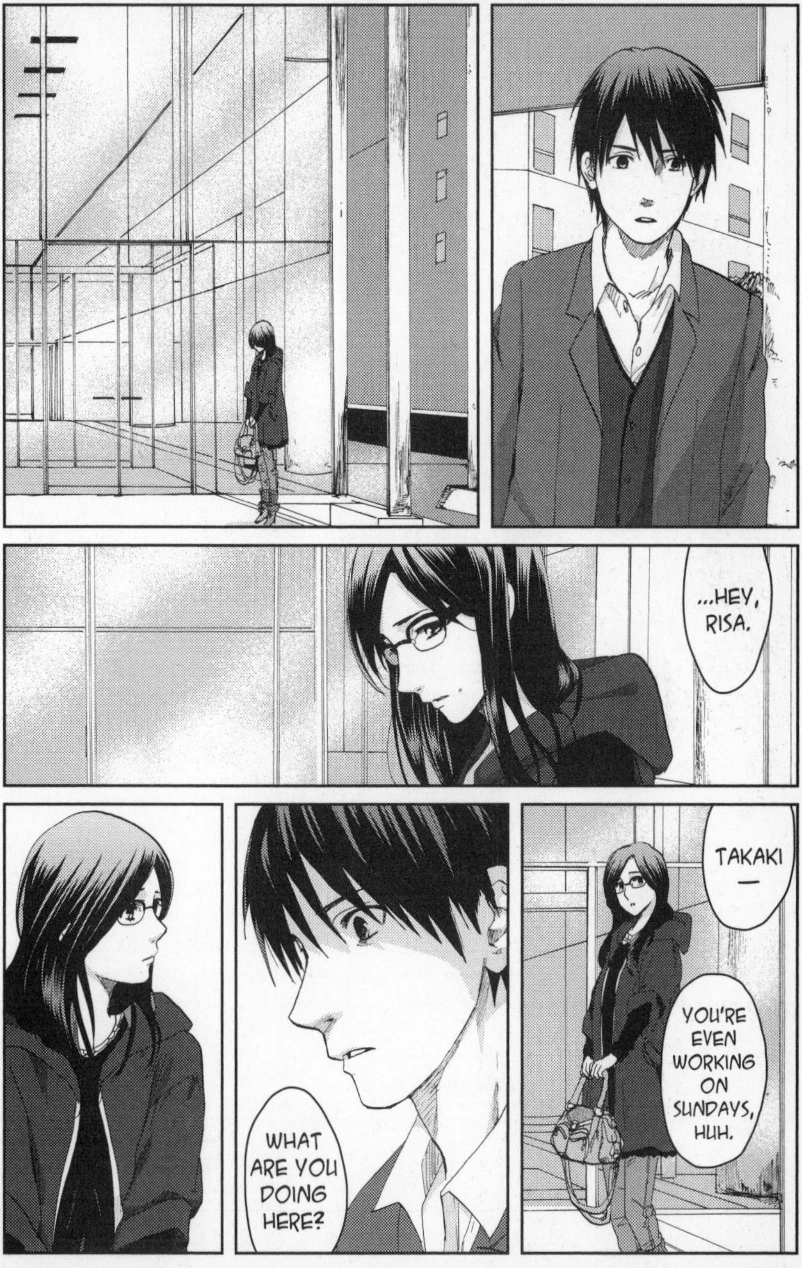
...HEY, RISA.
TAKAKI —
YOU'RE EVEN WORKING ON SUNDAYS, HUH.
WHAT ARE YOU DOING HERE?

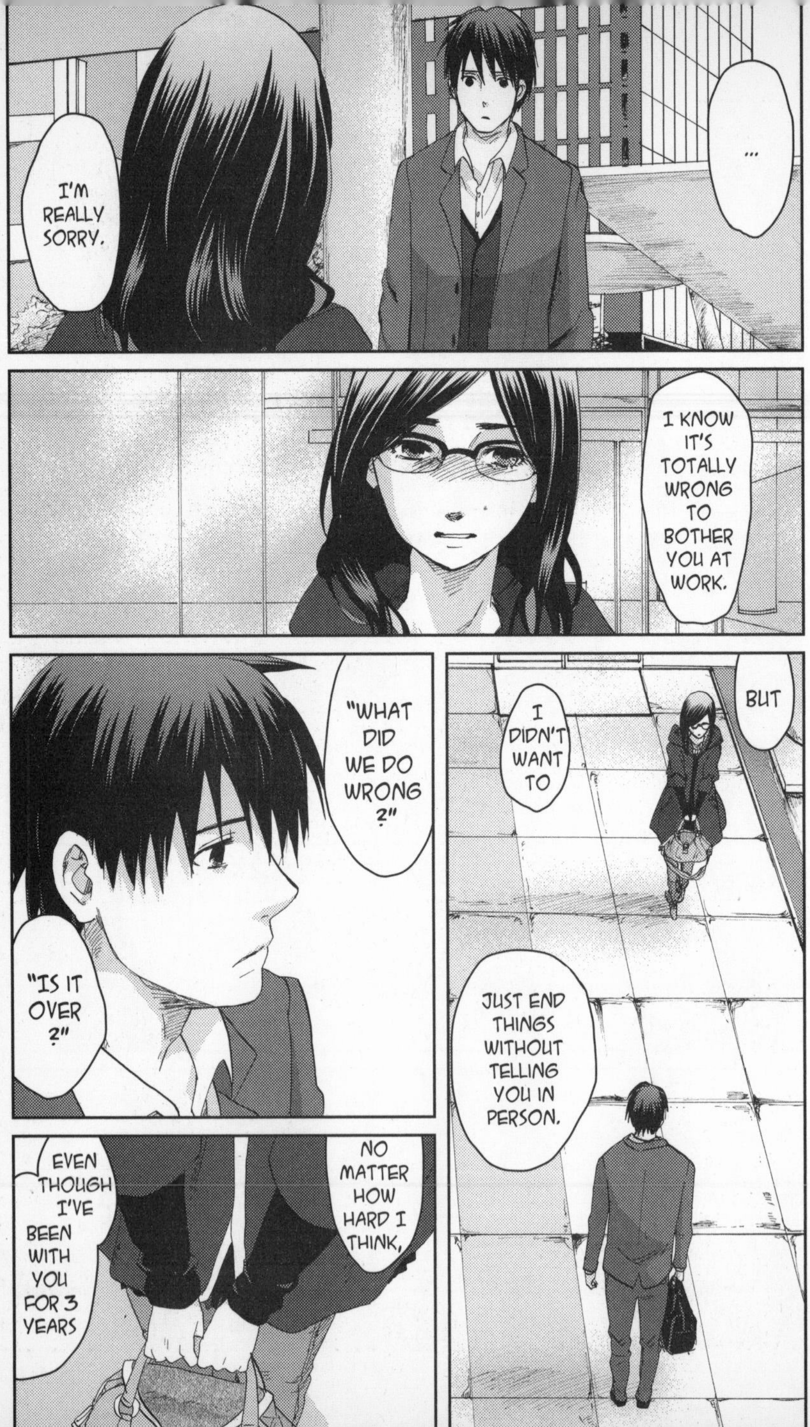
...
I'M REALLY SORRY.
I KNOW IT'S TOTALLY WRONG TO BOTHER YOU AT WORK.
BUT
I DIDN'T WANT TO
JUST END THINGS WITHOUT TELLING YOU IN PERSON.
"WHAT DID WE DO WRONG?"
"IS IT OVER?"
NO MATTER HOW HARD I THINK,
EVEN THOUGH I'VE BEEN WITH YOU FOR 3 YEARS

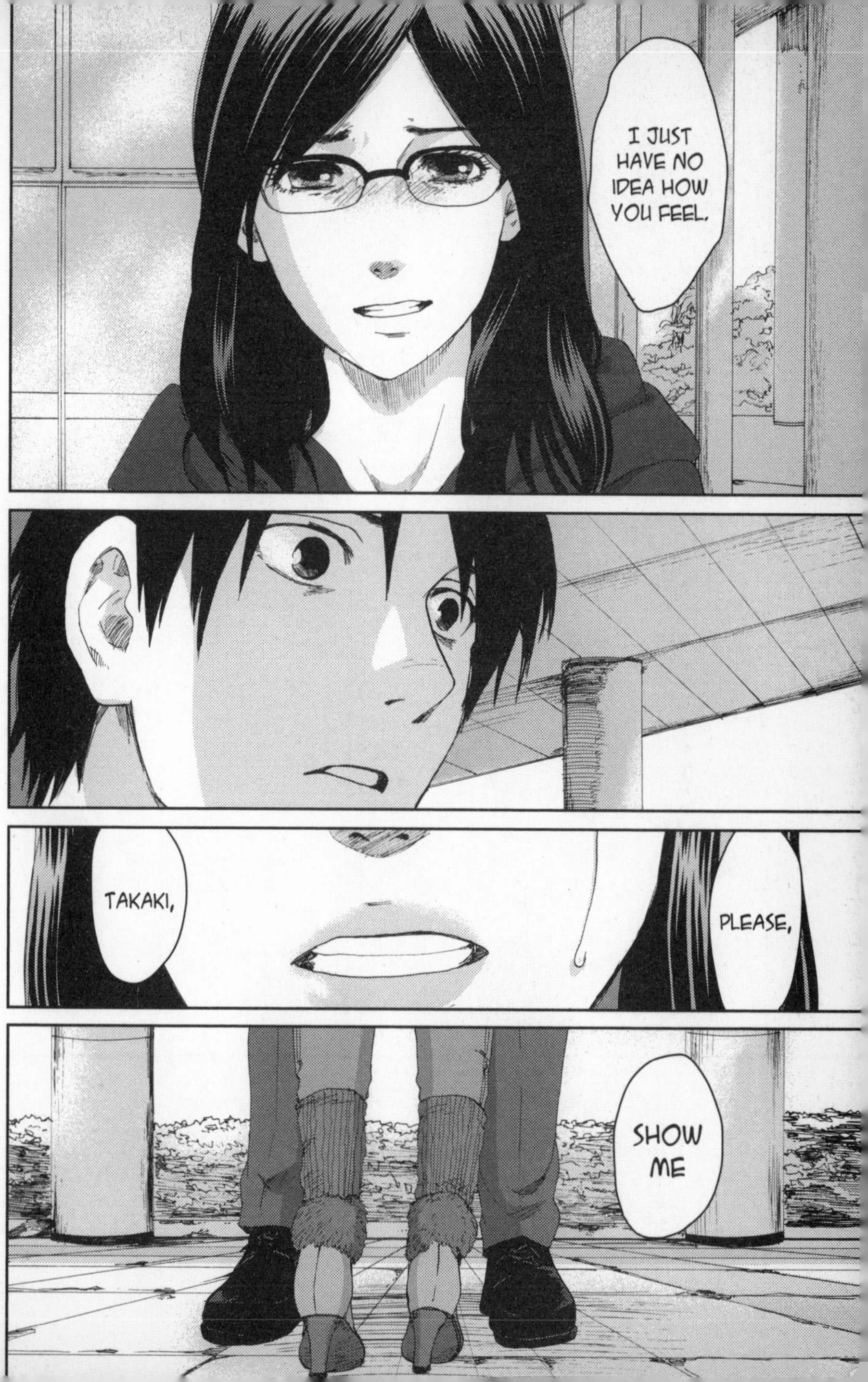
I JUST HAVE NO IDEA HOW YOU FEEL.
PLEASE,
TAKAKI,
SHOW ME

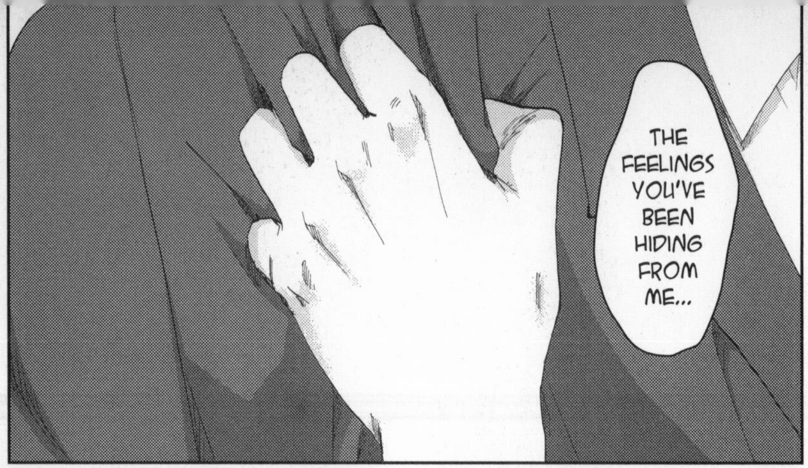
THE FEELINGS YOU'VE BEEN HIDING FROM ME...
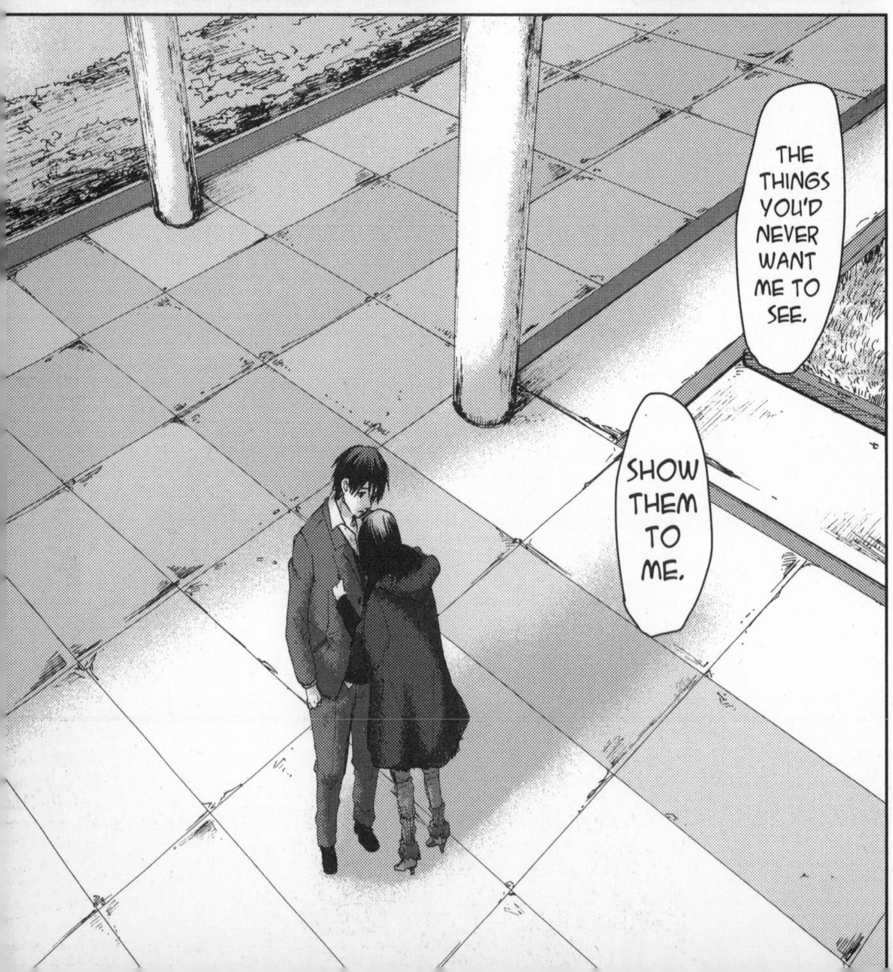
THE THINGS YOU'D NEVER WANT ME TO SEE.
SHOW THEM TO ME.

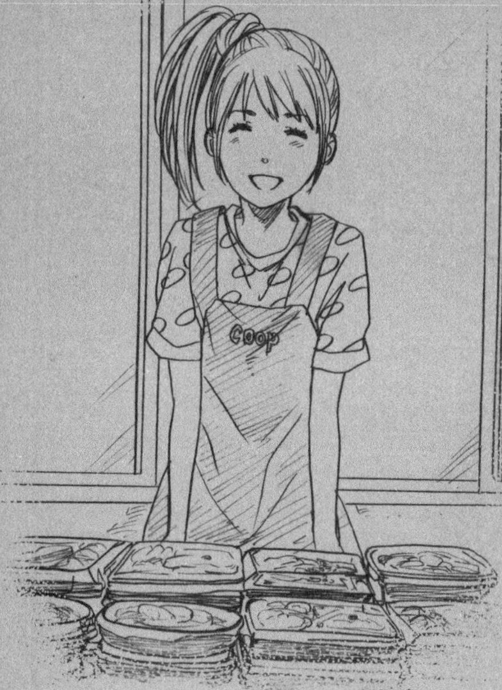
Coop
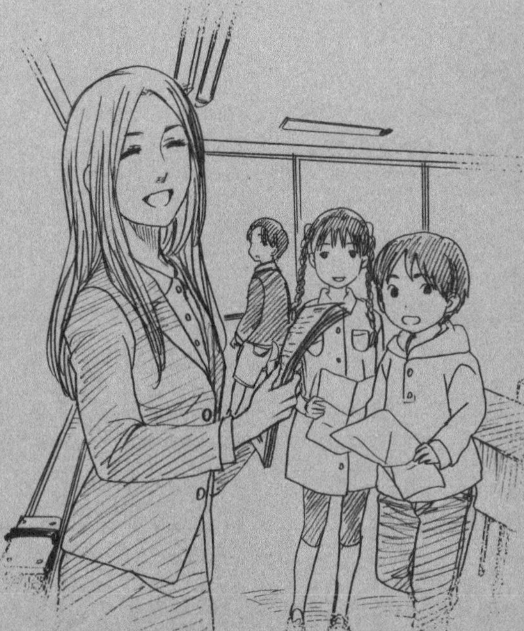

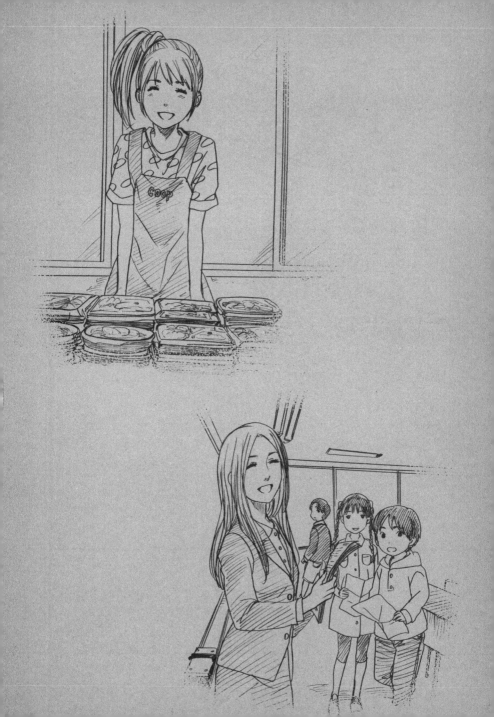

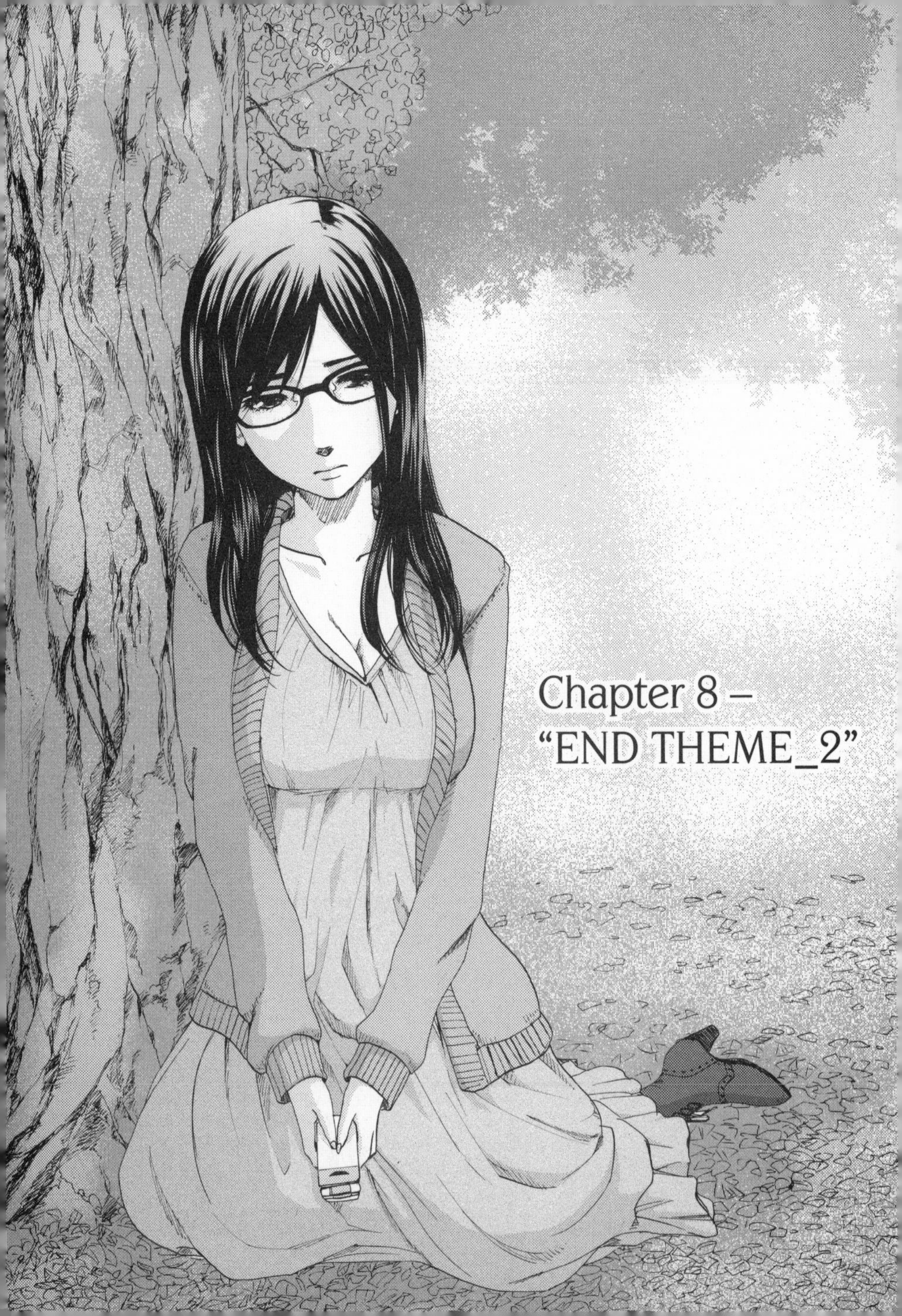

Chapter 8 – “END THEME_2”

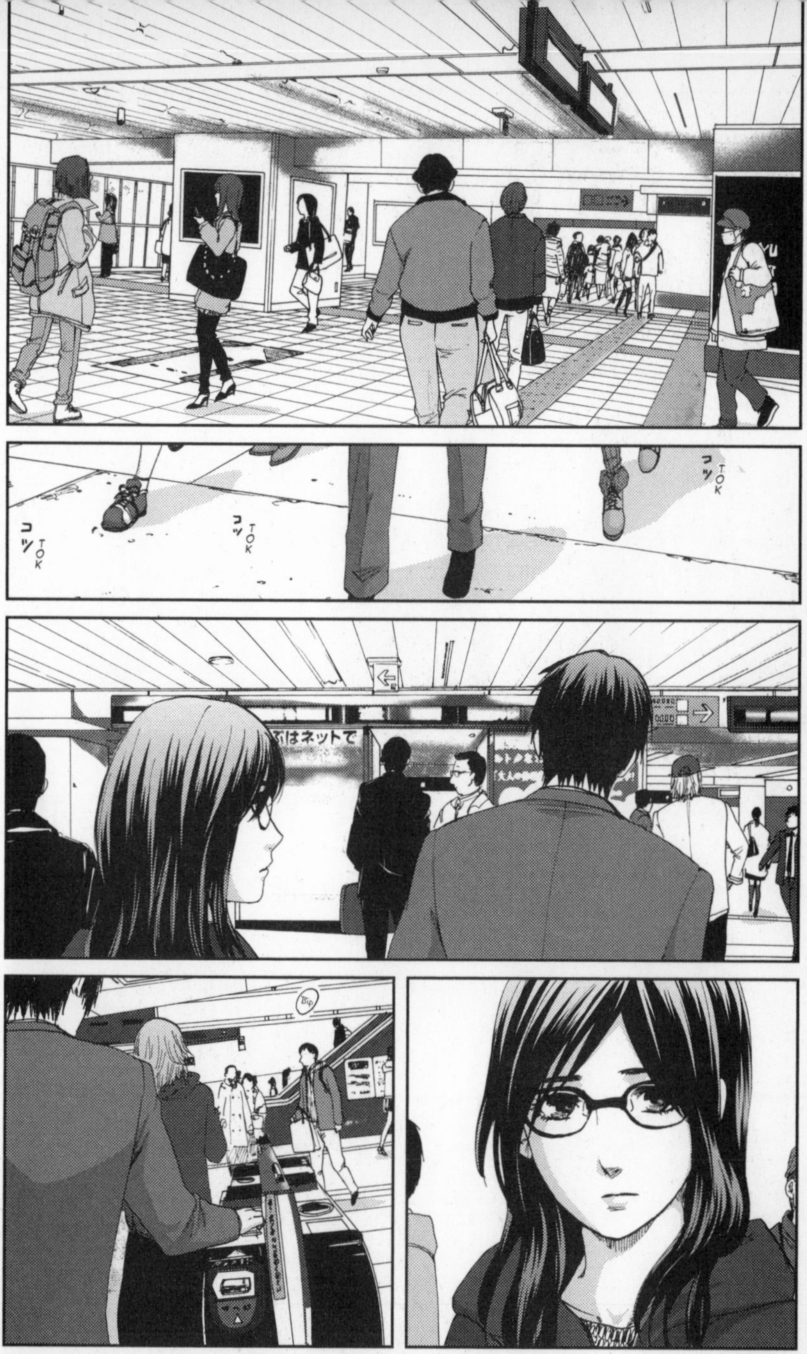
コッ TOK
コッ TOK
コッ TOK
ぶはネットで

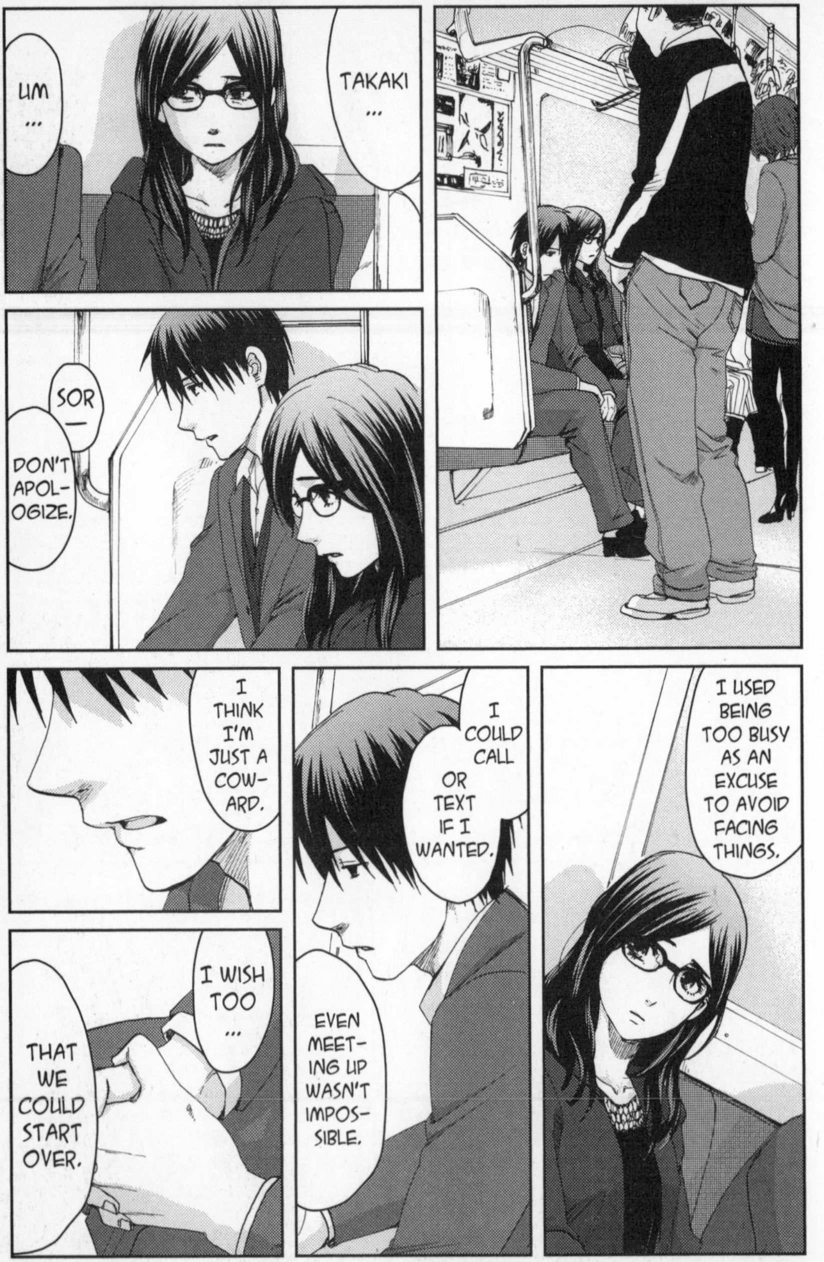
TAKAKI ...
UM ...
SOR —
DON'T APOL-OGIZE.
I USED BEING TOO BUSY AS AN EXCUSE TO AVOID FACING THINGS.
I COULD CALL
OR TEXT IF I WANTED.
EVEN MEET-ING UP WASN'T IMPOS-SIBLE.
I THINK I'M JUST A COW-ARD.
I WISH TOO ...
THAT WE COULD START OVER.

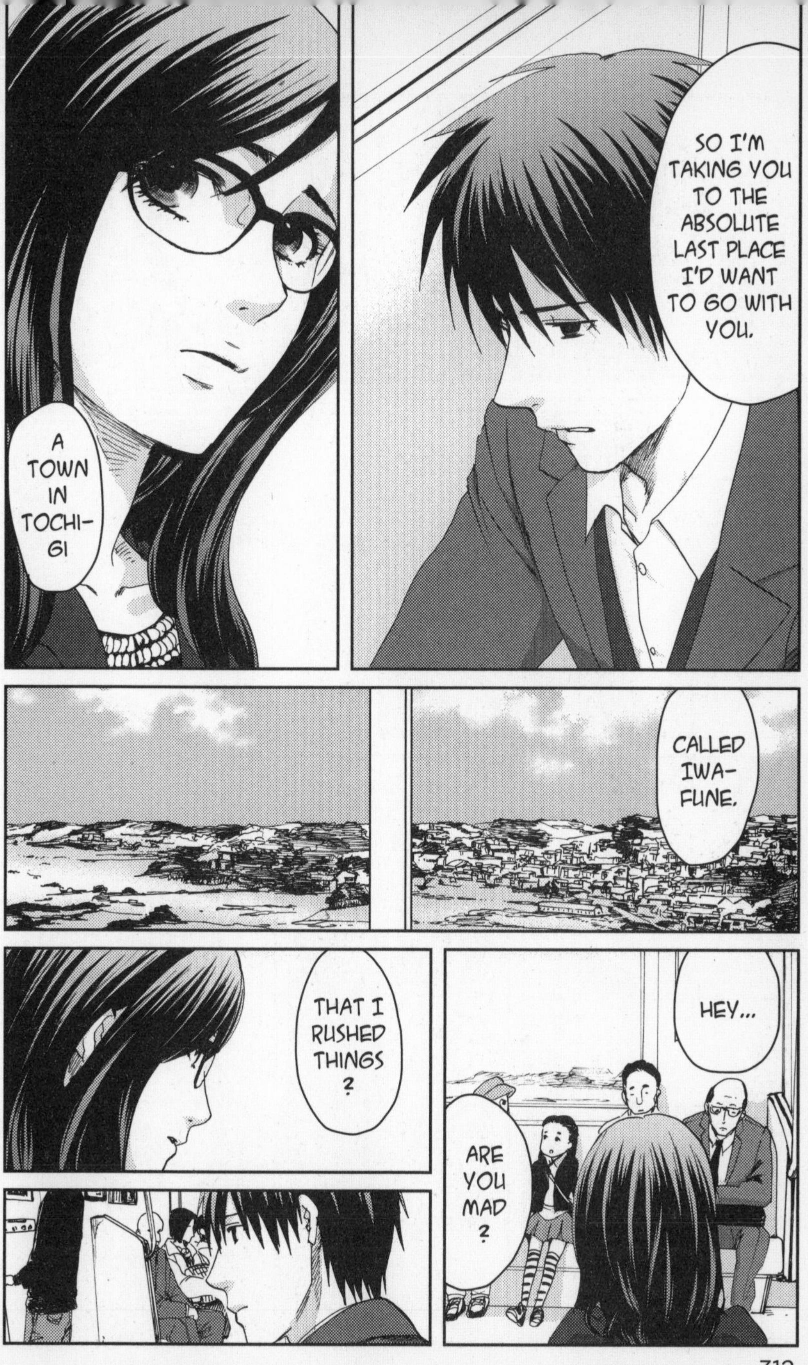
SO I'M TAKING YOU TO THE ABSOLUTE LAST PLACE I'D WANT TO GO WITH YOU.
A TOWN IN TOCHI-GI
CALLED IWA-FUNE.
HEY...
ARE YOU MAD?
THAT I RUSHED THINGS?

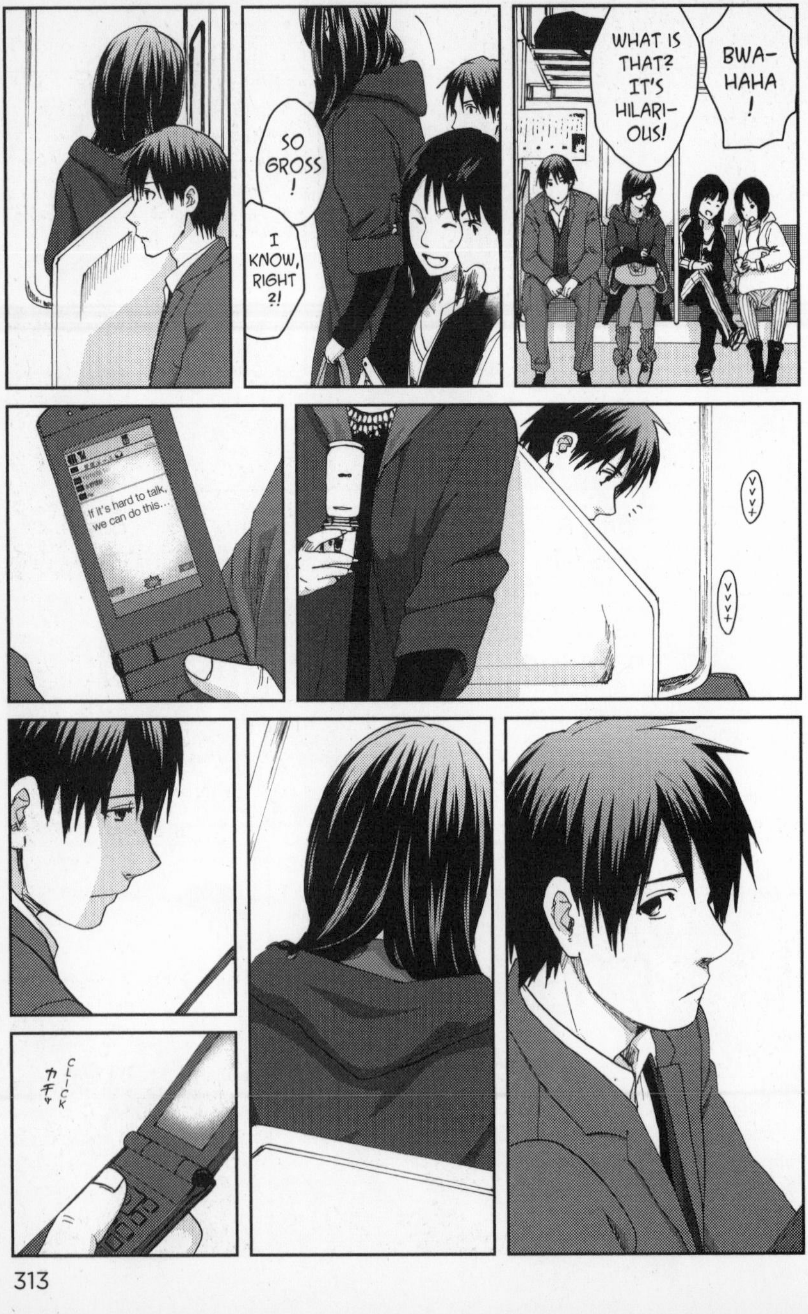
BWA-HAHA!
WHAT IS THAT? IT'S HILARIOUS!
SO GROSS!
I KNOW, RIGHT?!
If it's hard to talk, we can do this…
CLICK
カチャ

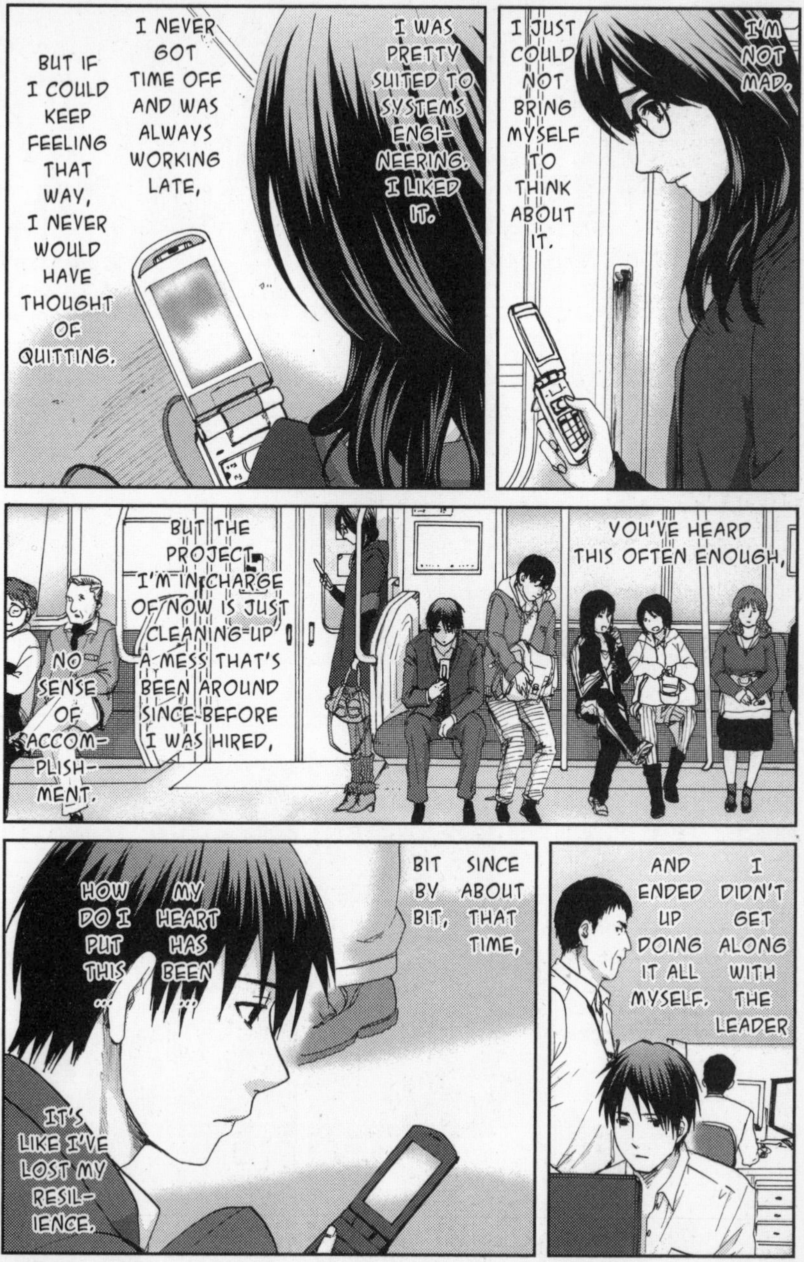
I'M NOT MAD.
I JUST COULD NOT BRING MYSELF TO THINK ABOUT IT.
I WAS PRETTY SUITED TO SYSTEMS ENGI-NEERING. I LIKED IT.
I NEVER GOT TIME OFF AND WAS ALWAYS WORKING LATE,
BUT IF I COULD KEEP FEELING THAT WAY, I NEVER WOULD HAVE THOUGHT OF QUITTING.
YOU'VE HEARD THIS OFTEN ENOUGH,
BUT THE PROJECT I'M IN CHARGE OF NOW IS JUST CLEANING UP A MESS THAT'S BEEN AROUND SINCE BEFORE I WAS HIRED,
NO SENSE OF ACCOM-PLISH-MENT.
I DIDN'T GET ALONG WITH THE LEADER
AND ENDED UP DOING IT ALL MYSELF.
SINCE ABOUT THAT TIME,
BIT BY BIT,
MY HEART HAS BEEN ...
HOW DO I PUT THIS ...
IT'S LIKE I'VE LOST MY RESIL-IENCE.

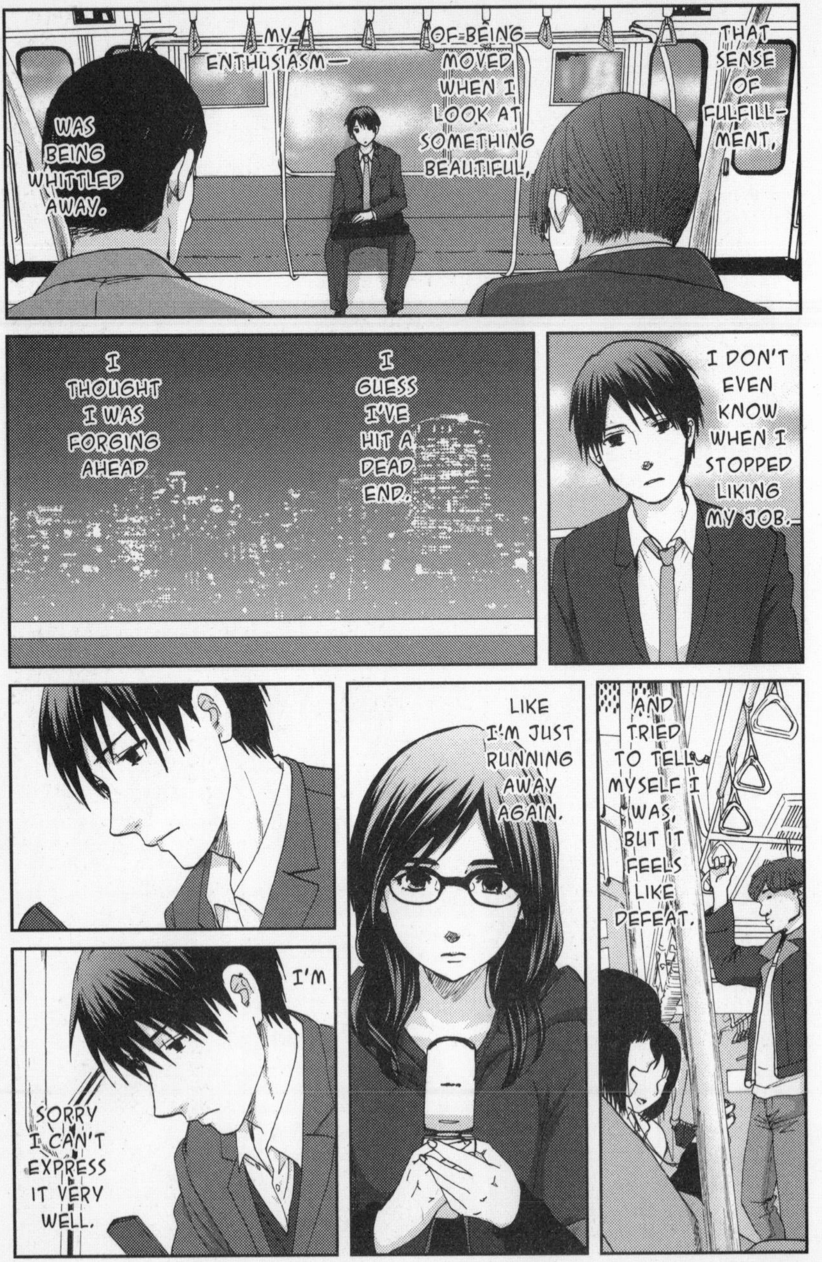
THAT SENSE OF FULFILLMENT,
OF BEING MOVED WHEN I LOOK AT SOMETHING BEAUTIFUL,
MY ENTHUSIASM—
WAS BEING WHITTLED AWAY.
I DON'T EVEN KNOW WHEN I STOPPED LIKING MY JOB.
I GUESS I'VE HIT A DEAD END.
I THOUGHT I WAS FORGING AHEAD
AND TRIED TO TELL MYSELF I WAS, BUT IT FEELS LIKE DEFEAT.
LIKE I'M JUST RUNNING AWAY AGAIN.
I'M
SORRY I CAN'T EXPRESS IT VERY WELL.

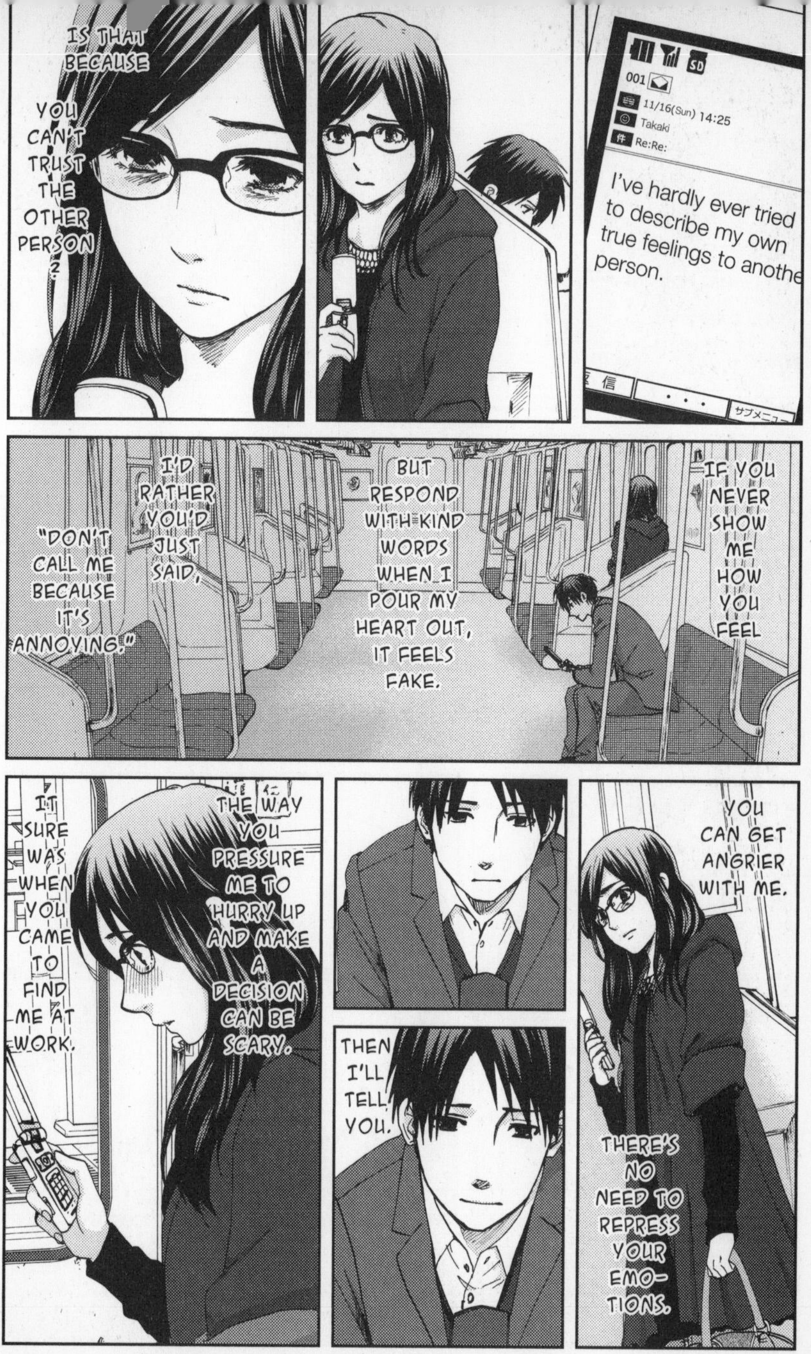
SD
001
11/16(Sun) 14:25
Takaki
Re:Re:
I've hardly ever tried to describe my own true feelings to anothe person.
IS THAT BECAUSE YOU CAN'T TRUST THE OTHER PERSON?
IF YOU NEVER SHOW ME HOW YOU FEEL
BUT RESPOND WITH KIND WORDS WHEN I POUR MY HEART OUT, IT FEELS FAKE.
I'D RATHER YOU'D JUST SAID,
"DON'T CALL ME BECAUSE IT'S ANNOYING."
YOU CAN GET ANGRIER WITH ME.
THERE'S NO NEED TO REPRESS YOUR EMOTIONS.
THEN I'LL TELL YOU.
THE WAY YOU PRESSURE ME TO HURRY UP AND MAKE A DECISION CAN BE SCARY.
IT SURE WAS WHEN YOU CAME TO FIND ME AT WORK.

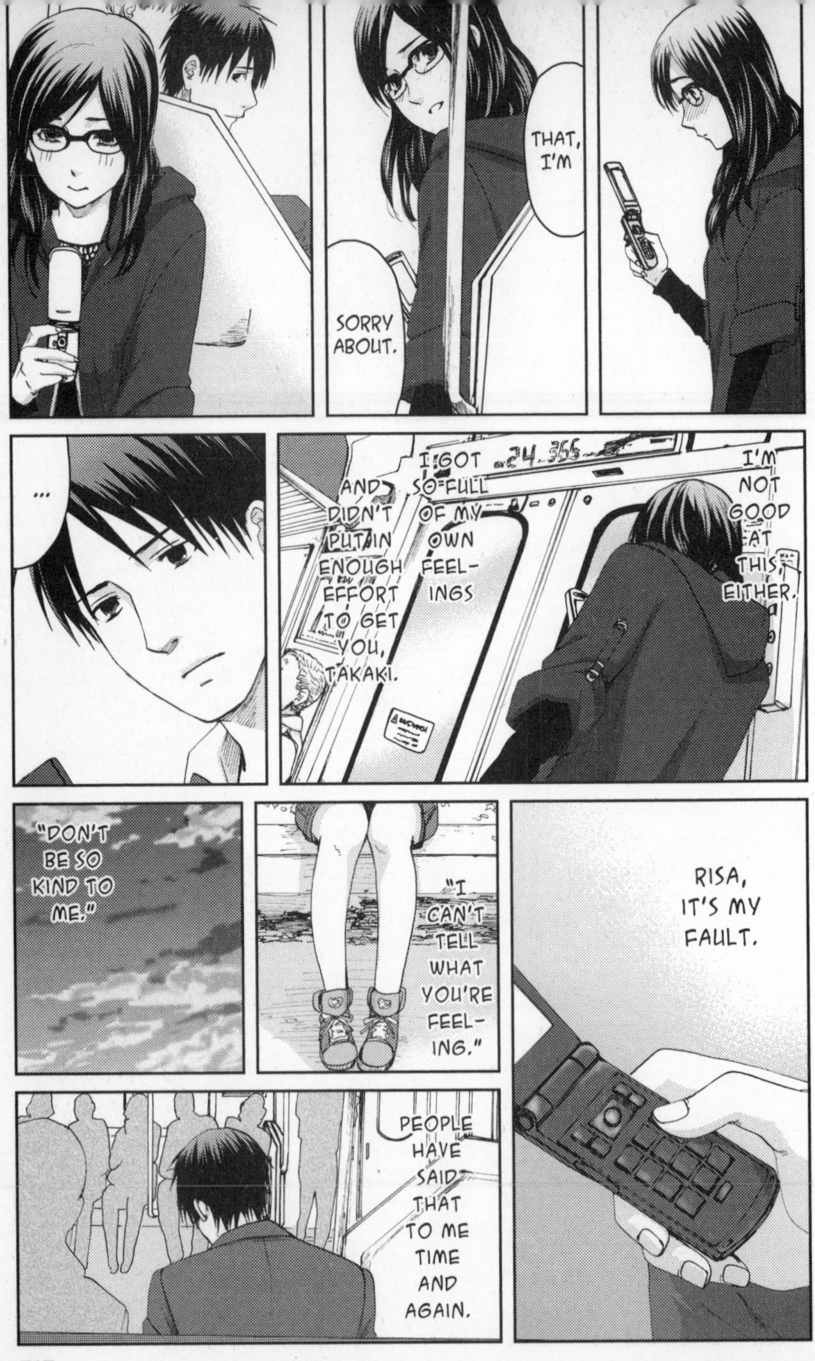
THAT, I'M
SORRY ABOUT.
I'M NOT GOOD AT THIS, EITHER.
I GOT SO FULL OF MY OWN FEEL- INGS
AND DIDN'T PUT IN ENOUGH EFFORT TO GET YOU, TAKAKI.
...
RISA, IT'S MY FAULT.
"I CAN'T TELL WHAT YOU'RE FEEL- ING."
"DON'T BE SO KIND TO ME."
PEOPLE HAVE SAID THAT TO ME TIME AND AGAIN.

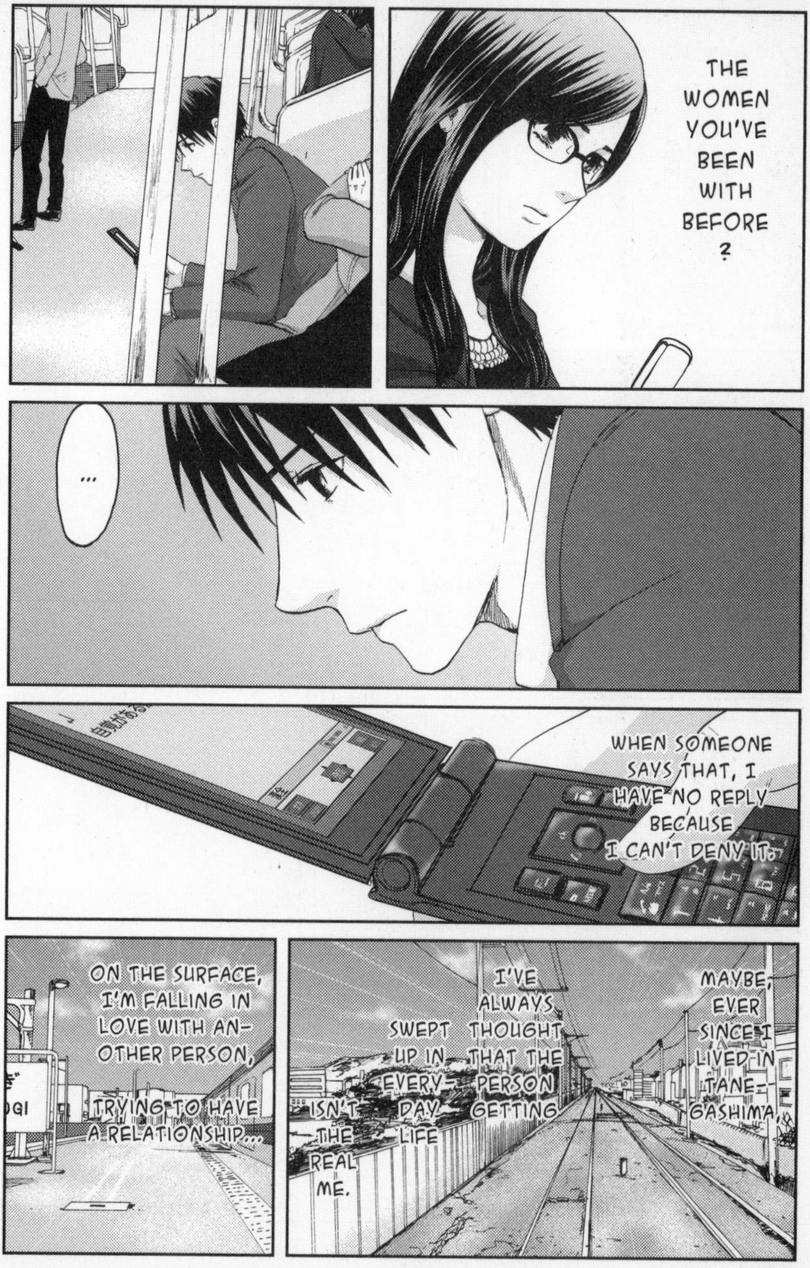
THE WOMEN YOU'VE BEEN WITH BEFORE ?
...
WHEN SOMEONE SAYS THAT, I HAVE NO REPLY BECAUSE I CAN'T DENY IT.
MAYBE, EVER SINCE I LIVED IN TANE-GASHIMA,
I'VE ALWAYS THOUGHT THAT THE PERSON GETTING
SWEPT UP IN EVERY-DAY LIFE
ISN'T THE REAL ME.
ON THE SURFACE, I'M FALLING IN LOVE WITH AN-OTHER PERSON,
TRYING TO HAVE A RELATIONSHIP...

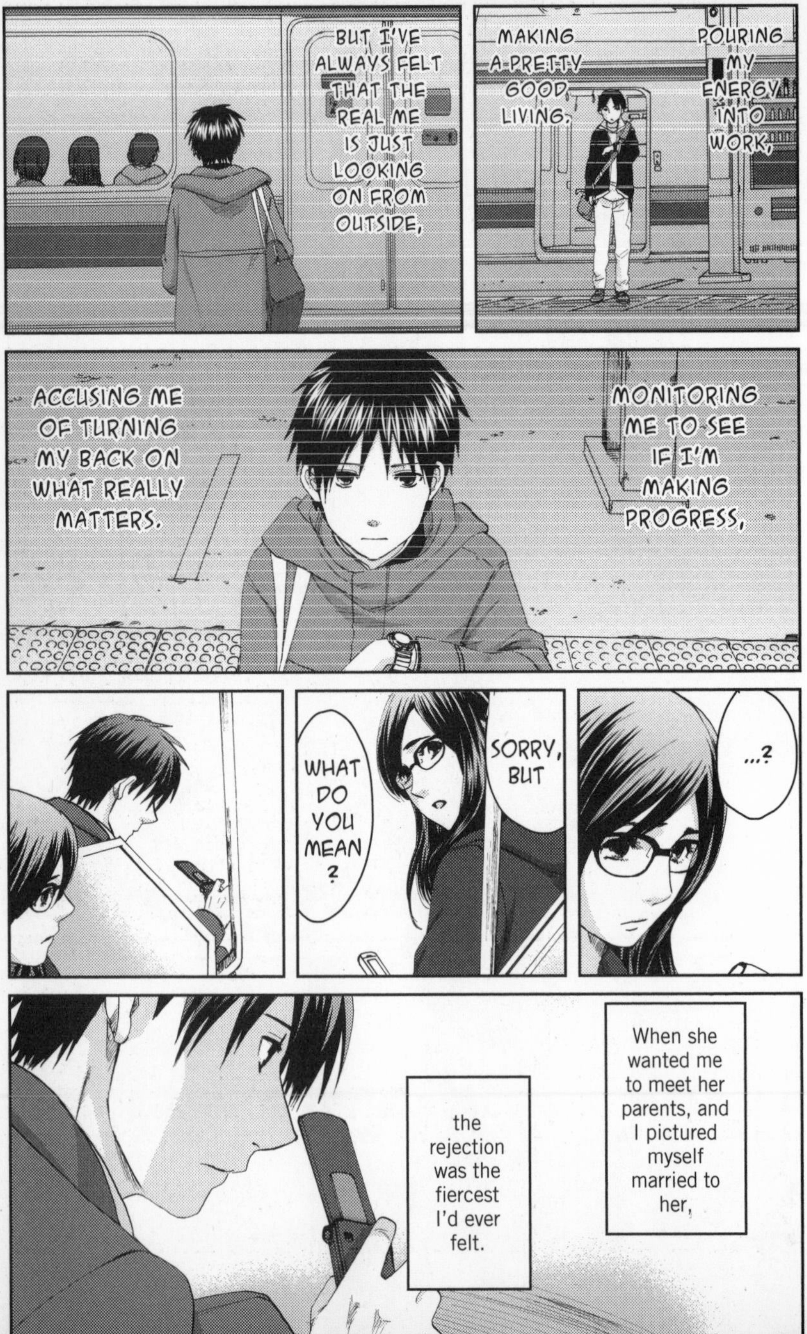
POURING MY ENERGY INTO WORK,
MAKING A PRETTY GOOD LIVING.
BUT I'VE ALWAYS FELT THAT THE REAL ME IS JUST LOOKING ON FROM OUTSIDE,
MONITORING ME TO SEE IF I'M MAKING PROGRESS,
ACCUSING ME OF TURNING MY BACK ON WHAT REALLY MATTERS.
...?
SORRY, BUT
WHAT DO YOU MEAN?
When she wanted me to meet her parents, and I pictured myself married to her,
the rejection was the fiercest I'd ever felt.

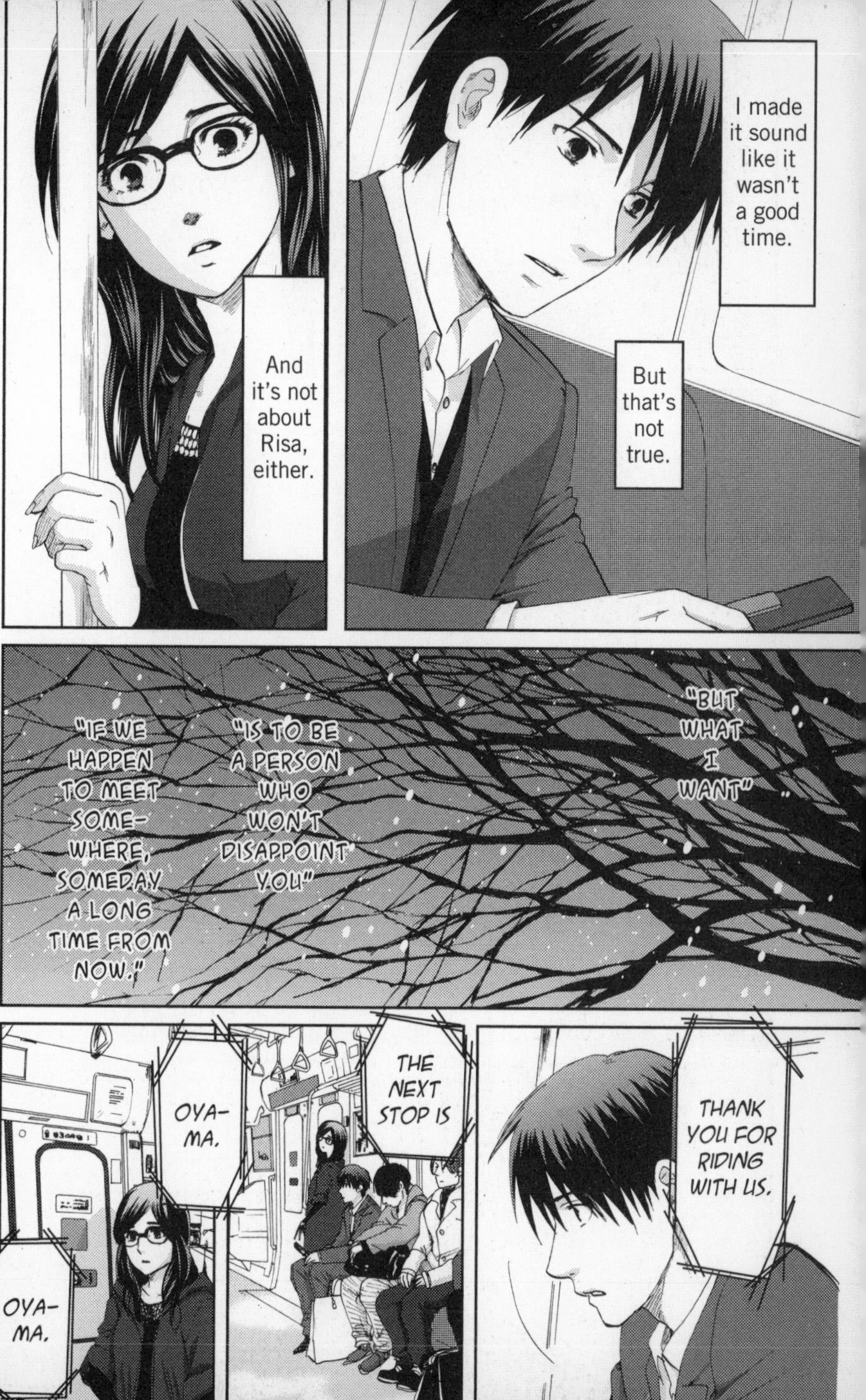
I made it sound like it wasn't a good time.
But that's not true.
And it's not about Risa, either.
"BUT WHAT I WANT"
"IS TO BE A PERSON WHO WON'T DISAPPOINT YOU"
"IF WE HAPPEN TO MEET SOME-WHERE, SOMEDAY A LONG TIME FROM NOW."
THANK YOU FOR RIDING WITH US.
THE NEXT STOP IS
OYA-MA.
OYA-MA.

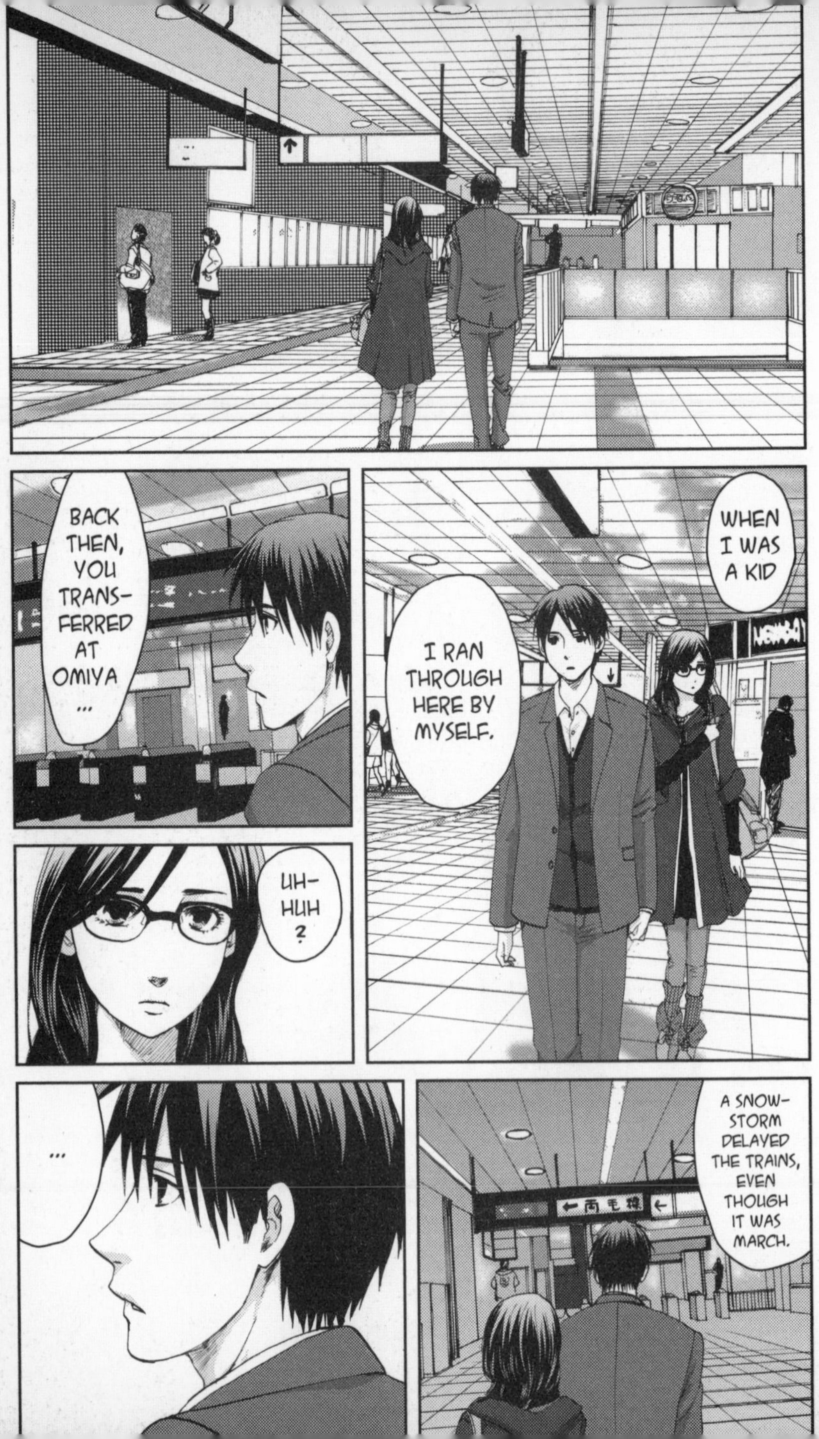
WHEN I WAS A KID
I RAN THROUGH HERE BY MYSELF.
BACK THEN, YOU TRANS-FERRED AT OMIYA ...
UH-HUH?
A SNOW-STORM DELAYED THE TRAINS, EVEN THOUGH IT WAS MARCH.
←両毛線←
...

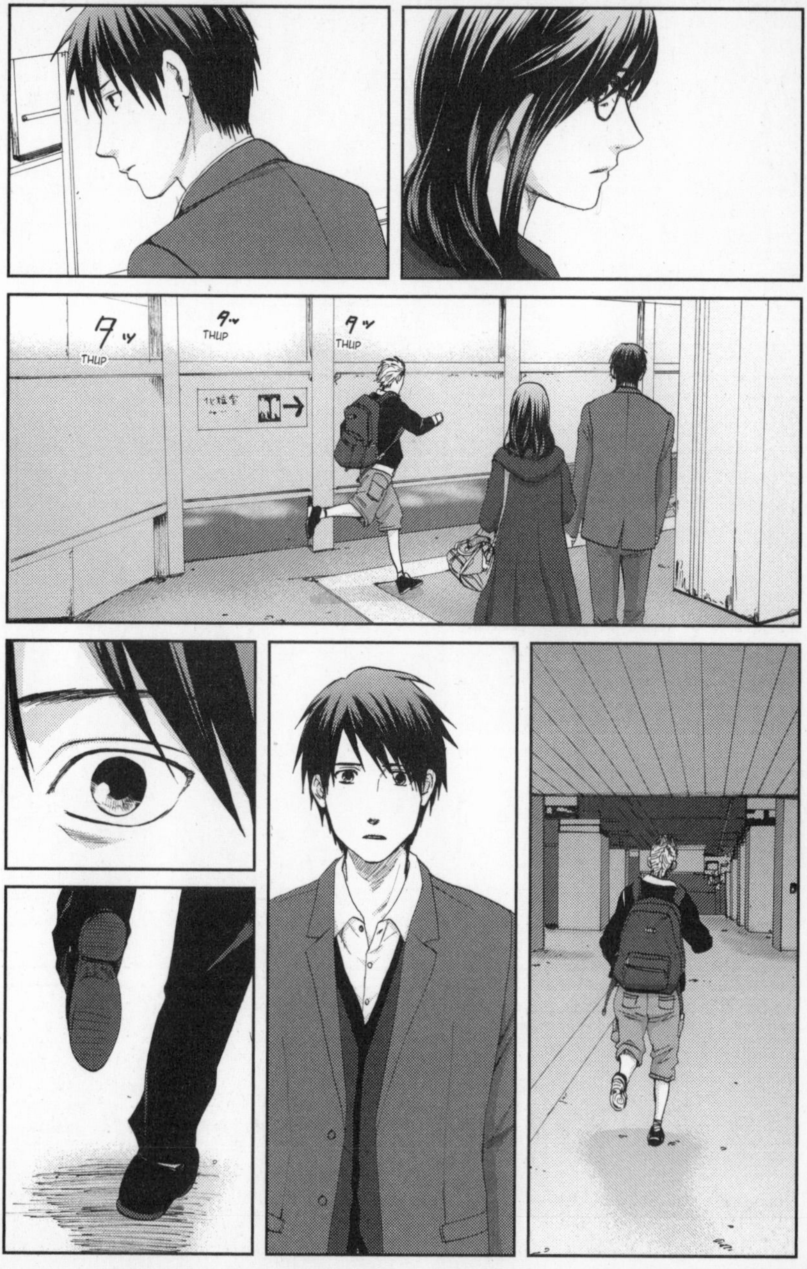
タッ
THUP
タッ
THUP
タッ
THUP

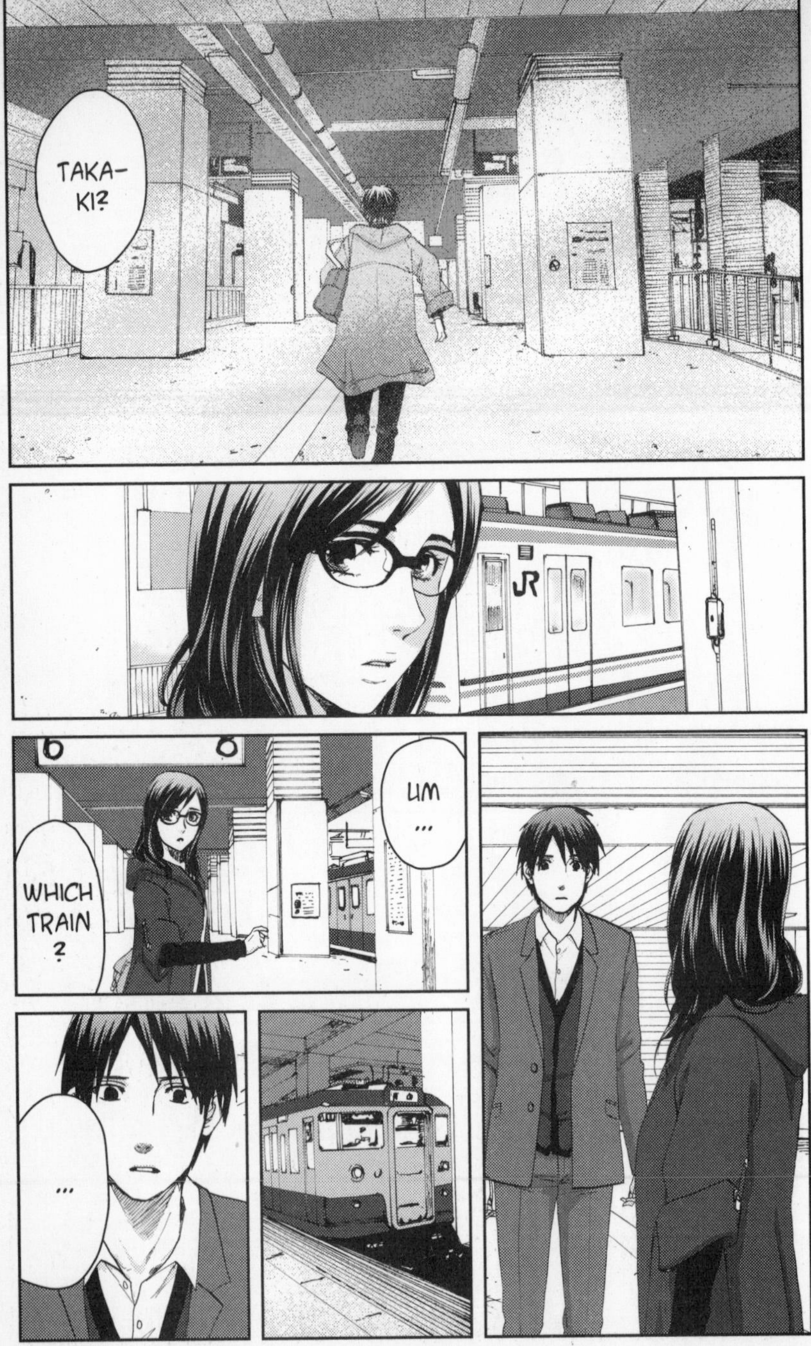
TAKA-KI?
UM ...
WHICH TRAIN ?
...

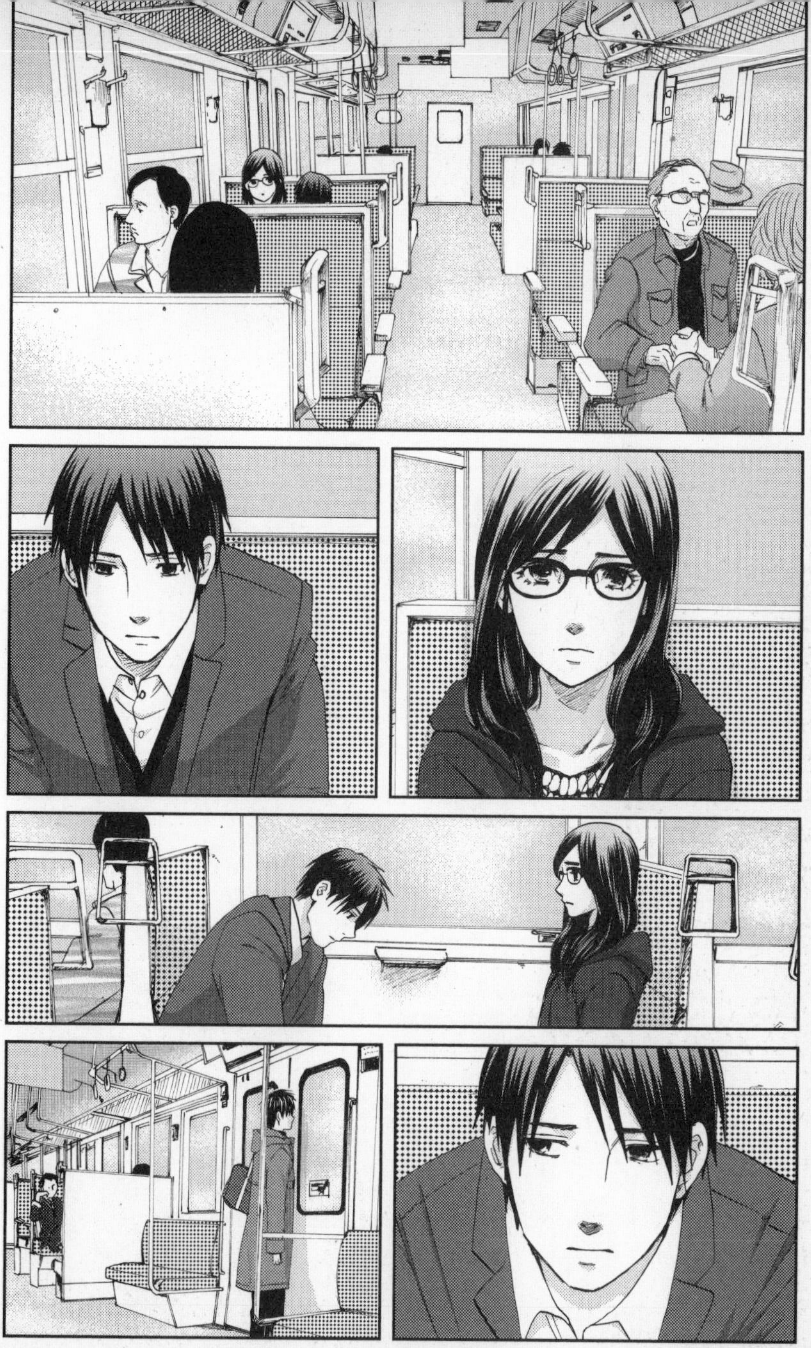

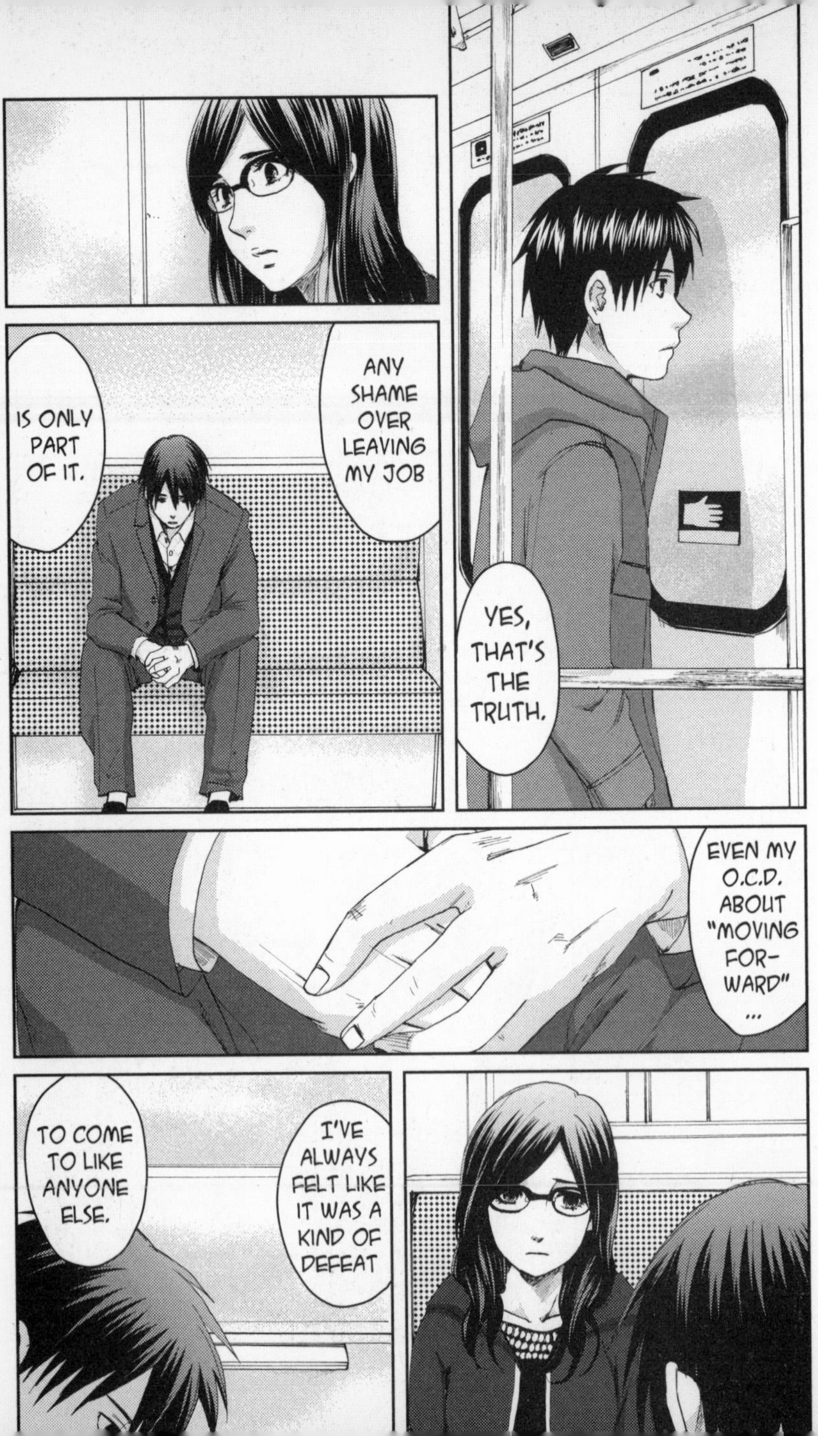
YES, THAT'S THE TRUTH.
ANY SHAME OVER LEAVING MY JOB
IS ONLY PART OF IT.
EVEN MY O.C.D. ABOUT "MOVING FOR-WARD" ...
I'VE ALWAYS FELT LIKE IT WAS A KIND OF DEFEAT
TO COME TO LIKE ANYONE ELSE.

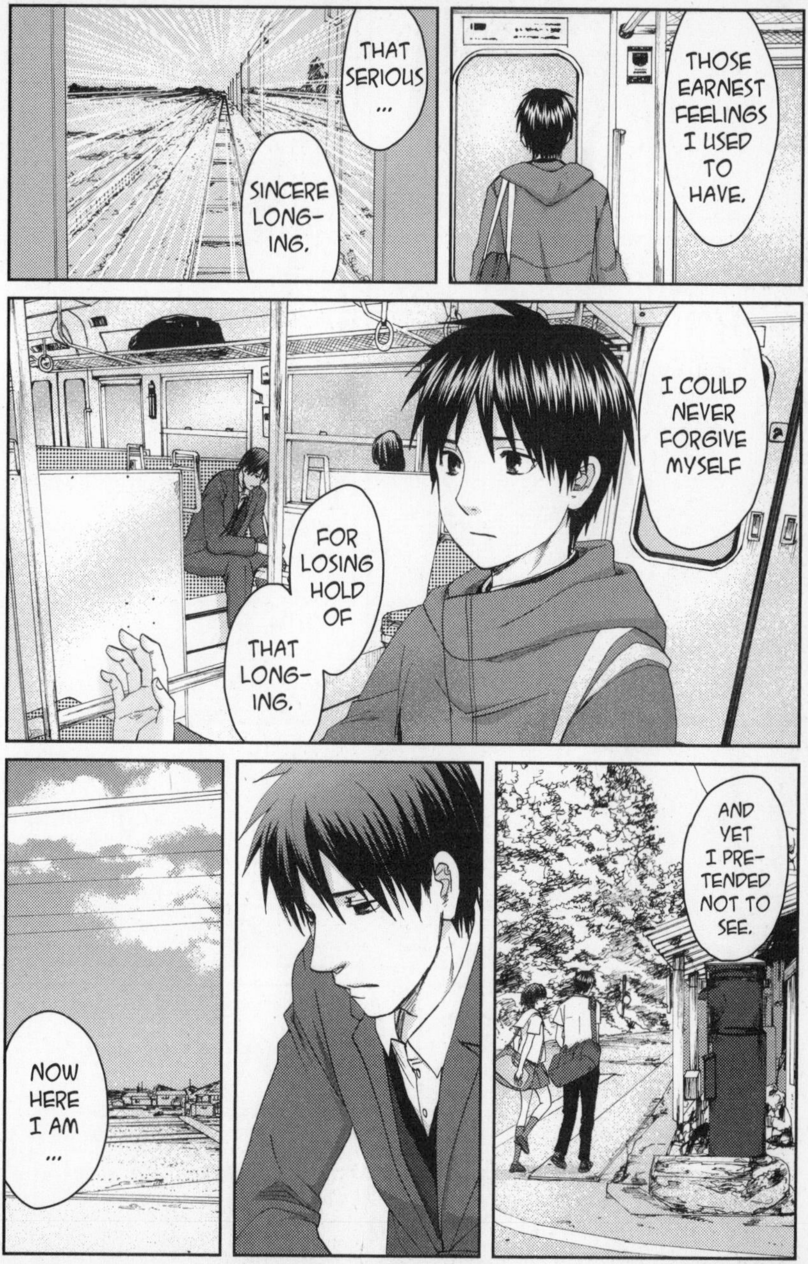
THOSE EARNEST FEELINGS I USED TO HAVE.
THAT SERIOUS...
SINCERE LONG-ING.
I COULD NEVER FORGIVE MYSELF
FOR LOSING HOLD OF
THAT LONG-ING.
AND YET I PRE-TENDED NOT TO SEE.
NOW HERE I AM...

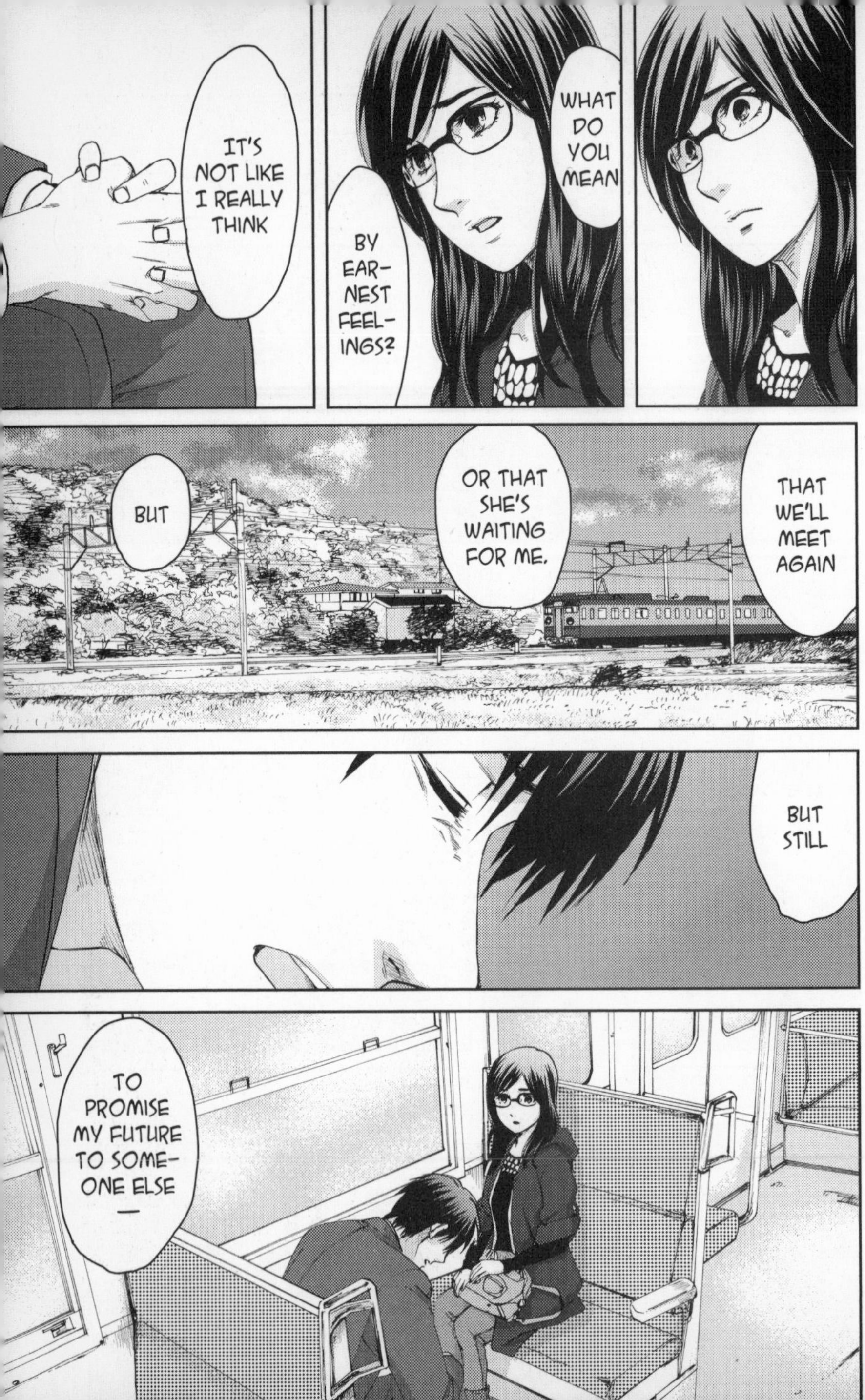
WHAT DO YOU MEAN
BY EAR-NEST FEEL-INGS?
IT'S NOT LIKE I REALLY THINK
THAT WE'LL MEET AGAIN
OR THAT SHE'S WAITING FOR ME.
BUT
BUT STILL
TO PROMISE MY FUTURE TO SOME-ONE ELSE —

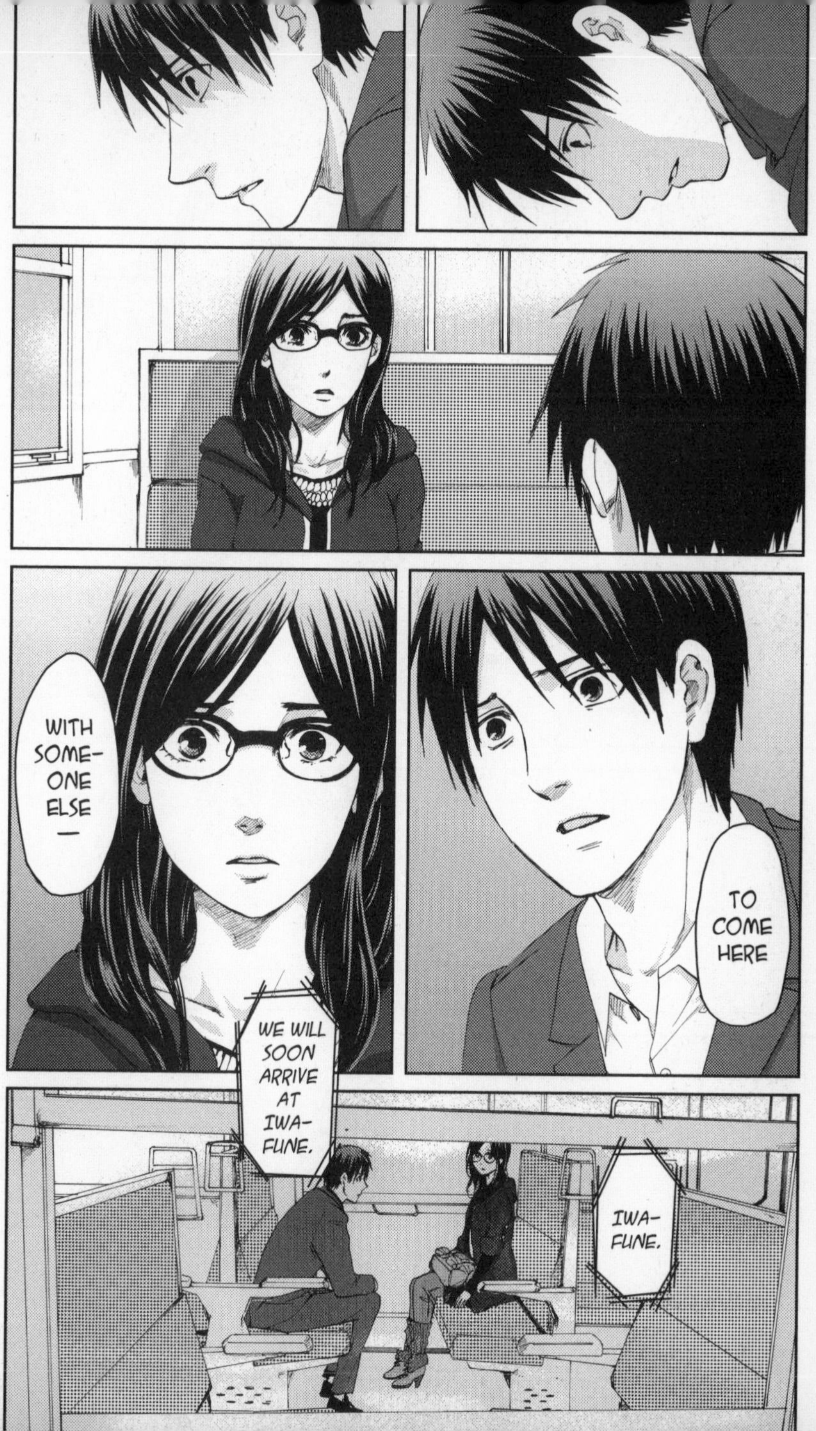
TO COME HERE
WITH SOME-ONE ELSE —
WE WILL SOON ARRIVE AT IWA-FUNE.
IWA-FUNE.

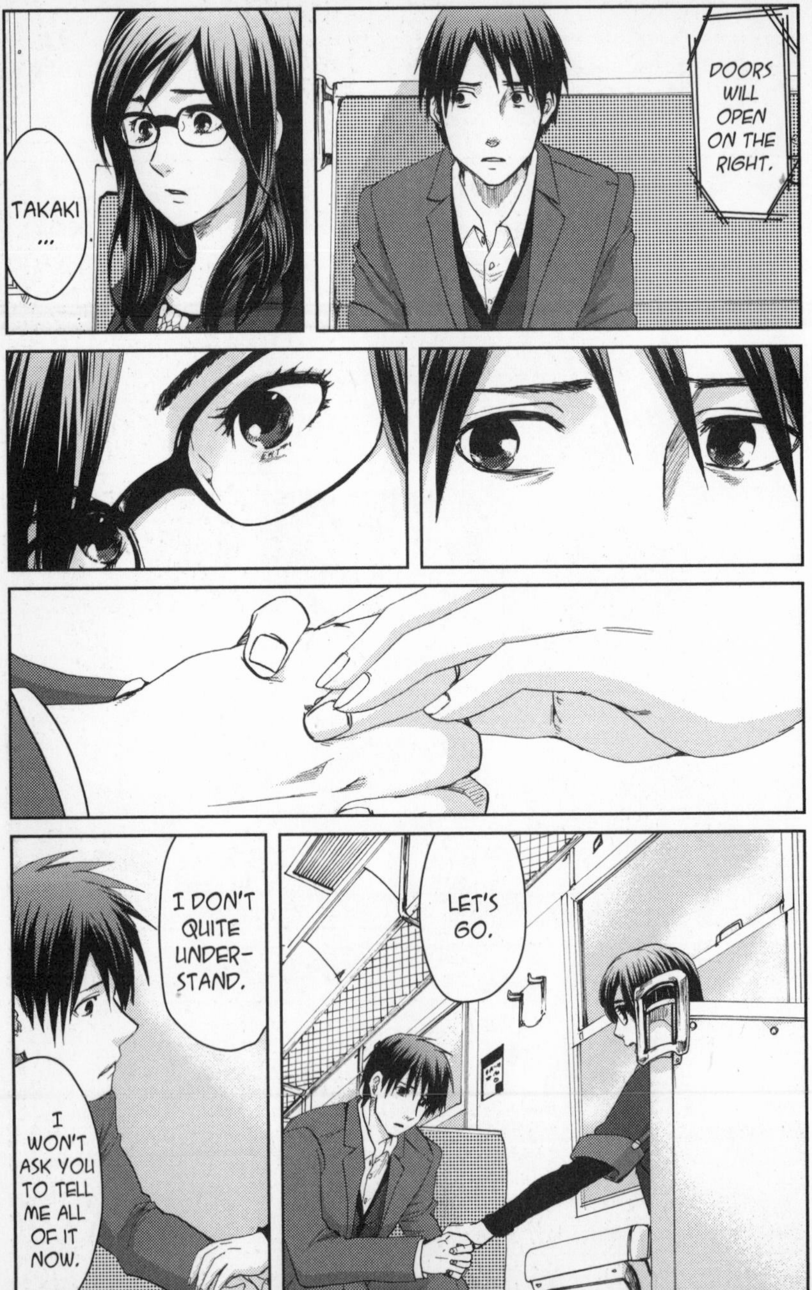
DOORS WILL OPEN ON THE RIGHT.
TAKAKI ...
LET'S GO.
I DON'T QUITE UNDER-STAND.
I WON'T ASK YOU TO TELL ME ALL OF IT NOW.

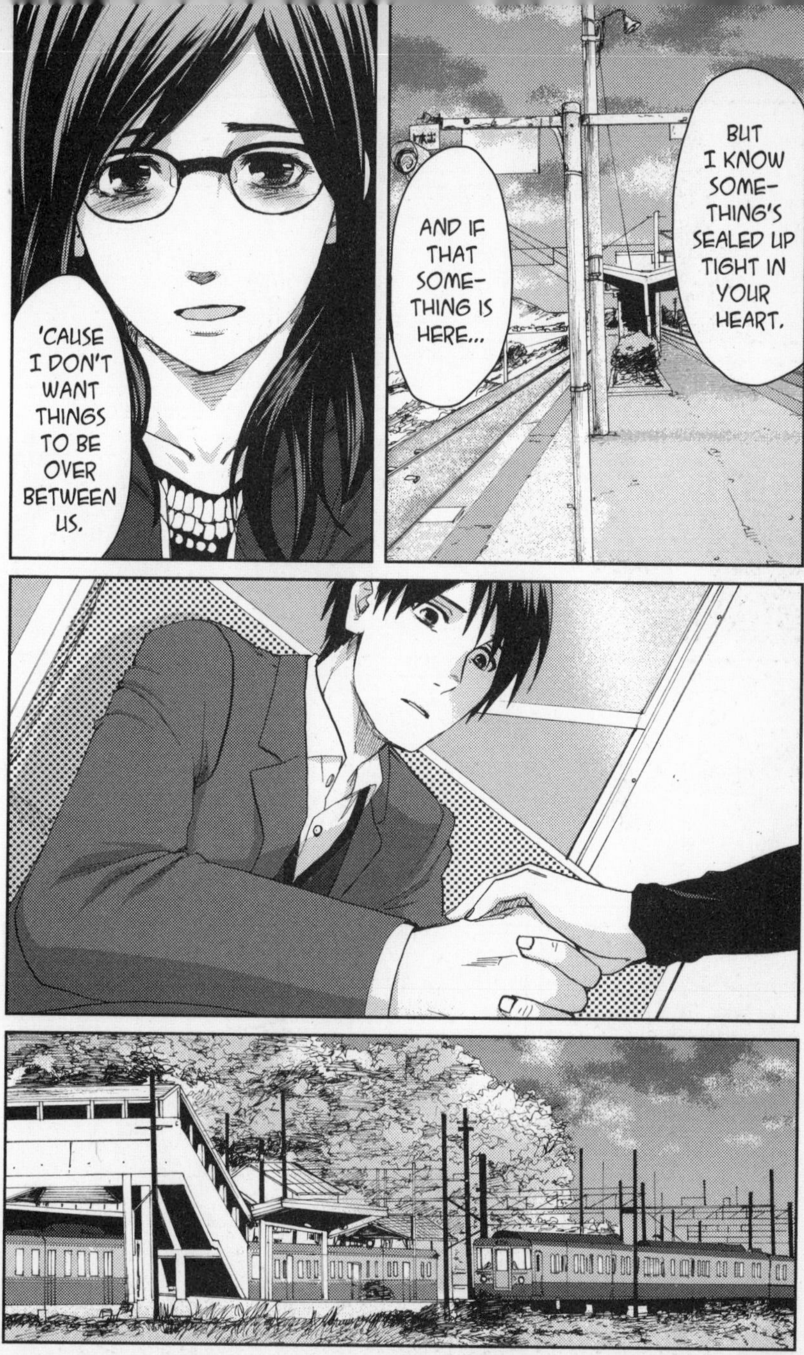
BUT I KNOW SOME-THING'S SEALED UP TIGHT IN YOUR HEART.
AND IF THAT SOME-THING IS HERE...
'CAUSE I DON'T WANT THINGS TO BE OVER BETWEEN US.

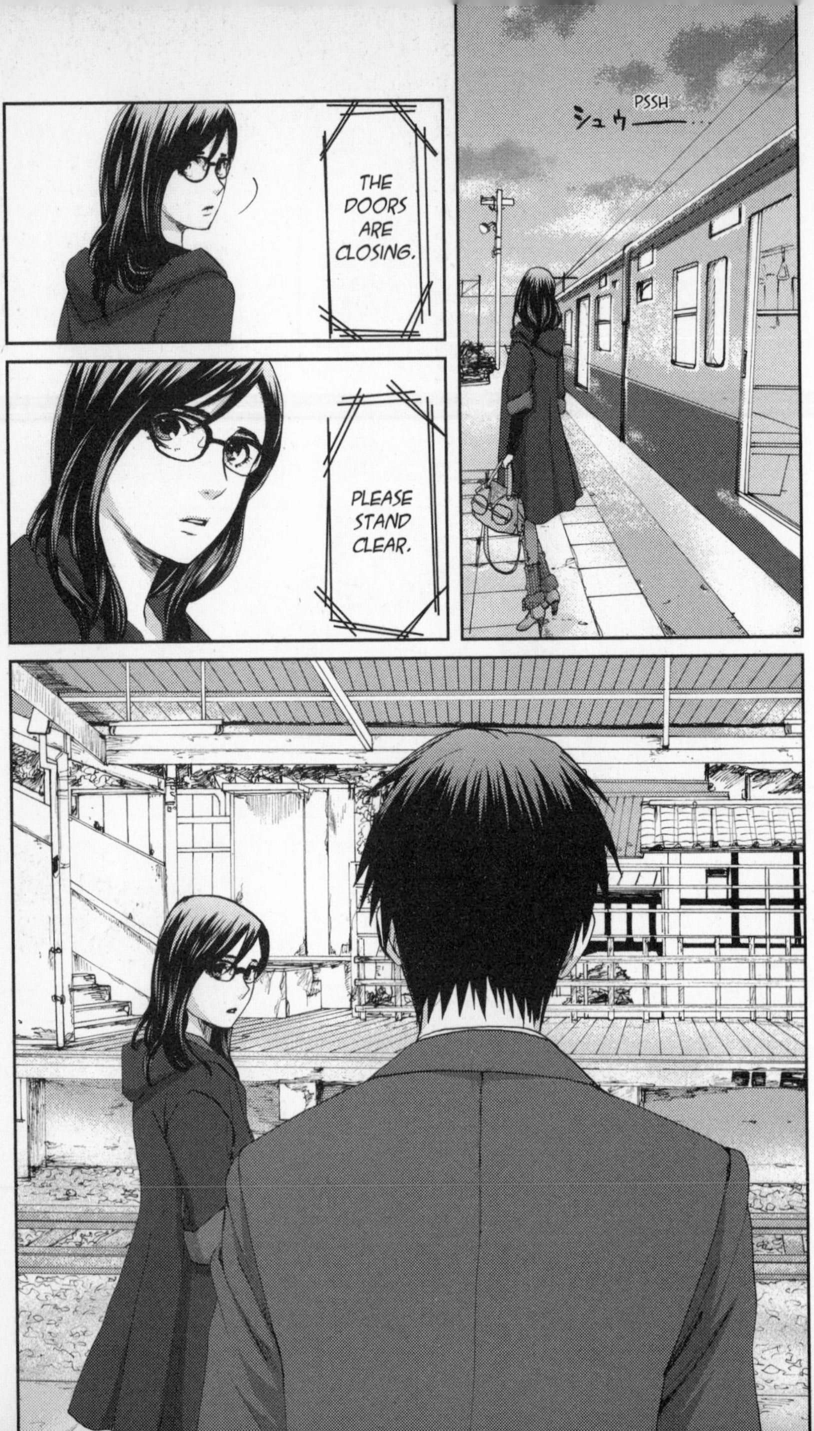
シュウー…
PSSH
THE DOORS ARE CLOSING.
PLEASE STAND CLEAR.

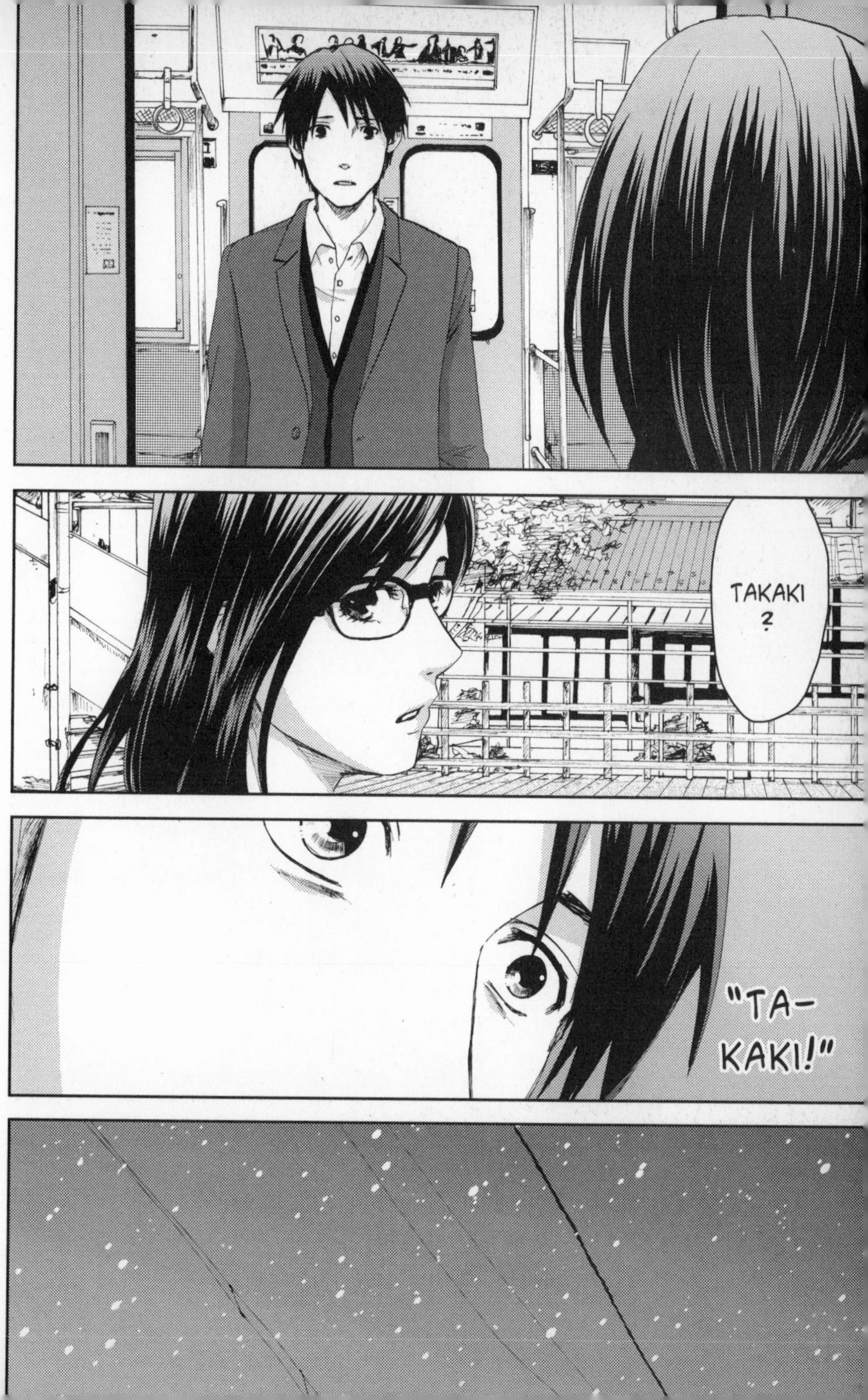
TAKAKI?
"TA-KAKI!"

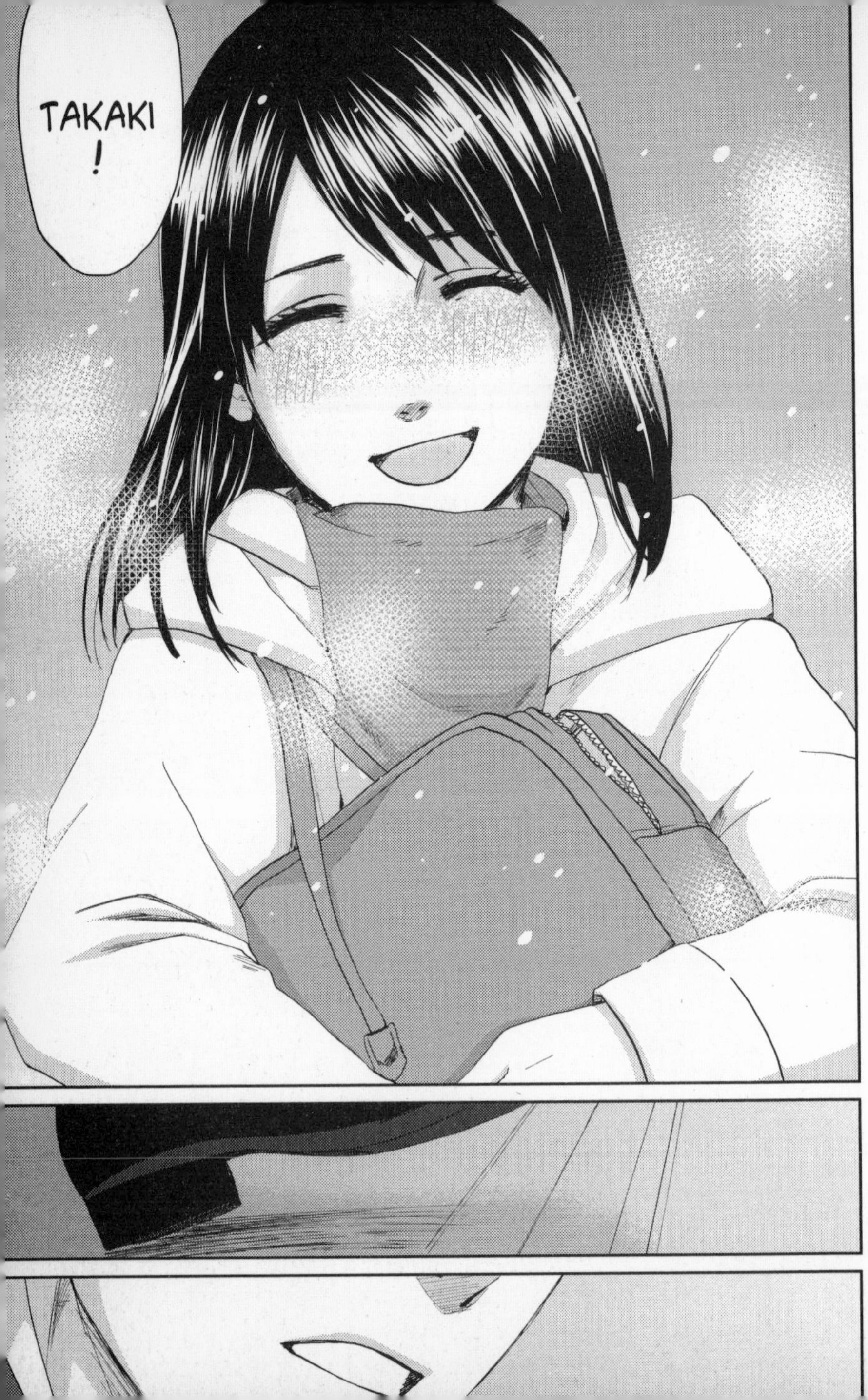
TAKAKI
!

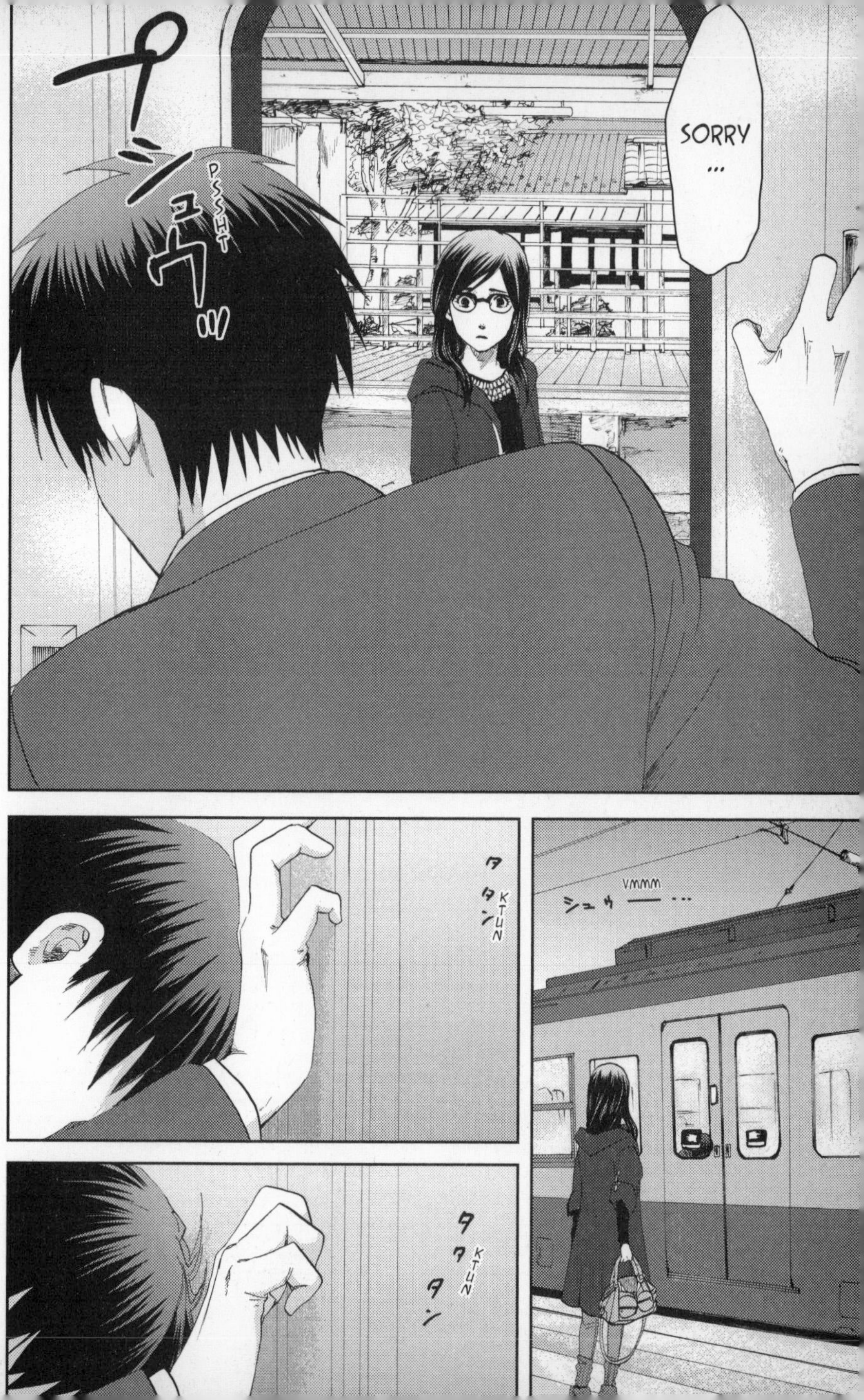
SORRY ...
プシュウッ
PSSHT
タタン
KTUN
シュゥ—— ...
VMMM
タタタン
KTUN

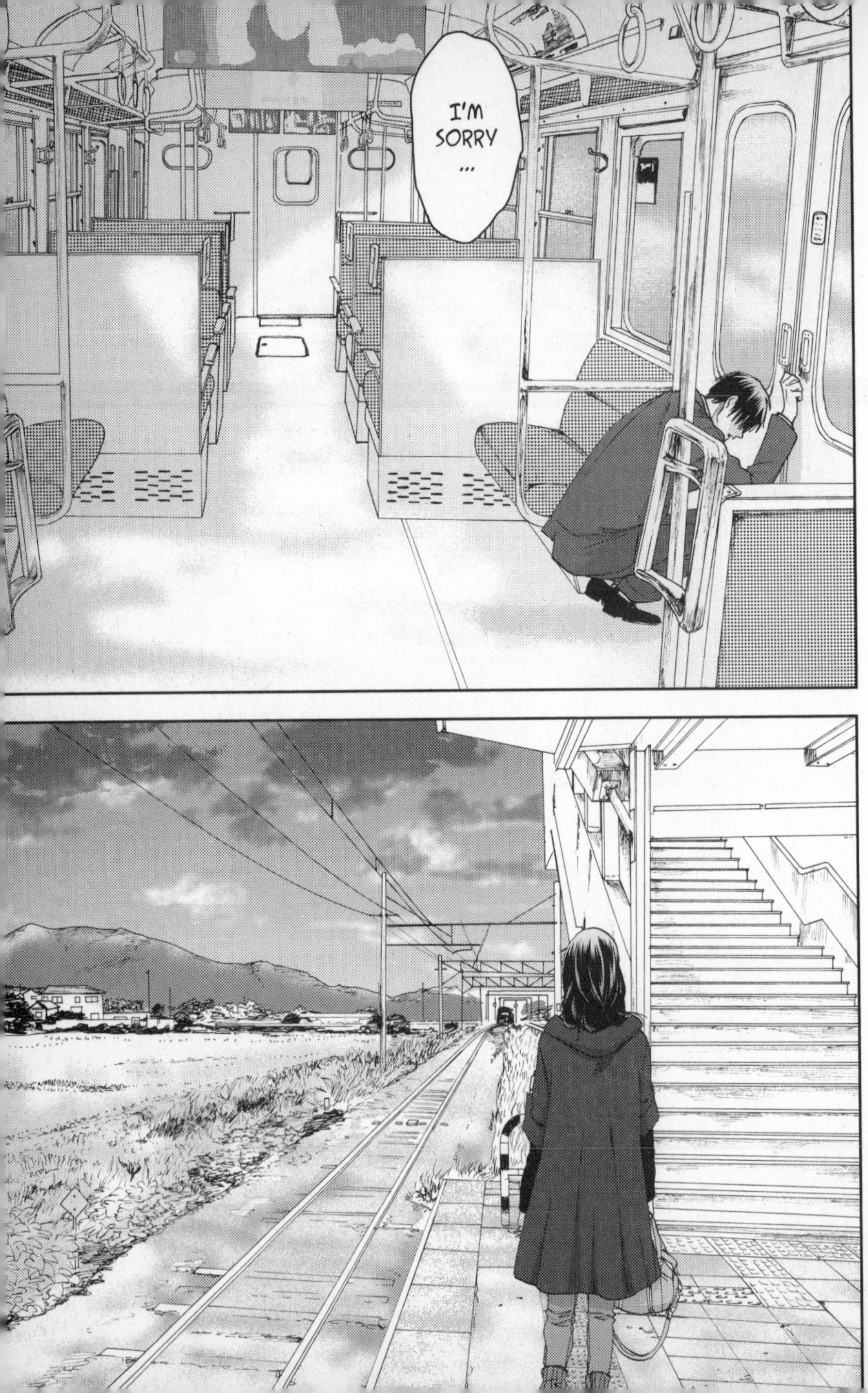
I'M SORRY ...

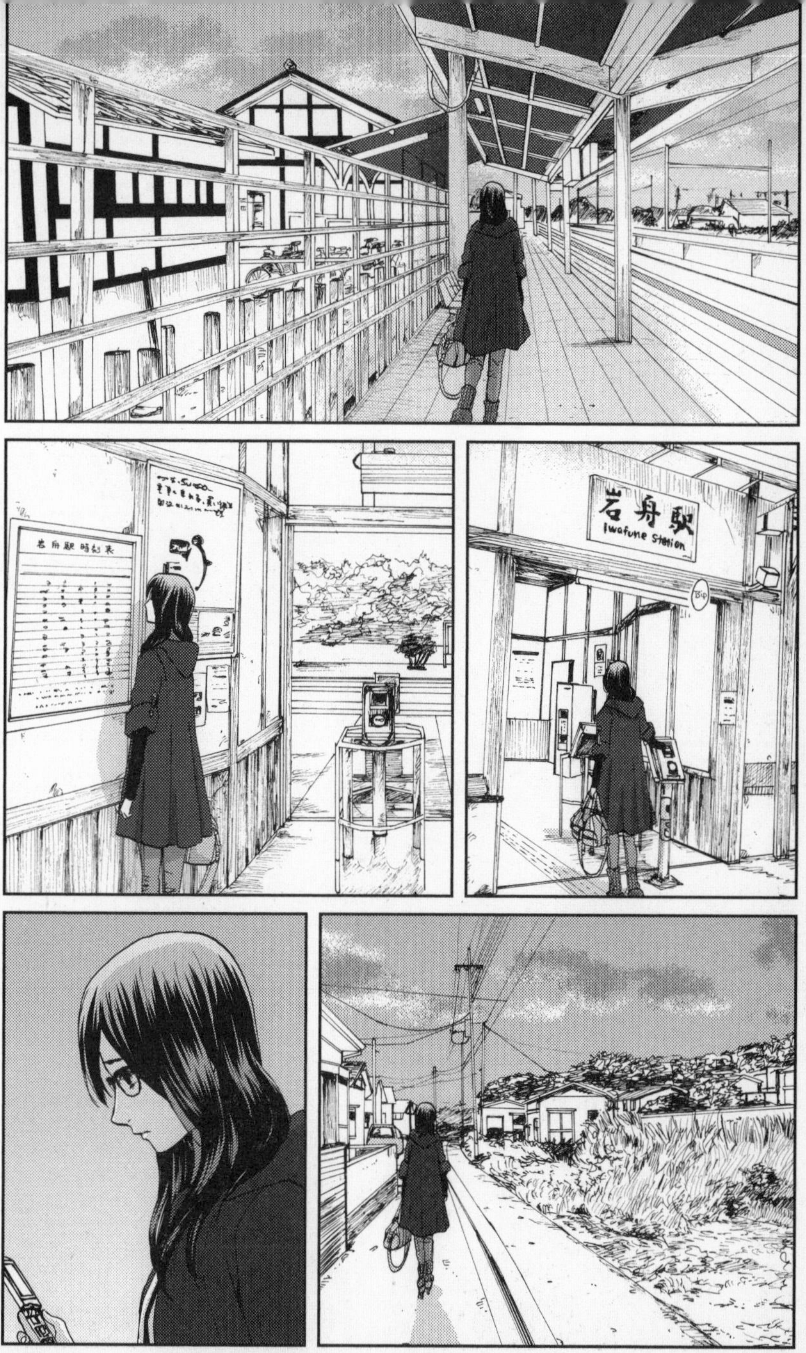
岩舟駅
Iwafune station
岩舟駅時刻表

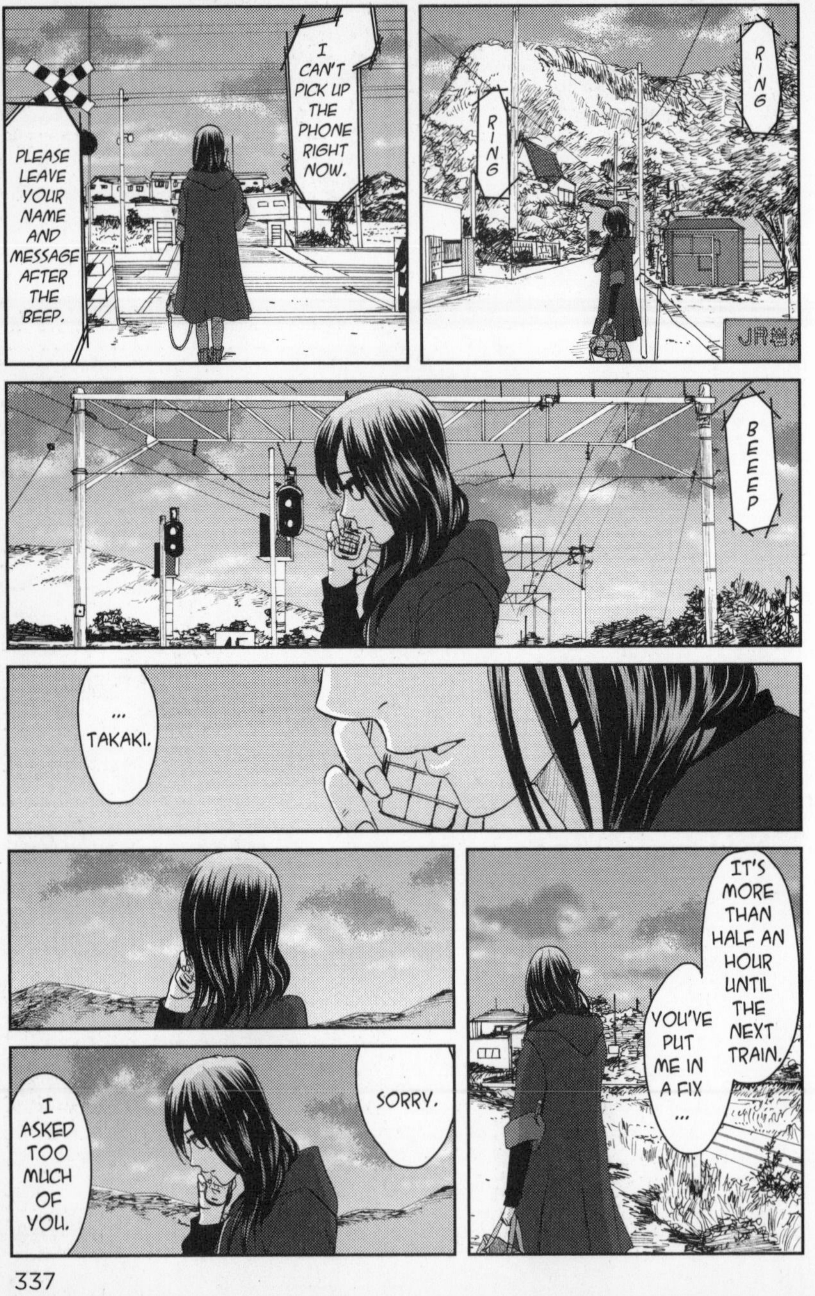
RING
RING
I CAN'T PICK UP THE PHONE RIGHT NOW.
PLEASE LEAVE YOUR NAME AND MESSAGE AFTER THE BEEP.
BEEEP
... TAKAKI.
IT'S MORE THAN HALF AN HOUR UNTIL THE NEXT TRAIN.
YOU'VE PUT ME IN A FIX ...
SORRY.
I ASKED TOO MUCH OF YOU.

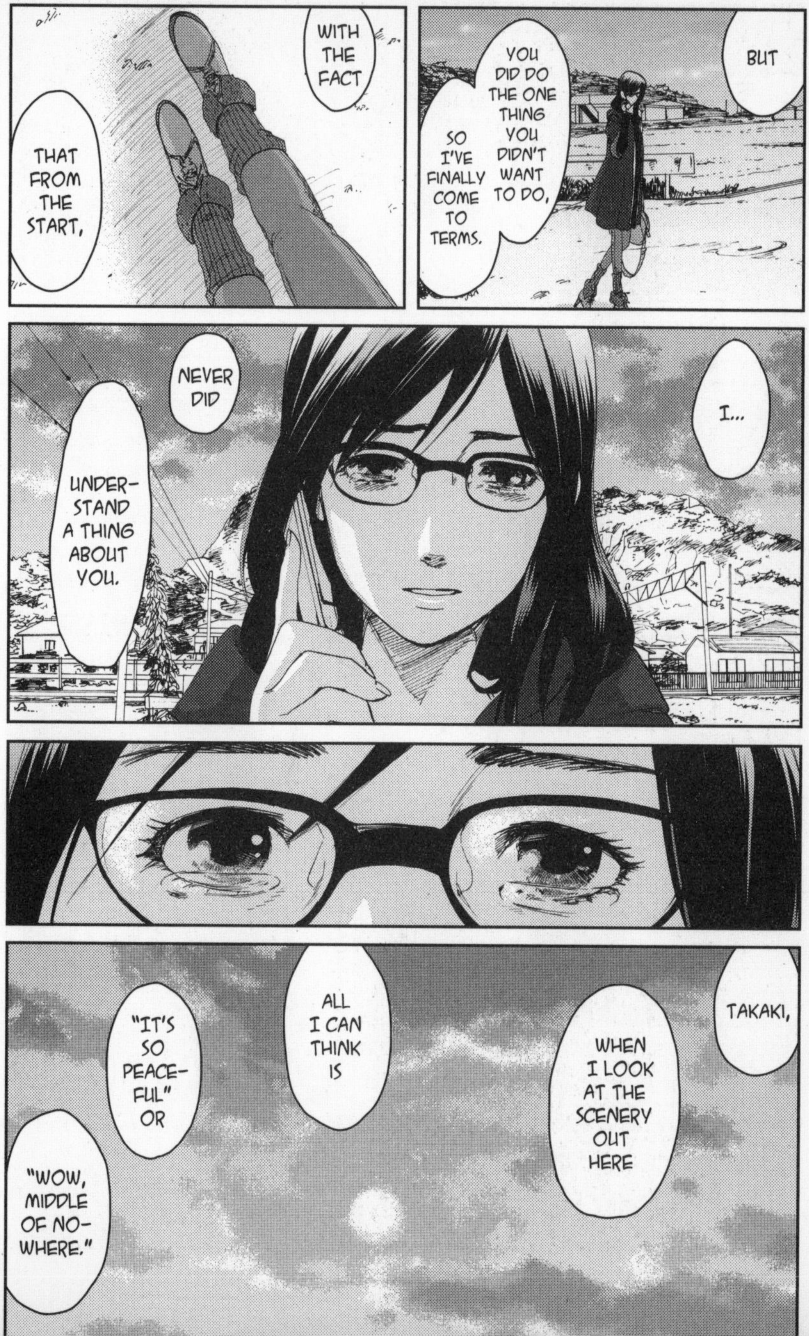
BUT
YOU DID DO THE ONE THING YOU DIDN'T WANT TO DO,
SO I'VE FINALLY COME TO TERMS.
WITH THE FACT
THAT FROM THE START,
I...
NEVER DID
UNDERSTAND A THING ABOUT YOU.
TAKAKI,
WHEN I LOOK AT THE SCENERY OUT HERE
ALL I CAN THINK IS
"IT'S SO PEACEFUL" OR
"WOW, MIDDLE OF NOWHERE."

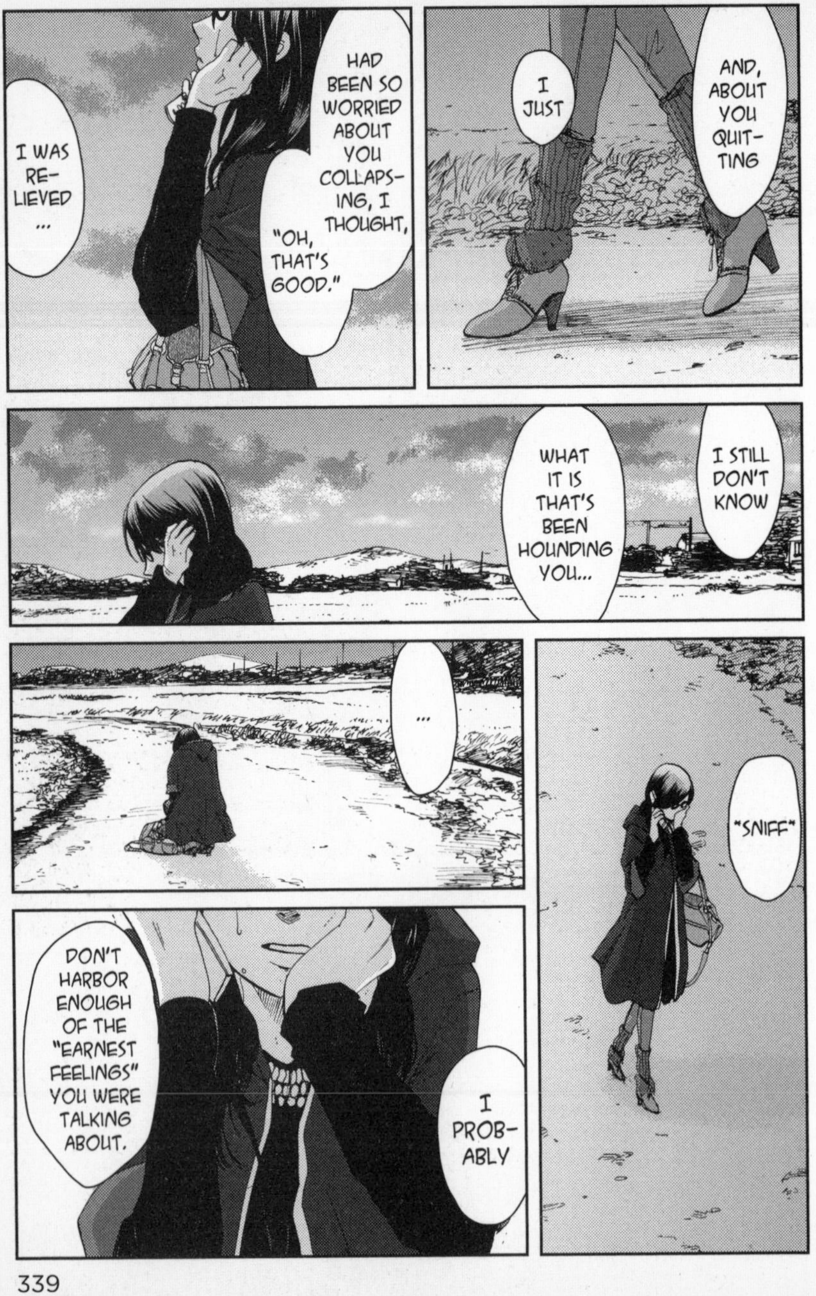
AND, ABOUT YOU QUIT-TING
I JUST
HAD BEEN SO WORRIED ABOUT YOU COLLAPS-ING, I THOUGHT, "OH, THAT'S GOOD."
I WAS RE-LIEVED ...
I STILL DON'T KNOW
WHAT IT IS THAT'S BEEN HOUNDING YOU...
"SNIFF"
...
I PROB-ABLY
DON'T HARBOR ENOUGH OF THE "EARNEST FEELINGS" YOU WERE TALKING ABOUT.

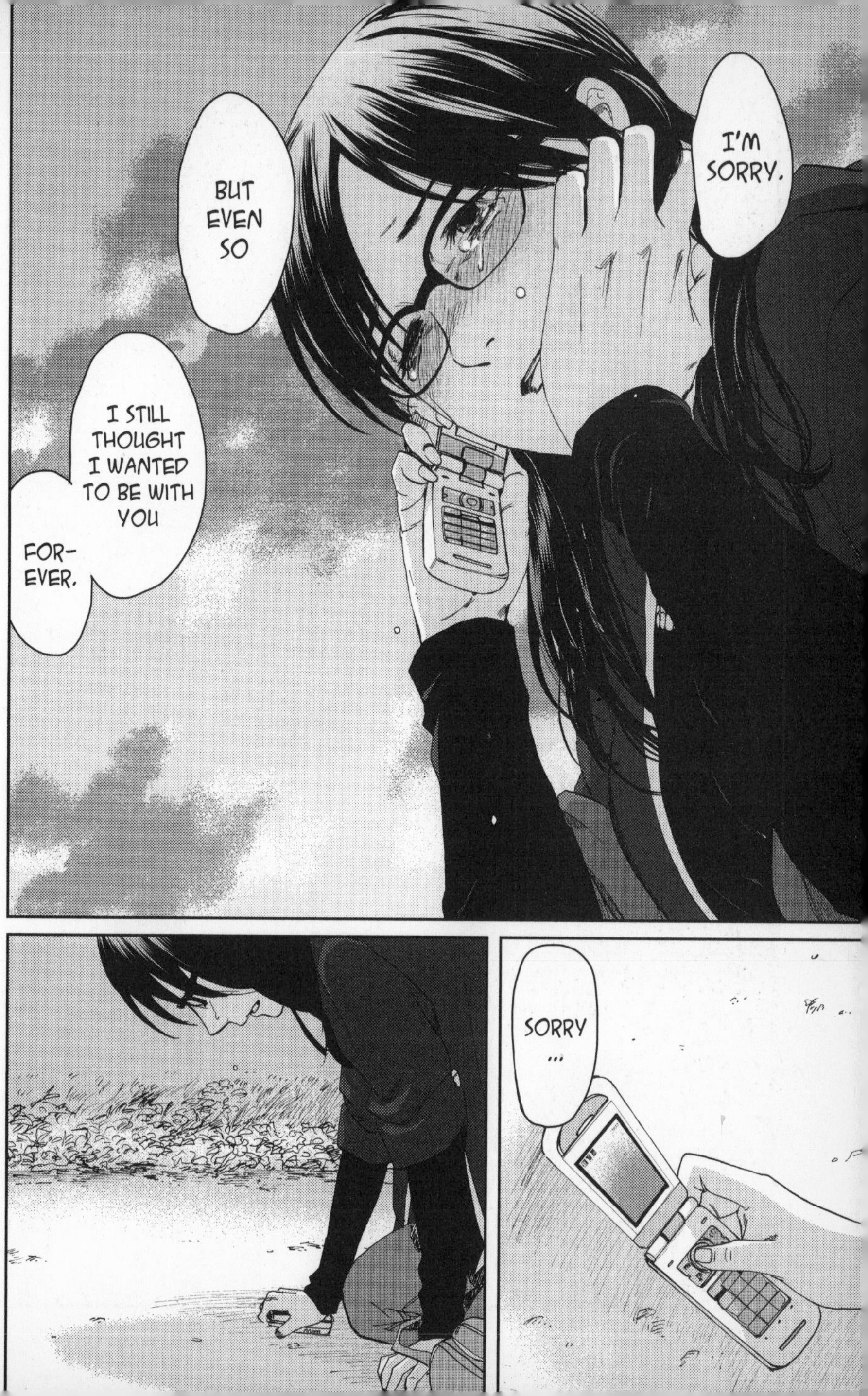
I'M SORRY.
BUT EVEN SO
I STILL THOUGHT I WANTED TO BE WITH YOU
FOR-EVER.
SORRY ...

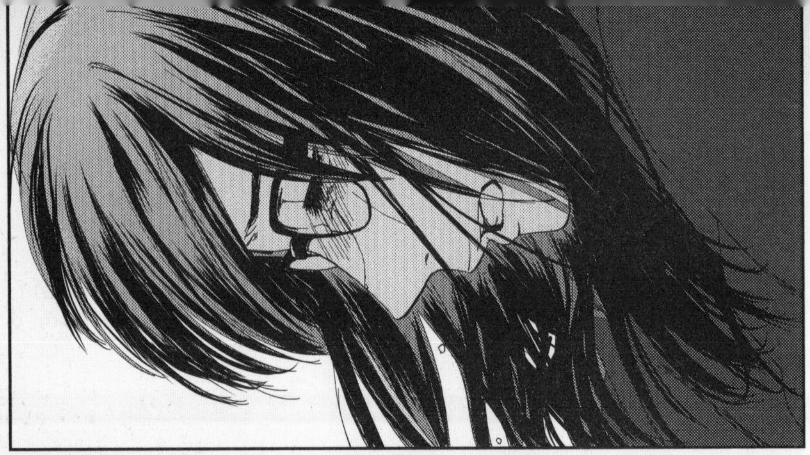
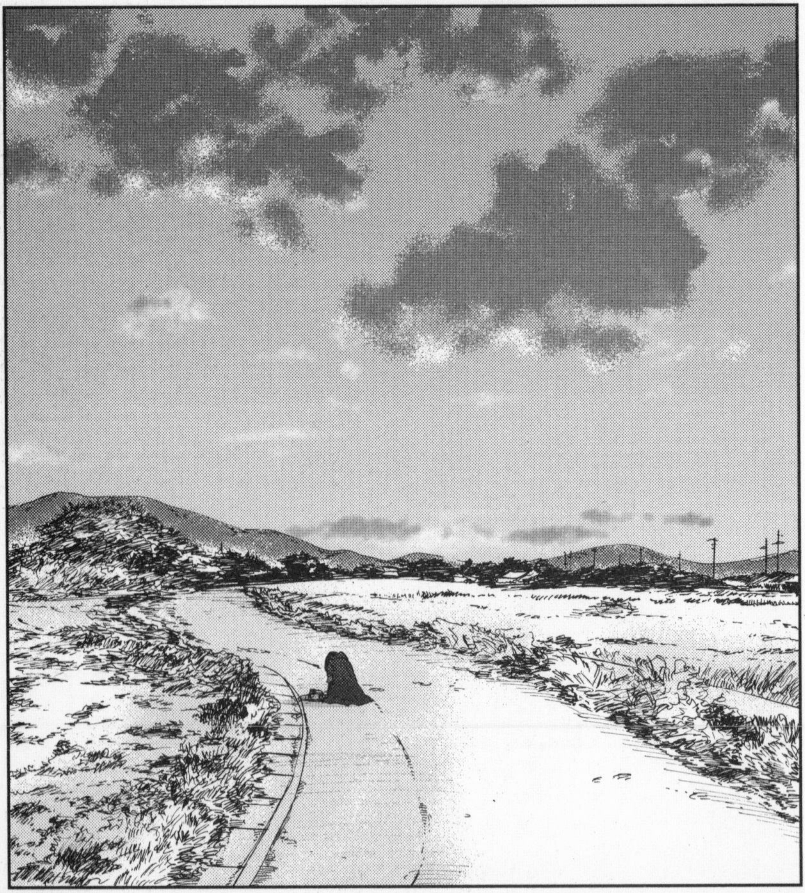

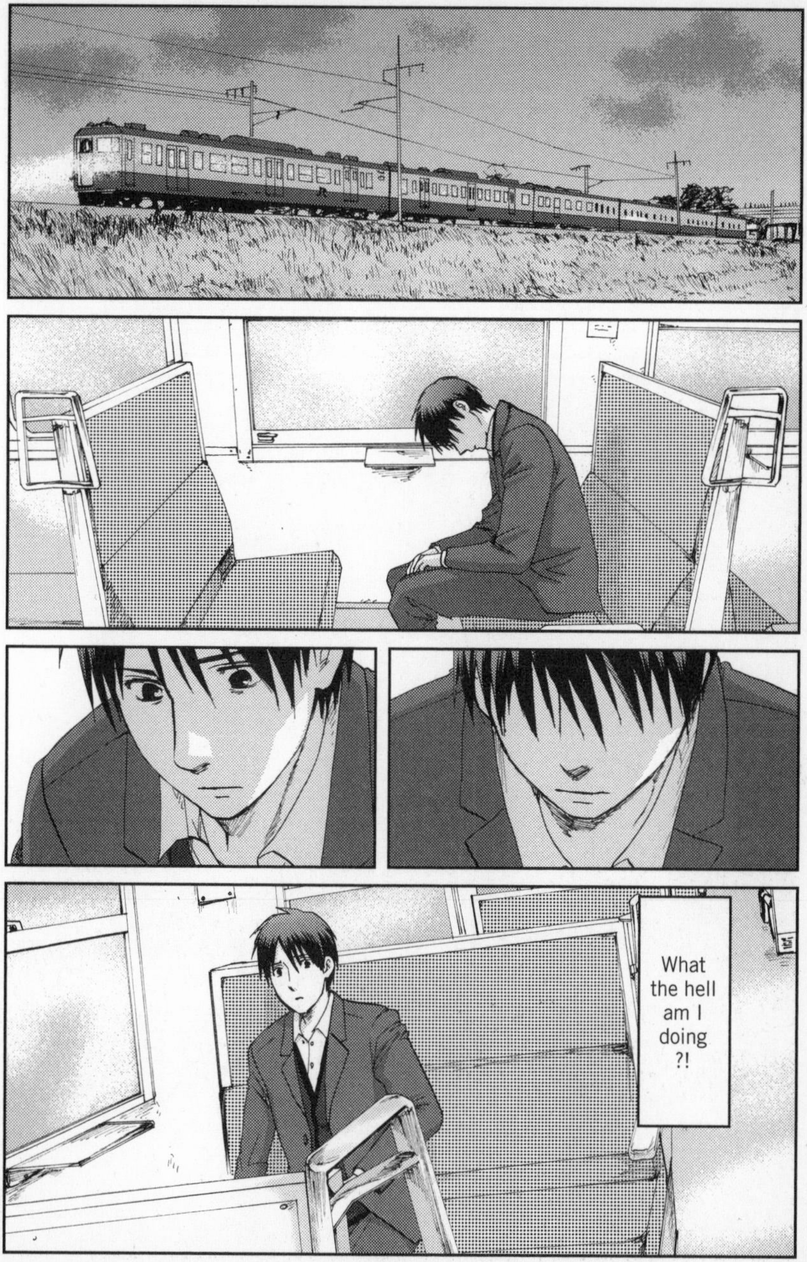
What the hell am I doing ?!

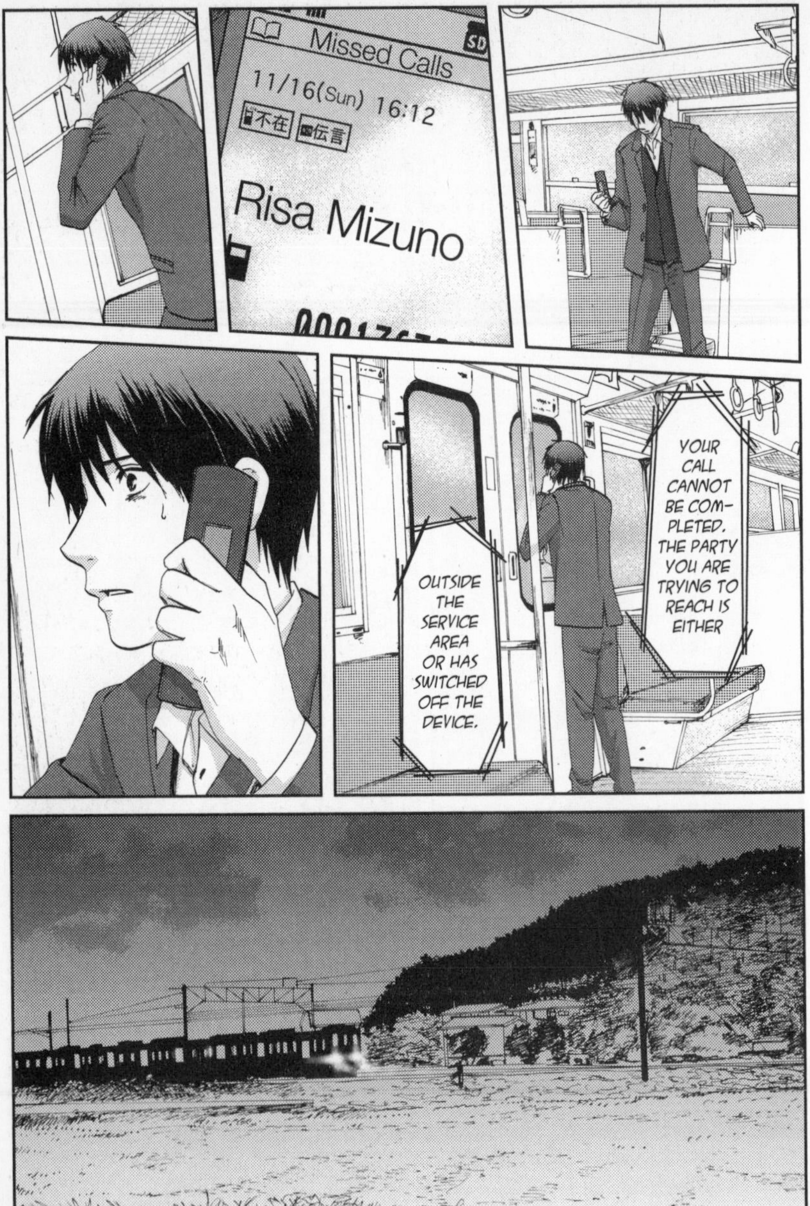
Missed Calls
11/16(Sun) 16:12
不在
伝言
Risa Mizuno
YOUR CALL CANNOT BE COM-PLETED. THE PARTY YOU ARE TRYING TO REACH IS EITHER
OUTSIDE THE SERVICE AREA OR HAS SWITCHED OFF THE DEVICE.

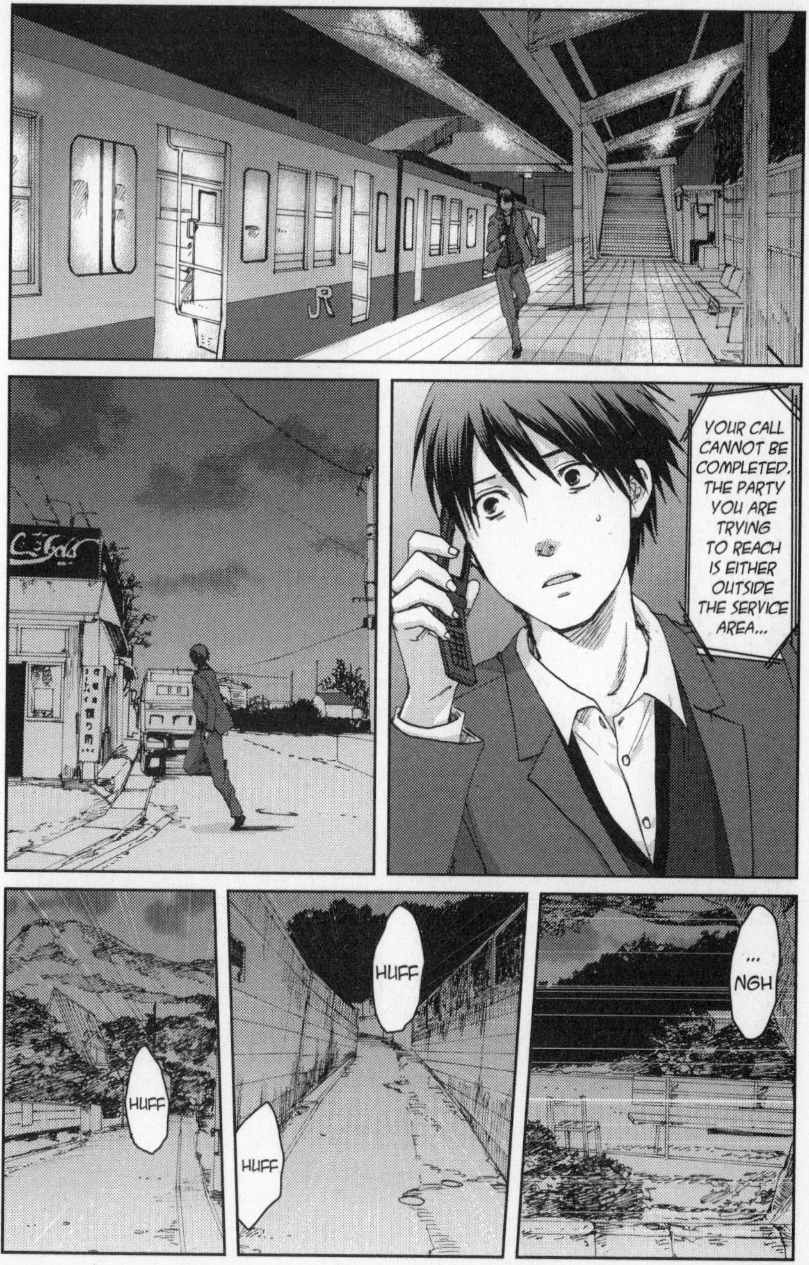
JR
YOUR CALL CANNOT BE COMPLETED. THE PARTY YOU ARE TRYING TO REACH IS EITHER OUTSIDE THE SERVICE AREA...
... NGH
HUFF
HUFF
HUFF

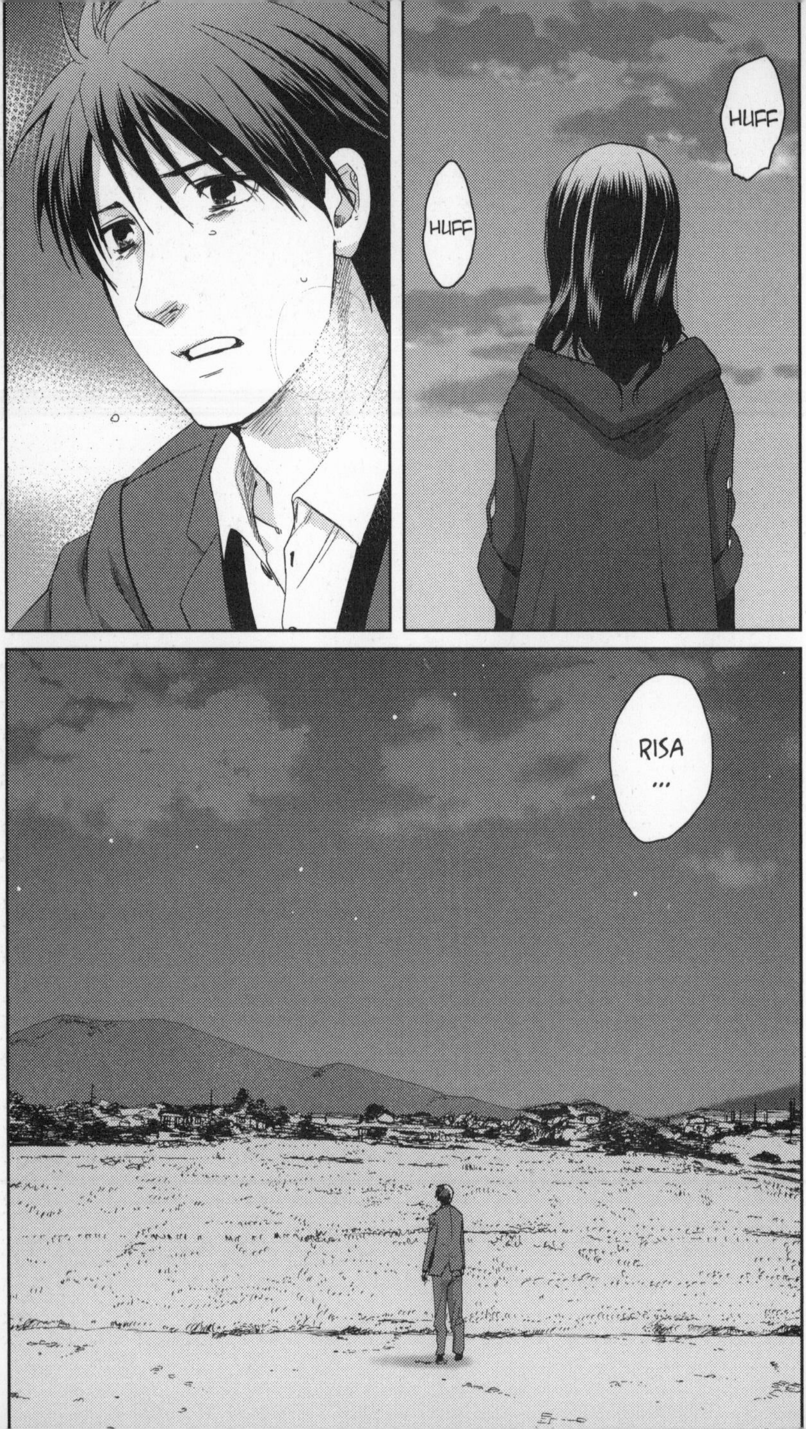
HUFF
HUFF
RISA ...

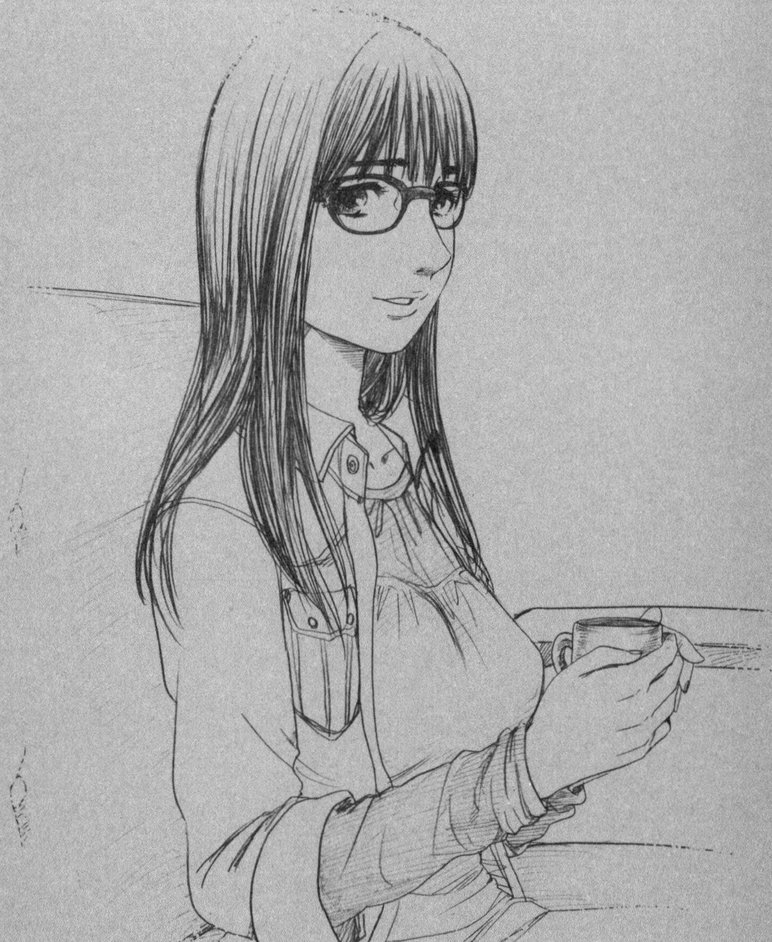

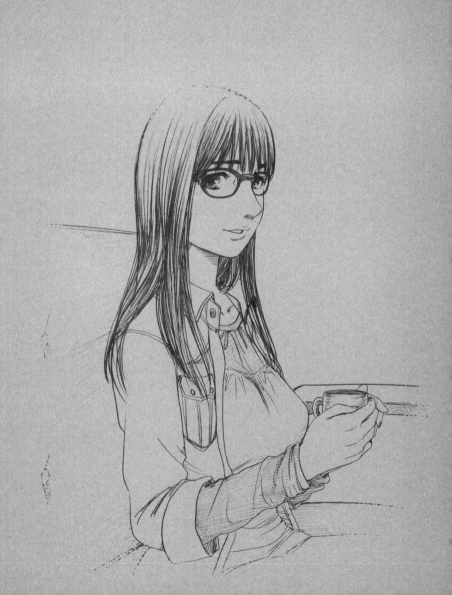

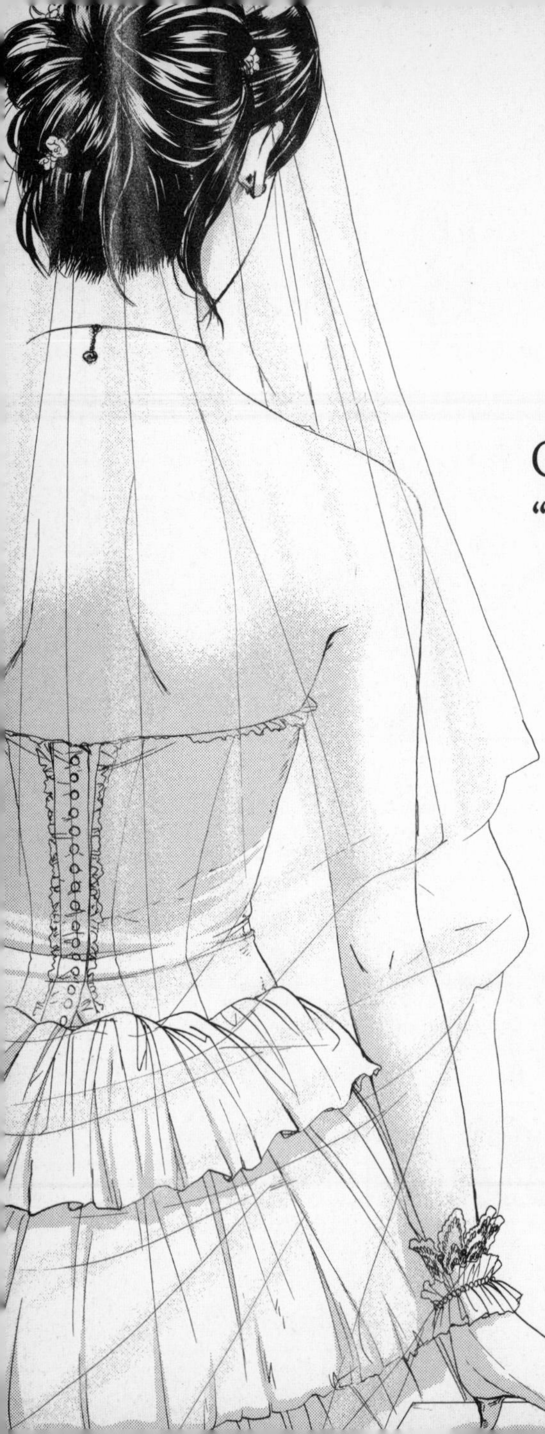

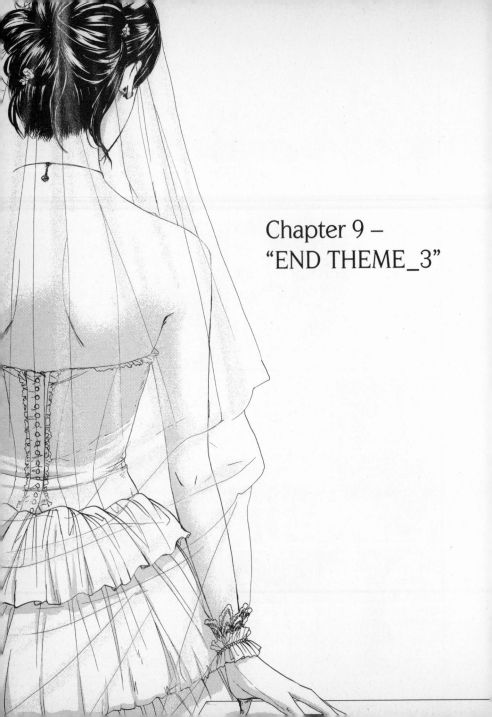

Chapter 9 –
“END THEME_3”

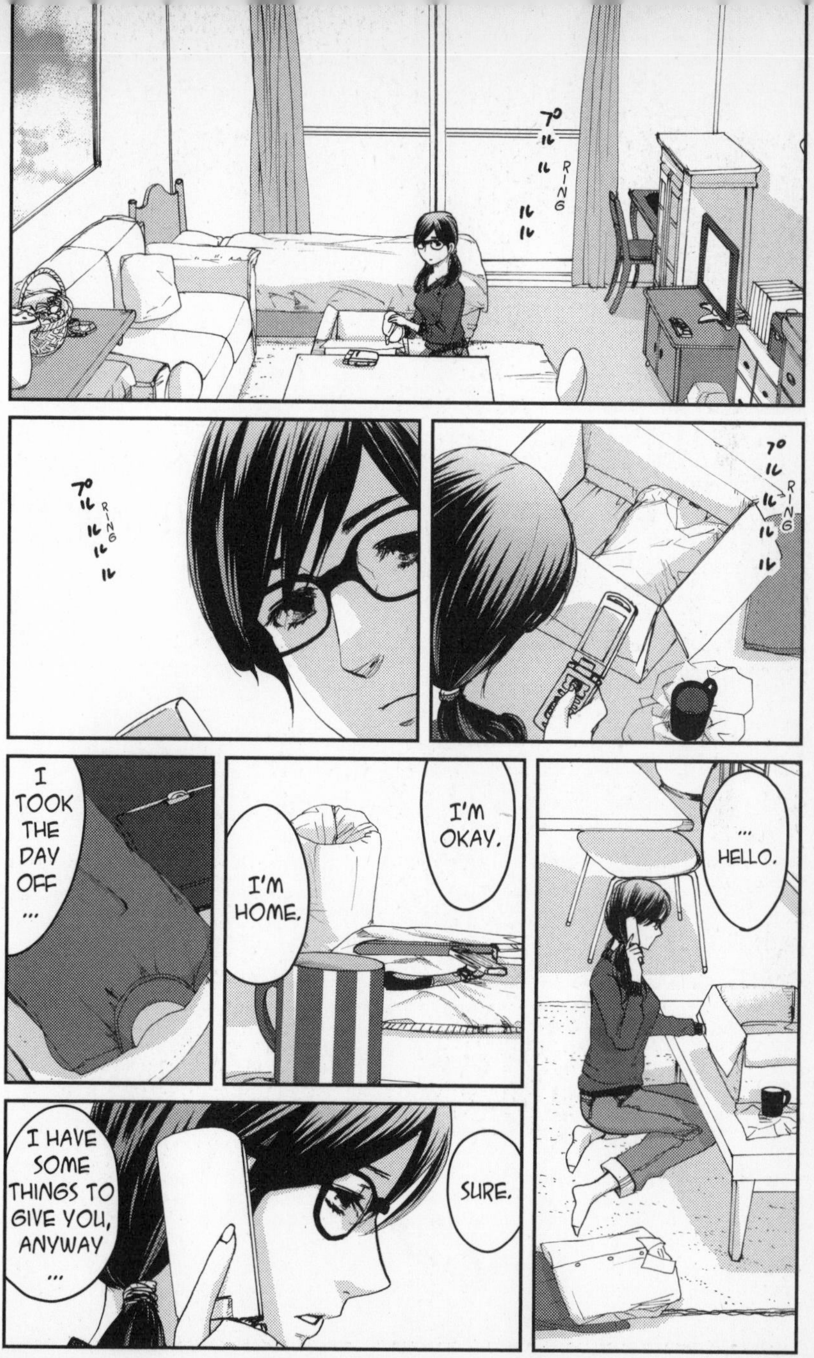

プルルルル
RING
プルルルル
RING
プルルルル
RING
... HELLO.
I'M OKAY.
I'M HOME.
I TOOK THE DAY OFF ...
SURE.
I HAVE SOME THINGS TO GIVE YOU, ANYWAY ...

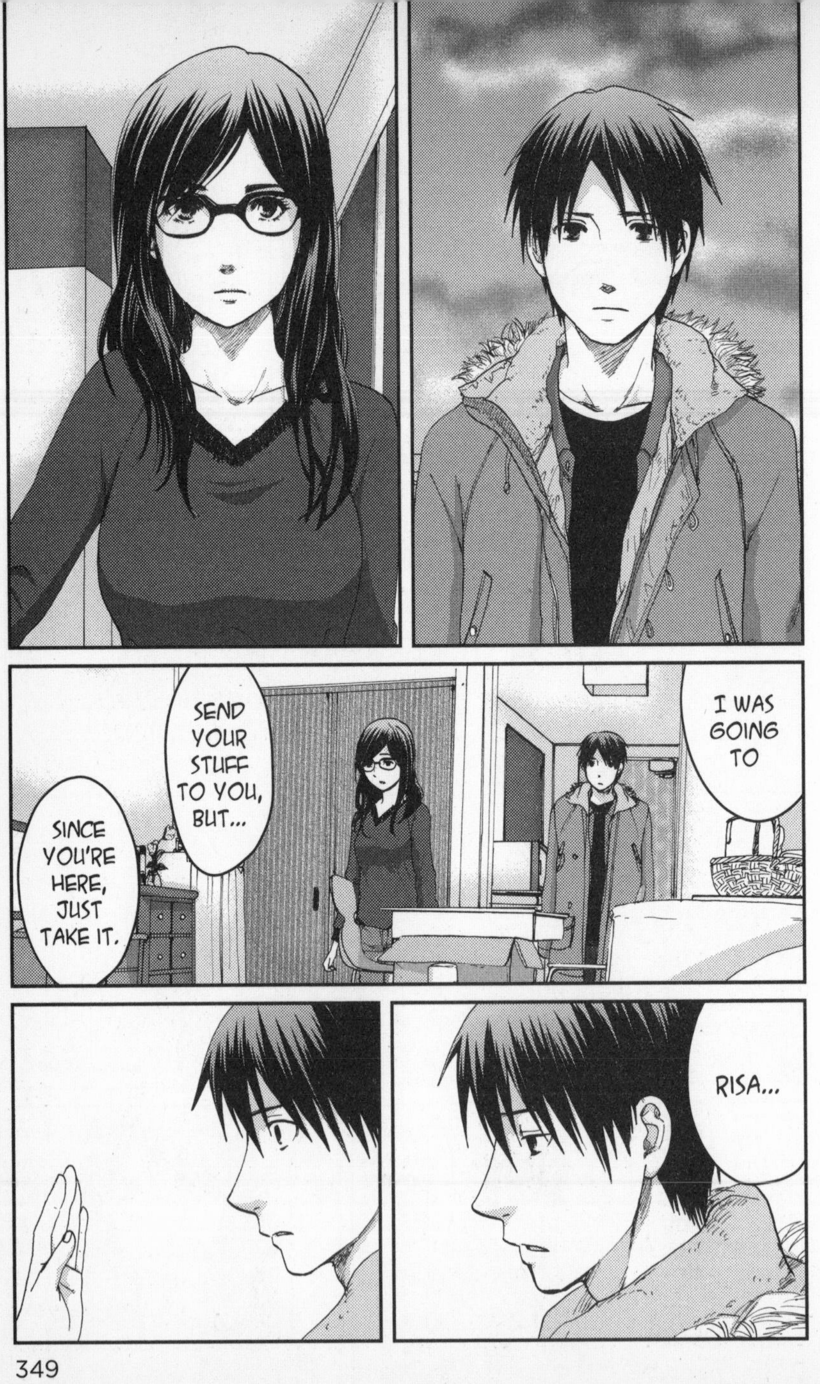
I WAS GOING TO
SEND YOUR STUFF TO YOU, BUT...
SINCE YOU'RE HERE, JUST TAKE IT.
RISA...

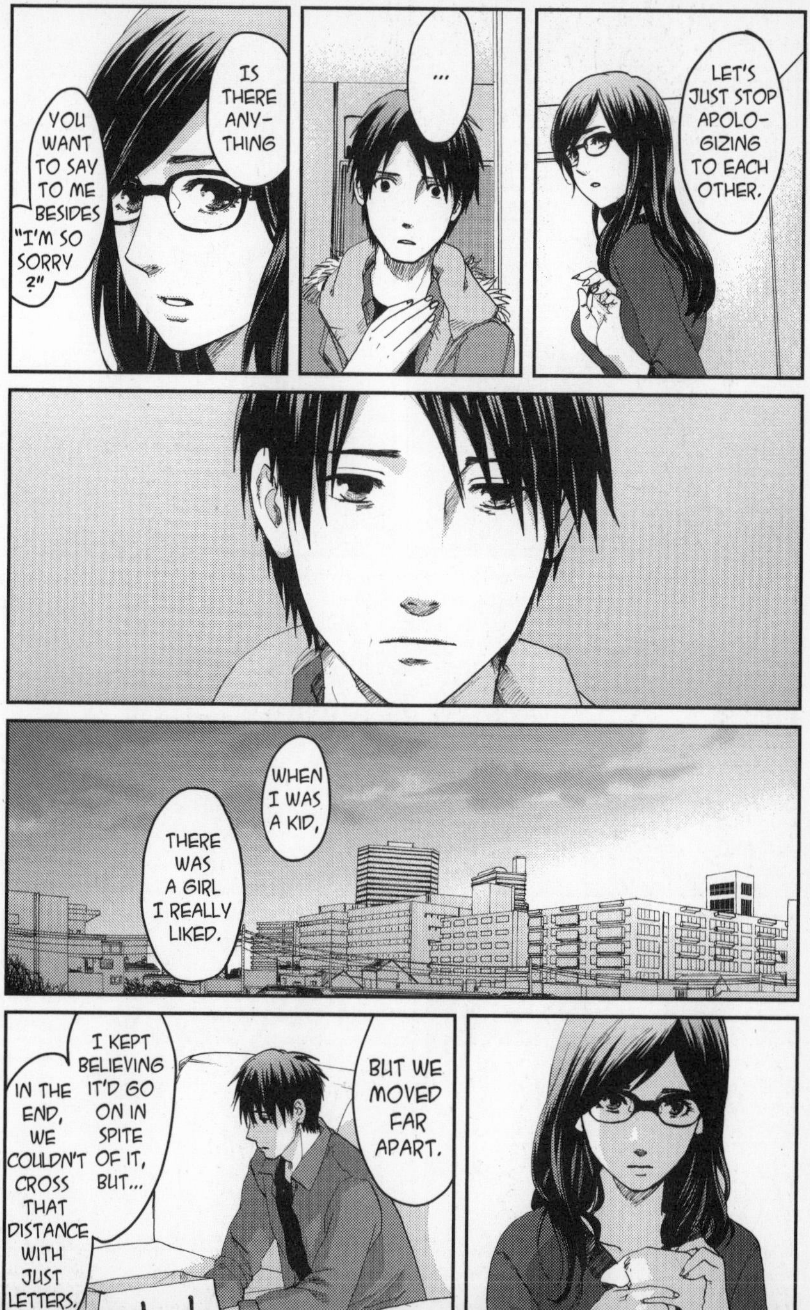
LET'S JUST STOP APOLOGIZING TO EACH OTHER.
...
IS THERE ANYTHING
YOU WANT TO SAY TO ME BESIDES "I'M SO SORRY?"
WHEN I WAS A KID,
THERE WAS A GIRL I REALLY LIKED.
BUT WE MOVED FAR APART.
I KEPT BELIEVING IT'D GO ON IN SPITE OF IT, BUT...
IN THE END, WE COULDN'T CROSS THAT DISTANCE WITH JUST LETTERS.

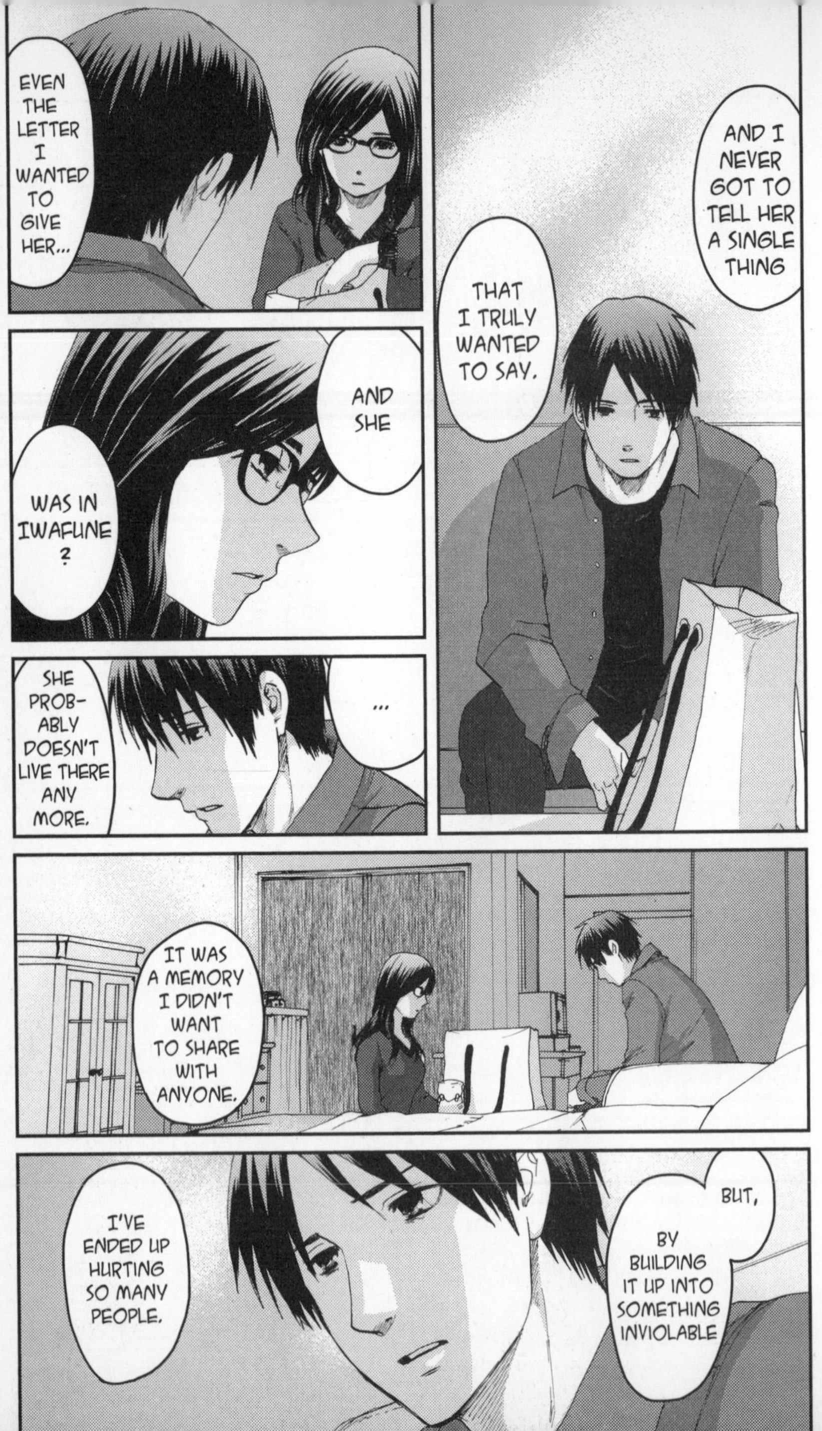
AND I NEVER GOT TO TELL HER A SINGLE THING
THAT I TRULY WANTED TO SAY.
EVEN THE LETTER I WANTED TO GIVE HER...
AND SHE
WAS IN IWAFUNE?
...
SHE PROB-ABLY DOESN'T LIVE THERE ANY MORE.
IT WAS A MEMORY I DIDN'T WANT TO SHARE WITH ANYONE.
BUT,
BY BUILDING IT UP INTO SOMETHING INVIOLABLE
I'VE ENDED UP HURTING SO MANY PEOPLE.

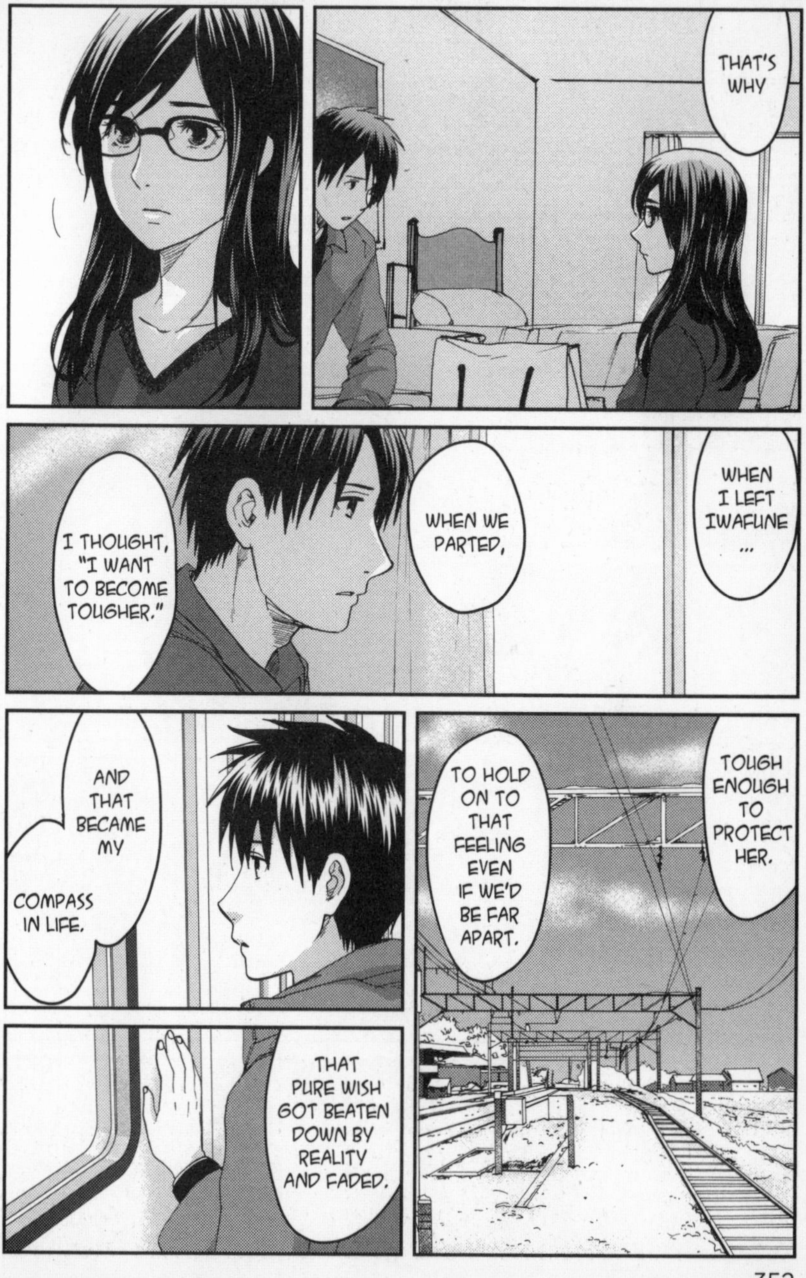
THAT'S WHY
WHEN I LEFT IWAFUNE ...
WHEN WE PARTED,
I THOUGHT, "I WANT TO BECOME TOUGHER."
TOUGH ENOUGH TO PROTECT HER.
TO HOLD ON TO THAT FEELING EVEN IF WE'D BE FAR APART.
AND THAT BECAME MY
COMPASS IN LIFE.
THAT PURE WISH GOT BEATEN DOWN BY REALITY AND FADED.

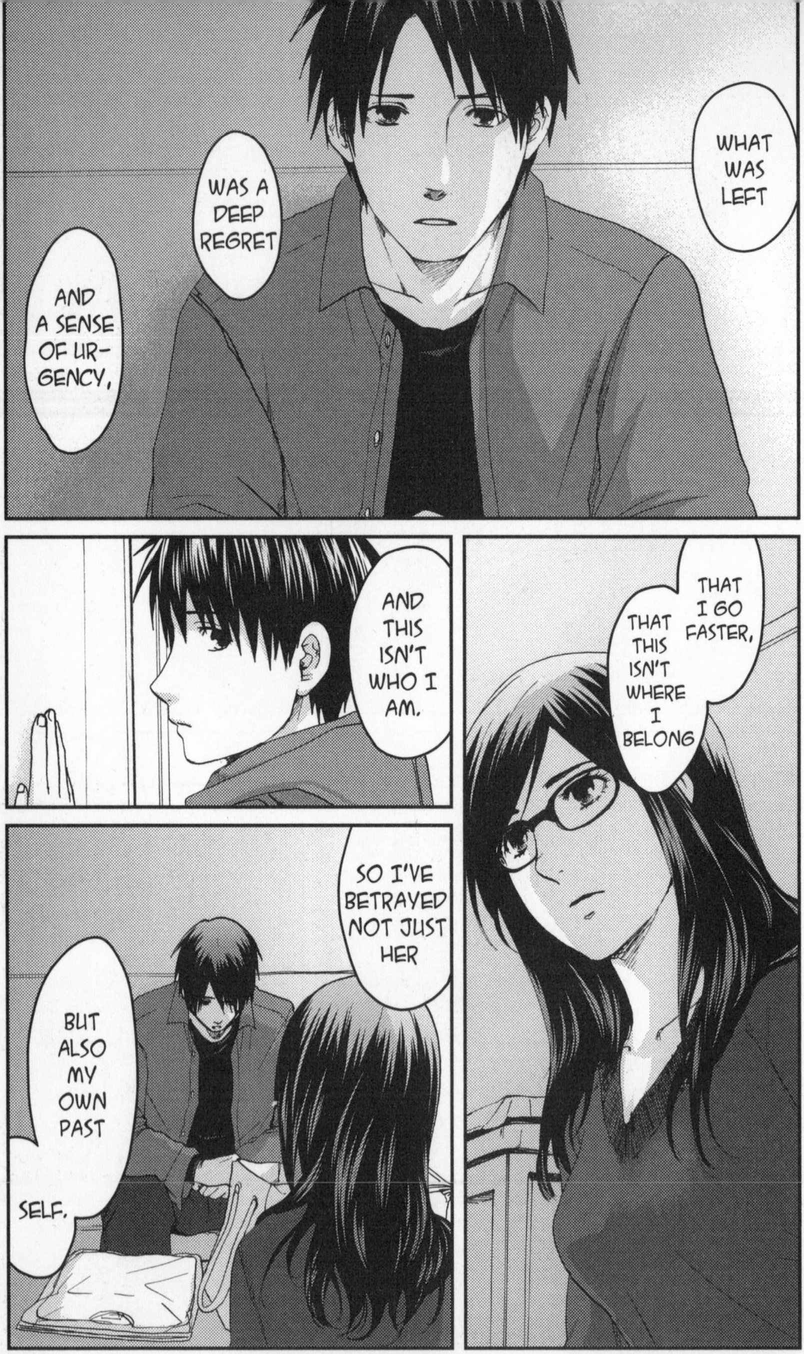
WHAT WAS LEFT
WAS A DEEP REGRET
AND A SENSE OF UR-GENCY,
THAT I GO FASTER,
THAT THIS ISN'T WHERE I BELONG
AND THIS ISN'T WHO I AM.
SO I'VE BETRAYED NOT JUST HER
BUT ALSO MY OWN PAST
SELF.

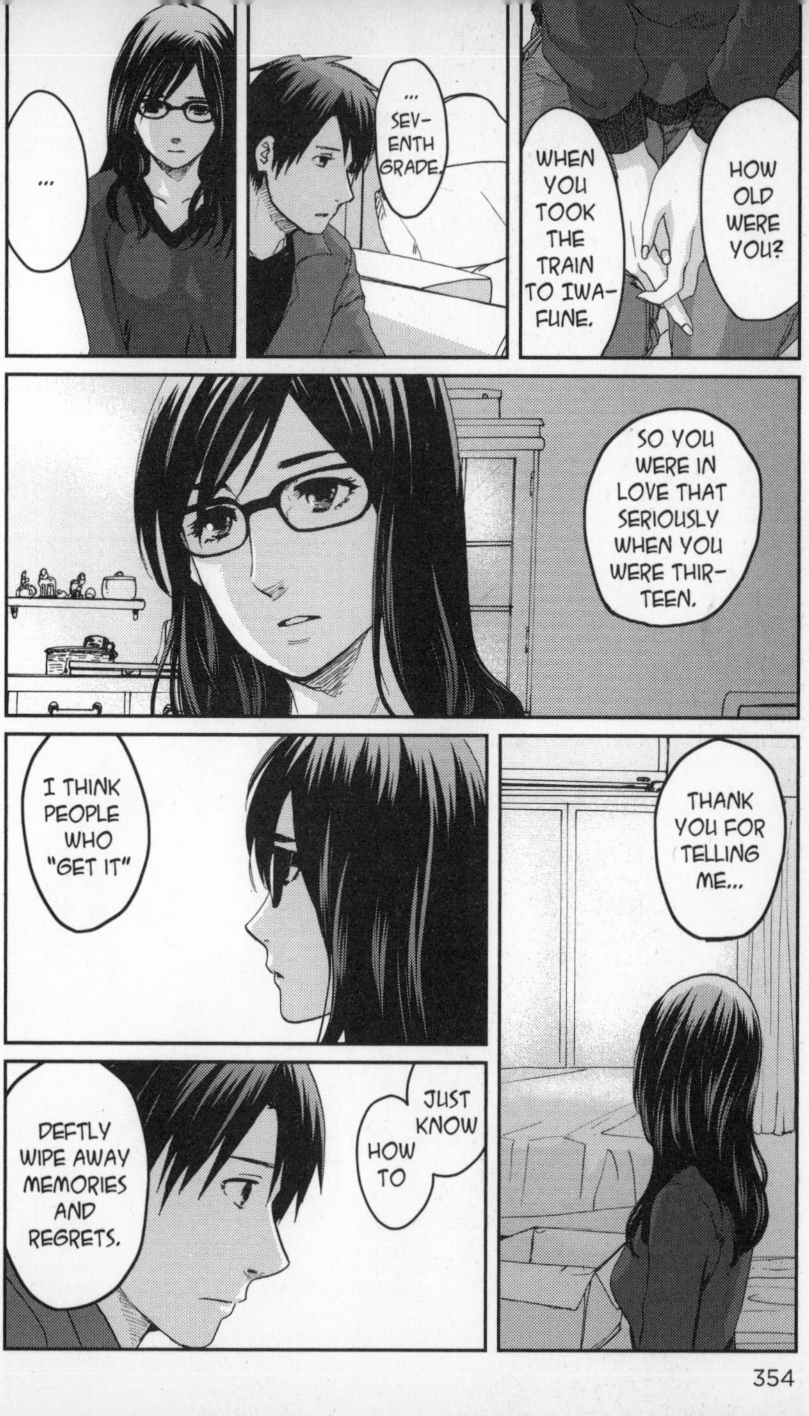
HOW OLD WERE YOU?
WHEN YOU TOOK THE TRAIN TO IWA-FUNE.
... SEV-ENTH GRADE.
...
SO YOU WERE IN LOVE THAT SERIOUSLY WHEN YOU WERE THIR-TEEN.
THANK YOU FOR TELLING ME...
I THINK PEOPLE WHO "GET IT"
JUST KNOW HOW TO
DEFTLY WIPE AWAY MEMORIES AND REGRETS.

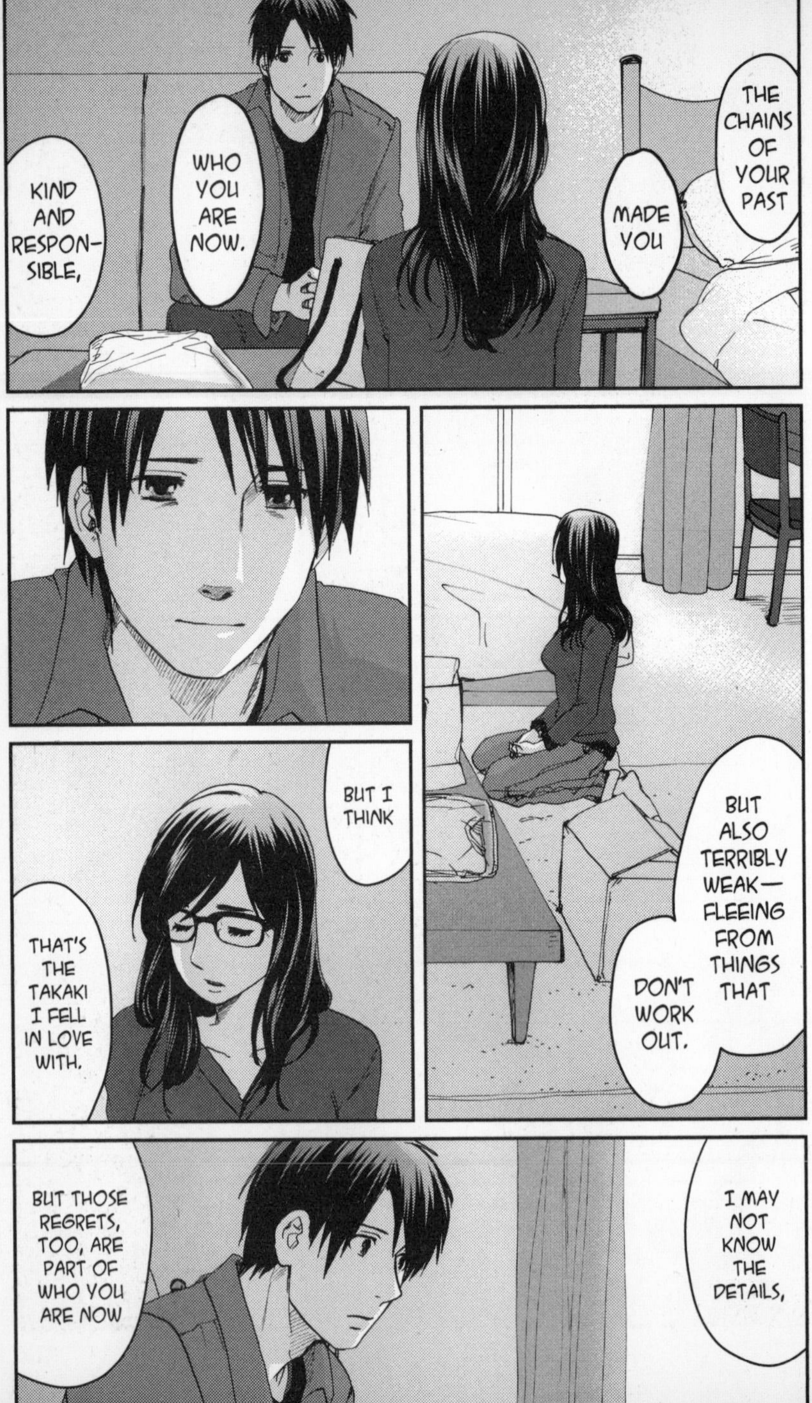
THE CHAINS OF YOUR PAST
MADE YOU
WHO YOU ARE NOW.
KIND AND RESPONSIBLE,
BUT ALSO TERRIBLY WEAK—FLEEING FROM THINGS THAT
DON'T WORK OUT.
BUT I THINK
THAT'S THE TAKAKI I FELL IN LOVE WITH.
I MAY NOT KNOW THE DETAILS,
BUT THOSE REGRETS, TOO, ARE PART OF WHO YOU ARE NOW

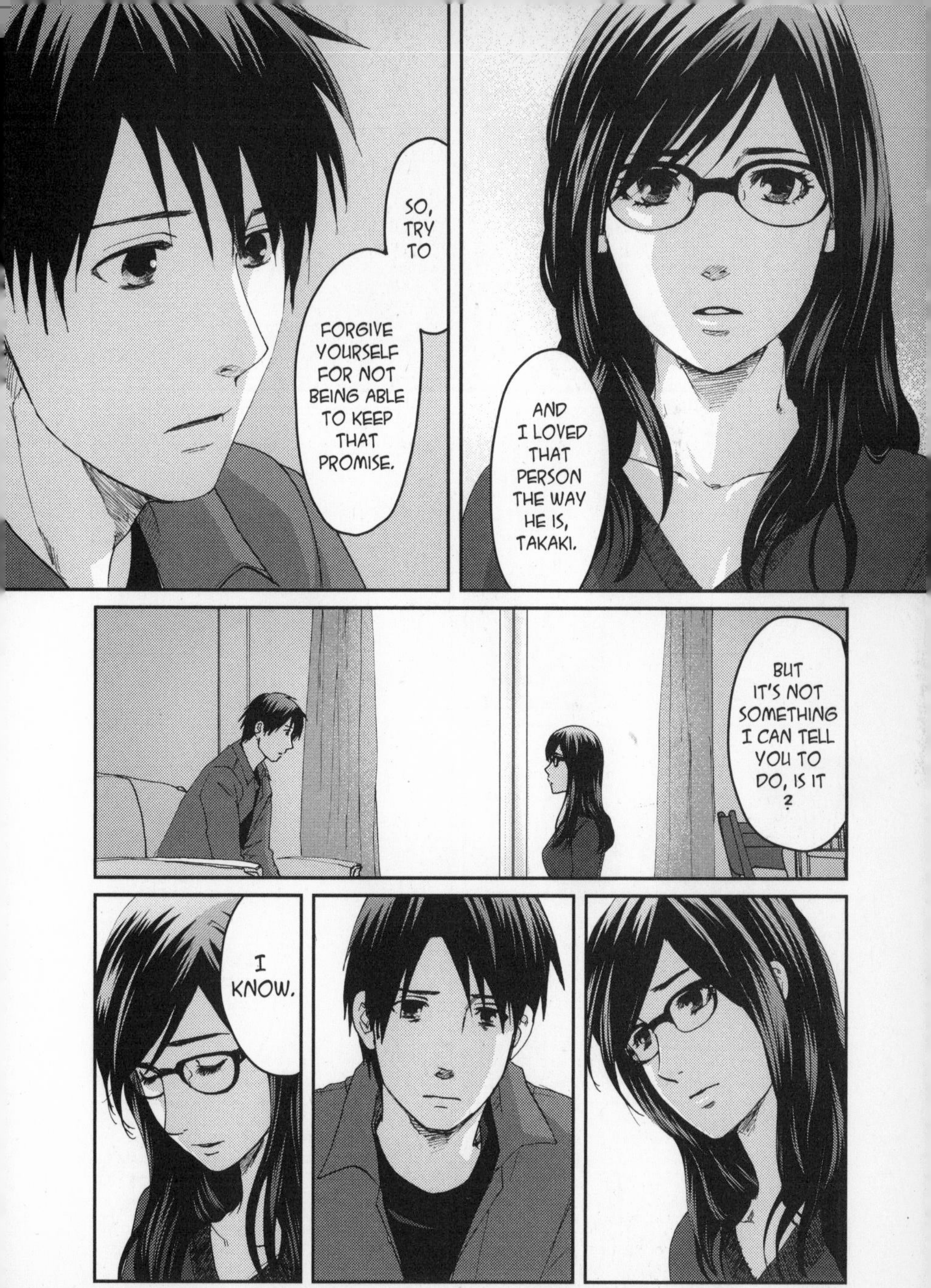
AND I LOVED THAT PERSON THE WAY HE IS, TAKAKI.
SO, TRY TO FORGIVE YOURSELF FOR NOT BEING ABLE TO KEEP THAT PROMISE.
BUT IT'S NOT SOMETHING I CAN TELL YOU TO DO, IS IT?
I KNOW.

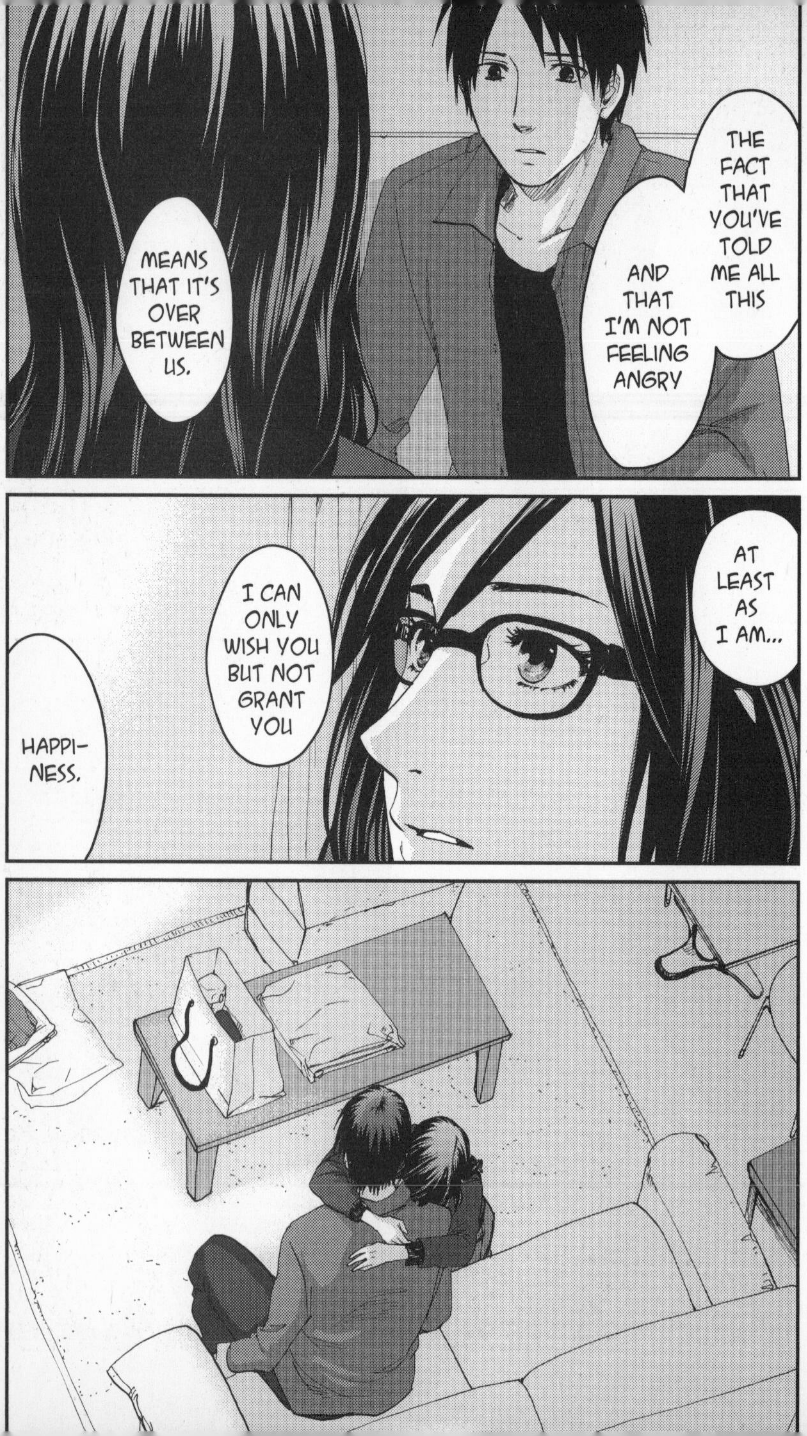
THE FACT THAT YOU'VE TOLD ME ALL THIS
AND THAT I'M NOT FEELING ANGRY
MEANS THAT IT'S OVER BETWEEN US.
AT LEAST AS I AM...
I CAN ONLY WISH YOU BUT NOT GRANT YOU
HAPPI- NESS.

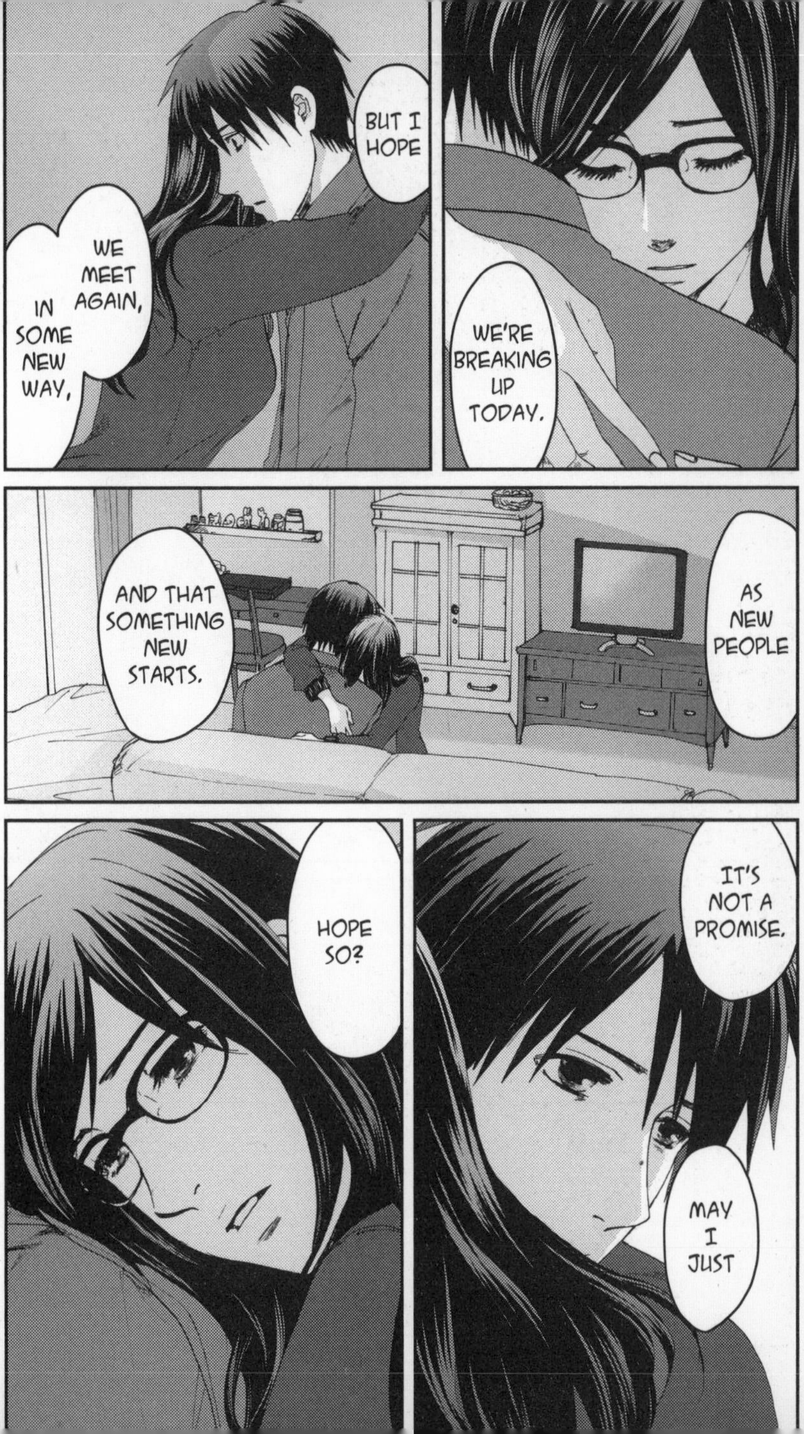
WE'RE BREAKING UP TODAY.
BUT I HOPE
WE MEET AGAIN,
IN SOME NEW WAY,
AS NEW PEOPLE
AND THAT SOMETHING NEW STARTS.
IT'S NOT A PROMISE.
MAY I JUST
HOPE SO?

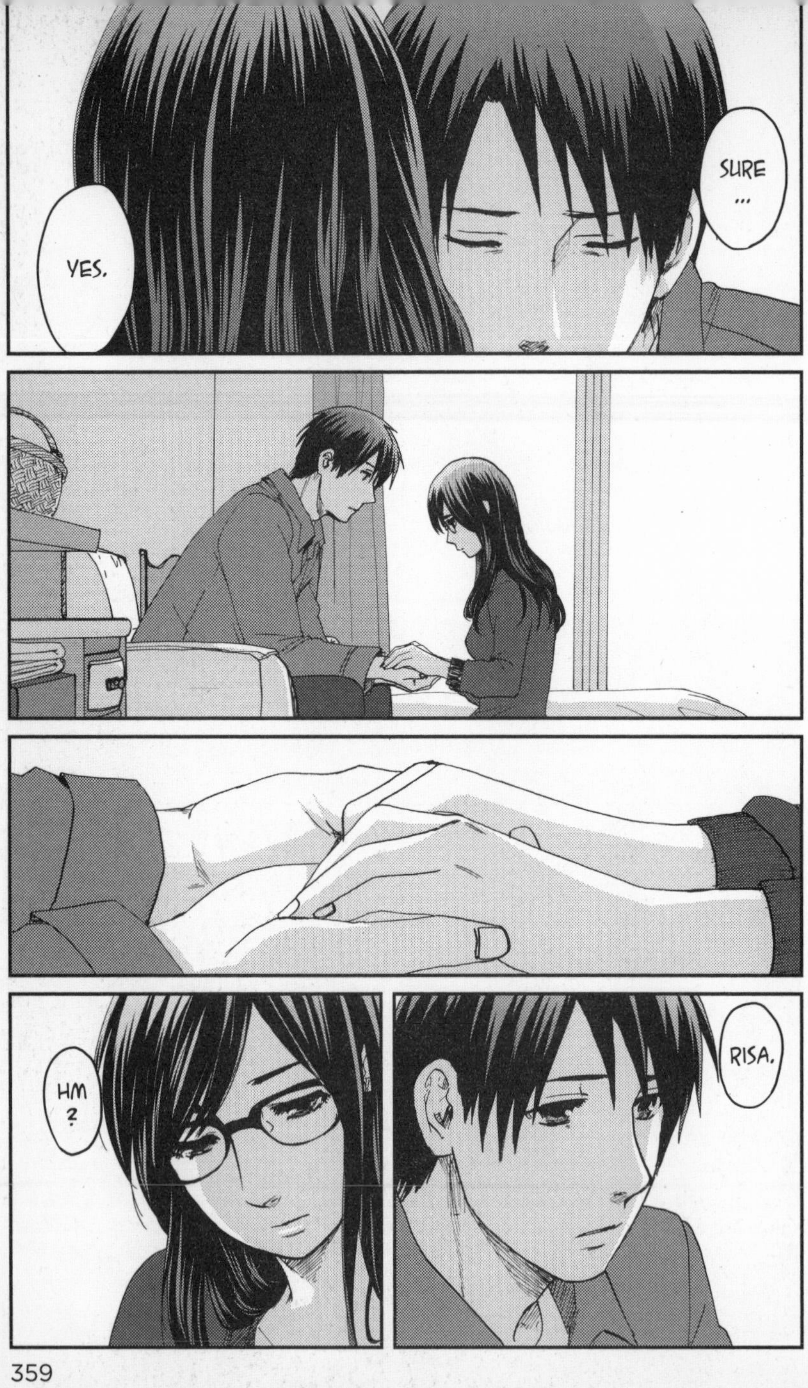
SURE ...
YES.
RISA.
HM ?

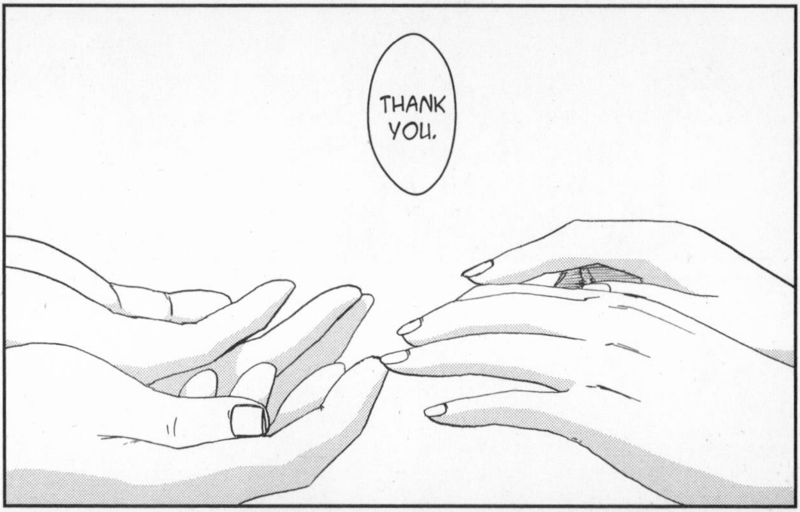
THANK YOU.
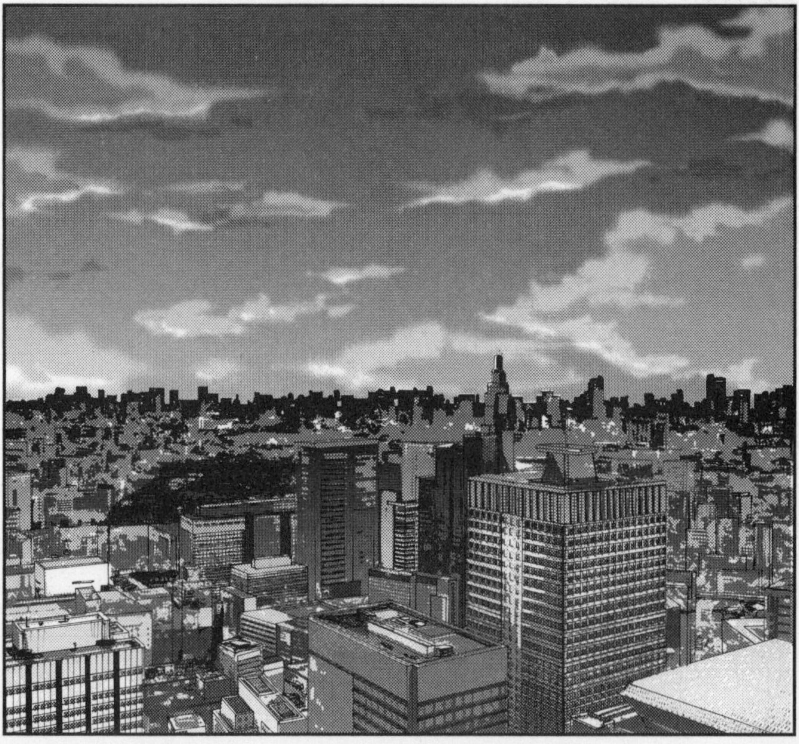

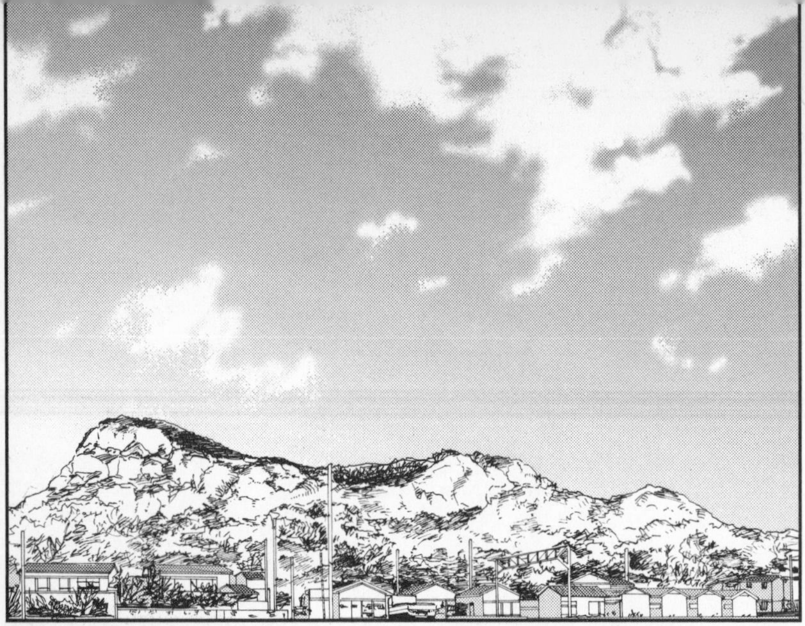

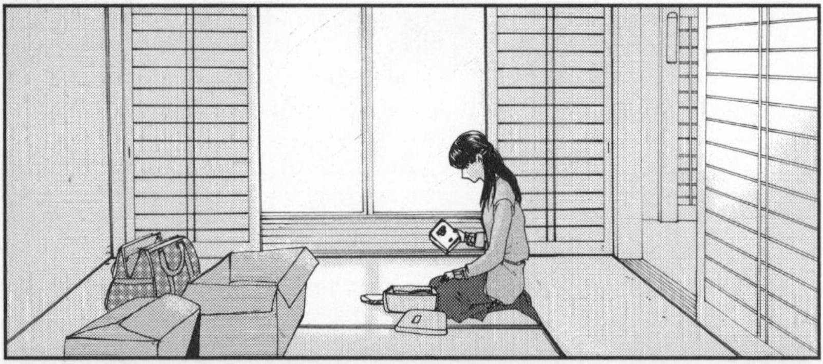

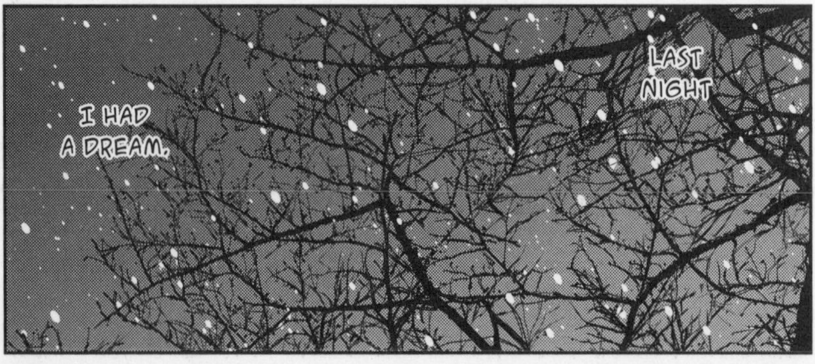
LAST NIGHT
I HAD A DREAM.

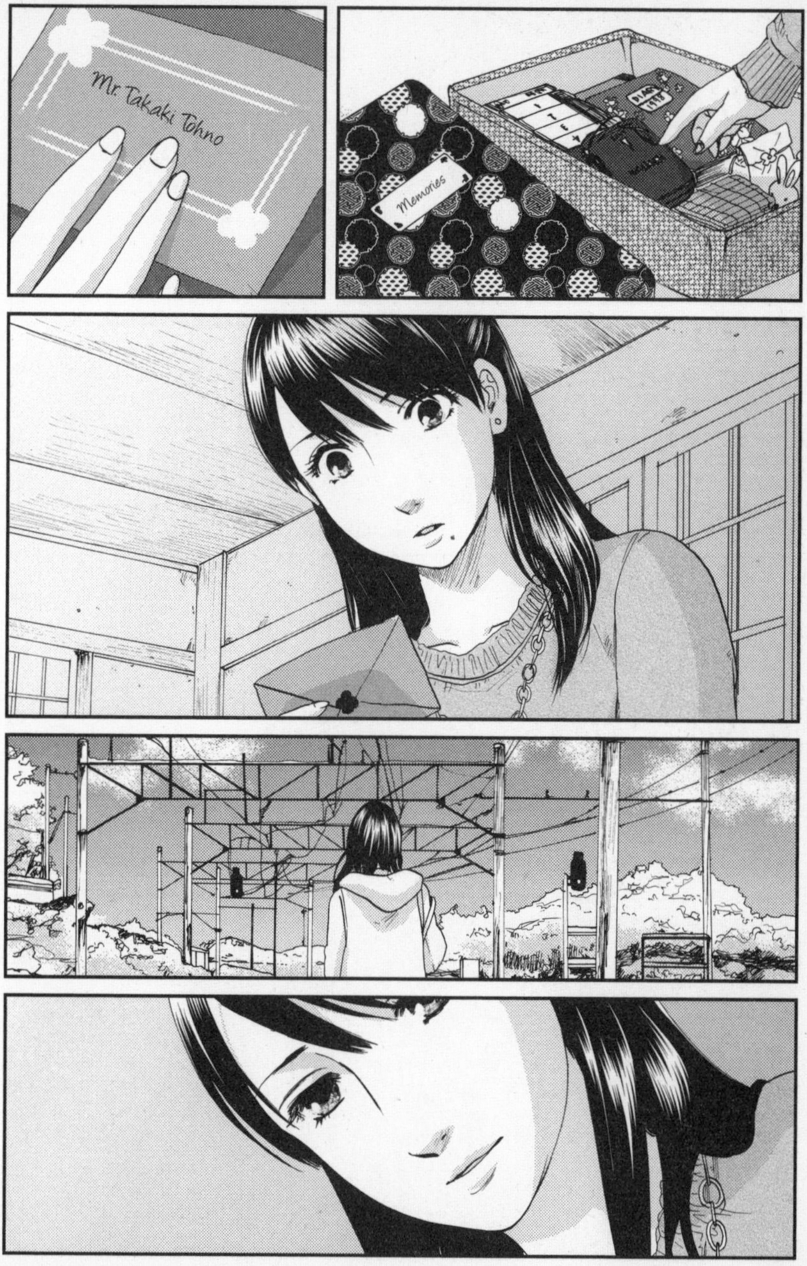
Memories
Mr. Takaki Tohno

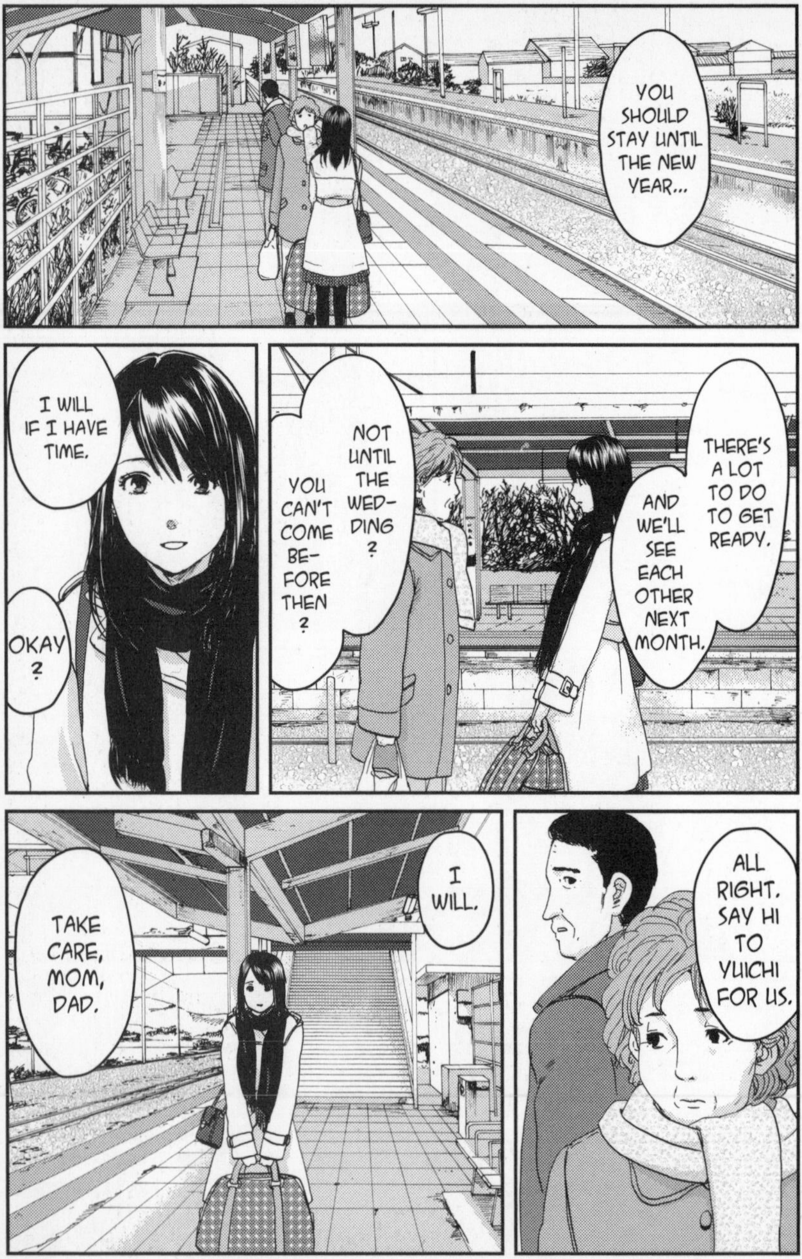
YOU SHOULD STAY UNTIL THE NEW YEAR...
THERE'S A LOT TO DO TO GET READY.
AND WE'LL SEE EACH OTHER NEXT MONTH.
NOT UNTIL THE WEDDING?
YOU CAN'T COME BEFORE THEN?
I WILL IF I HAVE TIME.
OKAY?
ALL RIGHT. SAY HI TO YUICHI FOR US.
I WILL.
TAKE CARE, MOM, DAD.

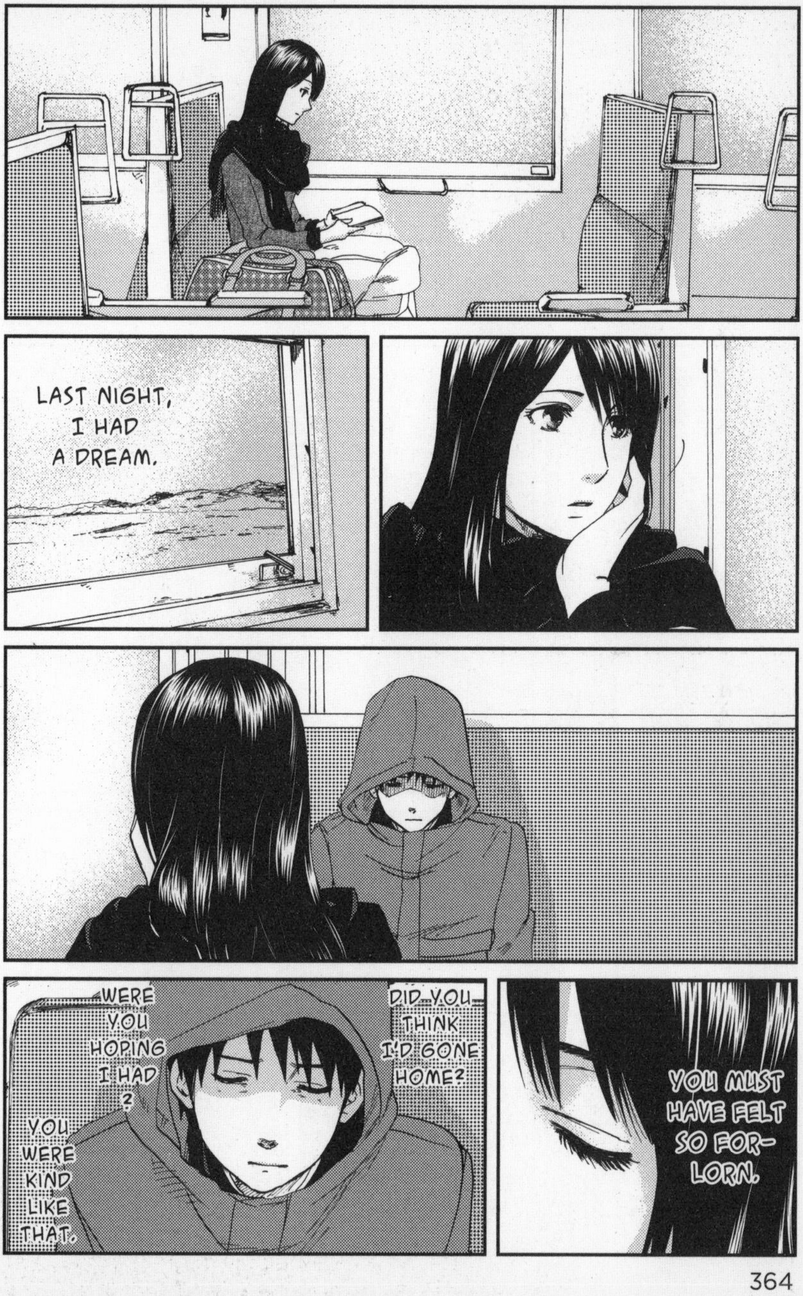
LAST NIGHT, I HAD A DREAM.
YOU MUST HAVE FELT SO FOR-LORN.
DID YOU THINK I'D GONE HOME?
WERE YOU HOPING I HAD?
YOU WERE KIND LIKE THAT.

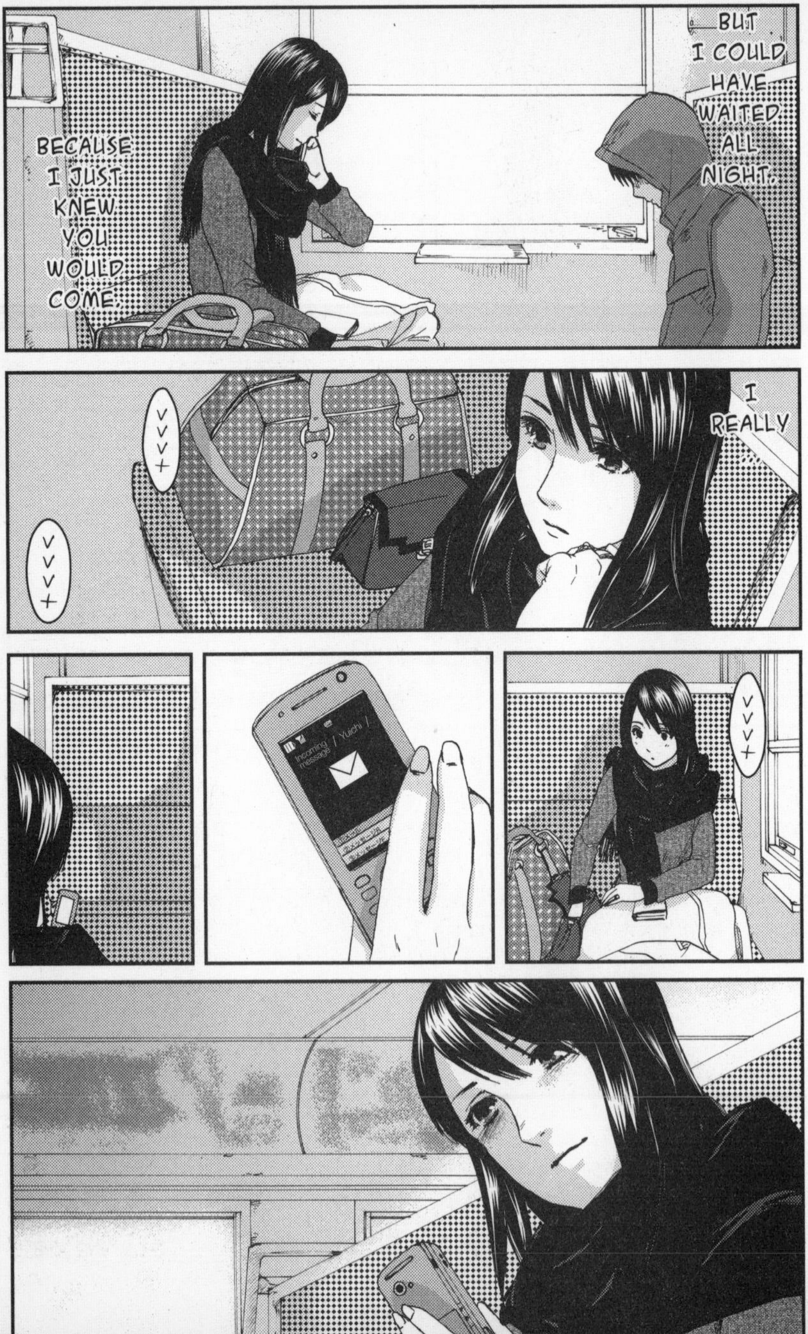
BUT I COULD HAVE WAITED ALL NIGHT.
BECAUSE I JUST KNEW YOU WOULD COME.
I REALLY ...
VVV+
VVV+
VVV+
Incoming message / Yuichi /

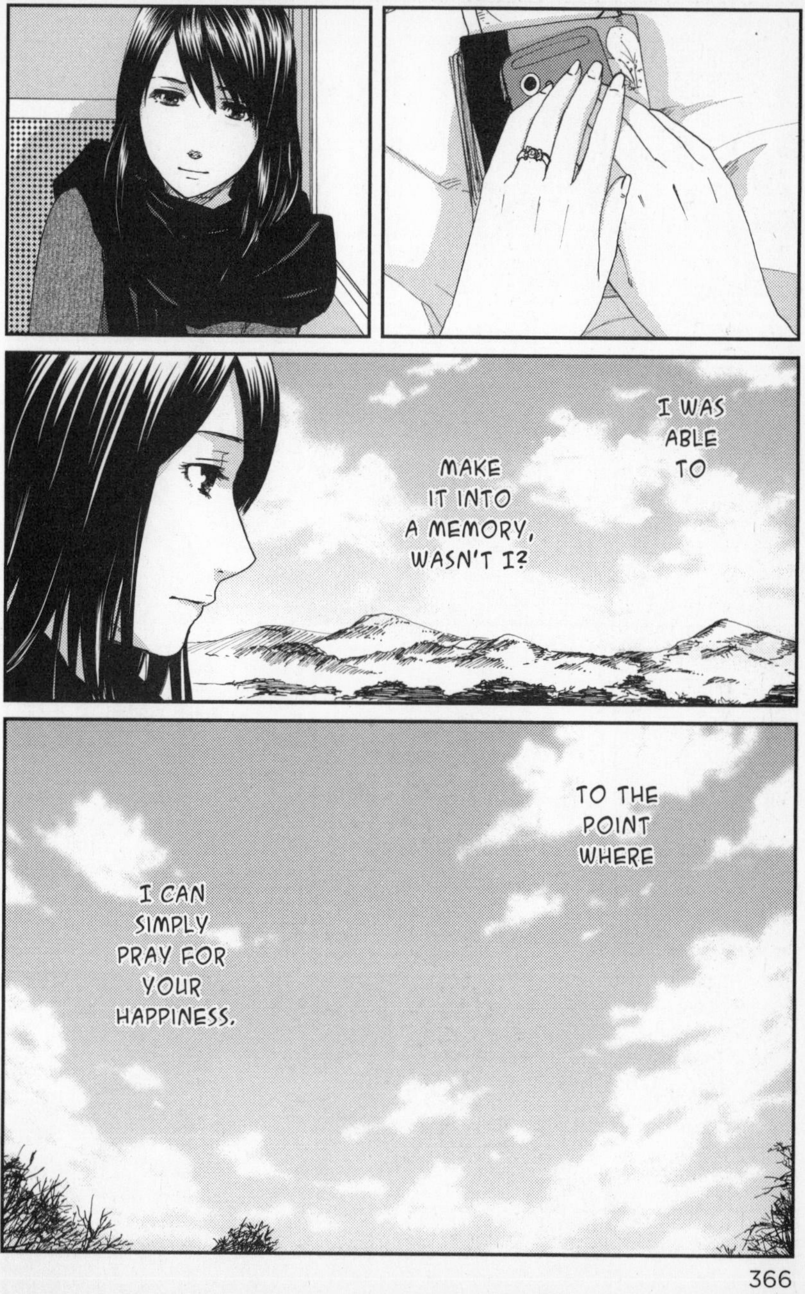
I WAS ABLE TO
MAKE IT INTO A MEMORY, WASN'T I?
TO THE POINT WHERE
I CAN SIMPLY PRAY FOR YOUR HAPPINESS.

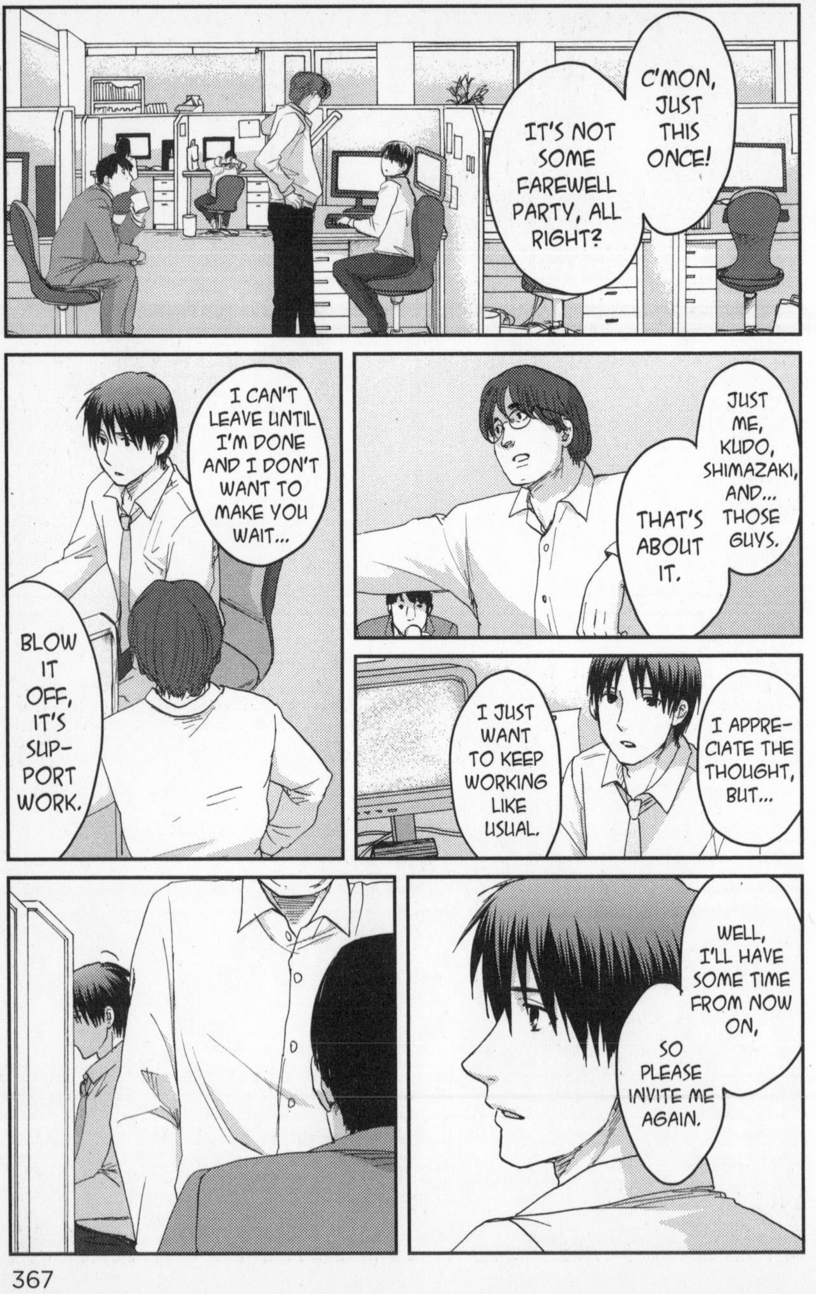
C'MON, JUST THIS ONCE!
IT'S NOT SOME FAREWELL PARTY, ALL RIGHT?
JUST ME, KUDO, SHIMAZAKI, AND... THOSE GUYS.
THAT'S ABOUT IT.
I APPRE-CIATE THE THOUGHT, BUT...
I JUST WANT TO KEEP WORKING LIKE USUAL.
I CAN'T LEAVE UNTIL I'M DONE AND I DON'T WANT TO MAKE YOU WAIT...
BLOW IT OFF, IT'S SUP-PORT WORK.
WELL, I'LL HAVE SOME TIME FROM NOW ON,
SO PLEASE INVITE ME AGAIN.

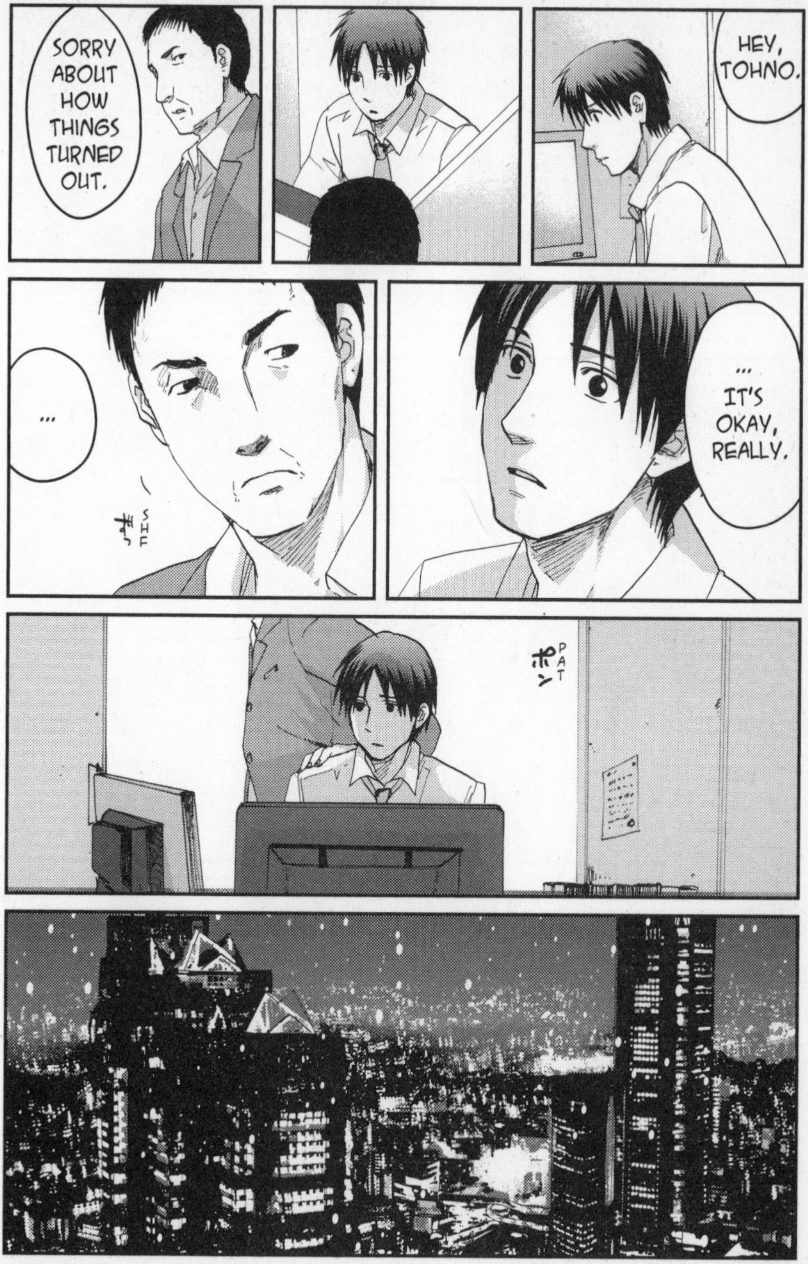
HEY, TOHNO.
SORRY ABOUT HOW THINGS TURNED OUT.
... IT'S OKAY, REALLY.
...
すっ SHF
ポン PAT

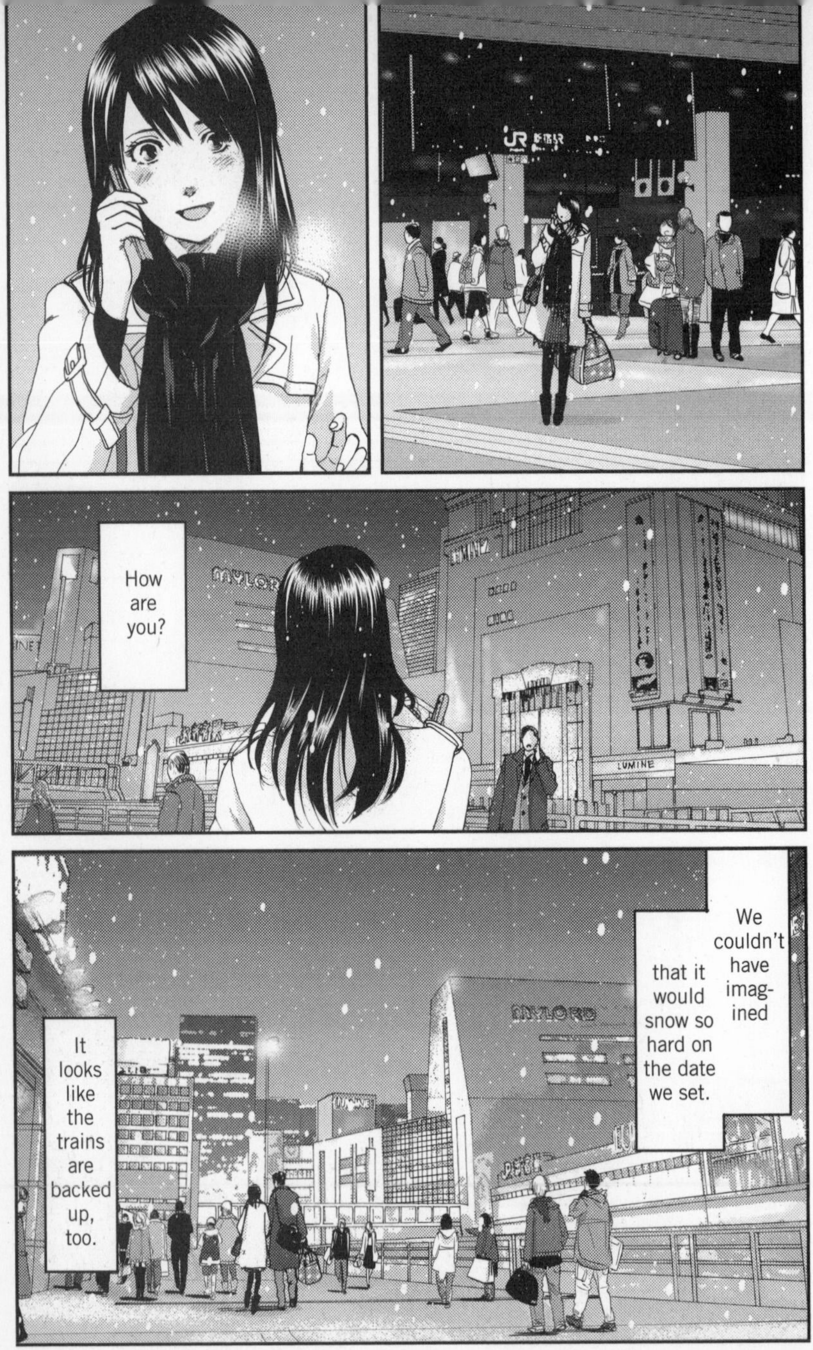
How are you?
LUMINE
We couldn't have imag-ined
that it would snow so hard on the date we set.
It looks like the trains are backed up, too.

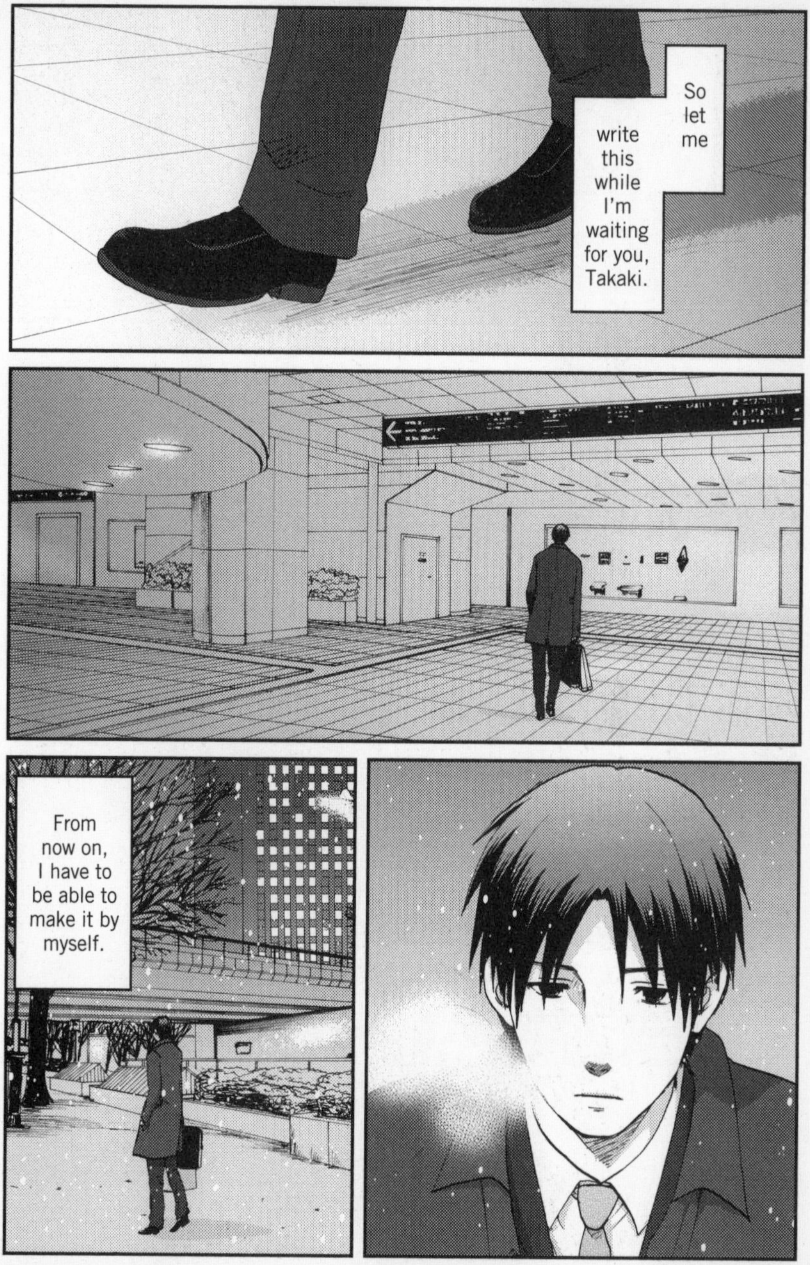
So let me write this while I'm waiting for you, Takaki.
From now on, I have to be able to make it by myself.

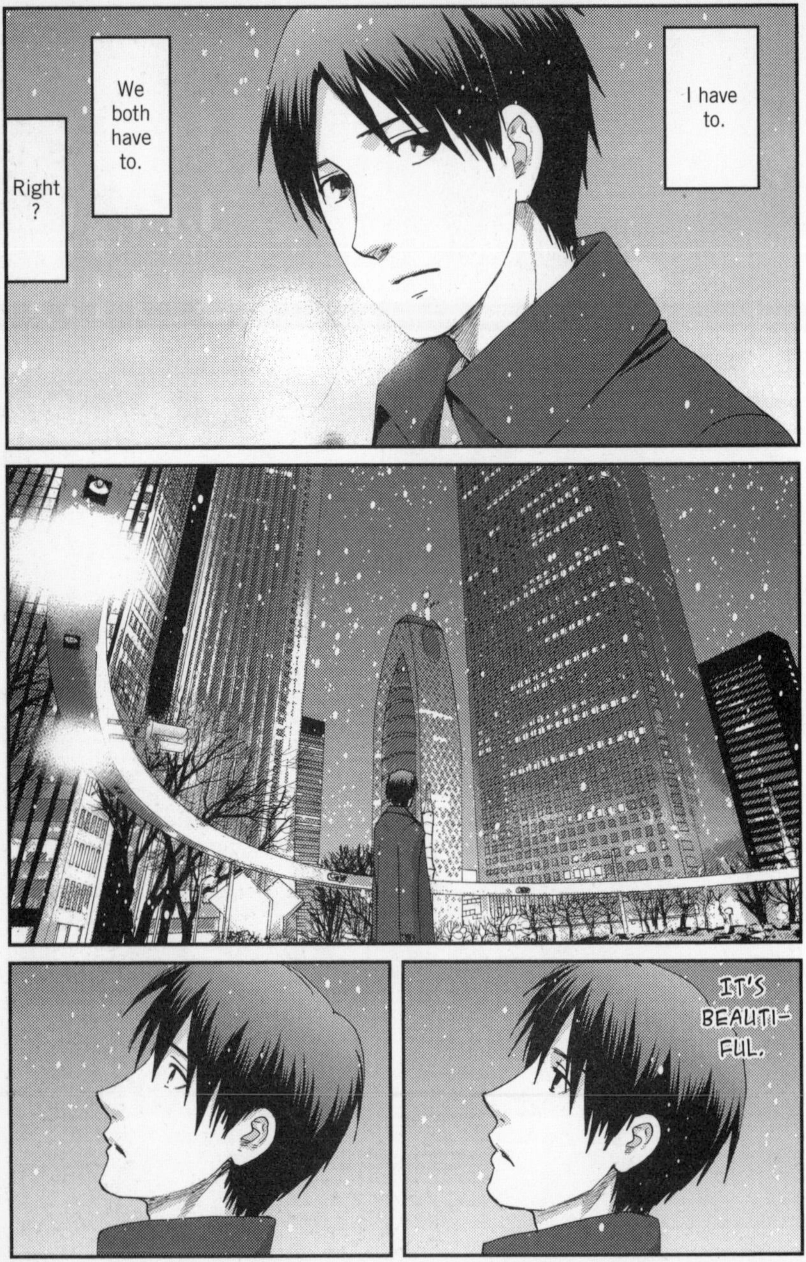
I have to.
We both have to.
Right?
IT'S BEAUTI-FUL.

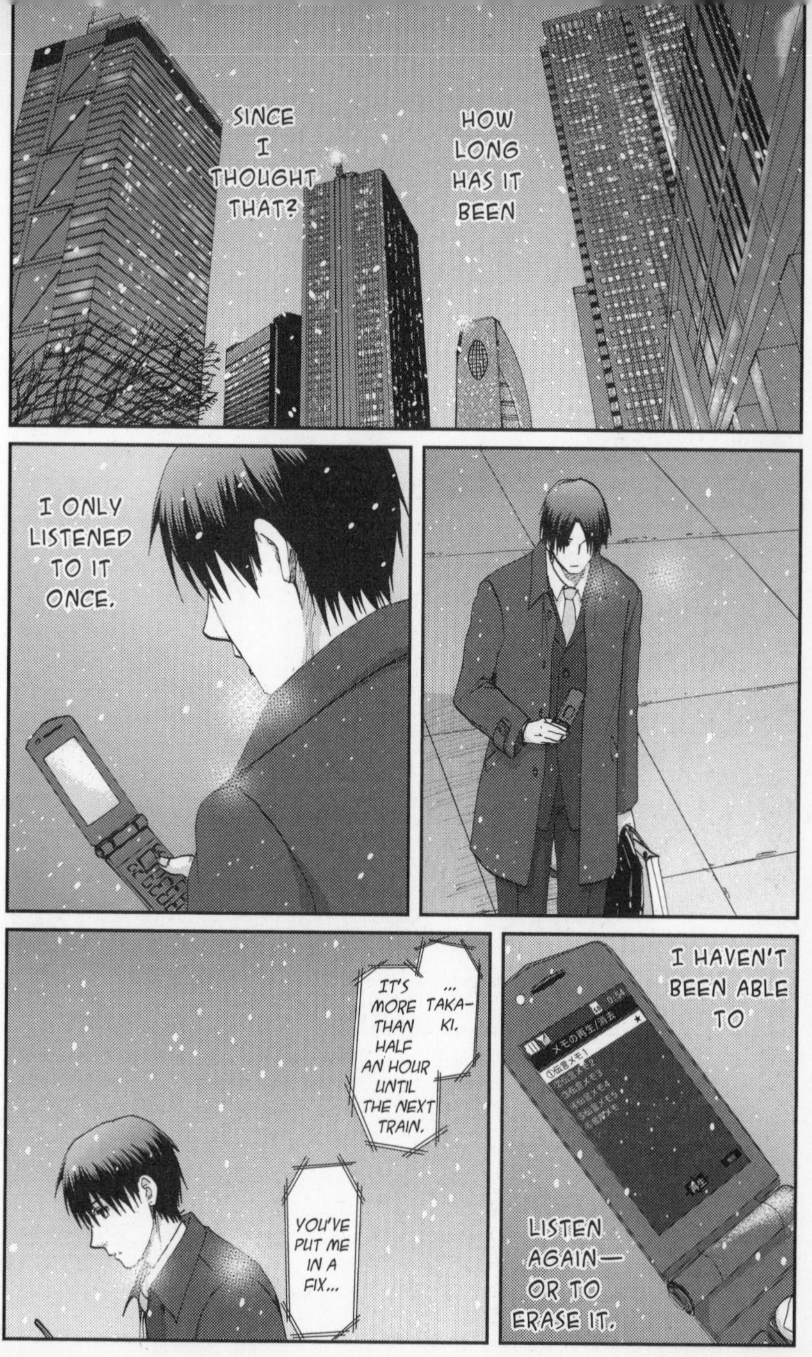
HOW LONG HAS IT BEEN
SINCE I THOUGHT THAT?
I ONLY LISTENED TO IT ONCE.
I HAVEN'T BEEN ABLE TO
LISTEN AGAIN— OR TO ERASE IT.
...TAKA-KI. IT'S MORE THAN HALF AN HOUR UNTIL THE NEXT TRAIN.
YOU'VE PUT ME IN A FIX...

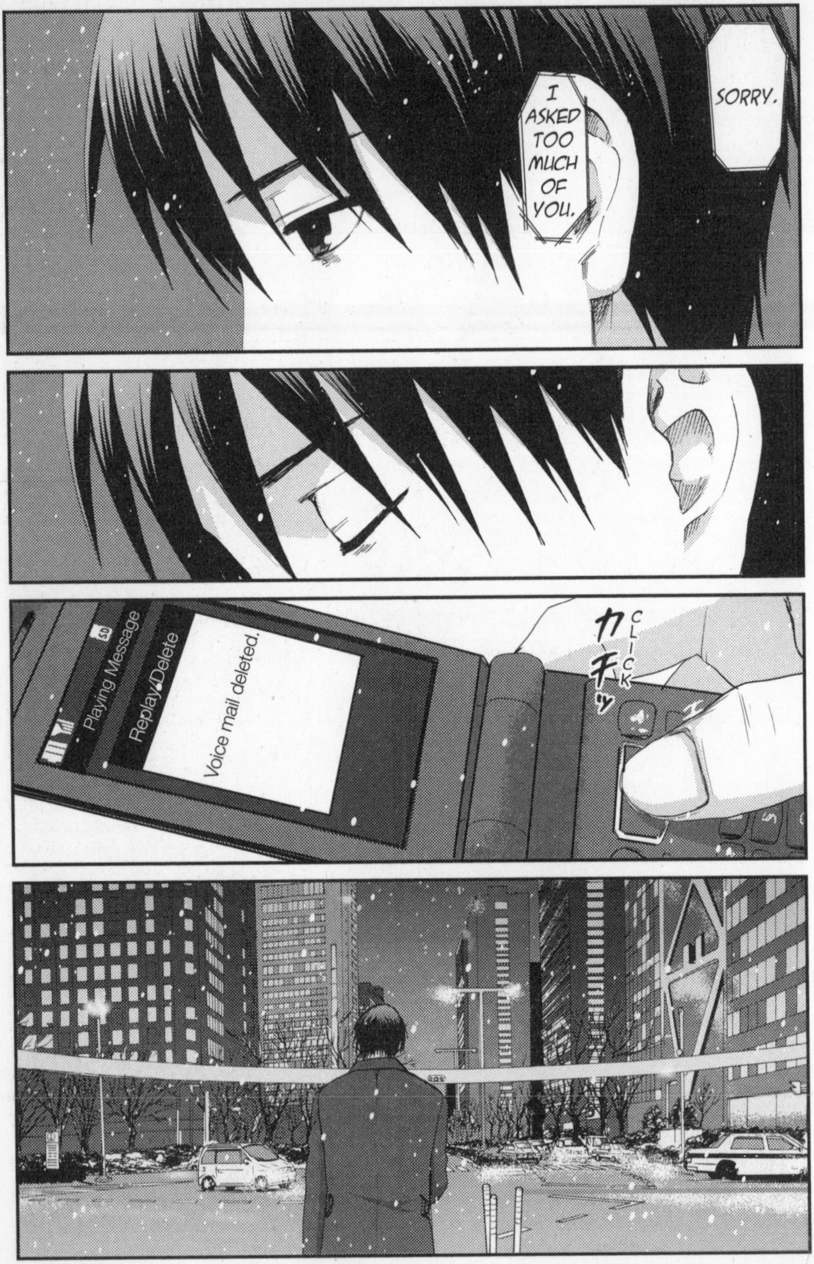
SORRY.
I ASKED TOO MUCH OF YOU.
Playing Message
Replay/Delete
Voice mail deleted.
カチッ
CLICK

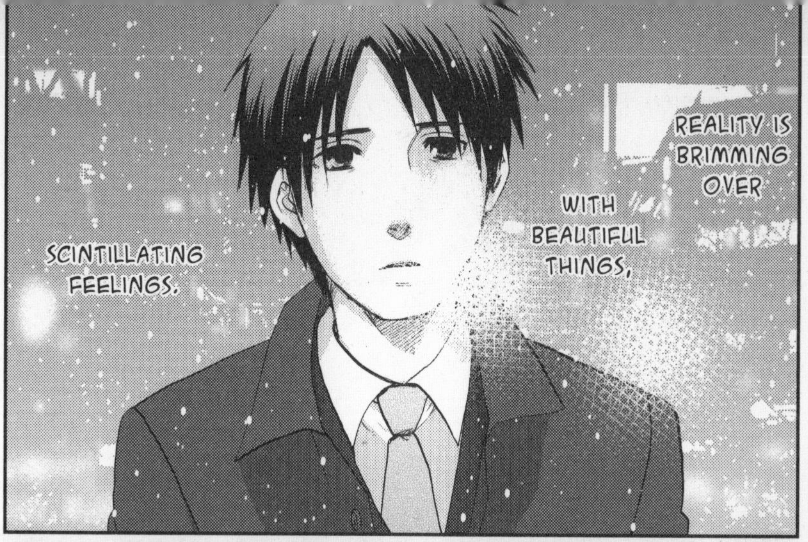
REALITY IS BRIMMING OVER
WITH BEAUTIFUL THINGS,
SCINTILLATING FEELINGS.

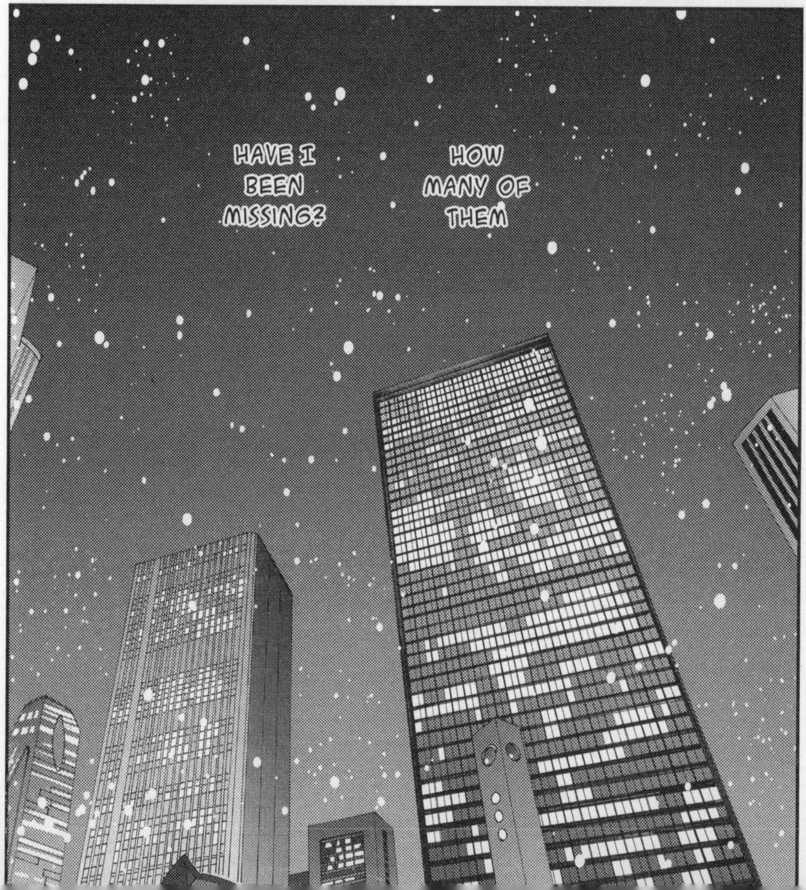
HOW MANY OF THEM
HAVE I BEEN MISSING?

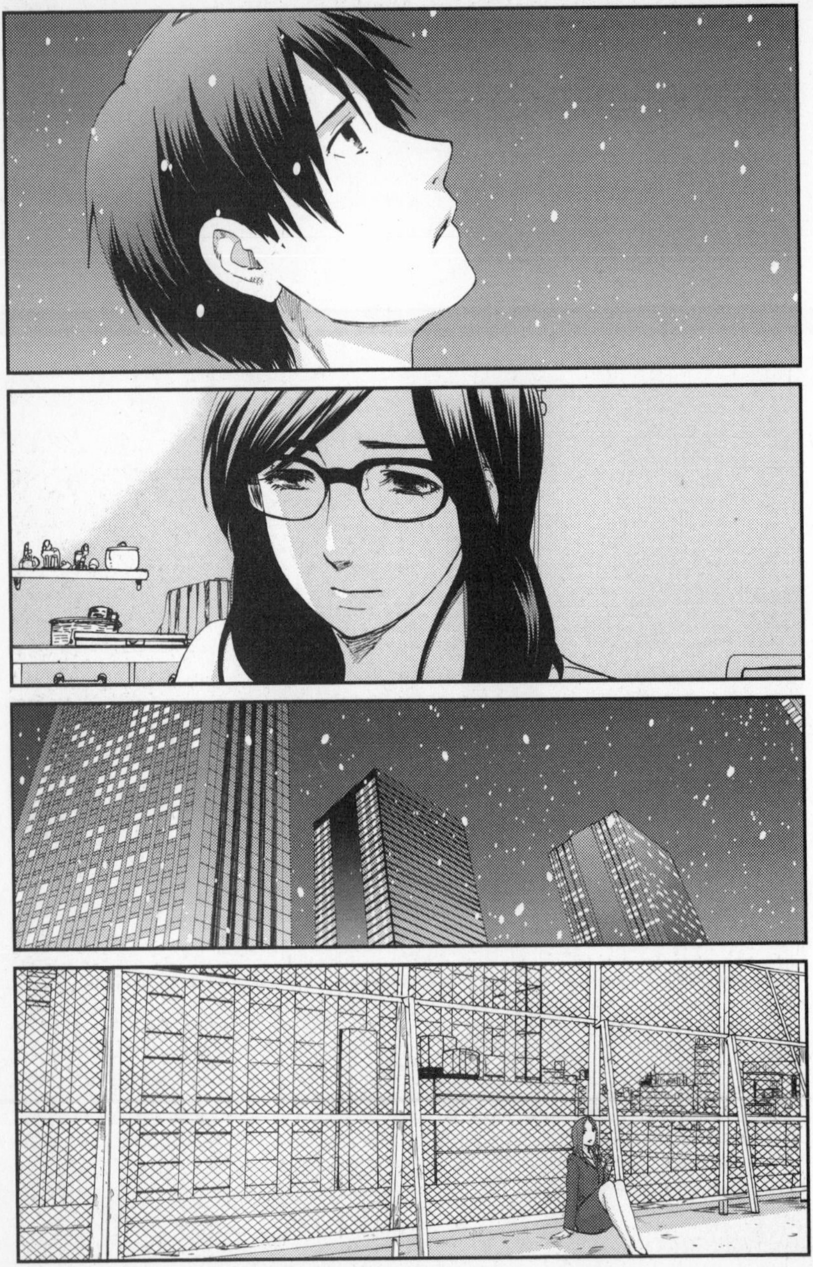

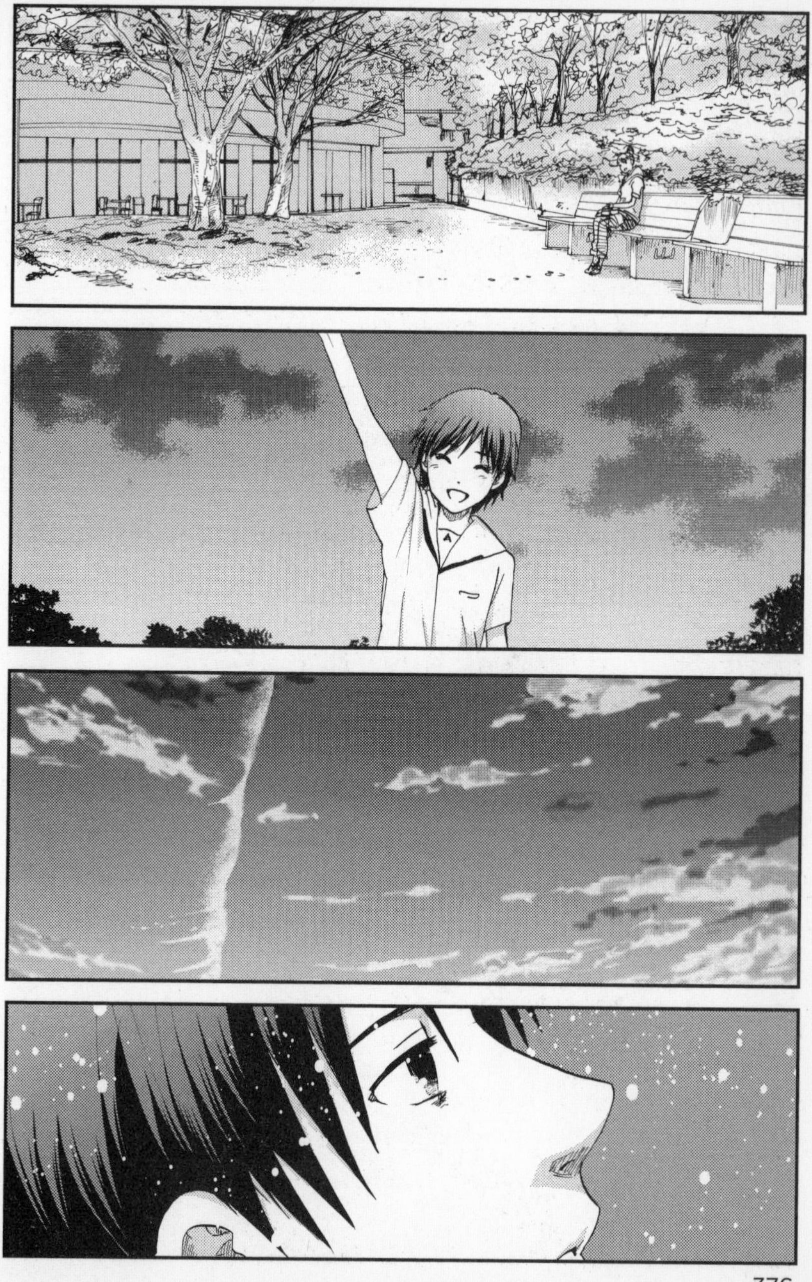

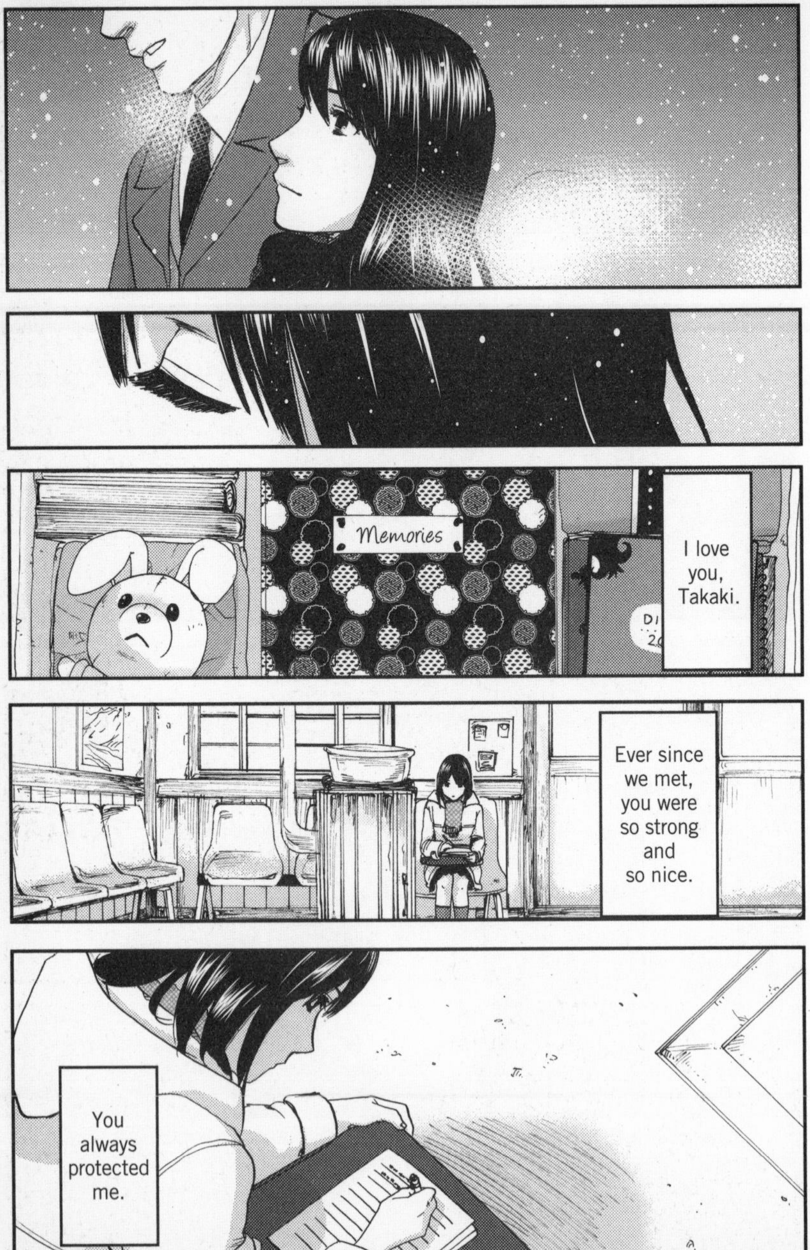
I love you, Takaki.
Memories
Ever since we met, you were so strong and so nice.
You always protected me.

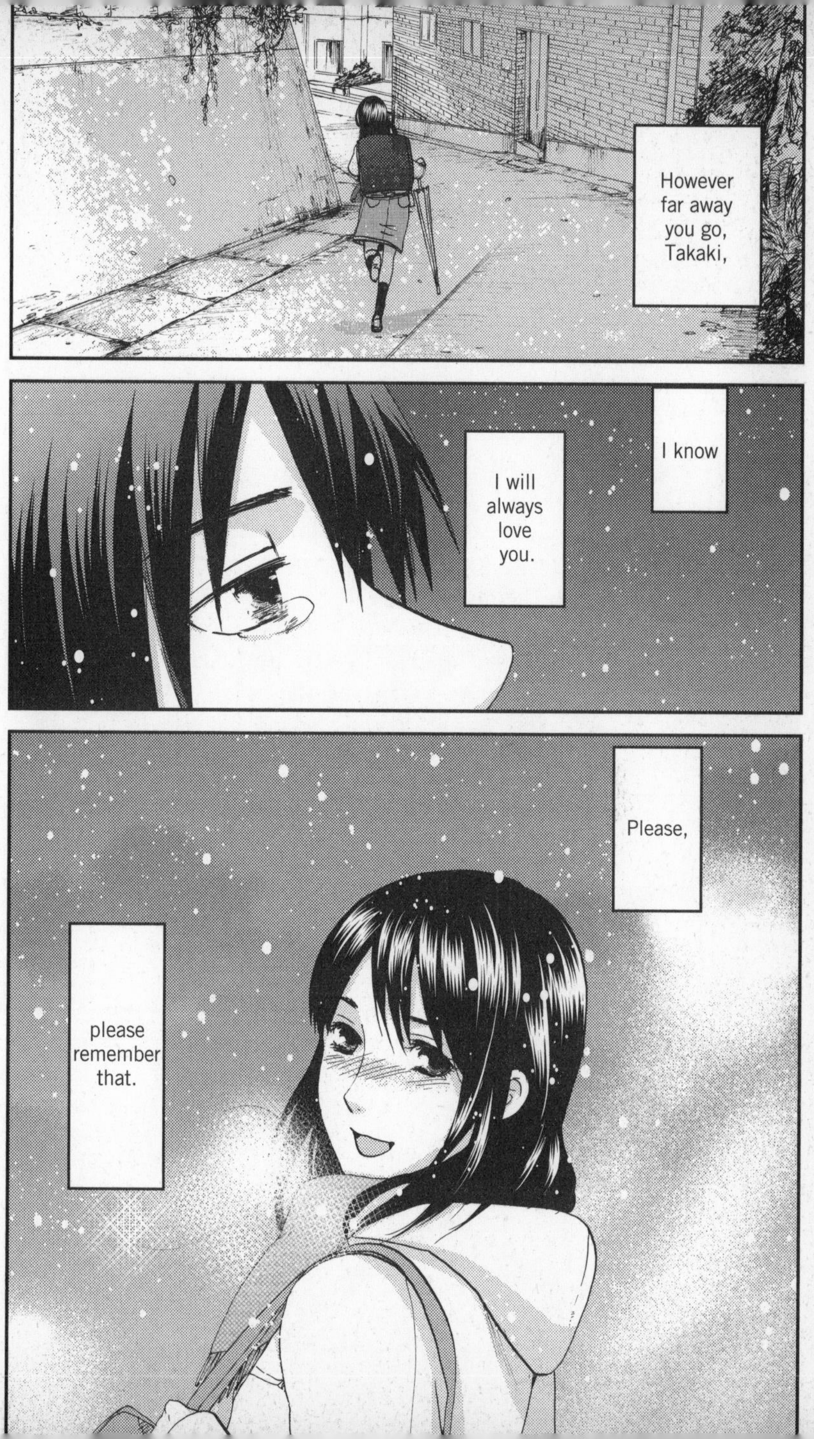
However far away you go, Takaki,
I know
I will always love you.
Please,
please remember that.

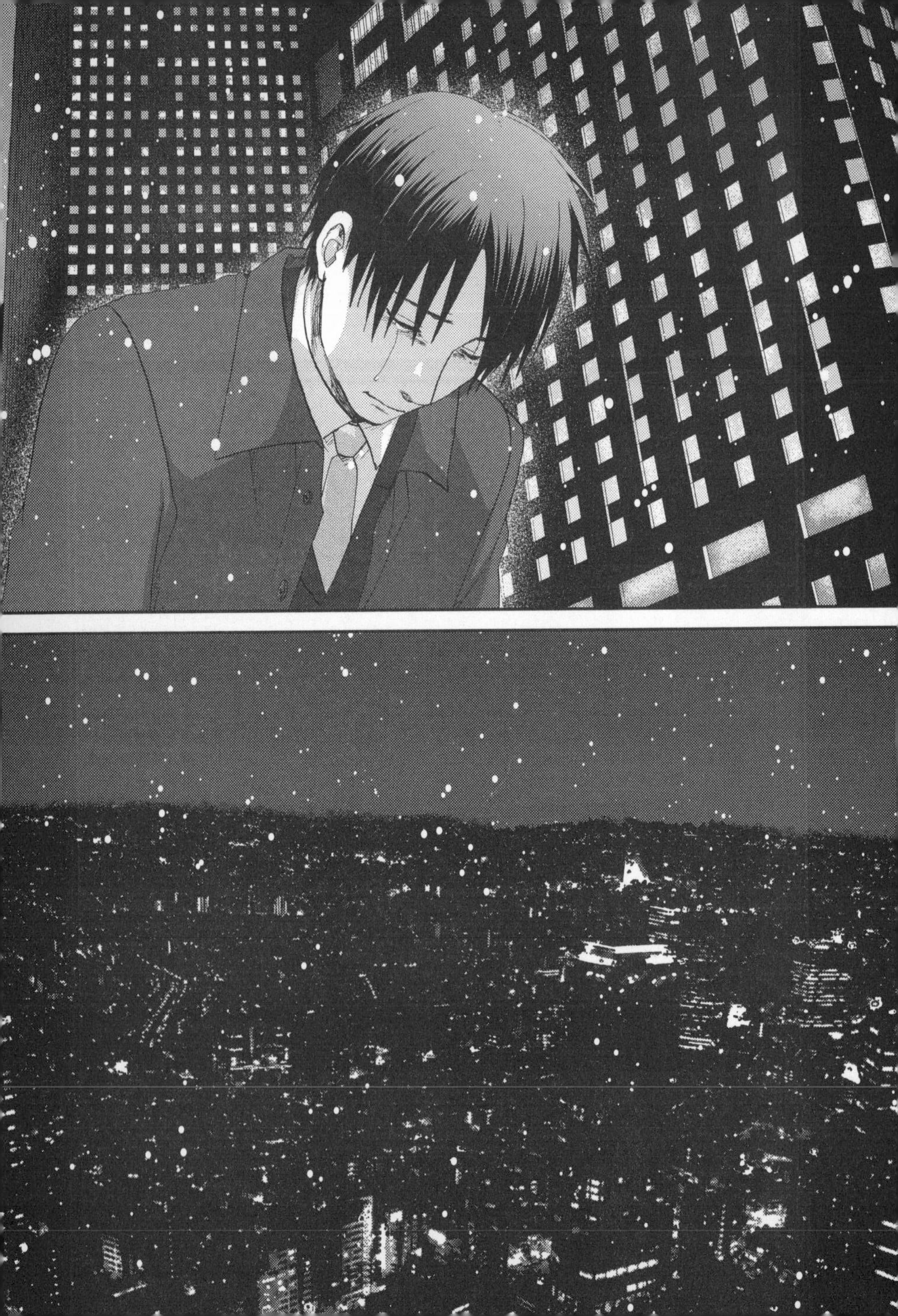

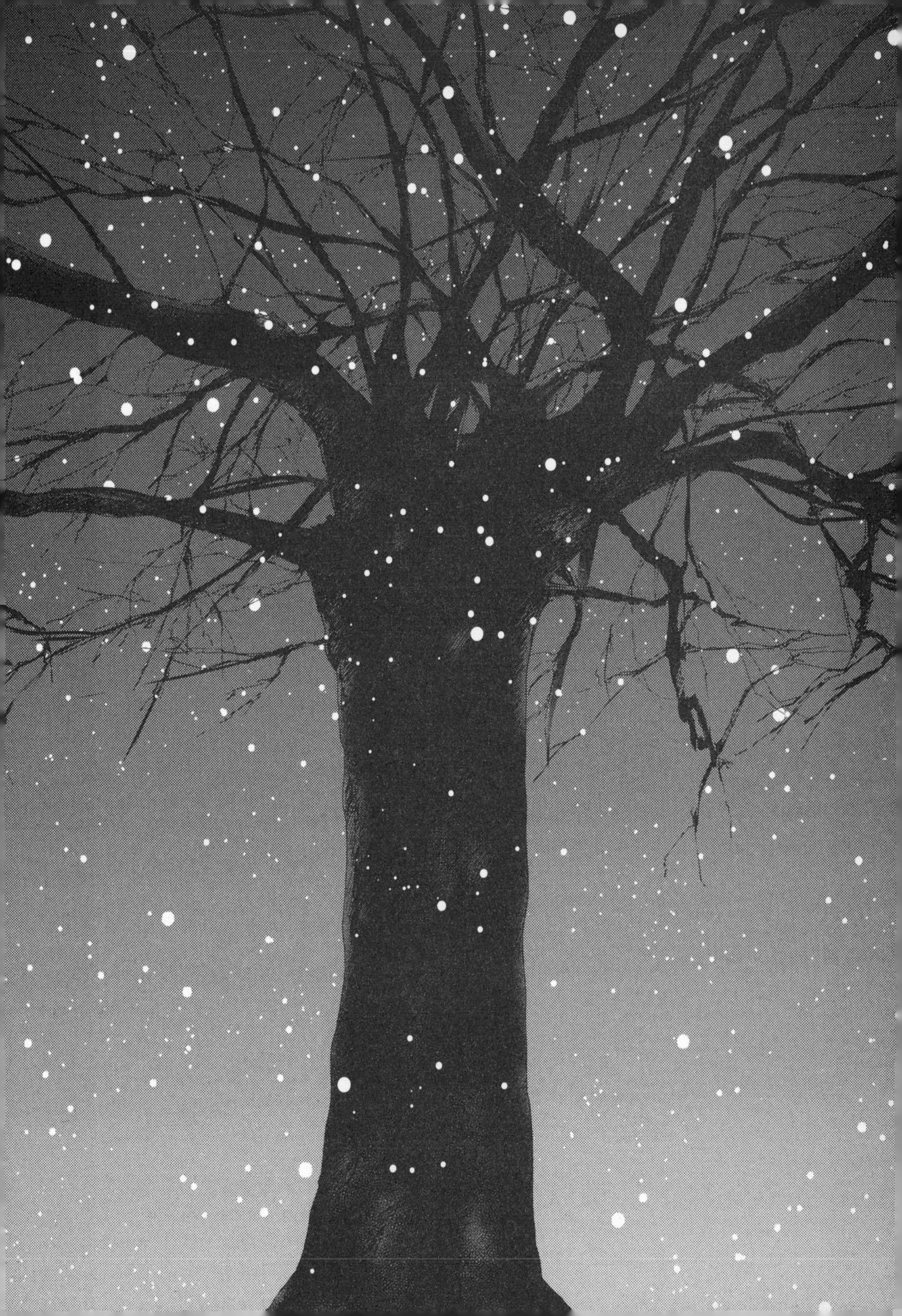

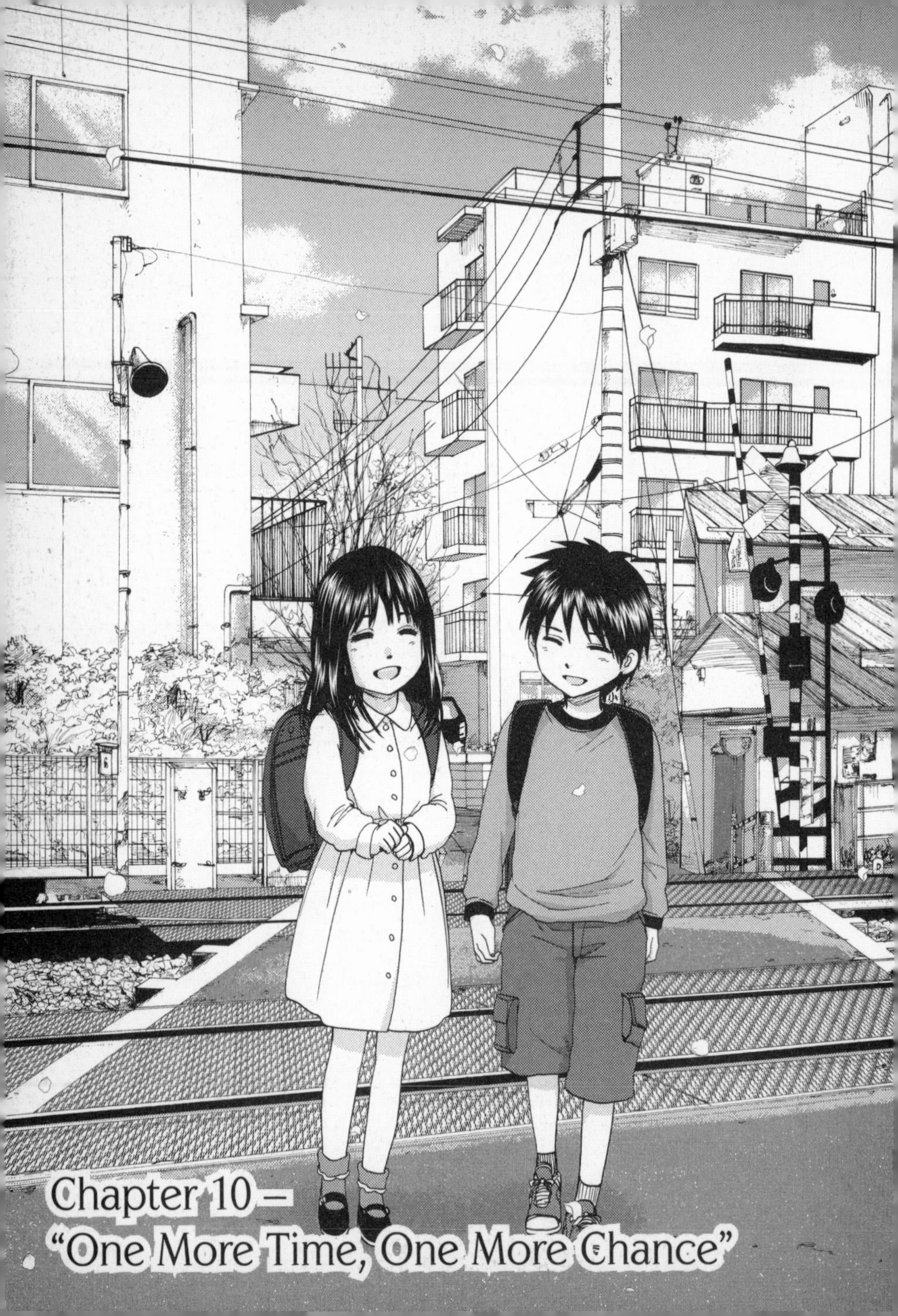

Chapter 10 – "One More Time, One More Chance"

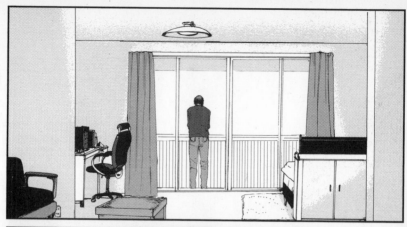

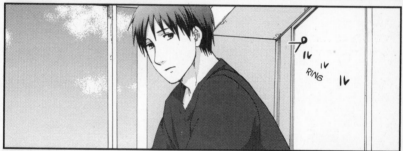

RING

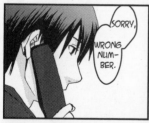

SORRY, WRONG NUMBER.

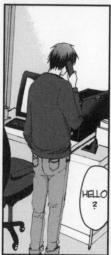

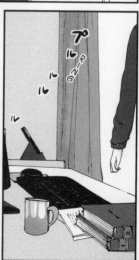

RING

HELLO?

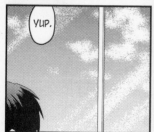

YUP.

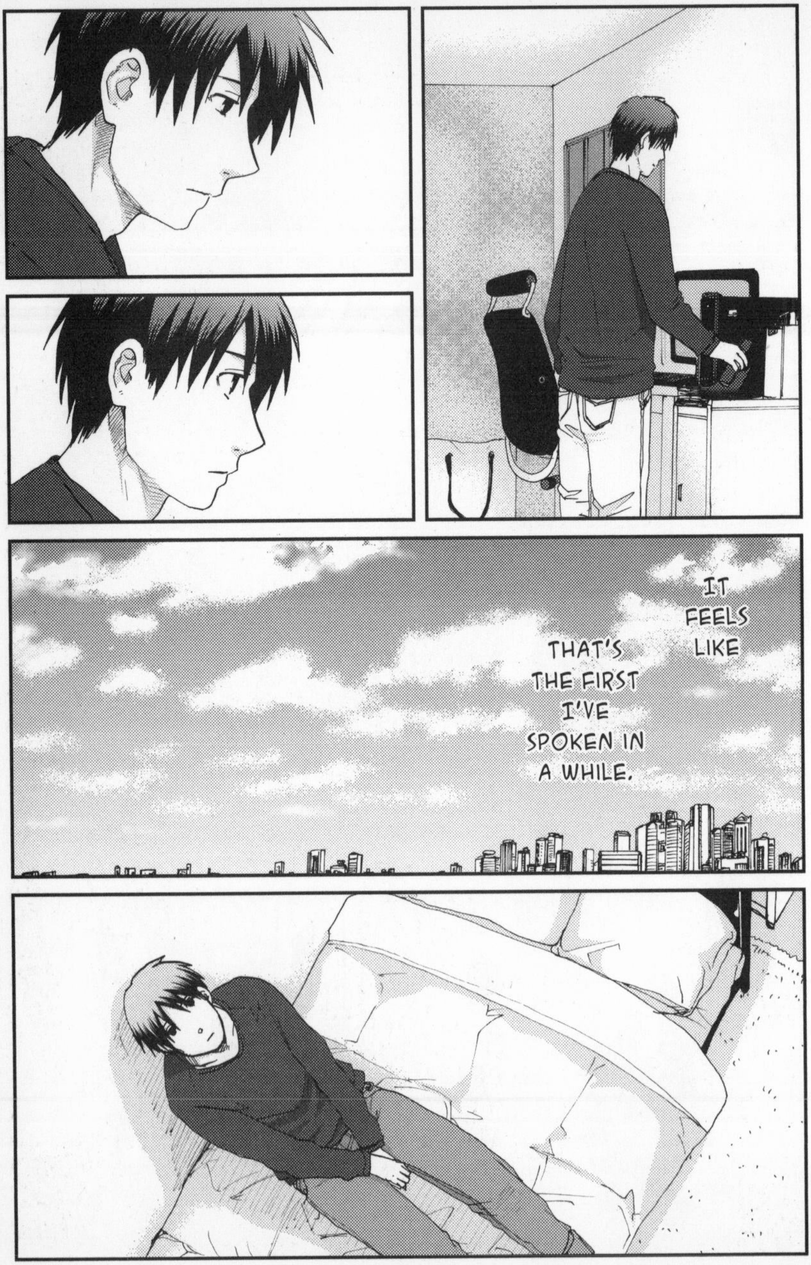
IT FEELS LIKE
THAT'S THE FIRST I'VE SPOKEN IN A WHILE.

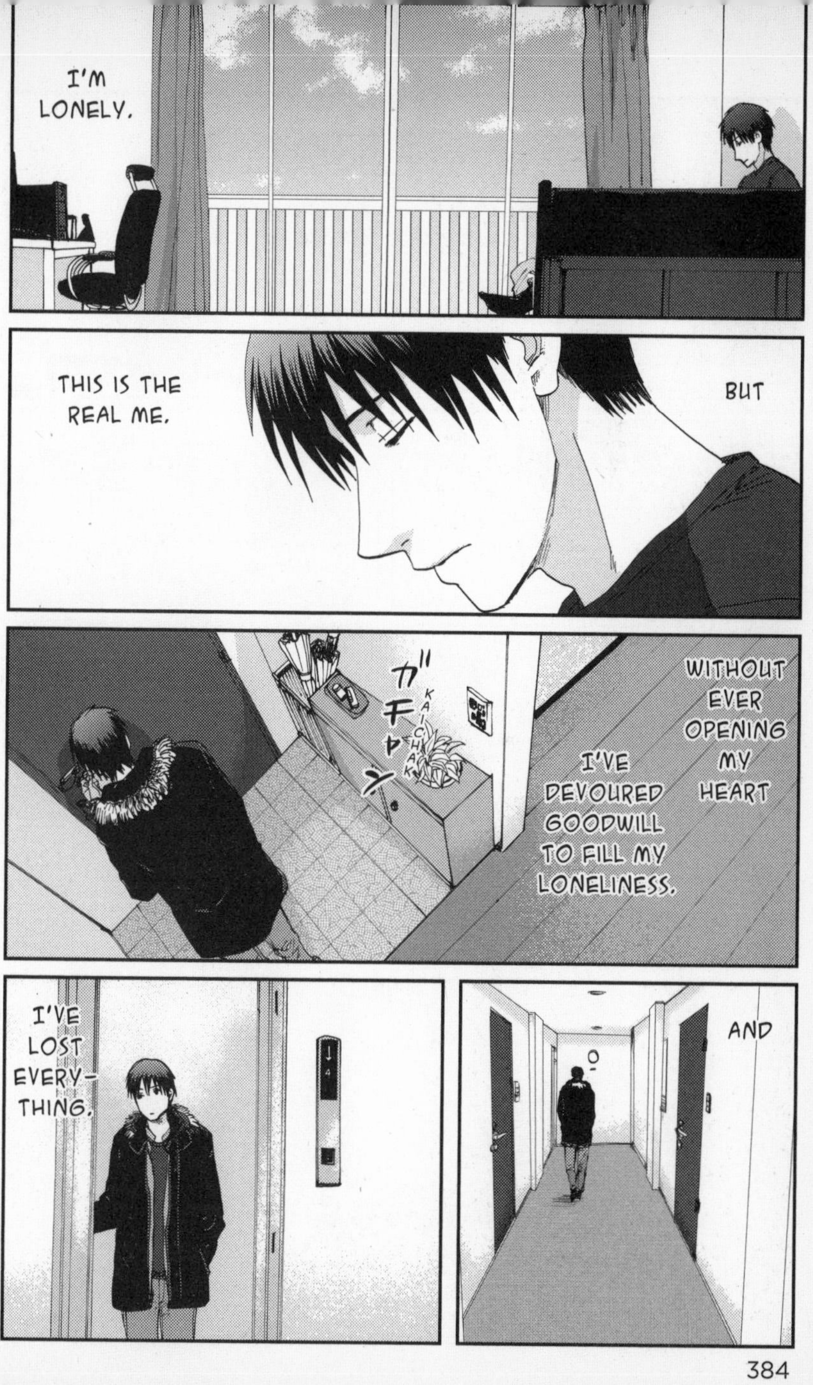
I'M LONELY.
THIS IS THE REAL ME.
BUT
WITHOUT EVER OPENING MY HEART
I'VE DEVOURED GOODWILL TO FILL MY LONELINESS.
ガチャン
KAICHAK
AND
I'VE LOST EVERY-THING.

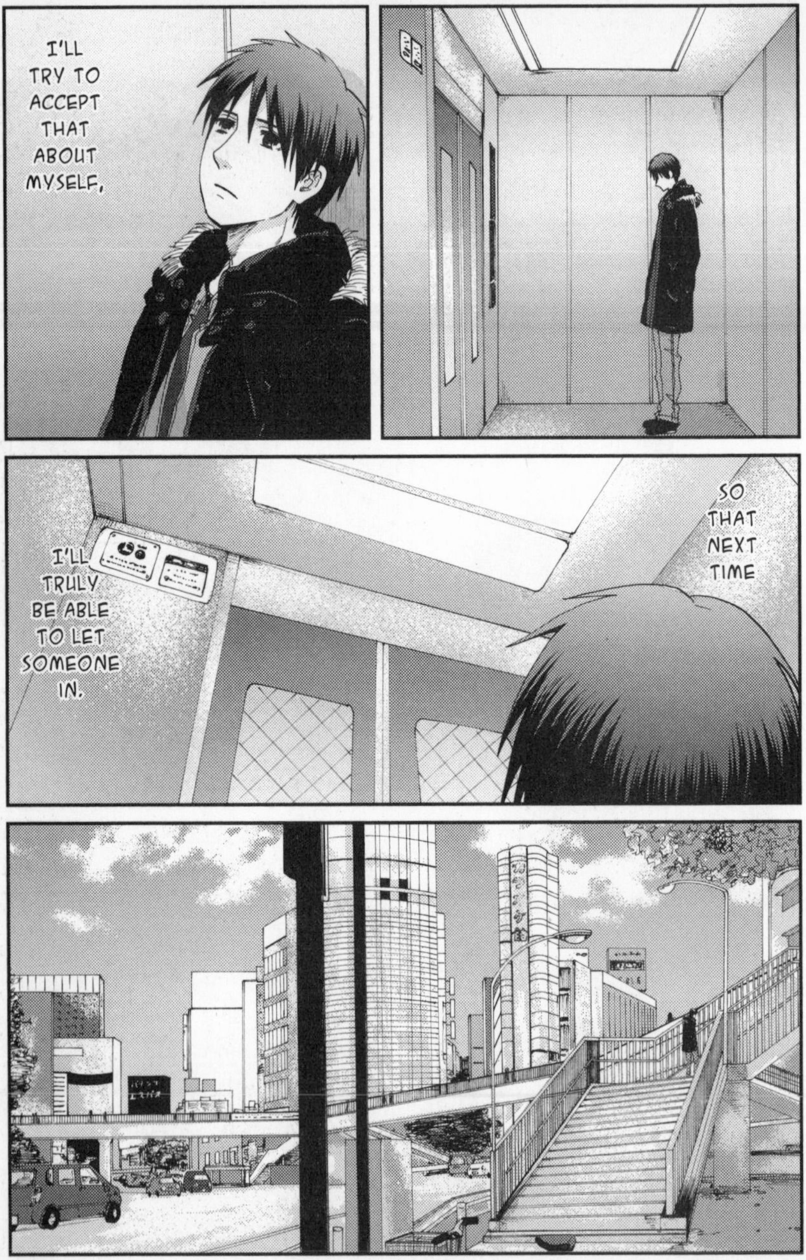
I'LL TRY TO ACCEPT THAT ABOUT MYSELF,
SO THAT NEXT TIME
I'LL TRULY BE ABLE TO LET SOMEONE IN.

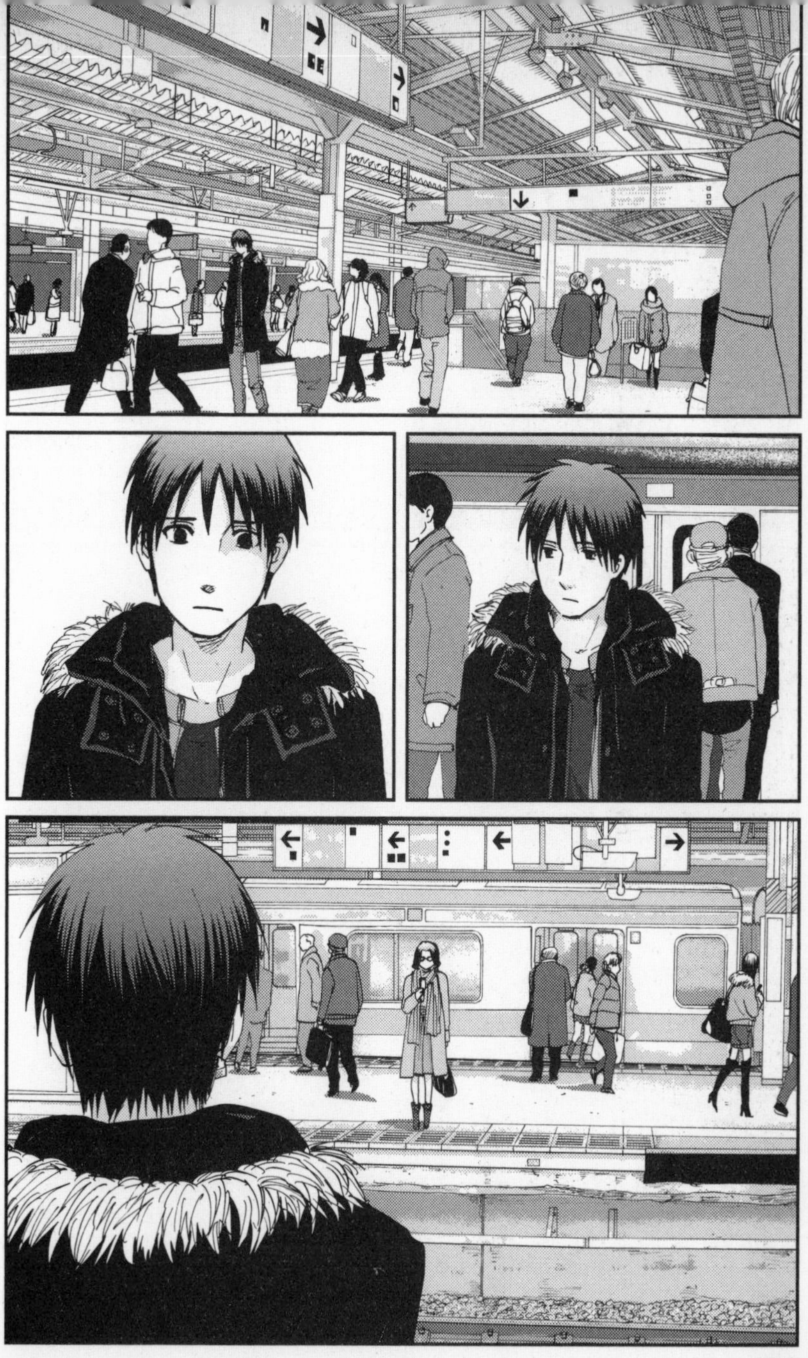

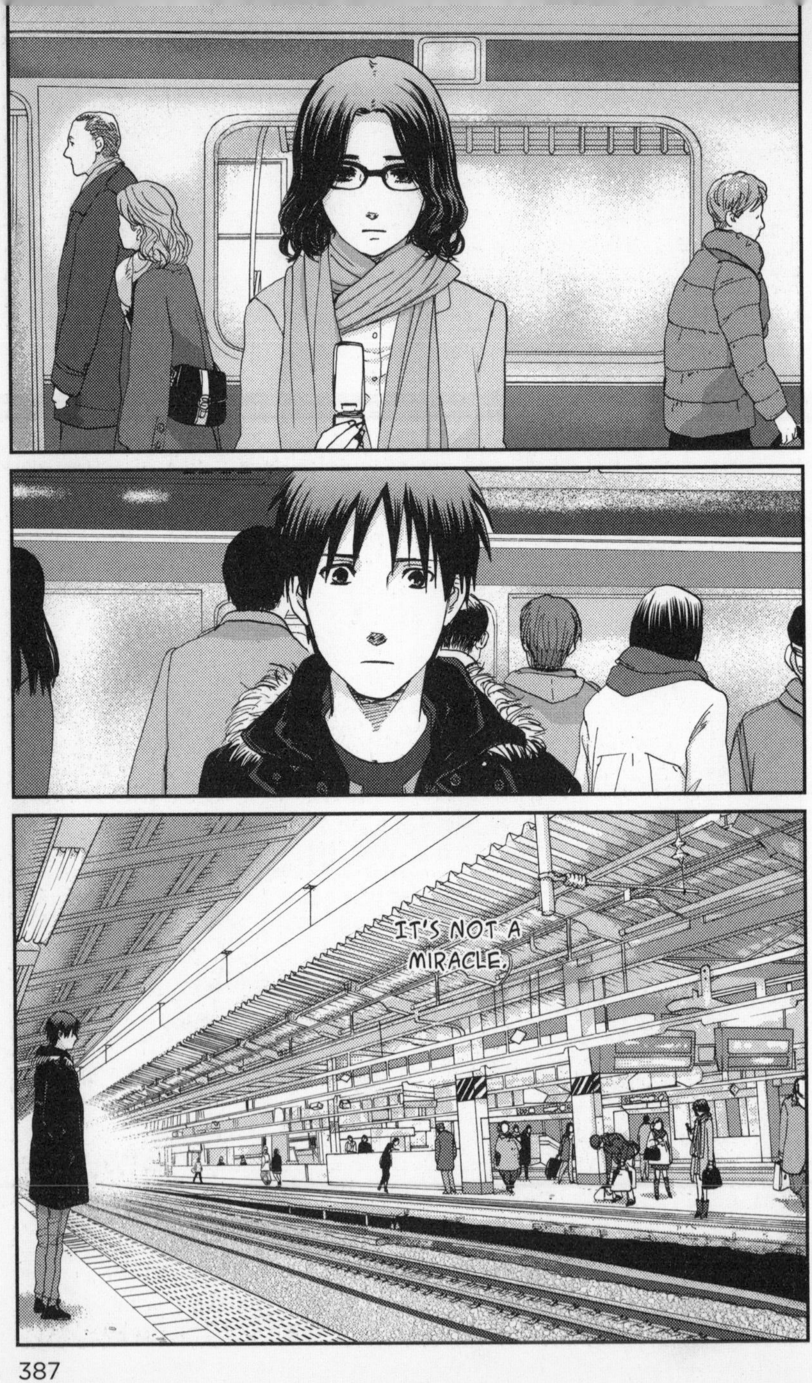
IT'S NOT A MIRACLE.

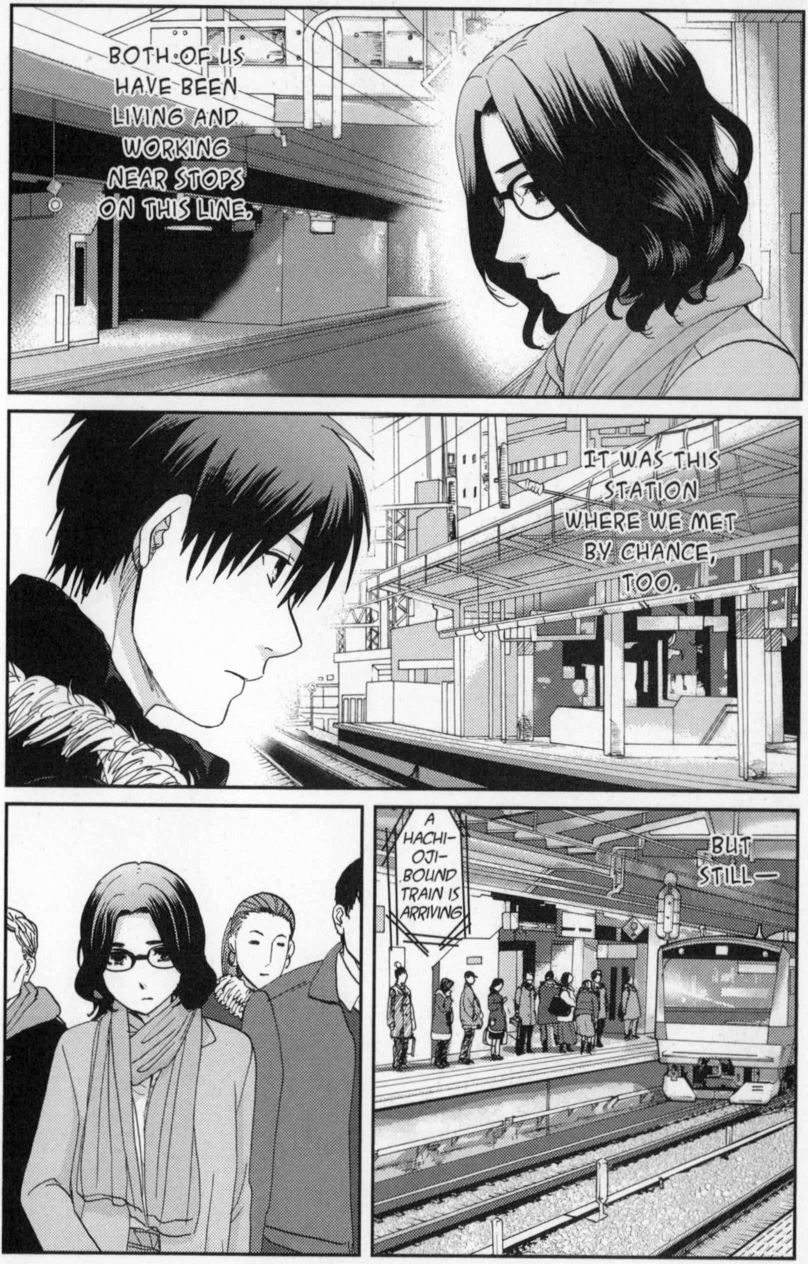
BOTH OF US HAVE BEEN LIVING AND WORKING NEAR STOPS ON THIS LINE.
IT WAS THIS STATION WHERE WE MET BY CHANCE, TOO.
BUT STILL—
A HACHI-OJI-BOUND TRAIN IS ARRIVING

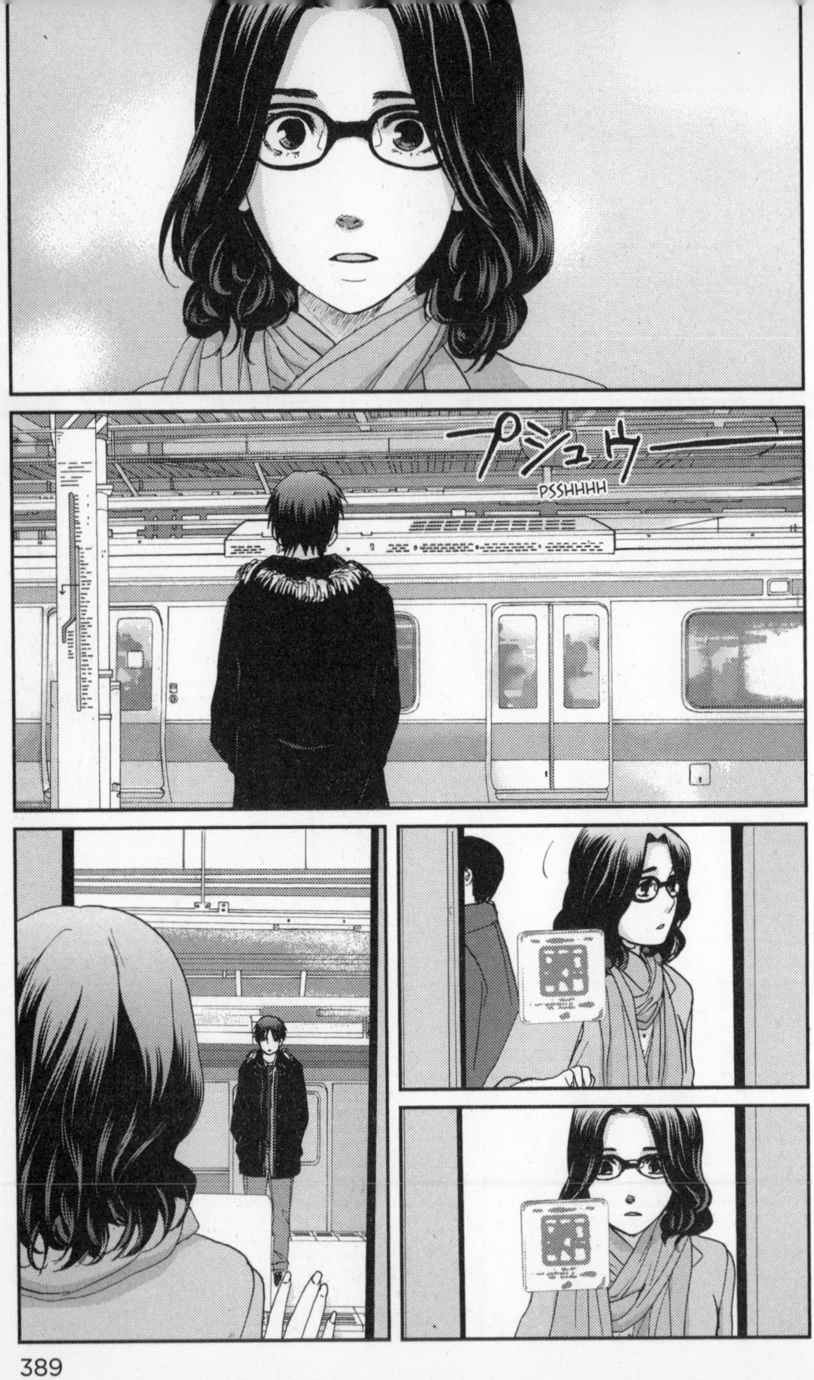
プシュウー
PSSHHHH

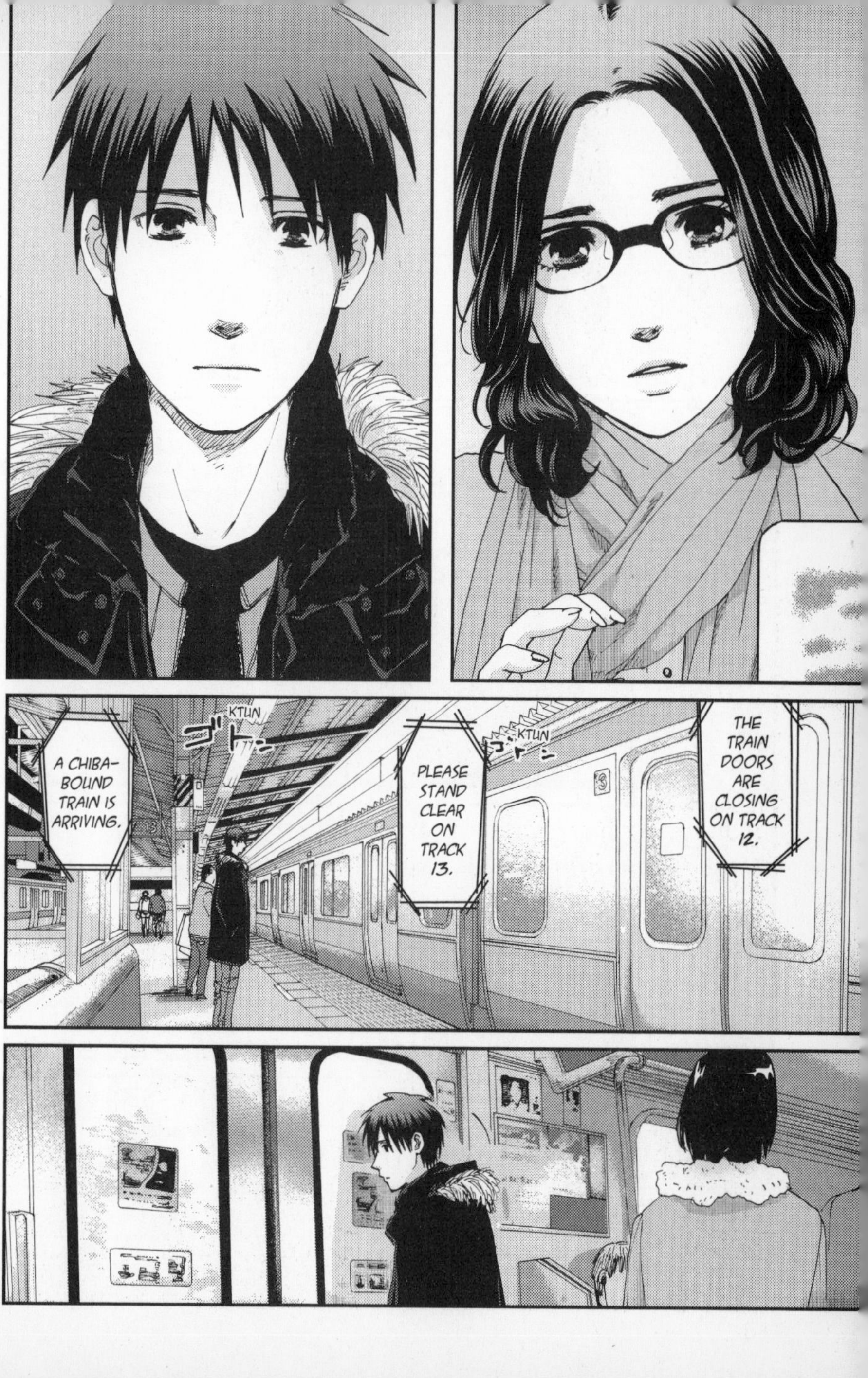
THE TRAIN DOORS ARE CLOSING ON TRACK 12.
KTUN
PLEASE STAND CLEAR ON TRACK 13.
KTUN
A CHIBA-BOUND TRAIN IS ARRIVING.

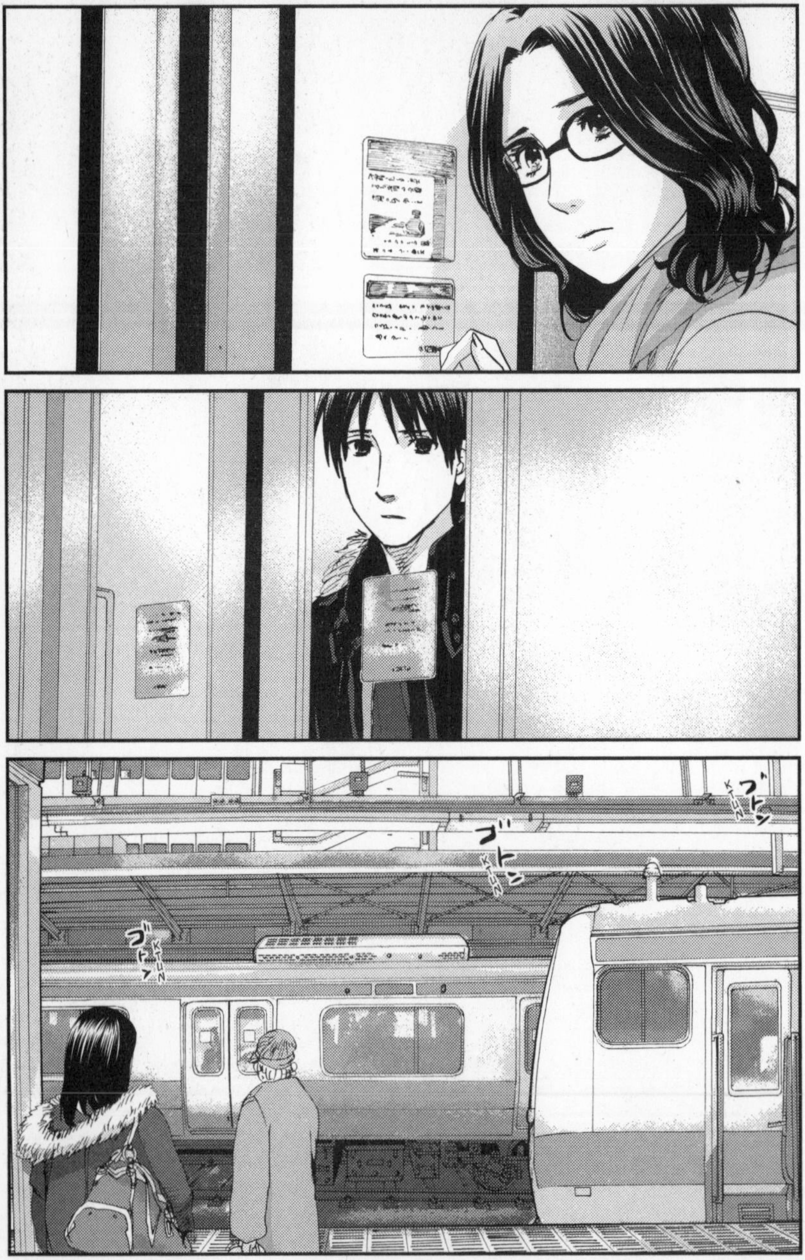

ゴトン
KTUN
ゴトン
KTUN
ゴトン
KTUN

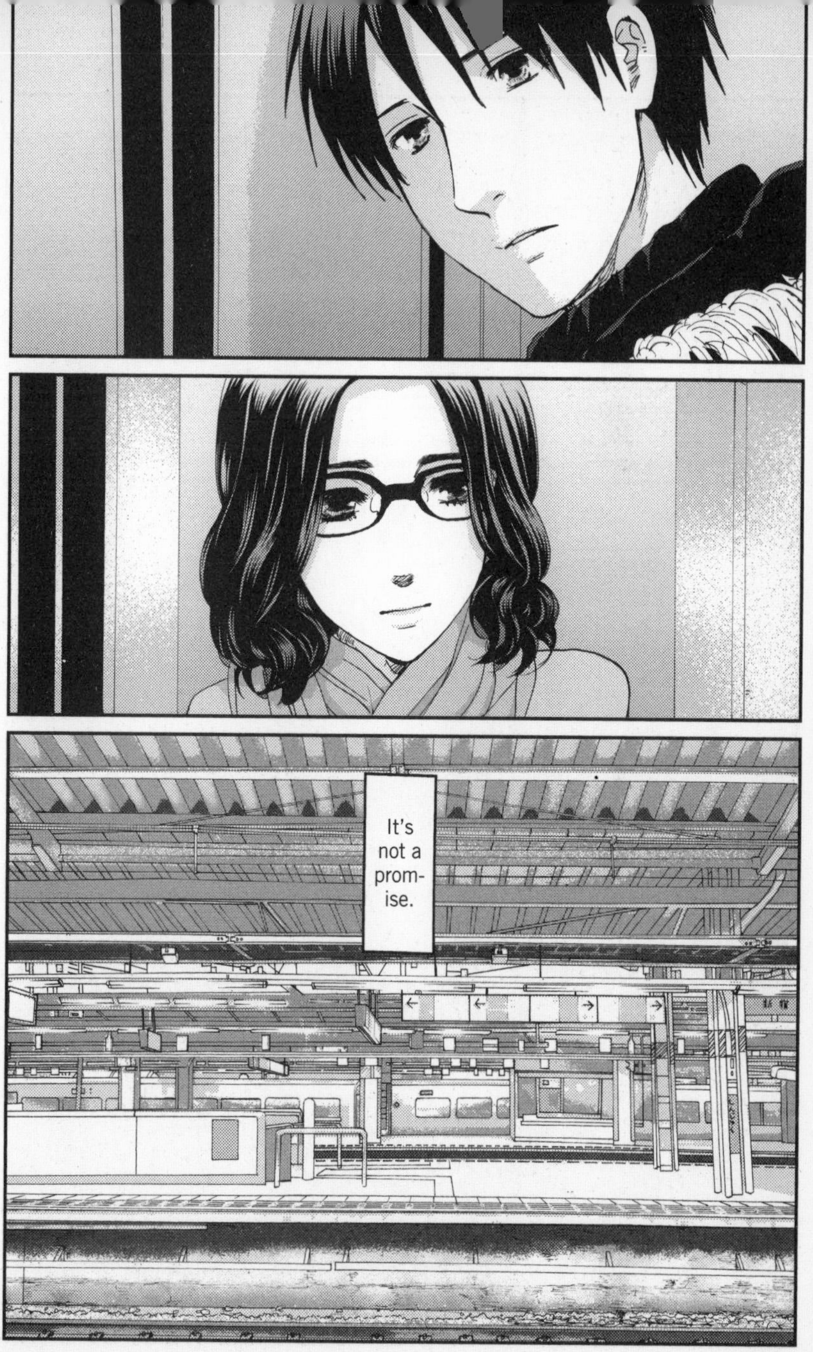
It's not a prom-ise.

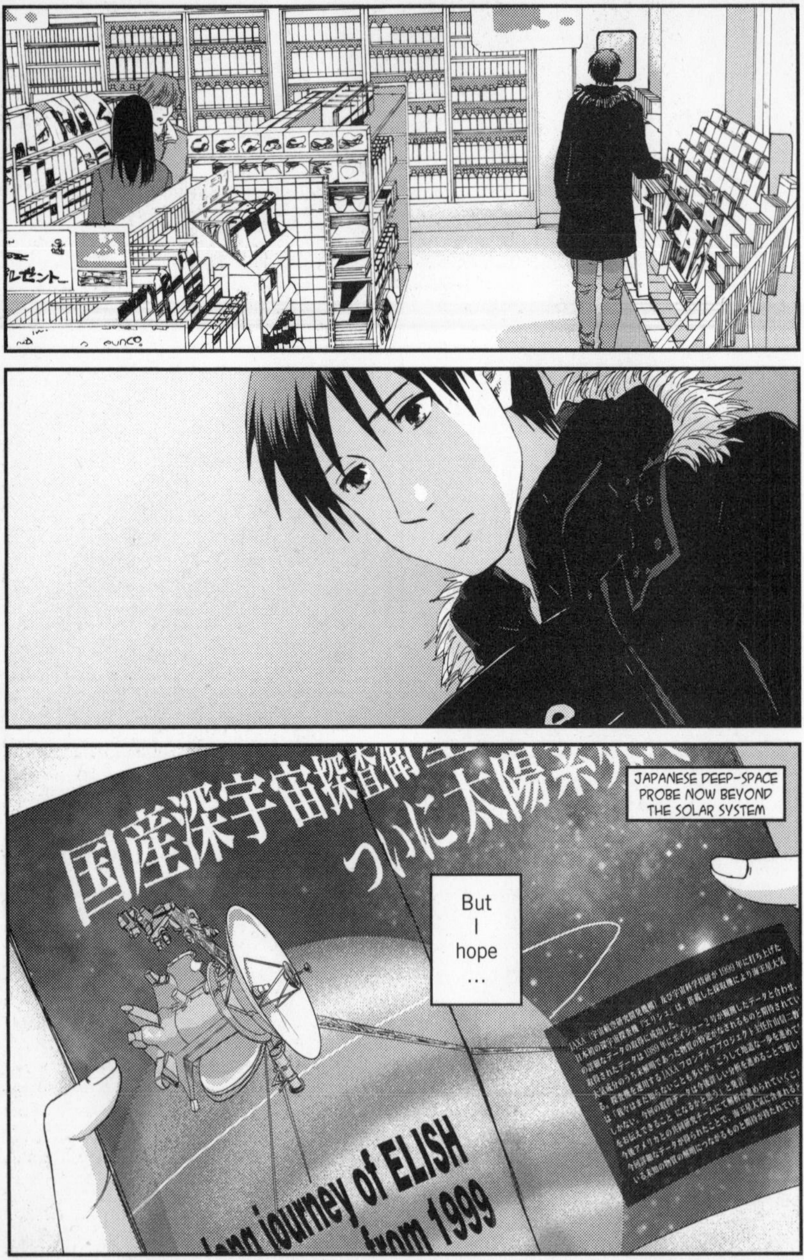
JAPANESE DEEP-SPACE PROBE NOW BEYOND THE SOLAR SYSTEM
国産深宇宙探査
ついに太陽系
But I hope ...
journey of ELISH
from 1999

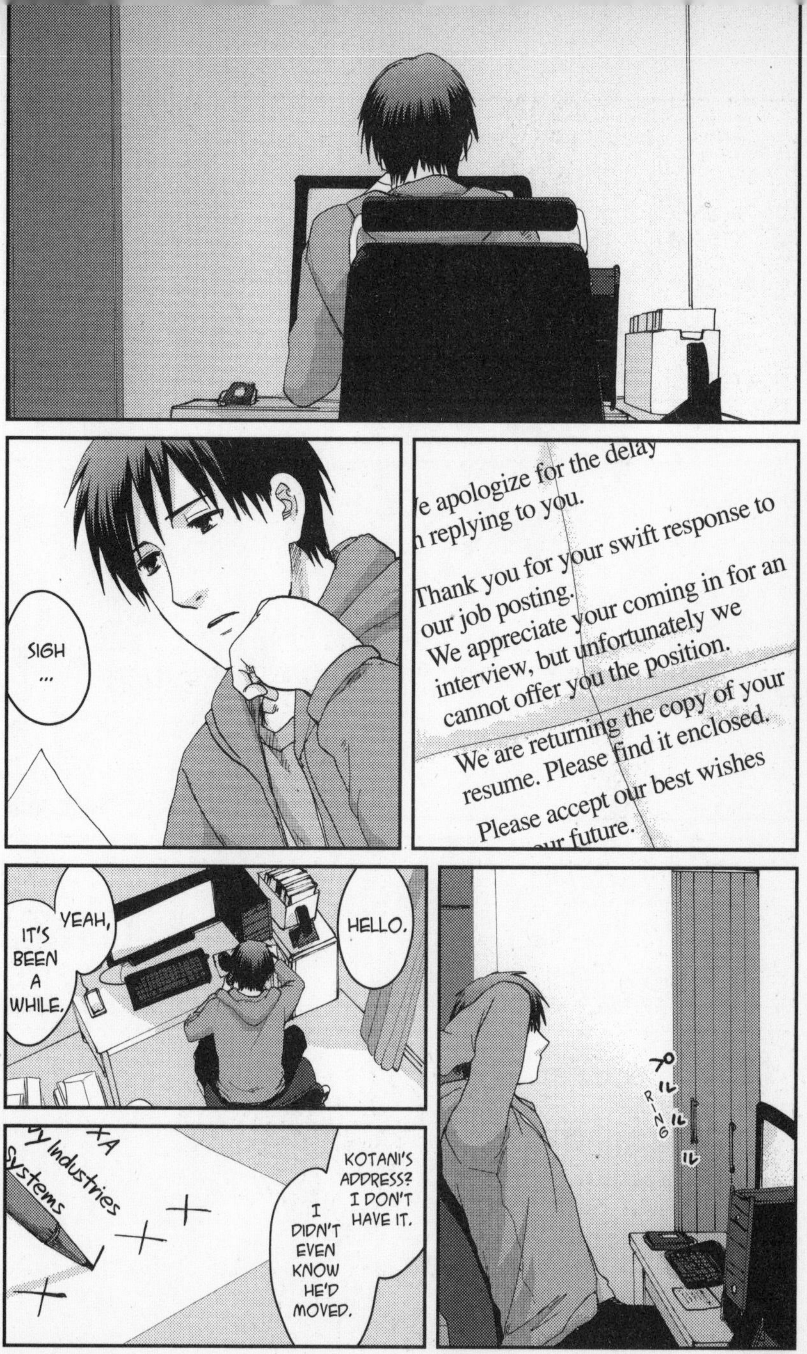
e apologize for the delay
n replying to you.
Thank you for your swift response to
our job posting.
We appreciate your coming in for an
interview, but unfortunately we
cannot offer you the position.
We are returning the copy of your
resume. Please find it enclosed.
Please accept our best wishes
our future.
SIGH ...
プルルル
RING
HELLO.
YEAH, IT'S BEEN A WHILE.
KOTANI'S ADDRESS? I DON'T HAVE IT.
I DIDN'T EVEN KNOW HE'D MOVED.
XA
y Industries
Systems

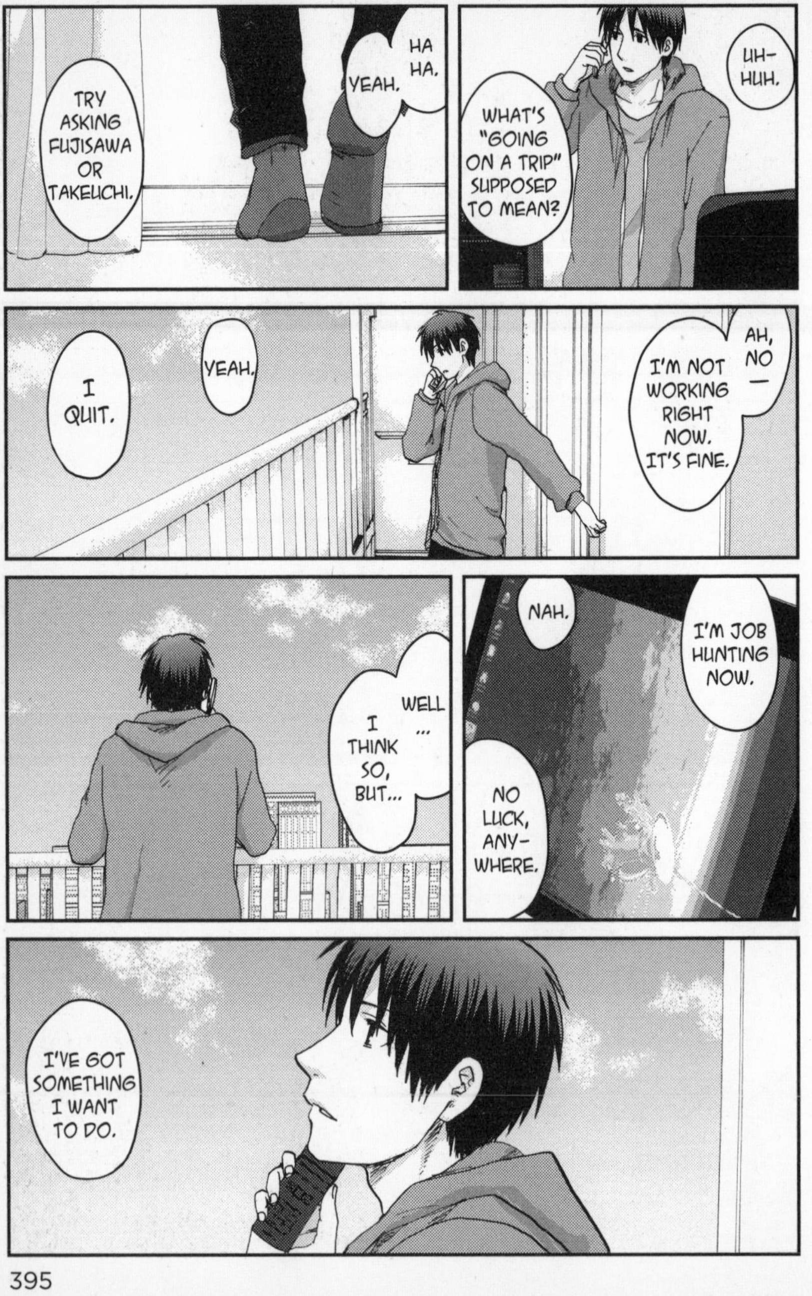
UH-HUH.
WHAT'S "GOING ON A TRIP" SUPPOSED TO MEAN?
HA HA.
YEAH.
TRY ASKING FUJISAWA OR TAKEUCHI.
AH, NO—
I'M NOT WORKING RIGHT NOW. IT'S FINE.
YEAH.
I QUIT.
NAH.
I'M JOB HUNTING NOW.
NO LUCK, ANY-WHERE.
WELL...
I THINK SO, BUT...
I'VE GOT SOMETHING I WANT TO DO.

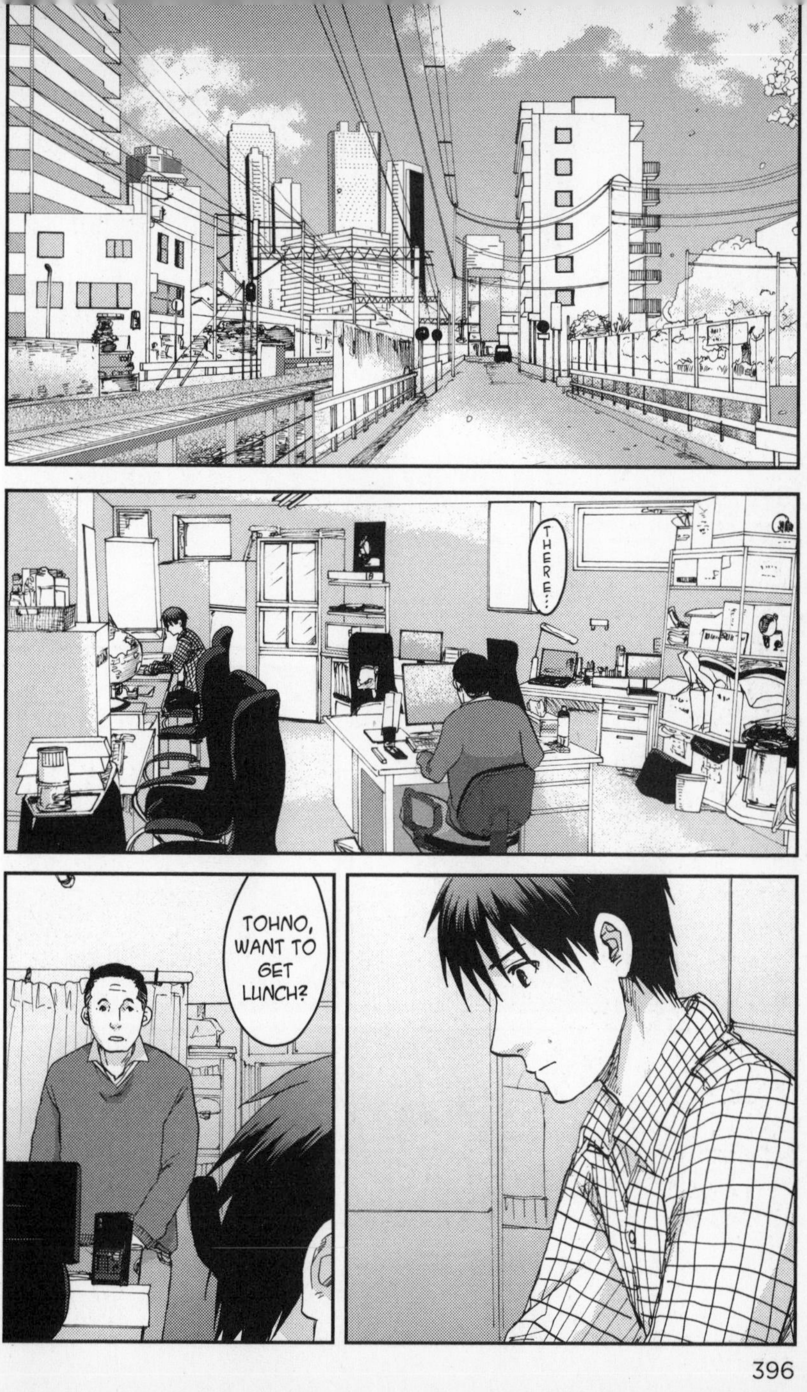
THERE...
TOHNO, WANT TO GET LUNCH?

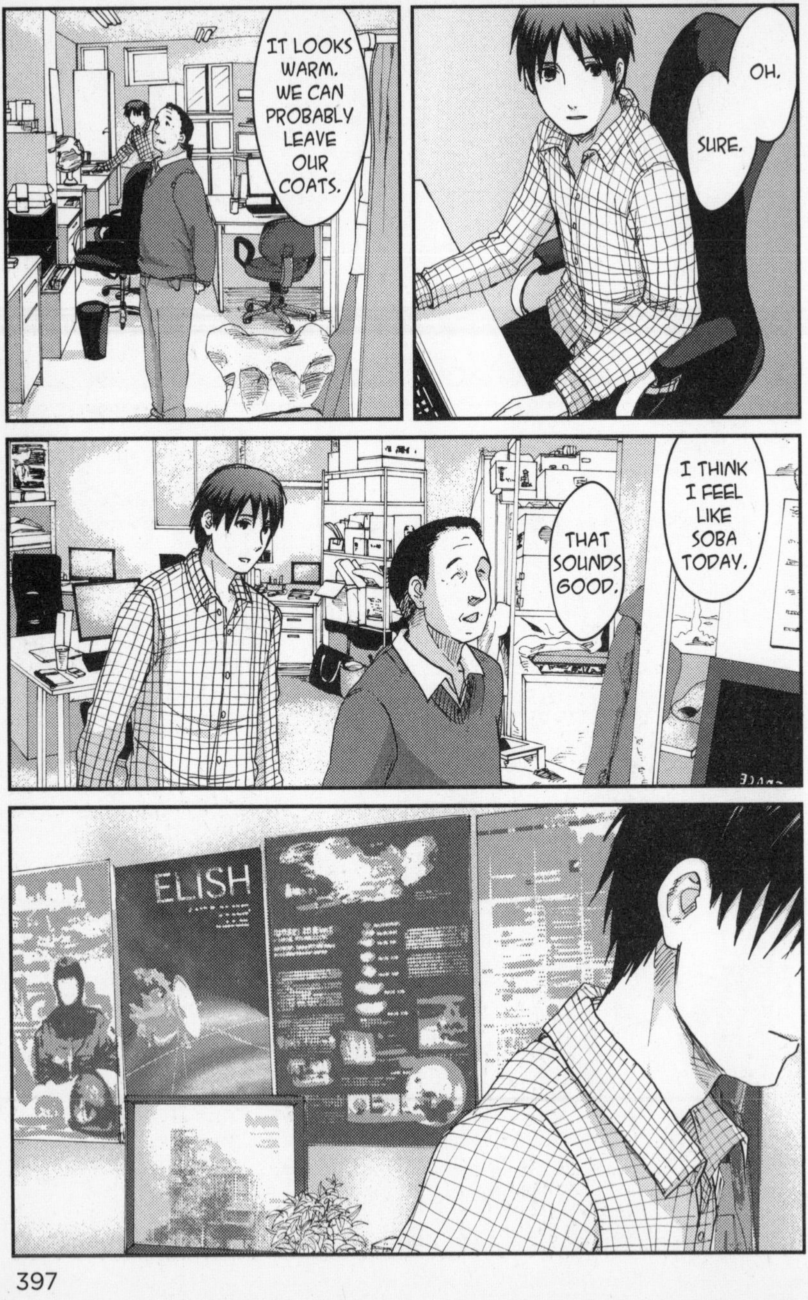

OH.
SURE.
IT LOOKS WARM. WE CAN PROBABLY LEAVE OUR COATS.
I THINK I FEEL LIKE SOBA TODAY.
THAT SOUNDS GOOD.
ELISH

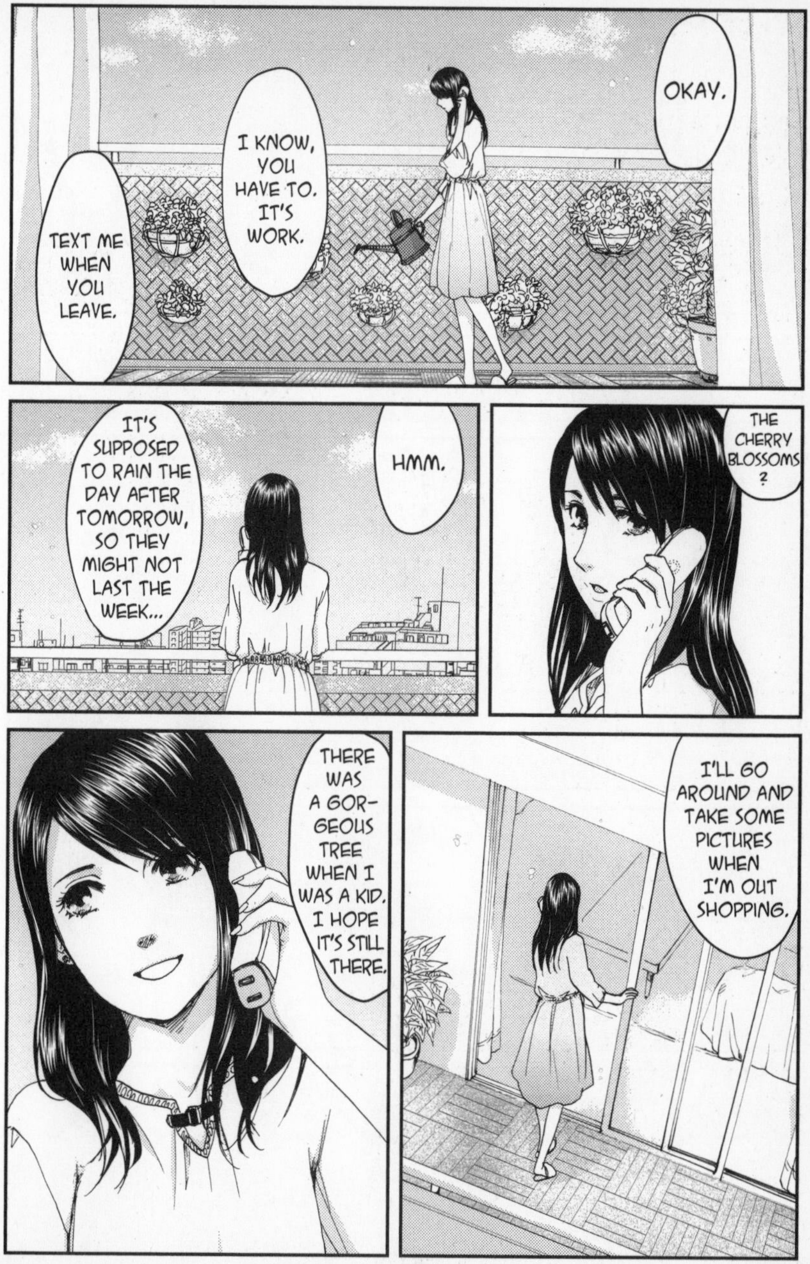
OKAY.
I KNOW, YOU HAVE TO. IT'S WORK.
TEXT ME WHEN YOU LEAVE.
THE CHERRY BLOSSOMS?
HMM.
IT'S SUPPOSED TO RAIN THE DAY AFTER TOMORROW, SO THEY MIGHT NOT LAST THE WEEK...
I'LL GO AROUND AND TAKE SOME PICTURES WHEN I'M OUT SHOPPING.
THERE WAS A GOR-GEOUS TREE WHEN I WAS A KID. I HOPE IT'S STILL THERE.

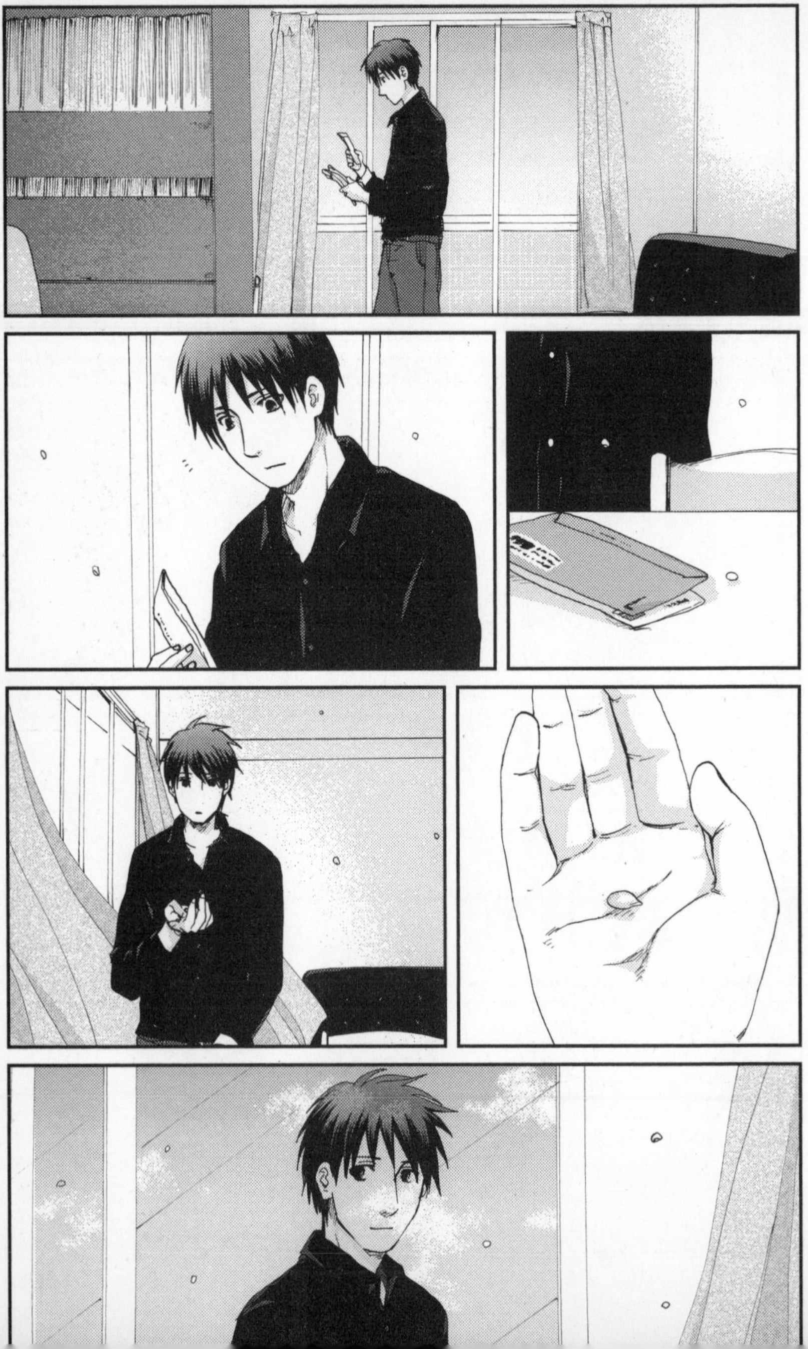

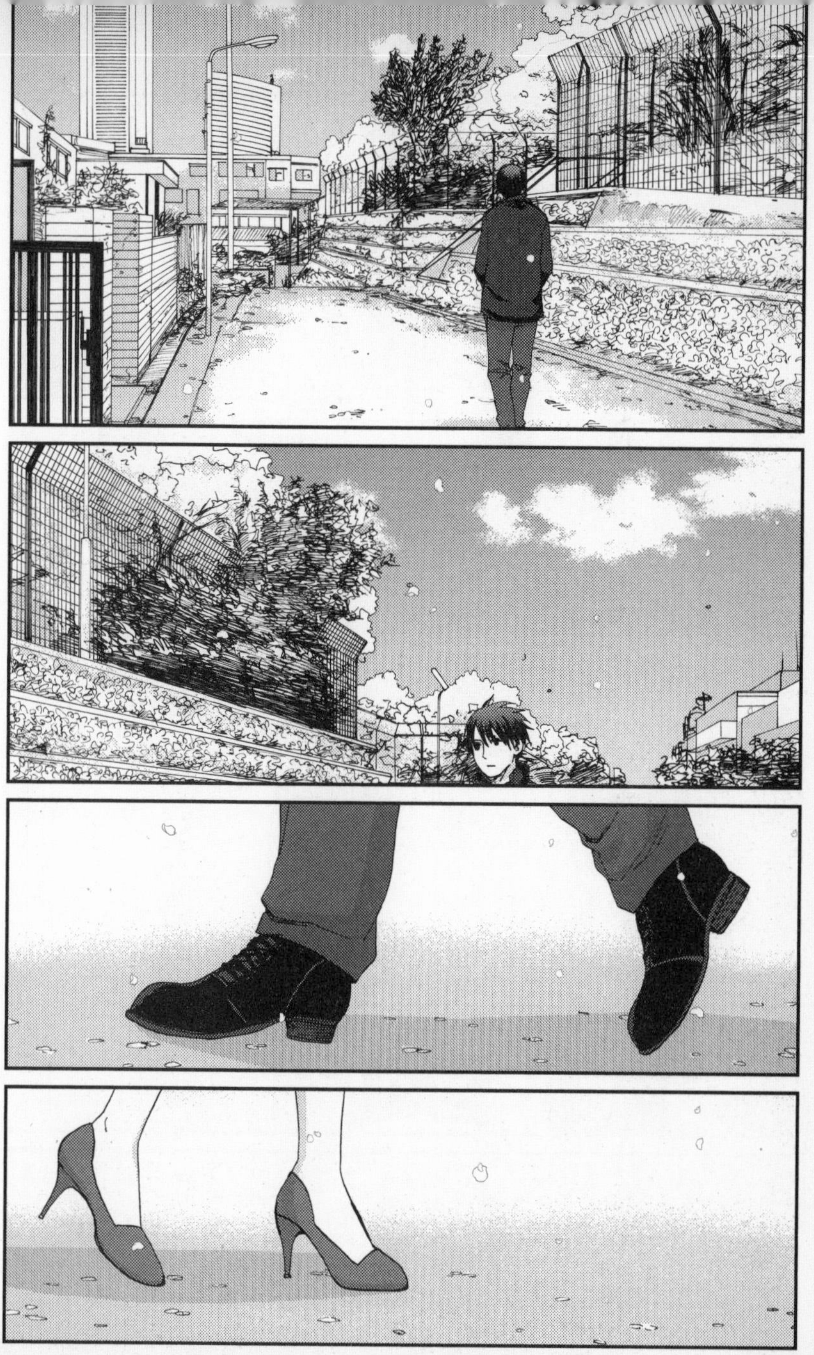

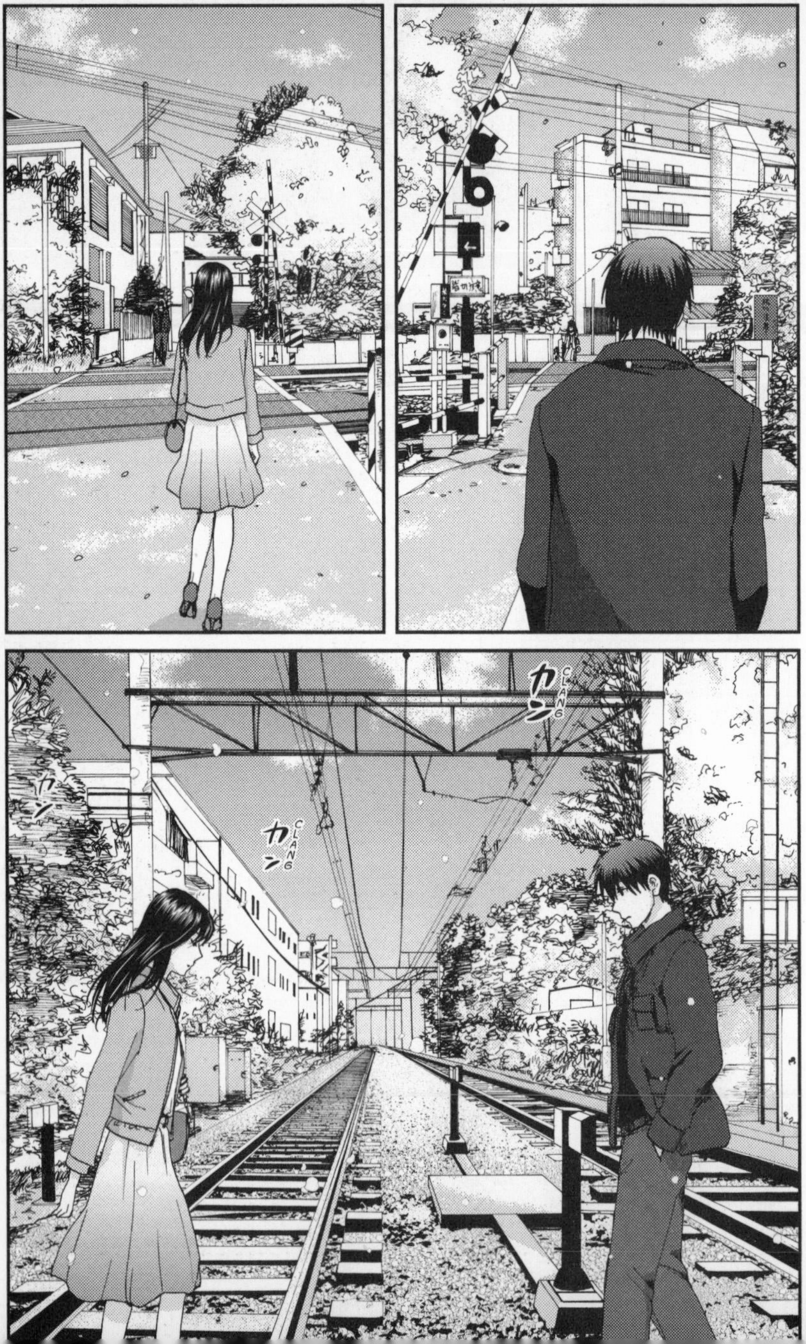
カーン
CLANG
カン
CLANG
カン

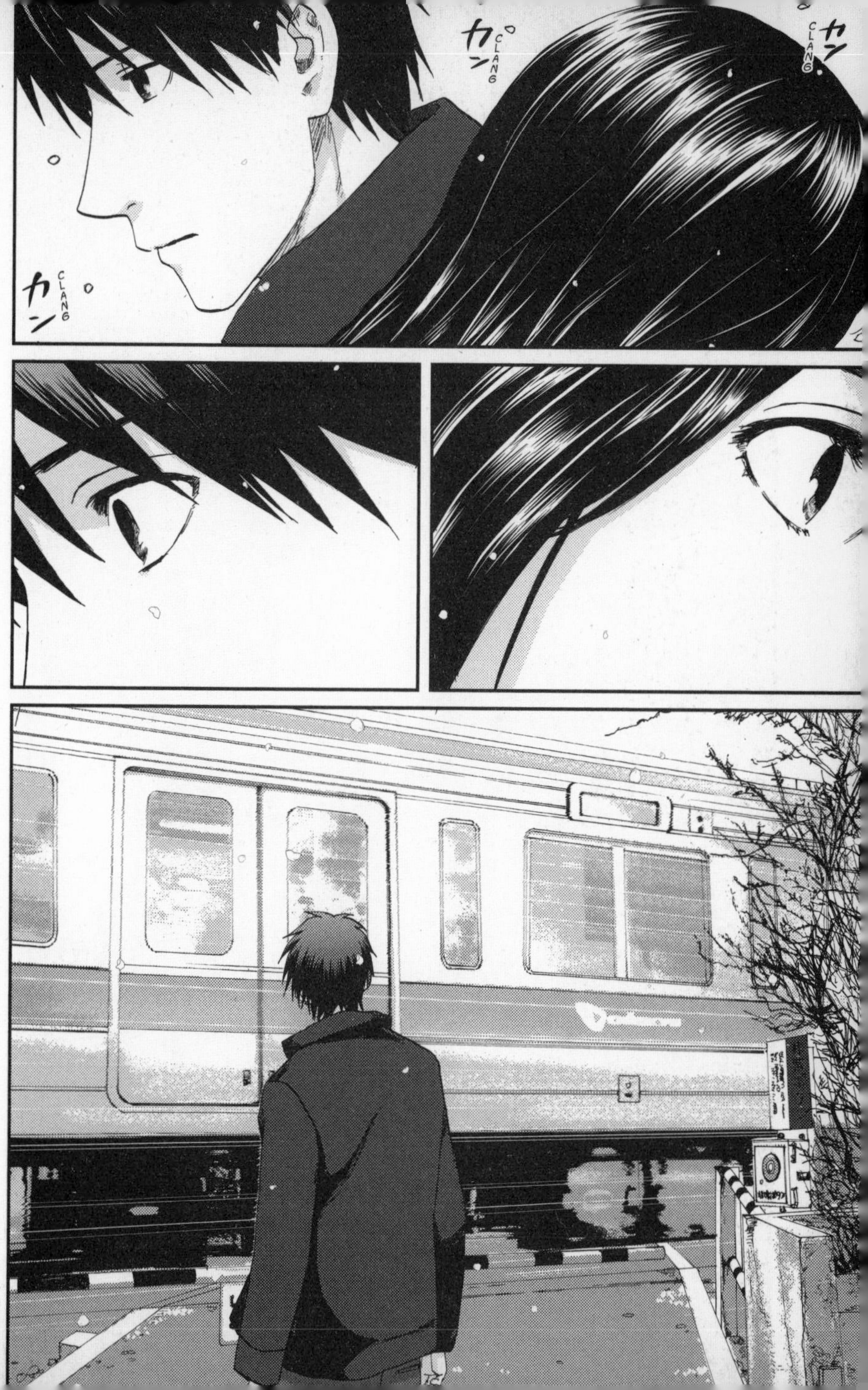
カン
CLANG
カン
CLANG
カン
CLANG

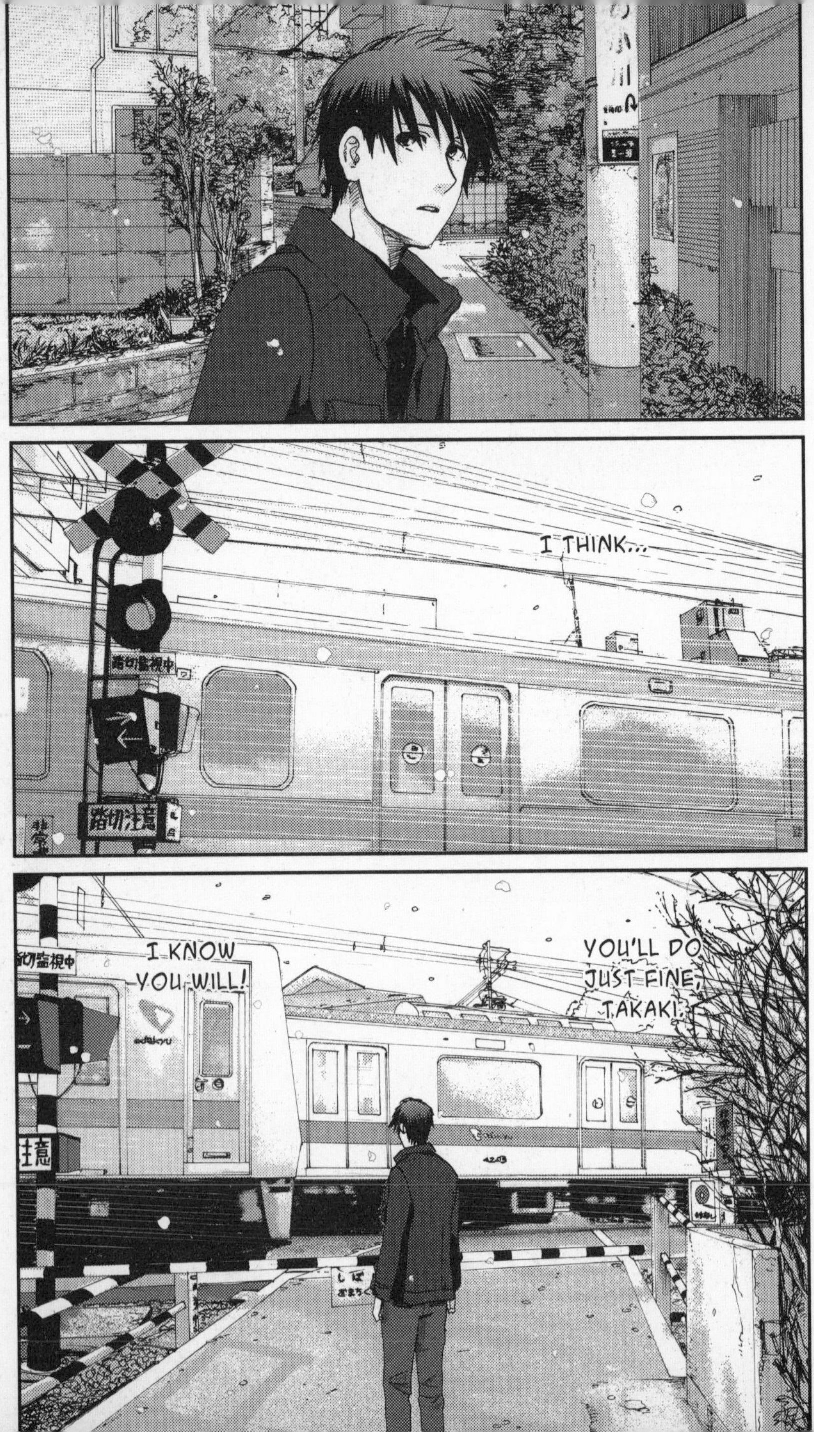
I THINK...
踏切監視中
踏切注意
YOU'LL DO JUST FINE, TAKAKI.
I KNOW YOU WILL!
踏切監視中

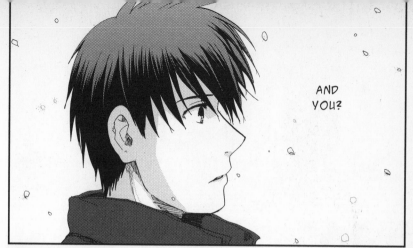

AND
YOU?

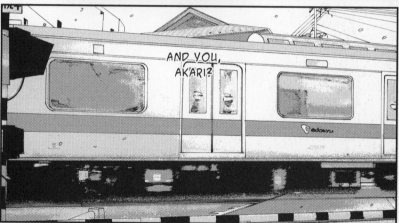

AND YOU,
AKARI?

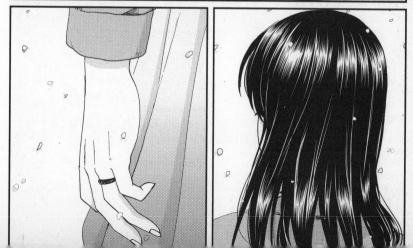

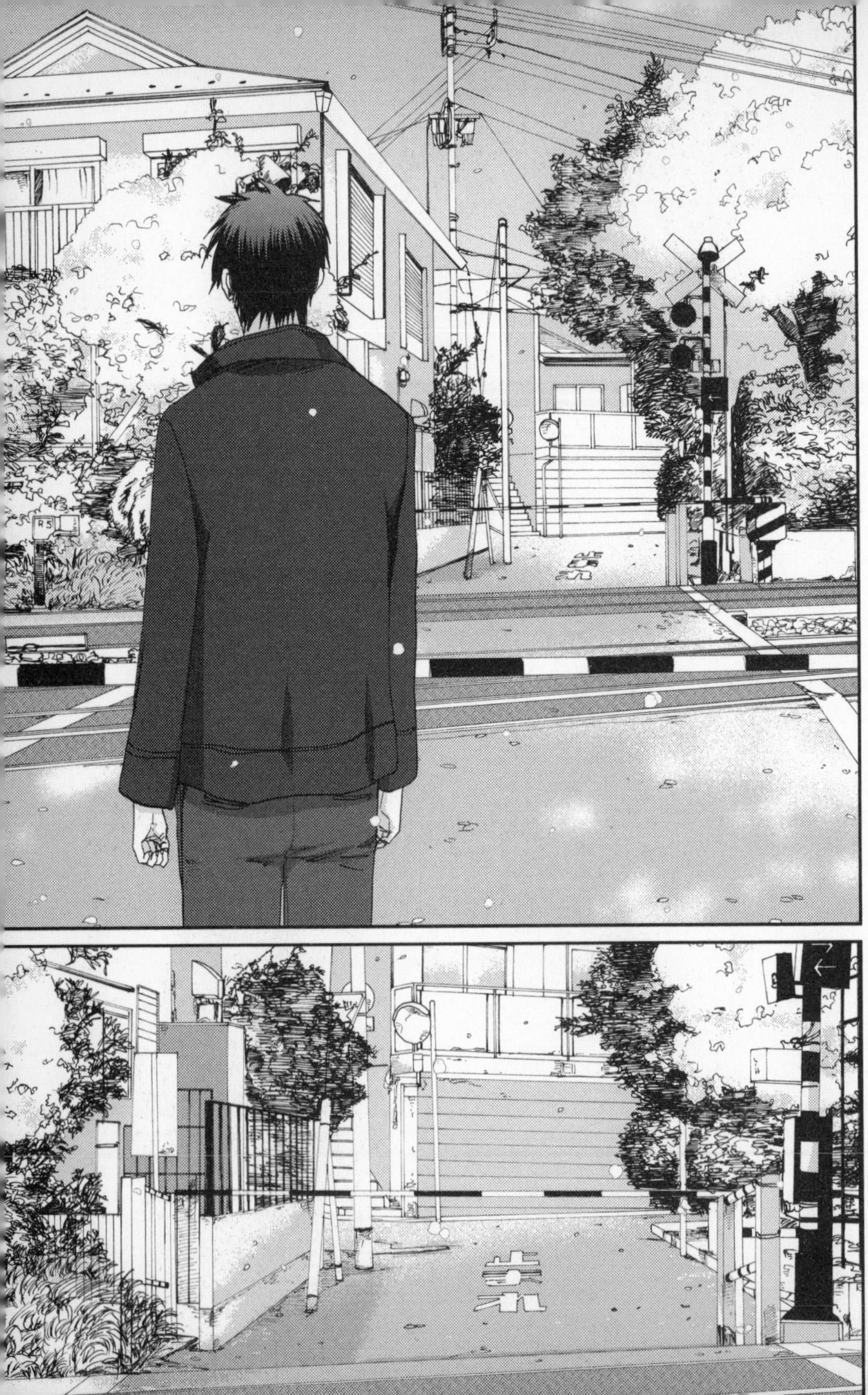

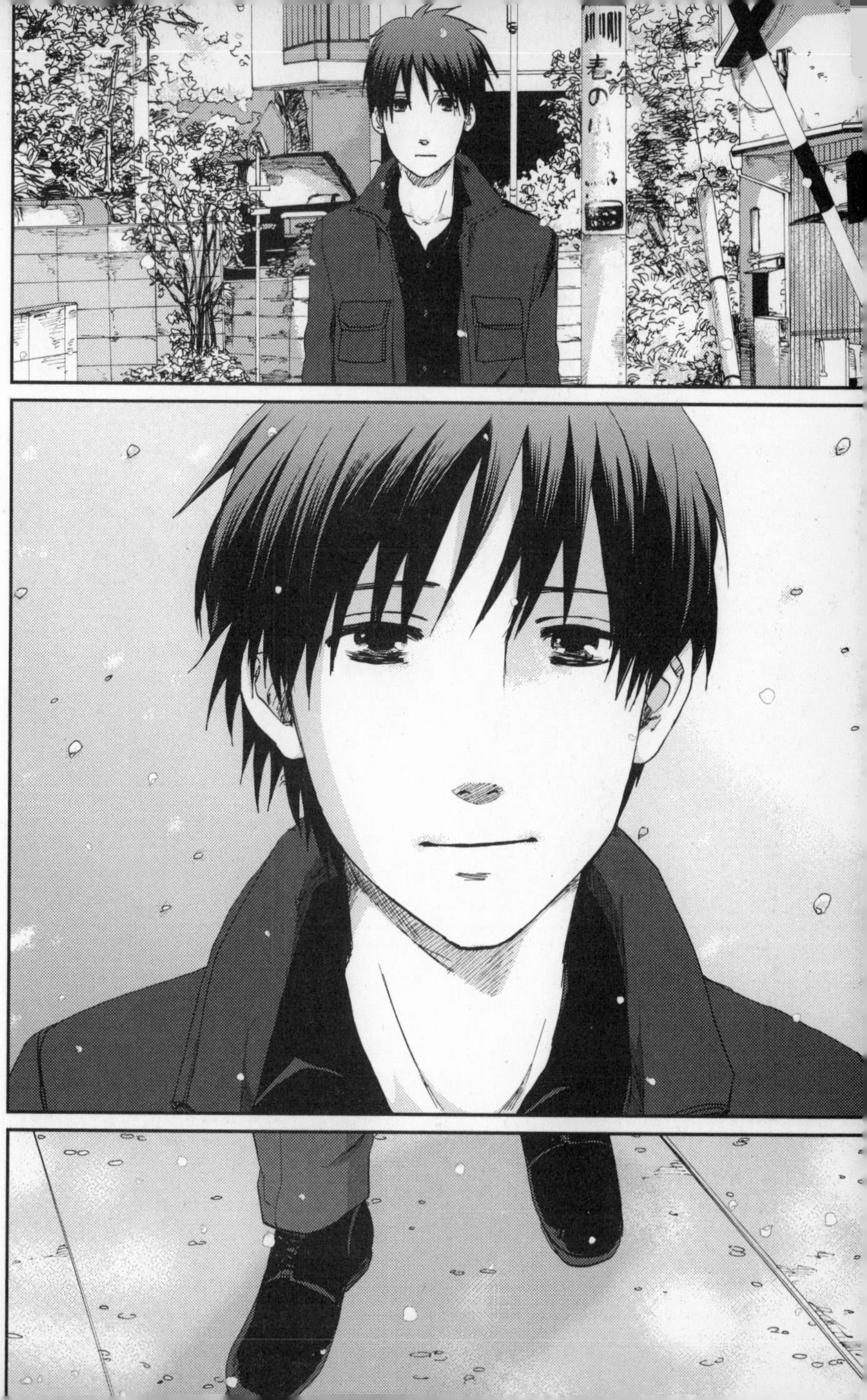

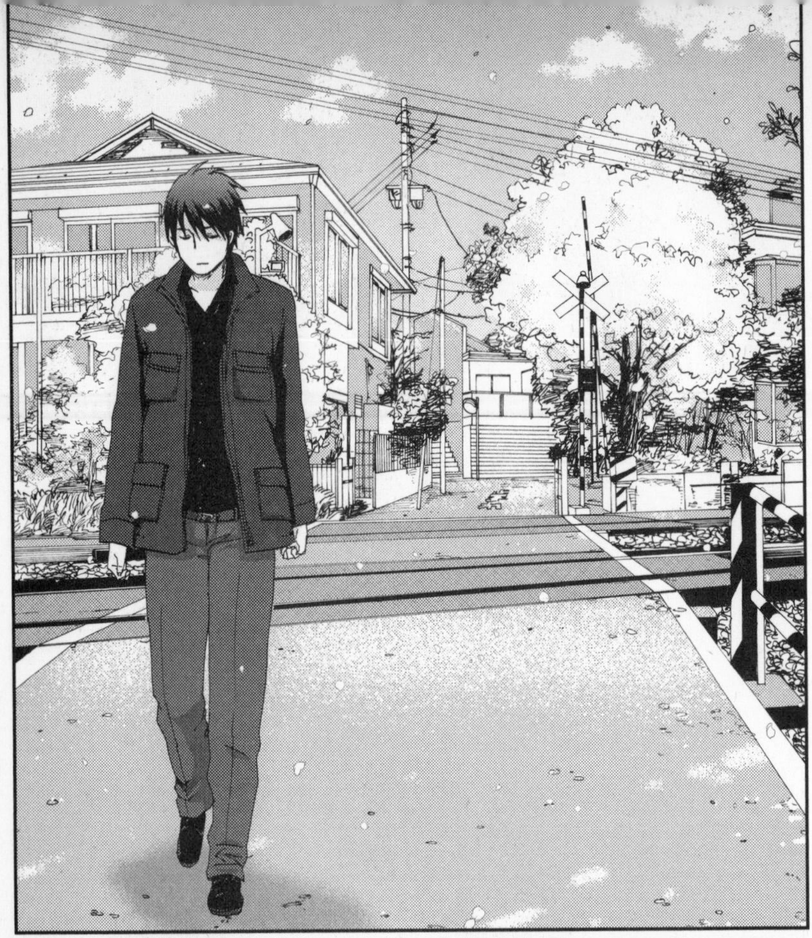

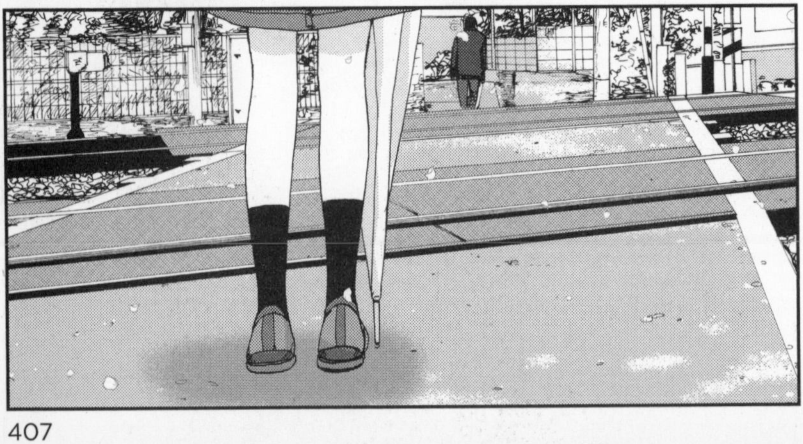

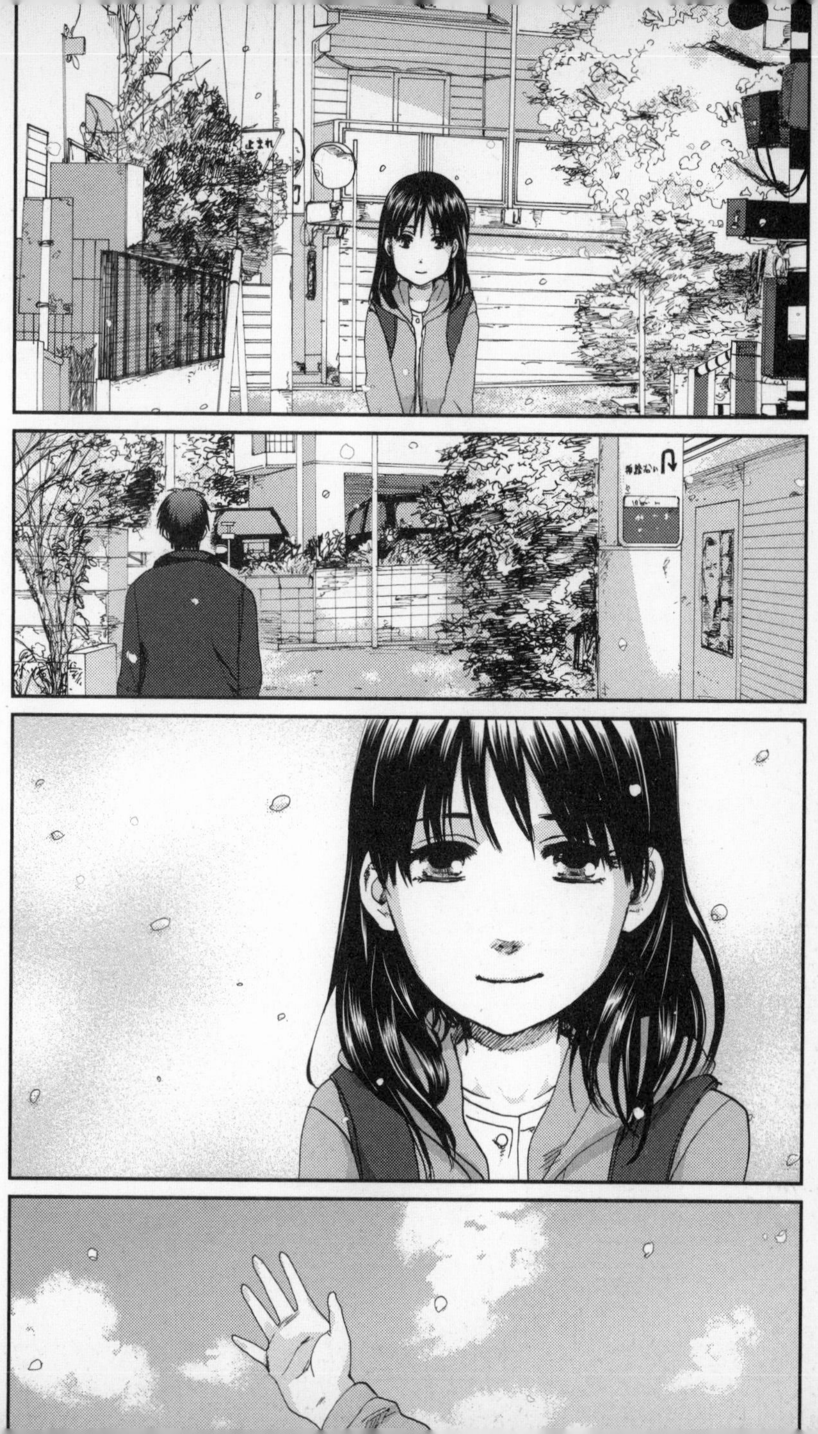
止まれ

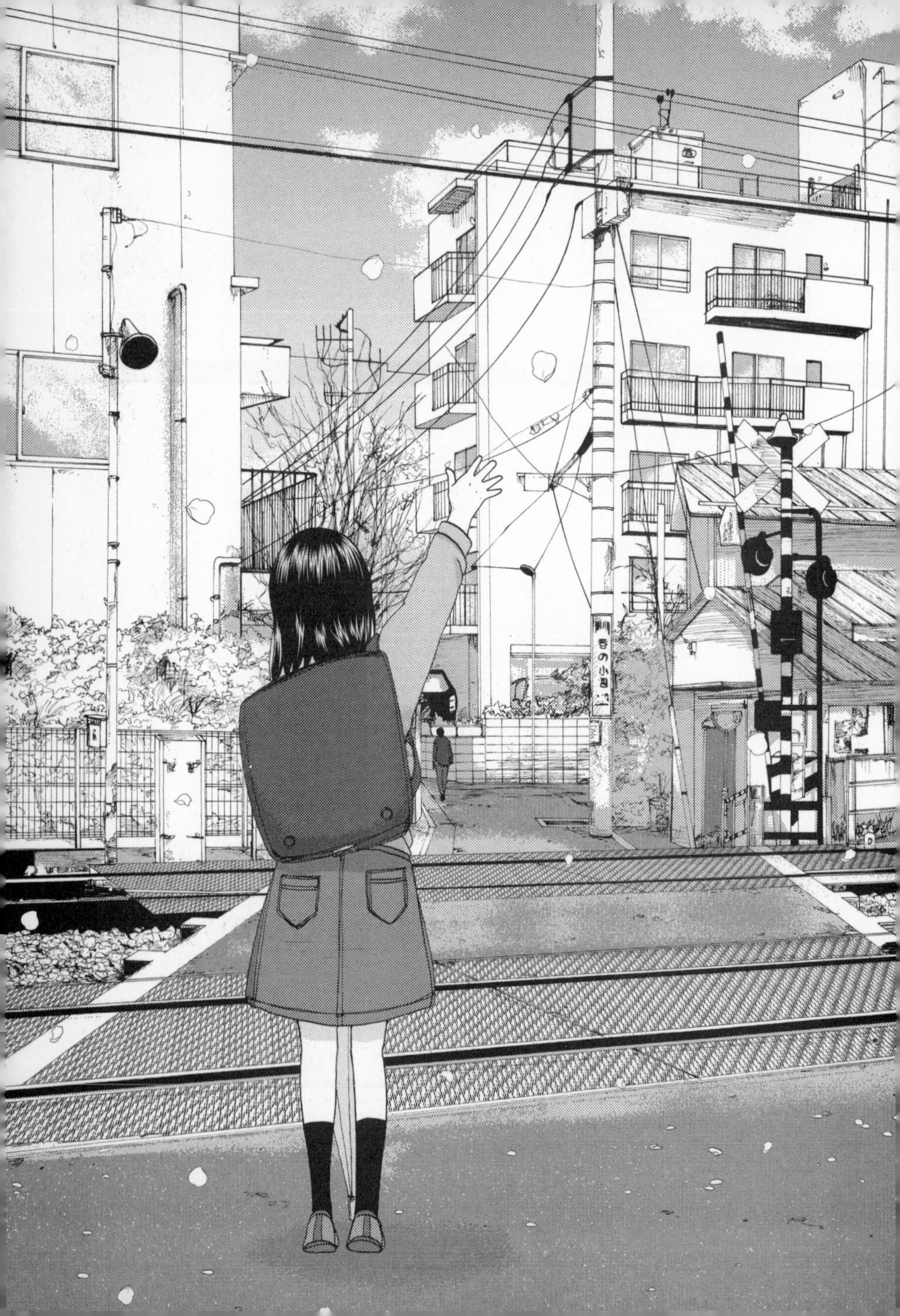
春の小道

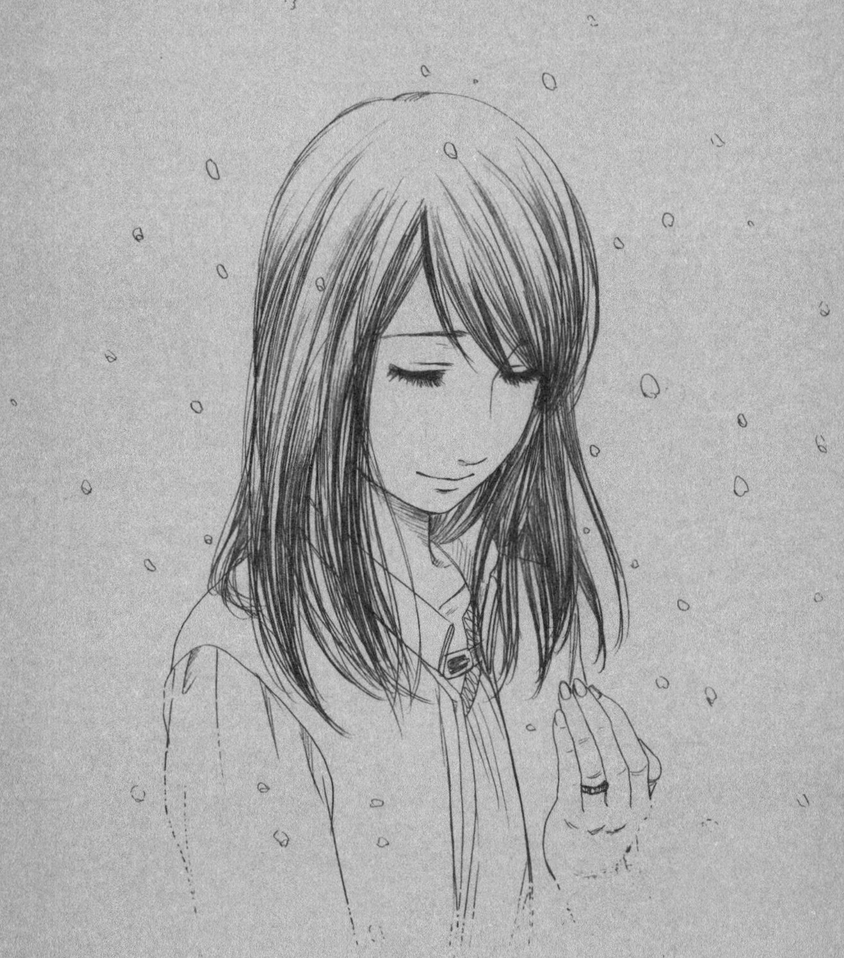

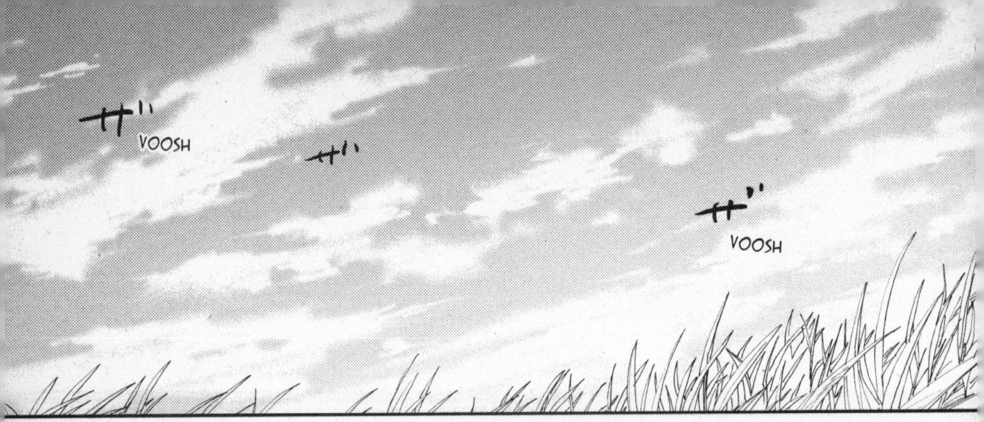
ザ
VOOSH
ザ
ザ
VOOSH
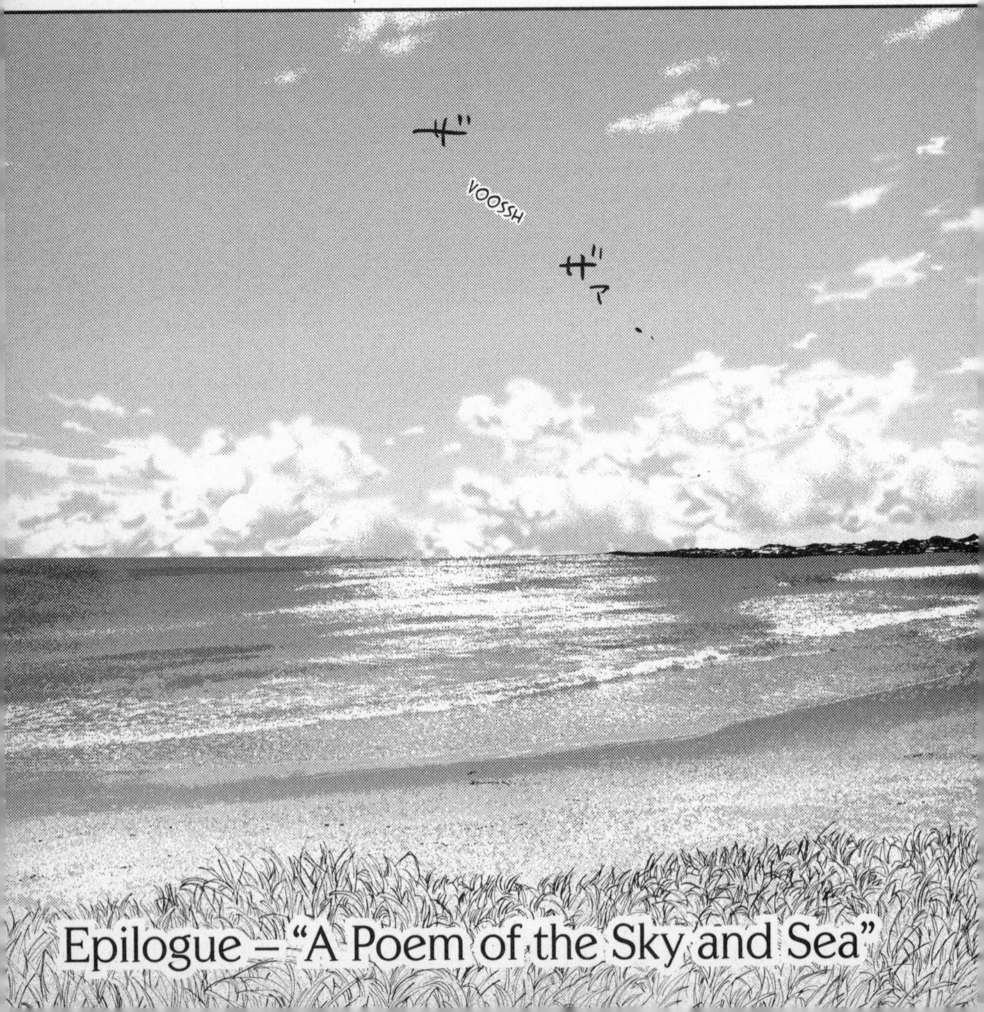
ザ
VOOSSH
ザァ
Epilogue – "A Poem of the Sky and Sea"

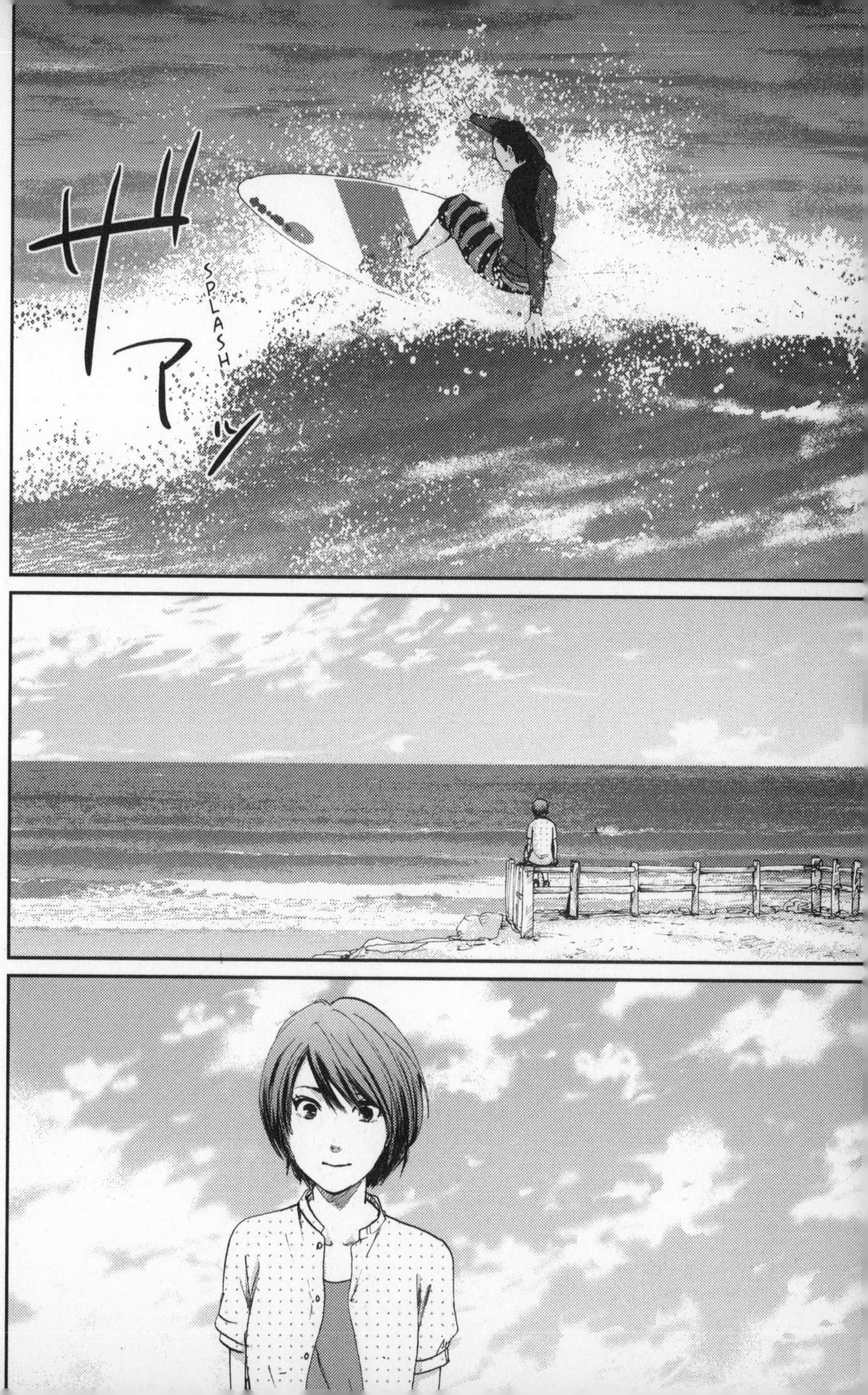
ザアッ
SPLASH

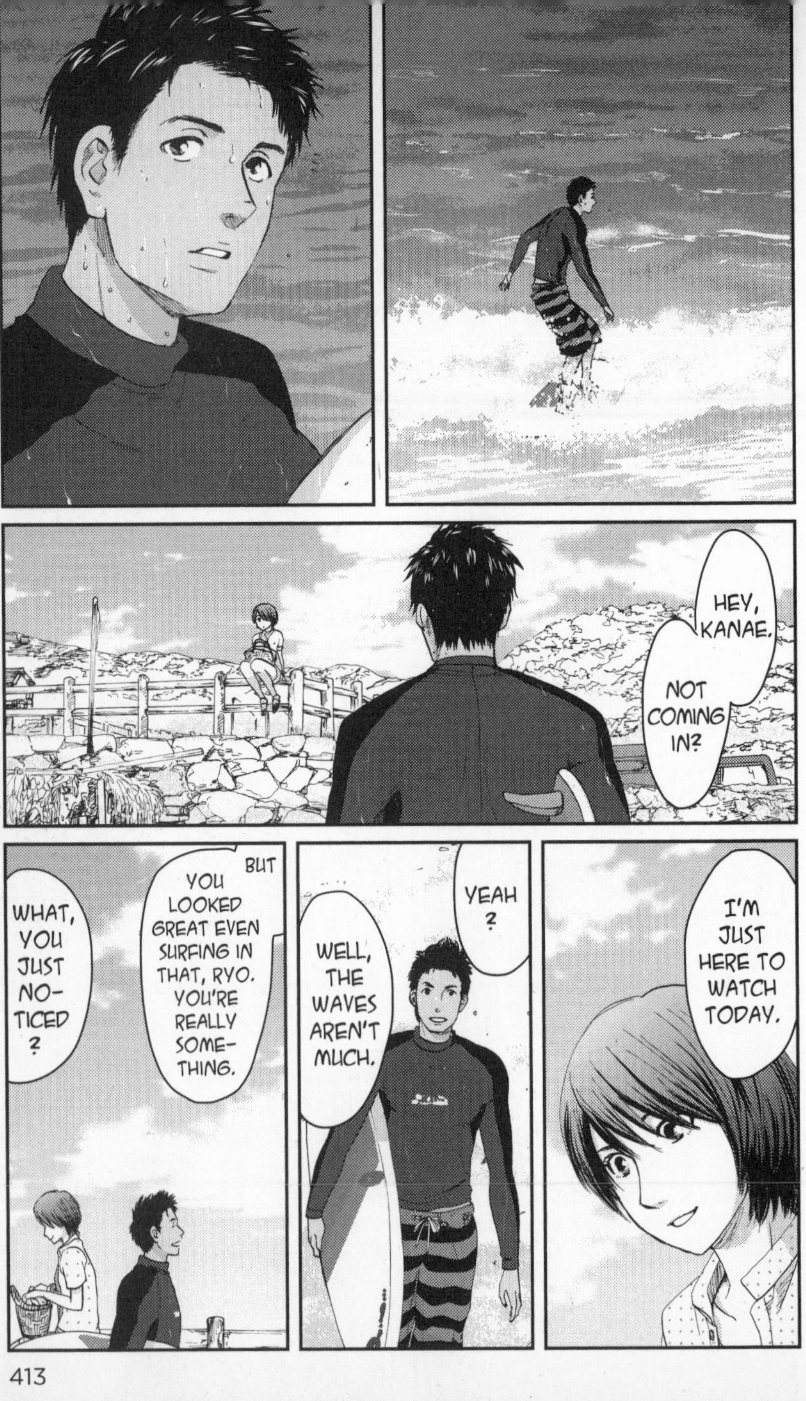
HEY, KANAE.
NOT COMING IN?
I'M JUST HERE TO WATCH TODAY.
YEAH?
WELL, THE WAVES AREN'T MUCH.
BUT YOU LOOKED GREAT EVEN SURFING IN THAT, RYO. YOU'RE REALLY SOME-THING.
WHAT, YOU JUST NO-TICED?

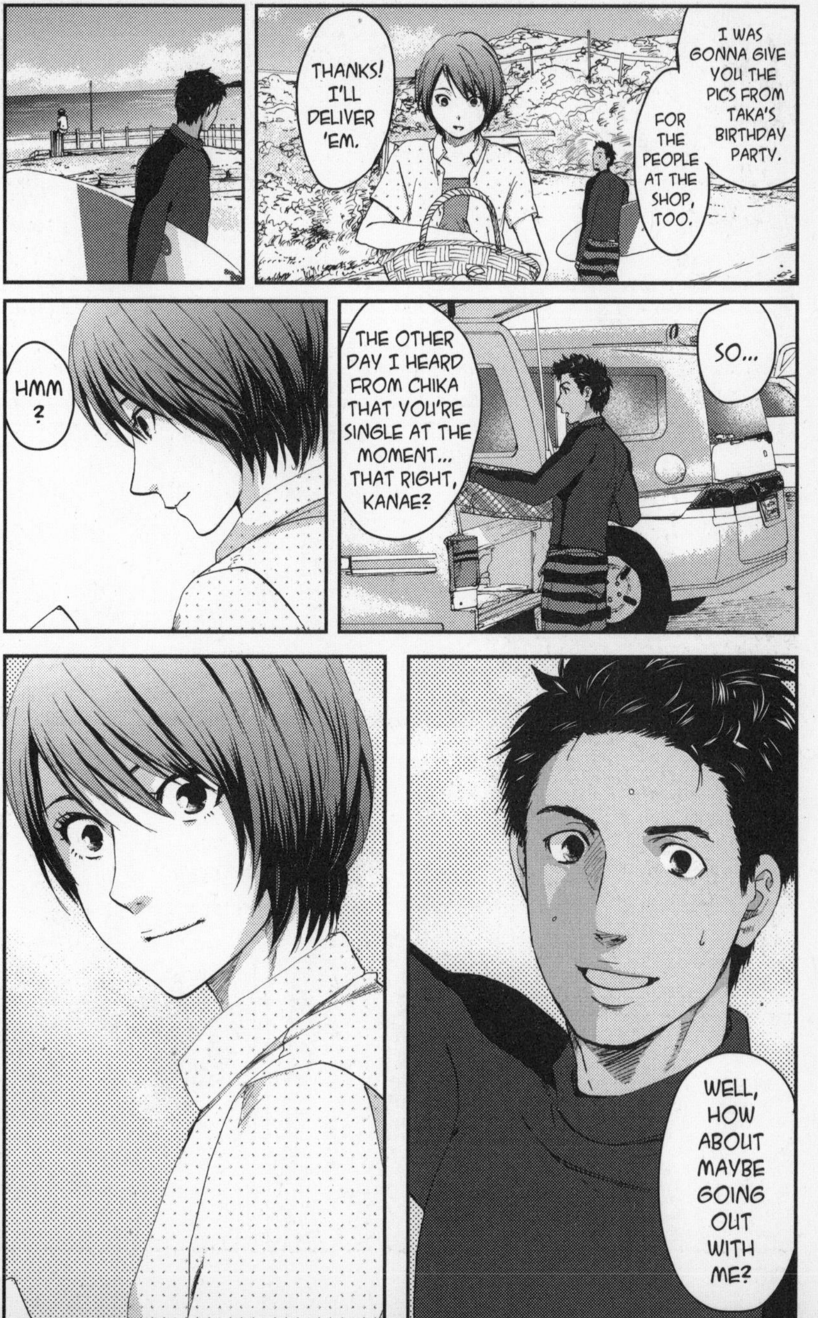
I WAS GONNA GIVE YOU THE PICS FROM TAKA'S BIRTHDAY PARTY.
FOR THE PEOPLE AT THE SHOP, TOO.
THANKS! I'LL DELIVER 'EM.
SO...
THE OTHER DAY I HEARD FROM CHIKA THAT YOU'RE SINGLE AT THE MOMENT... THAT RIGHT, KANAE?
HMM?
WELL, HOW ABOUT MAYBE GOING OUT WITH ME?

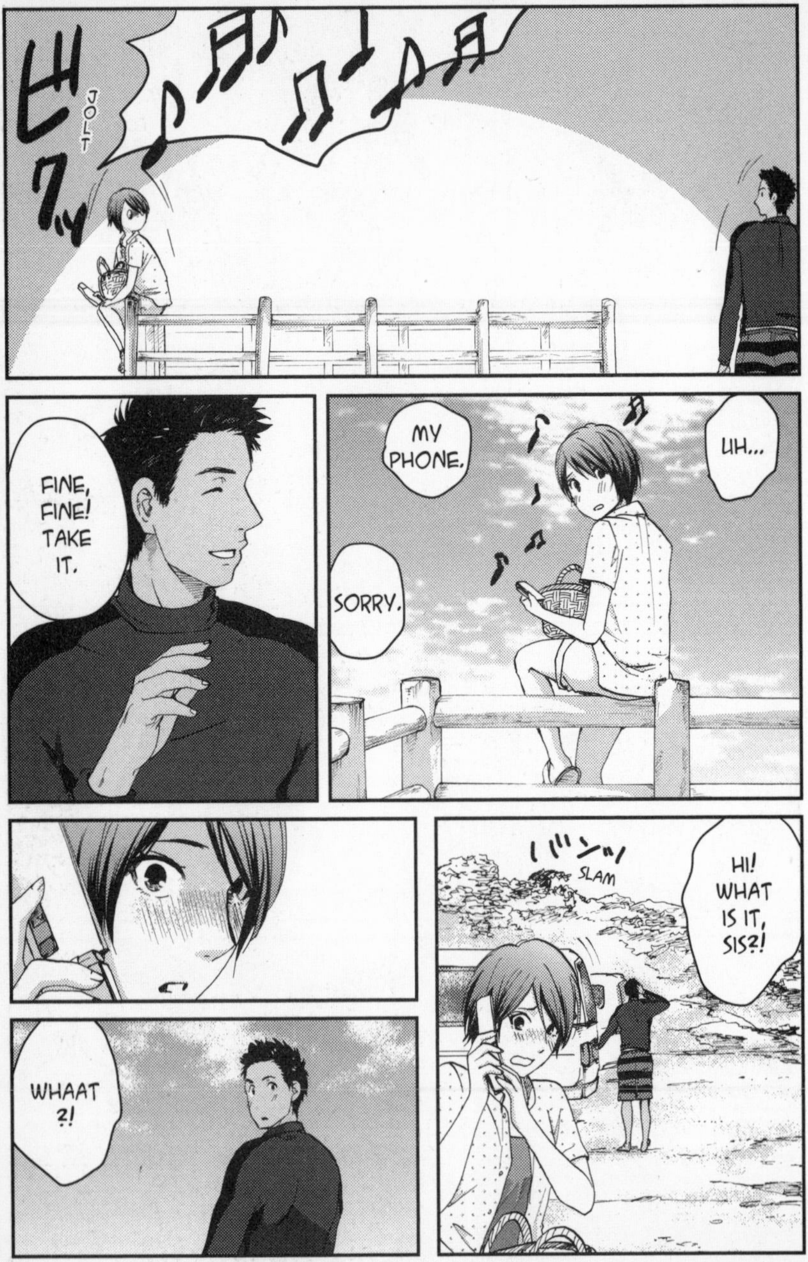
ビクッ
JOLT
UH...
MY PHONE.
SORRY.
FINE, FINE! TAKE IT.
バンッ
SLAM
HI! WHAT IS IT, SIS?!
WHAAT?!

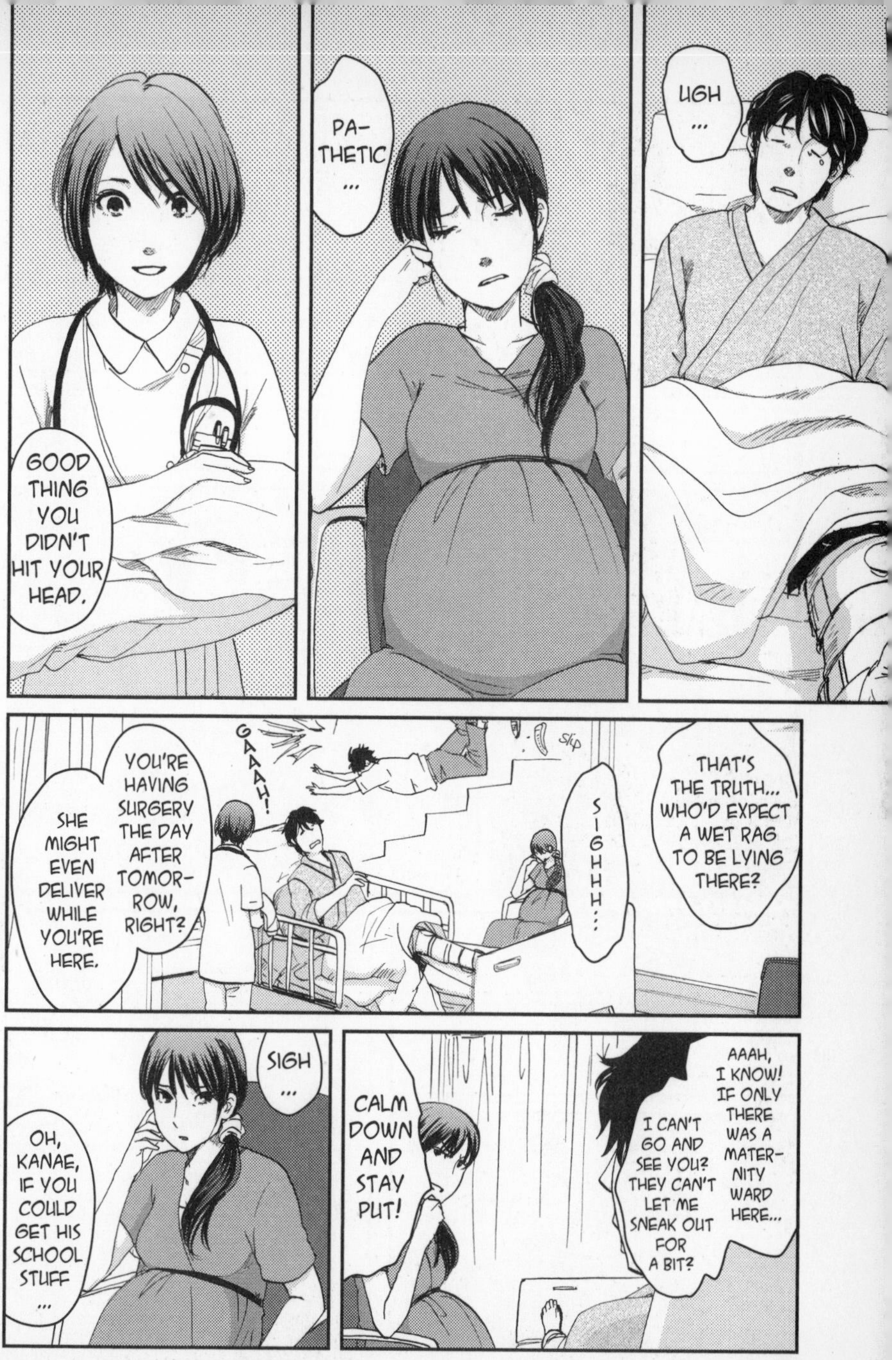
UGH ...
PA-THETIC ...
GOOD THING YOU DIDN'T HIT YOUR HEAD.
THAT'S THE TRUTH... WHO'D EXPECT A WET RAG TO BE LYING THERE?
slip
GAAAH!
SIGHHH...
YOU'RE HAVING SURGERY THE DAY AFTER TOMORROW, RIGHT?
SHE MIGHT EVEN DELIVER WHILE YOU'RE HERE.
AAAH, I KNOW! IF ONLY THERE WAS A MATERNITY WARD HERE...
I CAN'T GO AND SEE YOU? THEY CAN'T LET ME SNEAK OUT FOR A BIT?
CALM DOWN AND STAY PUT!
SIGH ...
OH, KANAE, IF YOU COULD GET HIS SCHOOL STUFF ...

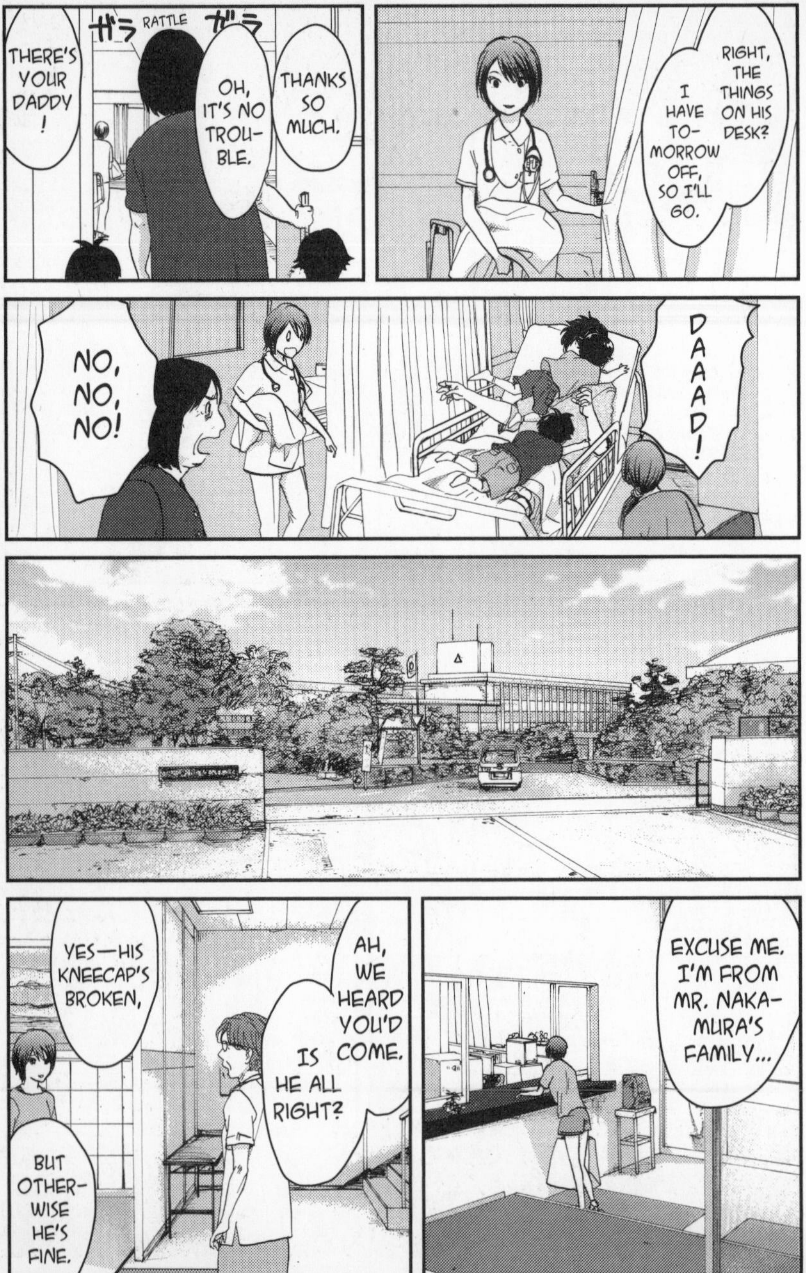
RIGHT, THE THINGS ON HIS DESK?
I HAVE TO-MORROW OFF, SO I'LL GO.
ガラ RATTLE ガラ
THANKS SO MUCH.
OH, IT'S NO TROUBLE.
THERE'S YOUR DADDY!
DAAAAD!
NO, NO, NO!
EXCUSE ME. I'M FROM MR. NAKA-MURA'S FAMILY...
AH, WE HEARD YOU'D COME.
IS HE ALL RIGHT?
YES—HIS KNEECAP'S BROKEN,
BUT OTHER-WISE HE'S FINE.

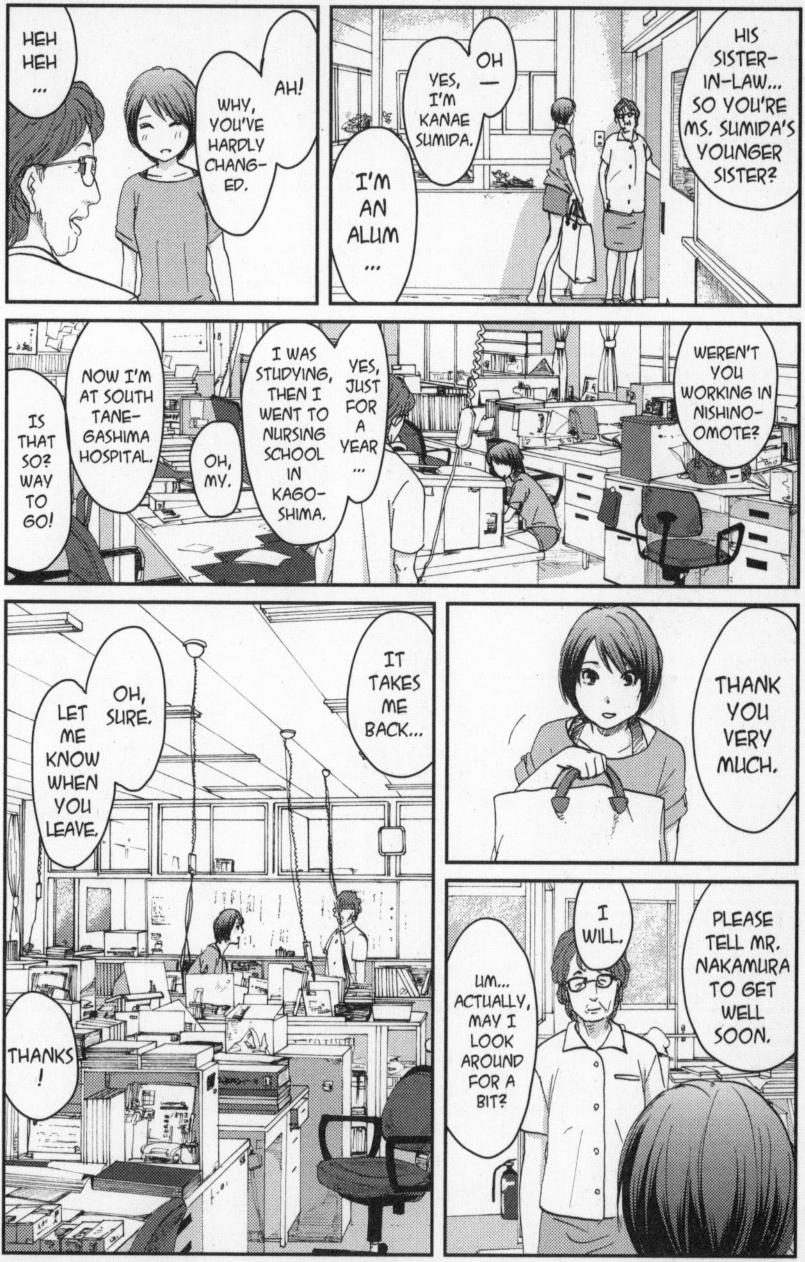
HIS SISTER-IN-LAW... SO YOU'RE MS. SUMIDA'S YOUNGER SISTER?
OH — YES, I'M KANAE SUMIDA.
I'M AN ALUM ...
AH! WHY, YOU'VE HARDLY CHANGED.
HEH HEH ...
WEREN'T YOU WORKING IN NISHINOOMOTE?
YES, JUST FOR A YEAR ...
I WAS STUDYING, THEN I WENT TO NURSING SCHOOL IN KAGOSHIMA.
OH, MY.
NOW I'M AT SOUTH TANEGASHIMA HOSPITAL.
IS THAT SO? WAY TO GO!
THANK YOU VERY MUCH.
PLEASE TELL MR. NAKAMURA TO GET WELL SOON.
I WILL.
UM... ACTUALLY, MAY I LOOK AROUND FOR A BIT?
IT TAKES ME BACK...
OH, SURE. LET ME KNOW WHEN YOU LEAVE.
THANKS!

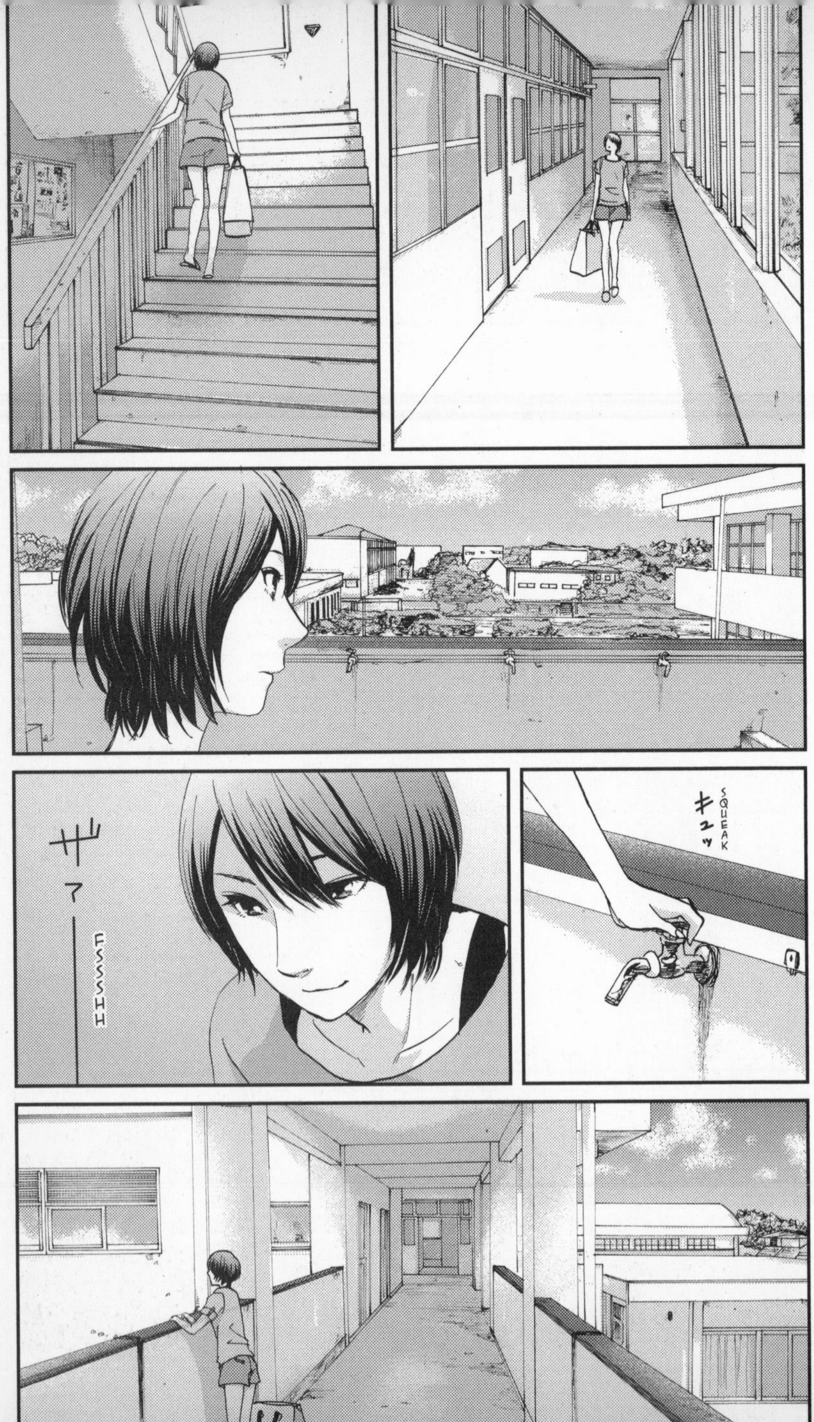
キュッ
SQUEAK
ザァー
FSSSHH

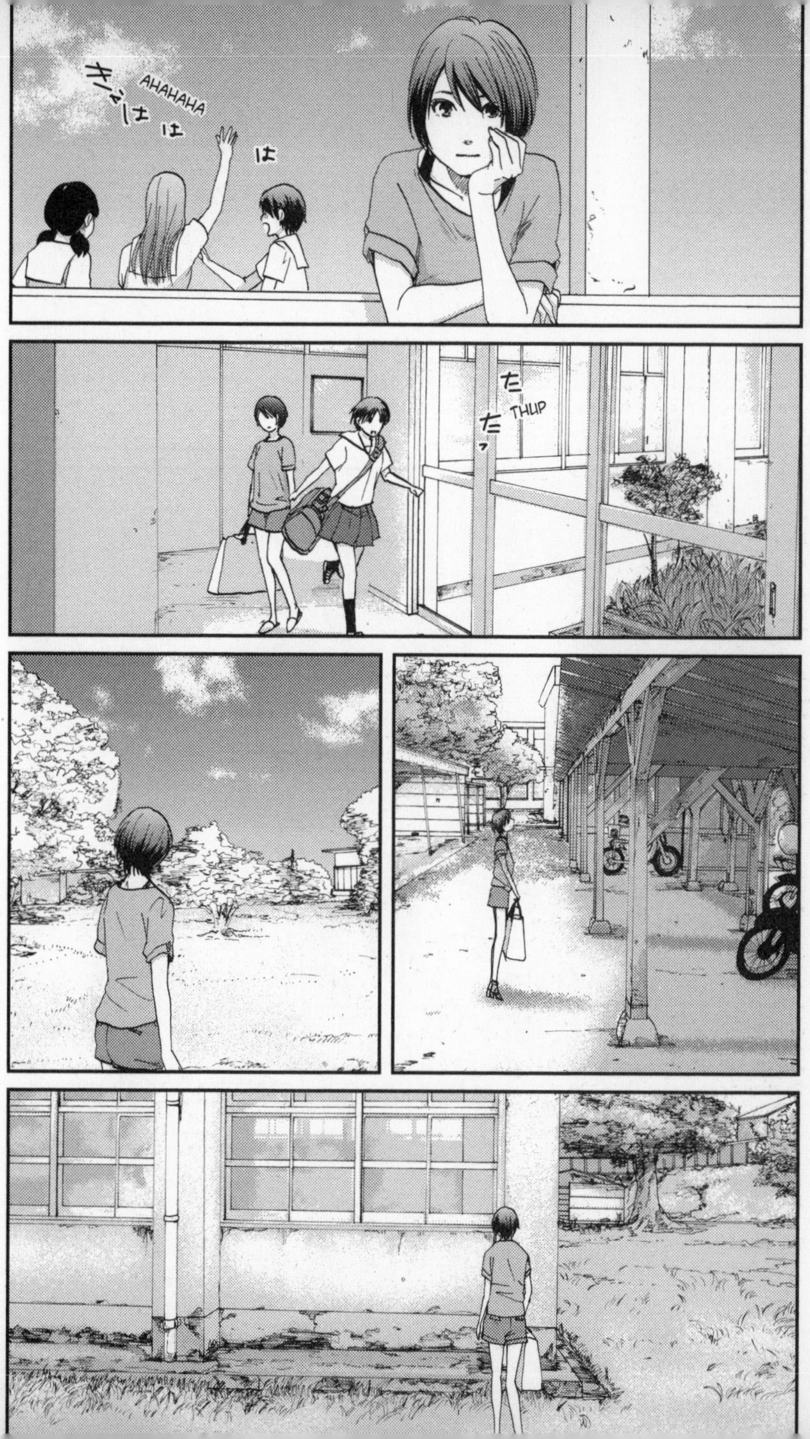

きゃはは
は
は
AHAHAHA
たたっ
THUP

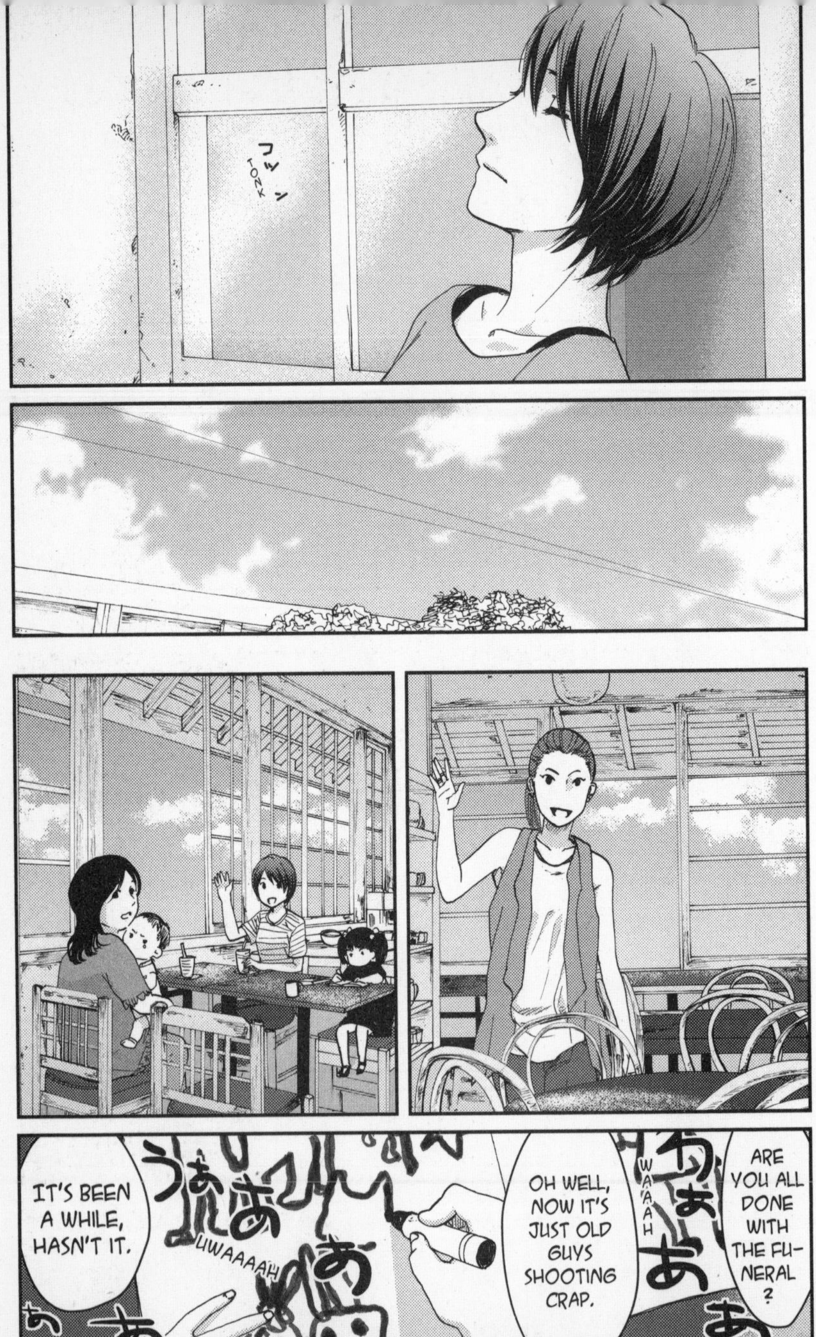
コッン
TONK
ARE YOU ALL DONE WITH THE FU-NERAL?
WAAAH
OH WELL, NOW IT'S JUST OLD GUYS SHOOTING CRAP.
UWAAAAH
IT'S BEEN A WHILE, HASN'T IT.

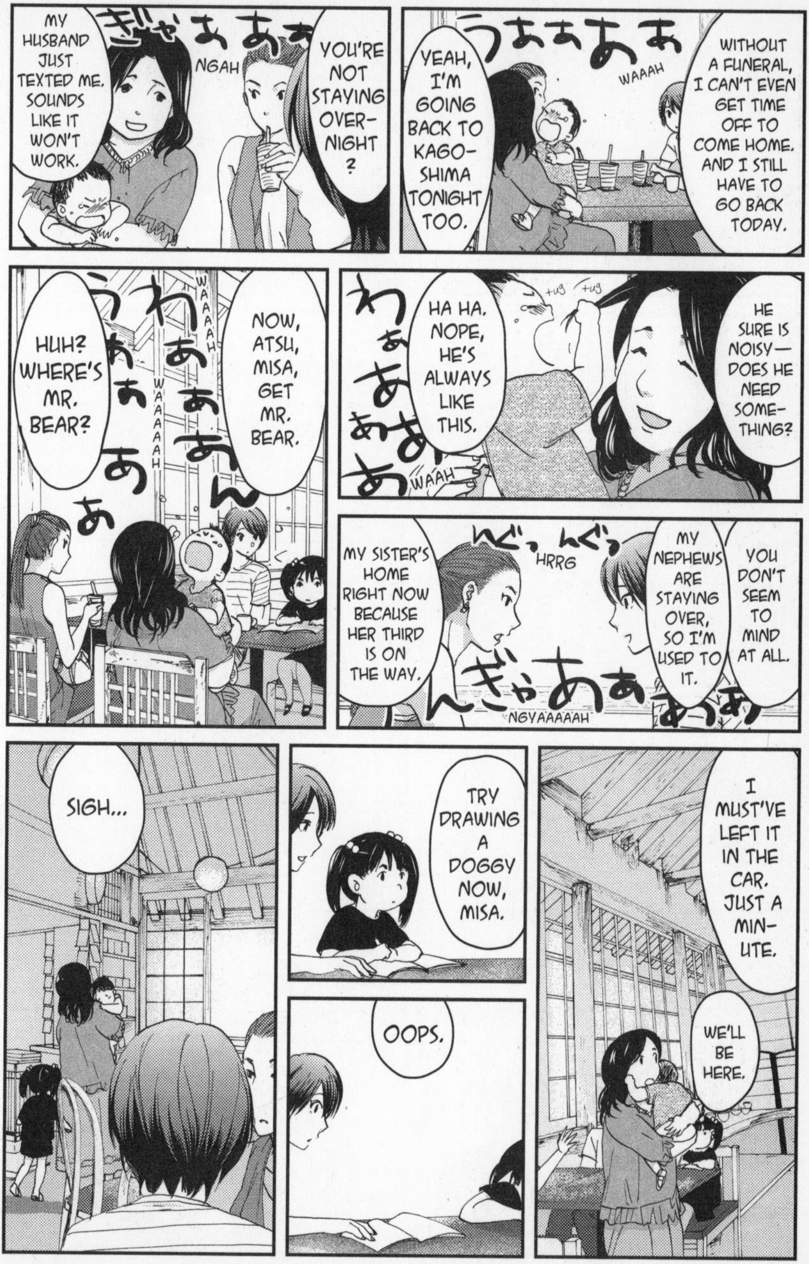
WITHOUT A FUNERAL, I CAN'T EVEN GET TIME OFF TO COME HOME. AND I STILL HAVE TO GO BACK TODAY.
うあぁぁぁ
WAAAH
YEAH, I'M GOING BACK TO KAGO-SHIMA TONIGHT TOO.
YOU'RE NOT STAYING OVER-NIGHT?
ぎゃあぁぁ
NGAH
MY HUSBAND JUST TEXTED ME. SOUNDS LIKE IT WON'T WORK.
HE SURE IS NOISY—DOES HE NEED SOME-THING?
tug tug
HA HA. NOPE, HE'S ALWAYS LIKE THIS.
わぁあぁあぁあ
WAAH
YOU DON'T SEEM TO MIND AT ALL.
MY NEPHEWS ARE STAYING OVER, SO I'M USED TO IT.
んぐっんぐっ
HRRG
MY SISTER'S HOME RIGHT NOW BECAUSE HER THIRD IS ON THE WAY.
んぎゃあぁあっあっ
NGYAAAAAH
NOW, ATSU, MISA, GET MR. BEAR.
WAAAAH
うわぁぁあぁあんあ
WAAAAAH
HUH? WHERE'S MR. BEAR?
I MUST'VE LEFT IT IN THE CAR. JUST A MIN-UTE.
WE'LL BE HERE.
TRY DRAWING A DOGGY NOW, MISA.
OOPS.
SIGH...

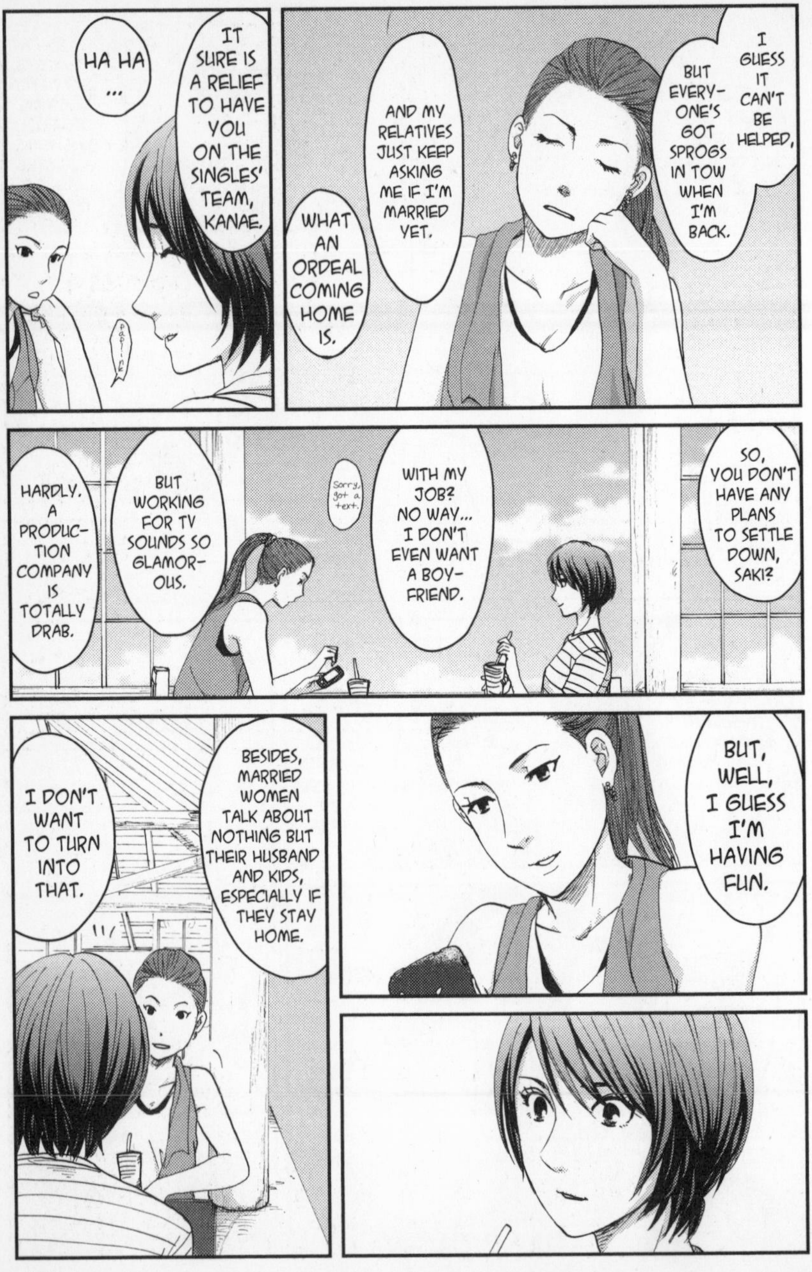
I GUESS IT CAN'T BE HELPED,
BUT EVERY-ONE'S GOT SPROGS IN TOW WHEN I'M BACK.
AND MY RELATIVES JUST KEEP ASKING ME IF I'M MARRIED YET.
WHAT AN ORDEAL COMING HOME IS.
IT SURE IS A RELIEF TO HAVE YOU ON THE SINGLES' TEAM, KANAE.
HA HA ...
SO, YOU DON'T HAVE ANY PLANS TO SETTLE DOWN, SAKI?
WITH MY JOB? NO WAY... I DON'T EVEN WANT A BOY-FRIEND.
Sorry, got a text.
BUT WORKING FOR TV SOUNDS SO GLAMOR-OUS.
HARDLY. A PRODUC-TION COMPANY IS TOTALLY DRAB.
BUT, WELL, I GUESS I'M HAVING FUN.
BESIDES, MARRIED WOMEN TALK ABOUT NOTHING BUT THEIR HUSBAND AND KIDS, ESPECIALLY IF THEY STAY HOME.
I DON'T WANT TO TURN INTO THAT.

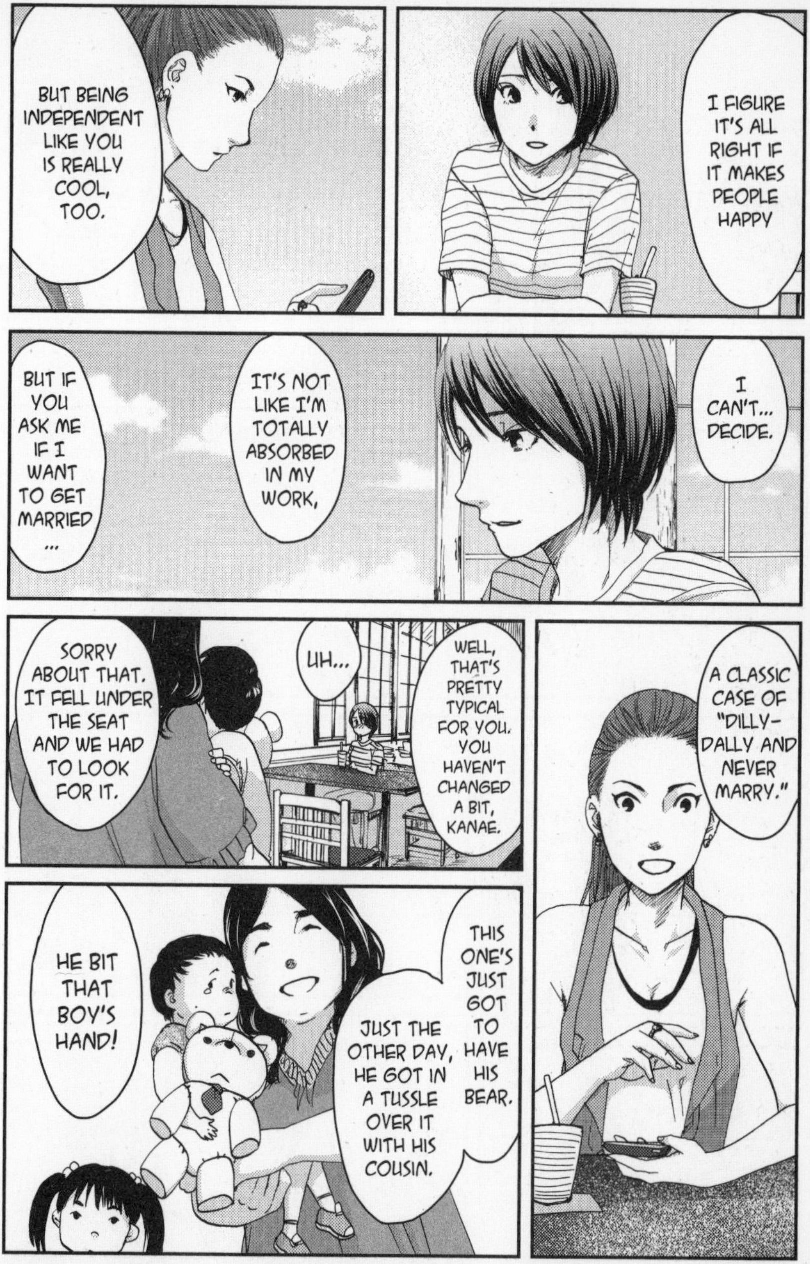
I FIGURE IT'S ALL RIGHT IF IT MAKES PEOPLE HAPPY
BUT BEING INDEPENDENT LIKE YOU IS REALLY COOL, TOO.
I CAN'T... DECIDE.
IT'S NOT LIKE I'M TOTALLY ABSORBED IN MY WORK,
BUT IF YOU ASK ME IF I WANT TO GET MARRIED...
A CLASSIC CASE OF "DILLY-DALLY AND NEVER MARRY."
WELL, THAT'S PRETTY TYPICAL FOR YOU. YOU HAVEN'T CHANGED A BIT, KANAE.
UH...
SORRY ABOUT THAT. IT FELL UNDER THE SEAT AND WE HAD TO LOOK FOR IT.
THIS ONE'S JUST GOT TO HAVE HIS BEAR.
JUST THE OTHER DAY, HE GOT IN A TUSSLE OVER IT WITH HIS COUSIN.
HE BIT THAT BOY'S HAND!

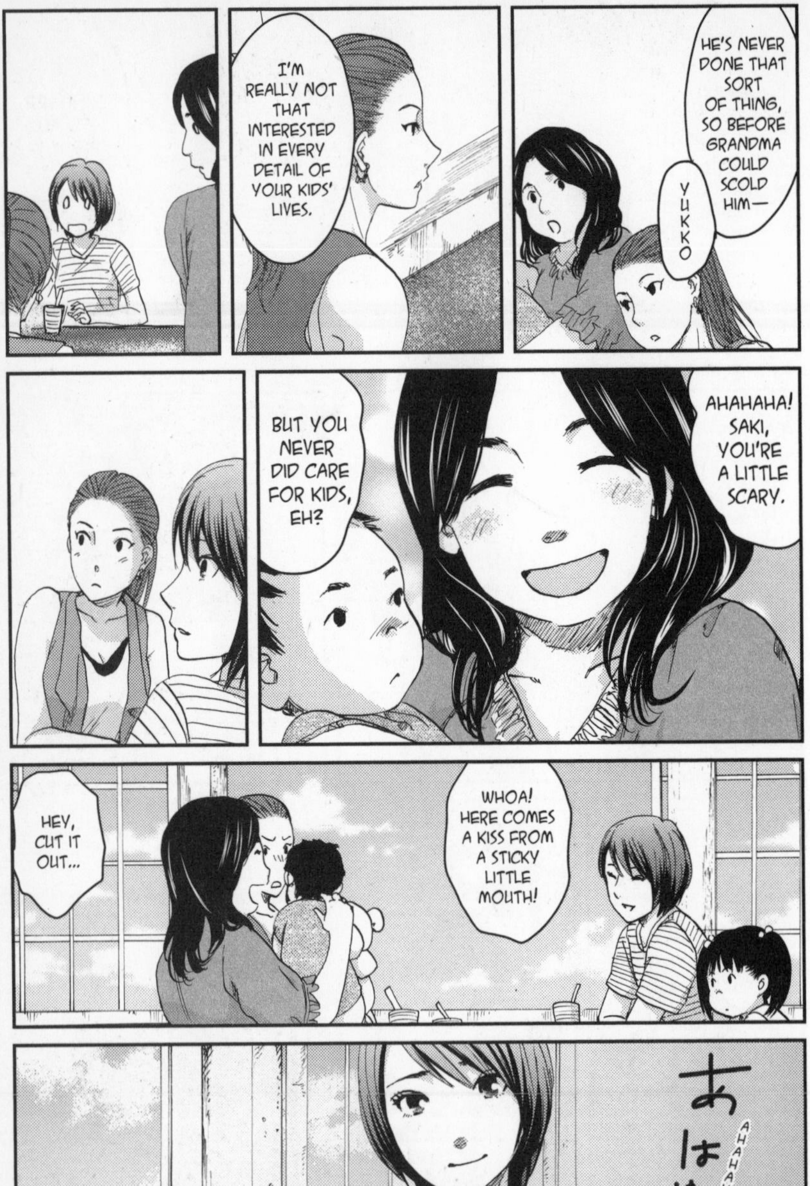
HE'S NEVER DONE THAT SORT OF THING, SO BEFORE GRANDMA COULD SCOLD HIM—
YUKKO
I'M REALLY NOT THAT INTERESTED IN EVERY DETAIL OF YOUR KIDS' LIVES.
AHAHAHA! SAKI, YOU'RE A LITTLE SCARY.
BUT YOU NEVER DID CARE FOR KIDS, EH?
WHOA! HERE COMES A KISS FROM A STICKY LITTLE MOUTH!
HEY, CUT IT OUT...
あはは
は
AHAHAHA

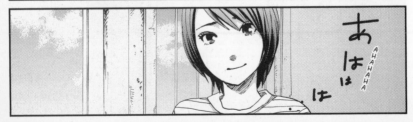

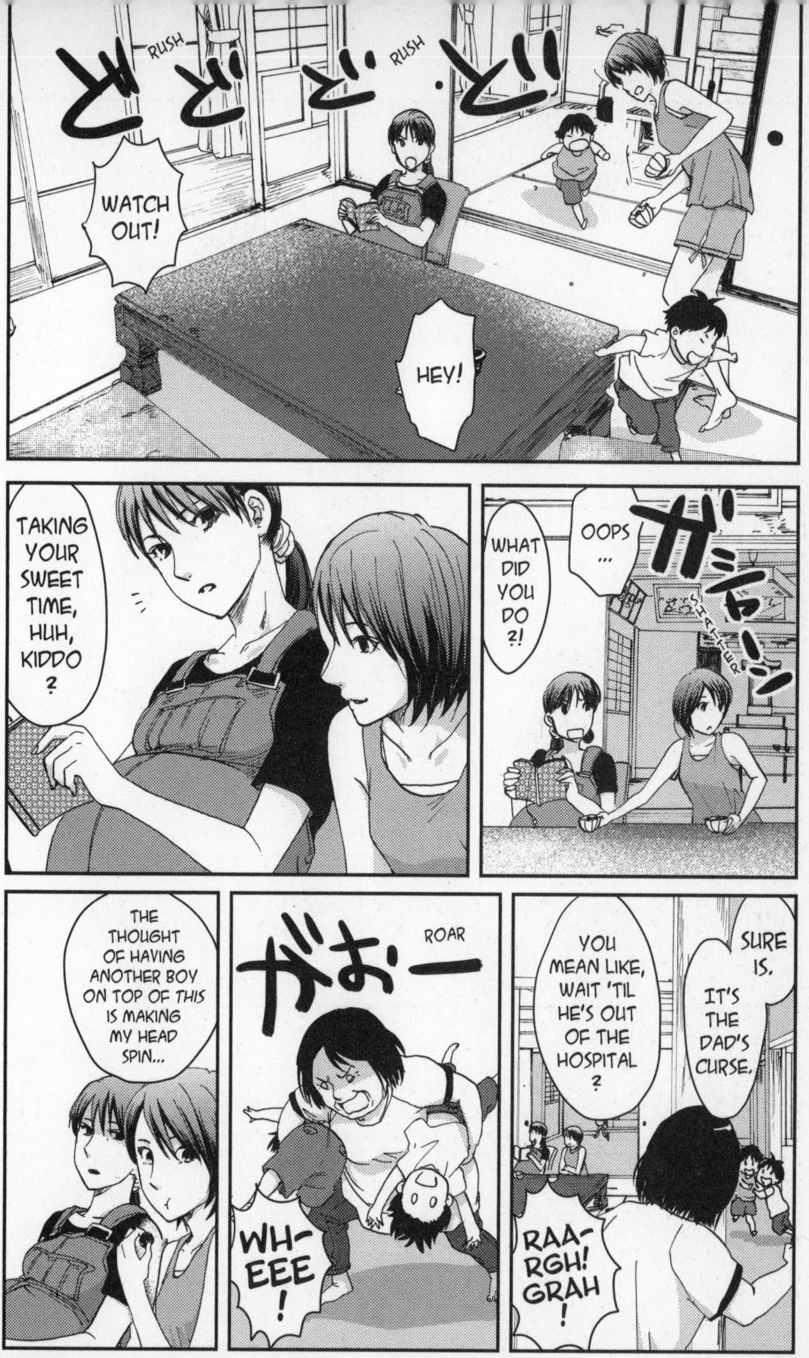
RUSH
RUSH
WATCH OUT!
HEY!
OOPS ...
WHAT DID YOU DO ?!
SHATTER
TAKING YOUR SWEET TIME, HUH, KIDDO ?
SURE IS. IT'S THE DAD'S CURSE.
YOU MEAN LIKE, WAIT 'TIL HE'S OUT OF THE HOSPITAL ?
RAA-RGH! GRAH !
がおー
ROAR
WH-EEE !
THE THOUGHT OF HAVING ANOTHER BOY ON TOP OF THIS IS MAKING MY HEAD SPIN...

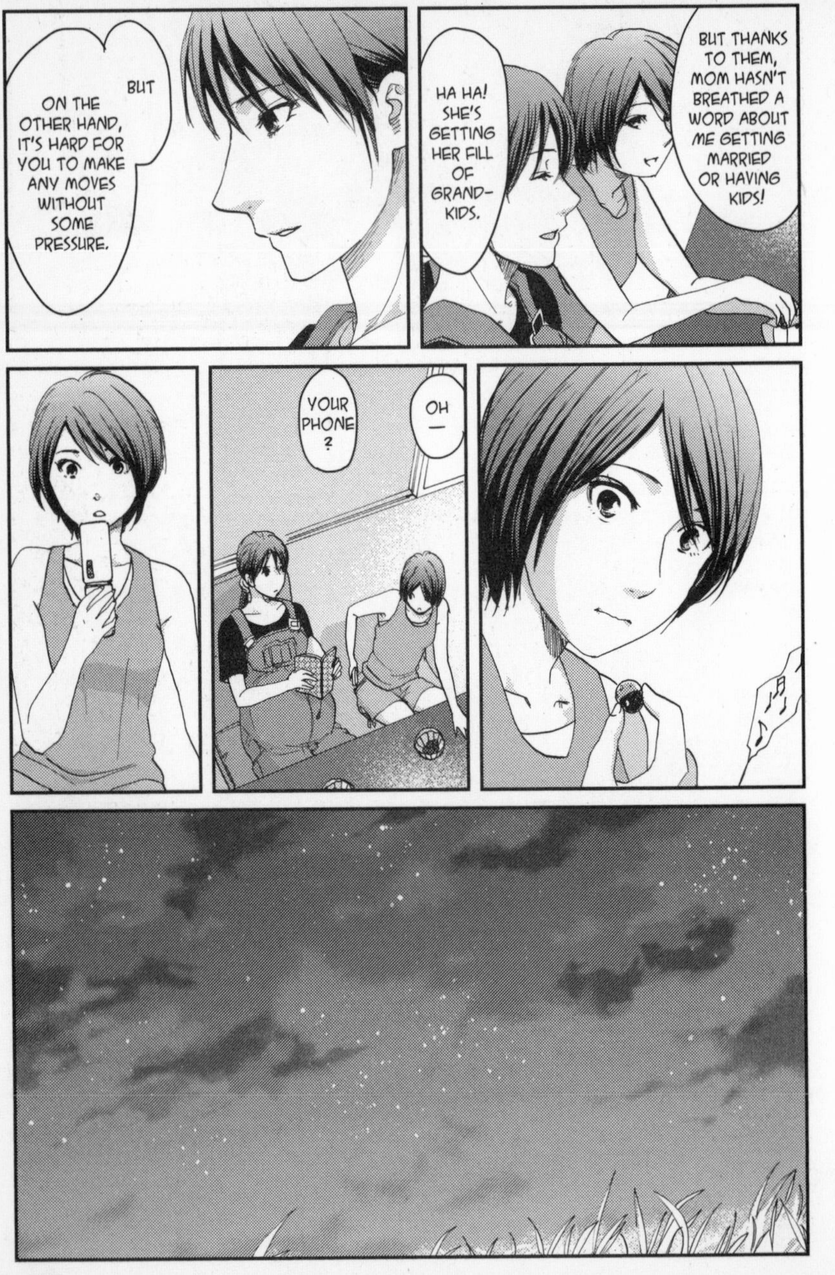
BUT THANKS TO THEM, MOM HASN'T BREATHED A WORD ABOUT ME GETTING MARRIED OR HAVING KIDS!
HA HA! SHE'S GETTING HER FILL OF GRAND-KIDS.
BUT ON THE OTHER HAND, IT'S HARD FOR YOU TO MAKE ANY MOVES WITHOUT SOME PRESSURE.
OH —
YOUR PHONE?

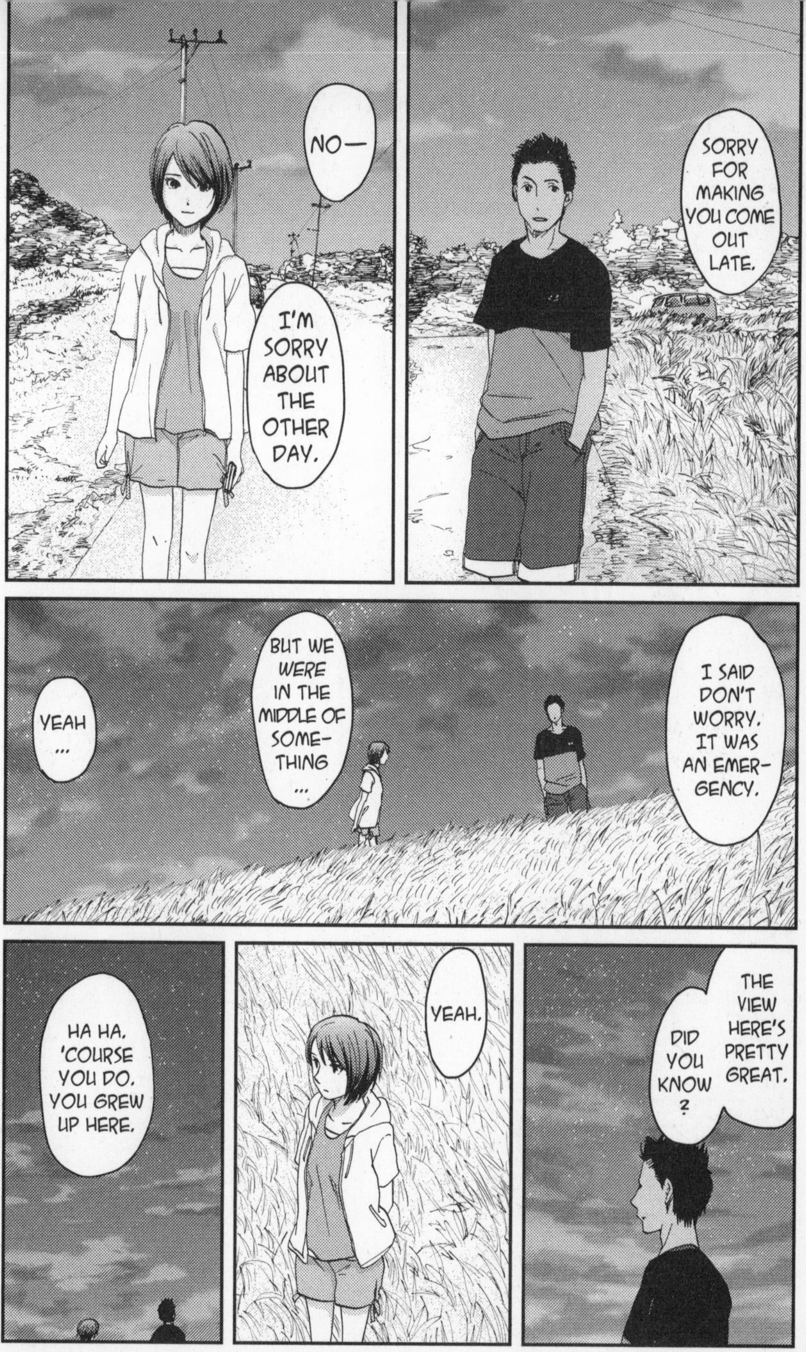
SORRY FOR MAKING YOU COME OUT LATE.
NO—
I'M SORRY ABOUT THE OTHER DAY.
I SAID DON'T WORRY. IT WAS AN EMER-GENCY.
BUT WE WERE IN THE MIDDLE OF SOME-THING ...
YEAH ...
THE VIEW HERE'S PRETTY GREAT.
DID YOU KNOW?
YEAH.
HA HA. 'COURSE YOU DO. YOU GREW UP HERE.

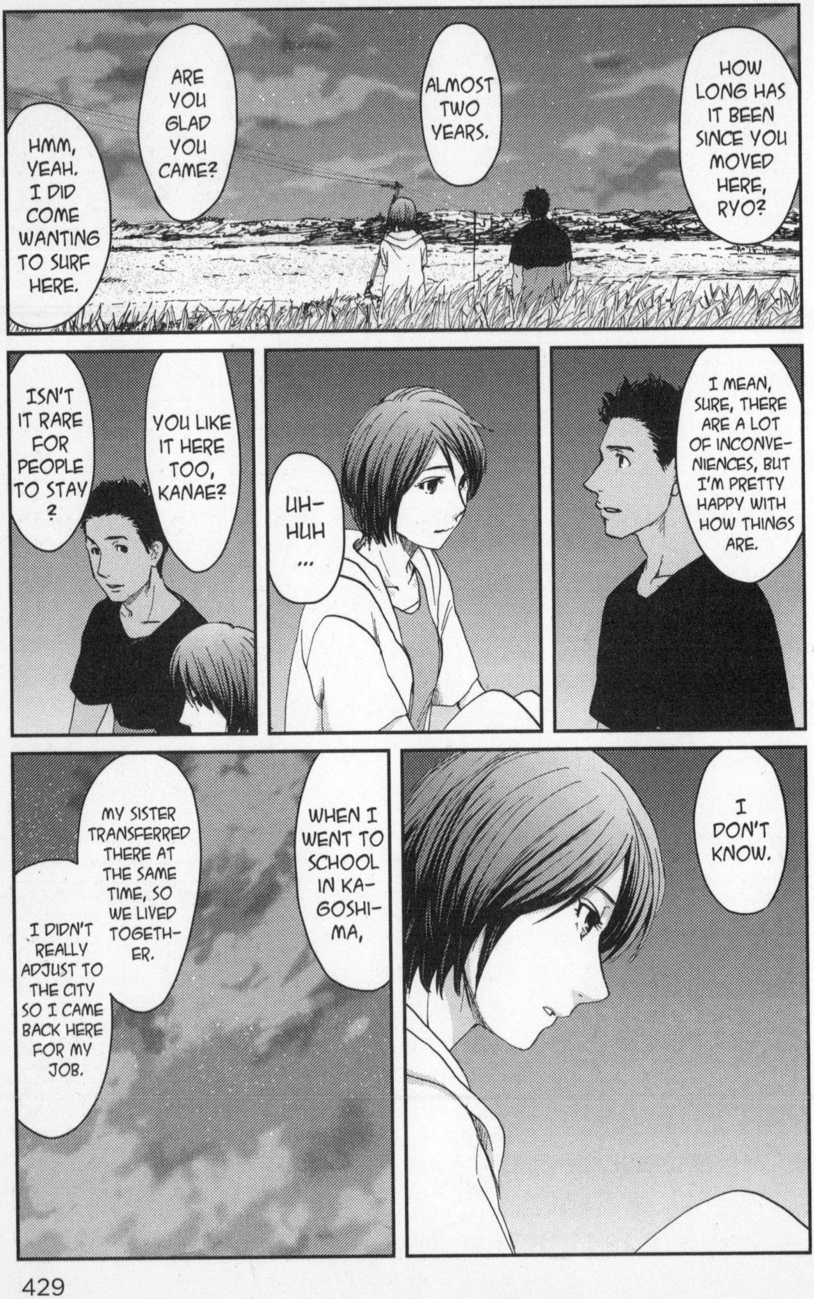
HOW LONG HAS IT BEEN SINCE YOU MOVED HERE, RYO?
ALMOST TWO YEARS.
ARE YOU GLAD YOU CAME?
HMM, YEAH. I DID COME WANTING TO SURF HERE.
I MEAN, SURE, THERE ARE A LOT OF INCONVE-NIENCES, BUT I'M PRETTY HAPPY WITH HOW THINGS ARE.
UH-HUH ...
YOU LIKE IT HERE TOO, KANAE?
ISN'T IT RARE FOR PEOPLE TO STAY?
I DON'T KNOW.
WHEN I WENT TO SCHOOL IN KA-GOSHI-MA,
MY SISTER TRANSFERRED THERE AT THE SAME TIME, SO WE LIVED TOGETH-ER.
I DIDN'T REALLY ADJUST TO THE CITY SO I CAME BACK HERE FOR MY JOB.

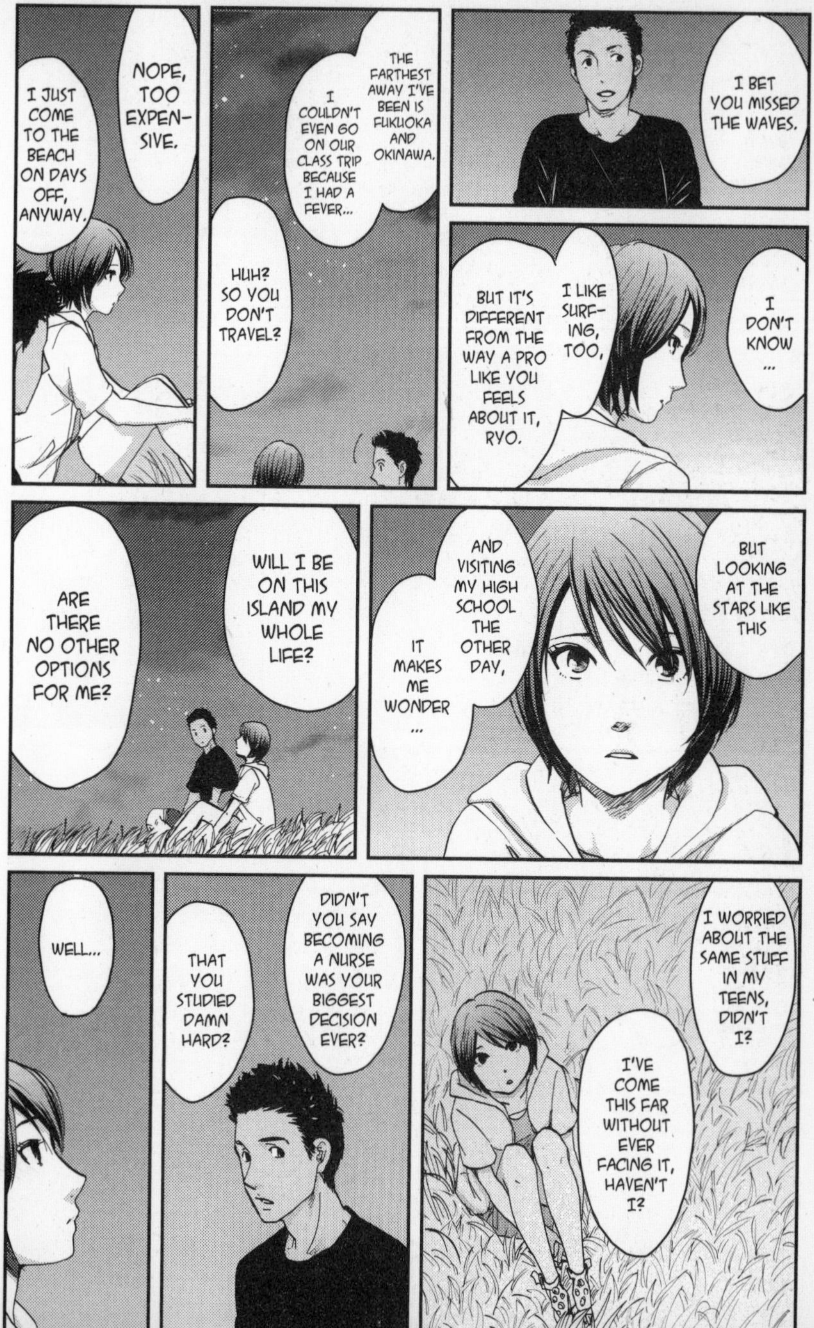
I BET YOU MISSED THE WAVES.
I DON'T KNOW ...
I LIKE SURF-ING, TOO,
BUT IT'S DIFFERENT FROM THE WAY A PRO LIKE YOU FEELS ABOUT IT, RYO.
THE FARTHEST AWAY I'VE BEEN IS FUKUOKA AND OKINAWA.
I COULDN'T EVEN GO ON OUR CLASS TRIP BECAUSE I HAD A FEVER...
HUH? SO YOU DON'T TRAVEL?
NOPE, TOO EXPEN-SIVE.
I JUST COME TO THE BEACH ON DAYS OFF, ANYWAY.
BUT LOOKING AT THE STARS LIKE THIS
AND VISITING MY HIGH SCHOOL THE OTHER DAY,
IT MAKES ME WONDER ...
WILL I BE ON THIS ISLAND MY WHOLE LIFE?
ARE THERE NO OTHER OPTIONS FOR ME?
I WORRIED ABOUT THE SAME STUFF IN MY TEENS, DIDN'T I?
I'VE COME THIS FAR WITHOUT EVER FACING IT, HAVEN'T I?
DIDN'T YOU SAY BECOMING A NURSE WAS YOUR BIGGEST DECISION EVER?
THAT YOU STUDIED DAMN HARD?
WELL...

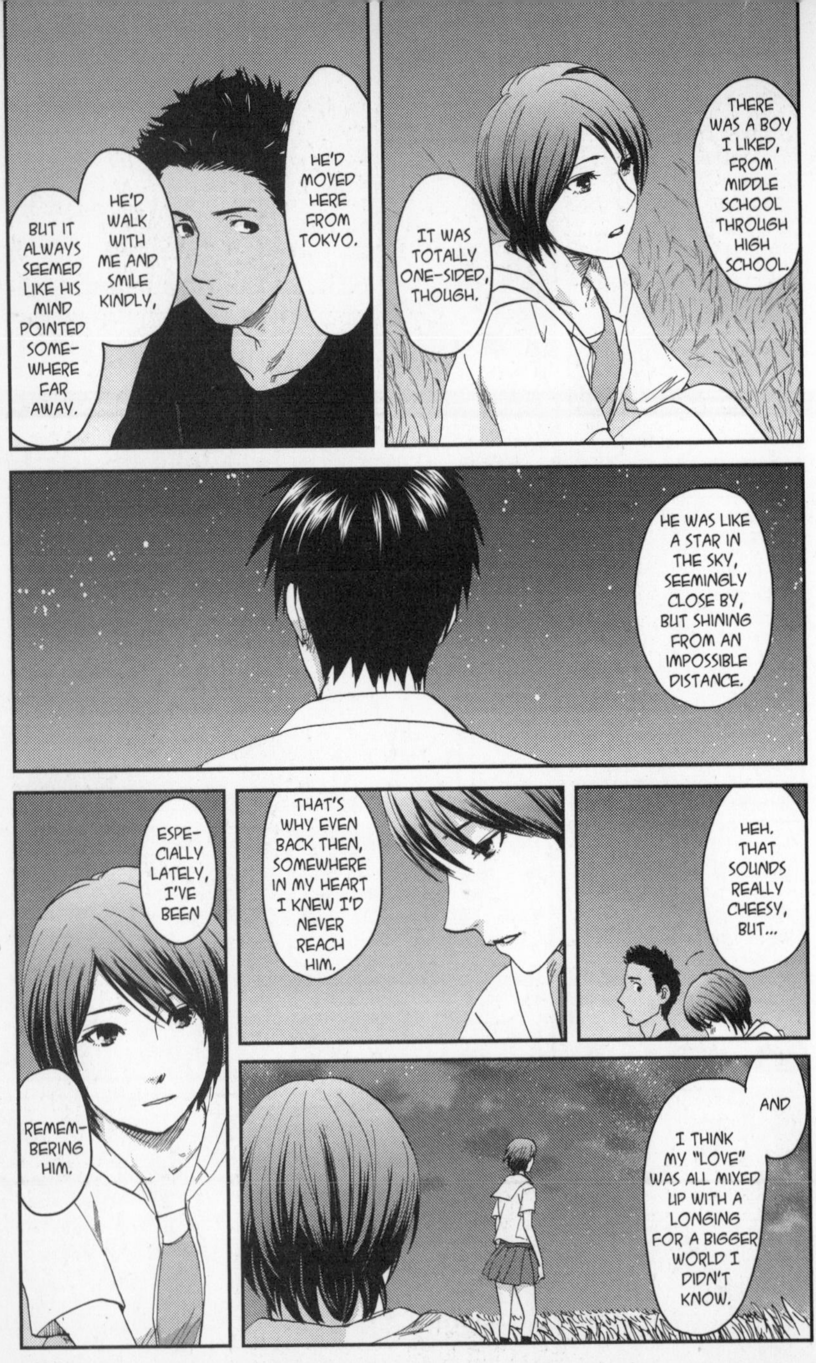
THERE WAS A BOY I LIKED, FROM MIDDLE SCHOOL THROUGH HIGH SCHOOL.
IT WAS TOTALLY ONE-SIDED, THOUGH.
HE'D MOVED HERE FROM TOKYO.
HE'D WALK WITH ME AND SMILE KINDLY,
BUT IT ALWAYS SEEMED LIKE HIS MIND POINTED SOME-WHERE FAR AWAY.
HE WAS LIKE A STAR IN THE SKY, SEEMINGLY CLOSE BY, BUT SHINING FROM AN IMPOSSIBLE DISTANCE.
HEH. THAT SOUNDS REALLY CHEESY, BUT...
THAT'S WHY EVEN BACK THEN, SOMEWHERE IN MY HEART I KNEW I'D NEVER REACH HIM.
AND
I THINK MY "LOVE" WAS ALL MIXED UP WITH A LONGING FOR A BIGGER WORLD I DIDN'T KNOW.
ESPE-CIALLY LATELY, I'VE BEEN
REMEM-BERING HIM.

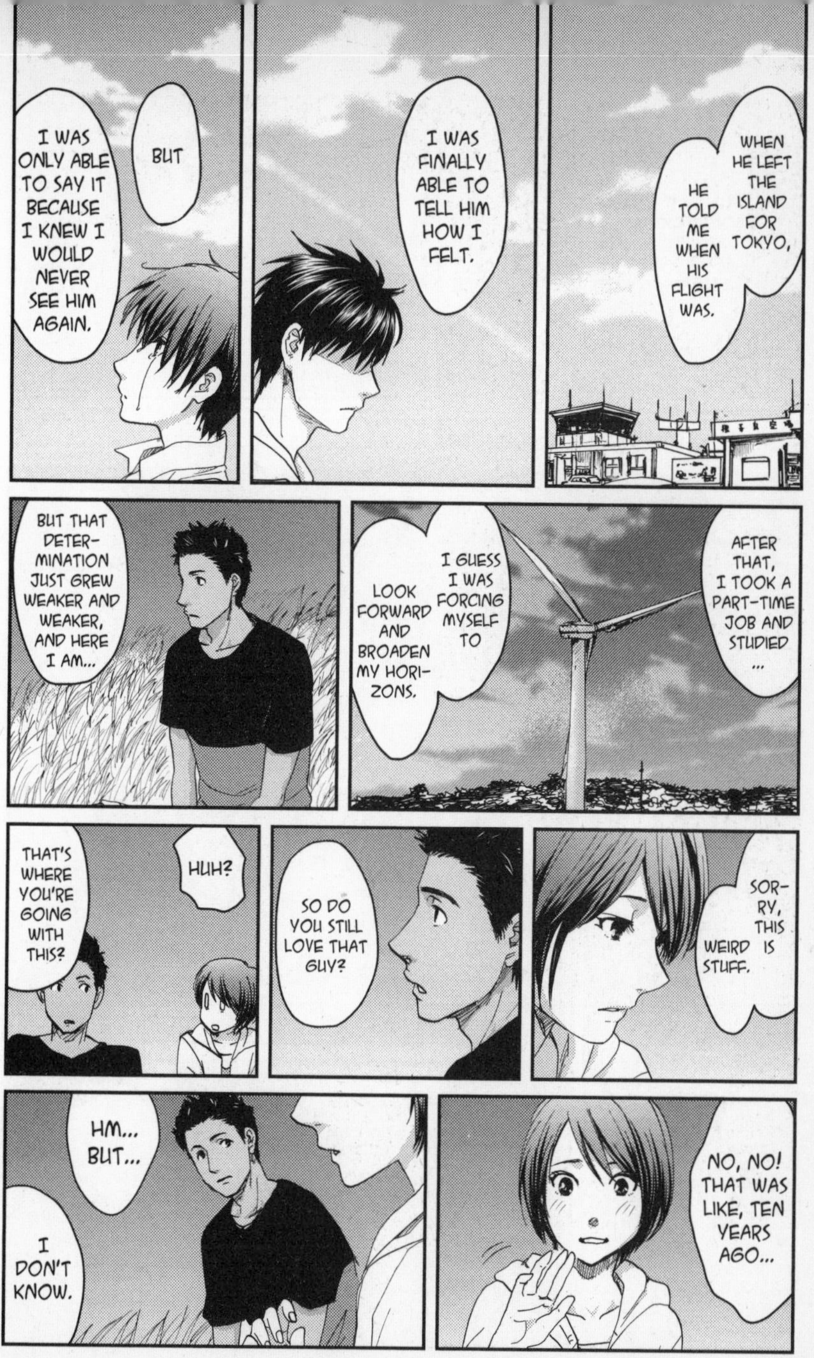
WHEN HE LEFT THE ISLAND FOR TOKYO,
HE TOLD ME WHEN HIS FLIGHT WAS.
I WAS FINALLY ABLE TO TELL HIM HOW I FELT.
BUT
I WAS ONLY ABLE TO SAY IT BECAUSE I KNEW I WOULD NEVER SEE HIM AGAIN.
AFTER THAT, I TOOK A PART-TIME JOB AND STUDIED ...
I GUESS I WAS FORCING MYSELF TO
LOOK FORWARD AND BROADEN MY HORIZONS.
BUT THAT DETERMINATION JUST GREW WEAKER AND WEAKER, AND HERE I AM...
SORRY, THIS IS WEIRD STUFF.
SO DO YOU STILL LOVE THAT GUY?
HUH?
THAT'S WHERE YOU'RE GOING WITH THIS?
NO, NO! THAT WAS LIKE, TEN YEARS AGO...
HM... BUT...
I DON'T KNOW.

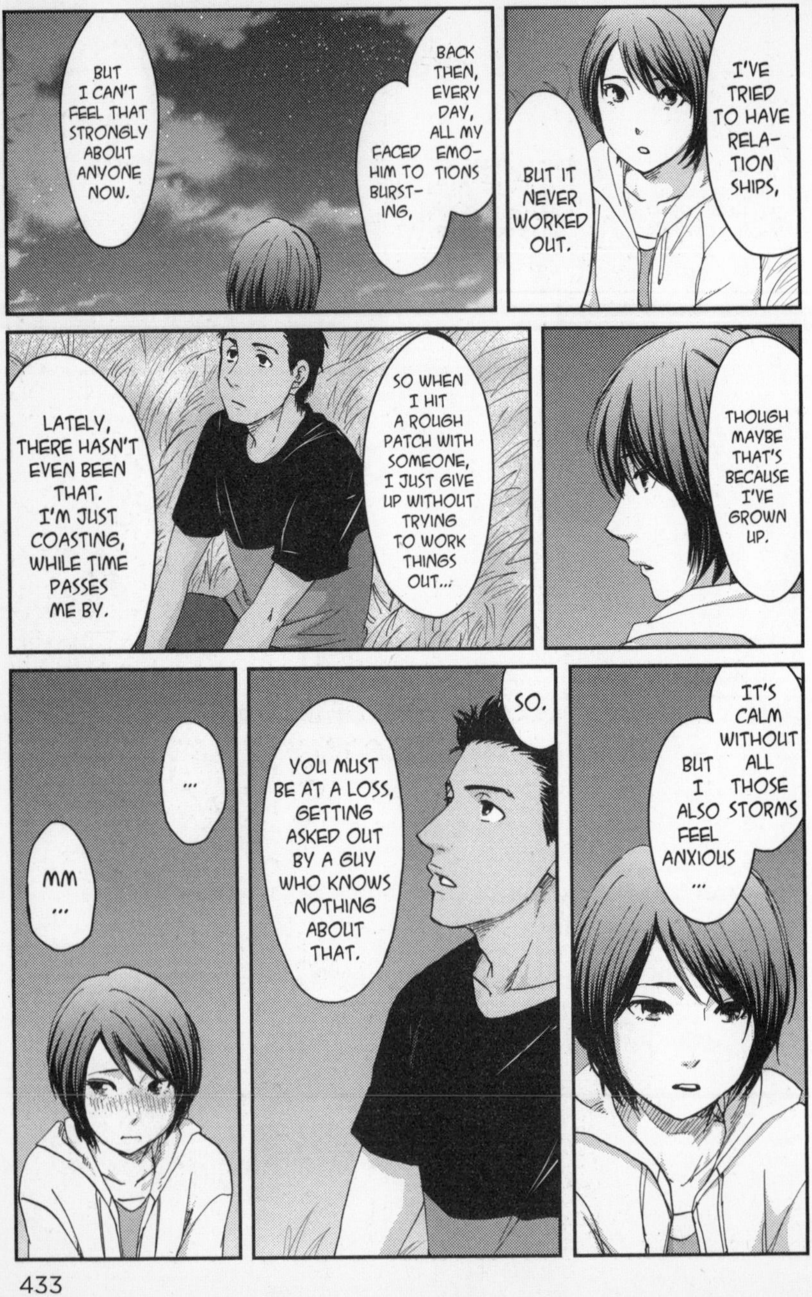
I'VE TRIED TO HAVE RELATIONSHIPS,
BUT IT NEVER WORKED OUT.
BACK THEN, EVERY DAY, ALL MY EMOTIONS
FACED HIM TO BURSTING,
BUT I CAN'T FEEL THAT STRONGLY ABOUT ANYONE NOW.
THOUGH MAYBE THAT'S BECAUSE I'VE GROWN UP.
SO WHEN I HIT A ROUGH PATCH WITH SOMEONE, I JUST GIVE UP WITHOUT TRYING TO WORK THINGS OUT...
LATELY, THERE HASN'T EVEN BEEN THAT. I'M JUST COASTING, WHILE TIME PASSES ME BY.
IT'S CALM WITHOUT ALL THOSE STORMS
BUT I ALSO FEEL ANXIOUS ...
SO.
YOU MUST BE AT A LOSS, GETTING ASKED OUT BY A GUY WHO KNOWS NOTHING ABOUT THAT.
...
MM ...

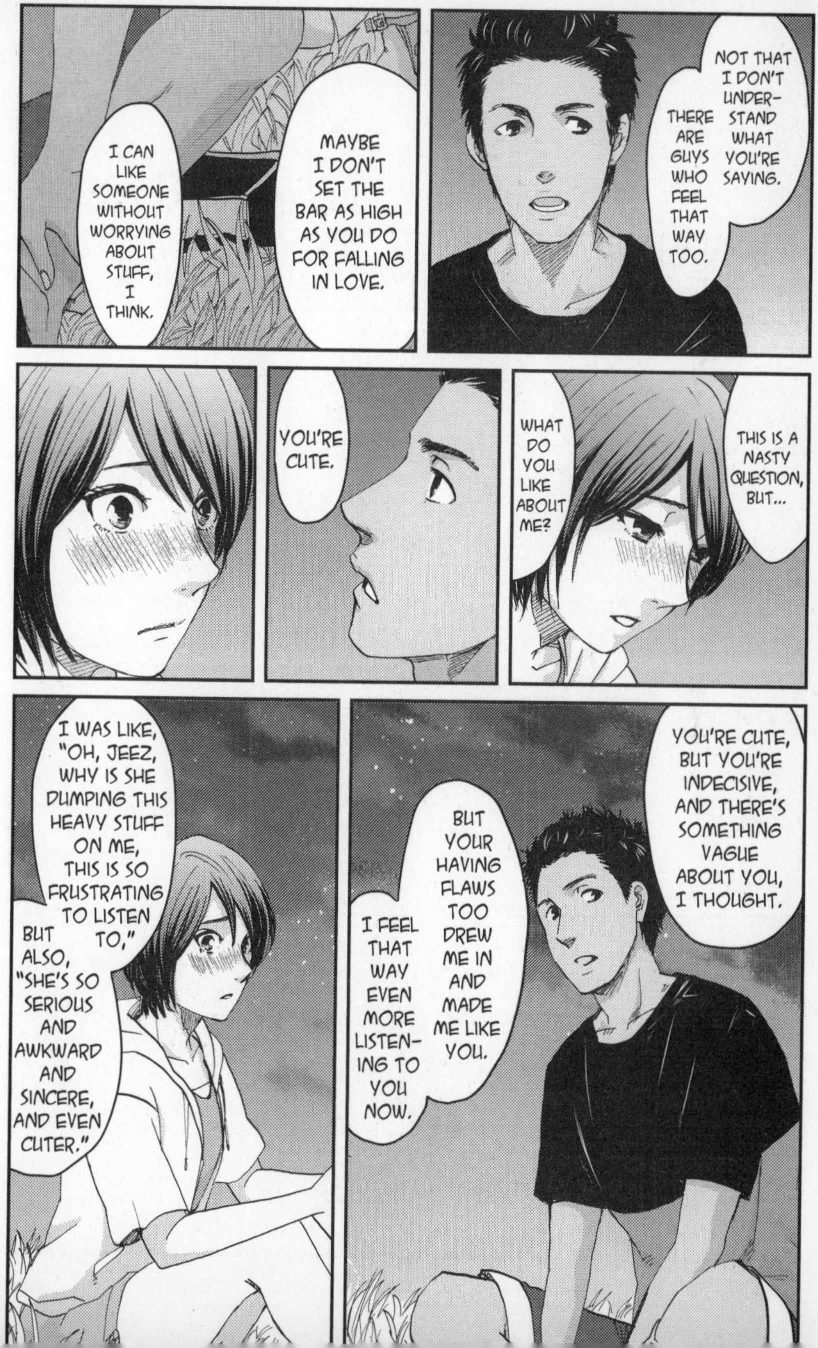
NOT THAT I DON'T UNDER-STAND WHAT YOU'RE SAYING.
THERE ARE GUYS WHO FEEL THAT WAY TOO.
MAYBE I DON'T SET THE BAR AS HIGH AS YOU DO FOR FALLING IN LOVE.
I CAN LIKE SOMEONE WITHOUT WORRYING ABOUT STUFF, I THINK.
THIS IS A NASTY QUESTION, BUT...
WHAT DO YOU LIKE ABOUT ME?
YOU'RE CUTE.
YOU'RE CUTE, BUT YOU'RE INDECISIVE, AND THERE'S SOMETHING VAGUE ABOUT YOU, I THOUGHT.
BUT YOUR HAVING FLAWS TOO DREW ME IN AND MADE ME LIKE YOU.
I FEEL THAT WAY EVEN MORE LISTENING TO YOU NOW.
I WAS LIKE, "OH, JEEZ, WHY IS SHE DUMPING THIS HEAVY STUFF ON ME, THIS IS SO FRUSTRATING TO LISTEN TO,"
BUT ALSO, "SHE'S SO SERIOUS AND AWKWARD AND SINCERE, AND EVEN CUTER."

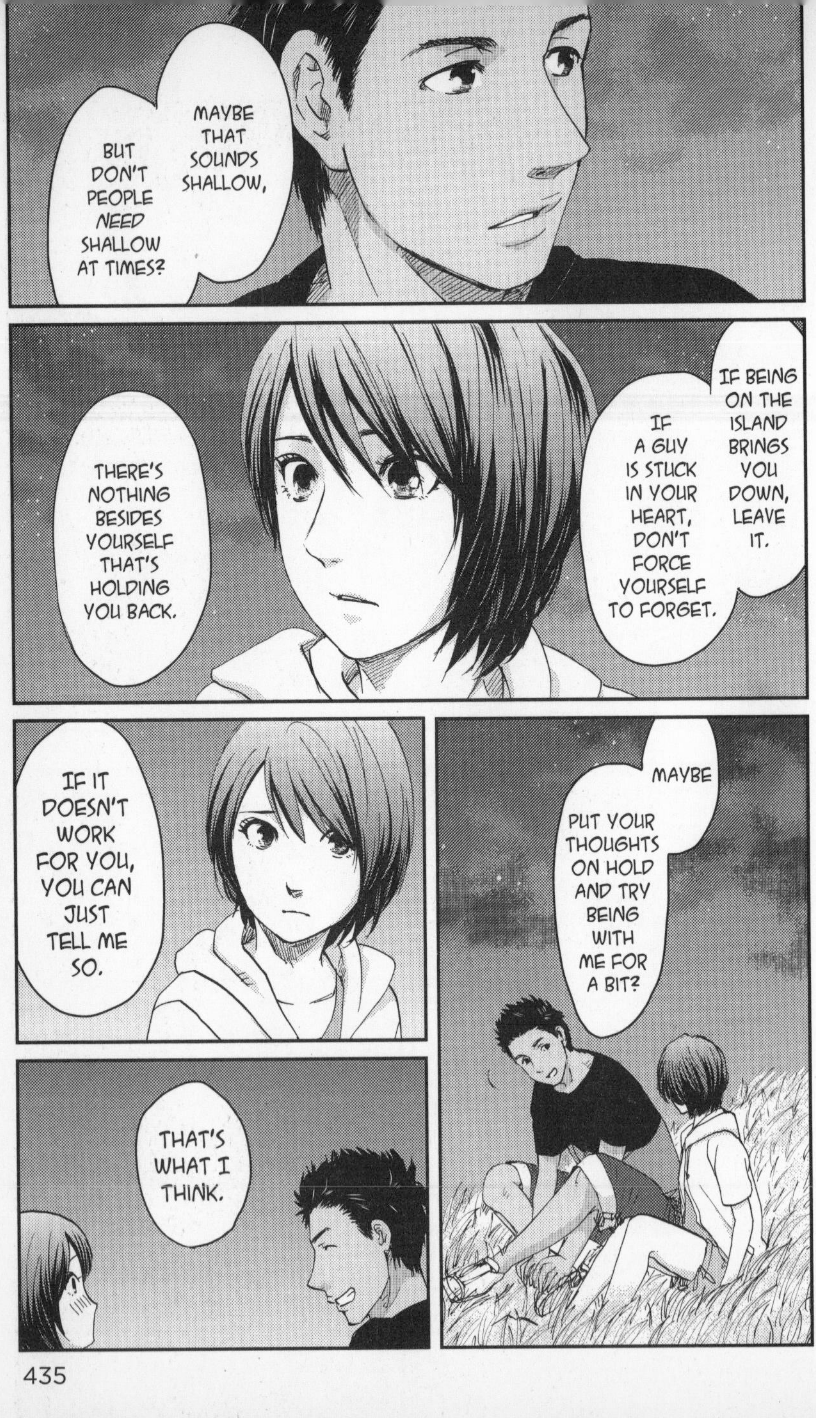
MAYBE THAT SOUNDS SHALLOW,
BUT DON'T PEOPLE NEED SHALLOW AT TIMES?
IF BEING ON THE ISLAND BRINGS YOU DOWN, LEAVE IT.
IF A GUY IS STUCK IN YOUR HEART, DON'T FORCE YOURSELF TO FORGET.
THERE'S NOTHING BESIDES YOURSELF THAT'S HOLDING YOU BACK.
MAYBE
PUT YOUR THOUGHTS ON HOLD AND TRY BEING WITH ME FOR A BIT?
IF IT DOESN'T WORK FOR YOU, YOU CAN JUST TELL ME SO.
THAT'S WHAT I THINK.

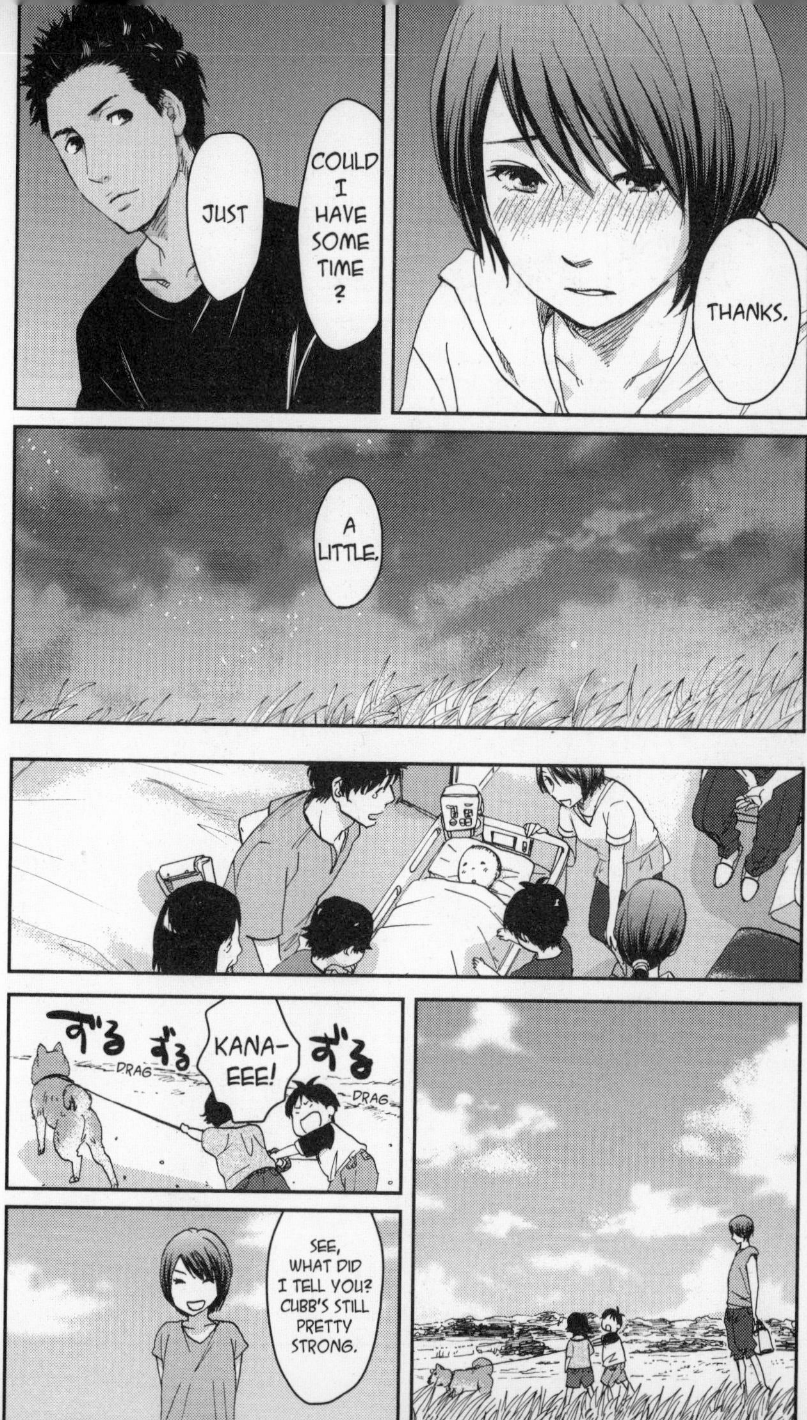
THANKS.
COULD I HAVE SOME TIME?
JUST
A LITTLE.
ずる
DRAG
KANA-EEE!
ずる
ずる
DRAG
SEE, WHAT DID I TELL YOU? CUBB'S STILL PRETTY STRONG.

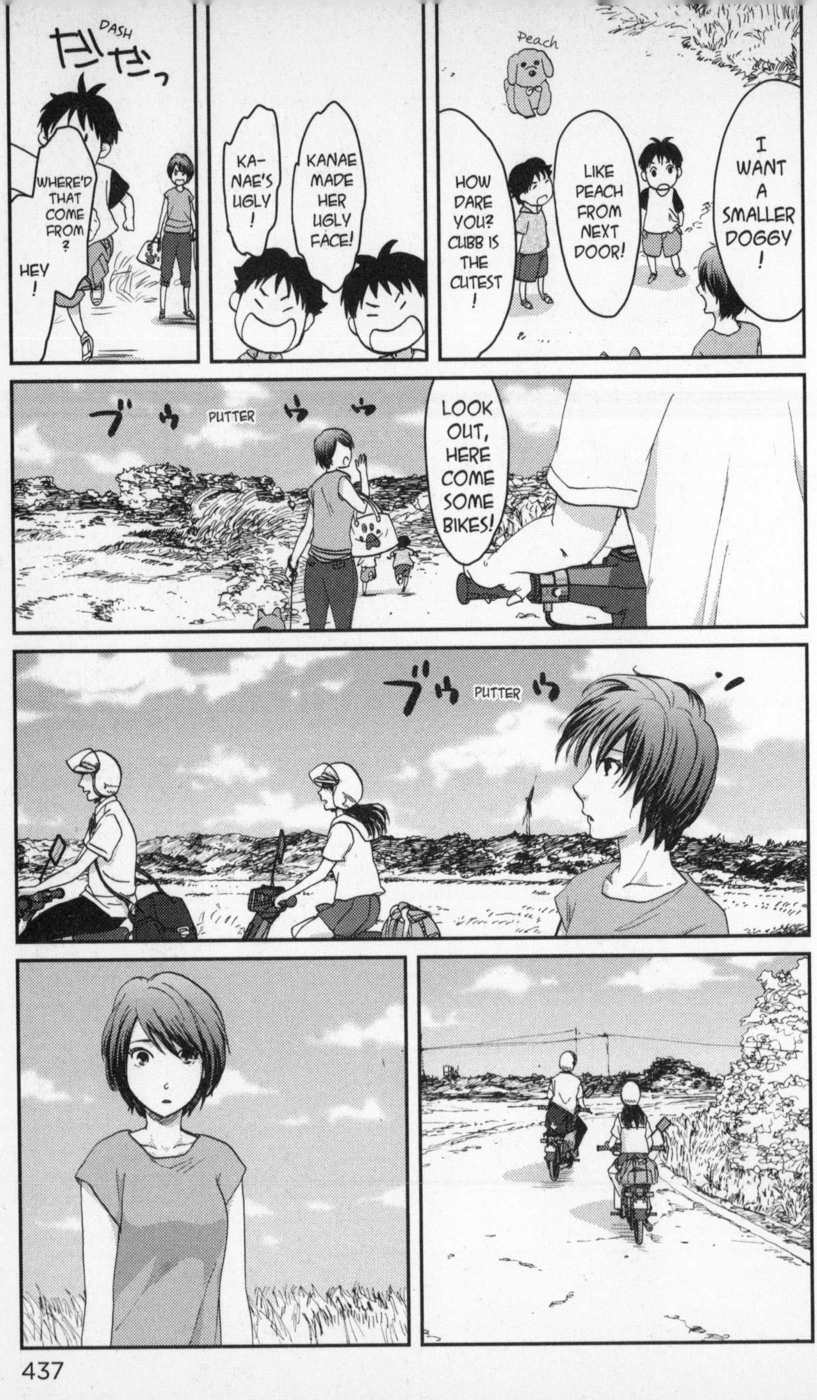

I WANT A SMALLER DOGGY!
Peach
LIKE PEACH FROM NEXT DOOR!
HOW DARE YOU? CUBB IS THE CUTEST!
KANAE MADE HER UGLY FACE!
KA-NAE'S UGLY!
DASH
WHERE'D THAT COME FROM?
HEY!
LOOK OUT, HERE COME SOME BIKES!
PUTTER
PUTTER

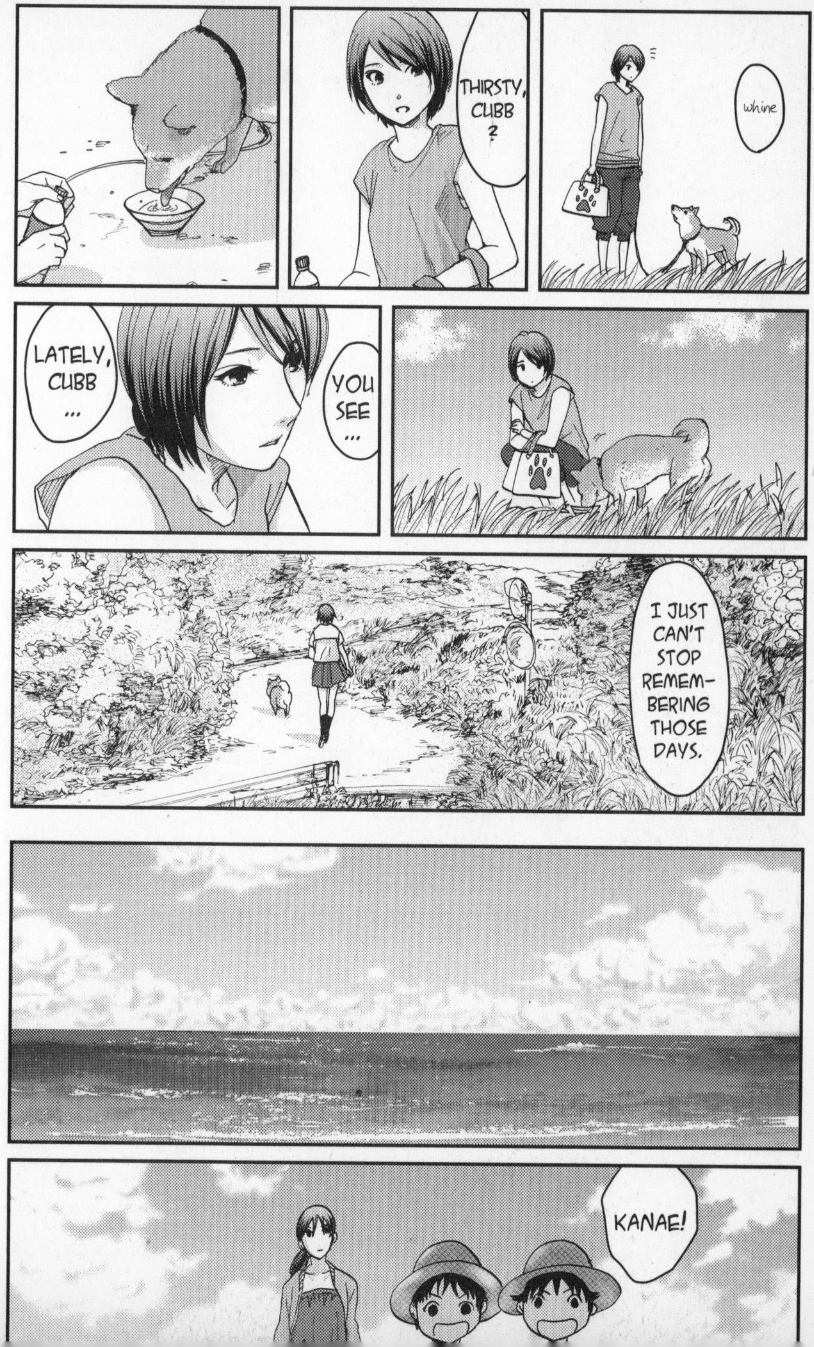
whine
THIRSTY, CUBB?
YOU SEE ...
LATELY, CUBB ...
I JUST CAN'T STOP REMEMBERING THOSE DAYS.
KANAE!

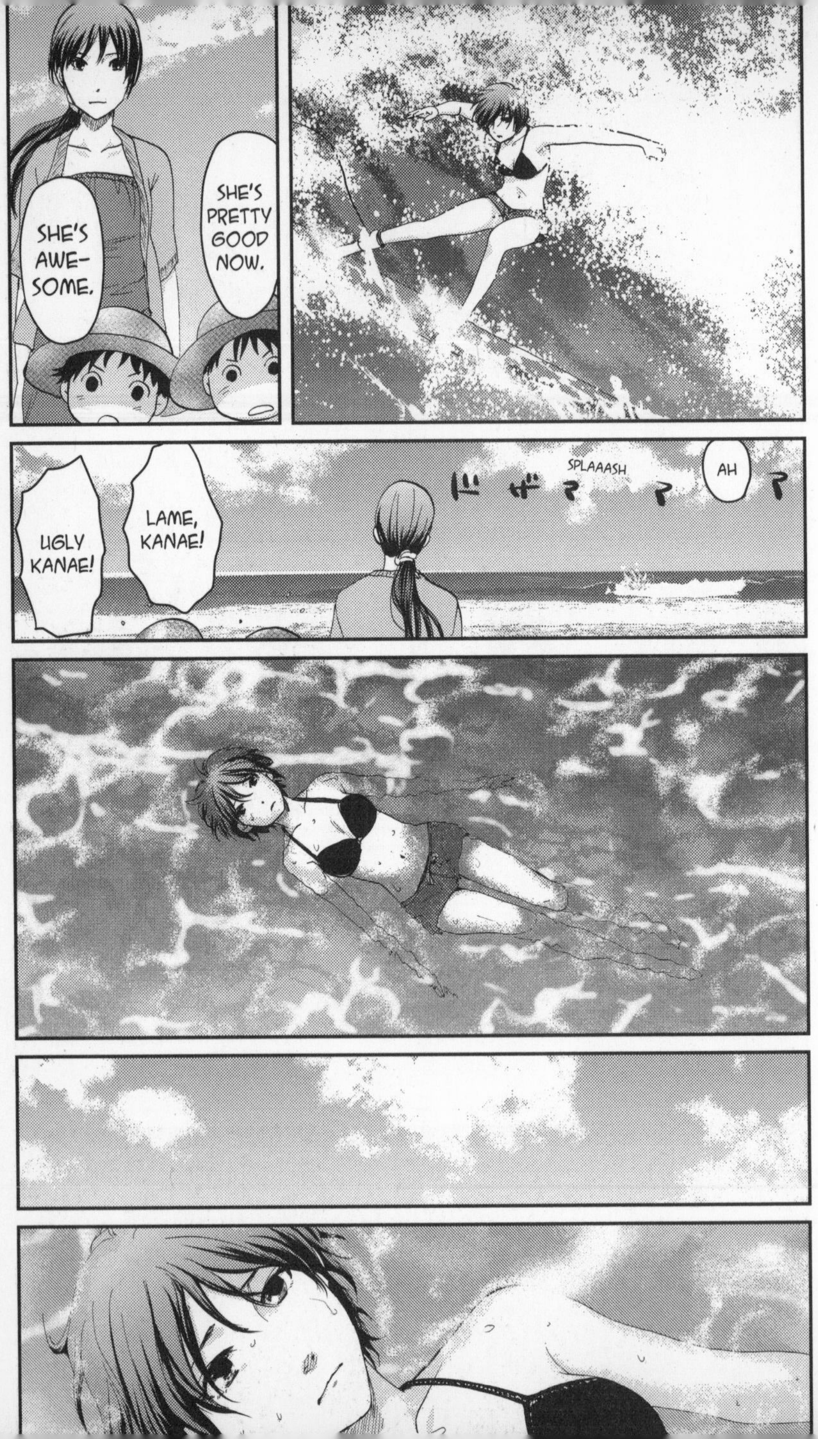
SHE'S PRETTY GOOD NOW.
SHE'S AWE-SOME.
AH
SPLAAASH
LAME, KANAE!
UGLY KANAE!

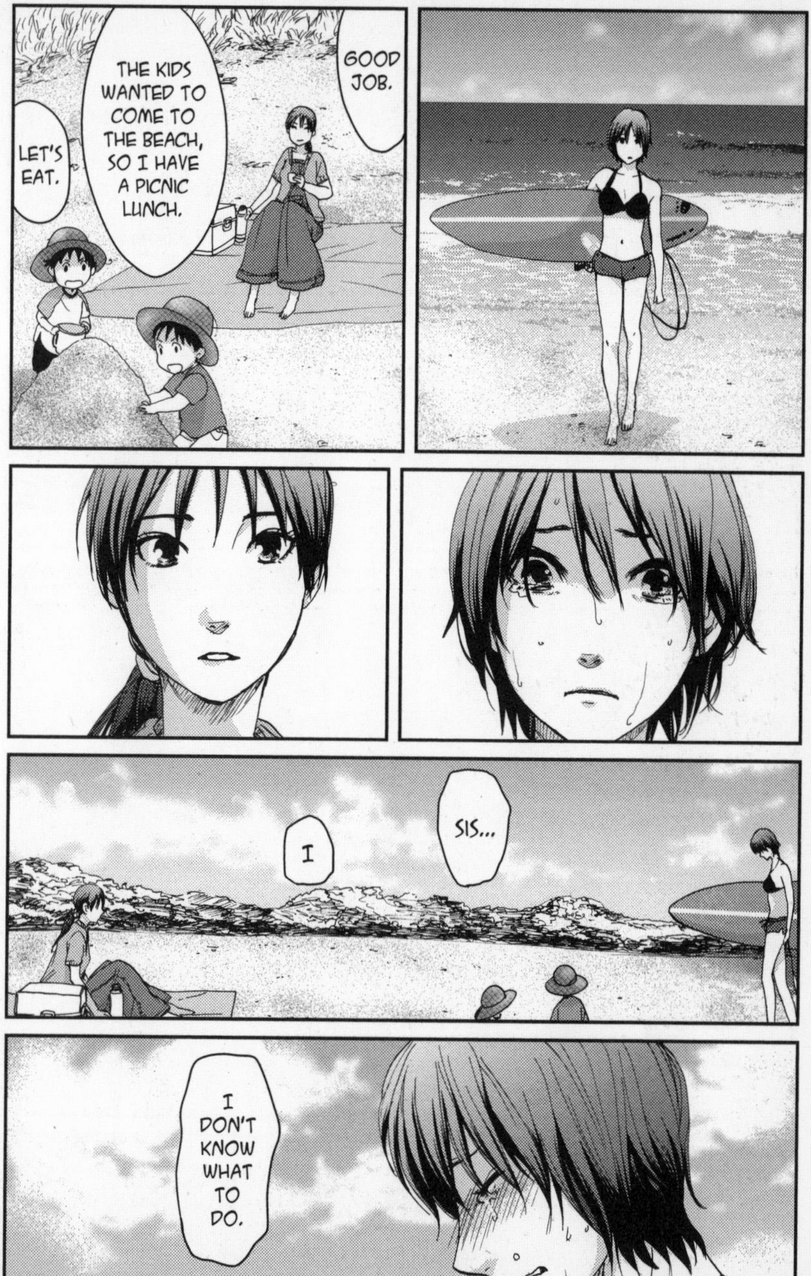
GOOD JOB.
THE KIDS WANTED TO COME TO THE BEACH, SO I HAVE A PICNIC LUNCH.
LET'S EAT.
SIS...
I
I DON'T KNOW WHAT TO DO.

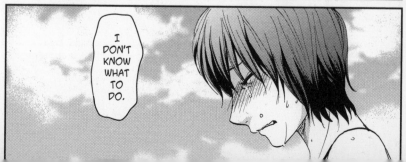

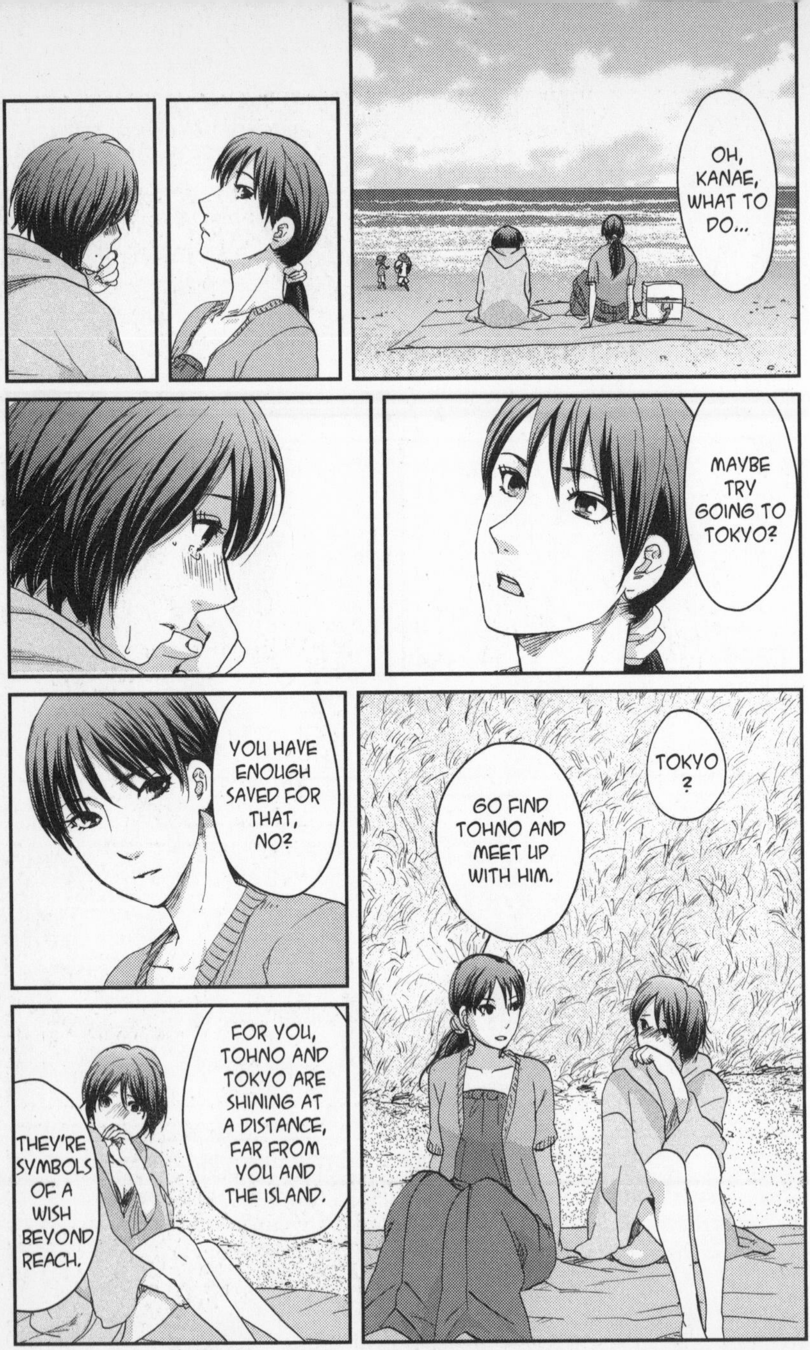
OH, KANAE, WHAT TO DO...
MAYBE TRY GOING TO TOKYO?
TOKYO?
GO FIND TOHNO AND MEET UP WITH HIM.
YOU HAVE ENOUGH SAVED FOR THAT, NO?
FOR YOU, TOHNO AND TOKYO ARE SHINING AT A DISTANCE, FAR FROM YOU AND THE ISLAND.
THEY'RE SYMBOLS OF A WISH BEYOND REACH.

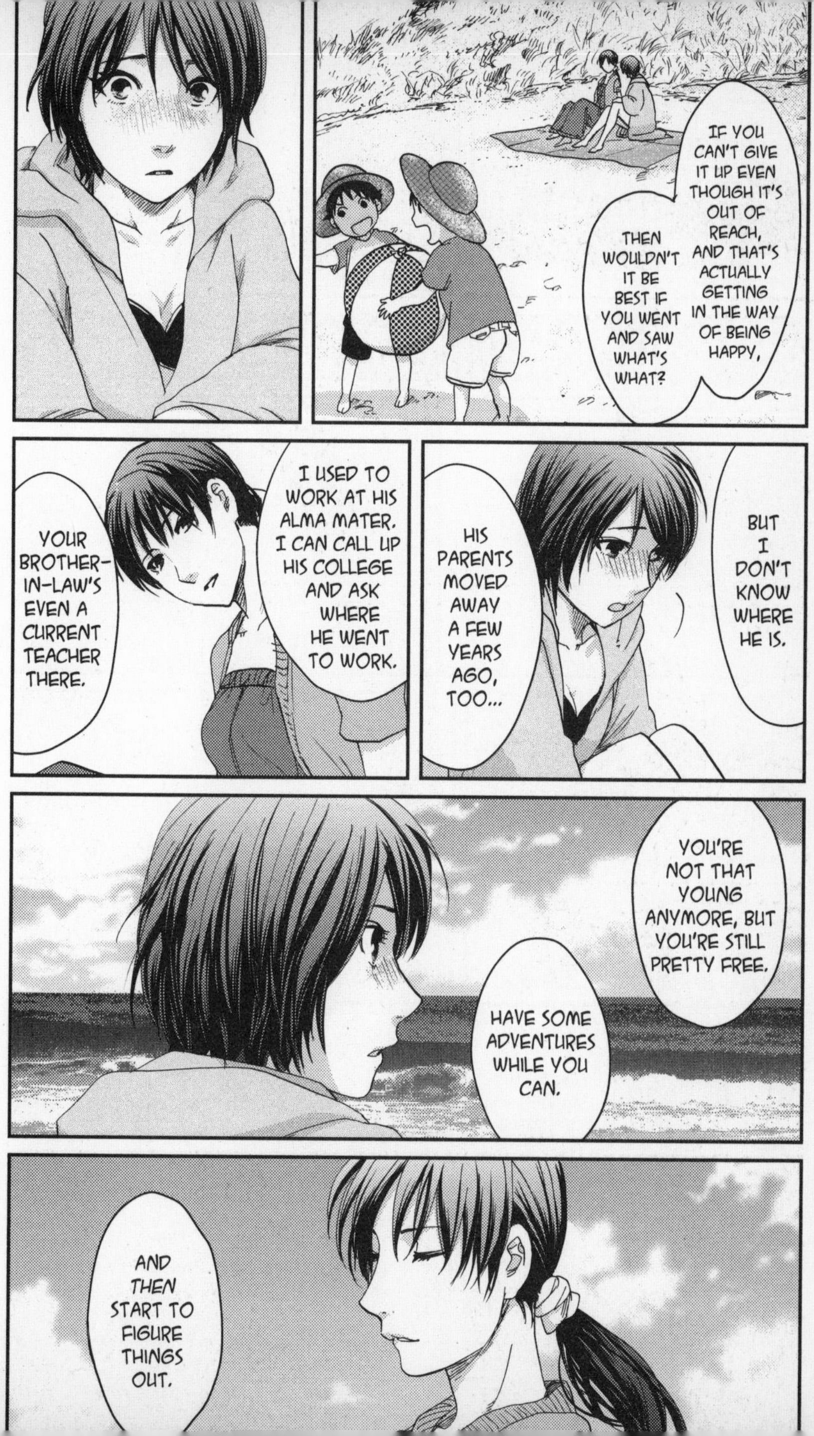
IF YOU CAN'T GIVE IT UP EVEN THOUGH IT'S OUT OF REACH, AND THAT'S ACTUALLY GETTING IN THE WAY OF BEING HAPPY,
THEN WOULDN'T IT BE BEST IF YOU WENT AND SAW WHAT'S WHAT?
BUT I DON'T KNOW WHERE HE IS.
HIS PARENTS MOVED AWAY A FEW YEARS AGO, TOO...
I USED TO WORK AT HIS ALMA MATER. I CAN CALL UP HIS COLLEGE AND ASK WHERE HE WENT TO WORK.
YOUR BROTHER-IN-LAW'S EVEN A CURRENT TEACHER THERE.
YOU'RE NOT THAT YOUNG ANYMORE, BUT YOU'RE STILL PRETTY FREE.
HAVE SOME ADVENTURES WHILE YOU CAN.
AND THEN START TO FIGURE THINGS OUT.

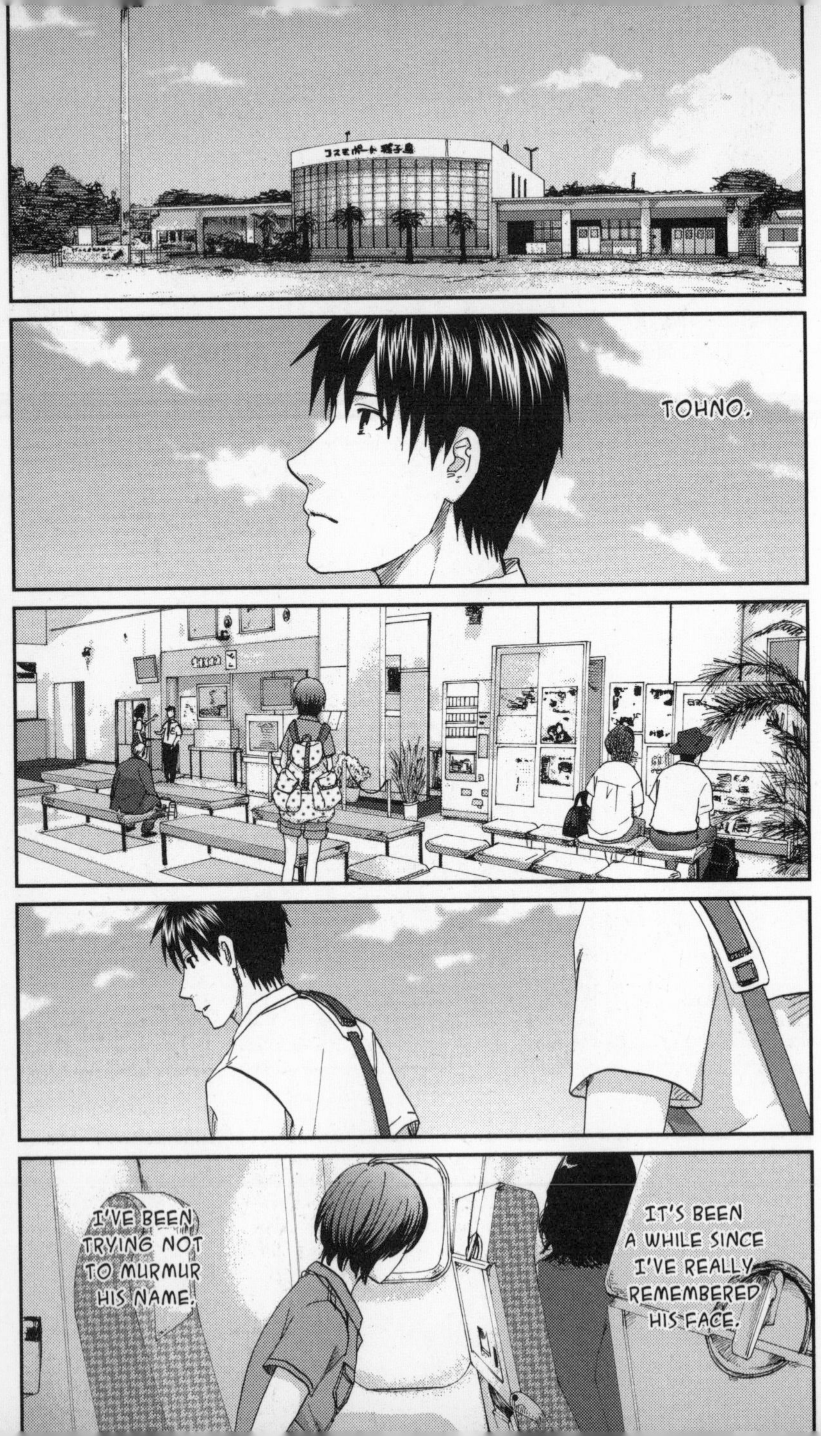
TOHNO.
IT'S BEEN A WHILE SINCE I'VE REALLY REMEMBERED HIS FACE.
I'VE BEEN TRYING NOT TO MURMUR HIS NAME.

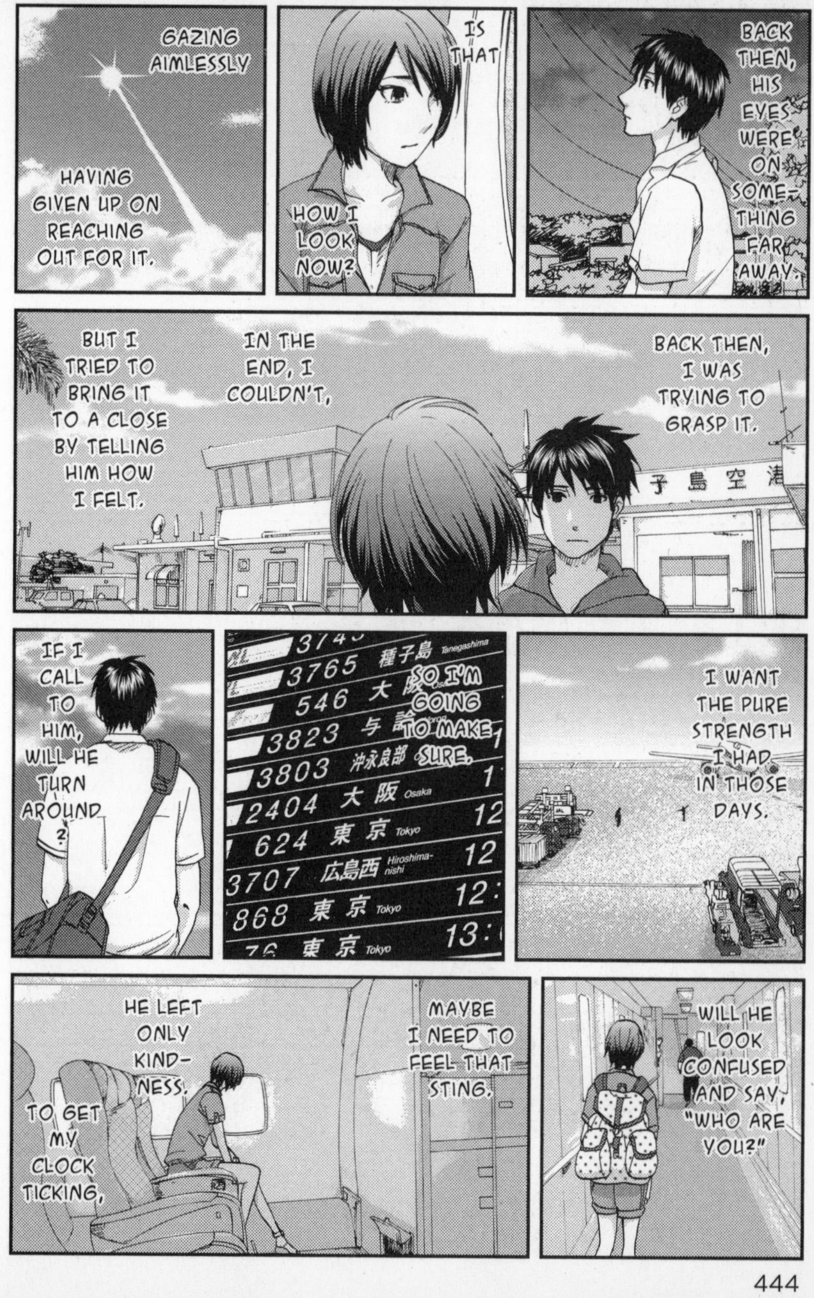
BACK THEN, HIS EYES WERE ON SOMETHING FAR AWAY.
IS THAT
HOW I LOOK NOW?
GAZING AIMLESSLY
HAVING GIVEN UP ON REACHING OUT FOR IT.
BACK THEN, I WAS TRYING TO GRASP IT.
IN THE END, I COULDN'T,
BUT I TRIED TO BRING IT TO A CLOSE BY TELLING HIM HOW I FELT.
I WANT THE PURE STRENGTH I HAD IN THOSE DAYS.
SO I'M GOING TO MAKE SURE.
3765 種子島 Tanegashima
546 大阪
3823 与論
3803 沖永良部
2404 大阪 Osaka
624 東京 Tokyo
3707 広島西 Hiroshima-nishi
868 東京 Tokyo
東京 Tokyo
IF I CALL TO HIM, WILL HE TURN AROUND?
WILL HE LOOK CONFUSED AND SAY, "WHO ARE YOU?"
MAYBE I NEED TO FEEL THAT STING.
HE LEFT ONLY KINDNESS.
TO GET MY CLOCK TICKING,

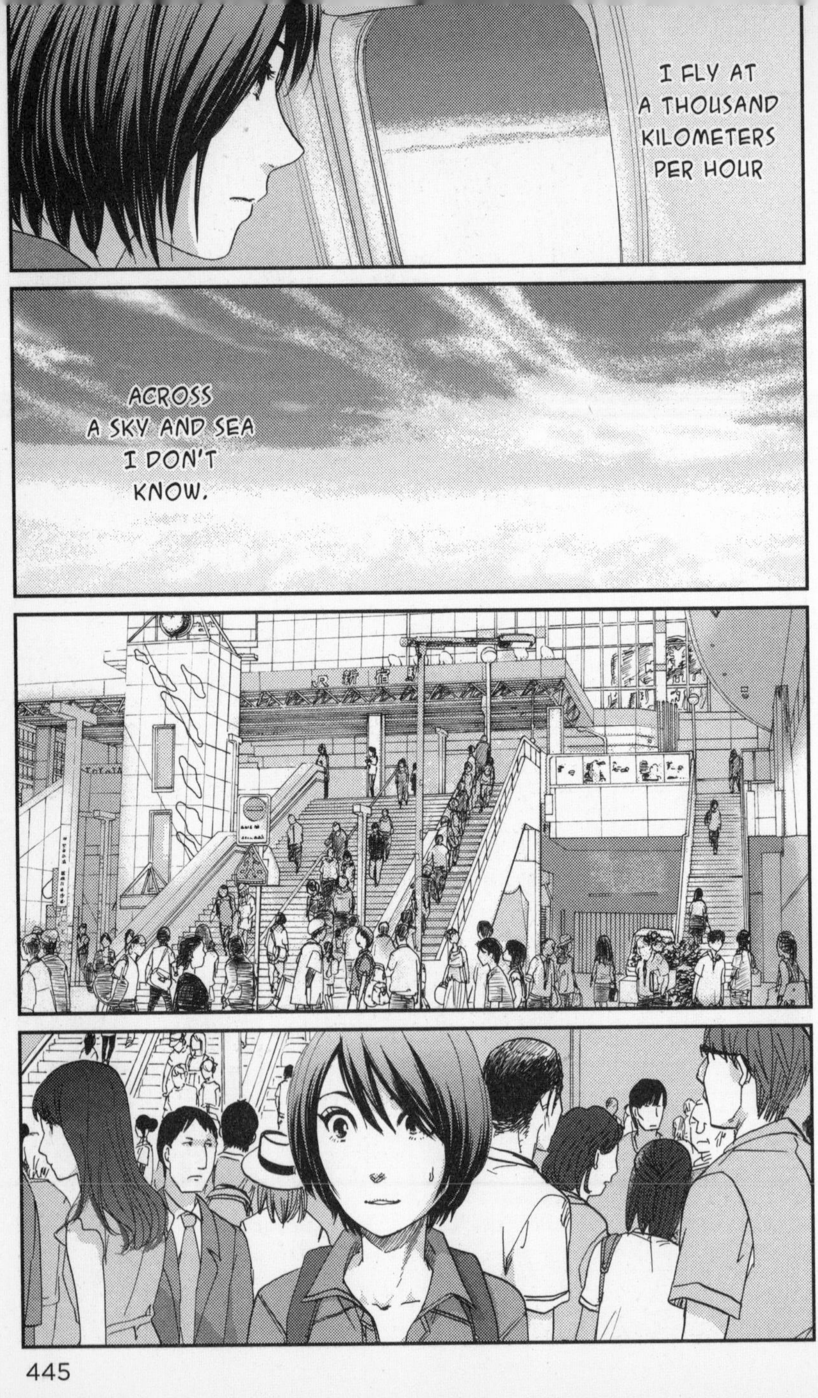
I FLY AT A THOUSAND KILOMETERS PER HOUR
ACROSS A SKY AND SEA I DON'T KNOW.

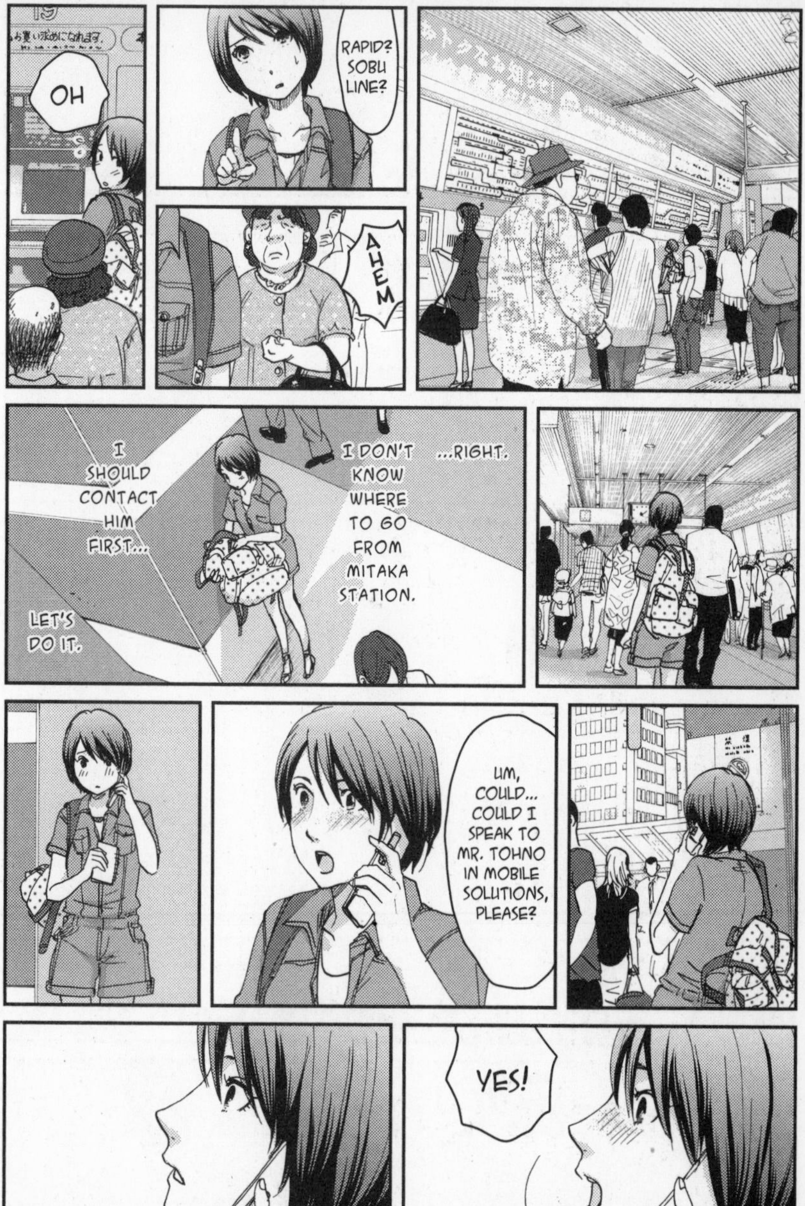
RAPID? SOBU LINE?
AHEM
OH
...RIGHT.
I DON'T KNOW WHERE TO GO FROM MITAKA STATION.
I SHOULD CONTACT HIM FIRST...
LET'S DO IT.
UM, COULD... COULD I SPEAK TO MR. TOHNO IN MOBILE SOLUTIONS, PLEASE?
YES!

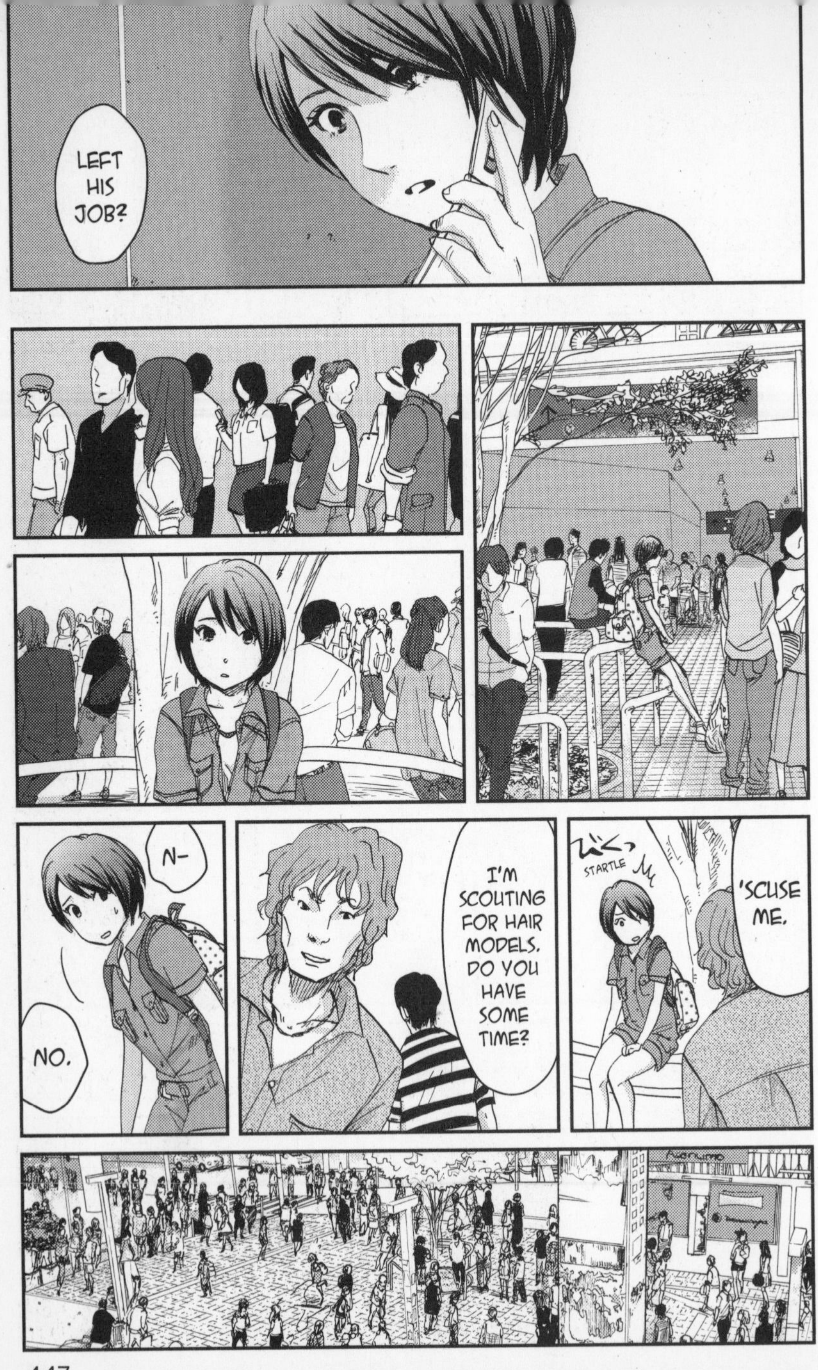
LEFT HIS JOB?
びくっ
STARTLE
'SCUSE ME.
I'M SCOUTING FOR HAIR MODELS. DO YOU HAVE SOME TIME?
N-
NO.

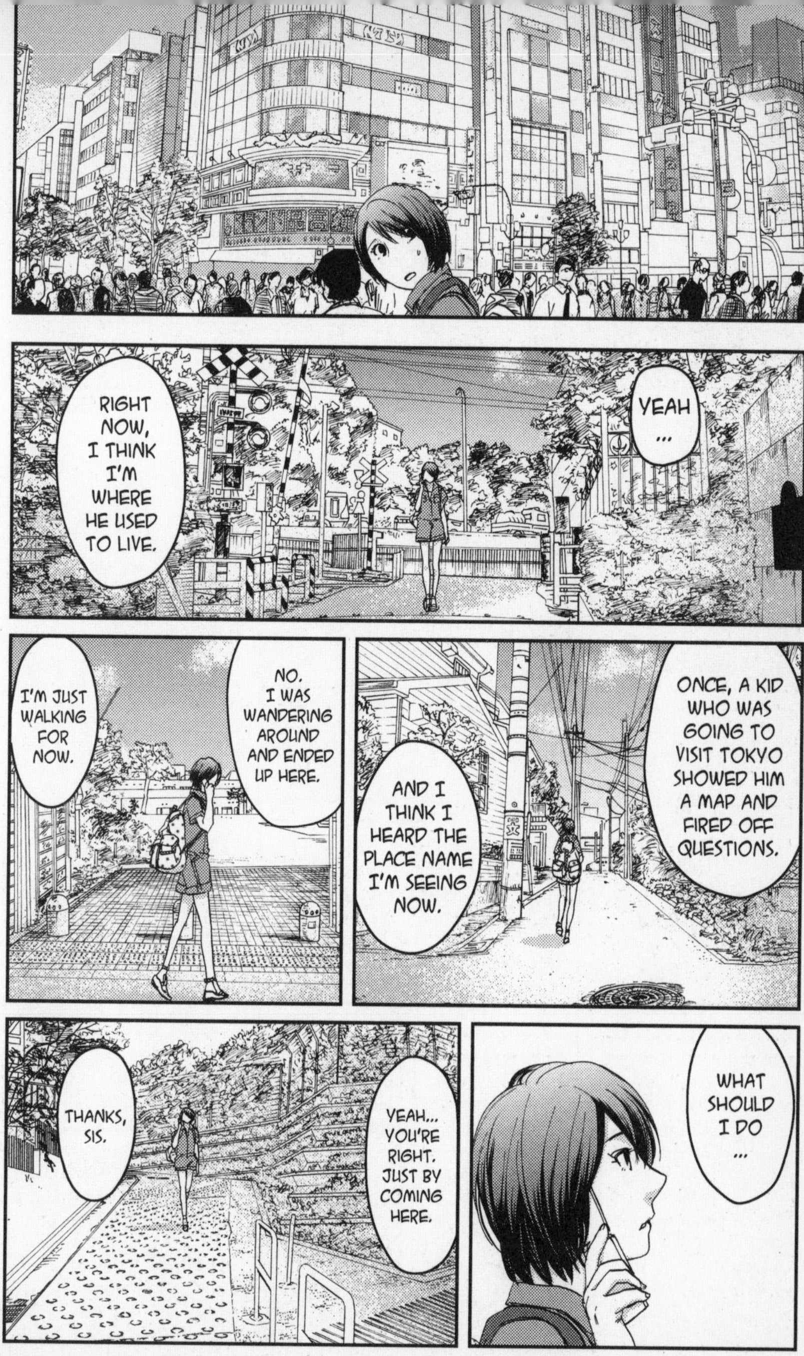
YEAH ...
RIGHT NOW, I THINK I'M WHERE HE USED TO LIVE.
ONCE, A KID WHO WAS GOING TO VISIT TOKYO SHOWED HIM A MAP AND FIRED OFF QUESTIONS.
AND I THINK I HEARD THE PLACE NAME I'M SEEING NOW.
NO. I WAS WANDERING AROUND AND ENDED UP HERE.
I'M JUST WALKING FOR NOW.
WHAT SHOULD I DO ...
YEAH... YOU'RE RIGHT. JUST BY COMING HERE.
THANKS, SIS.

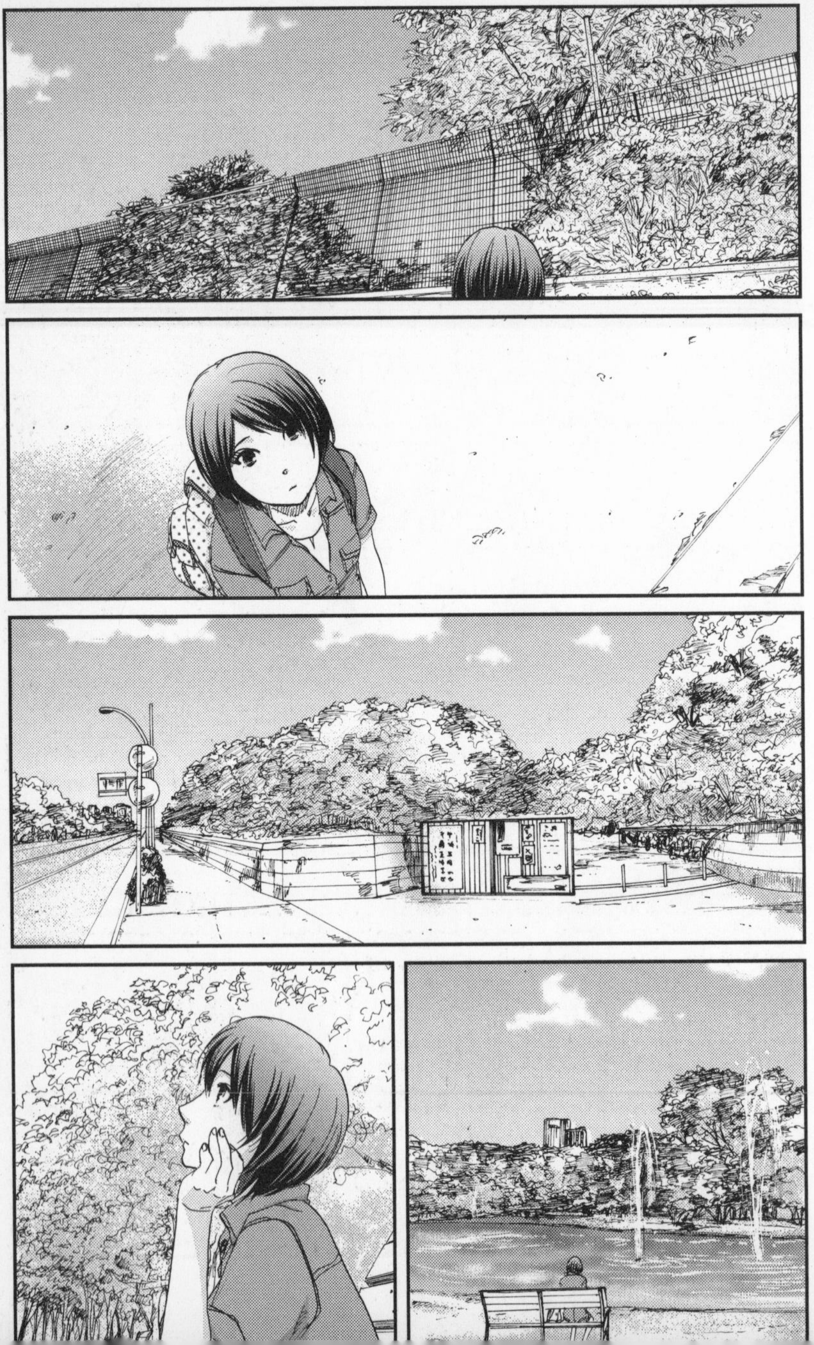

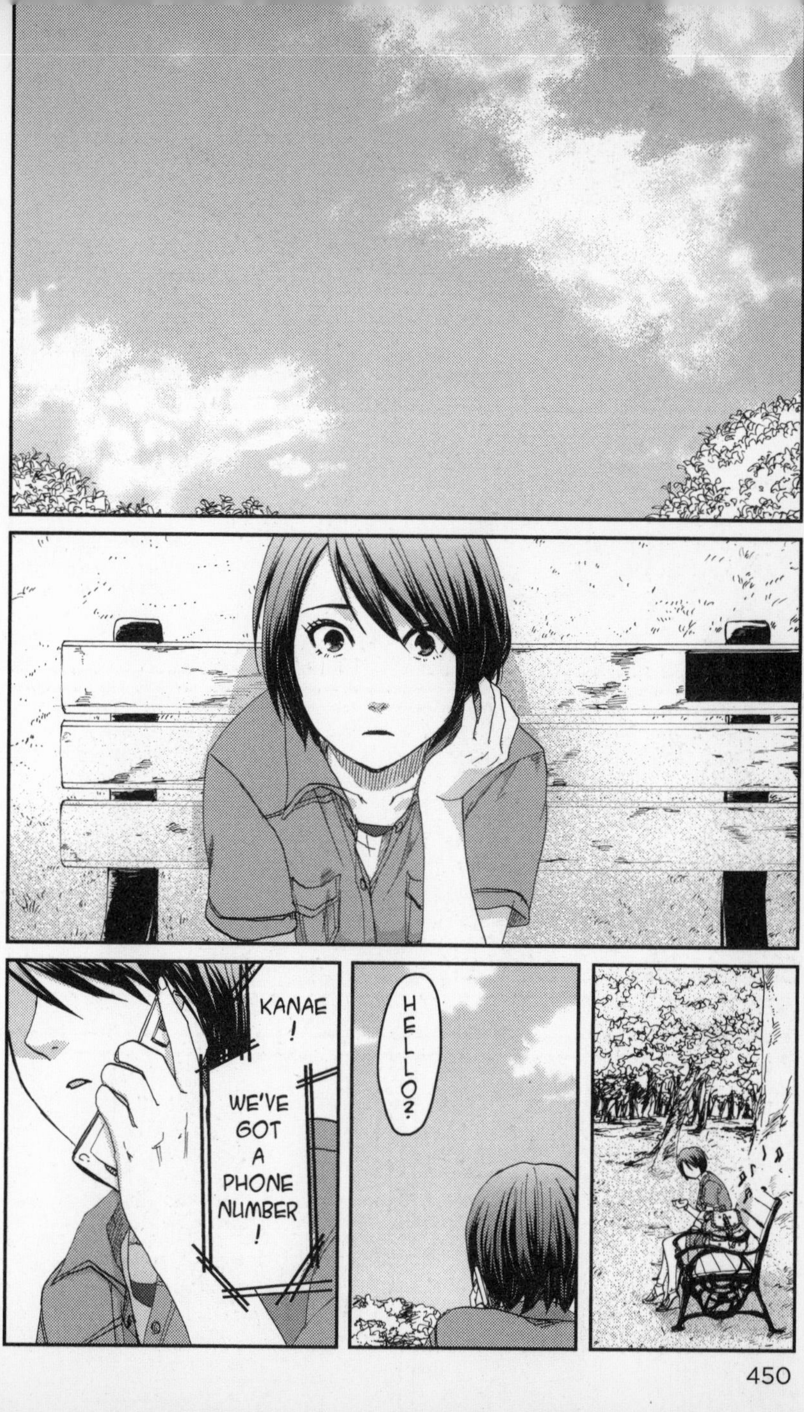
HELLO?
KANAE!
WE'VE GOT A PHONE NUMBER!

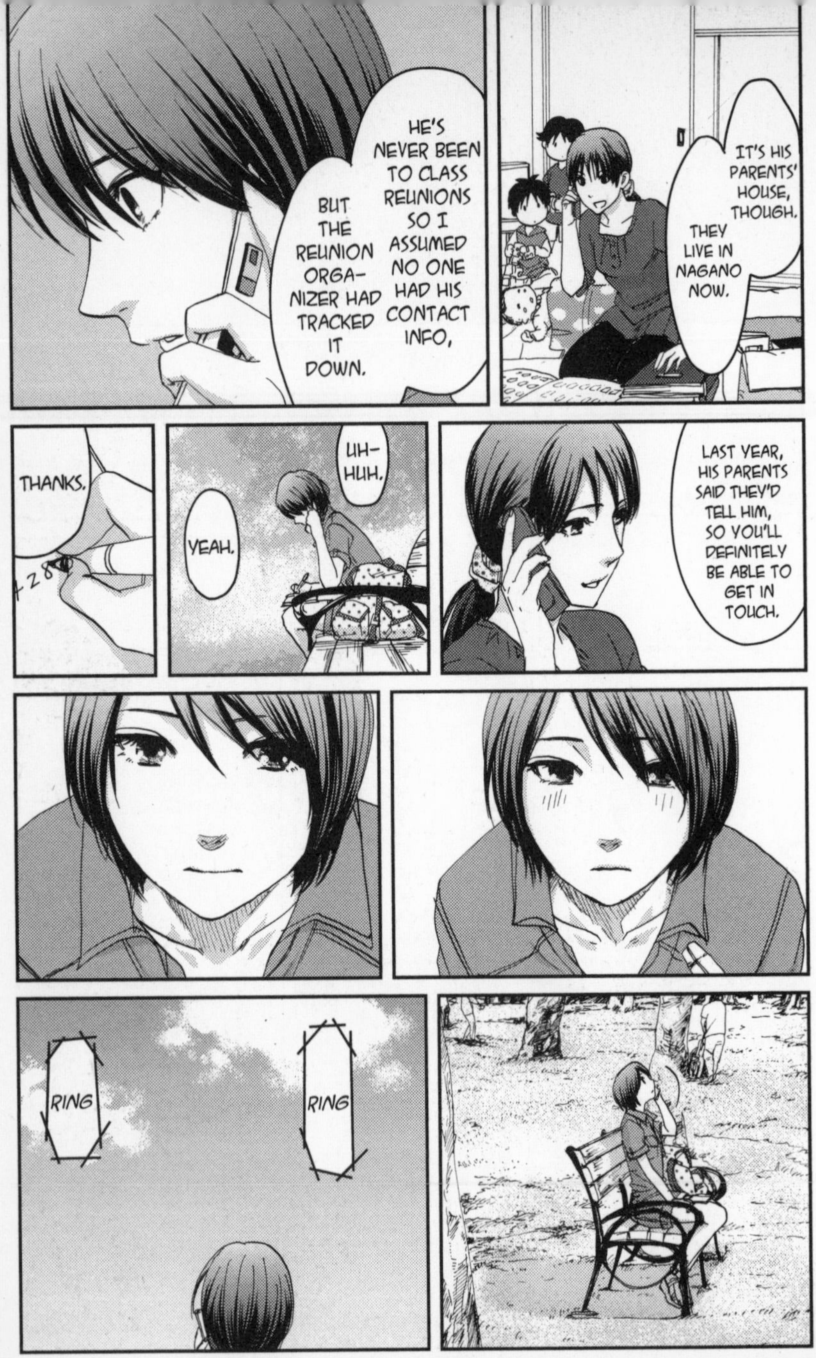
IT'S HIS PARENTS' HOUSE, THOUGH.
THEY LIVE IN NAGANO NOW.
HE'S NEVER BEEN TO CLASS REUNIONS SO I ASSUMED NO ONE HAD HIS CONTACT INFO,
BUT THE REUNION ORGA-NIZER HAD TRACKED IT DOWN.
LAST YEAR, HIS PARENTS SAID THEY'D TELL HIM, SO YOU'LL DEFINITELY BE ABLE TO GET IN TOUCH.
UH-HUH.
YEAH.
THANKS.
RING
RING

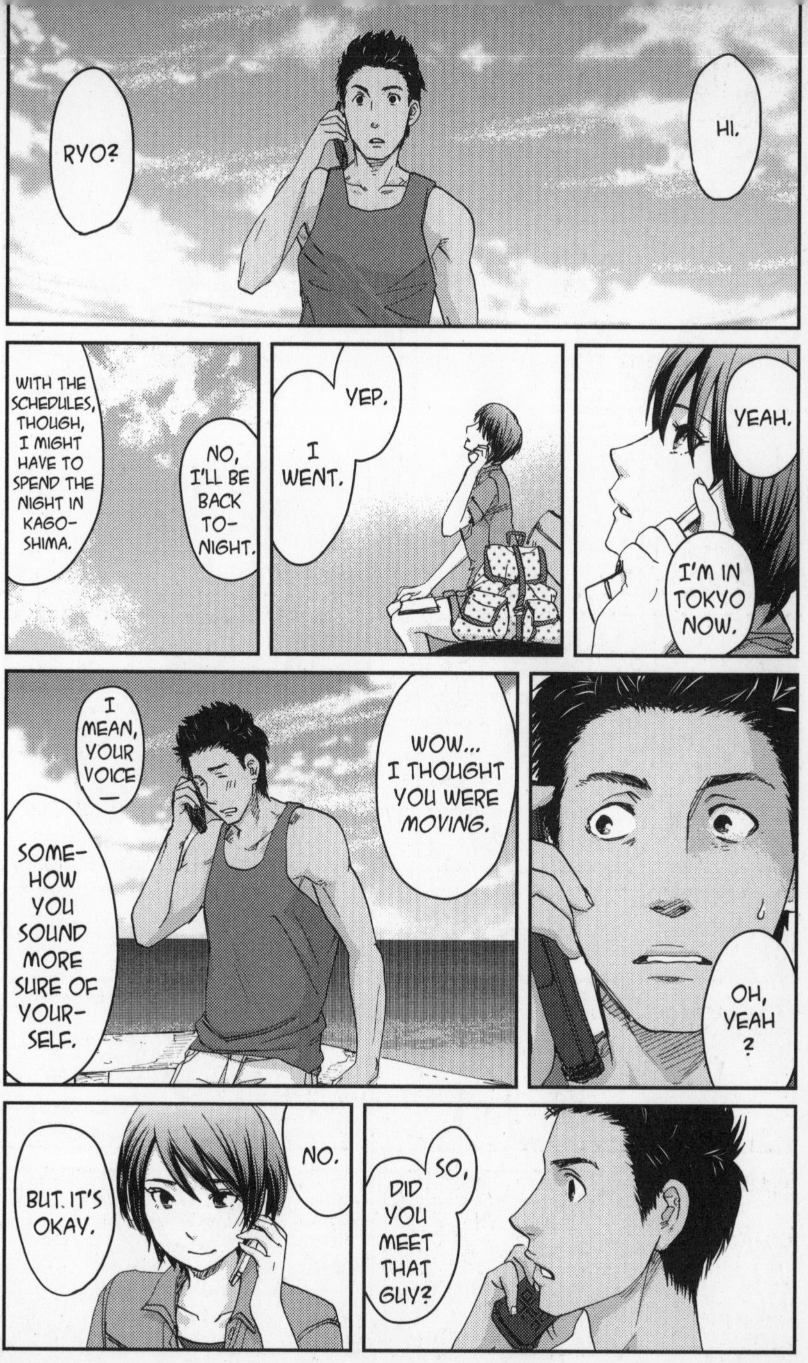
HI.
RYO?
YEAH.
I'M IN TOKYO NOW.
YEP.
I WENT.
NO, I'LL BE BACK TO-NIGHT.
WITH THE SCHEDULES, THOUGH, I MIGHT HAVE TO SPEND THE NIGHT IN KAGO-SHIMA.
OH, YEAH?
WOW... I THOUGHT YOU WERE MOVING.
I MEAN, YOUR VOICE—
SOME-HOW YOU SOUND MORE SURE OF YOUR-SELF.
SO, DID YOU MEET THAT GUY?
NO.
BUT. IT'S OKAY.

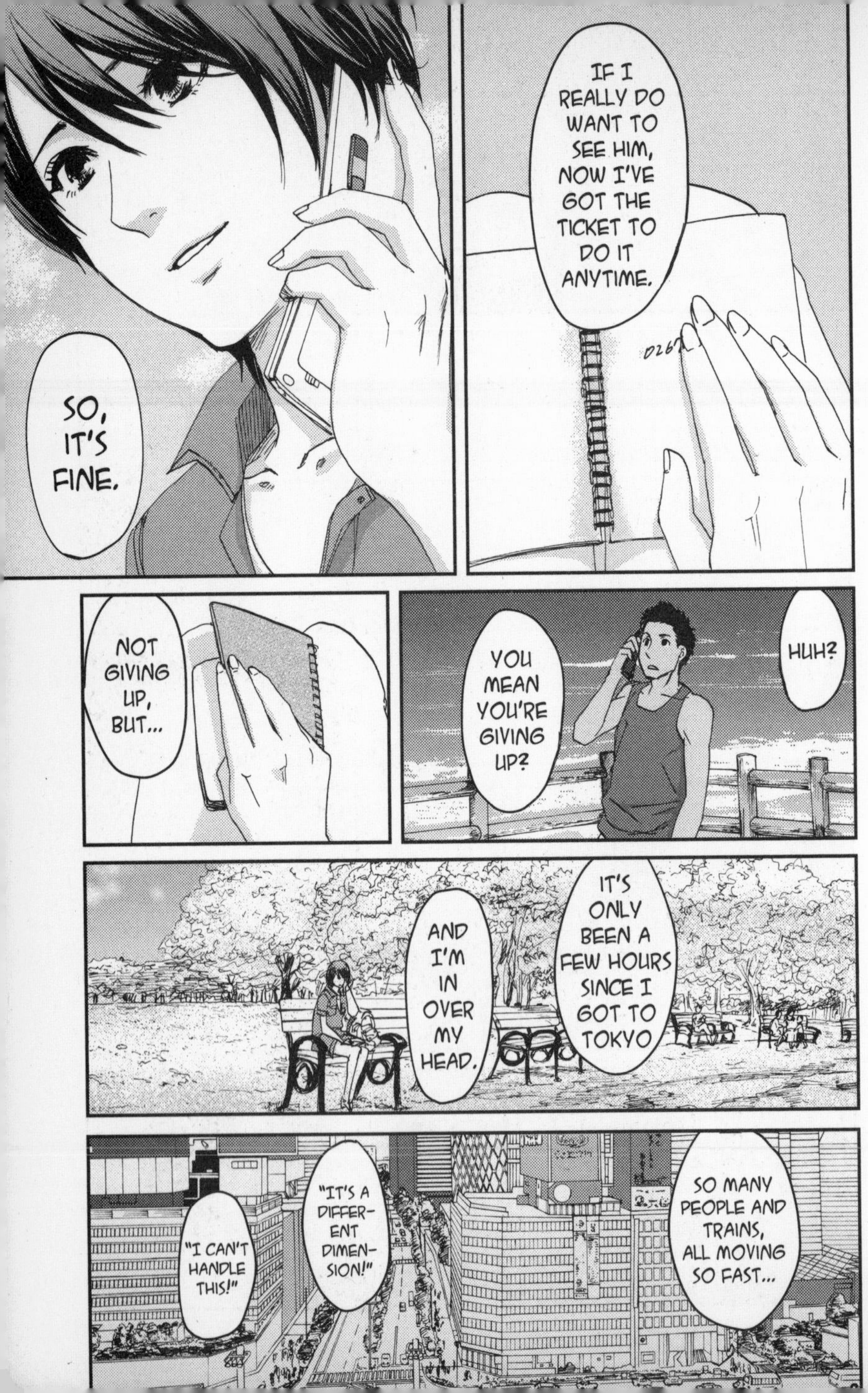
IF I REALLY DO WANT TO SEE HIM, NOW I'VE GOT THE TICKET TO DO IT ANYTIME.
SO, IT'S FINE.
HUH?
YOU MEAN YOU'RE GIVING UP?
NOT GIVING UP, BUT...
IT'S ONLY BEEN A FEW HOURS SINCE I GOT TO TOKYO
AND I'M IN OVER MY HEAD.
SO MANY PEOPLE AND TRAINS, ALL MOVING SO FAST...
"IT'S A DIFFER-ENT DIMEN-SION!"
"I CAN'T HANDLE THIS!"

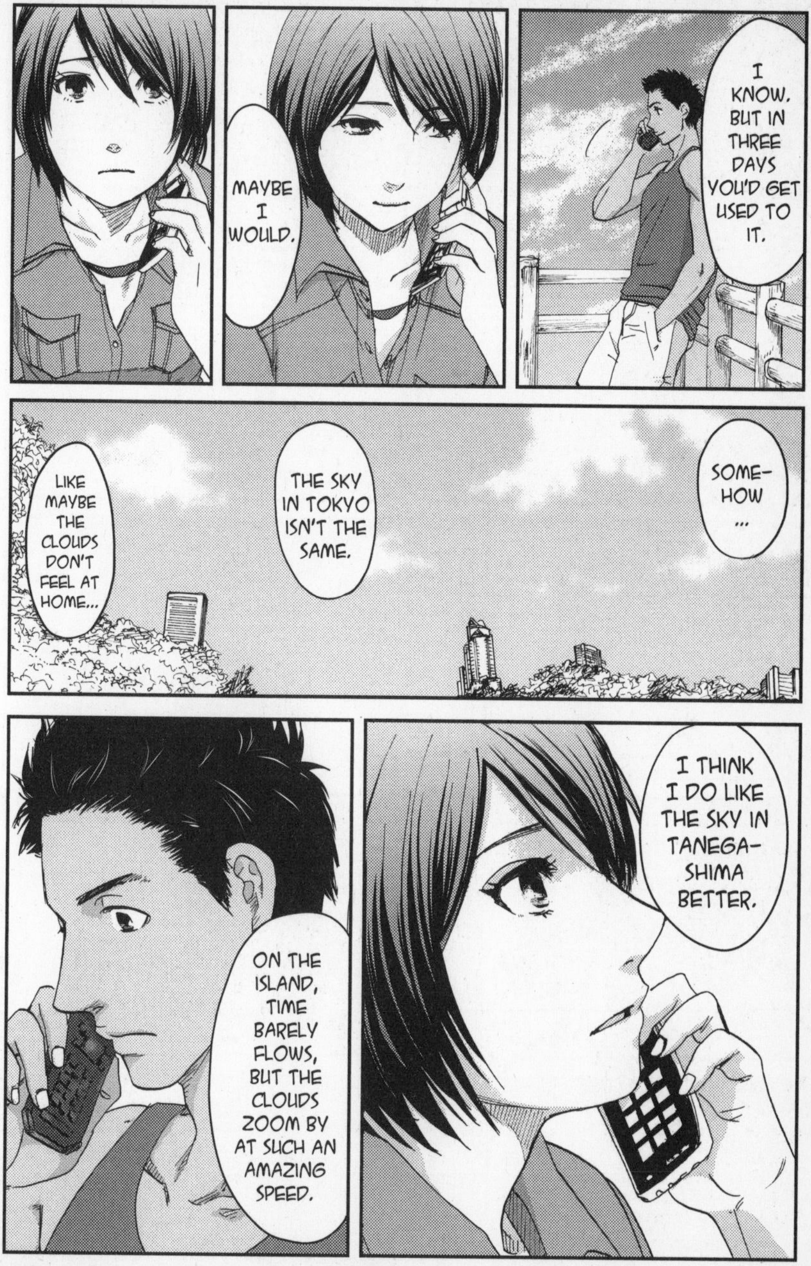
I KNOW. BUT IN THREE DAYS YOU'D GET USED TO IT.
MAYBE I WOULD.
SOME-HOW ...
THE SKY IN TOKYO ISN'T THE SAME.
LIKE MAYBE THE CLOUDS DON'T FEEL AT HOME...
I THINK I DO LIKE THE SKY IN TANEGA-SHIMA BETTER.
ON THE ISLAND, TIME BARELY FLOWS, BUT THE CLOUDS ZOOM BY AT SUCH AN AMAZING SPEED.

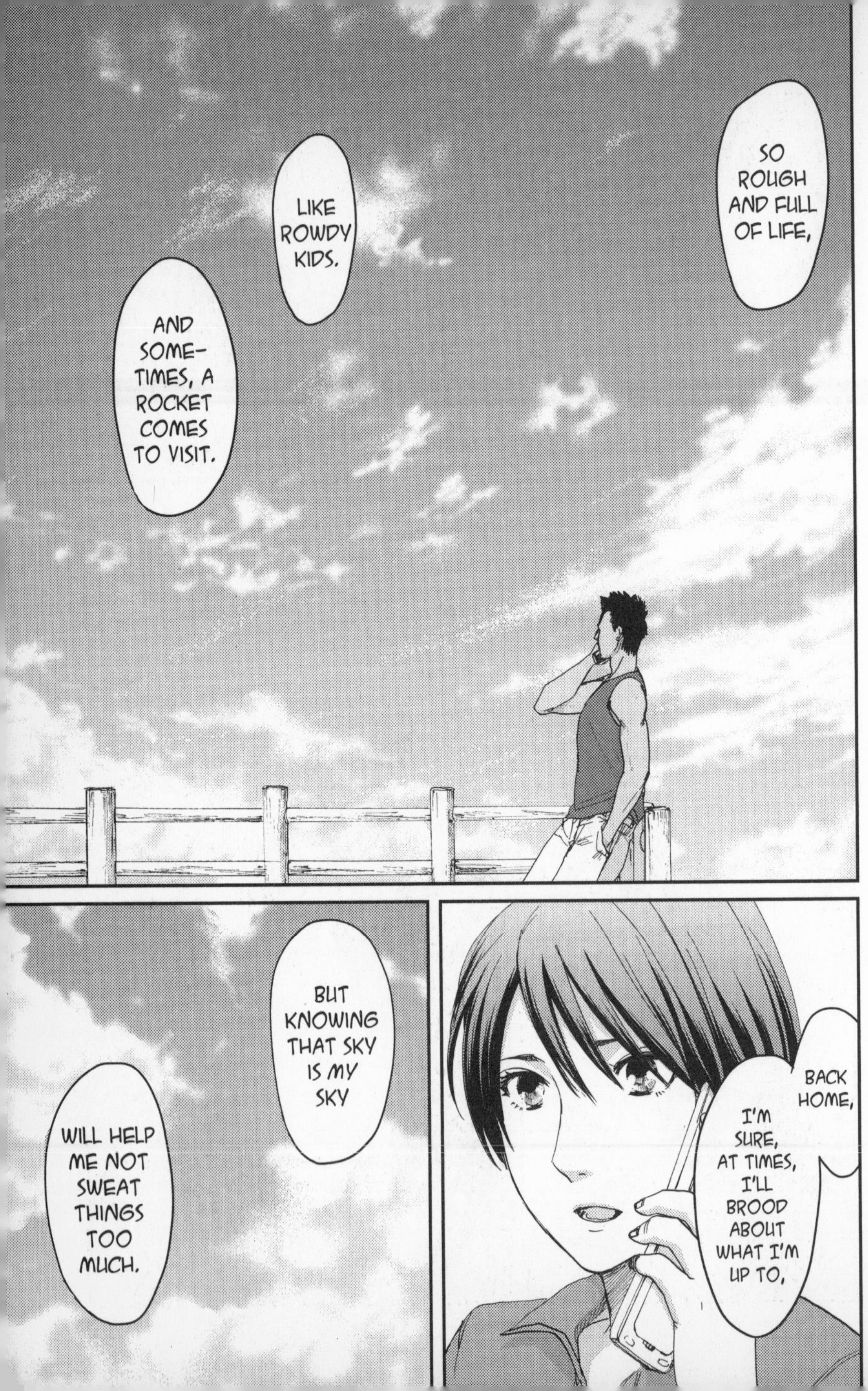
SO ROUGH AND FULL OF LIFE,
LIKE ROWDY KIDS.
AND SOME-TIMES, A ROCKET COMES TO VISIT.
BACK HOME,
I'M SURE, AT TIMES, I'LL BROOD ABOUT WHAT I'M UP TO,
BUT KNOWING THAT SKY IS MY SKY
WILL HELP ME NOT SWEAT THINGS TOO MUCH.

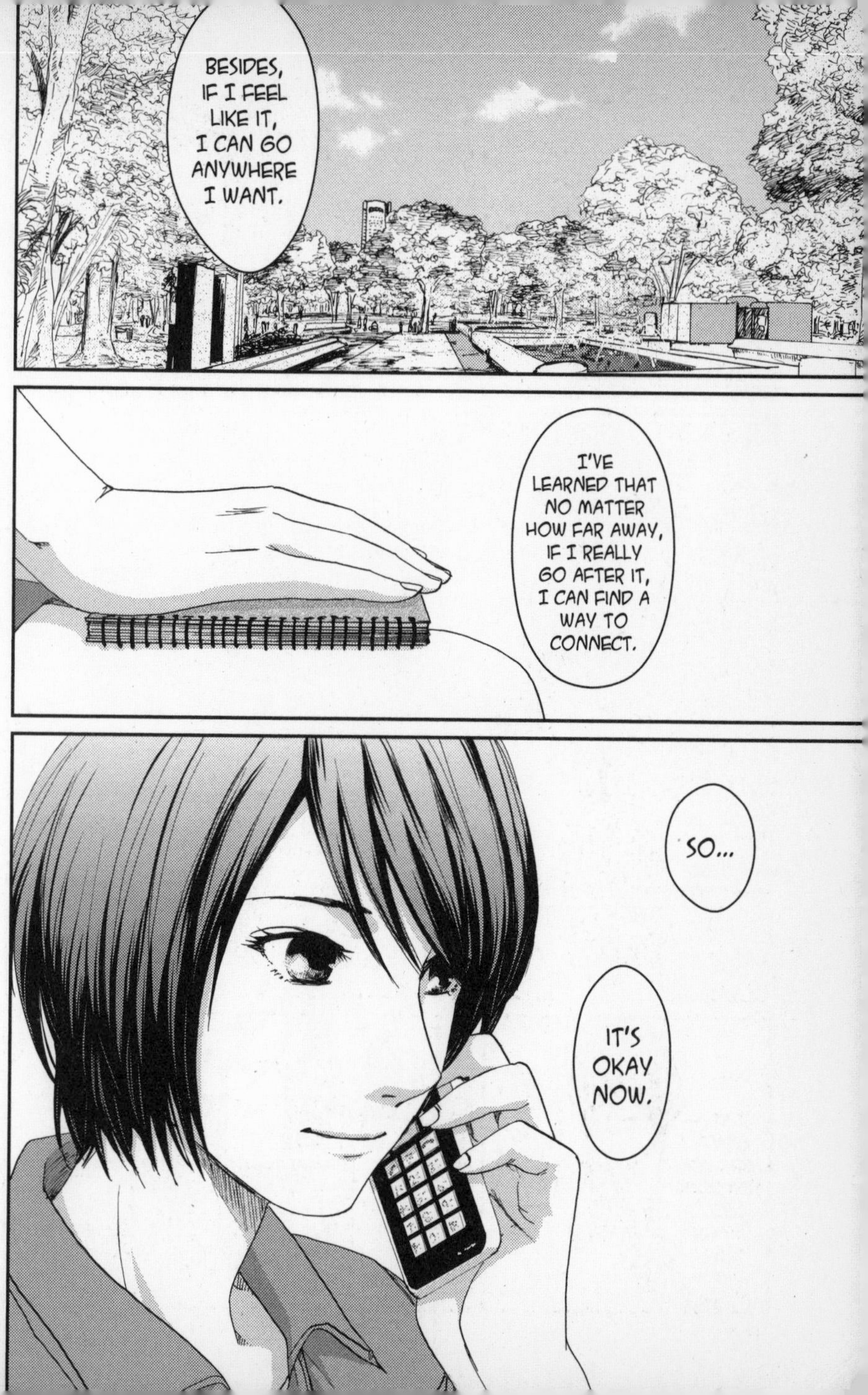
BESIDES, IF I FEEL LIKE IT, I CAN GO ANYWHERE I WANT.
I'VE LEARNED THAT NO MATTER HOW FAR AWAY, IF I REALLY GO AFTER IT, I CAN FIND A WAY TO CONNECT.
SO...
IT'S OKAY NOW.

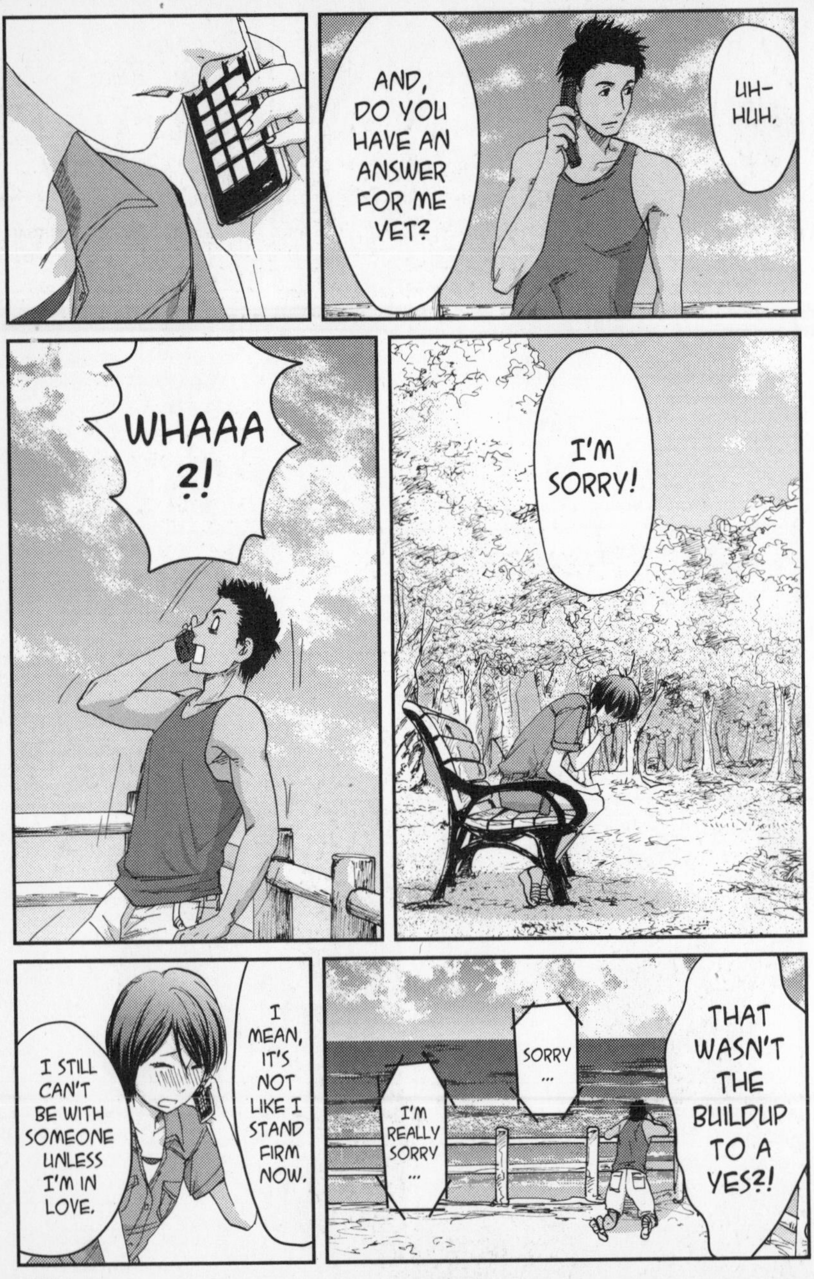
UH-HUH,
AND, DO YOU HAVE AN ANSWER FOR ME YET?
I'M SORRY!
WHAAA ?!
THAT WASN'T THE BUILDUP TO A YES?!
SORRY ...
I'M REALLY SORRY ...
I MEAN, IT'S NOT LIKE I STAND FIRM NOW.
I STILL CAN'T BE WITH SOMEONE UNLESS I'M IN LOVE.

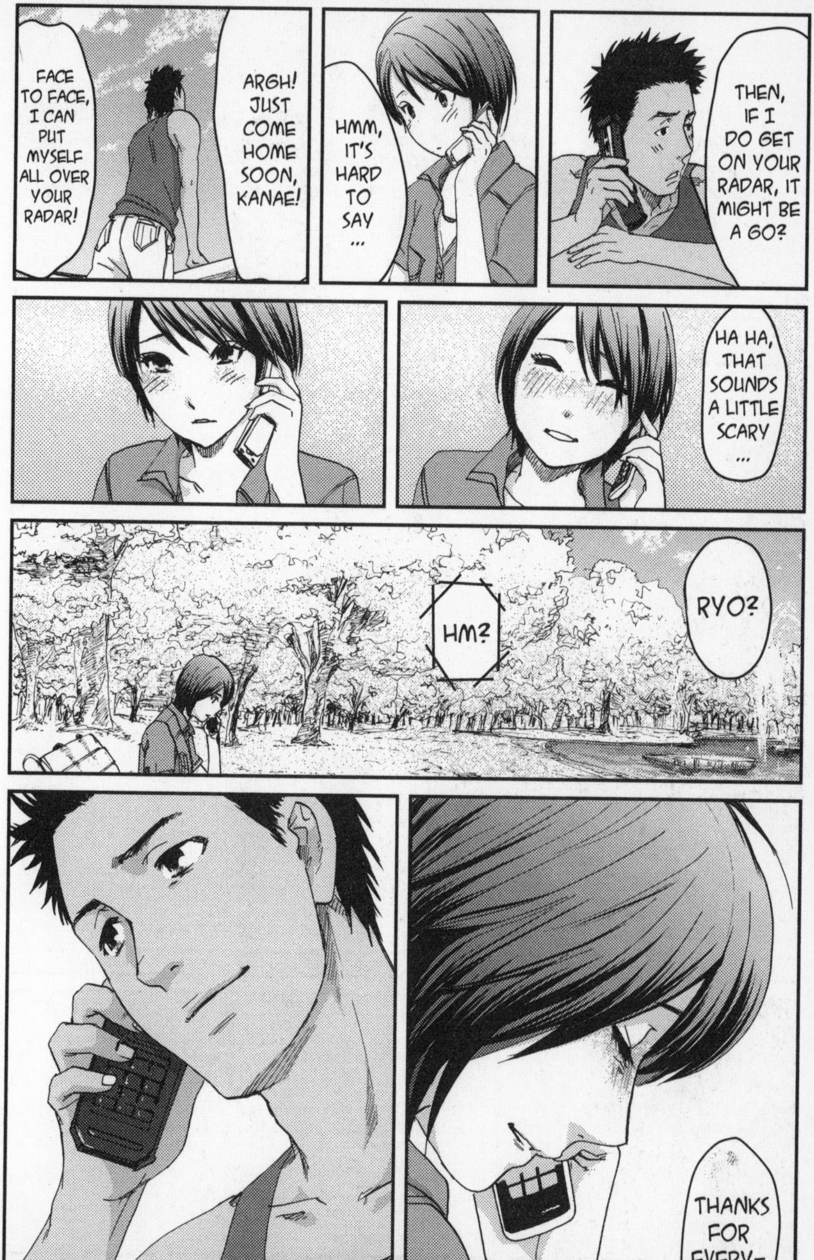
THEN, IF I DO GET ON YOUR RADAR, IT MIGHT BE A GO?
HMM, IT'S HARD TO SAY ...
ARGH! JUST COME HOME SOON, KANAE!
FACE TO FACE, I CAN PUT MYSELF ALL OVER YOUR RADAR!
HA HA, THAT SOUNDS A LITTLE SCARY ...
RYO?
HM?
THANKS FOR EVERY-THING.

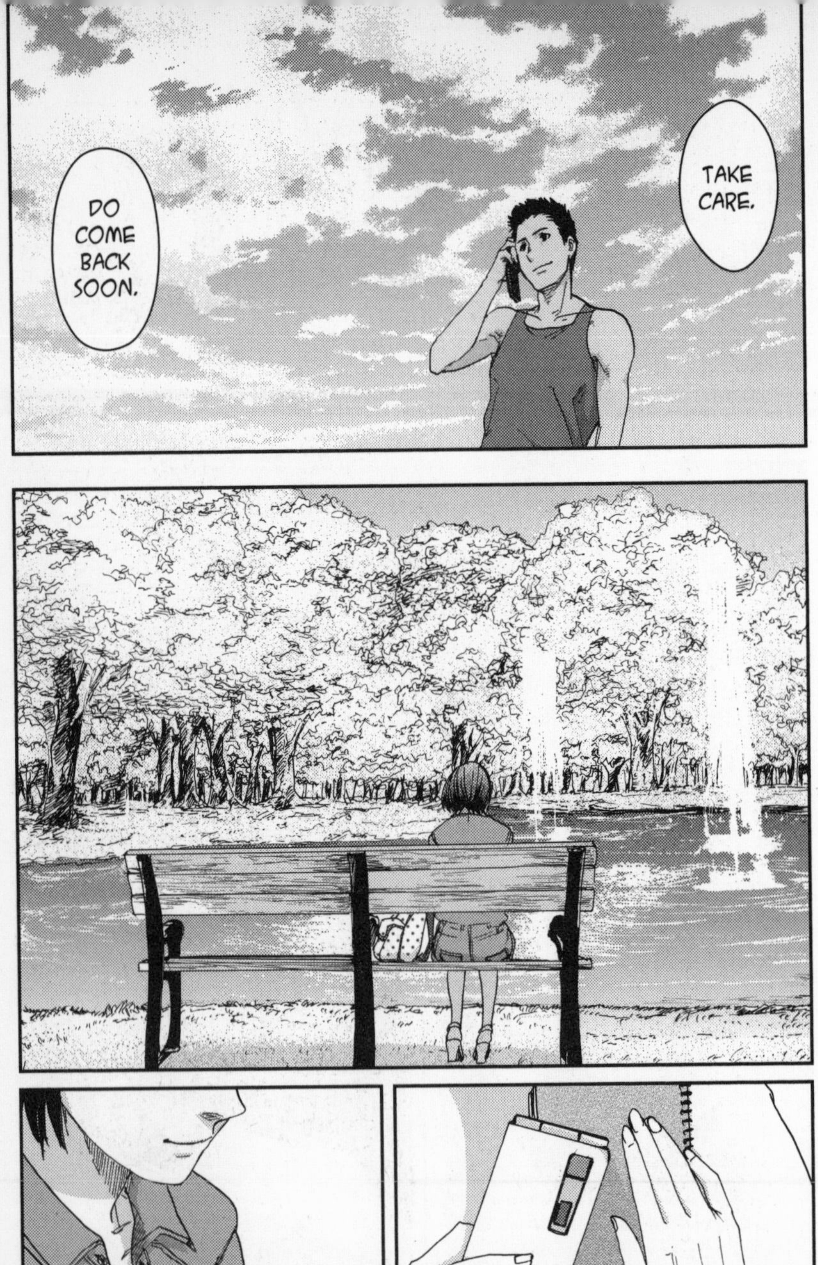
TAKE CARE.
DO COME BACK SOON.

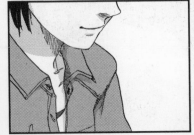

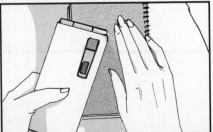

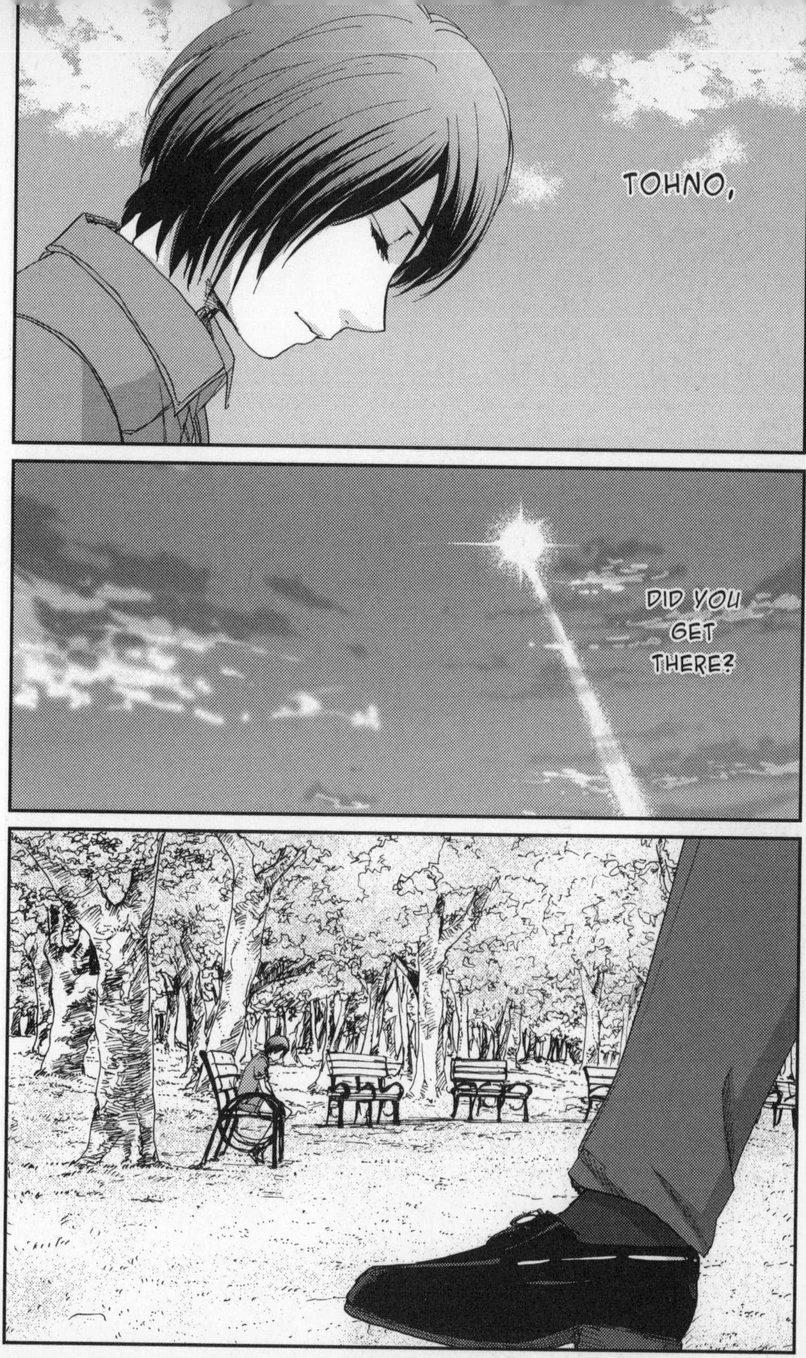
TOHNO,
DID YOU GET THERE?

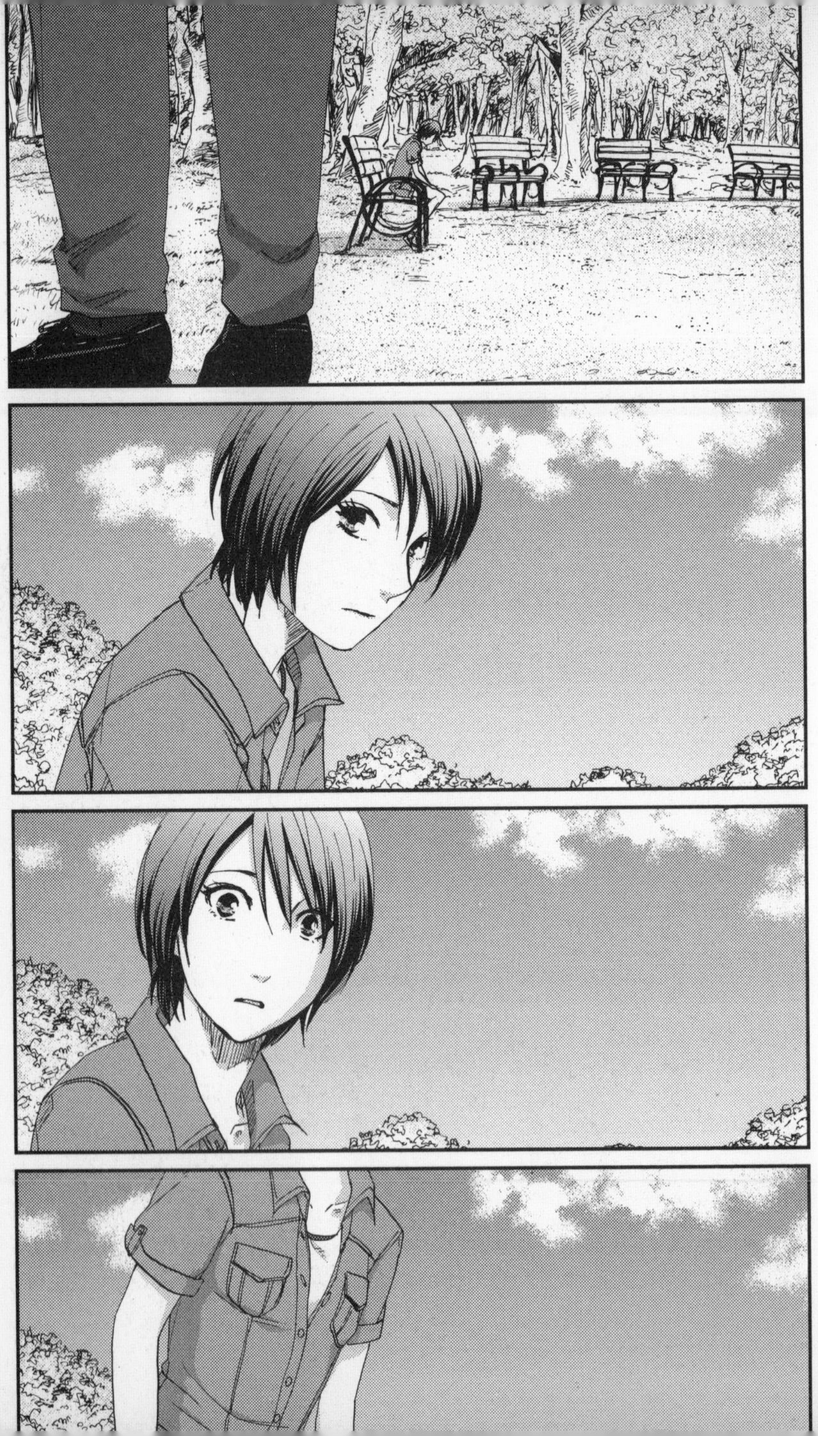

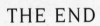

THE END

It's clearly a comedy, but when it takes a turn into drama, it doesn't feel unnatural. *14 Days in Shonan* looks like one of those series that can be brutally funny when it wants to be." —*Comics Alliance*

"I loved it... The most surprising thing about *14 Days in Shonan* is its ability to address serious social problems without devolving into an Afterschool Special." —*The Manga Critic*

"Suffice to say, the first chapter grabbed me almost immediately. It was the same *Great Teacher Onizuka* humor I remember, and most importantly, I reacted the same to it as I had when I was stuck in my college dorm on those long Syracuse winter nights." —*Japanator*

"Established fans will definitely get more out of it, but there's enough fun here to 'open the doors of all hearts,' as Onizuka himself would put it." —*Otaku USA*

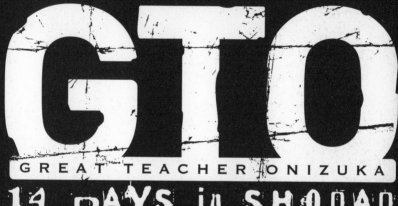

GTO
GREAT TEACHER ONIZUKA
14 DAYS in SHONAN
by TORU FUJISAWA

Completed only last year, this new arc in the saga of the most badass teacher ever requires no prior schooling in the franchise to move you (when you aren't laughing your head off).

VOLUMES 1 TO 6 AVAILABLE NOW!

200 pages, $10.95 each

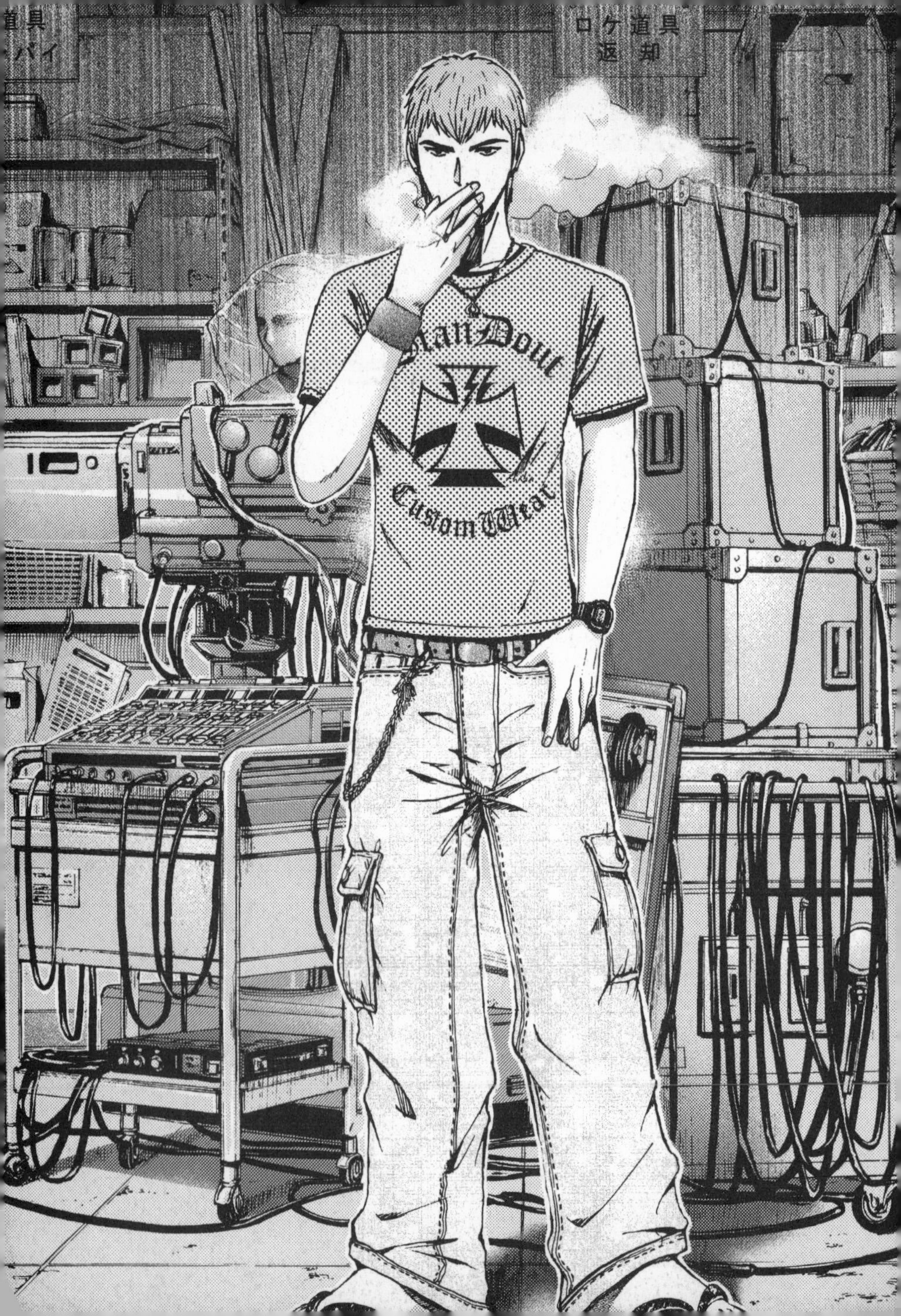
ロケ道具
返却
Custom Wear

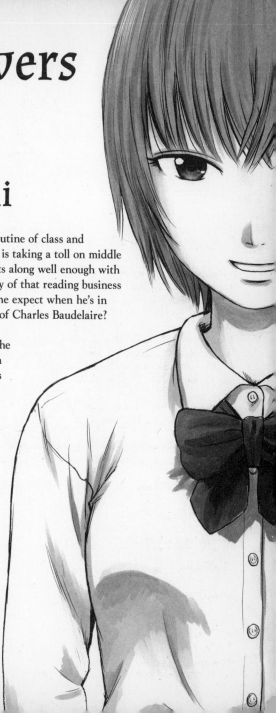

The Flowers of Evil

Shuzo Oshimi

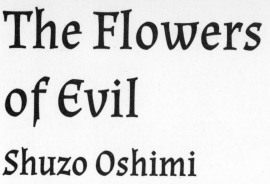

Nowhere to go. Nothing to do. The routine of class and endless stupidity in a provincial town is taking a toll on middle schooler Takao Kasuga. Though he gets along well enough with his peers, they'll never begin to dig any of that reading business that's his only true escape. What can he expect when he's in love with foreign stuff like the poems of Charles Baudelaire?

Yet, his life threatens to take a turn for the worse when he finds and takes home, in a moment of weakness, the gym clothes of pretty, sweet, and smart Nanako Saeki on whom he has a major crush. Witness to the theft is the oddest girl in class, who seems to consider the whole world a pile of excrement and to nurse a terribly sadistic streak...

Rising star Shuzo Oshimi, author of the hit apocalyptic series *Drifting Net Cafe*, finds his groove in an ever-so-slightly autobiographical work that grows more soulful with each volume. Nominated for the 2012 Manga Taisho (Cartoon Grand Prize).

5 Centimeters per Second

Translation: Melissa Tanaka
Production: Hiroko Mizuno
Nicole Dochych
Tomoe Tsutsumi

First published in Japan in 2010 by Kodansha, Ltd., Tokyo
Publication for this English edition arranged through Kodansha, Ltd., Tokyo
English language version produced by Vertical, Inc.

Translation provided by Vertical, Inc., 2012
Published by Vertical, Inc., New York

Originally published in Japanese as *Byousoku 5-senchimeetoru 1, 2* by Kodansha, Ltd., 2010-2011
Byousoku 5-senchimeetoru first serialized in Afteroon, Kodansha, Ltd., 2010-2011

ISBN: 978-1-932234-96-1

Manufactured in Canada

First Edition

Third Printing

Vertical, Inc.
451 Park Avenue South
7th Floor
New York, NY 10016
www.vertical-inc.com

WRONG WAY

Japanese books, including manga like this one,
are meant to be read from right to left.
So the front cover is actually the back cover, and vice versa.
To read this book, please flip it over
and start in the top right-hand corner.
Read the panels, and the bubbles in the panels,
from right to left,
then drop down to the next row and repeat.
It may make you dizzy at first,
but forcing your brain to do things backwards
makes you smarter in the long run.
We swear.